THE BEST PLAYS OF 1941-42

EDITED BY
BURNS MANTLE

THE BEST PLAYS OF 1899-1909
(*With Garrison P. Sherwood*)
THE BEST PLAYS OF 1909-19
(*With Garrison P. Sherwood*)
THE BEST PLAYS OF 1919-20
THE BEST PLAYS OF 1920-21
THE BEST PLAYS OF 1921-22
THE BEST PLAYS OF 1922-23
THE BEST PLAYS OF 1923-24
THE BEST PLAYS OF 1924-25
THE BEST PLAYS OF 1925-26
THE BEST PLAYS OF 1926-27
THE BEST PLAYS OF 1927-28
THE BEST PLAYS OF 1928-29
THE BEST PLAYS OF 1929-30
THE BEST PLAYS OF 1930-31
THE BEST PLAYS OF 1931-32
THE BEST PLAYS OF 1932-33
THE BEST PLAYS OF 1933-34
THE BEST PLAYS OF 1934-35
THE BEST PLAYS OF 1935-36
THE BEST PLAYS OF 1936-37
THE BEST PLAYS OF 1937-38
THE BEST PLAYS OF 1938-39
THE BEST PLAYS OF 1939-40
THE BEST PLAYS OF 1940-41
THE BEST PLAYS OF 1941-42
THE BEST PLAYS OF 1942-43
THE BEST PLAYS OF 1943-44
THE BEST PLAYS OF 1944-45
CONTEMPORARY AMERICAN
PLAYWRIGHTS (1938)

oto by Vandamm Studio.

"CANDLE IN THE WIND"

Madeline: Oh, I wonder—I wonder— How many chances we're given . . . How do we da
part, Raoul, knowing how all the chances are against us?
Raoul: Most lovers of the world are parting just that way these days.
(*Louis Borell, Helen Hayes*)

THE BEST PLAYS OF 1941-42

AND THE
YEAR BOOK OF THE DRAMA
IN AMERICA

EDITED BY
BURNS MANTLE

With Illustrations

DODD, MEAD AND COMPANY
NEW YORK - - - 1946

"In Time to Come," copyright, 1942, by Howard Koch (Revised)
Copyright, 1940, by Howard Koch under the title "Woodrow Wilson"
Copyright and published, 1942, by Dramatists' Play Service, New York
"The Moon Is Down," copyright, 1941, by John Steinbeck
Copyright and published as a novel, 1942, by The Viking Press, New York
"Blithe Spirit," copyright, 1941, by Noel Coward
Copyright and published, 1941, by Doubleday, Doran & Co., Garden City, New York
"Junior Miss," copyright, 1942, by Jerome Chodorov and Joseph Fields
Copyright and published, 1942, by Random House, Inc., New York
"Candle in the Wind," copyright, 1941, by Maxwell Anderson
Copyright and published, 1941, by Anderson House, Washington, D. C. Distributed through Dodd, Mead & Co., New York
"Letters to Lucerne," copyright, 1941, by Fritz Rotter and Allen Vincent
Copyright and published, 1942, by Samuel French, Inc., New York
"Jason," copyright, 1942, by Samson Raphaelson
Copyright and published, 1942, by Random House, Inc., New York
"Angel Street," copyright, 1939, by Patrick Hamilton
Copyright and published, 1941, by Constable & Co., Ltd., London, under title "Gaslight"
"Uncle Harry," copyright, 1941, by Thomas Job
Copyright and published, 1942, by Samuel French, Inc., New York
"Hope for a Harvest," copyright, 1940, by Sophie Treadwell
Copyright and published, 1942, by Samuel French, Inc., New York

COPYRIGHT, 1942,

BY DODD, MEAD AND COMPANY, INC.

CAUTION: Professionals and amateurs are hereby warned that the above-mentioned plays, being fully protected under the copyright laws of the United States of America, the British Empire, including the Dominion of Canada, and all other countries of the Copyright Union, are subject to a royalty. All rights, including professional, amateur, motion picture, recitation, public reading, radio broadcasting, and the rights of translation into foreign languages, are strictly reserved. In their present form these plays are dedicated to the reading public only. All inquiries regarding them should be addressed to their publishers or authors.

INTRODUCTION

IT was not a critics' year in the theatre. Burdened by their reasonably acquired high standards, depressed by the play output, confused by wartime problems and a little unhappy because not even a single playwriting genius appeared to comfort them, members of the New York Drama Critics' Circle could find no one drama of American authorship worthy of a citation as the best of the year. These professional playgoers voted, 11 to 6, against any attempt to accept what might be classified as a respectable substitute, and were equally firm in refusing to name a "second best." A critics' theatre is not a people's theatre, by any stretch of the imagination, but I daresay it has its value as a deterrent to crime in playwriting and play producing fields.

The Pulitzer Prize Committee followed the critics' lead, or at least agreed with that body, in refusing to name a "best" American play for the season. The Critics' Circle did find that Noel Coward's "Blithe Spirit" deserved a citation as the best of the plays imported from abroad during the year, and two American dramas were named by a protesting minority content with naming the best of a season's disappointing plays. "In Time to Come," a historical drama concerned with Woodrow Wilson's last fight for a League of Nations, written by Howard Koch, with John Huston serving as a friendly consultant, received four votes, and John Steinbeck's drama of the second World War as it has affected the occupied countries, "The Moon Is Down," was given two votes.

Admitting that, for a variety of very good reasons, this has been an abnormal year in the theatre there were, it seems to me, at least ten plays among the sixty dramas produced that not only provided intelligent entertainment in the theatre but are worthy of inclusion in this volume devoted to the season's record.

Your editor happens to be more deeply interested in the people's theatre than he is in the critics' theatre, believing that the theatre is, and always has been, a people's creation, a people's institution, reflecting social tastes and trends of the times it serves. The theatre has survived through its entertainment rather than because of its messages, but its greater morale-building and progress-stimulating influences are found in the better plays the people endorse and support. In their enthusiasm for leadership, in their pride of discovery, lies the strength and helpfulness of critics of any art form. And in their impatient refusal to conceal their contempt for the equally honest reactions of their potential followers lies their weakness. The human urge to dictate rather than to counsel is doubtless too firmly set in the universal ego to be dislodged. But it is well for playgoers and book readers, and every investigating member of the human family, to remember that it is there.

I have taken, in addition to the controversial "In Time to Come" and "The Moon Is Down," the Coward farce, "Blithe Spirit," which is the best example of what has been classified as "high farce" written the last several years. The Coward item, it seems to me, represents the entertainment value of the theatre quite perfectly.

"Junior Miss," which the Messrs. Jerome Chodorov and Joseph Fields chipped out of Sally Benson's sub-deb stories printed in the *New Yorker* magazine, is another comedy of wide appeal. Any family having enjoyed sub-deb experiences in the home, even any family that has imagined what they might be like, as I suspect the authors and Moss Hart, who staged the play, of doing in part, will find "Junior Miss" to their liking.

Maxwell Anderson had his say about Nazi character in conflict with American courage, and romance, in "Candle in the Wind." Helen Hayes, playing the heroine, served the drama as what is generally referred to as a tower of strength; but the Anderson text, as usual, and the Anderson feeling for character and drama, were helpful.

"Letters to Lucerne" happens to have been, to me, the most appealing of the newer war plays. Neither my colleagues nor any considerable portion of the playgoing public enjoyed the same positive reaction from the play. I suppose the demand for sympathy for an enemy heroine, for all she was an anti-Nazi enemy, had its influence.

"Jason" provides an interesting character study. A drama critic's reactions when he is faced with the problem of writing a fair review of a play authored by an erratic genius who is bent upon seducing his (the critic's) wife, provides the story background. But Samson Raphaelson's study of a critic of the drama who is completely unsympathetic toward practically all the people by whose lives all drama is inspired is the more interesting theme.

Patrick Hamilton's "Angel Street" and Thomas Job's "Uncle

Harry" are plays of the theatre written and staged with exceptional skill. In "Angel Street," which was known as "Gaslight" in London, Mr. Hamilton gained his effects by developing a most perfect suspense. Would the villain succeed in driving his innocent wife insane, or at least in having her committed as being insane, or would he not? For two hours even the most theatre-hardened of audiences sat upright in their seats awaiting the answer.

In Mr. Job's "Uncle Harry" a reverse technique is employed. Within ten minutes of curtain rise the audience knows who the murderer is. From then on its interest is tautly held while the circumstances leading up to the commission of the crime, and the distressful adventures of the murderer trying to break down the circumstantial evidence he had so carefully built up, are painstakingly revealed.

Sophie Treadwell's "Hope for a Harvest" is stronger in purpose than in theatre value. The story of a California that suffered from a gradual deterioration of native character that had made it a leader among the commonwealths, and is again threatened with later infiltrations of "Okies" and well-to-do loafers, is, your editor feels, a story of definite social value. The Treadwell message, as it reached the stage, even with the gifted Fredric and Florence Eldridge March to tell it, was more theatrical than convincing, but it still remains an important message to Americans in any theatre season.

So much for the best plays of a wartime theatre season in the theatrical capital of the country. It is not a record to set even a devoted theatre follower cheering, but it is a fair reflection of the times and the part the theatre played in them. It will, I hope, be of help to theatre historians in that brighter future to which, God helping us, we will fight through.

B. M.

Forest Hills, L. I., 1942.

CONTENTS

	PAGE
INTRODUCTION	v
THE SEASON IN NEW YORK	3
THE SEASON IN CHICAGO	15
THE SEASON IN SAN FRANCISCO	22
THE SEASON IN SOUTHERN CALIFORNIA	27
IN TIME TO COME, BY HOWARD KOCH AND JOHN HUSTON	34
THE MOON IS DOWN, BY JOHN STEINBECK	72
BLITHE SPIRIT, BY NOEL COWARD	109
JUNIOR MISS, BY JEROME CHODOROV AND JOSEPH FIELDS	145
CANDLE IN THE WIND, BY MAXWELL ANDERSON	180
LETTERS TO LUCERNE, BY FRITZ ROTTER AND ALLEN VINCENT	212
JASON, BY SAMSON RAPHAELSON	244
ANGEL STREET, BY PATRICK HAMILTON	282
UNCLE HARRY, BY THOMAS JOB	316
HOPE FOR A HARVEST, BY SOPHIE TREADWELL	349
THE PLAYS AND THEIR AUTHORS	385
PLAYS PRODUCED IN NEW YORK, 1941-42	391
DANCE DRAMA	456
OFF BROADWAY	458
STATISTICAL SUMMARY	462
LONG RUNS ON BROADWAY	463
NEW YORK DRAMA CRITICS' CIRCLE AWARD	464

CONTENTS

	PAGE
Pulitzer Prize Winners	465
Previous Volumes of Best Plays	466
Where and When They Were Born	479
Necrology	490
The Decades' Toll	496
Index of Authors	497
Index of Plays and Casts	501
Index of Producers, Directors and Designers	506

ILLUSTRATIONS

CANDLE IN THE WIND	*Frontispiece*
	FACING PAGE
IN TIME TO COME	36
THE MOON IS DOWN	84
BLITHE SPIRIT	116
JUNIOR MISS	148
LETTERS TO LUCERNE	212
JASON	244
ANGEL STREET	292
UNCLE HARRY	324
HOPE FOR A HARVEST	356

THE BEST PLAYS OF 1941-42

THE BEST PLAYS OF 1941-42

THE SEASON IN NEW YORK

THE tendency of Broadway commentators to juggle superlatives started most of them bragging shortly after the holidays that they were experiencing probably the worst theatre season in all the city's history. They may have been right. A comparison of many factors would be necessary to prove them either right or wrong. In the number of new productions tried the season was ten or twelve plays ahead of the seasons of 1940-41 and 1939-40. But in the matter of quality production it undoubtedly fell quite a ways behind. Wartime is not a time to inspire good creative work. As a result there were many revivals of past successes staged, and there promise to be even more of these next season.

When we arbitrarily closed the books on the theatre season of 1940-41, which was June 15, 1941, there were still sixteen theatre attractions playing on Broadway. Some of these were good, healthy stickers, too, like "Life with Father," which had come down from the season of 1939-40 and promises to go on for another year at least. "My Sister Eileen" and "Arsenic and Old Lace" were also making a run of it, and continued through the new season.

Then there were such items as "Panama Hattie," which ran from October, 1940, to January, 1942. And "The Corn Is Green," which began as far back as November, 1940, and kept Ethel Barrymore working until January, 1942. And "Watch on the Rhine," which began in April, 1941, and ran on until it went to the Coast to be made into a picture in February, 1942. And "Pal Joey," which, with one engagement and another, was here from December, 1940, to November, 1941. For that matter, "Hellzapoppin," having started in September, 1938, did not call it a run until December, 1941, though there were a couple of new editions added to the first bill during that time. Rose Franken's "Claudia," having started in February, 1941, ran a year, or into March, 1942, and then, after a short road tour, came back for another engagement at popular prices. When this record was prepared, Mrs. Franken's comedy was giving every indication of going through its second Summer with no sign of strain.

There was only one real Summer show in 1941—that was "It Happens on Ice" at the Center Theatre, which was reopened after a layoff. With a new cast of principals it ran from July 14, 1941, to April 26, 1942. There were two reopenings of importance in early September—"Lady in the Dark," which finally netted Gertrude Lawrence a total of 467 performances, and the aforementioned "Pal Joey."

The first of the new shows for the new season was Carl Allensworth's "Village Green." Tried successfully in the barn theatres, it was thought its minor weaknesses would be largely overcome by the presence of Frank Craven in the leading rôle. Mr. Craven was able to do a lot, and was notably assisted by his son John in the rôle of the juvenile, but they could not save the comedy. It was closed after thirty performances. Frederick Hazlitt Brennan's "The Wookey" appeared a week later. This was the season's first current war play and was variously received. The bombings of London in the blitz of 1940 were its background, and its sound effects were reproduced from recordings made on the spot by the British Broadcasting company. The effect was more stunning than dramatic. The story of a rebellious tugboat captain who was agin' the war until he was drawn into the retreat from Dunkirk had some little difficulty fighting its way through the noise and the confusion. The English actor, Edmund Gwenn, remembered for his "Laburnum Grove," scored a definite personal hit in the name part. "The Wookey" was played for 134 performances, being withdrawn shortly after our entrance into the war, which served to diminish interest in it.

The first of the escapist comedies was one called "Cuckoos on the Hearth," a completely mad but quite exciting satire on most of the mystery dramas, written by Parker Fennelly. It found a divided public following a divided press report of its attractions as entertainment. Some thought it great, others found it silly. Brock Pemberton, the producer, believed in it sufficiently to nurse it along for 128 performances.

A few more failures and then along came George Abbott's "Best Foot Forward." This one was interesting as a musical comedy, and also because Mr. Abbott had frankly combed the country as far west as Chicago for such youthful talent as would not be subject to the draft or to attacks of war fever for at least two years. His actors were mostly teen-age kids. His authors were John Cecil Holm, who did the book, and two youngsters, Hugh Martin and Ralph Blane, who furnished the music. They, having reached draft age, were shortly in the army or headed that way. The young stars included Maureen Cannon, Nancy Walker, Virginia Schools, Gil Stratton, Jr., and Jack Jordan, Jr., with the slightly more experienced Rosemary Lane of Hollywood to play the lead and Marty May in charge of the comedy. They all made good and "Best Foot Forward" played through the season.

The Theatre Guild thought to try a series of popular-priced revivals, starting with Eugene O'Neill's "Ah, Wilderness," with Harry Cary in the part George Cohan played so long. After a few weeks the Guild directors decided that either their scheme was wrong, or that the Cohan run had exhausted the popularity of this particular comedy and gave up. The Guild tried again, a month later, with Maxwell Anderson's "Candle in the Wind," the Playwrights' Company being joint producers. This serious study of the curse of Hitlerism superimposed upon an American actress' romance disappointed its critics, but, with the help of Helen Hayes, who played the heroine, found and interested a considerable public. After 95 performances in New York the play was taken on tour and played out the season.

Fairly picturesque failures of these early weeks of the season included a racial comedy called "Good Neighbor," backed and staged by Novelist Sinclair Lewis; "Anne of England," a rewriting of an English drama by Norman Ginsbury called "Viceroy Sarah," the new version being by Mary Cass Canfield and Ethel Borden of the upper social brackets, and "The Land Is Bright." With this last George S. Kaufman and Edna Ferber tried to do something to help make present generation Americans conscious of their grafting and greedy ancestors. Their hope, undoubtedly, was that they would inspire a healthy urge for reform with the generation moving into the problem-studded days ahead, but the melodrama got away from them, rather completely smothering the message. There was not enough audience-response to keep their play going after 79 showings.

The comedian, Danny Kaye, who in two seasons had lifted himself from the barn theatre circuit and the lesser nightclubs to the ranking of Broadway's newest favorite, got another big chance in a musicalized version of "Cradle Snatchers" called "Let's Face It." Cole Porter had furnished the songs and lyrics (with interpolations by Sylvia Fine Kaye and Max Liebman), and Vinton Freedley had hand-picked a supporting cast, including Eve Arden, Mary Jane Walsh and Benny Baker. "Let's Face It" turned out to be the season's riot.

Practically the same week George Jessel tried to capitalize the spirit and some of the humors of old-time burlesque in a piece called "High Kickers." Mr. Jessel had the red-hot mamma queen, Sophie Tucker, to help him, and they both worked with a will. But they missed what Michael Todd was able to give much later in the season in "Star and Garter." This was burlesque with a suggestion of class. "High Kickers" was carried through 171 performances, but failed when it took to the road.

A quick failure which some of us regretted, was "The Man with the Blond Hair," Norman Krasna's attempt to explain and stir sympathy for a Nazi war prisoner who had escaped from Canada and tried to hide out with a Jewish family on New York's East Side. After two days this fellow was so touched by the simple humanness of the American way of life that he was ready to pray for the salvation of his fuehrer's soul if not for his defeat. Drama critics, however, would have nothing to do with the idea, counting it preposterously far-fetched, and the play was withdrawn at the close of its first week.

Now came Noel Coward with one of the brightest and gayest of his farce comedies, written admittedly in the hope of taking London playgoers' minds away from the war effort for an hour or two. This was called "Blithe Spirit." It had to do with the complication resulting from the materialization of the spirit of a man's first wife to devil and disturb the home life of his second wife. It proved the comedy hit of the year, and was the only play to be awarded a citation by the New York Drama Critics' Circle. There were, it developed, four stars in the cast: Peggy Wood, Clifton Webb, Leonora Corbett (from England) and Mildred Natwick. They too, at the end of the season, were threatening to go on forever, or at least another year.

That favorite American comedienne, Grace George, was happy in finding a bright little comedy written by Isabel Leighton and Bertram Bloch called "Spring Again." Paired with the stalwart and veteran C. Aubrey Smith, she told the story of the wife of a much-publicized son of a hero. She was able finally to put him in his place without too shattering an effect upon their married life. It was the George performance, supported by those of C. Aubrey Smith and the Jewish comedian, Joseph Buloff, which helped "Spring Again" to the Theatre Club prize as the best play of the year by American authors.

Having been warned that "Macbeth" might prove too gory and war-torn a tragedy for these days, Maurice Evans went right ahead with his preparations for its revival. Again he proved his professional advisers wrong. With Judith Anderson as his Queen,

THE SEASON IN NEW YORK

she being generally accepted as the most impressive Lady Macbeth of recent years, Mr. Evans told the bloody story of the ambitious one for 131 performances in New York, and later met with a fine success on tour. When he brought his season to a close with performances for soldiers in camp, his success there was also great. Mr. Evans, having adopted American citizenship, promises to provide in the classic field a proper leadership for the native theatre for many seasons to come.

Cornelia Otis Skinner, seeking a vote of confidence on her ability as an actress capable of playing a sustained rôle, offered her devoted mono-drama public a glimpse of her as the heroine of a Somerset Maugham story called "Theatre." Guy Bolton whittled the play from the Maugham novel of the same title. Miss Skinner played a wondering actress who adventured in sin as a stimulation to her ego. After 69 performances the actress took her company on tour, further to convince her mid-Western following of her quality. She could not afford to play "Theatre" long, however. Successful though she was, she could make three times as much money with her one-woman show.

Jane Cowl was unhappy in her choice of a comedy called "Ring Around Elizabeth," by Charlotte Armstrong, and gave it up after two weeks. The stage was set for a real hit when "Junior Miss" arrived in mid-November. This comedy was assembled from incidents and characters introduced by Sally Benson in her sub-deb sketches. Jerome Chodorov and Joseph Fields did the assembling with marked cleverness, and the result is adolescent comedy that stirs most audiences to happy approval. You will find a digest of the play in later pages of this volume and some account of the producer's good fortune in finding Patricia Peardon, of the Navy Peardons, to play Judy Graves, the 14-year-old heroine. The fact that Patricia ran away from her career later in the season long enough to get herself duly married did not prevent her continuing this season, at least, to look 14.

The Theatre Guild suffered a failure with Sophie Treadwell's "Hope for a Harvest," despite the fact that Fredric March and Florence Eldridge March played it for them. It proved a purposeful drama builded out of a definite American social problem, and is also included in this volume. Charles Rann Kennedy tried to stir the faithful to a new declaration for Christian socialism with "The Seventh Trumpet," but found the faithful too busy to attend his call. An Italian family comedy, "Walk into My Parlor," written by a student dramatist, Alexander Greendale, was heavy with good character acting. A young actor named Nicholas

Conte contributed part of it. A few weeks later he was tapped for a leading rôle in Raphaelson's "Jason," and is now by way of becoming a leading juvenile. "Walk into My Parlor," however, was withdrawn after thirty performances. "Sunny River," with an attractive score by Sigmund Romberg but a heavy and uninspiring romantic book by Oscar Hammerstein, 2d, gave up after 36 costly performances, the Max Gordon production having been rich to the point of extravagance. (Whatever becomes of the good scores of bad musical comedies, do you suppose?)

"Hellzapoppin" having run its course after three full years, a successor was staged by the Messrs. Olsen and Johnson. "Sons o' Fun," they called this one. It proved a natural offspring of its papas' first collaboration, being filled again with surprises and noise, gags and gadgets, and decorated with Carmen Miranda and a goodly ensemble of dancing and singing beauties.

The surprise dramatic success of the season, as is also more fully related hereafter, was Patrick Hamilton's English melodrama entitled "Angel Street." It had been played in England as "Gaslight," and had been also tried in America in several barn theatres and in Hollywood. Shepard Traube finally raised enough money to bring it to New York. He feared the worst, hoped for the best, and the morning following the opening found himself with a very definite hit to cheer his immediate future. Vincent Price and Judith Evelyn are probably still playing it somewhere.

"Brooklyn, USA," was a murder play that undertook to reveal just how a murder trust managed to survive in that placid city for years, or until a certain courageous district attorney got after it. Exciting, but 57 performances were enough. John Bright and Asa Bordages wrote it.

"Letters to Luzerne," the best of the current war plays to date, it seemed to us, suffered the same handicap that had defeated "The Man with the Blond Hair." It asked sympathy for a representative of the enemy. The play, written by Fritz Rotter and Allen Vincent, was given a fine production by Dwight Deere Wiman, but was withdrawn after three weeks. It was, however, one of the better plays of the season and a digest is included in later pages of this record.

After being away thirteen years, Eddie Cantor came back to Broadway with a musicalized version of "Three Men on a Horse" called "Banjo Eyes." The John Cecil Holm-George Abbott script had been pepped up by a delegation of Mr. Cantor's gagmen, which did not help much. Eddie in person was wildly greeted. He ran on for 128 performances, and only closed then because of a physical backset which sent him to a hospital.

Clifford Odets also came back from the Pacific Coast with a new drama called "Clash by Night." Billy Rose produced it as his first experiment with drama, and Tallulah Bankhead, flanked by Joseph Schildkraut and Lee J. Cobb, played in it. It was a pattern melodrama, however, and even good acting failed to excite sufficient audience interest in it to pay expenses. Six weeks and it was gone.

The story of President Woodrow Wilson's fight for a League of Nations and a reasonably modified and sane Treaty of Versailles, at the close of World War I, reached the stage in a drama called "In Time to Come," written by Howard Koch and John Huston. As historical drama the play was dramatically revealing. As dramatic entertainment it was largely dependent upon the interest of politically informed audiences. Its severest critics admitted that it was an important contribution to the theatre season, but there was a falling off of popular support after five weeks and the drama was withdrawn. "In Time to Come" received four votes in the Drama Critics' Circle search for a play of American authorship worthy its approval, as against eleven tallies for a "no decision" vote.

The Theatre Guild tried again with "Papa Is All," a light domestic comedy about the Pennsylvania Dutch folk, written by Patterson Greene. With Jessie Royce Landis and Carl Benton Reed featured it ran for eight weeks. And again the Guild tried with a revival of "The Rivals," with Walter Hampden, Mary Boland and Bobby Clark, the burlesquer, playing Sir Anthony Absolute, Mrs. Malaprop and mischievous Bob Acres respectively. It was Mr. Clark who produced most of the humor, and consequently most of the business. The Sheridan classic ran on for 53 performances in town and afterward did very well on the road, until Miss Boland was forced out of the cast by illness in Chicago.

A piece about a dramatic critic, of all things, was "Jason," written by Samson Raphaelson, who has had his experiences with the breed. Mr. Raphaelson's critic, however, was a decent and rather interesting type, suffering a bit from a conscious supply of erudition and a slightly abnormal dislike of people. The critics were kind to "Jason," as "Jason" had been to them, and the playgoers developed quite an interest in him. He lasted for 125 performances.

A happy inspiration on the part of Cheryl Crawford was that of reviving the George Gershwin-DuBose Heyward operetta,

"Porgy and Bess." With a cast headed by the Todd Duncan and Anne Brown of the original cast, and a popular-price standard of prices, "Porgy and Bess" proved one of the outstanding hits of the year. It was still booming along in midsummer.

In "Cafe Crown" H. S. Kraft dramatized the lives and activities of a group of Yiddish actors who frequent a famous Yiddish restaurant on Second Avenue, New York. It was strong in its exposure of racial group comedy and of sufficiently wide appeal to please many audiences, thanks in no small part to the work of Sam Jaffe and Morris Carnovsky in leading rôles. Ben Hecht, novelist and scenarist extraordinary, tried a dramatization of one of his own short stories having to do with the spirits of certain cadavers picked up by the city guardians and deposited at the morgue. It proved a sometimes fascinating, sometimes depressingly gruesome tale of a ghostly missionary meeting that revealed the sordid lives and inner spiritual promptings of dispossessed and outcast humans. "Lily of the Valley" won little support from the press and was withdrawn after a week's trial.

"Solitaire," a story of a sweetly precocious child and a human but frustrated "okie," brought Patricia Hitchcock, the 12-year-old daughter of Alfred Hitchcock, Hollywood director, to the New York stage for her Broadway debut. Patricia was a promising success, but the play, though written by John Van Druten and handsomely staged by Dwight Deere Wiman, was a little too close to the theatre and a little too artificially removed from life, to satisfy its audiences. Mr. Wiman withdrew it after three weeks.

Katina Paxinou, a leader of the Greek theatre, decided to employ a new translation of Henrik Ibsen's "Hedda Gabler" for her American debut. This was presumably a simplification of former translations and was made by Ethel Borden and Mary Cass Canfield. It did not appear to add to the attractions of the play or character, but it did fit admirably the sultry and lightly repellent characterization of Miss Paxinou. The reviews were friendly but the public response was not.

Less than a month after Pearl Harbor the Boston Opera Company, a new organization of young people devoted to Gilbert and Sullivan, was singing "The Mikado." They were particular to change the lyric to read "We are *gangsters* of Japan," and this gave the audience an excuse to applaud rather than to hiss. It was an organization of pleasant voices, including those of Kathleen and Mary Roche, Margaret Roy and Morton Bowe, with veterans Florenz Ames, Bertram Peacock and Robert Pitkin to serve as professional ballast.

Marc Connelly wrote and staged a little drama of exalted purpose called "The Flowers of Virtue" (which are bound to bloom, even in a scorched-earth world), with Frank Craven again hopefully trying to build a weak leading rôle into one of commanding importance. This was the story of a tired American business man who seeks relaxation in deepest Mexico and runs into the conspiracy of a small-time Hitler trying to enslave his townsmen. The author's approach was timid and the result disappointing and regrettable.

The American Youth Theatre, helped out by Alexander Cohen, cooked up a topical revue which they called "Of V We Sing." Spotted with new talent, produced with a great deal of native enthusiasm, the young folk managed to play 76 performances. A misguided trio of authors and Sam Grisman thought to popularize a farce, "They Should Have Stood in Bed." This one attracted some attention to its title, derived from a sporting character's lament for having got up to attend a business conference that worked out badly, but none to its entertainment. Toni Canzoneri, one-time champ, played a bit part.

"Heart of a City" came from London. It was a realistic melodrama of the war written by Lesley Storm. It drew its inspiration from reactions of the theatrical troupe that bravely played "the little Windmill Theatre off Shaftesbury Avenue" all through the 1940 blitzing of London. It was well staged and directed by Gilbert Miller, and well played by a company headed by Gertrude Musgrove, a likable English actress; Margot Grahame and Richard Ainley, also from the other side; Beverly Roberts and Lloyd Gough, Bertha Belmore and Dennis Hoey. It wasn't a popular realism, that of a bombed city, and four weeks' uncertain trade was all the support it got.

Still another war drama, and the most fantastic of the lot, was called "Plan M," written by James Edward Grant of the movies. In this the German High Command substituted one of its own men for the head of the war office in London, and thus eased the way for an invasion of England which was thwarted in the end barely in the nick of time. More excitement than sense. Gone in a week.

A pleasant surprise hit sneaked in in late February. This was "Guest in the House." It was written by two Hollywood writers, Hagar Wilde and Dale Eunson, and produced by Stephen and Paul Ames, who were new to this business. The reviews were more encouraging than discouraging, but not too good. Yet

"Guest in the House," thanks to the boldly played characterization of a thoroughly unlovely brat of a heroine, ran on and on for 129 performances. Mary Anderson, also new to Broadway, was the brat. Audiences were not thrilled, but they were interested.

Cheryl Crawford had found audiences in Dennis, Mass., and Maplewood, N. J., greatly interested in her revival of Sir James M. Barrie's "A Kiss for Cinderella," with Luise Rainer in the rôle that Maude Adams played twenty-six years ago for more than 150 performances on Broadway and a season or two on tour. Miss Crawford, figuring that audiences are really much alike wherever you find them, brought "A Kiss for Cinderella" to Broadway. Here the reaction was practically the reverse of what it had been in the rural centers. Barrie's sentimental tale of the drudge and the London bobby in the last war was politely kidded out of the theatre, and that was that. Audience interest, however, did hold it for 48 performances.

Then came a sudden drive of vaudeville. Clifford C. Fischer, late of the Moulin Rouge, had an idea the time was ripe for a good vaudeville show. Lee Shubert, having empty theatres, agreed with him. Fischer organized one with Lou Holtz, Willie Howard, Phil Baker and Paul Draper as its four headliners, filled in with a variety of acrobats, musicians and such and announced "Priorities of 1942." There was a schedule of popular prices, a dollar top at the matinees, $2 at night performances. Public response was immediate and enthusiastic. Immediately Mr. Fischer decided the time was even riper than he had imagined and organized a second bill, this one headed by Victor Moore, William Gaxton, Hildegarde and the Hartmans. For one reason and another this bill, called "Keep 'Em Laughing," never quite caught up with the first, so there was an injection of new names—Gracie Fields, England's most popular music hall queen; Argentinita, the dancer; A. Robins, the banana clown; Al Trahan and others. This one was entitled "Keep 'Em Laughing." Still "Priorities" continued to lead the way.

The season was edging toward its close, and a lot of experiments were being tried. Showmen were convinced that with war-time organization of cantonments within reaching distance of Broadway; with gasoline being rationed and tires hard to get, this would prove an unusual theatre summer in New York. They were right.

"Johnny 2 x 4," a tough little melodrama of speakeasy days, found a limited public interested in night clubs and the lower

THE SEASON IN NEW YORK

cafe society brackets. It ran for eight weeks. "Nathan the Wise," which had been produced by the Students Theatre of the School for Social Research in Twelfth Street, was brought uptown to the Belasco for an additional four weeks.

John Steinbeck's dramatization of his own best-selling novel, "The Moon Is Down," seemed a most promising entrant for a summer run. Oscar Serlin, having invested a part of his "Life with Father" profits in the play, brought it to the Martin Beck. The reviews, as more fully appears in other pages, were mixed, the public's support uncertain. After fighting valiantly for the play for nine weeks Mr. Serlin decided this was not the season for it.

The Theatre Guild's final production of the season was that of Emlyn Williams' "Yesterday's Magic," a London success. Paul Muni came on from Hollywood to play the rôle of an old English actor who is protected by a crippled daughter, played by Jessica Tandy. Again it was a question of whether exceptional performances by gifted actors could save a fairly obvious and frankly sentimental theatre piece. The actors lost. Came a bad stretch of weather after seven weeks and "Yesterday's Magic" was sent to the storehouse for the Summer.

And now, as late as April 27, came the happiest event of all the sad new year. Sponsored by the American Theatre Wing War Service Katharine Cornell and Guthrie McClintic revived Bernard Shaw's "Candida" with what proved to be the greatest cast that stalwart comedy has ever been given—Miss Cornell in the name part, Raymond Massey playing Morell, Burgess Meredith the poet Marchbanks, Mildred Natwick the Prossy, Dudley Digges the Burgess and Stanley Mill the curate. The town's upper bracket playgoers, led by the play reviewers, were practically ecstatic. They had been patiently waiting all season for just one play and production worth cheering for, and here it was. The revival had been made for the benefit of the Army and Navy relief agencies and for special matinees only. Extensions were prayed for. Private Meredith's leave was extended. The play went on for another two weeks. And then for a week in Washington. The cheering continued until finally the close came when Massey and Digges both had to fill picture assignments.

Not much after that. Ed Sullivan and Noble Sissle organized a "Harlem Cavalcade" to take advantage of the turn to vaudeville. Their all Negro revue got 51 performances. There were two or three quick failures in late April and early May—a Brooklyn Dodgers play, "The Life of Reilly," by William Roos;

a comedy called "The Walking Gentleman," by Grace Perkins and Fulton Oursler, with Victor Francen; a Scotch "Wookey" called "The Strings, My Lord, Are False," by Paul Vincent Carroll.

Then a fair hit, Thomas Job's "Uncle Harry," with Eva Le Gallienne and Joseph Schildkraut renewing an acting partnership that they first enjoyed when they played "Liliom" for the Theatre Guild in 1926. This unusually interesting murder play ran well into the summer, stirring the hope that Miss Le Gallienne would find the urge and the money later to revive her Civic Repertory enterprise.

The last play of the season, counting the seasons as extending from one June 15 to another, was "By Jupiter," a musicalization of Julian Thompson's comedy "The Warrior's Husband" skillfully wrought by Lorenz Hart and Robert Rodgers. Ray Bolger was the star of "By Jupiter," playing the sissie Sapiens to the Amazonian Pomposia of Bertha Belmore, the Hippolyta of Benay Venuta and the Antiope of Constance Moore, a newcomer from the screen who was away to a flying start with this first Broadway assignment. Antiope, it will be recalled, was also the part that sent Katharine Hepburn flying out to the coast and a career as a movie star in 1931.

Because of war conditions previously mentioned, the summer promised to be much more active than any Broadway had known for some years. This promise, at the hour of skipping with this manuscript to the printer's, was being generously realized.

THE SEASON IN CHICAGO

By Cecil Smith
Drama Critic of the *Chicago Tribune*

IT is remarkable, and not a little shocking, to discover at each season's end how little the Chicago stage changes its habits and outlook from year to year. The differences between 1940-41 and the succeeding season of 1941-42 were primarily statistical in nature; the general structure of theatre business in the nation's second city remained virtually as it has been for the past ten years. Since the bank closings of 1932, when the theatres took a drubbing from which some never recovered, the city has subsisted on a minimum diet. Not more than six professional plays were ever on view at one time during the season which closed officially on May 31, 1942, and it was only during four weeks of the year that as many as six legitimate theatres were open.

During the year the face of Chicago's scattered Rialto underwent one major, and painful, operation. On June 14, 1941, the historic Auditorium Theatre on Congress Street closed its doors forever. The irony of the gods dictated that "Hellzapoppin" should be the last entertainment to light a house which gloried in more than a half century's memories of Patti, Caruso, Toscanini, Galli-Curci, Garden, Muzio and Chaliapin, of Duse, Pavlowa, Danilova and Massine. For a few months a listless "Save the Auditorium" campaign received some lip service, but after Pearl Harbor it became all too tragically apparent that the requisite $400,000 would have to be devoted to other more immediately compelling purposes. Nearly a year after the final performance of "Hellzapoppin" in the old house, the furnishings from backstage and out front were sold at public auction, and it was depressing to discover how few nostalgic bidders put in an appearance.

An important managerial transfer took place on July 1, 1941, when the Grand Opera House, which has a history almost as long and colorful as that of the Auditorium, passed from the control of the Shubert constellation back into the hands of the Hamlin estate, which originally built the theatre. For two years previously the theatre, which had prospered enormously in the days when it was known as Cohan's Grand, had been having hard sledding under the management of Sam Gerson, who operated it under some working arrangement, never too clearly defined in the public mind, with the Shuberts. Although the management representing the Hamlin estate redecorated the house handsomely, its year was anything but a success, for the United Booking office preferred to grant its most potent attractions to the established managements of the Selwyn, Harris and Erlanger Theatres. All three of these houses accordingly rolled up an exceptionally consistent record of occupancy, while the Grand was shuttered more than half the time.

The Blackstone Theatre, a handsome house which had been rescued from oblivion by the 66-week engagement of "Life with Father" which ended in May, 1941, remained empty until March. At that time a mildly successful return engagement of "Papa Is All" brought the theatre back into the active list, and the subsequent sensational success of "Good Night, Ladies" has undoubtedly re-established the Blackstone as a theatre popular enough to be attractive to bookers. The Studebaker and the Great Northern, both seriously in need of renovation in every department of decoration and equipment, cannot be said to have been satisfactorily restored to public favor, despite intermittent engagements in both theatres. The big Majestic, once the home of vaudeville, musical comedy and operetta, still looms dark and silent in its inconvenient Monroe Street location.

As has been the case for many years now, Chicago continues to be almost wholly dependent upon Broadway for all its desirable professional theatrical attractions. Two attempts at local production were made during the past season, and both failed abysmally. Lee Sloan and Clyde Elliott, taking a lease on the Great Northern Theatre, presented three unprofitable plays with mediocre casts before they became convinced that Chicago did not appreciate their efforts. For their opening lure, the ill-advised producers chose to present Jack Norworth in "Village Green," the New Hampshire comedy which had expired in New York only a few weeks earlier, for easily demonstrable reasons. This they followed with one of the most revolting farces of the past 25 years, the title of which—"Let's Have a Baby"—may give a sufficient explanation of my reticence in recounting the details of its subject matter. The obituary of this season was written by "Take My Advice," an ancient college wheeze farce which had been seen on Broadway many years ago, and which was advertised in Chicago with undated New York press quotations.

The second attempt at local production was an even sorrier

affair. Charles K. Freeman, who had presented a highly creditable performance of "Girls in Uniform" a number of years ago, brought together a home-written and home-acted musical revue, to which he gave the rather provocative title of "American Sideshow." The material was puerile, however, and so was the acting. After two performances "American Sideshow" was closed by Actors' Equity, since Mr. Freeman had grossly violated union rules in engaging his cast.

Chicago has a way, from time to time, of establishing surprise hits of its own, which sometimes fail when they are taken to New York later. John Barrymore's charade called "My Dear Children" was a typical case in point. The Spring of 1942 brought another quasi-phony Chicago hit into the national spotlight. From the west coast two little known producers, Howard Lang and Al Rosen, brought a rewritten and resexed version of the ancient Avery Hopwood farce, "Ladies' Night" (in a Turkish Bath). Retaining the general structure of the second act Turkish bath scene, the producers hired Cyrus Wood to create up-to-date dialogue and a variety of fresh situations. They engaged Buddy Ebsen and Skeets Gallagher, both expert practitioners of farce, and surrounded them with a small galaxy of astoundingly attractive Hollywood lovelies.

On the opening night of "Good Night, Ladies" Claudia Cassidy of the *Chicago Sun*, the city's only feminine reviewer, was fortunate in finding a conflicting engagement. The male instincts of the press were suitably aroused, and the first night performance, which was incontrovertibly extremely funny once the stylistic premises of the play were accepted, won a handsomely innuendo-filled batch of notices. The farce caught on at once, and entered into a Summer of sellout business. Miss Cassidy finally went to see it, and quite properly held out against the mass opinion of the male critics.

While "Good Night, Ladies" might bore a New York audience, on the other hand it might not, considering the success of various hokey revivals of vaudeville. To the credit of the producers, it must be said that they were shrewd enough to stage their production without any trace of shoddy economy, and—more remarkable still—that they did not hire a single beauty who did not possess at least a reasonable modicum of talent for acting and characterization. Indeed, the play probably owes its continuing business to the fact that it is more expertly presented than one might normally expect.

Four other plays with immediate Broadway aspirations were

tried out in Chicago. Only two—Cornelia Otis Skinner in Guy Bolton's transcription of Somerset Maugham's "Theatre," and the Theatre Guild production of "Papa Is All," reached New York. Charles Butterworth, seeking a stage comeback, appeared rather monotonously as an over-age telegraph messenger in a frail but not entirely unattractive farce named "Western Union, Please." It lasted a week. Later on another week of the season was graced by the presence of "They Can't Get You Down," an "intimate" musical comedy originating on the west coast, with the name of Dwight Deere Wiman inexplicably linked to the production. Its score was by Jay Gorney, who wrote the music for "Meet the People." But unfortunately the entire book of "They Can't Get You Down" contained about as much essential material as one sketch from the none too brilliant "Meet the People."

It has always been Chicago's fate to see a good many second companies in the reigning New York successes. Sometimes, as in the cases of "Life with Father," "Arsenic and Old Lace" and "My Sister Eileen" these second companies will stand comparison with the New York originals; indeed, Effie Afton in the Chicago company of "My Sister Eileen," which came back for a return engagement, is the best Ruth I have seen, not excluding the excellent Shirley Booth.

Four concurrent New York attractions were given in Chicago by second companies, in addition to "Arsenic and Old Lace" and "My Sister Eileen," which held over into the season we are considering. The first of these was "Hellzapoppin," which got along perfectly well with Eddie Garr and Billy House as its comics, though nobody in his right mind would compare the quality of their teamwork with that of Olsen and Johnson, who are past masters, whatever you think of their material.

After a much publicized still hunt for a young actress to take over the title rôle, John Golden, with the blessing of Rose Franken, the author, settled upon a newcomer named Phyllis Thaxter as the heroine of the Chicago company of "Claudia." I shall have to see Miss Thaxter in other assignments before I can allay my suspicion that she is not a completely schooled actress, but her natural attributes suited her to the part of Claudia, and her performance won many friends for her. Except for Marguerite Namara, who made a wonderfully splashy thing out of the prima donna character, and the excellent players in the servant rôles, the Chicago "Claudia" company was not the equal of the New York original.

In the case of "Blithe Spirit," the discrepancy between Chicago

THE SEASON IN CHICAGO

and New York performances was much greater. Even though I found Estelle Winwood's portrait of Madame Arcati much waftier and infinitely more amusing than Mildred Natwick's, and though Carol Goodner's second wife was at least as deftly conceived as Peggy Wood's, the general aspect of the ensemble was rather crude. The opening night was quite good in pace, and possessed the requisite light touch. When I returned a week or so later, however, the performance had already taken on a horrid road company obviousness, with Dennis King in particular working unashamedly for laughs. Then, too, the casting of Annabella as the spirit was a singularly unhappy mischance, for her inability to grasp an English drawing room style of delivery left her lines inert and sometimes even meaningless. The engagement of "Blithe Spirit" closed abruptly in May, and it was rumored that John C. Wilson, the producer, who had come out from New York, posted a closing notice as soon as he had seen a performance. Producers and stage directors should see their plays in Chicago much more frequently. They often lose thousands of dollars, simply because they do not realize that the performance has departed grievously from its original direction.

The Chicago company of "Angel Street" was considerably better than that of "Blithe Spirit," but it was still no match for the one in New York. Neither Victor Jory nor Sylvia Sidney really projected the eerie psychopathic horror which Vincent Price and Judith Evelyn are able to create so marvelously. Ernest Cossart, however, was a delight as the garrulous detective. The remarkable lighting effects, of course, were handled just as effectively in Chicago as in New York. But Chicago did not patronize "Angel Street" generously, and it lasted only eight weeks.

Some other plays, which had finished their New York careers, came to Chicago with important cast changes. "Mr. and Mrs. North," too frothy a piece to attain a long run, was most agreeably acted by Anita Louise, who seems to have real talent to go along with her looks, and Owen Davis, Jr., in his last assignment before entering military service. In "Panama Hattie" the replacement of Ethel Merman with Frances Williams was hurtful, since Miss Williams' old-fashioned type of extroversion does not jibe with Cole Porter's sophisticated style. Likewise "Pal Jocy" would have profited from the presence of Gene Kelly, though George Tapps danced well and made a creditable attempt at characterization. And then there was Phil Baker's attempt to make a go of "Charley's Aunt," back in July, 1941—an attempt which failed partly, I am sure, because of the searing heat in the uncooled Studebaker Theatre.

The Theatre Guild's revival of "The Rivals" provided some of the most animated incidents of the year. After two performances Mary Boland, the Mrs. Malaprop, left the cast abruptly and without warning, taking the train to California. She claimed that she had to leave because of illness. Since she refused to let a doctor appointed by Actors' Equity examine her, however, the Theatre Guild posted charges with Equity, charging Miss Boland with unprofessional conduct. In due season the case was closed fairly amicably, and the unsubstantiated, off-the-record charge was forgotten, to the effect that Miss Boland was aroused to anger because Bobby Clark received the lion's share of critical notice.

Upon Miss Boland's departure the understudy, Rosalind Ivan, took over the rôle of Mrs. Malaprop until the last night of the fortnight's engagement in Chicago. On the closing night Margaret Anglin demonstrated her resources of imagination and style, but unhappily kept forgetting her lines.

Some of the greatest acclaim of the season was awarded to Herman Shumlin's fine productions of "The Corn Is Green," with Ethel Barrymore and Richard Waring, and "Watch on the Rhine," with Paul Lukas and the rest of the New York cast. In the cast of both plays, however, Mr. Shumlin wounded Chicago's sensibilities by assuming that public support would be short-lived. Because of an inflexible touring schedule, both plays left the city before thousands of potential customers had been able to secure tickets.

In sum total, 31 plays of professional or allegedly professional caliber were presented in Chicago between June 1, 1941, and May 31, 1942. They may be classified as follows:

Dramas (5)—"Native Son," with Canada Lee; "The Corn Is Green"; "Candle in the Wind," with Helen Hayes; "Watch on the Rhine"; "Angel Street" (second company).

Comedies and farces (12)—"My Sister Eileen" (second company; held over from previous season; closed in September, 1941; returned in May, 1942, for second engagement at reduced prices); "Arsenic and Old Lace" (second company; held over from previous season); "Claudia" (second company); "Theatre"; "Western Union, Please"; "Mr. and Mrs. North" (touring company); "Village Green"; "Let's Have a Baby"; "Papa Is All"; "Take My Advice"; "Blithe Spirit" (second company); 'Good Night, Ladies."

Musical entertainments (7)—"Hellzapoppin" (second company; held over from previous season); "Louisiana Purchase"; "Pal Joey"; "Panama Hattie"; "They Can't Get You Down"; "American Sideshow"; "High Kickers."

Revivals of all kinds (7)—"Charley's Aunt," with Phil Baker; "The Doctor's Dilemma," with Katharine Cornell; "Blossom Time"; "The Student Prince"; "The Rivals"; "Macbeth," with Maurice Evans and Judith Anderson; "Accent on Youth," with Sylvia Sidney and Luther Adler.

The 22-week run of "Claudia" was the season's longest. By May 31, 1942, "My Sister Eileen" had played in Chicago for 35 weeks, but a large part of the total belongs to the record of 1940-41. "Good Night, Ladies," which is still playing as these paragraphs are written, may finally achieve a very long run, and the return engagement of "My Sister Eileen," also still in progress, gives evidence of considerable future prosperity. "Louisiana Purchase" was the leading musical, with 14 weeks to its credit. "Blithe Spirit" also ran for 14 weeks.

With a total playing time of 178¾ weeks, the overall tenancy of Chicago theatres fell slightly under the 1940-41 total of 191 weeks. It should be noted, however, that "Life with Father" alone accounted for 51 weeks in that season. Six more professional productions were seen in Chicago in 1941-42 than in the previous season.

Semi-professional and tributary theatre activity in Chicago did not flourish on a particularly praiseworthy level, with the single exception of a group known as the Actors Company of Chicago. This organization, which has a little theatre on the fourth floor of a Wabash Avenue office building, gave an exceptionally fine performance of Lillian Hellman's "The Children's Hour," which had not been produced in Chicago before. Under the direction of Minnie Galatzer, the acting approaches desirable professionalism more closely than that of any sub-professional group Chicago has possessed for a number of seasons.

THE SEASON IN SAN FRANCISCO

By Fred Johnson
Drama Editor, *The Call-Bulletin*

MIDWAY in their theatrical year, going to the theatre took on a new meaning for San Franciscans, differing for a geographical reason from the mental state of show-goers in other parts of the nation.

This condition of mind, as they looked across the footlights, was the same as elsewhere in the country-wide realization there was a bigger show going on in the shape of a world war, that December 7 was a date dividing the theatrical season in half and that the remembrance of Pearl Harbor had altered the course of show business, with disturbing effect on the minds of producers, managers and audiences alike.

But there was this difference: At this western extremity of the touring road the Spring of 1942 brought early signs of transportation difficulties for traveling companies—a scarcity of baggage cars at different points en route and uncertainty as to the class of accommodations a troupe would draw on its return journey.

Following a lean year in the number of Broadway and other touring attractions to reach this destination, the amusement prospect became still more discouraging to impresarios and patrons, who had been given promise of visitations by several of the long-awaited New York hits that had taken to the road.

The obvious vulnerability of this coast in the event of enemy attack was soon evident in the managerial mind, besides the thought of increasing obstacles to normal touring.

Later on, nervousness grew with the accepted belief San Francisco would be target No. 1 in a Japanese foray. And then came the first blackouts, descending on jittery audiences already in theatres and bringing the decision of potential theatre-goers that for a time, at least, they would venture less from their homes in search of entertainment. With decreasing alarm from the fewer ensuing alerts over the sight of planes that proved to be friendly, play-going in San Francisco returned to better than normal, despite the new obstacle of a rubber shortage, and an influx of service men figured conspicuously among the audiences.

The season became notable before the beginning of Summer

for its return of long-run engagements, with such wanted attractions as "My Sister Eileen" and "Life with Father" filling adjoining theatres for periods remindful of pre-depression days.

War and its blackouts took their first serious toll of the theatre in a casualty suffered by the redoubtable Henry Duffy and his historic Alcazar Playhouse, to which he had returned in the Spring of 1941 with a series of revivals and newer plays employing Hollywood stars and excellent supporting casts.

Beginning with Edward Everett Horton in "Springtime for Henry" and Billie Burke in "The Vinegar Tree," he had gone into the current season with Francis Lederer in "No Time for Comedy," with Rose Hobart and Doris Dudley as other principals; Joe E. Brown and Helen Chandler in "The Show-Off"; Dale Winter and Minna Gombell in "Quiet Please"; Otto Kruger, Ruth Matteson and Marjorie Lord in "The Male Animal" and Taylor Holmes in "The Man Who Came to Dinner."

All these were well patronized for satisfying runs with the exception of "Quiet Please," one of the four comedies of Hollywood life that had failed of success in the preceding Broadway season. There was hopefulness among the old Alcazar followers, and with good reason, that the house would be restored to its one time stability, as Duffy had chosen plays and casts that met with high favor.

But the war was yet to be reckoned with. Its alarms fell upon audiences during the run of "Patricia," a musical version of Duffy's old comedy hit, "The Patsy," and blackouts closed the play soon after December 7. A return engagement early in the new year failed to pick up where it had left off.

But Katharine Cornell was not to be dispossessed in any such fashion. Her engagement in "The Doctor's Dilemma" was one week old at the Curran when Pearl Harbor and its aftermath affected the theatre—with no defeat for this attraction, which continued playing to near-capacity for another six days without blackout hindrance.

Show world curiosity, however, then centered on the likelihood of her continuance with plans for the San Francisco premiere of her new Henri Bernstein play, "Rose Burke," scheduled for January 19. But after a desert vacation with Guthrie McClintic during the holidays and rehearsals under McClintic, with Bernstein in attendance, the curtain went up before critics and audience in pleased agreement over virtuoso performances by the star, Philip Merivale, Doris Dudley and Jeanne-Pierre Aumont, and as firmly agreed over the vehicle's discursiveness and general inadequacy.

A few nights later, darkness was officially decreed for the town if not the theatre, less than an hour before curtain time. But Miss Cornell found her way on foot through the blackened streets, joined others of the company and played before an audience of some 300 souls who had been early in reaching the theatre. Two weeks of fair patronage were credited mainly to magic of the Cornell name.

Early in the season Eugene O'Neill's "Anna Christie" was given an excellent presentation by the Hollywood-based Selznick Company under direction of John Houseman and Alfred de Liagre, Jr., Miss Bergman, interrupting her screen assignments for an impressive performance, was supported by J. Edward Bromberg, Jessie Busley and Damion O'Flynn for a fortnight's satisfying business.

Despite the absence from its cast of Olsen and Johnson, then filming their extravaganza in Hollywood, "Hellzapoppin" played three weeks to capacity, with Eddie Garr and Billy House as substitute stars. "Tobacco Road" made another successful return visit, again with John Barton and advertised as playing its farewell engagement here. The Katherine Dunham Dancers won raves in a single performance and returned for a less profitable single night. Magician Dante's "Sim Sala Bim" revue was a novelty show of surprising success, but Ruth Draper's return in character sketches lacked the usual support, presumably due to her repetition of sketches seen here during the last decade.

"Blossom Time," starring Everett Marshall, was again well received. Then "Good Night, Ladies," Cyrus Wood's rewrite of Avery Hopwood's "Ladies' Night in a Turkish Bath," made its sexy appeal to the town in exciting stages of undress by a flock of Hollywood starlets, featuring Buddy Ebsen and Skeets Gallagher. The critics' jibes, also conveying the word of this pulchritudinous exhibit, had the effect of packing the Curran for five weeks, which would not have ended the run but for an opening date in Chicago, where it fuller had opportunity for its record-breaking capacity.

The Geary Theatre, adjoining the Curran, was given over to road-show motion pictures until early Autumn, when Ethel Waters, a favorite in "Cabin in the Sky" and other San Francisco appearances, returned in a successful revival of "Mamba's Daughters," supported by Vincent Price and Fredi Washington. "My Sister Eileen," with Marcy Wescott, Effie Afton, Philip Loeb and

Guy Robertson, was first of the Broadway successes to entertain eager audiences, doing so well in its four weeks' Geary Theatre run that it returned from Hollywood for an added stay of five weeks at the Curran.

Meanwhile "Life with Father," co-starring Percy Waram and Margalo Gillmore, began its final touring engagement of the season at the Geary, extending to twelve weeks—a new long-run mark in recent years for this city. The company was engaged here while Louis Calhern and Dorothy Gish were teaming at Hollywood in the same vehicle.

Closing the San Francisco theatrical season as usual, the civic light opera associations of this city and Los Angeles wound up its most successful year with "Bitter Sweet," starring Muriel Angelus and John Howard; "The Vagabond King," with Bob Lawrence, Dorothy Sandlin, Marthe Errolle and Robert Stanford; "Hit the Deck," with Joan Roberts, June Preisser, Frank Albertson and Eddie Foy, Jr., and "Music in the Air," starring John Charles Thomas, Irra Petina, Francis Lederer, Al Shean and Fritz Leiber.

In early Winter another attempt was made to revive music at the historic Tivoli Theatre—home of Tetrazzini and other opera stars of the past. A civic light opera committee, briefly confused in some minds with the similar organization presenting the regular Spring festival, put on "The Firefly" and "The Merry Widow," but this project also met the fate of a literal blackout in mid-December. As the season ended it was followed in by "Varieties of 1942," a girl and vaudeville extravaganza, under the aegis of Homer Curran, of the theatre bearing his name.

Despite the uncertainty of touring conditions, there were in prospect, as Summer opened, the arrival of "Claudia," "Arsenic and Old Lace" and "Watch on the Rhine." Meanwhile Shipstad and Johnson's "Ice Follies of 1942" was filling in the entertainment void.

A single Summer theatre season outside the city was planned for the second year by the Del Monte Playhouse on the grounds of that resort at Monterey, under Equity rules. The opening bill was to be Francis Swann's comedy, "Out of the Frying Pan," followed by "Mr. and Mrs. North."

The Stanford (University) Players, under the direction of Hubert Heffner, was active during the year, with productions of "Marco Millions," "Knickerbocker Holiday," "Beggar's Opera" and "He Who Gets Slapped."

The University of California Little Theatre ("without a theatre") carried on in Wheeler Hall, with a new and closer affiliation with the university drama department in its directorial end and with productions still under the associated student body.

San Francisco's most enduring repertory theatre, The Wayfarers, again highlighted the season with its usual Shakespearean presentations. And the Berkeley Playmakers, in its eighteenth year, gave first productions of numerous one-act plays, besides launching a barnstorming division for the entertainment of service men at near-by posts. A national playwriting competition was opened, with William Saroyan as one of the judges, to obtain short plays suitable for soldier audiences.

THE SEASON IN SOUTHERN CALIFORNIA

By Edwin Schallert
Drama Editor of the *Los Angeles Times*

THE theatrical grab-bag—it was essentially that during 1941-42—yielded varied and odd contributions to add to the show world chronicle through the years in Southern California. Needless to say, in view of everything that happened—or didn't happen—in New York during the erratic twelve months, it wasn't an especially good season on the West Coast either. It wouldn't be fair, possibly, to say it was the worst, but the approach was close to depression times, and in those days there was at least more order about the enterprises that did come to fruition.

The public seemed but fitfully responsive to the attractions of even the best entertainment during 1941-42. It was a public, of course, that had the war on its mind almost continuously from December 7. To its imagination the menace sometimes seemed close to Pacific shores, again very remote. The first blackouts, and particularly the one when Coast guns actually boomed away at something supposedly in the Los Angeles area, were conducive to an abnormal excitement, which wasn't helpful to the theatrical business in any department. A greater sense of security prevailed after the initial baptisms, but it tended to waver whenever the news was not too favorable.

"Life with Father," in its engagement under Oscar Serlin supervision at the Music Box, was undoubtedly as good a barometer as any of popular interest in the stage. After many fits, starts and sputterings that made it look as if the play would close in about 10 or 12 weeks, it seemed finally to settle down to a run. Question of whether this run might compare with such offerings as "Abie's Irish Rose," "White Collars" and the musical entertainment, "Meet the People," was in abeyance at the close of the season, but the engagement was constantly being extended. There were hopes and expectations that it might bridge the dull spaces after the cream of theatre attendants was skimmed off, and that the populace in general would be drawn in large numbers to the attraction as its engagement continued.

Louis Calhern and Dorothy Gish of the so-called Boston company, which had gone touring, were the main principals in a cast that was also graced by the presence of the poet, Charles Hanson Towne, as the Episcopalian divine, and the company was unusually good throughout, the younger group appealing. It was a competent production, the only thing seriously missing being the rare atmosphere of the old Empire Theatre of the eastern Broadway.

Miss Gish's performance as Vinnie compared very favorably with Dorothy Stickney in the same rôle. Calhern gave a creditable delineation of the male parent of the title, though this writer inclines to Howard Lindsay in the same rôle. Miss Gish unfortunately had to leave the cast before the run was completed and her place was taken by Viola Frayne, but this young actress suffered no lack of approval for her work by those who viewed this part of the engagement.

"My Sister Eileen" did better than originally programed. Its run stretched several weeks beyond the normal fortnight, and it was rated a good popular hit. Here curiously enough was a show more local to New York by far than "Life with Father," yet it had sophisticated comedy elements which seemed to delight the audiences which viewed the play. Its run, of course, did not compare with "Life with Father," and was accomplished by cutting the price for seats during the later days of its residence.

Of the plays selected by Burns Mantle as the best during the 1941-42 season, none has showed up since its premiere in New York. "Angel Street" was seen in Hollywood briefly under the title "Gaslight" during 1940-41, and must be considered a different affair from the western offering, with the one exception that Judith Evelyn acted in the Coast production, ere she gained her terrific success in New York. The character of the staging, plus the novelty of the event, which apparently was unrecognized in a film colony theatre, proved vitalizing forces in the eastern debut of this period thriller by Patrick Hamilton. Basically, it was the same play, though, and was rather well carried out in its California incarnation.

On the horizon as the 1941-42 annum ended were glimmering some Mantle selections for the 1940-41 season, like "Claudia," with Dorothy McGuire; "Arsenic and Old Lace" and "Watch on the Rhine" with main members of the original Manhattan casts. Strictly speaking these belong to the Southern California season of 1942-43. "My Sister Eileen" was of the 1940-41 vintage, and "Life with Father" of 1939-40.

It is probable that from the 1941-42 season in New York the Coast will ultimately view "Junior Miss," and mayhap "Blithe

THE SEASON IN SOUTHERN CALIFORNIA 29

Spirit," on a professional basis, though most of the others are likely to mature either in Pasadena Community or other little theatre purlieus. There was little enough that was interesting in a transcontinental way in New York during the season recently closed.

Very much out of the grab-bag were producing manifestations in the Los Angeles district. Trends were difficult if not impossible to discern. Those who saw the plays liked very well what David O. Selznick attempted to do at Santa Barbara in the summer of 1941, though this was remote from the tortuous theatrical stem of Southern California's chief municipality. He tried one new full-length play, "Lottie Dundass," by Enid Bagnold, author of "Serena Blandish," the strongest interest being that it brought Geraldine Fitzgerald to the stage, and another, a curtain-raiser by William Saroyan, cleverly devised, called "Hello Out There."

Selznick also revived "Anna Christie" as a special vehicle for his star Ingrid Bergman. This was worth-while as a revival with this particular star, who was to the manor born, despite that audiences felt the allure of the Eugene O'Neill drama, revolutionary in its time, had paled. Selznick also presented George Bernard Shaw's "The Devil's Disciple" with Sir Cedric Hardwicke and Alan Marshall on the same program as "Hello Out There" as his best all-around bill at the Channel City playhouse, the Lobero. Regrettably, there are no signs of his renewing the activity, since motion pictures will probably claim all his attention again.

Mention of Saroyan brings to the forefront the fact that the Pasadena Community playhouse was one of the many such establishments to present his "Jim Dandy" during the season, which, naturally, was an interest-stirring premiere. Even more expressionistic than "Across the Board on Tomorrow Morning," which was given the previous year, this new exhibit had an effect on audiences almost as puzzling as the eccentric and brief Saroyan film career. The Pasadena Playhouse, as always, strove valiantly for artistic staging of the production, and the cast attained a very high level in their work for these offerings, but it appeared doubtful whether "Jim Dandy" would distinguish itself by making any new or important theatrical history. The more vague he becomes the less Saroyan seems to satisfy, which is probably an axiomatic result with dramatists who attempt to follow that course, or at any rate let themselves be led into it by inspiration or otherwise.

Pasadena had other premieres during the year, which seemed to provide more substance for the commercial theatre, and the likelihood that the exhibits might eventually reach New York. One was "A Riddle for Mr. Twiddle," written by Madison Goff, and the other "Escape to Autumn" by De Witt Bodeen. "A Riddle for Mr. Twiddle" partakes of that out-of-the-world character which individualizes "Blithe Spirit," solution of a mystery problem in the domain of the spirits being the main idea in the Goff stage piece. Maybe it will fit in with a new cycle, typical of this war time as it was of the last. "Escape to Autumn," which featured the European actress, Leopoldine Konstantin, had an authoress as its central figure, surrounded by a somewhat erratic family, progeny of several marriages, and may be tabulated as possessing a generic resemblance to "The Constant Nymph." There was an exhilarating aspect to these two ventures along new ways.

Traveling stars and troupes were notably conspicuous by their absence—no other season having attained quite such a low as this. Katharine Cornell had the courage to traverse the country in "The Doctor's Dilemma," a very poor play for her personally, but evaded Los Angeles with her new and short-lived "Rose Burke," which was premiered in San Francisco. "My Sister Eileen" was the Chicago company. "Blossom Time," with Everett Marshall, paid a visit. John Barton came back once again in "Tobacco Road." Ethel Waters who had been a star of the light opera season of 1941 in "Cabin in the Sky" tried this musical fantasy at the principal road theatre, and also appeared in a Coast production of "Mamba's Daughters." Close to the end of the season the Biltmore, which was the setting for a sparse list indeed, went over to vaudeville. It was also the locale early in the theatrical year for a presentation by Dante, the Magician, which scored a hit, and then moved to Hollywood.

During the year El Capitan Theatre on Hollywood Boulevard, originally opened with Charlot's Revue, and later acquired by Henry Duffy for his many successful plays, including "Ah, Wilderness" with Will Rogers, was transformed into a motion picture palace. But toward the close of the season a new El Capitan emerged under somewhat the same general management, with Sid Grauman, and various film personages interested too, where the Hollywood Playhouse was formerly located. This began its career with a vaudeville show, or revue, as it might more appropriately be styled.

Before its demise as a stage habitat El Capitan on the Boulevard housed a very effective rendition of "The Man Who Came to Dinner," with Laird Cregar, famous for his Oscar Wilde impersonation of a year or two ago, in the rôle of Sheridan Whiteside, previously played on the Coast by Alexander Woollcott, and incidentally George Kaufman. Cregar virtually duplicated the acclaim he won for his portrayal of the British poet of sensational fame.

At El Capitan were also offered "The Male Animal" with Otto Kruger starred, and "Springtime for Henry" with Edward Everett Horton, which carried over into the early war days briefly, when attention was distracted from practically all show-going for a time.

Entertainment that assures "release" seemed to take precedence over all others, topmost being the musical shows. Light opera had a flourishing four to five weeks, with "The Vagabond King," "Bitter Sweet," "Music in the Air" and "Hit the Deck" on the schedule. John Charles Thomas, mainstay as a star, was present for "Music in the Air," otherwise brightened by Irra Petina and Francis Lederer. "Bitter Sweet" with Muriel Angelus and John Howard was the best performance of this Noel Coward musical heard in the Los Angeles environs, notwithstanding Evelyn Laye took part in a J. J. Shubert presentation of several years ago. John Carradine was an interesting presence as Louis XI in "The Vagabond King."

Numerous efforts were put forth to obtain a show to rival "Meet the People," one even by the group associated with that production, Henry Myers, Edward Eliscu and Jay Gorney. Under the title "They Can't Get You Down," this attempted a satire on the musical play, collegiate type, with a happy ending. It had much originality but failed in actual construction. The purport of the plot was hazily brought out, and the audience's enjoyment was chiefly confined to the song numbers. Never catching on too well, "They Can't Get You Down" expired shortly after fatal December 7.

Popular among Summer and early Fall events of 1941 was "Jump for Joy," with all-Negro cast, and Duke Ellington and his band. This lasted for 10 weeks at the Mayan in downtown Los Angeles, and revealed any number of talented people in its ensemble.

Attempts were made to give life to "Rally Round the Girls," "Fun for the Money," "Music to My Ears," "Zis Boom Bah" and various others, but the production that outlived them all was the new Turnabout Theatre's combination of puppet shows and vaudeville, the latter adroitly titled "No Strings Revue." This held forth throughout the season, and was continuing. Elsa Lanchester, wife of Charles Laughton, with her sophisticated and characteristic songs, was its major star—a great favorite.

John Murray Anderson essayed entering the cafe-revue sphere with his "Silver Screen" production headed by Gitta Alpar and Cynda Glenn, and including many old-time film favorites, but that terrain still remains exclusively the possession of Earl Carroll with his two productions annually and N.T.G. of the Florentine Gardens. Carroll's lavish presentations survived both labor and war setbacks.

In passing, mention might be made of "Rose Marie" as produced at Hollywood Bowl with Allan Jones starred, and Nancy McCord feminine lead; the visit of "Hellzapoppin" (not included among Biltmore attractions previously cited) without Olsen and Johnson; the remarkable persistence of the play "She Lost It in Campeche," which has now passed the year mark despite its inferior attributes; the ever-living "Drunkard," which has now entered its tenth year, the abbreviated appearance of a very bad play, "To Live Again," with Ian Keith, who was good, and the resuscitation of vaudeville.

Vaudeville on the Coast really got off to a flying start through the endeavors of George Jessel, an excellent master of ceremonies, Jack Haley, Kitty Carlisle, Ella Logan, the De Marcos and others. Opening of their "Show Time" caused the rafters of the Biltmore to ring with applause. Entering on the scene shortly afterward was "Blackouts of 1942," headed by Ken Murray and Billy Gilbert, which also pleased audiences hugely. This may not be vaudeville as it was known in the halcyon days, but it evidently supplies a desired diversion.

Community and little theatres are gradually dwindling to a few regulars with evident rights to survivorship, though sporadic undertakings are perennial because of the chance of show-casting for the film studios. Aside from the Pasadena Community Playhouse, which has such an abundant tradition, stronger contenders for regularity included the Max Reinhardt Workshop, the Bliss-Hayden, Call Board, Hollytown and a few others. These are recognized as good try-out ground for plays, and often develop players either for stage or pictures.

The Pasadena Community continues its Summer festivals from year to year, having centered on modern American comedies in 1941, and the semi-historic American comedy for 1942. "Beggar on Horseback," "George Washington Slept Here," "Dinner at Eight," "Minick," "Once in a Lifetime," "You Can't Take It with You," "The Royal Family" and "The Man Who Came to Dinner" made up the series for 1941, and apart from plays al-

THE SEASON IN SOUTHERN CALIFORNIA

ready mentioned, the Community gave "Skylark," "Ladies in Retirement," "Flight to the West," "The Great American Family," "The Little Foxes," "The Male Animal," "The Far Off Hills," "Yellow Jacket," "The Philadelphia Story," "Much Ado About Nothing," "One Sunday Afternoon," "Out of the Frying Pan," "Lovely Miss Linley," "Mr. and Mrs. North," "Home from Home" and "Ladies in Waiting."

Aside from this, "Catch as Catch Can," by Ray Morris, which originated in a little theatre situation, played later professionally with Jeanine Crispin from France as star. "Murder in a Nunnery" was offered with its cast headed by Margaret Wycherly, Pedro de Cordoba, John McGuire and Christine Abel. This mystery play was authored by Emmet Lavery. "Don't Feed the Actors," by Jerry Horwin and Catherine Turney; "Bright Champagne," by De Witt Bodeen; "The Baby's Name Is Oscar" by Smith Dawless, with a Hollywood background, were a few among the many to be noted, but there is scarcely any chance or need to dwell in detail on the eternal fermentation in the little theatre realm, except to remark on its extensiveness.

IN TIME TO COME
A Drama in Prologue and Seven Scenes

By Howard Koch and John Huston

THE dramatic story of President Woodrow Wilson's fight for a world peace that would, in his belief, be strengthened and secured by a League of Nations, was first put into play form by Howard Koch and entitled "Woodrow Wilson." Later John Huston, who had worked with Mr. Koch on many successful scenarios in Hollywood, was called into consultation and the revised drama was retitled "In Time to Come."

The play was produced December 28, 1941, at the Mansfield Theatre in New York, by Otto L. Preminger. It met with a generally favorable critical reception, but one that was quite mixed so far as public support was concerned. Audiences made up largely of those who had lived through the Wilson tragedy following the First World War were definitely interested. A younger public, to which the play became largely a drama of historical significance, overlaid with political intrigue and debate, did not react as favorably as the older public had done, and after a shortened run of 40 performances the play was withdrawn. In the drama critics' Spring search for the best play of American authorship to represent the season of 1941-42 "In Time to Come" received four votes, as opposed to two for John Steinbeck's "The Moon Is Down" and eleven recommending that no choice of a best American play be made that year.

For those who liked the play Brooks Atkinson of the *New York Times* eloquently summed up the general impression when he wrote: "Mr. Koch and Mr. Huston have written a record of the greatest of the world's lost causes without rhetoric or recrimination. There, by the grace of God, went a chance to prevent the scourge of warfare that is now beating the aching back of the world. Although Woodrow Wilson is their hero, they have not averted their eyes from his defects of personality, his sharp temper and high-handed use of men. They have unfolded a great tragedy of ideals and the hero who stood for them, and they have not cheapened it. When Woodrow Wilson goes down in the last scene, you know that the ancient blackness is settling down over the world again."

IN TIME TO COME

"Because in dealing with such a subject they (the Messrs. Koch and Huston) have eschewed dramatic pyrotechnics of any sort," Richard Watts, Jr., wrote in the New York *Herald Tribune*, "they were vastly convincing in what they were saying, and 'In Time to Come' emerges as a dignified, arresting and remarkably convincing historical document."

When the curtain rises on "In Time to Come" the theatre is for a moment held in complete darkness. Gradually a single spotlight picks out the head and shoulders of the President of the United States, Thomas Woodrow Wilson. He is standing on the rostrum of the House of Representatives, addressing a joint session of House and Senate membership. The date is April 2, 1917; the occasion the message advising that the Congress declare war against the Imperial German Government in World War I. The President is reading from a paper dimly outlined on the stand in front of him. His voice is full and steady—

"With a profound sense of the solemn and even tragical character of the step I am taking, and of the grave responsibilities which it involves," he says, "I advise that the Congress declare the recent course of the German Government to be, in fact, nothing less than war against the Government and the people of the United States. The present German warfare is a warfare against mankind. It is a war against all nations. Each nation must decide for itself how it will meet it. The choice we make for ourselves must be made with a moderation of counsel and a temperateness of judgment befitting our character and our motives as a nation. There is one choice we cannot make, we are incapable of making, we will not choose the path of submission.

"Let us be very clear and make very clear to all the world what our motives and our objects are. We have no selfish ends to serve. We desire no conquests, no dominions. We seek no indemnities. We are glad now that we see the facts with no veil or false pretense about them to fight for the ultimate peace of the world and for the liberation of all its peoples, and the privilege of men to choose their way of life and of obedience. The world must be made safe for democracy. A steadfast concert for peace cannot be maintained except by a partnership of democratic nations. No autocratic government could be trusted to keep faith within it. It must be a league of honor, a partnership of opinion."

There is a brief pause. As the President proceeds to his conclusion his voice takes on a new fullness, a graver note of determination—

"It is a fearful thing to lead this great peaceful people into war," he is saying. "There are, it may be, many months of fiery trial and sacrifice ahead of us. But the right is more precious than peace and we shall fight for the things which we have always carried nearest our hearts. To such a task we can dedicate our lives and our fortunes, everything that we are and everything that we have, with the pride of those who know that the day has come when America is privileged to spend her blood and her might for the principles that gave her birth and happiness, and the peace which she has treasured. God helping her, she can do no other."

Slowly the lights fade and the figure of the President is dissolved in darkness. For a few seconds no sound comes from the darkness. Then from a distance the martial strains of a military band playing. The music increases in volume as the scene gradually lightens, revealing the President's study in the White House at Washington. It is about the middle of September, 1918.

"The room is furnished simply and with dignity. There are comfortable chairs and a small mahogany desk. Book shelves take up the entire rear wall, except for two tall windows."

The President is seated at the desk, pecking slowly at an old-fashioned typewriter, pausing frequently to frame a sentence. Near the desk Edith Bolling Wilson is sitting, knitting. She is "a woman about thirty-five years old, of charming appearance and gracious manner."

The music swells as the band nears the White House. The President would have Mrs. Wilson close the window. "The war creeps in even through the cracks and crevices," he says.

It is Mrs. Wilson's thought that he has been working long enough. It is time he stopped and they had their sherry. But the President wants to wait for Colonel House. He wants his wife and his close friend to be the first to hear what he has written.

Captain Stanley, the President's military aide, "a trim young man in uniform," is in with a personal cable from London, which Mrs. Wilson decodes for the President. It is from Ambassador Page, but there is nothing definite in it—

"I've tried to imagine what news of the armistice will look like . . ." the President murmurs as he drops the cable on the desk. "Will it ever come? . . ."

The Graysons, and some friends of theirs, are coming to dinner, Mrs. Wilson reports. She is tidying up the desk when she finds two large books. "Are you through with these?" she asks.

"IN TIME TO COME"

Wilson: ... Have you estimated the cost of maintaining an army big enough to prevent them from forming a bigger one? Can France support such an army?

Clemenceau: The Saar and the Rhineland will help. We will create a defensive barrier around France that will be impregnable.

Wilson: Such security is worthless, Monsieur Clemenceau. You may build a wall to keep destruction out and later find that you have fenced it in.

(Guy Sorel, Harold Young, Richard Gaines)

Photo by Fred Fehl

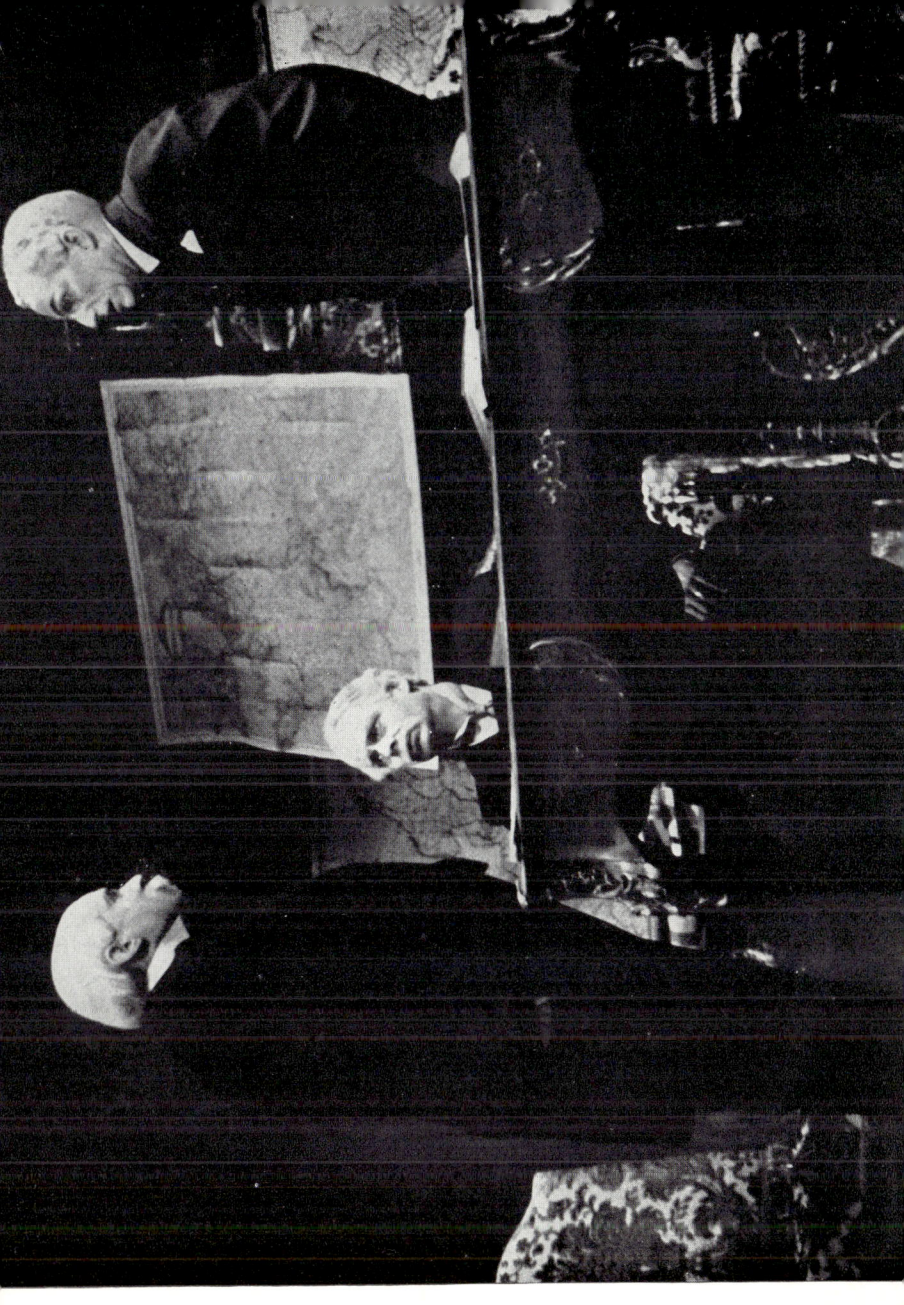

"Yes," he answers and adds reflectively—

"The more I read of the past, the more I realize history's full of good ideas that didn't work. I keep thinking of all the others who have tried to bring peace to the world. . . . That frightens me when I think of my responsibility."

"Have you told anyone yet about our plans?"

"Not yet."

"You're still not sure?"

"I've asked Brandeis to call this afternoon. If there's no legal objection to my going I'll tell House I've made up my mind."

A smile of satisfaction, almost a look of triumph, radiates from Mrs. Wilson's face. "The more I think of the trip, Woodrow, the more wonderful it seems," she says.

Joseph Tumulty, personal secretary to the President, "a man in his forties, of Irish descent, warm and alert," comes to announce the arrival of Colonel House. "There is no formality between Tumulty and the Wilsons," and the President is quick to sound out his secretary as to the thought that is troubling him. Seeing that no American President has ever left the country during his term of office, what does Tumulty think the people would say if one did?

"Suppose he went to Europe," ventures the President, and then, noting Tumulty's startled look he quickly adds—"I mean after the war and he had the best possible reason for going?"

"That sounds like a pretty good reason," answers Tumulty, without committing himself.

Colonel House, "a gentle, keen-appearing man of fifty-five," breaks the President's reverie. There is evidence of their warm bond of friendship and mutual respect in their greeting. House is just back from a New York trip and eager for news from overseas. There is none to give him, save the cable from Page, indicating that he feels the armistice is only a matter of days.

"That's the way Baruch felt," reports House. "I had lunch with him today. He believes Germany's internal situation is desperate."

"I hope he's right."

"Sir William Wiseman called this morning."

"Did you tell him our ideas on the League?"

"He thought very highly of them. Then, of course, he got back to the favorite British theme. They haven't dropped their objections to the freedom of the seas clause."

"I have their word the armistice will be based on the fourteen points—*all* of the fourteen points."

"I hope they'll keep their word."

"If necessary, I'll appeal to the British people," declares Wilson.

A brief knock on the door and Tumulty is back to announce that Senator Lodge has arrived with what he insists is an urgent inquiry to make. The President is irritated rather than interested. The Senator had no appointment.

Lodge may be the next Chairman of the Foreign Relations Committee, House suggests, and probably wants to talk over peace terms. The President feels that Lodge knows what those peace terms are, just as the whole world knows. He refuses to be stampeded into seeing anyone.

"It might do no harm, Governor, to let Lodge think he can force an issue," suggests Colonel House, tactfully. "An occasional concession of that kind might disarm him for more serious attacks on your policies."

"I don't agree with you," replies the President, a little stiffly. "Politicians regard concessions as a sign of weakness."

"That's true, Governor. You've been able to go over their heads to the people, and always with astonishing success, but those were domestic issues. This involves the whole world and you'll need your own country solidly on your side."

"If it were anyone but Lodge. He brings out all my defects. Each meeting has clarified our essential disagreement and confirmed our enmity. . . . Besides, I can't stand the man."

This declaration spreads a smile all around, and the next moment the President has his excuse. The phone rings and Justice Brandeis is announced. The President will see Brandeis and let Colonel House talk with Senator Lodge. "You handle him better than I can," he says to House.

Judge Brandeis, "an ascetic-appearing man of about sixty," finds this answer to the President's summons one of his "agreeable duties," and is eager to be of such service as he can. As to whether, from a purely legal standpoint, there are any reasons why the President of the United States should not attend the Peace Conference in person and assist in negotiating the treaty, Brandeis finds the question a bit difficult.

"As you know, the treaty-making power rests jointly with the President and the Senate," says Brandeis. "A treaty goes into effect when the President negotiates the treaty directly, in addition to signing it. He is in a sense representing himself and executing two functions, not one as contemplated by the Constitution."

"And would that fact make the procedure illegal?" The President is plainly impatient.

"There's no specific prohibition in the Constitution, or is there any precedent against it."

"Then I would be within my rights."

"It isn't quite that simple. In questions like this, there exists a No-Man's Land between legality and illegality. Such an assumption of power might be termed an adventure in which a man takes the law with him and extends it to new boundaries of action. If he fails in whatever his purpose might be, he is usually regarded as a usurper; if he succeeds, he becomes a benefactor."

The President has walked to the window. It is past sunset and the room is gradually darkening. After a considerable silence Justice Brandeis rises. "I'm sorry, sir, that I can't give you a more definite answer," he says, speaking with affection.

"You've given me the answer I wanted," the President says. "Now I know more than ever what I must do."

"Whatever that is, it has my blessing."

"Thank you, Brandeis. Thank you." They shake hands warmly.

Justice Brandeis has gone and Colonel House is back from his interview with Senator Lodge. He had found the Senator quite affable, but seriously interested in certain suggestions he had to make about peace aims. The Senator feels that they should be more concrete and has submitted a draft embodying his conclusions.

" 'Proposals to indemnify the United States for acts of German aggression,' " reads the President from a paper that House hands to him. By the time he has finished the paper the President's face has become white and stern—

"Did that man dare to suggest that these are the war aims of the American people?" he demands—

HOUSE—In so far as the Senate represents them.

WILSON—He lies. I could publish these right now and destroy him politically.

HOUSE—And show Europe we're of two minds? . . . Besides, the idea of forcing Germany to pay for the war isn't only Lodge's. He represents a very considerable opinion.

WILSON—A selfish minority.

HOUSE—Politics is the means by which the will of the few becomes the will of the many, and Senator Lodge is a very capable politician.

Wilson—House, if I thought this war were to end the way other wars have ended, I couldn't condone the loss of one more life. I'd sue Germany for peace today.

House—And be, impeached.

Wilson—That would be an honor compared to being a party to . . . anything like this. (*He crumples* Lodge's *memorandum and drops it on the desk.*) When it was over, what could I say to the widows? "Dear Mrs. Smith of Galena, Illinois . . . Experts have figured out your husband's life is worth seven thousand, eight hundred and seventy-two dollars, which you will receive in German marks."

House—*If* we can collect them.

Wilson—House, such a thing must never happen. Just today I've made up my mind to what length I'm prepared to go to be *sure* it doesn't happen. . . . But first I want to read you something . . .

"THE HIGH CONTRACTING PARTIES,
In order to promote international co-operation and to achieve international peace and security by the acceptance of obligations not to resort to war, by the prescription of open, just and honorable relations between nations, by the firm establishment of the understandings of international law as the actual rule of conduct among Governments, and by the maintenance of justice and a scrupulous respect for all treaty obligations in the dealings of organized peoples with one another, Agree to this Covenant of the League of Nations."

(*For a moment there is silence, as he puts the paper down.*) That's what we're fighting for—that and nothing else. (*He looks at* House.)

House—A constitution for the world. Governor, do you remember the advice Philip of Macedon gave his son, Alexander? "Never go to war for less than an empire" . . . It seems you have even more at stake.

A servant lets Mrs. Wilson through a door. She is carrying a tray with three glasses of sherry and is prepared to call a recess in the conference. They have been standing in the dark long enough. A moment later they are drinking "to an old custom." For a little their conversation is gay, but soon they are back considering more serious subjects. The President has decided that Colonel House should return to Europe at once. It would be well for him to be there even before an armistice is signed and before he (Wilson) arrives. As for the breaking of precedents the President is willing to take full personal responsibility—

"In the past there's been too much indirect negotiation," he says. "This time I feel the treaty should be drawn by those directly accountable to their people."

As to who should take care of things at home, there is Marshall—and Tumulty— But there are also political considerations, Colonel House insists. How about Lodge?

"Lodge again!" answers the President, a little stiffly. "I don't feel he's in a position to dictate my moves."

"But he's in a position to take advantage of them. Then there's the question of your prestige at the Conference. You've become the acknowledged spokesman for the principles of the Allied cause. With American opinion behind you, you'll have more influence in world affairs than any other man has . . . or perhaps ever had."

"That's my reason for going. . . ."

"Governor, there's one thing we must realize: here, you're an infallible oracle, speaking from Olympus. Over there, you'll be a man treating with other men. . . ."

"Colonel House, do you feel my husband isn't equal to the task?" demands Mrs. Wilson, sharply.

"No, I don't, Edith." A look of pained surprise steals over the Colonel's face. "I only wanted the Governor to consider every possibility."

The Graysons are announced and Mrs. Wilson goes to meet them. She would have Colonel House join them at dinner, but the Colonel has work to do and would prefer to have his dinner sent to his room, if that is agreeable. . . .

"Have you considered what delegates you're taking with you to Paris, Governor?" House would know.

WILSON—Oh, only in a general way. Lansing, of course; Bliss; Seymour—

HOUSE—What Republicans?

WILSON—Have you anyone in mind?

HOUSE—If you're only taking one, I'd suggest a prominent man, who'd have the support of his party—say Hughes, or Taft.

WILSON (*after deliberating*)—They'd have set ideas of their own. . . . Anyway, I'd prefer someone not in politics, like Henry White. (HOUSE *shrugs. It is evident he knows the subject is not one to be pressed. He continues his walk across the room, stops in front of the globe and looks down at it as he talks to* WILSON.)

HOUSE (*affectionately*)—Get in good shape for the trip. . . .

WILSON (*relieved*)—Thanks, Colonel. . . . (*Shakes hands.*) You know, I was afraid you were very much opposed to my going.

HOUSE (*very simply . . . quietly*)—I am. Take care of yourself while I'm gone, Governor. You'll have the world on your shoulders.

Wilson looks up and House meets his gaze. They shake hands. House walks out as the curtain falls.

The morning of December 14, 1918, the steamship *George Washington* was approaching the harbor of Brest. Outside the cabin suite assigned the President and Mrs. Wilson a half dozen newspaper correspondents are gathered. They are wearing overcoats and mufflers against the blustery weather. They represent various newspapers and news agencies and their names are Dillan, Smith, Price, Gordon and Terry. They alternate between leaning over the rail and stamping about the deck in an effort to shake off the chill.

The boys are growing a bit impatient, both with the President, who has apparently had very little news to give out: with the conferences which are always held in the open air, and with the trip, which has proved colorless and uninteresting.

Soon there is the distant shriek of whistles. The welcoming fleet apparently is approaching. "Boats, boys, boats—hundreds of boats," calls Dillan.

"Why not? Aladdin's coming with his peace lamp," answers Gordon, with the suggestion of a sneer. "Fourteen wishes in a black portfolio."

"Once a Republican, always a Republican," counters Price, solemnly shaking his head.

The laughter at this has barely faded when the door to the President's suite is opened. The President, in overcoat and cap, comes out on deck, followed by his physician, Dr. Cary Grayson.

The President smiles cheerfully at the correspondents, but underneath there is a noticeable gravity in his manner. He obviously would like to have the interview over as quickly as possible. Yes, he has had a good rest. As to his feelings on entering the harbor of Brest—

"I have a sense of our grave responsibility, which we can fulfill only with the aid of Providence," he says simply.

"Mr. Wilson, in the program you have in mind, do you anticipate the full co-operation of the other governments?" Correspondent Smith would know.

"Naturally," the President answers, looking at his interrogator sharply.

"Including the enemy country?" asks Dillan.

"There is no longer an enemy country."

"Is there any reason to suppose, sir, the Allied statesmen are going to take the same generous view?" There is a trace of irony in Smith's tone.

"Do you know any reason why they shouldn't?"

"There's been mention of certain previous agreements . . . private understandings among the Allies of a . . . somewhat different nature."

"Such understandings, if they exist, are not my concern. From now on, there are to be no secrets between governments and their people."

The growing tension is somewhat relieved when Correspondent Price cuts in with a question as to Mrs. Wilson's shopping plans in Paris. But the serious note is soon struck again when several of his questioners would know whether or not Colonel House has already started negotiations over the proposed League of Nations. Colonel House's actions have been left largely to his own discretion, replies the President.

The press will be informed in due time of what may have transcribed. He (the President) has been on the high seas for eight days and—despite the wireless—

"Have there been any cable communications from any of the Allied Governments?" Gordon would know.

There had been a cable from the English, the President confesses, suavely. This was a message of official greetings as he entered European waters. And that's all? That's all the President feels at liberty to divulge. Now, if there are no more questions he will continue his walk.

The correspondents are not too well pleased. "So that's the new diplomacy . . . ?" mutters Dillan. "Everyone gets the news but the newspapers."

"If you ask me, boys, for someone who's going to save humanity, he's a little lacking in the human touch," ventures Smith.

"The hell he is," answers Price, sharply. "He's put through more social reforms than any ten presidents before him."

"But here he's going to be up against something much tougher than he ever tackled at home."

"That's what they said when he went from Princeton to Trenton, and from Trenton to Washington: the idealistic college professor. But he fooled them all—Federal Reserve Act, Federal Trade Commission, Farm Loans, Eight Hour Day—"

"That's socialism."

"Aw, you."

The boys drift away—all but Smith. He has seen Henry White approaching the Wilson stateroom and lingers behind the others. Craftily Smith would get a statement from Mr. White by telling him the President has practically admitted the receipt of a cablegram from the English. Incidentally Smith would like to assure Mr. White of the kindly interest of Senator Lodge, with whom he had talked the night before the *George Washington* sailed. At this moment the door to the Wilson stateroom opens and a secretary hurries down the deck with a cablegram in his hand. Smith and White exchange significant glances. The noise of the distant ship whistles increases—

"Is it victory they are blowing for? Or peace? I wonder," wonders Smith.

"I was under the impression the greeting was for the President," drily replies Mr. White.

Again the newspaper man would strike up some sort of understanding with Mr. White, not as a member of the President's commission, but as an official representative of the Republican party. Surely Mr. White is aware of the informal poll taken in the Senate two weeks ago. He must, as a practical man, know that all practical men, in Europe and all over the world, want a practical peace—

"Except, possibly, Mr. Wilson," concludes Smith. "And in the interests of such a treaty, it's been suggested to me that this information might prove of interest to . . . certain Allied statesmen."

"In what way?"

"To acquaint them with the fact that the President's views on the treaty—and especially the League—are not entirely in accord with those of the majority of his countrymen."

The President's secretary is returning to the President's stateroom when Mr. White asks to be announced. Then he turns back to Smith and says, with unconcealed contempt—

"You made a slight error just now, young man. You called me an official representative of the Republican party. . . ."

"Well, aren't you?"

"As it happens, I'm here in another capacity—as a member

of the President's peace commission."

"I thought perhaps in view of Mr. Wilson's failure to divulge—"

"I don't care to discuss the matter further," says Mr. White, with curt finality. Smith bows, with a cold smile, and walks away.

Shortly the President joins Mr. White and, after formal pleasantries have been exchanged, their talk turns to the debated cable from the British Government. "Is it true," Mr. White would know, "that they've refused to participate in the conference unless the 'Freedom of the Seas' clause is dropped from our program?"

Mr. Wilson, resentful that not only are cables tapped by foreign powers, but even by his own commission, reluctantly admits the truth of Mr. White's information, whatever its source. His reason for not acquainting the Commission with this ultimatum was that whatever decision should be made he would have to make. The President had agreed to the British terms. Nor does he believe that such a decision will in any way undermine his program.

"Mr. White, 'Freedom of the Seas' refers to the rights of neutrals in wartime," explains the President. "In any future wars there will be no neutrals. After the League is in effect, all nations will be united against the aggressor."

The welcoming ships are setting up a terrific din as Mrs. Wilson comes from the stateroom. An exchange of greetings and Mr. White leaves them.

"Is this all for us?" Mrs. Wilson asks, as the noise increases.
"I think so, Edith."

EDITH—Some of them are warships.
WILSON (*betraying his annoyance as he looks*)—Probably English.
EDITH—Woodrow, what did Mr. White come to see you about?
WILSON—The cable. I think everyone knew it before I did.
EDITH (*quickly*)—You sent the reply, didn't you?
WILSON—Yes.
EDITH—You're still . . . worried about it?
WILSON—Edith, last night for a few hours after the cable came, I was on the point of ordering the Captain to reverse his course and return to America.
EDITH—My dear!
WILSON—Freedom of the seas was one of the fourteen points.

EDITH—That leaves thirteen. (*The whistles are now frantic, indicating the ship is entering the roads.*) I feel very proud of you, dear.

WILSON—I feel—a terrible isolation. I suppose anyone feels that who tries to read the destiny in the affairs of his fellow-men. (*She puts her hand in his.*) But I mustn't think of myself. It's the people I'm coming for. . . . (*Cheers and screaming whistles continue.*) Out there . . . and all over the world . . . it's the people speaking. If I could only tell them what's in my heart. . . . This time their voices will be heard and, God willing, their hopes will be fulfilled.

"By this time the ovation is a pandemonium of cheering shouts, distant bands and frantic whistles. Suddenly there is the ominous sound of a cannon beginning the Presidential salute. A startled look flashes across the President's face. Again the cannon shot reverberates until it overwhelms the rest of the sounds. The curtain comes slowly down and the last three reports of the cannon sound in the dark house after the curtain is down."

In January, 1919, the Wilsons are quartered in a house in Paris near the Parc Monceau. "It is ornately furnished in the manner of the Napoleonic period." The President is using two rooms as a reception room and office with study adjoining. Tall French windows look down on the street.

At the moment Colonel House is studying a map spread on a table before him, while Professor Seymour, one of the American experts on the Peace Commission, looks over his shoulder. The Colonel has evidently been in conference with Venezelos of Greece, and is a little disturbed when Prof. Seymour puts him right as to the possible results should Venezelos' demands be met.

The President's secretary, Stanley, reports that there are so many people waiting to see the President that he doesn't know where to put them. King Nikita of Montenegro heads the list. The King is there with two bodyguards who, to the distress of Stanley, "don't seem to sit on chairs." Monsieur Pichon of France is due at 11:30, the President is still conferring with Signor Orlando of Italy in the study and Lloyd-George is waiting in the drawing room downstairs. House will join Lloyd-George first and see King Nikita later.

Edith Wilson has brought a large bouquet of mimosa to the President's room and left orders that the butler should see that the President has his sherry and egg before he goes to the conference.

"It's hard to believe that it's really here, isn't it?" Mrs Wilson says to Stanley. "For two years the President's worked for this day . . . dreamed of it . . . and now it's come."

The rumble of Signor Orlando's voice coming through the study door reminds her of the Italian receptions for the President. "On the Corso they were lined up for miles, throwing flowers in front of our car," she remembers. . . .

From the study appears the President. He is followed by Signor Orlando and Signor Martino, an interpreter. Signor Orlando is practically overwhelming the President with his voluble Italian and the President, a little amused, is dividing his attention between the excitable histrionics of the speaker and the measured translations of Signor Martino.

Signor Orlando would have the President know that the Italian people realize full well how well he understands their problems. Signor Orlando would assure the President that the compulsory arbitration feature of the League of Nations need apply only to Europe and not to the American Continent. Signor Orlando would repeat that the President can count on Italy. After which there is an elaborate exchange of "Arrivedercis" and the signors retire.

The President is quite pleased to have found Signor Orlando so co-operative. He had brought up only one of the Italian claims—the Brenner Pass. "I must say he made a very plausible argument," ventures the President, noting the suggestion of anxiety in Colonel House's attitude. "He pointed out that with the breakdown of Austria, Italy would have the Germans on their frontier and could only defend herself against future aggression by controlling the Pass."

"You didn't commit yourself, Governor?"

"I told him frankly I'd been against most of the Italian demands, but I was inclined to favor this one."

Colonel House walks quickly to the table and picks up the house phone. He asks to have Prof. Seymour bring in the Brenner Pass figures. "I think you've made a mistake, Governor," he says, frankly, as he hangs up the phone. And, as Wilson winces, he adds—"Oh, perhaps nothing very serious, but I think you should have the facts."

"But Signor Orlando explained the situation fully."

"There are one or two things he may not have mentioned," says the Colonel and adds, as Seymour enters with a paper in his hand, "Seymour, what are the population figures on the Tyrol, south of the Brenner?"

"About 245,000. Fourteen percent Italian, eighteen percent mixed strains and sixty-eight percent dominantly German blood."

"Does that mean the majority is pro-Austrian?"

"At least they're anti-Italian."

"Is that a fact, Professor Seymour, or an opinion?"

"In a way, sir, all the facts over here are opinions."

House smiles at Seymour's sally, but the President does not. "I see. Thank you," he says, calmly. And adds: "I'll have another talk with Orlando."

Colonel House thinks that perhaps Orlando will be willing to make other concessions in exchange for the Wilson consent on the Brenner Pass, a distasteful thought to President Wilson.

"Governor, beginning this morning we'll be negotiating with self-interested men, without your high intentions. There may be times when we'll have to compromise, and we'll need all the bargaining points we've got."

"The English were already committed to Italy on the Brenner."

"Unwillingly. Now that the war's won they're counting on us to hold the Italians in check."

How does Colonel House know that? Because, while the President was conferring with Orlando, he had been talking with Lloyd-George. And why hadn't Lloyd-George waited? Because he had wanted to talk with Clemenceau before the conference.

"Hmmmm. . . . Did he have anything to say about the League?"

"Only that there's considerable public pressure to hasten peace, and he wondered if discussions of the League at this time might not delay the treaty."

"I'll negotiate no treaty that doesn't include the League. I hope you made that clear," flatly declares the President.

Colonel House confesses that he had let Lloyd-George do most of the talking. As for himself, as a Democrat, the Colonel is more interested in the situation at home at the moment. From what Tumulty has written, the opposition, under Senator Lodge, is beginning to come out openly against the League. There is danger in that situation. Frankly, Colonel House admits, he believes President Wilson should return to the United States as soon as he can. It is difficult for the President to believe that the Colonel is really serious.

"You suggest that I leave here on the day we're beginning our work—when in an hour we'll be in our first conference!"

House—You could outline your views on the treaty before you left.

Wilson—And what about the League?

House—Work would go ahead on the covenant . . . subject to your approval in Washington. In the meantime, we'd negotiate a temporary treaty on the same terms as the armistice.

Wilson—House, I've looked in the faces of thousands of people . . . here and on my trip. Everywhere is the same mute appeal in their eyes. They want no makeshift, patchwork Armistice. They want a peace that's final and enduring.

House—That may be true. But remember this: Once your leadership at home is questioned, the European Press will follow suit. The slightest false move . . . like the Brenner . . . and the pack'll be yapping at your heels.

Wilson—Then we'll bar the Press from the Conference . . . let nothing out until the treaty's finished. Clemenceau already suggested that.

House (*surprised*)—What about "open covenants openly arrived at"?

Wilson—I know; that's why I've refused to consider the subject up to now. But I counted on Press support.

House—You mean the Press would be welcome at the Conference as long as they were uncritical. (Wilson *stiffens noticeably.* House *recognizes the sign and hastens to make amends.*) I'm sorry, Governor. I'm only trying to point out dangers. . . . Once you get into conference anything can happen. Let me confer. Let me take the brunt of it. If I fail—if I make mistakes, you can disavow me. I beg you, Governor, think how much the whole world has at stake in the task we've assumed.

Wilson (*crossing the room thoughtfully, upset by* House's *plea, but impressed by its logic*)—I don't know. I'll have to think it over.

Monsieur Pichon, the French Foreign Secretary, has arrived to escort the American party to the Conference. . . . "He is a fussy little man, somewhat pompous and with a native alert shrewdness." Monsieur Pichon would also include Mrs. Wilson in the party, seeing that the first meeting will be merely a formal ceremony. He has walked to the window as he speaks. Pulling aside the curtains he looks down—

"This is a great day, Monsieur le President! Look at the people of France . . . how they are standing in the streets . . . for hours they are waiting there . . . many thousands of men and women . . . for one glimpse of you—the man who will save the world. Last week I have heard a story about a girl in the street. A little girl who tells her rosary. 'Hail Mary, Mother of Grace; Hail President Wilson, Father of Peace.' (*Solemnly.*) It is so, Monsieur le President . . . deep in our hearts."

The President is a little embarrassed, but is quick to answer when, a moment later, Monsieur Pichon suggests that there is one thought that is troubling the French people: How could it be that the President has been in France for two months and has not yet visited the battlefields?

"How can you understand us if you have not seen the sacrifice . . . the devastation," Monsieur would know. "And the countless graves of our dead. Crosses, everywhere crosses."

"Don't you feel we can best honor the dead by fulfilling our duty to the living?" demands the President, a little grimly.

"I beg your pardon. I do not . . ." Monsieur Pichon is puzzled.

"Then let me remind you it's nearly three months since the Armistice and no attempt has been made to relieve a starving people."

Still the Secretary does not understand and Colonel House seeks to explain: "The President refers to the Allied blockade of enemy ports."

"Ah, the enemy. . . . The Boche." Monsieur Pichon is quite indifferent.

"Monsieur Pichon, I'll be frank with you," continues the President, his temper rising. "I'm getting out of patience with this official indifference to the suffering of human beings we've promised to help."

"But what can I do? This question is not in my province. . . ."

"It seems to be in no one's province," snaps the President. "Everyone I talk to refers me to someone else. It's occurred to me that the people of France might consider it *their* province if I were to appeal directly to them."

"No, Mr. President. That is not necessary," quickly insists the alarmed Secretary. "We will talk with Monsieur Clemenceau again. He will find a way, I assure you."

Mrs. Wilson has come in with her hat and coat—and the President's sherry-and-egg. She is very happy about the orchids he has not forgotten to send her, in spite of all that is on his mind, and quite delighted with the friendliness of the French people. The President, however, is not happy. He doesn't like Paris. She would know why. For a little he will not say. Then he confesses—

"House wants me to go back home."

"He wants you to go home. . . . Now?"

"Yes."

"But your work here is just beginning. . . ."

"He was against my coming," recalls the President as he drinks his sherry.

"Yes, I remember."

"Oh, he means it for the best," admits the President, putting on his coat.

"Woodrow, don't let it spoil your day," she says, going to him. "You've made such a glorious start. Nothing can defeat you now . . . nothing!"

"My dear," he answers, taking her hand, "I needed to hear someone say that."

She has linked her arm in his, and is smiling up at him as they start for the door. The curtain falls.

Three months later, in April, 1919, the Big Four—Wilson, Clemenceau, Lloyd-George and Sonino—are meeting in closed conference in a room in the Quai d'Orsay. It is a bare room, with tall windows overlooking the street. The conference table is littered with papers, the walls hung with many maps.

"By now not only newspapermen, but even secretaries and interpreters are barred from these conferences. Clemenceau looks old and bored and heavy-lidded. Occasionally he goes off in a doze, but always manages to be awake when there is an opportunity for sarcasm or when the interests of France are touched upon in a discussion. Then he snarls out a comment like a tiger disturbed in a nap. Lloyd-George is Lloyd-George. Sonino is a stodgy man with a surly temper, who speaks English with an Italian accent. Wilson appears much more worn than in the previous scene. The strain of constant vigilance and excessive responsibility has taken its toll. It is soon evident that the formal stage of the Paris conference is over and by now these four men are familiar enough with each other to speak their minds plainly, without many concessions to station or dignity. They know each other's attitudes so well that for the most part they listen to each other's words with tolerant disinterest. If there is any progress apparent in their futile discussion, it is the progress of the Allied statesmen in slowly wearing Wilson down."

At the moment Sonino, having risen at the end of the table, is addressing President Wilson. Lloyd-George is looking on, Clemenceau is dozing, his chin resting on his chest. What has been going on may easily be judged by the spirit with which Sonino is speaking—

". . . And now I must tell you frankly, Mr. President, I am weary of your pretending ignorance of the pacts between our Allied governments . . . and of my pretending to believe you. We are not deceiving each other, so let us stop deceiving ourselves."

"Very well, Mr. Sonino," replies President Wilson, resuming his chair with great patience. "You have private agreements, but I am not a party to them. I came here in another capacity."

"In just what capacity, Mr. Wilson?" Clemenceau has roused himself momentarily.

"As a representative of the people."

"People? Of what people?"

"Of no *one* people."

Clemenceau shakes his head and goes back to his doze. "Mr. Wilson, possibly you're in a more fortunate position than the rest of us," ventures Lloyd-George, suavely. "It appears your authority is . . . unlimited. But Signor Sonino, Monsieur Clemenceau and I have our nationals to deal with. What we must do is not always what we would like to do."

"I must answer to my Government," interjects Sonino.

"Gentlemen, these secret treaties aren't within the scope of our discussion," calmly but earnestly answers President Wilson. "Our peoples didn't send us here to enforce bargains, but to establish rights."

"The possession of Fiume is our sacred right." Sonino's voice is shrill. "It was pledged to us when Italy entered the war. We paid for it with a million lives."

"Mr. Sonino, must we go over that again? What you say amounts to an admission you sacrificed men to gain territory. Did you tell your countrymen that when they were fighting? No, you told them they were fighting to put an end to aggression and preserve civilization."

Again Clemenceau comes to. "*You* told them that, Mr. Wilson."

"And I intend to keep my word," snaps the President, beginning to lose his patience.

Mr. Lloyd-George suggests quietly that they are getting away from their subject, which is the settlement of the Fiume and Adriatic claims. Mr. Sonino reiterates that unless the Fiume matter is settled to the satisfaction of his Government, Italy will not join the League. Mr. Wilson would point out that membership in the League is not to be looked upon as a bargain but as a privilege to be shared—

"It will give your country the right to interfere in our affairs, but you would not welcome our interference in yours," protests Sonino.

"We do not wish to interfere in Europe's politics," answers Wilson. "But we helped you fight a war and we have a right to insist on a settlement that will prevent such a thing from happening again."

LLOYD-GEORGE—That's what we want to do. But apparently we disagree on—

WILSON—Only on the terms, Mr. Lloyd-George—surely not on the necessity of maintaining the peace that we won. The League is the only guarantee we have that what we do here will be enduring.

LLOYD-GEORGE—But, Mr. Wilson, we are none of us infallible. We might make mistakes. We perhaps *have* made mistakes.

CLEMENCEAU (*with a half smile*)—The Brenner, Mr. Wilson.

WILSON—As you already know, the League has a provision for correcting any such mistakes.

LLOYD-GEORGE—Then if we are mistaken again in the case of Fiume, Mr. Wilson, we can rely on the League to make it right.

WILSON (*with a trace of humor*)—It's hardly a good excuse for doing a wrong that someone else may make it right.

CLEMENCEAU—Right and wrong are not in our province, Mr. Wilson. Let's leave something to God.

WILSON—I was under the impression that you didn't believe in God, Monsieur Clemenceau.

CLEMENCEAU—I don't. I am one old man who will enjoy sleeping in peace. (*And with that he closes his eyes again.*)

LLOYD-GEORGE—Gentlemen, of course none of us *wants* to do a wrong, but there arise questions of expediency. In a conversation with Colonel House it was his opinion we should consider the Adriatic question from the standpoint of . . .

WILSON (*interrupting*)—I don't care whose opinion it was. . . . (*As the others look at him, even* CLEMENCEAU *opens his eyes.*) I'm sure you misunderstood Mr. House. We've both made our positions sufficiently clear. Fiume is Austrian and Austrian it remains.

SONINO (*starting up*)—Mr. President, I want to tell you again. . . .

WILSON (*facing them to make a last plea*)—Don't you see, gentlemen, we're talking in terms of the past. That's all over with. We have more to gain for our countries than Fiume . . . more than if we could extend our national boundaries to cover these maps. . . . Forget for the moment our responsibilities to those we represent. Think, if you will, of our individual destinies. What will historians fifty—a hundred—years hence write next to our names? "These four men met in Paris in the year 1919 and divided the spoils of war"? "The peace they made lasted" . . . what shall I say . . . "twenty years"? Gentlemen, we have one life, one chance—in our case a grave decision—to do what others have done . . . a small thing that time will make smaller . . . or what has never been done before . . . a great thing that time will make greater. We can accomplish something new . . . something lasting. We're the representatives of Christian nations. We can make a Christian peace. We have it in our power to divide the tide of history. We can appoint a day in the affairs of men when conquest is to end and good will among all peoples to begin.

Mr. Wilson has said some very true things, Lloyd-George is willing to admit. Mr. Wilson is an excellent orator, agrees Clemenceau. Which brings the retort from Wilson that he was not making a speech. Neither is he a politician—

"It isn't that we lack faith in your League, Mr. President," explains Lloyd-George. "The Covenant raises a great hope in the world. Even Monsieur Clemenceau will not deny that. But a hope for the *future*. In the meantime our governments insist on . . . certain practical securities."

"The League is for mutual protection. We are all agreed that it should be made so strong, so armed with force and economic sanctions that no aggressor would dare to face the combined might of the League members. What more security can you ask?"

Again Sonino is demanding geographical barriers between enemies. Again President Wilson is protesting that they should have no enemies, now that they have signed the peace. The position of the United States is different, insists Clemenceau. With an ocean either side of her, America can afford to forgive her enemies. But, as for France— Fifty years ago Germany dictated her terms of peace, repeats Clemenceau. Now it is France's turn. No, France will not take German statesmanship as a model. She'll improve on it—

"Gentlemen, I loathe German militarism as much as you do," President Wilson is saying. "It was and still remains the most vicious threat to civilization. My country joined your effort to stamp it out, but we mustn't imitate the very thing we despise. A treaty of revenge will one day put those in power who will use revenge as the excuse for their own ambitions. I plead with you not to give them that excuse. We have broken the German military machine. We have deposed their rulers. We are now dealing with a people's government in Germany. Let's give this government a chance—a chance to break with the past."

CLEMENCEAU—The Germans never forgive defeat. I know that, Mr. Wilson—they are our enemies and shall always be our enemies.

WILSON (*sits in his chair*)—That depends on us. We can either cause that to happen or prevent it—here, by what we do now.

SONINO—Do you want to let the Germans go unpunished after the horrors of the last four years?

WILSON—No, I agree with you that the wrongs committed by Germany in this war have to be righted. I agree that the German people share the responsibility with their Government for their vicious and criminal aggression, and it ought to be burned into man's consciousness forever that no people should permit its government to do what the German Government did. But you cannot obliterate a nation of sixty million people—or do you advocate starving them to death?

CLEMENCEAU (*obviously bored*)—The blockade again!

WILSON—Yes, the blockade! Gentlemen, once more I demand the blockade be lifted and supply ships be permitted to enter German ports.

CLEMENCEAU—I told you I can do nothing. A military necessity.

WILSON—But I spoke to Marshal Foch and he says it's safe.

CLEMENCEAU—Foch is not a military pope. He may be mistaken. I prefer to follow the advice of Marshal Petain. Besides, Mr. Wilson, have you considered that if the German people suffer a little they may be more inclined to accept our peace terms?

WILSON—Monsieur Clemenceau . . .

LLOYD-GEORGE—Gentlemen, I'm afraid our discussion—interesting as it is—has no direct bearing on the Adriatic problem before us. I need hardly remind you that all Europe is becoming most anxious over our . . . somewhat lengthy deliberations.

The arguments are resumed. Mr. Sonino cannot go back to Italy without Fiume. With Italy it has become a matter of national honor. Only because feeling has been worked up by Italy's controlled press, answers President Wilson. Even the agreed upon secrecy of the treaty conferences has been violated. If these violations continue, President Wilson warns them, he will go to the press with a complete statement of all that has happened in the conferences, including Clemenceau's repeated threats to withdraw from the League unless he (Wilson) subscribes to his (Clemenceau's) treaty demands.

"I regret this information reached the press," regrets Sonino, "but you misunderstand its effect on my country. They do not resent concessions to our Allies, so long as similar benefits are bestowed upon Italy."

"From this point on I intend to call a halt on all such benefits," replies the President. Lloyd-George and Sonino exchange significant glances and turn to Clemenceau. The French premier is very much awake now and his temper is plainly rising. "Mr. Wilson, you have not begun to hear France's demands," says Clemenceau, with the suggestion of a low growl.

"I think before we proceed any further I should know the extent of all your demands," replies President Wilson very quietly.

Clemenceau accepts the challenge. France will accept no treaty that does not include the Saar Basin "and all the territory west of the Rhine." President Wilson can hardly believe that this statement is made seriously, but M. Clemenceau assures him that it is. France has won her right to dictate by winning the war. He is not at all concerned with the interests of the people living in the Saar territory. They can go live where they please. Armistice or no armistice, they had forfeited their rights in the war. "They are murderers," calmly announces Clemenceau.

"It is dangerous to pronounce a nation a murderer," warns President Wilson. "If the Germans accept the verdict they may act accordingly."

CLEMENCEAU—We will prevent that.

WILSON—How, Monsieur Clemenceau? If not through the League of Nations— (CLEMENCEAU *shrugs*.) Have you estimated the cost of maintaining an army big enough to prevent them from forming a bigger one? Can France support such an army?

CLEMENCEAU—The Saar and the Rhineland will help. We will create a defensive barrier around France that will be impregnable.

WILSON—Such security is worthless, Monsieur Clemenceau. You may build a wall to keep destruction out and later find that you have fenced it in.

CLEMENCEAU—Are you trying to frighten me, Mr. Wilson? I and my Government demand the Rhineland and the Saar Basin in the name of the French people!

WILSON—I doubt if you or your Government knows or cares what your people want.

LLOYD-GEORGE—Mr. Wilson! After all, Monsieur is the originator of the present French policy. Is there any better authority for what the French people want?

WILSON—Yes, the people themselves. Gentlemen, I suggest that we go to the Italian people and let them decide about Fiume.

SONINO—I protest!

WILSON—And that we go to the French people and ask them what kind of peace they want—

CLEMENCEAU—They don't want your kind, Mr. Wilson. I can tell you that! No, and not even your own people want it! Not even America—because you are pro-German and sympathize with our enemies.

WILSON (*his face livid*)—And you, Monsieur Clemenceau, are a thief!

LLOYD-GEORGE (*rising quickly*)—Gentlemen! (*There is a moment in which* CLEMENCEAU *and* WILSON *eye each other with defiance, and then* WILSON *turns stiffly and walks out the door.* CLEMENCEAU *quickly regains his composure.*)

SONINO—Now he will appeal to the people. . . .

CLEMENCEAU—Let him.

SONINO (*dubiously*)—I did not think you were going to mention the Rhineland so soon.

CLEMENCEAU—Fiume will appear a very slight concession now.

SONINO (*brightening*)—I see . . . But Mr. Wilson's League—this League of Nations—will it approve the terms of the treaty . . . our terms?

CLEMENCEAU—The League? Gentlemen— There is a story of an inventor who had a machine. Oh, a very remarkable machine that was to move perpetually. There were wheels and discs and cylinders . . . and all run by electric energy. On the paper it was perfect—not a flaw. Every possibility thought out. Every problem solved. Er—except one. . . . He couldn't get the machine to start. (SONINO *roars with laughter.*)

LLOYD-GEORGE (*standing at the window looking down*)—He's getting in his car. Funny—there are no crowds around him any more. He seems quite alone. (*Turns to his two allies.*) And to think, gentlemen, if he had appealed to these people two months ago, even one month ago, he could have overthrown any government in Europe.

CLEMENCEAU (*quietly*)—*If* . . .

The three are smiling at each other as the curtain falls.

Two months later, in the living room of the Wilson apartment in Paris, Colonel House and Henry White of the American Peace Commission are considering the Peace Treaty. The Germans have yet to sign, but Colonel House is sure they will accept. President Wilson, he reports, is not in sympathy with all the terms of the treaty; many of them, in fact, he had vigorously opposed, including that of the Fiume incident.

"How do you account for the change in the people's regard for the President?" asks Mr. White. "Just fickleness?"

"Misrepresentation on the part of the few, forgetfulness on the part of the many," replies Colonel House.

Mr. White has been called to this particular conference with the President, the Colonel explains, in the hope that even if he does not fully approve of the treaty which has been signed, that he will understand the difficulties under which it was made, and support it, says Colonel House—

"Mr. White, as unsatisfactory as the treaty may be, have you considered what kind of peace might have been made without the President's endeavor?"

"I suppose it's possible the terms would've been even more severe."

"There was enough organized hate in Europe to resume the war. You just referred to the treaty as one part hope. In that hope lies the means of its redemption. All its shortcomings we trust will eventually be corrected by the League of Nations, provided our country joins and throws its tremendous and isolated power in the balance."

"And until that happens?"

"We must all work together to achieve that as soon as possible. In this you can be of great service."

It would be a help, Colonel House suggests, if when he returns

IN TIME TO COME

to America, he would bring influence to bear on the leaders of his party. Mr. White is afraid his party influence at the moment is at pretty low ebb.

The outer door is heard to open. The President has let himself into the house. He has recently dispensed with servants, Colonel House explains, having become suspicious that those selected for him previously had been working in the interests of the French Government. The President has been under considerable strain, the Colonel also suggests, tactfully. It would be helpful if Mr. White would state such criticism of the treaty as he had in mind rather mildly.

As the President comes into the room with Mrs. Wilson he appears thin and extremely tense. "His eyes are restless; his whole manner bears evidence of resentment and disillusionment."

The Germans are still holding off signing the treaty, the President reports, because of the war guilt clause. If they persist in their refusal the French Army may have to take over again.

"Surely they wouldn't renew the war?" protests Mrs. Wilson.

"It's a question whether it ever stopped," answers House.

"Or ever will," adds Mr. White.

The President has asked Mr. White to this meeting hoping for his support of the treaty as signed. Mr. White will go no farther than to say that he hopes that what has been done is for the best. He will, he tells the President, support the treaty "to the extent that it fulfills your high purposes."

Mrs. Wilson returns with a sedative tablet for the President. Dr. Grayson has prescribed that. Mr. White is hopeful that the voyage home will give the Wilsons a needed rest. A moment later he takes his leave.

The President does not feel that he can depend on Mr. White for much support. "He's a party man, after all. I distrust all politicians. . . . I prefer that we have no further dealings with Mr. White," says the President.

"The crowds are beginning to collect in the street." Colonel House is at the window. "I wonder what's going through their minds. What are they waiting for? A miracle from heaven or a chance to get back in their civilian clothes? A new world or an excuse to spend a night in a cafe?"

"I believe in the people," mutters the President, his voice coming as from a great distance, quietly, and without any feeling.

"You've done all any man can do," says Colonel House, regarding his friend "with sorrow and with deep respect."

"Isn't it enough for you, either, House?" demands the President, his temper flaring. "Are you going to apologize for the treaty?"

"I know how you feel, Governor. A parent loves a sick child more than a well one."

It is the President's intention to take the treaty home with him, present it to the people and explain it to them. In view of this decision Colonel House would have the President know that there is a report that an American newspaper chain has secured a copy of the treaty. The news is alarming but the President does not believe any newspaper would risk a charge of treason by printing the treaty. Unless, Colonel House suggests, they could get it read into the Congressional Record. Then it would become news.

In any event, there is nothing to be done, unless, as Colonel House suggests, the President would be willing to try taking his enemies by surprise. He could make them his friends by taking men like Senator Lodge into his confidence. No doubt there would have to be compromises. But, seeing the President has already made many sacrifices for the treaty, why not one or two more?

"You want me to enter into political training?" demands the President.

"If the trades are in your favor, yes."

"Politics! I tell you I'll have no more haggling with politicians." The President's manner grows more excited. "Let them print the treaty. Let them attack it. I'll answer them—clause for clause—word for word. I'll show them up before the whole country. I'll go to the people—this time *my* people!"

"If that's your decision."

"It is."

A moment after the Colonel leaves Mrs. Wilson returns. She still is worried about her husband. These endless conferences are leaving him drained and depressed, unsure of himself and of his work. "Can you spare that energy? Do they accomplish so much?" she asks.

"We accomplished nothing. They're all against me."

"Never mind, dear." A slight look of satisfaction has come into her face. "You'll rest better now that it's over."

"If I could shut off my thoughts at night. But I carry them into my sleep. . . . Last night we were in a cemetery like the one we visited at Beaumont, and there were several men sitting around. We thought at first they were caretakers, but they had helmets on. They'd pulled up some of the crosses and they began to whittle. I spoke to them but they wouldn't look up.

They kept tearing loose the cross-sticks and putting sharp points on them."

Secretary Lansing has called by phone to report that Clemenceau has refused to strike out the war guilt clause. "He may live to see Germany throw those words in his face," mutters President Wilson.

"What will happen now, Woodrow?" asked Mrs. Wilson, sitting down beside him. "Will the Germans sign even so?"

WILSON—I think so.

EDITH—But you want them to sign?

WILSON (*dully*)—I want to get it over with. So this is the treaty . . . This is the best we could do.

EDITH—But the League's part of it, Woodrow—the important part.

WILSON—Yes, there's still the League.

EDITH (*looking at him with great sympathy and taking his arm to lead him out*)—Darling, lie down for a while. I'll bring you in any news.

WILSON (*putting his hand over hers*)—My dear, you've been so kind. I'm afraid I haven't been as thoughtful of you.

EDITH—All I ask is to help you in the little ways I can.

WILSON (*smiles, touching the document*)—The little things are part of the big things . . . From now on this is *our* Covenant, Edith . . . between ourselves and with the world. We'll take it back to our people . . . They'll understand what it means . . . that we've made a beginning and with their help, we'll never rest until it's done. (*They look at each other for a moment. Then suddenly a bell begins to toll—the deep somber tones of Notre Dame. They stand for a moment looking toward the window. Then against the resonant sound of the Cathedral bells comes the insistent tinkle of the telephone. The* PRESIDENT *hurries over to answer it.*) Yes? . . . Yes. . . . Thank you. (*He puts the receiver down, turns to* EDITH, *who looks at him eagerly.*) The Germans have accepted. (*She smiles. Now from a remote point comes the faint boom of a cannon as an army post salutes the peace. A shadow crosses* WILSON'S *face for a brief instant, then a triumphant acceptance of whatever is and whatever is to come.*)

The curtain falls.

In late August, 1919, the Wilsons are back in the White House. At the moment, in his study, the President is giving dictation to

Joe Tumulty, his secretary. "He still has a harried look, but appears more spirited and defiant." The letter he is dictating is to Colonel House.

"My dear Colonel House: In response to your letter, I appreciate your interest and advice, but . . ." He cannot go on with this and Tumulty crosses it out. "My dear Colonel House: I have already made arrangements to meet Senator Lodge to discuss our . . . our differences before receiving yours of the same date advising me to do so. I look forward to an understanding with Mr. Lodge but without any of the—concessions you think advisable." No, that will not do either. In the end he decides not to send any letter.

Mrs. Wilson is in for a moment. Senator Lodge's secretary has telephoned that the Senator is on the way. She hopes that in their talk the President will be careful—

"Edith, if I'd stump the country, if I'd talk in every city, I could still bring him to his knees instead of ask him favors."

"You must put that out of your mind."

"I promised our soldiers, when I asked them to risk their lives, that it was a war to end wars, and I must do all in my power to put the treaty into effect."

"There's a limit to what anyone can do. You know what Cary Grayson said."

"Taking my life in my hands . . . Yes, I suppose I can better afford my pride. (*Presses her hand.*) Don't worry, my dear. For the Covenant I'll even do this."

When Senator Lodge arrives his manner is "frigidly polite." "Underneath his formality there is a dangerous undertone of suspicion and hostility."

The weather having been discussed and dismissed, the reasons and excuses for the meeting are taken up. It was the President's impression that it was mutually desirable. It is the Lodge idea that the appointment was entirely at the President's request. "It is evident he has no intention of sparing the President any possible humiliation."

There are a number of points that have come up in relation to the peace treaty on which he would like the Senator's advice, the President admits. The Senator is a little surprised. He has a feeling that any advice he may have to give would have been more timely before the President went to Europe, but the President feels that he was well acquainted with the Senator's point of view at that time. True, whenever the Senator had tried to see the President before it was Colonel House who had received him, but now the President has decided to give the matter his personal attention.

It is the President's earnest wish that they may be able to come to an understanding on the League of Nations. Because a copy of the treaty had been secured by bribery and published in opposition newspapers to embarrass the President before his return from Paris, the League Covenant had been misrepresented from the start—

"Senator, I'm sure we have one purpose in common—to serve the best interests of the American people," ventures the President.

"But apparently very different ideas as to what constitutes their best *interests*," sharply replies Senator Lodge.

WILSON—In that case, shouldn't we at least try to reconcile them?

LODGE—Very well. If you want my opinion, this is it: The American people want most of all to forget the war and its problems and to return to normal conditions of living.

WILSON—Normal conditions wait on one thing only . . . the peace.

LODGE—The treaty would have been approved by Congress weeks ago if it weren't attached to your League.

WILSON—It isn't my League, Senator. The Covenant is the expression of the world's enduring hope. I'm merely one of its proponents.

LODGE—And you've stated your case before the Foreign Relations Committee. Since then I've replied to your arguments. What more is there for us to say?

WILSON—What we said on those occasions was for the public record. I thought that in a private conversation such as this, we might reach a more frank . . . collaboration.

LODGE—Collaboration? Just a moment, Mr. Wilson. You're not suggesting that you're prepared to deed me a half interest in your idealistic venture? If you are, I can assure you there was never a more unwilling grantee.

WILSON (*stiffening*)—Mr. Lodge, may I ask that your personal feeling toward me be kept out of our discussion?

LODGE—You're mistaken, sir, if you believe any personal feeling has influenced my opposition to the League of Nations. I've stated my objections. I'm utterly opposed to the pledge of American arms and economic sanctions to preserve the territorial integrity of all other nations.

WILSON—As I've already pointed out, such obligations would

be moral and not legal ones—and within the jurisdiction of Congress to pass upon.

LODGE—Mr. President, I'm not currently known as an idealist but I do have a very deep respect for moral obligations and I wouldn't like to commit my country to a course of action which she could avoid only by a dishonorable repudiation of her accepted responsibilities.

WILSON—She wouldn't try to avoid her obligations when they were justly called upon.

LODGE—And that, Mr. Wilson, would mean war. War every time an ambitious ruler in Europe or Asia tries to extend his influence at the expense of a neighbor. War every time one state covets the land or resources of another. We'd be constantly embroiled in quarrels that would be none of our business.

WILSON—The peace of every part of the world is the business of every civilized person and every civilized state.

LODGE (*behind his chair*)—Mr. Wilson, you have a great liking for high phrases. I confess I'm no match for you in the verbiage of idealism. But I too have my ideals. And one of them is peace —but a realistic peace that we can surely maintain on our own continent. I realize it's not fashionable to quote Washington these days but that was his farewell advice to the American people.

WILSON—Washington spoke for his own time. We're living in a smaller world. In our own lifetime the conditions that face a laborer in a Wisconsin mill or a cotton grower in Georgia may depend upon policies in Roumania or Poland. Whether we wish it or not, we can no longer separate our national destiny from the common problems of mankind.

The tension is not relieved by Senator Lodge's declaration that if it is his advice rather than his conversion that the President seeks he will give it: "Accept Senate reservations to the treaty and keep out of European affairs unless in an advisory capacity."

In the eyes of the Allied statesmen, President Wilson feels, that would be a retreat from the purposes of the United States in fighting the war. If Senator Lodge had watched these men toil over the treaty as he had he would be less quick to question their motives.

Seeing this is an "off the record" conversation, Senator Lodge would like to ask the President a few relevant questions: Was Mr. Wilson entirely satisfied with the motives of the Council of Four when they took the Province of Shantung away from China and gave it to Japan? The President was satisfied with the motives, but opposed the action of the Council.

If Japan had been refused Shantung, would she have accepted the League? Mr. Wilson does not know. Did Mr. Wilson contest French occupation of the Saar, and Italian control of Fiume? He did. And gained a modification in both instances. Would Italy and France have entered the League if he had not? The President considers that query irrelevant. Very well. Did he seek to limit German indemnities to a reasonable sum? He did.

"But in spite of that, the Treaty calls for reparations beyond Germany's capacity to pay," thunders the Senator. "That's true, isn't it?"

"Reparations were *your* idea in the first place, Mr. Lodge, as I remember," replies the President with a faint smile.

Senator Lodge's face is flushed, but he continues the attack. Had the President opposed the annexation of the German colonies? He had, as far as he could, but he had found reason to approve the Treaty despite his objections. Were these reasons influenced by his discovery of the secret treaties of other nations? The President does not feel that he is at liberty to answer that question—

"I believe I quote you correctly that 'The hearts of Clemenceau and Lloyd-George beat with the heart of the world.' At the time these provisions were discussed in the Council, were you equally convinced of their lofty idealism?"

"Mr. Lodge, at this point the motives of the allied statesmen aren't important. Perhaps we made mistakes—all of us, but regardless of the Treaty and what we think of it, or of those who made it, the League is attached to it. And the League of Nations is the only hope we have to avoid wars in the future. I beg you to consider that. I beg you to help me save that hope."

"Do you admit, then, Mr. Wilson, that they forced a vicious treaty down your throat in exchange for the League of Nations?"

"I consider that question an impertinence!"

"Mr. Wilson, I've always been able to guess the processes of thought behind your actions. Let me venture another. You've got the world saddled with a Treaty you despise for the sake of a Covenant no one else really wants. And you're beginning to realize that you're desperate. Your conscience can't face the prospect of losing what you've paid such a price for. So you'd even enlist me to salvage it. . . . But I want no part of the League. It's yours, Mr. Wilson. Take it down in history with you—the history you've got your heart set on making. You're little concerned with the kind of peace so long as your name's attached to it. You don't care about your country's welfare, but your own personal glory!"

"Mr. Lodge, the President has no further business with you."

For a moment the two men stare at each other with implacable hate. Then Senator Lodge turns his back and walks to the door. "The President makes no move until his caller has left. Then a tremor runs through his body. He sits, and his eyes glance about the room as if he were just waking from a sleep and getting his bearings. They come to rest on the wall map of the United States. A resolve is taking inflexible form in his mind."

Tumulty comes to ask if there is anything he can do. "Yes . . . you can start making arrangements for my trip," the President answers. "There's only one way left . . . I'm going to the people."

"No, that's out of the question, Governor. Grayson's absolutely certain it would be . . . well, as much as your life's worth."

WILSON—Even if that's true, can I ask any less of myself than I've asked of thousands of others.

TUMULTY—But it isn't the same thing. You're needed here. You can't afford to take any risks.

WILSON—I can't afford not to . . . Joe, there will come a day when the world will call our memories to account . . . for what we did and what we left undone. Whatever happens we must preserve our faith in us or they may lose their faith in the things that inspired us. (*His mood changes to business as he crosses to the map.*) Here's the route I have in mind. We begin in Cleveland . . . then Detroit . . . (*With his pencil he begins to trace on map connecting lines between dots.*) Chicago . . . St. Paul . . . Topeka . . . across to Salt Lake City . . . Sante Fe . . . Pueblo . . . That's eight . . . Let's see—about five more. We'll decide on them later.

TUMULTY—Thirteen stops. That's a lot of speaking, Governor.

WILSON—I must reach as many people as I can and I've got to do it quickly. . . . Joe, if you'll take down some notes I'll work them into my speeches.

TUMULTY—Yes, Governor. (TUMULTY *sits down with a pad and pencil.* WILSON *starts to dictate.*)

WILSON (*pacing*)—"There's only one honorable course when you have won a cause—to see that it stays won" . . . That's the note I must keep hitting—see that the war stays won. . . . "The hatreds of the world have not cooled" . . . No, make that rivalries . . . "The rivalries of the world have not cooled."

TUMULTY—Yes, sir.

WILSON—"Victory has been won over a particular group of nations but not over the passions of those nations" . . . That's not enough. Add "or over the passions of those nations that were set against them."

TUMULTY—That hits close to home.

WILSON—That's what I mean it to do. (*Goes on dictating.*) "We have not made the weak nations strong by making them independent. If you leave those nations to take care of themselves, Germany will yet have her will upon them, and we shall have committed the unpardonable sin of undoing the victory which our boys won." (*Now warming up to his speech.*) "You cannot establish freedom without force and the only force you can substitute for an armed mankind is the concerted force of the combined action of mankind through the instrumentality of all the enlightened governments of the world. . . ."

The President is still dictating as the curtain falls.

It is the following March 4. In the President's study Joe Tumulty is half heartedly emptying letters from the desk into a file. Dr. Grayson comes from an adjoining room. President Wilson, he reports, has come through the inaugural ceremony much better than he had expected. "He won't stop fighting until he's—dead," says Grayson.

"I wonder if he'll stop then. . . . I was proud of him this morning, Doc. He walked out of here President of the United States. He sat there straight as a poker while they gave the oath to Harding. And when he came back, by God, he was still President."

"To us, Joe."

"I watched his eyes while Harding spoke. I never saw pain before—not like that. It was the whole world crying—without a tear being shed."

Dr. Grayson is remembering the inaugural and quoting bitterly from the Harding address: " 'America's present need is not heroics but healing, not revolution but restoration, not surgery but serenity, not nostrum but normalcy.' . . . Those are the words they cheered for. That's what the crowd wanted to hear."

"Let the politicians, the practical men take over," says Tumulty with Irish fire in his eyes. "Give them the world and see what they can do with it. They've beaten him down, maybe they've killed him. But they haven't killed what he stood for and they never will. Some day it will rise up again and sweep their kind off the earth. . . . I'd rather go down in history as Wilson's office boy than the twenty-ninth President of the United States!"

It is Dr. Grayson's opinion that Tumulty himself had better have a care. Let him continue as he has been going much longer and he, too, will stand in danger of a collapse. If the President had listened to his doctor before he stumped the country— But the Tumulty mind finds it hard to readjust itself.

"I'll never forget that speech in Pueblo," the worried secretary is saying. "His body was shaking when he went on the platform. He could hardly speak above a whisper. But that audience never missed a word. . . . The last of what he had went out of him that night."

Nor is Tumulty so sure that his President needs him any longer. There is a certain look that has come into the Wilson eye that Tumulty has seen once before. Colonel House was in his mind then.

"No, Joe, that's different," says Dr. Grayson, with an attempt at reassurance. "House shared his dream, so House is the reminder of all he lost. That's more than any man in his condition could bear."

"Funny, I never thought of it that way. . . . Look here, Grayson. I'll black his shoes if he lets me stay. But if he—doesn't want me around, for *any* reason or for *no* reason, I can understand. See? . . . Don't let it make any difference to you."

"All right, Joe."

Mrs. Wilson comes in. There are the last orders to be given that everything may be left ready for Mr. Harding. Dr. Grayson takes the opportunity to suggest that perhaps Washington is not the best place for the Wilsons to live after they leave the White House, but Mrs. Wilson thinks it is. Her husband will want to keep in touch with things, and as for forgetting—he couldn't do that in Alaska any better than he could here. "He will go on as long as he can," she says, "and I'll go on with him."

"Edith, you're a very great woman," Grayson says, seriously.

"Cary! You're no judge of that. You've known me too long."

"I wonder if you realize that for six months when he was so ill, you were for all intents and purposes President of the United States? And a damn good one!"

"No. I was only carrying out his wishes. Even when he couldn't speak to me, I knew what he wanted and how he wanted it done. You learn that from—loving a man. But *he* was still the President."

Colonel House is announced. He is downstairs and would like to pay his respects to the President. Mrs. Wilson is about to send the Colonel word that the President is not well enough to see anyone, but changes her mind. She sends word to the President instead.

It is a changed Wilson who shortly comes into the room. He has become "an old man, shrunken, white-haired, one paralyzed arm held still against his body. Only his eyes are alive, and they have a terrible brightness." Mrs. Wilson tells the President that Colonel House has come to pay him a visit and is waiting downstairs.

President Wilson looks slowly from his wife to Grayson, to Tumulty and back to his wife "as if expecting someone to deny her words. Then he appears suddenly to forget the people as he notices trifling changes in the room. He begins to put things back in their accustomed places as if he could only pull his forces together under conditions entirely familiar. Crossing to the file, he opens a section and carries some papers to his desk. Next he observes that the globe has been packed. Glancing at Tumulty with almost childish resentment, he takes the globe from the box and returns it to its standard. Then, seated at his desk, he removes objects from the drawer—a pen, a paper-weight, an inkstand, a blotter—and very carefully puts them back on the top of his desk in the precise positions they originally stood. Now he appears more satisfied, more in command. Again he is the President at his desk. During this long interim, the others have remained so still while they waited, that even their breathing seemed to be suspended. Time did not pass—it stopped and resumes again as Wilson brings the focus of his mind back to their presence. . . . He speaks directly to Tumulty with his voice under tight restraint."

"Please thank Colonel House for calling and tell him I . . . regret that I'm unable to see him."

"Governor, are you sure that you—" The President's eyes have become steel. Tumulty bites his lip, turns and goes.

"Edith," says the President, "I've been thinking over the question of a secretary. As soon as we move, I feel we should procure a new one."

"You mean—in place of Tumulty?"

"Yes."

"Very well, Woodrow. Just as you wish."

The President has returned to the rearrangement of his desk, looking in the drawers for other familiar objects. Hereafter, he says, he does not wish to have anything touched that is on his desk. Mrs. Wilson will see to that. She is sure he is going to like their new house, and with more leisure they will be able to do many things again that they had had to give up. They will resume their rides into Virginia again, and Cary will go with them—

Tumulty is back. "Colonel House asked me to convey his affectionate regards to you both," he says. As the President looks up with a harsh: "Well?" Tumulty goes on: "Governor, he thought your . . . health might be such that you wouldn't be able to see him, so he brought along this letter, which he asked me to give you."

The President looks down at the envelope in his hand for a long time and then deliberately tears through it and lets the pieces fall unopened to the floor. Suddenly he looks up, startled. There is a gun firing in the distance, he insists, and begins mumblingly to count the reports only he can hear.

"It's over! Why don't they stop!" he cries out in anguished protest. "Why must they keep shooting? Why? Why?"

They would have him lie down before he tries to go on with the article he feels he still has to prepare on the Covenant. He will be better able to work after a rest—

"I think I shall begin very simply," the President is saying, as Mrs. Wilson is helping him back to his room, "like this: 'The people of the world desire peace. We must strive on to make their will effectual. . . . We must never stop until . . . Peace can be secured only by the unity of nations against aggression. This unity must be achieved.'"

They have disappeared through the doorway. Tumulty stands alone in the room. Presently his eyes stray to the torn letter on the floor. He picks it up as Dr. Grayson comes back into the room. Tumulty tears open the envelope and puts the pieces of the letter together, smoothing them out on the desk. He glances at Grayson, who nods, and Tumulty begins to read—

"'Dear Governor: Forgive me for taking this liberty. There is something that is much on my mind. You may think me of the opinion, Governor, that things would be different if you had followed certain ideas of mine regarding the Treaty . . . in short, that, in my judgment, time has borne me out. Believe me, this is not the case. The conviction has grown in me that what happened had to be, and is perhaps even for the best.

"'For we must not underestimate this first great step. What may seem a failure at this time will one day find its justification as a model for what must never be allowed to happen again. Surely the day will come when your idea of the nations united to preserve the peace of the world will be put forward anew. And our people will know then, as we know now, the nature of the forces that operated against us—and that knowledge will be their weapon to achieve the fulfillment of your idea.

" 'For those who call themselves practical men—those whose creed it is to avoid their responsibility to the world—have seemed to prevail over us. But *in time to come they and their kind will be found impractical, and yours will be the final victory.*

" 'Men in the future will ask God to bless you, Governor, as I do now. . . . Ever your friend, House.' "

"Tumulty lifts his head, looks at Grayson, who answers his gaze. Their faces seem to reflect a renewal of courage and faith."

THE CURTAIN FALLS

THE MOON IS DOWN
A Drama in Two Parts

By John Steinbeck

IT was April 7 before Oscar Serlin, the producer, got John Steinbeck's drama of the military invasion of a neutral country, "The Moon Is Down," on a New York stage. The book of the same title already had gone through innumerable printings, and had caused as startling an explosion of superlatives in book review circles as any work of the year. Quite reasonably great things were expected of the drama.

To the disappointment of the book-enthused supporters the reception of the play was considerably less ecstatic. A majority of the drama critics agreed that "The Moon Is Down" was a good play insofar as it was competently acted, clearly spoken and well staged. But several of them were inclined to qualify their evaluations by declaring that they found it singularly unconvincing. If Mr. Steinbeck's Nazi officer class, which this group was obviously intended to represent, was true, then the popular belief in stories of Nazi brutality, and the deliberate and sustained cruelties of Nazi invasions of the occupied countries, must have been grossly exaggerated. If it were the author's hope that "The Moon Is Down" would be accepted as an inspiriting message from the heart of an occupied country saying the freemen were standing firm and would win in the end, that hope, they argued, was smothered by a more compelling suggestion that the true nobility of the higher and better German character was being unfairly attacked by Nazi enemies, including ourselves.

"By making his invaders more sinned against than sinning," Richard Lockridge wrote in the *New York Sun*, "Mr. Steinbeck has dissipated his drama. The drama needs two hostile forces face to face. Here are pleasant, reasonable people on one side and on the other only disembodied orders from 'the capital.' Mr. Steinbeck proves himself tolerant to a fault and his play suffers. So, I suspect, does his argument."

The debate spread until it included again the book reviewers, who returned to defend their belief in both play and novel, and drew into it such outraged enemies of Hitler Naziism as Dorothy Thompson, who thought to restate her faith in the basic virtues of the German people as represented by the better side of these gentler Nazi officers.

Public support of the drama strengthened, wavered and finally fell away to such an extent that Mr. Serlin decided to withdraw "The Moon Is Down" after fifty-five performances. Later a road company was organized with Conrad Nagel at its head. Some changes were made in the direction of the play and it was received with marked enthusiasm in the West.

The action of "The Moon Is Down" is in the present. The locale is not specifically designated, save as that of "a small mining town." The first scene reveals the drawing room of the Mayor's house. "The room is poor but has about it a certain official grandeur; tarnished gold chairs with worn tapestry seats and backs, and the slight stuffiness of all official rooms. . . . Altogether it is a warm room, which, trying to be stiff and official, has from use become rather comfortable and pleasant." Glass-paned doors let into a vestibule from which stairs to the upper rooms ascend. A small coal fire is burning in the grate, about which comfortable chairs are grouped. A long sofa, with small tables at either end, is in the center of the room. The Mayor's desk and chair stand at the side against the wall, near the door leading to his bedroom. Doors to dining room and kitchen are opposite.

It is nearing 11 o'clock in the morning. In the Mayor's drawing room Dr. Winter, "bearded, simple and benign," is sitting on the sofa waiting to see the Mayor. "He is the town historian and physician, and is dressed in a dark suit and very white linen, but his shoes are heavy and thick-soled. He sits rolling his thumbs over and over in his lap."

Joseph, the Mayor's serving man, tall, spare, properly humble, but definitely an individual, is straightening up the furniture and finding little things to change to keep himself within gossiping range of the Doctor.

Invaders are expected. Their note has said that they will arrive at 11 and they, being a time-minded people, as the Doctor notes, will be there. "They hurry to their destiny as though it wouldn't wait." The Mayor, it appears, is being dressed for the occasion by his wife, who has been insistent that he shall look his best, even to the point of having the hair trimmed out of his ears—

Dr. Winter is amused by the picture. "We're so wonderful. Our country is invaded and Madame is holding the Mayor by the neck and trimming the hair from his ears."

"He was getting shaggy, sir," Joseph reports, quite seriously.

"His eyebrows, too. His Excellency is even more upset about having his eyebrows trimmed than his ears. He says that hurts."

There is a knock at the door. The invaders are early. A moment later a soldier steps into the room, makes a cursory survey of the situation and steps aside. He is followed by Captain Bentick. They are both wearing plain uniforms, the Captain's rank modestly indicated by a shoulder tab. They wear helmets not quite like those of any known military force. "Captain Bentick is a slightly overdrawn picture of an English gentleman. He has a slouch. His face is red, long nose, but rather pleasant, and he seems as unhappy in his uniform as most British General Officers are."

The Captain is looking for the Mayor. He and his Sergeant have come to search for weapons before the Commanding Officer arrives. The Sergeant proceeds first to search Dr. Winter and Joseph, but with the Captain's apologies. According to the card given him there are also firearms in the house.

"Do you know where every gun in the town is?" inquires the interested Doctor.

"Nearly all, I guess," affably answers the Captain. "We had our people working here for quite a long time."

"Working here? Who?"

"Well, the work is done now. It's bound to come out. The man in charge here is named Corell."

"George Corell?"

"Yes."

"I don't believe it. I can't believe it. Why, George had dinner with me on Friday. Why, I've played chess with George night after night. You must be wrong. Why, he gave the big shooting match in the hills this morning—gave the prizes—"

"Yes—that was clever—there wasn't a soldier in town."

The Mayor and Mrs. Orden have come from the Mayor's bedroom. "He is a fine looking man of about sixty-five and he seems a little too common and too simple for the official morning coat he wears and the gold chain of office around his neck. His hair has been fiercely brushed, but already a few hairs are struggling to be free. He has dignity and warmth. Behind him Madame enters. She is small and wrinkled and fierce, and very proprietary. She considers that she created this man, and ever since he has been trying to get out of hand. She watches him constantly as the lady shower of a prize dog watches her entry at a dog show."

Captain Bentick explains his duty call, the Sergeant searches the Mayor for weapons, again with the Captain's apologies, and the matter of firearms in the house is taken up. Yes, the Mayor has a shotgun and a sporting rifle. They are, he thinks, in the back of the cabinet in his bedroom. He hasn't used them in a long time. The guns recovered, the Captain and the Sergeant politely withdraw. Colonel Lanser may be expected shortly.

Madame Orden is worried. How many officers should they expect? Should she offer them tea or a glass of wine? She asks the Doctor.

"It's been so long since we've been invaded, or invaded anyone else," the Doctor admits, "I just don't know what's correct."

"We won't offer them anything," announces the Mayor. "I don't think the people would like it. *I* don't want to drink wine with them."

Still Madame Orden is not satisfied. Why shouldn't they keep the proper decencies alive?

MAYOR ORDEN—Madame, I think with your permission we will not have wine! The people are confused. We have lived at peace so long they don't quite believe in war. Six town boys were murdered this morning. We will have no hunt breakfast. The people do not fight wars for sport.

MADAME—Murdered?

MAYOR ORDEN (*bitterly*)—Our twelve soldiers were at the shooting match in the hills. They saw the parachutes and they came back. At the bend in the road by Toller's farm the machine guns opened on them and six were killed.

MADAME (*excitedly*)—Which ones were killed? Annie's sister's boy was there.

MAYOR ORDEN—I don't know which ones were killed. (*He looks at* DR. WINTER.) I don't even know how many soldiers are here. . . . Do you know how many men the invader has?

DR. WINTER (*shrugging*)—Not many, I think. Not over two hundred and fifty. But all with those little machine guns.

MAYOR ORDEN—Have you heard anything about the rest of the country? Here there were parachutes, a little transport. It happened so quickly. Was there no resistance anywhere?

DR. WINTER—I don't know. The wires are cut. There is no news.

MAYOR ORDEN—And our soldiers . . . ?

DR. WINTER—I don't know.

JOSEPH (*entering*)—I heard . . . that is, Annie heard . . . six of our men were killed by the machine guns. Annie heard

three were wounded and captured.
  MAYOR ORDEN—But there were twelve.
  JOSEPH—Annie heard three escaped.
  MAYOR ORDEN (*sharply*)—Which ones escaped?
  JOSEPH—I don't know, sir. Annie didn't hear.

Madame Orden has time to give Joseph final instructions as to how he shall act in the presence of the invaders; how he should pass the cigarettes in the little silver conserve box and then leave the room. There is a sound of marching men outside and the command "Company, halt!" rings through the room. A moment later a helmeted Corporal has entered to announce that Colonel Lanser requests an audience with His Excellency. The Colonel follows a second later.

Colonel Lanser's rank is also indicated by his shoulder tab. He is "a middle-aged man, gray and hard and tired-looking. He has the square shoulders of a soldier, but his eyes lack the blank wall of a soldier's mind."

The introductions are formal and pleasant. Presently George Corell appears and with some show of confidence disposes of his hat and coat. The Colonel assumes that they all know Mr. Corell. Yes, indeed—they know him. But not until Dr. Winter tells them do the Mayor and Madame Orden suspect that George Corell is a traitor. Even being told, they find it hard to believe.

"He prepared for this invasion," the Doctor reports. "He sent our troops into the hills so they would be out of the way. He listed every firearm in the town. God knows what else he has done. . . ."

"Doctor, you don't understand," protests Corell, a nervous shifty little man. "This thing was bound to come. It's a good thing. You don't understand it yet, but when you do, you will thank me. The democracy was rotten and inefficient. Things will be better now. Believe me. (*Almost fanatic in his belief.*) When you understand the new order you will know I am right."

"George Corell—a traitor—?" It is hard for the Mayor to adjust his mind to this thought.

"I work for what I believe in. That's an honorable thing."

"This isn't true—George—" the Mayor is saying, almost pleadingly. "George—you've sat at my table—on Madame's right—we've played chess together. This isn't true, George—?"

"I work for what I believe in," repeats George. "You will agree with me when you understand."

There is a long silence. The Mayor's face "grows tight and

formal." "I don't wish to speak in this gentleman's presence," he says, firmly.

Colonel Lanser is understanding. He asks Corell to leave. Corell would protest, but the Colonel shuts him up, and out, with authoritative curtness. Before he can resume the investigation Annie, the maid, has come a little violently from the kitchen. There are soldiers standing on her porch, looking in. The Colonel would explain that this is only in the course of duty. Annie thinks it is because they have smelled the coffee.

"We want to get along as well as we can," the Colonel is saying, asking their permission to sit down. "You see, sir, this is more a business venture than anything else. We need your coal mine here and the fishing. We want to get along with just as little friction as possible."

"We've had no news," answers the Mayor. "Can you tell me —what about the rest of the country? What has happened?"

COLONEL LANSER—All taken. It was well planned.

MAYOR ORDEN (*insistently*)—Was there no resistance . . . anywhere?

COLONEL LANSER (*looking at him almost compassionately*)— Yes, there was some resistance. I wish there hadn't been. It only caused bloodshed. We'd planned very carefully.

MAYOR ORDEN (*sticking to his point*)—But there *was* resistance?

COLONEL LANSER—Yes. . . . And it was foolish to resist. Just as here, it was destroyed instantly. It was sad and foolish to resist.

DR. WINTER (*who has caught some of the* MAYOR'S *anxiousness*)—Yes . . . foolish, but they resisted.

COLONEL LANSER—Only a few and they are gone. The people as a whole are quiet.

DR. WINTER—But the people don't know yet what has happened.

COLONEL LANSER (*a little sternly*)—They are discovering now. They won't be foolish again. (*His voice changes, takes on a business-like tone.*) I must get to business. I am very tired. Before I can sleep, I must make my arrangements. The coal from this mine must come out of the ground and be shipped. We have the technicians with us. The local people will continue to work the mine. Is that clear? We do not wish to be harsh.

MAYOR ORDEN—Yes, that's clear enough. But suppose we don't want to work the mine?

COLONEL LANSER (*tightly*)—I hope you will want to, because you *must*.

MAYOR ORDEN—And if we won't?

COLONEL LANSER (*rising*)—You MUST! This is an orderly people. They don't want trouble. (*He waits for the* MAYOR'*s reply.*) Isn't that so, sir?

MAYOR ORDEN—I don't know. They're orderly under our government. I don't know what they'll be under yours. We've built our government over a long time.

COLONEL LANSER (*quickly*)—We know that. We're going to keep your government. You will still be the Mayor. You will give the orders, you will penalize and reward. Then we won't have any trouble.

MAYOR ORDEN (*looking helplessly at* WINTER)—What do you think?

DR. WINTER—I don't know. I'd expect trouble. This might be a bitter people.

MAYOR ORDEN—I don't know either. (*He turns to the* COLONEL.) Perhaps you know, sir. Or maybe it might be different from anything you know. Some accept leaders and obey them. But my people elected me. They made me and they can unmake me! Perhaps they will do that, when they think I've gone over to you.

COLONEL LANSER (*ominously*)—You will be doing them a service if you keep them in order.

MAYOR ORDEN—A service?

COLONEL LANSER—It's your duty to protect them. They'll be in danger if they are rebellious. If they work they will be safe.

MAYOR ORDEN—But suppose they don't want to be safe?

COLONEL LANSER—Then you must think for them.

MAYOR ORDEN (*a little proudly*)—They don't like to have others think for them. Maybe they are different from your people.

Now it is Joseph who has come from the kitchen in a state of excitement. It's Annie again. Annie still doesn't like soldiers on her porch. She doesn't like to be stared at, even if they are only carrying out orders. Annie is getting angry. But, at Madame Orden's request, Joseph will return and tell Annie to mind her temper, though he is not at all confident she will.

It is Colonel Lanser's suggestion that he and his staff will stay at the Mayor's house. It has been found, because of the suggested collaboration, to work better that way. The Mayor would protest, if he could. He is sure the people will not like it.

"Always the people!" snaps the Colonel, as though he were speaking to a recalcitrant child. "The people are disarmed. They have no say in this."

Again Joseph must break in with more excited news. It's Annie again. From the kitchen come distressed sounds, and excited words. "Look out!" "It's boiling!" "Jump!" There is a splash of water, the clang of a pan, and the cry of a distressed soldier. Quickly Madame Orden runs to the kitchen. Now there is a confused jumble of orders to Annie, from Madame, and orders to each other from the soldiers. "Grab her!" "Let go of me!" And then the sharp thud of someone being thrown to the floor, followed by the cry of a soldier who has been bitten.

"Have you no control over your servants, sir?" angrily demands Colonel Lanser.

"Very little," admits the Mayor, smiling. "Annie is a good cook when she's happy."

"We just want to do our job," wearily repeats the Colonel. And later, after he has ordered the soldiers to release Annie and go outside, he adds: "I could lock her up. I could have her shot."

"Then we'd have no cook," mildly protests the Mayor.

COLONEL LANSER—Our instructions are to get along with your people. I'm very tired, sir. I must have some sleep. Please co-operate with us for the good of all.

MAYOR ORDEN (*thoughtfully*)—I don't know. The people are confused and so am I!

COLONEL LANSER—But will you try to co-operate?

MAYOR ORDEN—I don't know. When the town makes up its mind what it wants to do I will probably do that.

COLONEL LANSER—You're the authority.

MAYOR ORDEN—Authority is in the town. That means we cannot act as quickly as you can . . . but when the direction is set . . . we act all together. I don't know . . . yet!

COLONEL LANSER—I hope we can get along together. I hope we can depend on you to help. Look at it realistically. There's nothing you can do to stop us. And I don't like to think of the means the military must take to keep order.

MADAME (*coming from the kitchen*)—She's all right.

MAYOR ORDEN (*taking cup of coffee she has brought*)—Thank you, my dear.

COLONEL LANSER—I hope we can depend on you.
MAYOR ORDEN—I don't know—yet.

Colonel Lanser bows and goes out the door, followed by the Corporal. Madame Orden is sitting on the sofa beside the Mayor straightening his hair as the curtain falls.

SCENE II

It is a few days later. The Mayor's drawing room is a changed place. Piled military equipment and canvas-wrapped bundles are lying around. The larger pieces of furniture, the wall pictures and the draperies have been removed. There are military maps, a microphone, samples of ore on the Mayor's desk.

Major Hunter, second in command to Colonel Lanser, "a short wide-shouldered mining engineer, a man of figures and a formula . . ." is balancing his drawing board against the table and against his lap. Lieutenant Prackle, "an undergraduate; a snotnose; a lieutenant trained in the politics of the day; a devil with women," has come from the bedroom with his tunic off, his face half covered with lather.

The Major would have the Lieutenant find him a tripod for his drawing board. The Lieutenant is not certain he can, but will try.

Captain Loft, "a truly military man; he lives and breathes his Captaincy; he believes that a soldier is the highest development of animal life, and if he considers God at all, he thinks of him as an old and honored General, retired and gray, living among remembered battles"—Captain Loft, complete with equipment, is back from a tour that has revealed Captain Bentick going on duty wearing a fatigue cap in place of his helmet. Such carelessness is certain to have a bad effect on the people. Every soldier should be familiar with Manual X12 on deportment in occupied countries, in which the leaders have considered everything. Major Hunter isn't so sure.

Lieutenant Tonder, "a different kind of sophomore; a dark and bitter and cynical poet, who dreams of the perfect ideal love of elevated young men for poor girls," has drifted in with a cup of coffee and shortly becomes interested in the bridge that Major Hunter is sketching. It is not a military bridge, it appears, but a toy bridge that the Major expects one day to add to the model railroad line which he is building in his backyard at home. . . .

Colonel Lanser has arrived. He would like to have Captain

Loft go to relieve Captain Bentick, who isn't feeling very well. Captain Loft is responsive to the order, though he would like it to be noted that he has but recently returned from a tour of duty. Such reports, going through to headquarters, are a help in acquiring those little danglers on the chest which "are the milestones in a military career."

"There is a born soldier," says Colonel Lanser, when Captain Loft has left.

"A born ass," amends Major Hunter.

"No. He is being a soldier the way another man would be a politician. He'll be on the General Staff before long. He'll look down on the war from above and so he'll always love it."

The staff renews its contact with the Colonel in different moods. Lieutenant Prackle is eager to know when the war is likely to be over. The Colonel wouldn't know that. Well, if it is quiet around Christmas, Lieutenant Prackle is wondering if there might not be furloughs. The Colonel wouldn't know about that, either. The orders will have to come from home.

Lieutenant Tonder, for his part, has been looking the country over and thinking that if the victors continue the occupation, there are a number of nice little farms around there that a fellow might pick up; might throw four or five of them together, in fact.

"Ah, well. We still have a war to fight," observes the Colonel, as though tired of talking to children. "We still have coal to ship. Suppose we wait until it is over, before we build up estates. Hunter, your steel will be in tomorrow. You can get your tracks started this week."

George Corell is outside seeking an audience. The Colonel has him sent in. Corell is wearing his dark business suit. A patch of white bandage is stuck into his hair with a cross of adhesive tape. He radiates good will and good fellowship, and is glad to meet the boys of Colonel Lanser's staff. They had, he tells them, done a good job, for which he had been careful to prepare the way.

"You did very well," admits Colonel Lanser, and adds: "I wish we hadn't killed those six men, though."

"Well, six men isn't much for a town like this, with a coal mine, too," suggests Corell.

"I don't mind killing people if that finishes it," says the Colonel. "But sometimes it doesn't finish it."

Corell would like to see the Colonel alone, but is obliged to put up with Major Hunter, who, the Colonel assures him, hears nothing when he is working. Noting the patch on Corell's head, the Colonel is solicitous. Corell is quite sure no one had thrown the rock that had hit him. It had fallen from a cliff in the hills. His people are not a fierce people, Corell insists. They haven't had a war for a hundred years.

"Well, you've lived among them, you ought to know," says the Colonel. "But if you are safe, these people are different from any in the world. I've helped to occupy countries before. I was in Belgium twenty years ago and in France."

The Colonel again compliments Corell on the work he has done and is prepared to send him to the Capitol if he wants to go. Corell doesn't want to go. He wants to stay there and he doesn't need a bodyguard. He wants to stay and help with the civil administration. The Colonel will be needing a Mayor he can trust. Corell is sure if Orden were to step down that he (Corell) and the Colonel could work very well together.

No, Corell admits, he has not had much contact with the people since the invaders arrived. He doesn't really know what they think of him. Of course, they have had a shock, but they will be all right. If it should develop, as Colonel Lanser suggests, that not alone will he do no more business at his store, but that he will also come in time to know the people's hatred, Corell feels that he will be able to stand it.

"You will not even have *our* respect," warns the Colonel, after a long moment of silence.

"The Leader has said all branches are equally honorable," insists Corell, jumping to his feet.

"I hope the Leader is right," answers Colonel Lanser, quietly. "I hope he can read the minds of the soldiers." With an effort he pulls himself together. "Now. We must come to exactness. I am in charge here. I must maintain order and discipline. To do that I must know what is in the minds of these people. I must anticipate revolt."

CORELL—I can find out what you wish to know, sir. As Mayor here, I will be very effective.

LANSER—Orden is more than Mayor. He *is* the people. He will think what they think. By watching him I will know them. He must stay. That is my judgment.

CORELL—My place is here, sir. I have made my place.

LANSER—I have no orders about this. I must use my own judgment. I think you will never again know what is going on here. I think no one will speak to you. No one will be near to you, except those people who live on money. I think without a bodyguard you will be in great danger. I prefer that you go back to the Capitol.

CORELL—My work, sir, merits better treatment than being sent away.

LANSER (*slowly*)—Yes, it does. But to the larger work I think you are only in the way. If you are not hated yet, you will be. In any little revolt you will be the first to be killed. I suggest that you go back.

COR ELL (*rising, stiffly*)—You will, of course, permit me to wait for a reply from the Capitol?

LANSER—Of course. But I shall recommend that you go back for your own safety. Frankly . . . you have no further value here. But . . . well, there must be other plans in other countries. Perhaps you will go now to some new town, win new confidence . . . a greater responsibility. I will recommend you highly for your work here.

CORELL (*his eyes shining*)—Thank you, sir. I have worked hard. Perhaps you are right. But I will wait for the reply from the Capitol.

LANSER (*his voice tight and his eyes slitted*)—Wear a helmet. Keep indoors. Do not go out at night and above all, do not drink. Trust no woman or any man. You understand?

CORELL (*smiling*)—I don't think you understand. I have a little house, a country girl waits on me. I even think she is fond of me. These are peaceful people.

LANSER—There are no peaceful people. When will you learn it? There are no friendly people. Can't you understand that? We have invaded this country. You, by what they call treachery, prepared for us. (*His face grows red and his voice rises.*) Can't you understand that we are at war with these people?

CORELL (*a little smugly*)—We have defeated them.

LANSER—A defeat is a momentary thing. A defeat doesn't last. We were defeated and now we are back. Defeat means nothing. Can't you understand that? Do you know what they are whispering behind doors?

CORELL—Do you?

LANSER—No.

There is a sudden snap of the catch on the door as it is closed. Corell goes to the door, opens it, looks out and then returns to face the Colonel—

CORELL (*insinuatingly*)—Are you afraid, Colonel? Should our Commander be afraid?

LANSER (*sitting down heavily in armchair*)—Maybe that's it. (*He says disgustedly.*) I am tired of people who have not been at war who know all about it. (*He is silent for a moment.*) I remember a little old woman in Brussels. Sweet face, white hair . . . Delicate old hands. (*He seems to see the figure in front of him.*) She used to sing our songs to us in a quivering voice. She always knew where to find a cigarette or a virgin. (LANSER *catches himself as if he had been asleep.*) We didn't know her son had been executed. When we finally shot her, she had killed twelve men with a long black hat pin.

CORELL (*eagerly*)—But you shot her.

LANSER—Of course, we shot her!

CORELL—And the murders stopped?

LANSER—No . . . the murders didn't stop. And when finally we retreated, the people cut off the stragglers. They burned some. And they gouged the eyes from some. And some they even crucified.

This may not be the way he should talk, or think, Colonel Lanser admits. He does not talk that way to his young officers. They would not believe him if he did. He has talked as he has to Corell because Corell's work is done.

The door is thrown open. Captain Loft, "rigid and cold and military," comes into the room. There has been trouble. Captain Bentick has been hurt. Two stretcher bearers carry Bentick's body, covered with blankets, into the bedroom, Colonel Lanser following. A moment later the Colonel is back.

"Who killed him?" he demands.

"A miner. . . . I was there, sir. . . . I had just relieved Captain Bentick as the Colonel ordered. Captain Bentick was about to leave to come here, when I had some trouble with a miner. He wanted to quit. When I ordered him to work, he rushed at me with his pick. Captain Bentick tried to interfere."

"You captured the man?"

"Yes, sir."

The Colonel has walked slowly to the fireplace. When he speaks it is as though he were talking to himself.

"So it starts again. We'll shoot this man and make twenty new enemies. It's the only thing we know. The only thing we know."

"What did you say, sir?"

"Nothing. Nothing at all, I was just thinking. Please give

"THE MOON IS DOWN"

There is the sound of marching men outside and the command "Company, halt!", rings through the room. A moment later a helmeted Corporal has entered to announce that Colonel Lanser requests an audience with His Excellency. The Colonel follows.

(Whitford Kane, Edwin Gordon, Otto Kruger, Ralph Morgan, Leon Powers)

Photo by Vandamm Studio.

my compliments to Mayor Orden and my request that he see me at once."

Captain Loft turns and leaves the room. Major Hunter, looking up from his drawing board, dries his inking pen carefully and puts it away in its velvet lined box as the curtain falls.

Scene III

Two days have passed. The Orden drawing room has undergone further changes, being stripped of more pictures and furniture. The chairs have been pushed back against the wall, leaving the center quite bare.

Joseph and Annie are bringing in a dining room table. It is so large they have considerable difficulty maneuvering it through the door. The Colonel had ordered the table. They are going to hold some sort of trial there, Joseph has heard. It's all crazy to Annie. Why can't they hold their trials at the City Hall? What do they want to hold trials for, anyway?

Joseph tries haltingly to explain that there is a report of trouble at the mine. Alex Mordon, they say, had got into some kind of trouble. They say he hit a soldier. Annie doesn't believe that. She knows the girl Alex married, and she wouldn't have married a man who hit people. The soldiers must have done something to Alex.

"I don't know," says Joseph. "Nobody seems to know what happened." Becoming suspicious, he tiptoes over to the door, opens it slowly, looks out, and then closes it carefully. "I heard that William Deal and his wife got away last night in a little boat and I heard that somebody hit that man Corell with a rock."

"Uneasy," echoes Annie. "You should see my sister. Her boy, Robbie, got away when they killed the other soldiers. Christine thinks she knows where he'd go back in the hills, but she can't find out if he was hurt or anything. She's going crazy worrying. She even wanted me to ask His Excellency to try to find out. He might be hurt. I can't ask His Excellency."

The door has opened quietly. Mayor Orden starts into the room. Hearing himself mentioned he stops in the doorway. "I know," Joseph is saying. "People in the town are worried about His Excellency. They don't know where he stands—soldiers in his house and he hasn't said anything. And you know—everybody liked Corell and then he was for the soldiers. People are worried about His Excellency."

Mayor Orden is followed into the room by Dr. Winter. Joseph

and Annie are embarrassed at being caught gossiping. The Mayor is quick to assure them that he is, in fact, still the Mayor.

Now Joseph and Annie have gone and Mayor Orden seeks counsel of Dr. Winter as to his position. Whether it were better for him to be thrown out of control or to remain and have the people suspect him. Dr. Winter believes that the Mayor can keep control and be with the people too.

"I don't know why they have to bring this trial in here," the Mayor protests. "They are going to try Alex Morden here for murder. You know Alex. He has that pretty wife, Molly."

"I remember. She taught in a grammar school before she was married. Yes, I remember her. She was so pretty she hated to get glasses when she needed them. Well, I guess Alex killed an officer all right. Nobody has questioned that."

"Of course, no one questions it," answers the Mayor, bitterly. "But why do they try him? Why don't they shoot him? We don't try them for killing our soldiers. A trial implies right or wrong, doubt or certainty. There is none of that here. Why must they try him—and in my house."

"I would guess it is for the show. There is an idea about that if you go through the form of a thing you have it. They'll have a trial and hope to convince the people that there is justice involved. Alex did kill the Captain."

"Yes, I know."

"And if it comes from your house, where the people have always expected justice . . ."

They are interrupted by Molly Morden, Alex's wife. "She is about thirty, is quite pretty and is dressed simply." Molly has come excitedly to see the Mayor about Alex. Is it true that Alex will be tried and shot? Surely the Mayor wouldn't do that. Alex is not "a murdering man!"

The Mayor understands. No, he wouldn't sentence Alex. But he would know, from Molly, how the people feel. Do they want to be free? Do they want order? Do they know what methods to use against an armed enemy?

"No, sir," admits Molly. "But I think the people want to show these soldiers that they aren't beaten."

Now Molly has gone, fighting hysteria. She knows, even though the Mayor will not sentence Alex, that the others will and that he will be shot. The Mayor sends Madame Orden after Molly, to stay with her and comfort her. The house and servants are unimportant, now. . . .

Colonel Lanser has come. He has on a new pressed uniform,

with a little dagger at the belt. There are things he would like to talk over with the Mayor. He is plainly disturbed. "I'm very sorry about this," he says to the Mayor, pausing at the end of each sentence hoping for an answer, and getting none. "I wish it hadn't happened. I like you, and I respect you. I have a job to do. You surely recognize that. We don't act on our own judgment. There are rules laid down for us. Rules made in the Capitol. This man has killed an officer."

"Why didn't you shoot him then? That was the time to do it," the Mayor says, finally, turning slowly to face the Colonel.

LANSER—Even if I agreed with you, it would make no difference. You know as well as I that punishment is for the purpose of preventing other crimes. Since it is for others, punishment must be publicized. It must even be dramatized.

ORDEN (*going to his desk*)—Yes—I know the theory—I wonder whether it works.

LANSER—Mayor Orden, you know our orders are inexorable. We must get the coal. If your people are not orderly, we will have to restore that order by force. (*His voice grows stern.*) We must shoot people if it is necessary. If you wish to save your people from hurt, you will help us to keep order. Now . . . it is considered wise by my government that punishments emanate from the local authorities.

ORDEN (*softly*)—So . . . the people did know, they do know — (*Speaks louder.*) You wish me to pass sentence of death on Alexander Morden after a trial here?

LANSER—Yes. And you will prevent a great deal of bloodshed later if you will do it.

ORDEN (*drumming his fingers on the desk*)—You and your government do not understand. In all the world, yours is the only government and people with a record of defeat after defeat for centuries, and always because you did not understand. (*He pauses for a moment.*) This principle does not work. First, I am the Mayor. I have no right to pass sentence of death under our law. There is no one in this community with that right. If I should do it I would be breaking the law as much as you.

LANSER—Breaking the law?

ORDEN—You killed six men when you came in and hurt others. Under our law you were guilty of murder, all of you. Why do you go into this nonsense of law, Colonel? There is no law between you and us. This is war. You destroyed the law when you came in, and a new cruel law took its place. You know you'll have to kill all of us or we in time will kill all of you.

LANSER—May I sit down?

ORDEN—Why do you ask? That's another lie. You could make *me* stand if you wanted.

LANSER—No. . . . I respect you and your office, but what I think—I, a man of certain age and certain memories—is of no importance. I might agree with you, but that would change nothing. The military, the political pattern I work in, has certain tendencies and practices which are invariable.

ORDEN—And these tendencies and practices have been proven wrong in every single test since the beginning of the world.

LANSER (*laughing bitterly*)—I, a private man—with certain memories—might agree with you. Might even add that one of the tendencies of the military mind is an inability to learn. An inabilty to see beyond the killing which is its job. (*He straightens his shoulders.*) But I am not a private man. The coal miner must be shot . . . publicly, because the theory is that others will then restrain themselves from killing our men.

ORDEN—Then we needn't talk any more.

LANSER—Yes, we must talk. We want you to help.

ORDEN (*smiling*)—I'll tell you what I'll do. How many men were on the machine guns that killed our soldiers?

LANSER—About twenty.

ORDEN—Very well. If you will shoot them, I will usurp the power to condemn Morden.

LANSER—You are not serious?

ORDEN—I am serious.

LANSER—This can't be done, you know it. This is nonsense.

ORDEN—I know it. And what you ask can't be done. It is nonsense too.

LANSER (*sighing*)—I suppose I knew it. Maybe Corell will have to be Mayor after all. (*He looks up quickly.*) You'll stay for the trial?

ORDEN (*with warmth*)—Yes, I'll stay. Then he won't be alone.

LANSER (*smiling sadly*)—We've taken on a job, haven't we?

ORDEN—Yes. The one impossible job in the world. The one thing that can't be done.

LANSER—Yes?

ORDEN—To break a man's spirit . . . permanently.

The Mayor's head has sunk a little toward the table. The room has become quite dark. The curtain slowly falls.

Scene IV

The court martial is in session. Colonel Lanser and Mayor Orden are at the center of the table. Lieutenant Tonder is standing at attention back of the table. Captain Loft, with his papers before him, is at the Colonel's end of the table, Lieutenant Prackle is at the other end. The doors are guarded by helmeted soldiers standing like wooden images, with bayonets fixed.

Alex Morden, "a big young man with a wide, low forehead," stands near the guards, his manacled hands clasping and unclasping in front of him. "He is dressed in black trousers, a blue shirt, a dark blue tie, and a dark coat shiny with wear."

Captain Loft reads the charges mechanically: "When ordered back to work, he refused to go. And when the order was repeated, the prisoner attacked Captain Loft with a pickax. Captain Bentick interposed his body . . ."

Mayor Orden interrupts to tell Alex to sit down. There is objection from Captain Loft, but Colonel Lanser permits Alex to be seated.

"These facts have been witnessed by several of our soldiers, whose statements are attached," continues Captain Loft. "This military court finds the prisoner is guilty of murder and recommends the death sentence. Does the Colonel wish me to read the statements of the soldiers?"

The Colonel is satisfied. He takes over the interrogation of the prisoner. Does Alex deny that he killed the Captain? Alex admits that he struck him. Whether he killed him or not he doesn't know. "I only hit him . . . and then somebody hit me," says Alex.

"Do you want to offer any explanation?" wearily asks Colonel Lanser.

"I respectfully submit that the Colonel should not have said that," breaks in Captain Loft. "It indicates that the court is not impartial."

"Have you any explanation?" the Colonel repeats, looking at Mayor Orden.

"I was mad, I guess," says Alex, trying to gesture with his right hand, but finding it attached to his left. "I have a pretty bad temper and when he said I had to go to work . . . I got mad and I hit him. I guess I hit him hard. It was the wrong man. (*He points at* Loft.) That is the man I wanted to hit. That one."

It doesn't matter who he wanted to hit. Is he sorry? "It

would look well in the record if he were sorry," the Colonel points out to Loft and Hunter.

No, Alex is not sorry. Loft had ordered him to go to work. He was a free man. He used to be an Alderman. He didn't want to go to work. If the sentence should be death would he be sorry? No, Alex doesn't think so.

"Put in the record that the prisoner is overcome with remorse," orders Colonel Lanser. And then, turning to Alex: "Sentence is automatic, you understand. The court has no leeway. The court finds you guilty and sentences you to be shot immediately. I do not see any reason to torture you with this any more. Now, is there anything I have forgotten?"

"You have forgotten me," quietly says Mayor Orden, getting up from his chair and going to Alex. "Alexander, I am the Mayor —elected."

ALEX—I know it, sir.

ORDEN—Alex, these men have taken our country by treachery and force.

LOFT (*rising*)—Sir, this should not be permitted.

LANSER (*rising*)—Be silent. Is it better to hear it, or would you rather it were whispered?

ORDEN (*continuing*)—When the enemy came, the people were confused and I was confused. Yours was the first clear act. Your private anger was the beginning of a public anger. I know it is said in the town that I am acting with these men. I will show the town that I am not. . . . But you . . . you are going to die. (*Softly.*) I want you to know.

ALEX (*dropping his head and then raising it*)—I know it. I know it, sir.

LANSER (*loudly*)—Is the squad ready?

LOFT (*rising*)—Outside, sir.

LANSER—Who is commanding?

LOFT—Lieutenant Tonder, sir. (TONDER *raises his head, and his chin is hard but his eyes are frightened.* LANSER *looks at his watch.*)

ORDEN (*softly*)—Are you afraid, Alex?

ALEX—Yes, sir.

ORDEN—I can't tell you not to be. I would be, too. And so would these . . . young gods of war.

LANSER (*facing the table*)—Call your squad.

TONDER—They're here, sir.

ORDEN—Alex, go knowing that these men will have no rest

... no rest at all until they are gone ... or dead. You will make the people one. It's little enough gift to you, but it is so ... no rest at all.

Alex has shut his eyes tightly. The Mayor leans over and kisses him upon the cheek: "Good-by, Alex," he says. The guards step forward and guide Alex through the door. They can be heard as orders are given and they march toward the Square. "I hope you know what you're doing," Mayor Orden mutters. "Man, whether we know it or not, it is what must be done," snaps the Colonel.

A silence falls on the room and each man listens tensely. After a little the orders come floating back from the Square: "Ready! Aim! Fire!" followed by the blast of a machine gun. The reverberation has barely ceased when there is another shot from outside the window, followed by a crash of glass. Lieutenant Prackle wheels about. He has been hit in the shoulder. Hunter and Loft have jumped away from the table and reached for their revolvers. Colonel Lanser takes command.

"Captain Loft—find the man who fired that shot! There should be tracks in the snow! Major Hunter, take Lieutenant Tonder and a detail. Search every house in the town for weapons. Shoot down any resistance. Take five hostages for execution. You, Mayor Orden, are in protective custody!"

"A man of certain memories," muses the Mayor.

"A man of no memories. We will shoot five—ten—a hundred for one!" The Colonel is pacing the room now. "So it starts again."

"It's beginning to snow," reports the Mayor at the window.

"We'll have to have that glass fixed. The wind blows cold through a broken window."

The curtain falls.

PART II

It is two months later. The Mayor's drawing room is bare and uncomfortable now. "A kind of discomfort will have crept in; a slight mess, due not to dirt as much as to the business of the men." There are blackout curtains, drawn tight. There are no electric lights. Two gasoline lanterns on the dining room table throw a hard, white light. On the wall there is a line drawing of Major Hunter's rail line from the mine to the dock. A Maxim machine gun is pointed out a window, with the cartridge belt in place. There is an army cot where the Mayor's desk used to stand, and a Tommy gun hangs from a nail driven into the wall. Outside the wind is blowing a small gale. The men are wearing their coats to keep warm.

Major Hunter is again at his drawing board. Lieutenant Prackle, sitting in one chair with his feet in another, is reading an illustrated paper. Lieutenant Tonder is having difficulty trying nervously to compose a letter. The atmosphere is fairly tense.

Lieutenant Prackle is recalling happier scenes, his memory spurred by the illustrations in his paper. There was a certain waitress in a certain restaurant who floats into the picture. "She had the strangest eyes—has, I mean—always kind of moist looking, as though she had just been laughing or crying. . . . I hope they aren't rationing girls at home."

"It'll probably come to that, too," grouches Tonder.

"You don't care much for girls, do you? Not much you don't!" twits Prackle.

"I like them for what girls are for," answers Tonder, putting down his pen. "I don't let them crawl around my other life."

"Seems to me they crawl all over you all the time," taunts Prackle.

To change the subject, Tonder would complain about the lights. When is Major Hunter going to get the dynamo fixed. And what has he done about the man who wrecked it this time? It could have been any one of five men, the Major explains. He had got all five. The lights will be on shortly. And they are. That helps.

Joseph comes in, quietly, with a bucket of coal for the fire. Tonder, with mounting nervousness, would know if he can get them any wine. Or brandy? Joseph shakes his head. "Answer, you swine! Answer in words!" shouts Tonder. There is neither wine nor brandy, Joseph reports. Coffee? Yes, there is coffee. He'll bring that.

"Had you shouting. That's what he wanted to do," observes Major Hunter, wisely.

"I'm all right," insists Tonder, a little shakily. "Sometimes they drive me a little crazy. You know they're always listening behind doors. (*Softly*.) I'd like to get out of this God-forsaken hole!"

It was Tonder, Prackle recalls, who thought he would like to live there after the war—putting four or five farms together to make a nice little place. " 'Nice, pleasant people—beautiful lawns and deer and little children.' " Prackle is imitating Tonder maliciously.

"Don't talk like that," shrieks Tonder, holding his hands to his temples. "These horrible people! They're cold! They never look at you, never speak. They answer like dead men. They obey. And the girls frozen—frozen."

Joseph has brought the coffee. Tonder pours himself a cup, tastes it doubtfully and finds it bitter.

"Now let's stop this nonsense," commands Major Hunter sharply. "The coffee is good or it isn't. If it is good, drink it. If it isn't, don't drink it. Let's not have this questioning."

"There's no rest from it, day or night," protests Tonder. His hands are pressing his temples again; his voice has "a soft tenseness of controlled hysteria." "No rest off duty." His voice breaks. "I'd like to go home. I want to talk to a girl. There's a girl in this town. I see her all the time. I want to talk to that girl."

The lights go out again. The room is in darkness. Major Hunter is relighting the lanterns. Everybody in town seems to be taking a crack at his dynamo. "You know, the other day a little boy shinnied up a pole and smashed a transformer," says the Major, and adds: "What can you do with children?" Then he turns to Tonder, and his tone becomes paternal. "Tonder, do your talking to us, if you have to talk. There's nothing these people would like better than to know that your nerves are getting thin. Don't let the enemy hear you talk this way."

"That's it! The enemy—everywhere. Every man and woman. Even children. Waiting. The white faces behind the curtains, listening. We've beaten them. We've won everywhere and they wait and obey and they wait. Half the world is ours. Is it the same in other places, Major?"

"I don't know."

"That's it. We don't know. The reports—'everything under control, everything under control.' Conquered countries cheer our soldiers. Cheer the new order. (*His voice changes and grows softer.*) What do the reports say about us? Do they say we're cheered, loved, flowers in our paths?"

"Now that's off your chest, do you feel better?" Captain Hunter speaks as to a child.

Tonder does not reply, but, rising quickly, he leaves the room. "He shouldn't talk that way," protests Prackle, miserably. "Let him keep things to himself. He's a soldier, isn't he? Let him be a soldier."

Captain Loft is back, well bundled up against the cold. At the mine, he reports, there has been more of the same old trouble—

the slow-down. Also a wrecked dump car. He had shot the wrecker. As for the slow-down, he had told the men that unless the coal came out as it should, there would be no more food for their children. They (the miners) would be fed at the mine. That would keep them in working condition and give them no chance to divide their food with their families. No coal, no food for the kids.

Lieutenant Tonder comes back into the room. Seeing Captain Loft, he questions him excitedly. What news is there from home? Is everything all right? Are the British defeated yet? And the Russians? Isn't the war just about won?

Captain Loft reports that everything has been going wonderfully. Successes everywhere. True, the British are still trying a few air raids. But it's all over with the Russians. When will they be going home? Well, the Captain has an idea it will take a long time to get the New Order working properly.

"All our lives, perhaps," suggests Tonder.

Captain Loft doesn't like the tone of that query. He faces Tonder angrily. He doesn't like the suggestion of doubt in Tonder's voice. Major Hunter tries to intervene. Tonder, he says, is tired, as they all are. "I'm tired, too," says Loft, "but I don't let doubt get in."

Major Hunter would know what Colonel Lanser is doing. He's making his report and asking for reinforcements, Captain Loft reports. This is a bigger job than they thought it was. The chance of reinforcements starts Tonder up again. Maybe there will also be replacements. Maybe they will be able to go home for awhile. "I could walk down the street and people would say 'Hello,' and they'd like me," says Tonder.

"Don't start talking like that," warns Prackle.

TONDER—There would be friends about and I could turn my back to a man without being afraid.

LOFT (*disgustedly*)—We've enough trouble without having the staff go crazy.

TONDER (*insistently*)—You really think replacements will come, Captain?

LOFT—Certainly. Look, Lieutenant, we've conquered half the world. We must police it for awhile.

TONDER—But the other half?

LOFT—It will fight on hopelessly for awhile.

TONDER—Then we must be spread out all over.

LOFT—For awhile.

TONDER (*breaking over*)—Maybe it will never be over. Maybe it can't be over. Maybe we've made some horrible mistake.

HUNTER—Shut up, Tonder!

LOFT (*rigid, with set jaw and squinted eyes*)—Lieutenant—if you had said this outside this room, I should prefer a charge of treason against you. Treason, not only against the Leader but against your race. Perhaps you are tired. That is no excuse. We are all tired, but we do not forget the destiny of our race. Make no mistake, Lieutenant, we shall conquer the world. We shall impose our faith and our strength on the world. And any weakness in ourselves, we shall cut off. I will not bring the charge this time. But I will be watching you. Weakness is treason— do not forget it.

TONDER (*looking up at him*)—Weakness?

LOFT—Weakness is treason!

TONDER—Weakness is treason?

PRACKLE (*nervously*)—Stop it! (*To* HUNTER.) Make him stop it!

TONDER (*to himself*)—Treason?

HUNTER—Be quiet, Tonder!

TONDER (*like a man a little out of his head*)—I had a funny dream. I guess a dream. Maybe it was a thought. Or a dream.

PRACKLE—Stop it!

TONDER—Captain, is this place conquered?

LOFT—Of course.

TONDER (*a little hysterical*)—Conquered and we are afraid. Conquered and we are surrounded. I had a dream. Out in the snow with the black shadows. And the cold faces in doorways. I had a thought. Or a dream.

PRACKLE—Stop it!

TONDER—I dreamed the Leader was crazy.

HUNTER (*trying to make a joke of it*)—The Leader crazy!

LOFT—Crazy! The enemy have found out how crazy.

TONDER (*still laughing*)—Conquest after conquest. (*The others stop laughing.*) Deeper and deeper into molasses. Maybe the Leader's crazy. Flies conquer the fly paper. Flies capture two hundred miles of new fly paper. (*His laughter is hysterical now.*)

LOFT (*steps close to* TONDER, *pulls him up out of his chair and slaps him in the face*)—Lieutenant! Stop it! Stop it!

The laughter stops. Tonder, amazed, feels his bruised face with his hand. He looks at his hand, sits in the chair and is sobbing, "I want to go home!" as the curtain falls.

Scene II

The evening of the next day, in the living room of her house, Molly Morden is cutting a piece of woolen material with a pair of scissors. It is "a pleasant, small room, rather poor and very comfortable." There is a window covered with blackout curtains, a door leading to the outside through a storm passage, and another door to the kitchen.

Molly "is pretty, and young, and neat. Her golden hair is done on top of her head, tied up with a blue bow." It is a quiet night, but there is a wind outside. Presently there is a rustle at the door, followed by three sharp knocks. A moment later Molly has let Annie, the Mayor's cook, into the room. Annie has come with a message. The Mayor is going to meet the Anders boys in Molly's cottage. The boys are sailing for England. Their brother Jack had been shot for wrecking a dump car and the invaders are looking for the other men of the family. The Anders will be there in half an hour.

Annie is barely out of the house before there is more knocking at the door. When Molly would know who it is, a man's voice answers her. "I come to—I don't mean any harm." A moment later Tonder has forced his way into the room, still protesting the innocence of his visit. "Miss, I only want to talk. That's all. I want to hear you talk. That's all I want."

"I don't want to talk to you!"

"Please, Miss. Just let me stay a little while. Then I'll go. Please. Just for a little while, couldn't we forget the war? Couldn't we talk together? Like people, together? Just for a little while?"

Molly relents a little. She sees that her visitor does not know who she is. He is just a lonely boy. Funny that it is as simple as that. She will let him stay for a moment. He starts as the house creaks, but it is only the snow on the roof. Molly has no man now to push it down. No, she will not let Tonder have it removed in the morning. "The people wouldn't trust me any more," she explains.

"I see. You *all* hate us. But I'd like to help you if you'd let me."

MOLLY (*her eyes narrowing a little cruelly*)—Why do you ask? You are the conqueror. Your men don't *ask*. They *take* what they want.

TONDER—No. That's not what I want. That's not the way I want it.

MOLLY (*cruelly*)—You want me to like you, don't you, Lieutenant?

TONDER (*simply*)—Yes. You are so beautiful. So warm. I've seen no kindness in a woman's face for so long.

MOLLY (*turning to him*)—Do you see any in mine?

TONDER (*looking closely at her*)—I want to.

MOLLY (*she drops her eyes*)—You are making love to me, aren't you, Lieutenant?

TONDER (*clumsily*)—I want you to like me. Surely I want you to like me. I want to see it in your eyes. I've watched you in the street. I've even given orders you must not be molested. Have you been molested?

MOLLY (*quietly*)—No, I've not been molested.

TONDER—They told us the people would like us here. Would admire us. And they don't. They only hate us. (*He changes the subject as though he works against time.*) You are so beautiful.

MOLLY—You are beginning to make love to me, Lieutenant. You must go soon.

TONDER—A man needs love. A man dies without love. His insides shrivel, and his chest feels like a dry chip. I'm lonely.

MOLLY (*looking away from him*)—You'll want to go to bed with me, Lieutenant.

TONDER—I didn't say that. Why do you talk that way?

MOLLY (*turns to him—cruelly*)—Maybe I am trying to disgust you! I was married once. My husband is dead.

TONDER—I only want you to like me.

MOLLY—I know. You are a civilized man. You know that love-making is more full and whole and delightful if there is liking too.

TONDER—Don't talk that way.

Molly has gone to him. She is not to be stopped now. They are a conquered people. She is hungry. Two sausages would be her price. She is hungry—and she hates him.

Again the Lieutenant would have her stop talking that way. She fills everything with hatred. These things she is saying cannot be true.

"Don't hate me," pleads Tonder, taking her hand and putting it to his cheek. "I'm only a soldier. I didn't ask to come here.

You didn't ask to be my enemy. I am only a man, not a conquering man."

"I know," she says, stroking his head.

"We have some little right to life." She has put her cheek against his head. "I'll take care of you," he says. "We have some right to life in all the killing—"

Suddenly Molly has straightened up. Her body is rigid. She is staring with wide eyes as though she had seen a vision. She draws away from Tonder. She does not hear his anxious: "What's the matter? What have I done?"

She is looking away from him now. Her voice is a haunted voice. "I dressed him in his best clothes, like a little boy for his first day of school. I buttoned his shirt and tried to comfort him. But he was beyond comfort. And he was afraid."

"What are you saying?"

"I don't know why they let him come home." She is staring straight ahead, as though she were seeing what she is describing. "He didn't know what was happening. He didn't even kiss me when he went. He was afraid. And very brave. Like a little boy on his first day at school."

"That was your husband?"

"And then—he marched away—not very well nor steadily, and then you took him out—and shot him. It was more strange than terrible then. I didn't quite believe it then."

"Your husband?"

"Yes, my husband. And now in the quiet house I believe it. Now with the heavy snow on the roof I believe it. And in the loneliness before day-break, in the half-warmed bed, I know it then."

Tonder has picked up his helmet. His face is full of misery. "Good night," he says at the door. "May I come back?"

"I don't know."

"Please let me come back."

"No."

Molly is sitting quietly on the settee, still in a daze, when Annie comes from the kitchen. A moment later Will and Tom Anders have come in—two tall, blonde young men. "They are dressed in pea-jackets and turtle-necked sweaters. They have stocking caps on their heads."

Then Mayor Orden comes. He sends Annie into the storm passage to warn them when the patrol passes. He will talk with the boys. He has a plan—

"What I have to say won't take long," the Mayor is saying.

"I want to speak simply. This is a little town. Justice and injustice are in terms of little things. The people are angry and they have no way to fight back. Our spirits and bodies aren't enough."

"What can we do, sir?"

"We want to fight them and we can't. They are using hunger on the people now. Hunger brings weakness. You boys are sailing for England. Tell them to give us weapons."

There is a quick knock on the door. The patrol is passing at the double quick, evidently after someone. Will and Tom are eager to be going.

"Do you want guns, sir? Shall we ask for guns?"

ORDEN—No. Tell them how it is. We are watched. Any move we make calls for reprisal. If we could have simple weapons, secret weapons. Weapons of stealth. Explosives. Dynamite to blow out rails. Grenades if possible. Even poison. (*He speaks angrily.*) This is no honorable war. This is a war of treachery and murder. Let us use the methods they have used on us. Let the British bombers drop their great bombs on the works, but let them also drop little bombs for us to use. To hide. To slip under rails. Under tracks. Then we will be secretly armed, and the invader will never know which of us is armed. Let the bombers bring us simple weapons. We'll know how to use them.

WILL—I've heard that in England, there are still men in power who do not dare to put weapons in the hands of common people.

ORDEN—Oh. (*As though the wind had been knocked out of him.*) I hadn't thought of that. Well, we can only see. If such people still govern England and America, the world is lost anyway. Tell them what we say if they will listen. We must have help. But if we get it—(*His face grows hard.*) we will help ourselves. Then the invader can never rest again, never. We will blow up his supplies. (*Fiercely.*) We will fight his rest and his sleep. We will fight his nerves and his certainties.

TOM—If we get through, we'll tell them. Is that all, Sir?

ORDEN—Yes, that's the core of it.

TOM—What if they won't listen?

ORDEN—We can only try as you are trying the sea tonight.

ANNIE (*coming in quickly*)—There's a soldier coming up the path. (*She looks suspiciously at* MOLLY. MOLLY *rises. The others look at* MOLLY.) I locked the door. (*There is a gentle knocking on the outside door.*)

ORDEN (*rising in wonder*)—Molly, what is this? Are you in trouble?

MOLLY—No— No. Go out the back way. You can get out through the back. Hurry. (*She moves to the entrance.* TOM *and* WILL *hurry through the kitchen.*)

ORDEN—Do you want me to stay, Molly?

MOLLY—No. It will be all right.

ANNIE (*cold with suspicion*)—It's the same soldier.

MOLLY—Yes.

ANNIE—What's he want?

MOLLY—I don't know.

ANNIE—Are you going to tell him anything?

MOLLY (*wonderingly*)—No. (*Then sharply turning to her.*) No!

ANNIE (*quietly*)—Good night then.

MOLLY—Good night, Annie. Don't worry about me.

ANNIE—Good night.

Molly stands watching her as the knocking is resumed. As she sits on the settee her hand falls on the scissors she had been working with. "She picks them up and looks at them intently. Again the knocking comes. She rises and places the scissors in her hand dagger fashion. Then turns to the lamp on the table, turns it low and the room becomes nearly dark. The knocking is repeated."

At the door Molly stands for a second. Her voice is stricken. "I'm coming, Lieutenant—I'm coming!" she calls. She is about to open the door when the curtain falls.

SCENE III

Three weeks later, Annie has just come from the Mayor's bedroom into the drawing room, where she faces Captain Loft. The room is now barren and disorderly. There is no comfort in it any more. It looks like a business office in which men have been relaxing. There are empty beer bottles, tin cups, cigarette butts and playing cards on the table.

Captain Loft would know what Annie is doing there. When she tells him she had thought to clean up, he orders her to leave things as they are and get out.

There is a soldier at the door with several small blue packages. From the packages strings dangle, and at the ends of the strings there are pieces of cloth. Dismissing the soldier, Captain Loft goes to the table, picks up one of the packages and, with a look of distaste, holds it by the cloth attachment above his head. When he drops it the cloth opens to a tiny parachute and the package floats to the floor.

Colonel Lanser, followed by Major Hunter, comes into the room. They, too, fall to examining the packages on the table. Hunter, stripping off the cover of one, finds two items: A tube and a square. He rubs the material he finds in the square between his fingers.

"It's silly. It's commercial dynamite," he says. "I don't know what per cent nitroglycerine until I test it."

In the tube he finds an ordinary dynamite cap, fulminate mercury and about a one-minute fuse. "Very cheap. Very simple."

"How many do you think were dropped?" Colonel Lanser would know.

"I don't know, sir. We picked up about fifty. But we found ninety more parachutes with nothing on them. The people must have hidden those packages."

"It doesn't really matter. They can drop as many as they want. We can't stop it. And we can't use it back against them. They haven't conquered anybody."

"We can beat them off the face of the earth," says Loft.

They have found another smaller package inside the blue wrapper. This is revealed as a piece of chocolate. Very good chocolate, Colonel Lanser discovers by tasting it. Everybody, including his own soldiers, will be looking for those packages. . . .

"We must stop this thing at once, sir," Captain Loft is saying. "We must arrest and punish the people who pick these things up. We must get busy so that they won't think we are weak."

"Take it easy. Let's see what we have first and then we'll think of the remedies." He has picked up one of the packages of dynamite. "How effective is this, Hunter?"

"Very effective for small jobs. Dynamite with a cap and a one-minute fuse. Good if you know how to use it. No good if you don't."

"Listen to this. They'll know how to use it," says Colonel Lanser, reading from the inside of the wrapper. "To the Unconquered People. Hide this. Do not expose yourself. Do not try to do large things with it.' (*He begins to skip through.*) Now here: 'Rails in the country—work at night—tie up transportation.' Now here instructions: 'Rails. Place stick under rail, close to joint and tight against tie. Pack mud or hard-packed snow around it so that it is firm. When fuse is lighted, you have a slow count of sixty before it explodes.' "

Again Captain Loft is anxious that something be done. Colonel Lanser is not clear in his mind as to what it should be. He knows if he seeks advice from Headquarters what the reply will be— "Set booby traps. Poison the chocolate." The leaders, observes the Colonel, always think they're dealing with stupid people. And what will happen?

"One man will pick one of these and get blown to bits by our booby trap. One kid will eat chocolate and die of strychnine poisoning. And then—they'll poke them with poles or lasso them before they touch them. They'll try the chocolate on the cat. God damn it! These are intelligent people. Stupid traps won't catch them twice."

". . . Always before it was possible to disarm people and keep them in ignorance," the Colonel points out. "Now they listen to their radios and we can't stop them. They read handbills. Weapons drop from the sky for them. Now it's dynamite. Soon grenades. Then poison."

True, they haven't dropped poison yet, but they will. And what will Captain Loft think of that? How would he like to be struck in the back with one of those little game darts, coated with cyanide? However, if there is an organization they must find it and stamp it out, ferociously. Let Captain Loft take one detail, Lieutenant Prackle another, and start a search. But let there be no shooting unless there be an overt act.

The Colonel is tired. He admits as much to Major Hunter, who is anxious about him. But there is nothing to do but go on. The shortage of officers is still great. Orders from Headquarters do not change. "Take the leaders. Shoot the leaders. Take hostages. Shoot the hostages. Take more hostages. Shoot them." His voice sinks almost to a whisper. "And the hatred growing. And the hurt between us deeper and deeper."

Major Hunter, leaving, passes Lieutenant Prackle in the doorway. Lieutenant Prackle's face is sullen and belligerent. The Colonel notices and understands. "Don't talk for a moment," he says. "I know what it is. You didn't think it would be this way."

"They hate us. They hate us so," says the Lieutenant.

"I wonder if I know what it is." The Colonel is smiling wryly. "It takes young men to make good soldiers. Young men need young women, is that it? Does she hate you?"

"I don't know, sir," admits Prackle, a little amazed. "Sometimes she's only sorry."

"Are you pretty miserable?"

"I don't like it here, sir."

"No. You thought it would be fun. Lieutenant Tonder went to pieces. And then he went out and got himself killed. I could send you home. Do you want to be sent home, knowing we need you here?"

"No, sir."

"Good. Now, I'll tell you. And I hope you'll understand. You're not a man any more. You're a soldier. Your comfort is of no importance and your life not very much. If you live you will have memories. That's about all you will have. You must take orders and carry them out. Most of them will be unpleasant. But that's not your business. I will not lie to you, Lieutenant. They should have trained you for this. Not for cheers and flowers. (*His voice hardens. He gets to his feet.*) But you took the job. Will you stay with it, or quit it? We cannot take care of your soul."

"Thank you, sir." The Lieutenant is on his feet, ready to leave. "And the girl, Lieutenant," the Colonel adds. "You may rape her or protect her or marry her. That is of no importance, as long as you shoot her when it is ordered. You may go now."

Mr. Corell is shown in. He is a changed man. His expression is no longer jovial or friendly. His face is sharp and bitter. He would have come before, he reports, had Colonel Lanser's attitude been more co-operative. The Colonel had refused him a position of authority. He had left Mayor Orden in office, contrary to Mr. Corell's advice.

Colonel Lanser is of the opinion that there might have been more disorder than there has been with Mayor Orden where he is. Mr. Corell does not think so. To him Mayor Orden is the leader of a rebellious people who has been in constant contact with every happening in the community. He believes the Mayor knows where the girl who murdered Lieutenant Tonder is hiding, and it probably is he who is back of the parachute showers. Now will Colonel Lanser listen?

"What do you suggest?" the Colonel would know.

"These suggestions are a little stronger than suggestions, Colonel. Orden must now be a hostage. And his life must depend on the peacefulness of this community. His life must depend on the lighting of one single fuse." With that Corell reaches into his pocket and brings out a small black book of identification. He flips it open. "This was the answer to my report, sir."

Colonel Lanser looks at the book. "Um—you really did go over my head, didn't you?" says he quietly. There is frank dislike in his eyes.

CORELL—Now, Colonel, must I suggest more strongly than I have that Mayor Orden must be held hostage.

LANSER—He's here. He hasn't escaped. How can we hold him more hostage than we are? (*In the distance there is an explosion, and both men look in the direction from which it comes.*)

CORELL—There it is. If this experiment succeeds, there will be dynamite in every conquered country.

LANSER—What do you suggest?

CORELL—Orden must be held against rebellion.

LANSER—And if rebellion comes and we shoot Orden?

CORELL—Then that doctor's next. He's the next in authority.

LANSER—He holds no office. Well, suppose we shoot him—What then?

CORELL—Then rebellion is broken before it starts.

LANSER (*shakes his head a little sadly*)—Have you ever thought that one execution makes a hundred active enemies where we have passive enemies? Even patriotism is not as sharp as personal hurt, personal loss. A dead brother, a dead father—that really arms an enemy.

CORELL—Your attitude, sir, may lead you to trouble. It is fortunate that I am—your friend.

LANSER—I can see your report almost as though it were in front of me—

CORELL (*quickly*)—Oh! But you are mistaken, sir. I haven't—

LANSER (*turns to him*)—This war should be for the very young. They would have the proper spirit, but unfortunately they are not able to move guns and men about. I suffer from civilization. That means I can know one thing and do another. I know we have failed—I knew we would before we started. The thing the Leader wanted to do cannot be done.

CORELL (*excitedly*)—What is this? What do you say?

LANSER (*quietly*)—Oh! Don't worry. I will go about it as though it could be done and do a better job than the zealots could. And when the tide turns, I may save a few lives, from knowing how to retreat.

CORELL—They shouldn't have sent a man like you here!

LANSER—Don't worry—as long as we can hold, we will hold. I can act quite apart from my knowledge. I will shoot the Mayor. (*His voice grows hard.*) I will not break the rules. I will shoot the doctor. I will help tear and burn the world. I don't like you, Corell. I am licking my wounds surely. And— I am giving you wounds to lick. Sergeant!

SERGEANT (*entering*)—Sir?

LANSER (*slowly*)—Place Mayor Orden and Dr. Winter under arrest!

The Sergeant leaves. Colonel Lanser turns and follows him. "Corell looks after them, then turns back to the table, looks at it, places his hands on it, then slowly seats himself in the chair Lanser vacated." The curtain falls.

SCENE IV

A half hour later Mayor Orden is standing at the window of what was his drawing room looking out. He would have the soldier on guard at the door announce him, but the soldier pays no attention. Presently Dr. Winter appears in the doorway, followed by a second soldier.

"Well, Your Excellency, this is one time you didn't send for me." The Doctor is smiling.

"Well, we've been together in everything else. I suppose it was bound to come. They're afraid of us now. I'm glad it's come."

"They think that because they have only one leader and one head that we are like that. They know that ten heads lopped off would destroy them. But we are a free people. We have as many heads as we have people. Leaders pop up like mushrooms in a time of need."

"Thank you. I knew it, but it's good to hear you say it. The people won't go under, will they?"

"No. They'll grow stronger with outside help."

Quite seriously the Mayor admits that he has been thinking of his own death. "I am a little man in a little town," he is saying. "But there must be a spark in little men that can burst into flame. At first I was afraid. I thought of all the things I might do to save my own life. And then that went away and now I feel a kind of exaltation, as though I were bigger and better than I am. It's like—well, do you remember in school, a long time ago, I delivered Socrates' denunciation? I was exalted then, too."

Dr. Winter remembers the Orden oration and how he bellowed at the school board until their faces grew red with their efforts to keep from laughing. And the oration, how did it go?

" 'And now, O men.' " Dr. Winter can remember so much of it. The Mayor goes on:

" 'And now, O men who have condemned me—
I would fain prophesy to you—
For I am about to die—' "

The door has opened quietly and Colonel Lanser has stepped in. He stops as he hears the Mayor's words and stands listening. The Mayor is gazing intently at the ceiling, trying to remember—

" 'And—in the hour of death—
Men are gifted with prophetic power.
And I—prophesy to you, who are my murderers,
That immediately after my—my death' "

"Departure," prompts the Doctor. "The word is departure, not death. You made the same mistake before."

"No. It's death." He turns to Colonel Lanser, who is putting his helmet on the table. "Isn't it death?"

" 'Departure. Immediately after my departure,' " corrects the Colonel.

"You see. That's two to one. Departure is the word." Dr. Winter is quite pleased. And the Mayor, "looking straight ahead, his eyes in memory, seeing nothing outward" goes on:

" 'I prophesy to you who are my murderers,
That immediately after my departure,
Punishment far heavier than you have inflicted on me
Will surely await you.
Me, you have killed because you wanted to escape the accuser
And not to give an account of your lives . . .'
(*Softly*)
" 'But that will not be as you suppose—far otherwise.
(*His voice grows stronger.*)
For I say that there will be more accusers of you than there are now.
Accusers whom hitherto I have restrained.
If you think that by killing men, you can prevent someone from censoring your lives—you are mistaken.' "

The Mayor pauses. That is all he can remember, he admits, a little apologetically. "It's very good, after forty-six years," the Doctor assures him.

LANSER—Mayor Orden, I have arrested you as a hostage. For the good behavior of your people. These are my orders.
ORDEN (*simply*)—You don't understand. When I become a hindrance to the people, they'll do without me.
LANSER—The people know you will be shot if they light another fuse. (*Turns to him.*) Will they light it?
ORDEN—They will light the fuse.
LANSER—Suppose you ask them not to.
ORDEN (*looking at him slowly*)—I am not a very brave man, sir. I think they will light it anyway. I hope they will. But if I ask them not to, they will be sorry.
LANSER—But they will light it?
ORDEN—Yes, they will light it. I have no choice of living or dying, you see, sir. But—I do have a choice of how I do it. If I tell them not to fight, they will be sorry. But they will fight. If I tell them to fight, they will be glad. And I, who am not a very brave man, will have made them a little braver. (*He smiles apologetically.*) It's an easy thing to do, since the end for me is the same.
LANSER—If you say yes, we will tell them you said no. We will tell them you begged for your life.
WINTER (*angrily*)—They would know. You don't keep secrets. One of your men got out of hand one night and he said the flies had conquered the fly paper. Now the whole nation knows his words. They have made a song of it. You do not keep secrets.

Colonel Lanser is convinced that a proclamation from Mayor Orden would save many lives, but the Mayor is unconvinced. "You will be destroyed and driven out," he says, with finality. "The people don't like to be conquered, sir. And so they will not be. Free men cannot start a war. But once it is started, they can fight on in defeat. Herd men, followers of a leader, they cannot do that. And so it is always that herd men win battles, but free men win wars. You will find it is so, sir."

"My orders are clear. Eleven o'clock is the deadline. I have taken my hostages. If there is violence I will execute them."

Madame Orden has come in. She can't understand what all the nonsense is about. They can't arrest the Mayor. "No, they can't arrest the Mayor," her husband agrees. "The Mayor is an idea conceived by free men. It will escape arrest."

Colonel Lanser has adjusted his helmet. Now he stands before Mayor Orden. "Your Excellency!" He clicks his heels and bows. The front door is heard to slam as he goes out.

On the other side of the kitchen door Annie has been listening. She comes now, as the Mayor calls her. She is, he tells her, to stay with Madame Orden. "I'll take care of her, Your Excellency," Annie promises as he kisses her upon the forehead.

"Doctor, how did it go about the flies?"

"The flies have conquered the fly paper." The Mayor is chuckling to himself as he repeats: " 'The flies have conquered the fly paper.' "

Madame Orden is back with the Mayor's chain of office. He is always forgetting that. She places it around his neck. His arm is around her shoulder as he kisses her upon the cheek. "My dear—my very dear."

A noise in the kitchen has distracted her. She will have to see what Annie and Joseph are up to. She kisses the Mayor, straightens his hair, and is gone.

Lieutenant Prackle appears in the door. The soldiers snap to attention and shoulder their bayoneted rifles. The Mayor looks at his watch. "Eleven o'clock," he says.

"A time-minded people," Dr. Winter admits.

The Mayor takes his watch and chain and gives them to the Doctor. They have clasped hands now, and stand looking steadily at each other for a moment. " 'Crito, I owe a cock to Ascalaepius,' " recites the Mayor, as he turns to go. " 'Will you remember to pay the debt?' "

" 'The debt shall be paid.' "

"I remembered that one," chuckles the Mayor.

"Yes. You remembered it." The Doctor's voice is very soft. "The debt will be paid!"

The Mayor has turned and walked slowly toward the door, as another explosion is heard. It is closer this time. Lieutenant Prackle goes before him through the door. The soldiers follow them out.

THE CURTAIN FALLS

BLITHE SPIRIT

An Improbable Farce

By Noel Coward

OF all those playwrights who sought diligently for escapist drama inspirations during the early, depressing months of the Second World War, both in England and America, Noel Coward was the most successful. He had been devoting several months to war work in various parts of the world when he returned to London in 1940. He was, he afterward confessed, deeply moved to find his people bravely gay in the face of awful months of a battering blitzkrieg and repeated threats of an invasion.

"It isn't merely gallantry and putting on a brave face," he wrote to his American representative. "It's very real and infinitely stimulating. Realizing that this particular feeling was more important than anything else, I decided to write a farce."

"Blithe Spirit" was developed from that decision. Improbable to a degree, utterly fantastic and wholly without so much as a smidge of reference to any serious problem, "Blithe Spirit" set Londoners laughing merrily. It ran on and on and finally a second company, sent into the provinces, carried laughter into and through Coventry and Plymouth and all those other towns where lived the brave survivors of air raids and casualty lists.

Early in the new theatre season in New York, on November 5, to be exact, "Blithe Spirit" was revealed. Here the London experience was repeated. With the exception of Leonora Corbett, an English actress who came on from Hollywood to play a principal ghost, the company was recruited in New York and headed by Clifton Webb and Peggy Wood. Broadway audiences proceeded to roar you a roar as hearty as any heard in England, and the play reviewers, with one or two modest exceptions, tossed in their best superlatives in Master Coward's favor. A second company was also organized on this side and proceeded gustily to carry laughter through the Middle West to the Pacific Coast. "Blithe Spirit" was a happy incident of the war years which the theatre will not soon forget.

As "Blithe Spirit" opens the Charles Condomines are having cocktails in the living room of their house in Kent, England. It is a light, attractive living room, with French windows at one side, a fireplace at the other and a comfortable assortment of tables and chairs. Ruth Condomine, "a smart-looking woman in the middle thirties," who "is dressed for dinner, but not elaborately," is giving the maid, Edith, a few last-minute instructions respecting her conduct this particular evening. This is made necessary because Edith is new and has a habit of galloping through her tasks.

"Mme. Arcati, Mrs. Bradman and I will have our coffee in here after dinner," Mrs. Condomine is saying, "and Mr. Condomine and Dr. Bradman will have theirs in the dining-room—is that quite clear?"

"Yes'm."

"And when you're serving dinner, Edith, try to remember to do it calmly and methodically."

"Yes'm."

Charles Condomine, "a nice-looking man about forty, wearing a loose-fitting velvet smoking jacket," comes to take charge of the cocktails, which are to be dry Martinis, although Ruth thinks it possible Mme. Arcati may fancy something a little sweeter.

Ruth, in fact, is quite worried about this evening. She has a feeling that it may turn out to be quite awful. Charles admits that it may be funny, but he hardly thinks it will be awful. The evening, it transpires, is to be given over to a séance at which Mme. Arcati is to preside as medium. Charles, being a novelist, has an idea for a story to be called "The Unseen," and he is in search of contributing material. He remembers quite vividly how enormously he was helped with the idea for "The Light Goes Out" when he and Ruth had suddenly come upon "that haggard, raddled woman in the hotel at Biarritz," and they had sat up half the night talking about her—

"Used Elvira to be a help to you—when you were thinking something out, I mean?" asks Ruth.

"Every now and then—when she concentrated—but she didn't concentrate very often," Charles answers, pouring himself another cocktail.

RUTH—I do wish I'd known her.

CHARLES—I wonder if you'd have liked her.

RUTH—I'm sure I should—as you talk of her she sounds enchanting—yes, I'm sure I should have liked her because you know I have never for an instant felt in the least jealous of her—that's a good sign.

CHARLES—Poor Elvira.

RUTH—Does it still hurt—when you think of her?
CHARLES—No, not really—sometimes I almost wish it did—I feel rather guilty—
RUTH—I wonder if I died before you'd grown tired of me if you'd forget me so soon?
CHARLES—What a horrible thing to say . . .
RUTH—No—I think it's interesting.
CHARLES—Well, to begin with I *haven't* forgotten Elvira—I *remember* her very distinctly indeed—I remember how fascinating she was—and how maddening—(*sitting down*) I remember how badly she played all games and how cross she got when she didn't win—I remember her gay charm when she had achieved her own way over something and her extreme acidity when she didn't—I remember her physical attractiveness, which was tremendous—and her spiritual integrity which was nil . . .
RUTH—You can't remember something that was nil.
CHARLES—I remember how morally untidy she was . . .
RUTH—Was she more physically attractive than I am?
CHARLES—That was a very tiresome question, dear, and fully deserves the wrong answer.
RUTH—You really are very sweet.
CHARLES—Thank you.
RUTH—And a little naive, too.
CHARLES—Why?
RUTH—Because you imagine that I mind about Elvira being more physically attractive than I am.
CHARLES—I should have thought any woman would mind—if it were true. Or perhaps I'm old-fashioned in my views of female psychology . . .
RUTH—Not exactly old-fashioned, darling, just a bit didactic.
CHARLES—What do you mean?
RUTH—It's didactic to attribute to one type the defects of another type—for instance, because you know perfectly well that Elvira would mind terribly if you found another woman more attractive physically than she was, it doesn't necessarily follow that I should. Elvira was a more physical person than I—I'm certain of that—it's all a question of degree.
CHARLES (*smiling*)—I love you, my love.
RUTH—I know you do but not the wildest stretch of imagination could describe it as the first fine careless rapture.
CHARLES—Would you like it to be?
RUTH—Good God, no!
CHARLES—Wasn't that a shade too vehement?

RUTH—We're neither of us adolescent, Charles. We've neither of us led exactly prim lives, have we? And we've both been married before—careless rapture at this stage would be incongruous and embarrassing.

CHARLES—I hope I haven't been in any way a disappointment, dear.

RUTH—Don't be so idiotic.

There is still a suggestion of uncertainty in Ruth's continued probing of Charles' feelings toward the first Mrs. Condomine, but Charles is in no mood to satisfy it.

"I was devoted to Elvira," he freely admits. "We were married for five years. She died. I missed her very much. That was seven years ago. I have now, with your help, my love, risen above the whole thing."

"Admirable. But if tragedy should darken our lives, I still say—with prophetic foreboding—poor Ruth!"

A ring at the doorbell heralds the Bradmans, he "a pleasant-looking middle-aged man," she "fair and rather faded." They may have, they think, passed Mme. Arcati and her bicycle on the way. They are both extremely curious to meet the lady, never having had that experience before—

"She certainly is a strange woman," admits Charles, serving more cocktails. "It was only a chance remark of the Vicar's about seeing her up on the knoll on Midsummer Eve dressed in sort of Indian robes that made me realize that she was psychic at all. Then I began to make inquiries—apparently she's been a professional in London for years."

MRS. BRADMAN—It is funny, isn't it? I mean anybody doing it as a profession.

DR. BRADMAN—I believe it's very lucrative.

MRS. BRADMAN—Do you believe in it, Mrs. Condomine—do you think there's anything really genuine about it at all?

RUTH—I'm afraid not—but I do think it's interesting how easily people allow themselves to be deceived . . .

MRS. BRADMAN—But she must believe in it herself, mustn't she—or is the whole business a fake?

CHARLES—I suspect the worst. A real professional charlatan. That's what I am hoping for anyhow—the character I am planning for my book must be a complete impostor, that's one of the most important factors of the whole story.

DR. BRADMAN—What exactly are you hoping to get from her?

BLITHE SPIRIT

CHARLES (*handing* DR. *and* MRS. BRADMAN *cocktails*)—Jargon, principally—a few of the tricks of the trade—it's many years since I went to a séance. I want to refresh my memory.

DR. BRADMAN—Then it's not entirely new to you?

CHARLES—Oh, no—when I was a little boy an aunt of mine used to come and stay with us—she imagined that she was a medium and used to go off into the most elaborate trances after dinner. My mother was fascinated by it.

MRS. BRADMAN—Was she convinced?

CHARLES (*getting cocktail for himself*)—Good heavens, no—she just naturally disliked my aunt and loved making a fool of her.

DR. BRADMAN (*laughing*)—I gather that there were never any tangible results?

CHARLES—Oh, sometimes she didn't do so badly. On one occasion when we were all sitting round in the pitch dark with my mother groping her way through Chaminade at the piano, my aunt suddenly gave a shrill scream and said that she saw a small black dog by my chair, then someone switched on the lights and sure enough there was.

MRS. BRADMAN—But how extraordinary.

CHARLES—It was obviously a stray that had come in from the street. But I must say I took off my hat to Auntie for producing it, or rather for utilizing—even Mother was a bit shaken.

MRS. BRADMAN—What happened to it?

CHARLES—It lived with us for years.

RUTH—I sincerely hope Madame Arcati won't produce any livestock—we have so very little room in this house.

Another ring at the doorbell. Both Edith and Charles go to meet Mme. Arcati, whose voice, very high and clear, can be heard in the hallway assuring them that if no one touches her bicycle, which she has leant against a small bush, it will be perfectly all right.

Mme. Arcati "is a striking woman, dressed not too extravagantly but with a decided bias toward the barbaric. She might be any age between forty-five and sixty-five."

The Madame is volubly chipper. She is sorry if she is late; that would be because she went back to get her bicycle pump, fearing a puncture. Certainly she will have a cocktail—if it is a Martini. "If it is a concoction, no. Experience has taught me to be very wary of concoctions," the Madame explains. Bicycling she finds stimulating, after her sedentary London life. Books? Yes, she is writing another book to catch the Christmas sale.

"It's mostly about very small animals, the hero is a moss beetle," she says, and adds quickly, as Mrs. Bradman is threatened with laughter, "I had to give up my memoir of Princess Palliatini because she died in April—I talked to her about it the other day and she implored me to go on with it, but I really hadn't the heart."

"You *talked* to her about it the other day?" Mrs. Bradman doesn't understand.

"Yes, through my control, of course. She sounded very irritable."

"It's funny to think of people in the spirit world being irritable, isn't it? I mean, one can hardly imagine it, can one?"

"We have no reliable guarantee that the after life will be any less exasperating than this one, have we?" ventures Charles.

"Oh, Mr. Condomine, how can you?" Now Mrs. Bradman is laughing freely.

A moment later Edith announces dinner, and the party starts for the dining room.

"No red meat, I hope?" chirps Mme. Arcati, putting down her glass.

"There's meat, but I don't think it will be very red—would you rather have an egg or something?" Ruth would be reassuring.

"No, thank you—it's just that I make it a rule never to eat red meat before I work—it sometimes has an odd effect . . ."

"What sort of effect?"

They have disappeared through the doorway as the lights fade out.

When the lights are raised again dinner is over. Mme. Arcati, returning to the living room with Mrs. Bradman and Mrs. Condomine, is doing what she can, and cheerfully, to explain her attitude toward, and her experience with, the little known forces of the spirit world. The fact that she prefers to have a child control instead of an Indian, for example, she explains by saying that Indians are really not to be trusted. "For one thing, they're frightfully lazy and also, when faced with any sort of difficulty, they're rather apt to go off into their own tribal language which is naturally unintelligible—that generally spoils everything and wastes a great deal of time. No, children are undoubtedly more satisfactory, particularly when they get to know you and understand your ways. Daphne has worked for me for years."

"And she still goes on being a child—I mean, she doesn't show signs of growing any older?" Mrs. Bradman is most curious.

"Time values on the 'Other Side' are utterly different from ours," explains the psychic.

Mme. Arcati has been a medium, she discloses, ever since she was a child. "I had my first trance when I was four years old and my first protoplasmic manifestation when I was five and a half—what an exciting day that was."

Charles and Mr. Bradman have joined the ladies and with a gay "Heigho, heigho, to work we go" the Madame's preparations for the séance move forward. First there must be a few deep breaths of fresh air. These take her to the window, which she opens with a flourish. The others, she insists, should go right on talking while she inhales—which she does "deeply and a trifle noisily."

Now they have gathered around a table, hands outstretched, their fingers touching, and Mme. Arcati is looking for a record to play on Charles' electric gramophone.

"Daphne is really more attached to Irving Berlin than anybody else," she explains, shuffling the records; "she likes a tune she can hum—ah, here's one—'Always'—"

The selection is plainly disturbing to Charles, but he decides not to do anything about it.

"Now there are one or two things I should like to explain, so will you all listen attentively?" Mme. Arcati is asking. "Presently, when the music begins, I am going to switch out the lights. I may then either walk about the room for a little or lie down flat—in due course I shall draw up this dear little stool and join you at the table—I shall place myself between you and your wife, Mr. Condomine, and rest my hands lightly upon yours—I must ask you not to address me or move or do anything in the least distracting—is that quite, quite clear?"

CHARLES—Perfectly.

MADAME ARCATI—Of course I cannot guarantee that anything will happen at all—Daphne may be unavailable—she had a head cold very recently, and was rather under the weather, poor child. On the other hand, a great many things might occur—one of you might have an emanation, for instance, or we may contact a poltergeist which would be extremely destructive and noisy . . .

RUTH (*anxiously*)—In what way destructive?

MADAME ARCATI—They throw things, you know.

RUTH—No—I didn't know.

MADAME ARCATI—But we must cross that bridge when we come to it, mustn't we?

CHARLES—Certainly—by all means.

MADAME ARCATI—Fortunately an Elemental at this time of the year is most unlikely. . . .

RUTH—What do Elementals do?

MADAME ARCATI—Oh, my dear, one can never tell—they're dreadfully unpredictable—usually they take the form of a very cold wind . . .

MRS. BRADMAN—I don't think I shall like that—

MADAME ARCATI—Occasionally reaching almost hurricane velocity—

RUTH—You don't think it would be a good idea to take the more breakable ornaments off the mantelpiece before we start?

MADAME ARCATI (*indulgently*)—That really is not necessary, Mrs. Condomine—I assure you I have my own methods of dealing with Elementals.

RUTH—I'm so glad.

MADAME ARCATI—Now then—are you ready to empty your minds?

DR. BRADMAN—Do you mean we're to try to think of nothing?

MADAME ARCATI—Absolutely nothing, Dr. Bradman. Concentrate on a space or a nondescript color. That's really the best way . . .

DR. BRADMAN—I'll do my damnedest.

MADAME ARCATI—Good work!—I will now start the music.

During the playing of "Always" Mme. Arcati walks a little aimlessly about the room, skipping into an abortive dance step occasionally, and finally stopping abruptly to rush across the room and turn off the lights. The circle moves uneasily. "Is there anyone there?" queries Mme. Arcati. "One rap for yes—two raps for no—now then—is there anyone there?"

After a short pause the table gives a little bump. Further questioning on the part of Mme. Arcati establishes the fact that Daphne has arrived, but is not taking her assignment too seriously. Frequently Daphne has to be cautioned to behave herself.

Presently it appears that there is someone there who would like to speak to someone here, but it is not easy to discover whom. Finally the choice settles on Mr. Condomine. Charles would prefer that his visitor should leave a message, but this flippancy is quickly sat upon.

Has Charles known anyone who has passed over recently? Only a cousin in the Civil Service. There are two quick bumps on the table to dismiss cousin. Nor is it old Mrs. Plummet, who

"BLITHE SPIRIT"

Ruth: See what?
Charles: Elvira.
Ruth (staring at him incredulously): Elvira!
Charles (with an effort at social grace): Yes— Elvira, dear, this is Ruth—Ruth, this is Elvira.

(*Leonora Corbett, Clifton Webb, Peggy Wood*)

Photo by Vandamm Studio.

had died on Whit Monday. Mme. Arcati is afraid she will have to go into her trance if anything is to come of the meeting.

Now she puts "Always" back on the gramophone, again to Charles' annoyance, and presently she has returned solemnly to her seat near the circle. Presently, with a loud scream, Mme. Arcati falls off her stool onto the floor. Before anything can be done about this the table begins to bump violently. It is all the four of them can do to hold it down. Now it has got away from the circle and fallen with a crash to the floor.

Then, while the Bradmans are fussing as to whether the table should be picked up or left alone, a charming, but perfectly strange voice is heard to advise from the darkness—

"Leave it where it is."

Charles is the only one who has heard the voice. Questioned individually each denies having heard anything.

"Good evening, Charles," continues the voice.

And again Charles is the only one who hears. Now the others are beginning to look at him suspiciously. "It's you who are playing the tricks, Charles," charges Ruth; "you're acting to try to frighten us. . . ."

"I'm not—I swear I'm not," protests Charles, breathlessly.

Again comes the strange voice, clearly to Charles. "It's difficult to think of what to say after seven years, but I suppose good evening is as good as anything else."

"Who are you?" demands Charles, intensely.

"Elvira, of course—don't be so silly," answers the voice.

"I can't bear this another minute," shouts Charles, a little violently. "Get up, everybody—the entertainment's over—"

In the confusion that follows Mme. Arcati is discovered lying on her back on the floor, her feet on the stool on which she was sitting. She is completely unconscious. Excitedly Charles insists that she should be aroused. He himself would shake her into consciousness, but Dr. Bradman protests that he should go easy. Charles is in no mood for that. Brandy! That's what he would give Mme. Arcati. Lift her into a chair and give her brandy! They try that and finally, with a slight shiver, Mme. Arcati comes to.

She knows nothing about what has happened. She is feeling quite fit, as she always does after a trance. She is only puzzled by the strange taste in her mouth. Brandy? Why did they give her brandy? Dr. Bradman at least should have known better than that.

". . . Brandy on top of a trance might have been catastrophic," protests the Madame, with some vehemence. "Take it away, please—I probably shan't sleep a wink tonight as it is."

Mme. Arcati would like to know about the séance. Was everything satisfactory? Did anything happen?

They try to tell her nothing much happened. Charles, says Ruth, pretended to hear voices, but there was nothing else; no apparitions; no protoplasm. Mme. Arcati is not satisfied. Something assures her that there have been manifestations. "I am prepared to swear that there is someone else psychic in this room apart from myself," says she, with conviction. . . .

Mme. Arcati is going. "Next time we must really put our backs into it," she calls with a wave of the hand, when Charles takes her to the door.

Ruth and the Bradmans are immediately sunk in spasms of laughter. The Madame, they are agreed, is as mad as a hatter. Dr. Bradman even has a scientific explanation for a certain form of hysteria that would explain much—

"I do hope Mr. Condomine got all the atmosphere he wanted for his book," hopes Mrs. Bradman.

"He might have got a great deal more if he hadn't spoiled everything by showing off. . . . I'm really very cross with him."

At which moment Elvira walks in through the closed French windows. "She is charmingly dressed in a sort of negligee. Everything about her is gray: hair, skin, dress, hands, so we must accept the fact that she is not quite of this world. She passes between Dr. and Mrs. Bradman and Ruth while they are talking. None of them sees her. She goes upstage and sits soundlessly on a chair. She regards them with interest, a slight smile on her face."

"I suddenly felt a draught—there must be a window open," says Ruth.

"No—they're shut," Dr. Bradman reassures her.

Soon the Bradmans are going. As Charles sees them into the hall Elvira continues silently interested in the scene. Ruth passes quite close to her in going to the fire to turn over a log. Presently Charles returns. He is, he admits, reasonably satisfied with the way the evening turned out. As he turns, with a drink, to join Ruth by the fire he sees Elvira. With a startled "My God!" he drops the drink.

"That was very clumsy, Charles dear," says Elvira, sweetly.

"Elvira!—then it's true—it was you!"

"Of course it was."

Ruth is worried. What has happened to Charles—her darling

Charles? What is he talking about? But Charles keeps on talking, his gaze fixed on Elvira.

CHARLES (*to* ELVIRA)—Are you a ghost?
ELVIRA—I suppose I must be—it's all very confusing.
RUTH (*becoming agitated*)—Charles—what do you keep looking over there for? Look at me—what's happened?
CHARLES—Don't you see?
RUTH—See what?
CHARLES—Elvira.
RUTH (*staring at him incredulously*)—Elvira!!
CHARLES (*with an effort at social grace*)—Yes—Elvira dear, this is Ruth—Ruth, this is Elvira.
RUTH (*with forced calmness*)—Come and sit down, darling.
CHARLES—Do you mean to say you can't see her?
RUTH—Listen, Charles—you just sit down quietly by the fire and I'll mix you another drink. Don't worry about the mess on the carpet—Edith can clean it up in the morning. (*She takes him by the arm.*)
CHARLES (*breaking away*)—But you must be able to see her—she's there—look—right in front of you—there—
RUTH—Are you mad? What's happened to you?
CHARLES—You can't see her?
RUTH—If this is a joke, dear, it's gone quite far enough. Sit down for God's sake and don't be idiotic.
CHARLES (*clutching his head*)—What am I to do—what the hell am I to do!
ELVIRA—I think you might at least be a little more pleased to see me—after all, you conjured me up.
CHARLES—I didn't do any such thing. I did nothing of the sort.
ELVIRA—Nonsense, of course you did. That awful child with the cold came and told me you wanted to see me urgently.
CHARLES—It was all a mistake—a horrible mistake.
RUTH—Stop talking like that, Charles—as I told you before, the *joke's* gone far enough.
CHARLES (*aside*)—I've gone mad, that's what it is—I've just gone raving mad.
RUTH (*going to the table and quickly pouring him out some neat brandy*)—Here—let me get you a drink.
CHARLES (*mechanically—taking it*)—This is appalling!
RUTH—Relax.

CHARLES—How can I relax? I shall never be able to relax again as long as I live.

Ruth thinks brandy may help. She insists on his taking two or three drinks of it, which Elvira cautions him is not good, considering he always did have a weak head. It is Elvira's thought that Charles should get rid of Ruth so he and she can enjoy a peaceful talk. But that isn't easy. Ruth is getting fed up with Charles' actions. It is quite all right for him to dramatize any situation he may think will help him with his book, but enough's enough.

"I refuse to be used as a guinea pig unless I'm warned beforehand what it's all about," announces Ruth. . . . "I'm going up to bed now. I'll leave you to turn out the lights. I shan't be asleep—I'm too upset—so you can come in and say good night to me if you feel like it."

"That's big of her, I must say," chirps Elvira.

"Be quiet—you're behaving like a guttersnipe," snaps Charles.

Ruth turns at the door. "That is all I have to say. Good night, Charles," says she icily.

With Ruth gone Elvira is perfectly happy. She can't remember when she has enjoyed a half hour more. As to what she is going to do she doesn't know. How long she is going to stay she doesn't know either. It all seems a little like a dream. But she doesn't think Charles should make such a fuss about it. It is only a matter of adjustment. Could it be that Charles doesn't love her any more?

"I shall always love the memory of you," Charles assures her.

ELVIRA (*rising and walking about*)—You mustn't think me unreasonable, but I really am a little hurt. You called me back —and at great inconvenience I came—and you've been thoroughly churlish ever since I arrived.

CHARLES (*gently*)—Believe me, Elvira, I most emphatically did not send for you—there's been some mistake.

ELVIRA (*irritably*)—Well, somebody did—and that child said it was you—I remember I was playing backgammon with a very sweet old Oriental gentleman—I think his name was Genghis Khan—and I'd just thrown double sixes, and then that child paged me and the next thing I knew I was in this room . . . perhaps it was your subconscious.

CHARLES—Well, you must find out whether you are going to stay or not, and we can make arrangements accordingly.

ELVIRA—I don't see how I can.
CHARLES—Well, try to think—isn't there anyone that you know, that you can get in touch with over there—on the other side, or whatever it's called—who could advise you?
ELVIRA—I can't think—it seems so far away—as though I'd dreamed it. . . .
CHARLES—You must know somebody else beside Genghis Khan.
ELVIRA—Oh, Charles . . .
CHARLES—What is it?
ELVIRA—I want to cry, but I don't think I'm able to . . .
CHARLES—What do you want to cry for?
ELVIRA—It's seeing you again—and you being so irascible like you always used to be . . .
CHARLES—I don't mean to be irascible, Elvira . . .
ELVIRA—Darling—I don't mind really—I never did.
CHARLES—Is it cold—being a ghost?
ELVIRA—No—I don't think so.
CHARLES—What happens if I touch you?
ELVIRA—I doubt if you can. Do you want to?
CHARLES—Oh, Elvira . . . (*He buries his face in his hands.*)
ELVIRA—What is it, darling?
CHARLES—I really do feel strange, seeing you again . . .
ELVIRA—That's better.
CHARLES (*looking up*)—What's better?
ELVIRA—Your voice was kinder.
CHARLES—Was I ever unkind to you when you were alive?
ELVIRA—Often . . .
CHARLES—Oh, how can you! I'm sure that's an exaggeration.
ELVIRA—Not at all—you were an absolute pig that time we went to Cornwall and stayed in that awful hotel—you hit me with a billiard cue—
CHARLES—Only very, very gently . . .
ELVIRA—I loved you very much.
CHARLES—I loved you too . . . (*He puts out his hand to her and then draws it away.*) No, I can't touch you—isn't that horrible?
ELVIRA—Perhaps it's as well if I'm going to stay for any length of time. . . .
CHARLES—I feel strangely peaceful—I suppose I shall wake up eventually . . .
ELVIRA—Put your head back.
CHARLES (*doing so*)—Like that?
ELVIRA (*stroking his hair*)—Can you feel anything? . . .

122 THE BEST PLAYS OF 1941-42

CHARLES—Only a very little breeze through my hair. . . .
ELVIRA—Well, that's better than nothing.
CHARLES (*drowsily*)—I suppose if I'm really out of my mind they'll put me in an asylum.
ELVIRA—Don't worry about that—just relax—
CHARLES (*very drowsily indeed*)—Poor Ruth . . .
ELVIRA (*gently and sweetly*)—To hell with Ruth.
The curtain falls.

ACT II

It is nine-thirty next morning before Charles reaches the breakfast table. Ruth is already there, reading the *Times*. Their greetings are formal and friendly, save for a suggestion of iciness on the part of Ruth. With a few spirited passages this glacial attitude transfers itself to Charles and finally, when the discussion turns to the happenings of the evening before, Ruth is frank in insisting that practically everything can be explained by the fact that Charles was drunk—

"You had four strong dry Martinis before dinner," Ruth is saying; "a great deal too much burgundy at dinner—heaven knows how much port and kummel with Dr. Bradman while I was doing my best to entertain that madwoman—and then two double brandies later—I gave them to you myself—of course you were drunk."

"So that's your story, is it?"

"You refused to come to bed and finally when I came down at three in the morning to see what had happened to you I found you in an alcoholic coma on the sofa with the fire out and your hair all over your face."

"I was not in the least drunk, Ruth. Something happened to me—you really must believe that—something very peculiar happened to me."

"Nonsense."

"It isn't nonsense—I know it looks like nonsense now in the clear, remorseless light of day, but last night it was far from being nonsense—I honestly had some sort of hallucination—"

Try as he will Charles cannot convince Ruth, first, that he was not drunk, and, second, that he really believed that he saw and heard Elvira in that room. Protesting this honest conviction, Charles finally works himself into such a state of anger that he is prepared to forswear the entire feminine sex. Considering what his life with the women who have dominated him has been

Ruth is willing to agree that probably it is about time for a change.

"The only woman in my whole life who's ever attempted to dominate me is you—you've been at it for years," almost shouts Charles.

"That is completely untrue," answers Ruth.

CHARLES—Oh, no, it isn't. You boss me and bully me and order me about—you won't even allow me to have an hallucination if I want to.

RUTH—Alcohol will ruin your whole life if you allow it to get a hold on you, you know.

CHARLES—Once and for all, Ruth, I would like you to understand that what happened last night was nothing whatever to do with alcohol. You've very adroitly rationalized the whole affair to your own satisfaction, but your deductions are based on complete fallacy. I am willing to grant you that it was an aberration, some sort of odd psychic delusion brought on by suggestion or hypnosis. I was stone cold sober from first to last and extremely upset into the bargain.

RUTH—*You* were upset indeed! What about me?

CHARLES—You behaved with a stolid, obtuse lack of comprehension that frankly shocked me!

RUTH—I consider that I was remarkably patient. I shall know better next time.

CHARLES—Instead of putting out a gentle, comradely hand to guide me you shouted staccato orders at me like a sergeant-major.

RUTH—You seem to forget that you gratuitously insulted me.

CHARLES—I did not.

RUTH—You called me a guttersnipe—you told me to shut up—and when I quietly suggested that we should go up to bed you said, with the most disgusting leer, that it was an immoral suggestion.

CHARLES (*exasperated*)—I was talking to Elvira!

RUTH—If you were I can only say that it conjures up a fragrant picture of your first marriage.

CHARLES—My first marriage was perfectly charming and I think it's in the worst possible taste for you to sneer at it.

RUTH—I am not nearly so interested in your first marriage as you think I am. It's your second marriage that is absorbing me at the moment—it seems to be on the rocks.

CHARLES—Only because you persist in taking up this ridiculous attitude.

Ruth—My attitude is that of any normal woman whose husband gets drunk and hurls abuse at her.

Charles (*shouting*)—I was not drunk!

It is Ruth's stubborn conviction that if his belief in hallucinations persists Charles should send for Dr. Bradman. If not Dr. Bradman, then a nerve specialist. If not a nerve specialist a psychoanalyst. But Charles will have none of these, especially the psychoanalyst—

"I refuse to endure months of expensive humiliation only to be told at the end of it that at the age of four I was in love with my rocking horse," snaps Charles.

Charles is calmer now, even though his appeal for Ruth's understanding sympathy has been denied him. He thought for a time he might be going mad, but now, aside from being worried, he feels quite normal. He is neither hearing nor seeing anything in the least unusual. But at that moment in walks Elvira from the garden, her arms full of roses as gray as the rest of her.

"You've absolutely ruined that border by the sundial—it looks like a mixed salad," says Elvira, by way of cheerful greeting.

"Oh, my God!" exclaims the newly startled Charles.

"What's the matter now?" Ruth would know.

"She's here again!" wails Charles.

The mystery and the misunderstanding start all over again. Charles is plainly frightened. He would in some way placate Elvira, who has become insistently critical of Ruth and the way she is letting her house and her garden go, but he would also plead with Ruth please to understand something of what is happening to him.

Ruth—I've done everything I can to help—I've controlled myself admirably—and I should like to say here and now that I don't believe a word about your damned hallucinations—you're up to something, Charles—there's been a certain furtiveness in your manner for weeks— Why don't you be honest and tell me what it is?

Charles—You're wrong—you're dead wrong—I haven't been in the least furtive—I—

Ruth—You're trying to upset me—for some obscure reason you're trying to goad me into doing something that I might regret—I won't stand for it any more— You're making me utterly miserable— (*She bursts into tears and collapses on the sofa.*)

Charles—Ruth—please— (*Sits on sofa beside her.*)

Ruth—Don't come near me—
Elvira—Let her have a nice cry—it'll do her good.
Charles—You're utterly heartless!
Ruth Heartless!
Charles (*wildly*)—I was not talking to you—I was talking to Elvira.
Ruth—Go on talking to her then, talk to her until you're blue in the face but don't talk to me—
Charles—Help me, Elvira—
Elvira—How?
Charles—Make her see you or something.
Elvira—I'm afraid I couldn't manage that—it's technically the most difficult business—frightfully complicated, you know—it takes years of study—
Charles—You are here, aren't you? You're not an illusion?
Elvira—I may be an illusion but I'm most definitely here.
Charles—How did you get here?
Elvira—I told you last night—I don't exactly know—
Charles—Well, you must make me a promise that in future you only come and talk to me when I'm alone—
Elvira (*pouting*)—How unkind you are—making me feel so unwanted— I've never been treated so rudely—
Charles—I don't mean to be rude, but you must see—
Elvira—It's all your own fault for having married a woman who is incapable of seeing beyond the nose on her face—if she had a grain of real sympathy or affection for you she'd believe what you tell her.
Charles—How could you expect anybody to believe this?
Elvira—You'd be surprised how gullible people are—we often laugh about it on the other side.

Ruth has stopped crying and is staring at Charles in horror. Suddenly she gets up and goes to him. Her manner now is tenderly solicitous and reassuring. She is beginning to understand. If Charles will just come to bed and let her send for Dr. Bradman everything will be all right—
"She'll have you in a strait jacket before you know where you are," warns Elvira.
"Help me—you must help me—" Charles has turned to Elvira for aid now.
"My dear, I would with pleasure, but I can't think how—"
Charles has thought of a way. Pleading with Ruth to sit down, just for five minutes, he promises then to go to bed as

she asks. When Ruth humors him he repeats his earnest wish that she will believe him when he says that the ghost, or shade, or whatever she wants to call it, of his first wife, Elvira, is in the room at the moment. Then he turns to Elvira and asks her for help. Will she do what he asks. That, replies Elvira, depends upon what he asks. He turns back to Ruth—

CHARLES—Ruth—you see that bowl of flowers on the piano?
RUTH—Yes, dear—I did it myself this morning.
ELVIRA—Very untidily if I may say so.
CHARLES—You may not.
RUTH—Very well—I never will again—I promise.
CHARLES—Elvira will now carry that bowl of flowers to the mantelpiece and back again. You will, Elvira, won't you—just to please me?
ELVIRA—I don't really see why I should—you've been quite insufferable to me ever since I materialized.
CHARLES—Please.
ELVIRA—All right, I will just this once—not that I approve of all these Herman the Great carryings on. (*She goes over to the piano.*)
CHARLES—Now, Ruth—watch carefully.
RUTH (*patiently*)—Very well, dear.
CHARLES—Go on, Elvira—bring it to the mantelpiece and back again. (ELVIRA *does so, taking obvious pleasure in doing it in a very roundabout way. At one moment she brings it up to within an inch of* RUTH'S *face.* RUTH *shrinks back with a scream and then jumps to her feet.*)
RUTH (*furiously*)—How dare you, Charles! You ought to be ashamed of yourself!
CHARLES—What on earth for?
RUTH (*hysterically*)—It's a trick—I know perfectly well it's a trick—you've been working up to this—it's all part of some horrible plan—
CHARLES—It isn't—I swear it isn't—Elvira—do something else for God's sake—
ELVIRA—Certainly—anything to oblige.
RUTH (*becoming really frightened*)—You want to get rid of me—you're trying to drive me out of my mind—
CHARLES—Don't be so silly.
RUTH—You're cruel and sadistic and I'll never forgive you— (ELVIRA *lifts up a light chair and waltzes solemnly round the room with it, then she puts it down with a bang. Making a dive*

for the door.) I'm—I'm not going to put up with this any more.
CHARLES (*holding her*)—You must believe it—you must—
RUTH—Let me go immediately—
CHARLES—That was Elvira—I swear it was—
RUTH (*struggling*)—Let me go—
CHARLES—Ruth—please— (RUTH *breaks away from him and runs toward the windows.* ELVIRA *gets there just before her and shuts them in her face.* RUTH *starts back appalled.*)
RUTH (*looking at* CHARLES *with eyes of horror*)—Charles—this is madness—sheer madness! It's some sort of auto-suggestion, isn't it—some form of hypnotism, swear to me it's only that? Swear to me it's only that.
ELVIRA (*taking an expensive vase from the mantelpiece and crashing it into the grate*)—Hypnotism my foot! (RUTH *gives a scream and goes into violent hysterics as the curtain falls.*)

It is late the following afternoon. Ruth is impatiently awaiting the arrival of Mme. Arcati. Presently the Madame, "wearing a tweed coat and skirt and a great many amber beads," arrives. She is glad to come, and tremendously eager to hear of the more recent adventures in the Condomine home.

Ruth finds a description of what has happened a bit difficult. The facts are so fantastic—

"Facts very often are," observes Mme. Arcati. "Take creative talent, for instance, how do you account for that? Look at Shakespeare and Michael Angelo! Try to explain Mozart snatching sounds out of the air and putting them down on paper when he was practically a baby—facts—plain facts. I know it's the fashion nowadays to ascribe it all to glands but my reply to that is fiddledeedee."

"Yes, I'm sure you're quite right," Ruth agrees.

"There are more things in heaven and earth than are dreamt of in your philosophy, Mrs. Condomine."

It is probable, thinks Mme. Arcati, that Ruth has heard strange noises in the night, or the creaking of boards, or the slamming of doors, or a subdued moaning in the passages. No? Nor any gusts of cold wind? No. What then?

Ruth recounts the adventure of Elvira's materialization to Charles. Mme. Arcati is thrilled. What a triumph! Nothing so exciting has happened to her in years. She paces the room in her exultation and refuses to sit down.

"I appreciate fully your pride in your achievement," says Ruth firmly, "but I would like to point out that it has made my position in this house untenable and that I hold you entirely responsible."

Ruth has sent for Mme. Arcati, she explains, to try to induce her to send Elvira back to where she came from. Mme. Arcati would like to oblige, but fears that will be easier said than done. First she must make a report to the Psychical Research Society, for which purpose she produces a note book.

Ruth is not at all interested in Mme. Arcati's report, nor is she able to help greatly with it. She did not know the first Mrs. Condomine, nor does she have any idea why Elvira wanted to return at this time. It is Madame's opinion that Elvira had been anxious to return and had put herself on the waiting list. There must have been strong influences at work. . . . Still nothing is to be gained by Ruth's upsetting herself.

"It's all very fine for you to talk like that, Madame Arcati," Ruth is saying; "you don't seem to have the faintest realization of my position."

"Try to look on the bright side," suggests the madame.

RUTH—Bright side indeed! If your husband's first wife suddenly appeared from the grave and came to live in the house with you, do you suppose you'd be able to look on the bright side?

MADAME ARCATI—I resent your tone, Mrs. Condomine, I really do.

RUTH—You most decidedly have no right to—you are entirely to blame for the whole horrible situation.

MADAME ARCATI—Kindly remember that I came here the other night on your own invitation.

RUTH—On my husband's invitation.

MADAME ARCATI—I did what I was requested to do, which was to give a séance and establish contact with the other side— I had no idea that there was any ulterior motive mixed up with it.

RUTH—Ulterior motive?

MADAME ARCATI—Your husband was obviously eager to get in touch with his former wife. If I had been aware of that at the time I should naturally have consulted you beforehand— after all "Noblesse oblige"!

RUTH—He had no intention of trying to get in touch with anyone—the whole thing was planned in order for him to get material for a mystery story he is writing about a homicidal medium.

MADAME ARCATI (*drawing herself up*)—Am I to understand

that I was only invited in a spirit of mockery?

Ruth—Not at all—he merely wanted to make notes of some of the tricks of the trade.

Madame Arcati (*incensed*)—Tricks of the trade! Insufferable! I've never been so insulted in my life. I feel we have nothing more to say to one another, Mrs. Condomine. Goodby—

Ruth—Please don't go—please—

Madame Arcati—Your attitude from the outset has been most unpleasant, Mrs. Condomine. Some of your remarks have been discourteous in the extreme and I should like to say without umbrage that if you and your husband were foolish enough to tamper with the unseen for paltry motives and in a spirit of ribaldry, whatever has happened to you is your own fault, and, to coin a phrase, as far as I'm concerned you can stew in your own juice! (*She goes majestically from the room.*)

Ruth (*left alone, walks about the room*)—Damn—damn—damn!

Charles and Elvira are coming in as Mme. Arcati is going out. She sweeps past them. Charles would like to know what the Madame has been doing there. Elvira knows. Ruth has sent for Mme. Arcati to have her (Elvira) exorcised. "There's a snake in the grass for you," says Elvira. . . .

"I admit I did ask Mme. Arcati here with a view to getting you exorcised and I think that if you were in my position you'd have done exactly the same thing—wouldn't you?"

"I shouldn't have done it so obviously."

Ruth—What did she say?

Charles—Nothing—she just nodded and smiled.

Ruth (*with a forced smile*)—Thank you, Elvira—that's generous of you. I really would so much rather that there were no misunderstandings between us—

Charles—That's very sensible, Ruth—I agree entirely.

Ruth (*to* Elvira)—I want, before we go any further, to ask you a frank question. Why did you really come here? I don't see that you could have hoped to have achieved anything by it beyond the immediate joke of making Charles into a sort of astral bigamist.

Elvira—I came because the power of Charles's love tugged and tugged and tugged at me. Didn't it, my sweet?

Ruth—What did she say?

CHARLES—She said she came because she wanted to see me again.

RUTH—Well, she's done that now, hasn't she?

CHARLES—We can't be inhospitable, Ruth.

RUTH—I have no wish to be inhospitable, but I should like to have just an idea of how long you intend to stay, Elvira?

ELVIRA—I don't know—I really don't know! (*She giggles.*) Isn't it awful?

CHARLES—She says she doesn't know.

RUTH—Surely that's a little inconsiderate?

ELVIRA—Didn't the old spiritualist have any constructive ideas about getting rid of me?

CHARLES—What did Madame Arcati say?

RUTH—She said she couldn't do a thing.

ELVIRA (*moving gaily over to the window*)—Hurray!

CHARLES—Don't be upset, Ruth dear—we shall soon adjust ourselves, you know—you must admit it's a unique experience—I can see no valid reason why we shouldn't get a great deal of fun out of it.

RUTH—Fun? Charles, how can you—you must be out of your mind!

CHARLES—Not at all—I thought I was at first—but now I must say I'm beginning to enjoy myself.

RUTH (*bursting into tears*)—Oh, Charles—Charles—

ELVIRA—She's off again.

Charles is a little disappointed in Elvira. She should be more considerate of Ruth's feelings. Elvira is not impressed. She feels that Charles must have had quite a time living with the second Mrs. Condomine, considering her temper and everything.

Ruth continues to find the situation intolerable. Presently she has arrived at a definite conclusion—

"I've been making polite conversation all through dinner last night and breakfast and lunch today—and it's been a nightmare—and I am not going to do it any more. I don't like Elvira any more than she likes me and what's more I'm certain that I never could have, dead or alive. If, since her untimely arrival here the other evening, she had shown the slightest sign of good manners, the slightest sign of breeding, I might have felt differently towards her, but all she has done is try to make mischief between us and have private jokes with you against me. I am now going up to my room and I shall have my dinner on a tray. You and she can have the house to yourselves and joke and gossip with each other to your heart's content. The first thing in the morning I am going up to London to interview the Psychical Research Society and if they fail me I shall go straight to the Archbishop of Canterbury—"

Ruth has flounced out of the room. Charles would follow and comfort her, but Elvira holds him back. If Ruth wants to be disagreeable let her get on with it. Elvira feels that she has some rights, too. After all she has not seen Charles for seven years. Why shouldn't she want to have some time alone with him?

Charles has gone to dress for dinner. Elvira thinks his dressing is silly too, but— "I should like to watch you eat something really delicious," she admits.

"Be a good girl now—you can play the gramophone if you want to," answers Charles, smiling and kissing his hand to her as he goes out.

Elvira goes to the gramophone closet and takes out the record of "Always." She is waltzing lightly around the room to the music when Edith comes to fetch the tea tray. Edith stops the gramophone and puts the record back, but she barely has time to pick up the tray before Elvira has recovered the record and set it playing again. With a shriek Edith drops the tray and runs wildly from the room. Elvira has resumed her waltzing as the curtain falls.

It is evening several days later when the curtain rises. Outside it is raining. Inside Ruth has just been telling Mrs. Bradman of the chapter of fantastic accidents that have happened since they last met. Dr. Bradman is upstairs looking after Charles, who has an injured arm. Edith, too, has had a fall and is suffering from concussion.

When Dr. Bradman comes down it is to report that Charles' arm injury is slight, but he is a little worried about his nervous condition. Thinks he should go away for a couple of weeks. Symptoms? Well, Charles is showing a certain air of strain—an inability to focus his eyes on the person he is talking to—a few rather marked irrelevancies in his conversation.

"Can you remember any specific examples?" Ruth asks.

"Oh, he suddenly shouted, 'What are you doing in the bathroom?' and then, a little later, while I was writing him a prescription, he suddenly said, 'For God's sake behave yourself!'"

"He often goes on like that—particularly when he's immersed in writing a book—"

Charles comes in with his left arm in a sling just as the Bradmans are leaving. Elvira follows after and sits quietly by the fire. Charles still can't think the arm sprain is serious, and he would like to drive into Folkstone as he had planned. Both the doctor and Ruth would dissuade Charles if they could, but the doctor finally gives consent if he will promise to drive slowly and carefully. The roads are very slippery. It would be better if Ruth were to go too, and do the driving, but Ruth has her house chores—and Edith—to look after.

"You really are infuriating, Elvira—surely you can wait and go to the movies another night," says Ruth, when Charles has gone to the door with the Bradmans.

Elvira gives a gay little laugh, takes a rose from the vase, tosses it at Ruth's feet and romps through the French windows. "And stop behaving like a school girl—you're old enough to know better."

Ruth is still muttering when Charles comes back to tell her that Elvira isn't even in the room. "She was a minute ago—she threw a rose at me," protests Ruth.

If they are alone there is something that Ruth would like to talk about. "This is a fight, Charles—a bloody battle—a duel to the death between Elvira and me. Don't you realize that?"

CHARLES—Melodramatic hysteria.

RUTH—It isn't melodramatic hysteria—it's true. Can't you see?

CHARLES—No, I can't. You're imagining things—jealousy causes people to have the most curious delusions.

RUTH—I am making every effort not to lose my temper with you, Charles, but I must say you are making it increasingly difficult for me.

CHARLES—All this talk of battles and duels—

RUTH—She came here with one purpose and one purpose only —and if you can't see it you're a bigger fool than I thought you.

CHARLES—What purpose could she have had beyond a natural desire to see me again? After all, you must remember that she was extremely attached to me, poor child.

RUTH—Her purpose is perfectly obvious. It is to get you to herself forever.

CHARLES—That's absurd—how could she?

RUTH—By killing you off of course.

CHARLES—Killing me off? You're mad!

RUTH—Why do you suppose Edith fell down the stairs and

nearly cracked her skull?

CHARLES—What's Edith got to do with it?

RUTH—Because the whole of the top stair was covered with axle grease. Cook discovered it afterwards.

CHARLES—You're making this up, Ruth—

RUTH—I'm not. I swear I'm not. Why do you suppose when you were lopping that dead branch off the pear tree that the ladder broke? Because it had been practically sawn through on both sides.

CHARLES—But why should she want to kill me? I can understand her wanting to kill you, but why me?

RUTH—If you were dead it would be her final triumph over me. She'd have you with her forever on her damned astral plane and I'd be left high and dry. She's probably planning a sort of spiritual remarriage. I wouldn't put anything past her.

Ruth has a plan to circumvent her ghostly guest. Charles is not to let Elvira know that he suspects a thing. Ruth will go find Mme. Arcati and force her, if necessary, into another trance that they may all be rid of Elvira. Charles can explain to Elvira that she (Ruth) has gone to see the Vicar.

Before Ruth can get away Elvira has floated back from the garden. Discovering that she is there Ruth turns on Elvira to tell her frankly that she has been trying to prevail upon Charles not to drive her into Folkstone that evening. However, so long as he seems determined to place Elvira's interests first she has given way and she hopes they will enjoy themselves. With which statement she flounces out.

Now Elvira is worried. She fears Charles has lost interest in taking her. Charles hasn't but he is not going to hurry. He is going to drink a glass of sherry first. And if she doesn't stop criticizing Ruth and behave herself he will not take her into Folkstone ever—

"Besides," he adds, sipping his sherry, "the car won't be back for a half hour at least."

"What do you mean?" demands Elvira, sharply.

CHARLES—Ruth's taken it—she had to go and see the Vicar—

ELVIRA (*Jumping up—in extreme agitation*)—What!!

CHARLES—What on earth's the matter?

ELVIRA—You say *Ruth's* taken the car?

CHARLES—Yes—to go and see the Vicar—but she won't be long.

ELVIRA (*wildly*)—O, my God! O, my God!
CHARLES—Elvira!—
ELVIRA—Stop her! You must stop her at once—
CHARLES—Why—what for?—
ELVIRA (*jumping up and down*)—Stop her—go out and stop her immediately!
CHARLES—It's too late now—she's gone already.
ELVIRA (*backing away towards window*)—Oh! Oh! Oh! Oh!!!
CHARLES—What are you going on like this for? What have you done?
ELVIRA (*frightened*)—Done?—I haven't done anything—
CHARLES—Elvira—you're lying—
ELVIRA (*backing away from him*)—I'm not lying. What is there to lie about?
CHARLES—What are you in such a state for?
ELVIRA (*almost hysterical*)—I'm not in a state—I don't know what you mean—
CHARLES—You've done something dreadful—
ELVIRA (*backing away*)—Don't look at me like that, Charles—I haven't—I swear I haven't—
CHARLES (*striking his forehead*)—My God, the car!
ELVIRA—No, Charles—no—
CHARLES—Ruth was right—you did want to kill me—you've done something to the car—
ELVIRA (*howling like a banshee*)—Oh—oh—oh—oh!—
CHARLES—What did you do—answer me. (*At this moment the telephone rings.* CHARLES *stops dead; then with slow steps goes to it.*) Hallo—hallo—yes, speaking—I see—the bridge at the bottom of the hill—thank you. No. I'll come at once—(*He slowly puts back the receiver. As he does so the door bursts open.*)
ELVIRA (*obviously retreating from someone*)—Well, of all the filthy, low-down tricks— (*She shields her head with her hands and screams.*) Ow—stop it—Ruth—let go—

Elvira "runs out of the room and slams the door. It opens again immediately and slams again. Charles stares aghast" as the curtain falls.

ACT III

It is evening a few days later. Charles, in full mourning, is standing in front of his fireplace drinking his after dinner coffee. A moment later he has selected a book and settled comfortably into an easy chair for a quiet evening at home. A ring at the door quite plainly irritates him. Mme. Arcati is calling. She had felt a tremendous urge, like a rushing wind, the Madame reports, and just had to come. For days her conscience has been troubling her. She had, she feels, been unfair to the late Mrs. Condomine and she has come to do what she can to make amends. She trusts they are alone—

"My first wife is not in the room," Charles assures her; "she's upstairs lying down, the funeral exhausted her. I imagine that my second wife is with her but of course I have no way of knowing for certain."

"You have remarked no difference in the texture of your first wife since the accident?"

"No, she seems much as usual, a little under the weather perhaps, a trifle low-spirited, but that's all."

"Well, that washes that out."

"I'm afraid I don't understand."

"Just a little theory I had. In the nineteenth century there was a pretty widespread belief that a ghost who participated in the death of a human being disintegrated automatically—"

"How do you know that Elvira was in any way responsible for Ruth's death?"

"It came to me last night, Mr. Condomine—it came to me in a blinding flash—I had just finished my Ovaltine and turned the light out when I suddenly started up in bed with a loud cry—'Great Scott, I've got it!' I said—after that I began to put two and two together. At three in the morning—with my brain fairly seething—I went to work on my crystal for a little but it wasn't very satisfactory—cloudy, you know—"

"I would be very much obliged if you would keep any theories you have regarding my wife's death to yourself, Madame Arcati. . . ."

"My one desire is to help you. I feel I have been dreadfully remiss over the whole affair—not only remiss but untidy."

"I am afraid there is nothing whatever to be done."

Mme. Arcati, to the contrary, is quite hopeful. She has found a formula in Edmondston's "Witchcraft and Its Byways" which she is sure will do the work. If Mr. Condomine is still anxious to dematerialize his first wife it probably can be accomplished quite simply. Mme. Arcati may not even have to go into a trance. All that will be required of Charles is complete concentration.

Now Elvira has come floating into the room. She quickly

resents Mme. Arcati's presence. If the Madame is the one who got her there in the first place let her get her back as soon as she can. Elvira is sick of the whole business.

Mme. Arcati is thrilled to hear that Elvira is present, and eager to talk with her. But Elvira will have nothing to do with the Madame. "Tell the silly old bitch to mind her own business," orders Elvira. "She's dotty." Only on his promise to send Madame Arcati into the other room does Elvira agree to confirm her presence to the medium. Then she blows gently into Mme. Arcati's ears, which throws that delighted lady into a frenzy of excitement.

When she and Charles are alone Elvira is very unhappy and shortly gives way to ghostly tears. Her coming back has been a complete failure, and she had started out with such high hopes—

"I sat there on the other side, just longing for you day after day," wails Elvira. "I did really—all through your affair with that brassy-looking woman in the South of France I went on loving you and thinking truly of you—then you married Ruth and even then I forgave you and tried to understand because all the time I believed deep inside that you really loved me best . . . that's why I put myself down for a return visit and had to fill in all those forms and wait about in draughty passages for hours—if only you'd died before you met Ruth everything might have been all right—she's absolutely ruined you—I hadn't been in the house a day before I realized that. Your books aren't a quarter as good as they used to be either."

"That," answers Charles, sharply, "is entirely untrue . . . Ruth helped me and encouraged me with my work which is a damned sight more than you ever did."

"That's probably what's wrong with it."

Soon they are in the midst of a violently amusing quarrel. It carries them back to the evening that Elvira had gone out in a punt with Guy Henderson and got soaked to the skin. Which was the same evening that Charles had spent his entire time making sheep's eyes at Cynthia Cheviot. It includes their present memories of a completely blasted honeymoon at Budleigh Salterton and Elvira's flirtation with Captain Bracegirdle, a flirtation, insists Elvira, that had grown out of her state of complete boredom. The spat ends with their agreement that they both had been cheated in their marital adventure and Charles' sense of relief that he at last is well rid of Elvira.

". . . You're dead and Ruth's dead," Charles is saying, a

little exultantly; "I shall sell this house, lock, stock and barrel, and go away."

"I shall follow you," calmly announces Elvira.

CHARLES—I shall go a long way away—I shall go to South America—you'll hate that, you were always a bad traveler.

ELVIRA (*at the piano*)—That can't be helped—I shall have to follow you—you called me back.

CHARLES—I did *not* call you back!

ELVIRA—Well, somebody did—and it's hardly likely to have been Ruth.

CHARLES—Nothing in the world was further from my thoughts.

ELVIRA—You were talking about me before dinner that evening.

CHARLES—I might just as easily have been talking about Joan of Arc but that wouldn't necessarily mean that I wanted her to come and live with me.

ELVIRA—As a matter of fact she's rather fun.

CHARLES—Stick to the point.

ELVIRA—When I think of what might have happened if I'd succeeded in getting you to the other world after all—it makes me shudder, it does honestly . . . it would be nothing but bickering and squabbling forever and ever and ever. . . . I swear I'll be better off with Ruth—at least she'll find her own set and not get in my way.

CHARLES—So I get in your way, do I?

ELVIRA—Only because I was idiotic enough to imagine that you loved me, and I sort of felt sorry for you.

CHARLES—I'm sick of these insults—please go away.

ELVIRA—There's nothing I should like better—I've always believed in cutting my losses. That's why I died.

Charles has called Mme. Arcati from the dining room and explained to her that he and Elvira are agreed that Elvira should go back immediately. Mme. Arcati proceeds enthusiastically to put the formula she has acquired from the witch book into practice. First there must be a little pepper and salt sprinkled in the center of the table, and a few snapdragons added. Then they must have the same record put back on the gramophone.

Elvira, who has been sniffling and making rude remarks about Mme. Arcati, is first at the gramophone cabinet and finds the record, while Mme. Arcati looks on, startled and entranced—

"Oh, if only that Mr. Emsworth of the Psychical Research Society could see this," she gurgled, "he'd have a fit, he would really."

Now she would have Charles seated at the table again, warning him to be careful of the salt and pepper, in which she has made certain mystic tracings. She will turn out the lights herself, but she would like to have Elvira lie down on the sofa and relax, breathing steadily, while Charles is concentrating at the table.

Now Mme. Arcati darts swiftly across the room and turns out the lights. Suddenly Charles gives a healthy sneeze—

"Oh, dear—it's the pepper," giggles Elvira.

"Damn!" explodes Charles.

"Hold on to yourself—concentrate—" commands Mme. Arcati. In a sing-song voice she recites—

> "Ghostly specter—ghoul or fiend
> Never more be thou convened
> Shepherd's Wort and Holy Rite
> Banish thee into the night."

ELVIRA—What a disagreeable little verse.

CHARLES—Be quiet, Elvira.

MADAME ARCATI—Shhh! (*There is silence.*) Is there anyone there? . . . Is there anyone there? . . . One rap for yes—two raps for no. Is there anyone there? . . . (*The table gives a loud bump.*) Aha! Good stuff! Is it Daphne? . . . (*The table gives another bump.*) I'm sorry to bother you, dear, but Mrs. Condomine wants to return. (*The table bumps several times very quickly.*) Now then, Daphne . . . Did you hear what I said? (*After a pause the table gives one bump.*) Can you help us? . . . (*There is another pause, then the table begins to bump violently without stopping.*) Hold tight, Mr. Condomine—it's trying to break away. Oh! Oh! Oh— (*The table falls over with a crash.*)

CHARLES—What's the matter, Madame Arcati? Are you hurt?

MADAME ARCATI (*wailing*)—Oh! Oh! Oh—

CHARLES (*turning on lights*)—What on earth's happening? (MADAME ARCATI *is lying on the floor with the table upside down on her back.* CHARLES *hurriedly lifts it off. Shaking her.*) Are you hurt, Madame Arcati?

ELVIRA—She's in one of her damned trances again and I'm here as much as ever I was.

CHARLES (*shaking* MADAME ARCATI)—For God's sake wake up.

BLITHE SPIRIT

Madame Arcati (*moaning*)—Oh! Oh! Oh—
Elvira—Leave her alone—she's having a whale of a time. If I ever do get back I'll strangle that bloody little Daphne. . . .
Charles—Wake up!
Madame Arcati (*sitting up suddenly*)—What happened?
Charles—Nothing—nothing at all.
Madame Arcati (*rising and dusting herself*)—Oh, yes, it did—I know something happened.
Charles—You fell over—that's all that happened.
Madame Arcati—Is she still here?
Charles—Of course she is.
Madame Arcati—Something must have gone wrong.
Elvira—Make her do it properly. I'm sick of being messed about like this.
Charles—She's doing her best. Be quiet, Elvira.
Madame Arcati—Something happened—I sensed it in my trance—I felt it—it shivered through me. (*Suddenly the window curtains blow out almost straight and* Ruth *walks into the room. She is still wearing the brightly colored clothes in which we last saw her but now they are entirely gray. So is her hair and her skin.*)
Ruth—Once and for all, Charles, what the hell does this mean?
The lights fade.

Several hours have elapsed when the lights are turned up. "The whole room is in slight disarray. There are birch branches and evergreens laid on the floor in front of the doors and crossed birch branches pinned rather untidily onto the curtains."

Mme. Arcati has stretched herself out on the sofa, and lies with her eyes closed. Elvira is sitting despondently at the table. Ruth is standing by the fireplace and Charles is pacing restlessly about the room.

Evidently Ruth and Elvira have been exchanging comments, but not compliments, and things have reached a point at which Ruth feels some future course of action should be agreed upon.

"We have all agreed that as Elvira and I are dead that it would be both right and proper for us to dematerialize again as soon as possible," says Ruth. "That I admit. We have allowed ourselves to be subjected to the most humiliating hocus-pocus for hours and hours without complaining—"

"Without complaining?"

"We've stood up—we've lain down—we've concentrated.

We've sat interminably while that tiresome old woman recited extremely unflattering verses at us. We've endured five séances —we've watched her fling herself in and out of trances until we were dizzy and at the end of it all we find ourselves exactly where we were at the beginning. . . ."

"Well, it's not my fault," protests Charles.

"Be that as it may," continues Ruth; "the least you could do is to admit failure gracefully and try to make the best of it— your manners are boorish to a degree."

"I'm just as exhausted as you are. I've had to do all the damned table tapping, remember."

"If she can't get us back, she can't and that's that. We shall have to think of something else."

Charles is as firm as ever about their going back. Nor is he greatly impressed by their charges of ingratitude, based on the fact that they had devoted their lives to him and he has done nothing but try to get rid of them ever since he called them back.

Finally it is agreed that Mme. Arcati must be called upon again. The medium is awakened and found eager for another séance.

"I might be able to materialize a trumpet if I tried hard enough," Mme. Arcati promises. "I feel as fit as a fiddle after my rest."

"I don't care if she materializes a whole symphony orchestra— I implore you not to let her have another séance." Elvira is both excited and firm.

Charles, too, feels that something else should be tried. Also he refuses to accept gracefully his wives' repeated charge that he alone is responsible for their being there—

"Love is a strong psychic force, Mr. Condomine—it can work untold miracles," affirms Mme. Arcati. "A true love call can encompass the universe—"

"I am sure it can," admits Charles, hastily; "but I must confess to you frankly that although my affection for both Elvira and Ruth is of the warmest I cannot truthfully feel that it would come under the heading that you describe."

Still, Mme. Arcati is not convinced. "Neither of them could have appeared unless there had been somebody—a psychic subject—in the house, who wished for them. . . ."

Suddenly Mme. Arcati is again reminded of her success in the Sudbury case years before—

"It was the case that made me famous, Mr. Condomine," the Madame explains. "It was what you might describe in theatrical parlance as my first smash hit! I had letters from all over the world about it—especially India."

"What did you do?"

"I dematerialized old Lady Sudbury after she'd been firmly entrenched in the private chapel for over seventeen years."

The Sudbury formula—that's what Mme. Arcati will try now. A moment later she is gazing intently into her crystal. What she sees startles her. It is a white bandage—let them hold on to that. A white bandage—and she begins to recite—

> "Be you in nook or cranny answer me
> Do you in Still-room or closet answer me
> Do you behind the panel, above the stairs
> Beneath the eaves—waking or sleeping
> Answer me!

That ought to do it or I'm a Dutchman."

Mme. Arcati has picked up one of the birch branches and is waving it solemnly to and fro. Suddenly the door opens and Edith, the maid, comes into the room. "She is wearing a pink flannel dressing gown and bedroom slippers. Her head is bandaged."

"Did you ring, sir?" asks Edith, plaintively.

"The bandage! The white bandage!" cries Mme. Arcati.

"I'm sorry, sir—I could have sworn I heard the bell—or somebody calling—I was asleep—I don't rightly know which it was. . . ."

Mme. Arcati takes charge. She would question Edith. Who does Edith see in the room? At first the frightened girl can see no one save her master and the medium, but soon she is trapped into admitting that there are others standing over by the fireplace. With this encouragement Mme. Arcati takes a position in front of Edith and begins calling—"Cuckoo—cuckoo—cuckoo—"

"Oh, dear—what is the matter with her? Is she barmy?" pleads Edith, tremulously.

"Here, Edith—this is my finger—look— (*She waggles it.*) Have you ever seen such a long, long, long finger? Look now it's on the right now it's on the left—backwards and forwards it goes—see—very quietly backwards and forwards—tic-toc—tic-toc—tic-toc."

"The mouse ran up the clock," finishes Elvira.

"Be quiet—you'll ruin everything," protests Ruth.

Mme. Arcati is whistling a little tune close to Edith's face. Then she snaps her fingers sharply. Edith is looking stolidly into space without flinching.

"Well—so far so good—she's off all right," announces Mme. Arcati. "She's a Natural—just the same as the Sudbury case—it really is the most amusing coincidence. Now then—would you ask your wives to stand close together please?"

Ruth and Elvira are herded into position, despite their protests. "You know what you have to do now, don't you, Edith?"

"Oh, yes, Madame."

Elvira would call a halt if she could. There is something else she wants to tell Charles. Ruth, too, would like a last word. Mme. Arcati has dashed across the room and switched off the lights. Edith is softly singing "Always" in a very high Cockney voice—

"I saw Captain Bracegirdle again, Charles—several times," calls Elvira, out of the dark; "I went to the Four Hundred with him twice when you were in Nottingham. And I must say I couldn't have enjoyed it more."

"Don't think you're getting rid of us quite so easily, my dear," calls Ruth; "you may not be able to see us but we will be here all right—I consider that you have behaved atrociously over the whole miserable business. And I should like to say here and now—"

Ruth's voice has faded into a whisper and then disappeared altogether—

"Splendid! Hurrah! We've done it!" shouts Mme. Arcati, and adds: "That's quite enough singing for the moment, Edith."

Charles has pulled back the curtains. The room is flooded with daylight. "They've gone—they've really gone!" he shouts.

"Yes—I think we've really pulled it off this time," agrees Mme. Arcati.

A moment later the medium has awakened Edith and sent her, wonderingly, back to bed.

"Golly, what a night! I'm ready to drop in my tracks," sighs Mme. Arcati.

The grateful Charles would have her stay the night, but Mme. Arcati prefers to pedal off home. Nor will she let him think of settling her account. The experience has been a great pleasure to her. When he comes back, she will be delighted to lunch with him.

"Come back?" Charles doesn't understand.

"Take my advice, Mr. Condomine, and go away immediately."

CHARLES—But, Madame Arcati! You don't mean that . . . ?

MADAME ARCATI (*clearing her stuff from the table*)—This

must be an unhappy house for you—there must be memories both grave and gay in every corner of it—also— (*She pauses.*)

CHARLES—Also what?

MADAME ARCATI (*thinking better of it*)—There are more things in heaven and earth, Mr. Condomine. (*She places her finger to her lips.*) Just go—pack your traps and go as soon as possible.

CHARLES (*also in lowered tones*)—Do you mean that they may still be here?

MADAME ARCATI (*nodding and then nonchalantly whistling a little tune*)—Quien sabe, as the Spanish say. (*She collects her bag and her crystal.*)

CHARLES (*looking furtively round the room*)—I wonder—I wonder. I'll follow your advice, Madame Arcati. Thank you again.

MADAME ARCATI—Well, good-by, Mr. Condomine—it's been fascinating—from first to last—fascinating. Do you mind if I take just one more sandwich to munch on my way home? (*Comes to table for sandwich.*)

CHARLES—By all means. (MADAME ARCATI *goes to the door.* CHARLES *follows to see her safely out.*)

MADAME ARCATI (*as they go*)—Don't trouble—I can find my way. Cheerio once more and good hunting! (CHARLES *watches her into the hall and then comes back into the room. He prowls about for a moment as though he were not sure that he was alone.*)

CHARLES (*softly*)—Ruth—Elvira—are you there? (*A pause.*) Ruth—Elvira—I know damn well you're here— (*Another pause.*) I just want to tell you that I'm going away so there's no point in your hanging about any longer—I'm going a long way away—somewhere where I don't believe you'll be able to follow me. In spite of what Elvira said I don't think spirits can travel over water. Is that quite clear, my darlings? You said in one of your more acid moments, Ruth, that I had been hag-ridden all my life! How right you were—but now I'm free, Ruth dear, not only of Mother and Elvira and Mrs. Winthrop-Lewellen, but free of you too, and I should like to take this farewell opportunity of saying I'm enjoying it immensely— (*A vase crashes into the fireplace.*) Aha—I thought so—you were very silly, Elvira, to imagine that I didn't know all about you and Captain Bracegirdle—I did. But what you didn't know was that I was extremely attached to Paula Westlake at the time! (*The clock strikes sixteen viciously and very quickly.*) I was reasonably faithful to you, Ruth, but I doubt if it would have lasted much longer—you were becoming increasingly domineering, you know, and there's nothing more off putting than that, is there? (*A large picture falls down with a crash.*) Good-by for the moment, my dears. I expect we are bound to meet again one day, but until we do I'm going to enjoy myself as I've never enjoyed myself before. You can break up the house as much as you like—I'm leaving it anyhow. Think kindly of me and send out good thoughts— (*The overmantel begins to shake and tremble as though someone were tugging at it.*) Nice work, Elvira—persevere. Good-by again—parting is such *sweet* sorrow! (*He goes out of the room just as the overmantel crashes to the floor and the curtain pole comes tumbling down.*)

THE CURTAIN FALLS

JUNIOR MISS
A Comedy in Three Acts

By Jerome Chodorov and Joseph Fields

NEW YORK playgoers had prayed pretty desperately for a comedy hit through the early weeks of the 1941-42 season. The dramas had been disappointing and musical plays, however good, never completely satisfy your serious theatre follower. Then, on November 18, along came "Junior Miss," written by the Messrs. Chodorov and Fields, who had contributed "My Sister Eileen" the season before. The playgoers' prayers were answered. Here was a hit. A little quibbling here and there, perhaps, as usually happens, but in the main a sizable hit. And Moss Hart did the directing.

The Messrs. Chodorov and Fields extracted their material from the collection of sub-deb sketches contributed to the *New Yorker* magazine by Sally Benson. Concerning the adventures of a 14-year-old and her girl chum, the producer's first concern, quite naturally, was the finding of proper young actresses to play the two chief rôles. Adolescent heroines in the theatre have always been a little difficult to cast. If the actress is young enough to look the part she is too young to play it with anything resembling authority. If she is old enough and sufficiently experienced to have acquired authority she is likely to be much too mature to suggest convincingly the adolescent mood and reactions.

During Mr. Hart's search Patricia Peardon, the 16-year-old daughter of Commander Roswell Peardon, USN, was sitting in the ante-room of the Max Gordon offices waiting for a young actor who was applying for a part. She was wearing a sweater, skirt and low shoes, she reports, and had no thought of looking for a part for herself. A passing stage manager asked her if she were an actress; she said yes, promptly, because in fact she had done some work both on the stage and in radio. He suggested that she come back at 4 o'clock.

Patricia, a little excited by this time, dashed home and changed both her get-up and her make-up so that at 4 she might look more as she thought a grown-up actress should look. When she reappeared she was a young lady indeed. Mr. Hart gave her one look and handed her the rôle of Lois, the debutante sister of the "Junior Miss" heroine. Patricia read it and was about to be dismissed when Mr. Hart, a mite suspicious of her high heels and rouged cheeks, suggested that she read the rôle of Judy. Then she figuratively descended from her high heels and became herself. Two days later she was given the part and, as Broadway historians have recorded, scored the hit of her still young life in it. Sometimes it happens that way, even outside press agent stories.

"Junior Miss" was also fortunate in the casting of Judy's pal, Fuffy Adams, which went to Lenore Lonergan, daughter of the second Lester Lonergan and grand-daughter of the first Lester Lonergan and his wife, Amy Ricard, long-time favorites in an older theatre.

The scenes of "Junior Miss" are played in the Harry Graves' apartment, which is located in Manhattan's upper Sixties, and in a building that is definitely post-first-war and "has reached the sand-blasting stage." The living room, into which we are ushered, is comfortably furnished and in reasonably good taste, with a fairly familiar assortment of easy chairs, end tables and a sofa. "The total effect is middle-class, of people who have a fairly steady struggle to maintain their position."

On this particular mid-December evening Harry Graves, the head of the house, is comfortably settled in an easy chair with his feet on one of the end tables. "He is a good-looking sort of man of about 38, with the remains of an athletic physique."

A ring at the doorbell announces Joe, the elevator boy, who has come to bring Judy Graves' roller skates from the lobby. It would be a help, intimates Joe, if Mr. Graves would instruct his daughter not to leave her skates in the lobby. The janitor had recently slipped on one of them and gone right across the lobby with an armful of garbage. What a mess!

There is a telephone call for Lois, but it is so involved Mr. Graves gives it up. Let Lois straighten it out. She will know whether Ralph or Henry or Charlie is to call for her instead of Merrill, and probably why.

There are further disturbing complications for Mr. Graves when Mrs. Graves (an attractive young matron of 35) comes to hurry him into his evening clothes for a bridge date at the Bakers'. Nor is he made any happier when he discovers there are no ice cubes for a drink. Lois has taken the ice to make a pack to rub on her facial muscles to tighten them.

Lois Graves "is a pretty girl of 16, slim and straight, and wears a sweater and skirt and not quite high-heeled shoes. Her hair is held back by a circular comb. Lois is a very sophisticated woman of the world with a permanently detached air."

At the moment Lois is concerned with her evening's date and somewhat fussed that her father was not able to get Charlie's message straight, but she gains some little comfort from her mother's sympathetic understanding, and agrees to fetch the ice and glasses.

And now Judy Graves appears, a thoughtful look on her face, a school pad in her hand and a pencil stuck behind her ear. Judy is "thirteen years old, tall for her age and heavily built. From her shoulders to her knees, she is entirely shapeless, which gives her a square, broad look in spite of her height. Below her skirt, which is too short for her, her legs are hard, muscular and covered with scratches. Her dress, a soft blue one, smocked at the sleeves, is supposed to hang gracefully from the shoulders in a straight fold, but instead it is pulled, as though she had been stuffed into it. Her little round stomach bulges over a belt drawn tightly beneath it. On her fingers are a pair of cheap rings, and she wears three charm bracelets of a brassy color, and a locket and chain, so tight around her neck it seems to strangle her. Her dark brown hair keeps straight below her ears, and is held in place by numerous bobbie-pins and two ready-made bows."

Judy is at the moment in the throes of composing her autobiography for her English teacher. She would like to have a few outstanding events from her parents, seeing she is using them as a sort of background. Her mother would gladly oblige, but she is busy dressing. Her father is hooked—

"Well," begins Mr. Graves, "I was born in Brooklyn Heights—" Then he catches the expression of disappointment on Judy's face. "Sorry, Judy, I *wish* it was Shanghai—then I went to public school there until I went to Kent. Then when I got through Kent, I went to Yale. I met your mother at Smith, and a few years after the war I married her."

JUDY—Yes? Go on—
HARRY—That's about all.
JUDY—Gee, that's not much of a life.
HARRY—Well, I'm very sorry. Who do you want for a father —Rasputin?
JUDY—Fuffy's father had a very wild youth.
HARRY—Well, I'm having a very wild middle age.

JUDY—What about Mom? Anything happen to her?

HARRY—Well, she was born in Kansas City, Missouri. Your grandfather was Vice-President of some wholesale dry-goods store there.

JUDY—I wonder why he stayed in Kansas City? All the best people used to push on farther West.

HARRY (*annoyed*)—He had a darned good business—a *darned* good business! He managed to send all his girls to Smith. So it's just as well for you that he *didn't* push on West.

LOIS (*entering with tray and glasses, looking at* JUDY *superciliously*)—*Now* what'd she do?

JUDY (*flatly*)—Charming Lois . . .

HARRY—Judy's writing her autobiography, and I'm giving her some facts about the family.

LOIS—Not about Uncle Willis, I hope! (HARRY *gives her a warning look.*)

JUDY—There she goes again! Daddy, I don't think it's a bit fair for her to hold that over my head!

HARRY—What?

JUDY—Uncle Willis. . . . What is there about Uncle Willis that I can't know too!

LOIS—Must you know everything?

HARRY—Oh, for God's sake!

JUDY (*icily*)—I'm not addressing you—I'm addressing the man who happens to be our father. (*Pleadingly.*) Won't you please tell me about Uncle Willis, Daddy. My lips will be sealed —I promise.

HARRY (*irritably*)—There's nothing to tell. Your Uncle Willis has been away for a long time. Now let's drop the subject— I don't want you to discuss this in front of your mother.

JUDY (*agonized*)—Dad, it isn't fair!

LOIS—When you're old enough, dear. . . .

Mrs. Graves is dressed and ready for the party. While they are waiting she suggests that Judy read the important parts of her biography—the parts about Judy—and Judy is delighted.

It proves a fairly lurid and highly imaginative account, beginning "It was a wild stormy night and our family doctor fought his way through the terrible rain to reach the bedside of my mother who hovered between life and death. . . ."

" 'David Copperfield!' " sneers Lois.

"You were born in a very nice little private hospital on Cen-

"JUNIOR MISS"

Judy: Good night, Mother dear Don't wait up.
Grace: Have a nice time, darling.
Judy (shrugging her shoulders): Well you know Fartie....

(Jack Davis, Patricia Peardon, Philip O'yer, Barbera Robbins)

Photo by Lucas-Pritchard.

tral Park West," corrects Mrs. Graves. "It's been torn down since."

Facts are of no particular interest to Judy. She has a job to do and she is going to make it as interesting as possible. There are continued sneers from Lois, and further corrections from Mrs. Graves, but Judy reads blithely on. Finally Mr. Graves puts in a correction or two. After all, this is to be an account of Judy's life—not of the lives of her parents. But again Mrs. Graves comes to Judy's rescue. The parts about Lois are also fairly extravagant, arousing a good deal of big sister resentment. Finally, to Judy's expressed disgust, the whole thing is put over till the next day, when Mrs. Graves promises to help find a lot of interesting facts for the biography.

There is a peculiar knock on the door—two long and three short taps. That would be Fuffy Adams, who bounces in energetically. "She is the same age and height as Judy, dressed in a very similar manner, and overflowing with animal spirits. She is blonde and not quite so lumpy."

Fuffy has been working on her autobiography, too, and is it a "killer-diller!" She'd like to read it to them, and would, if Mrs. Graves didn't suggest that perhaps she had better read it to her parents first, instead of trying to surprise them.

Fuffy is full of news. She has got all her Christmas shopping done, including her present for Judy. They always tell each other what they're giving to be sure it's something they want.

Fuffy also has a problem. It's about hers and Judy's escorts for Mary Caswell's New Year's dance. Escorts! The idea is preposterous to Lois. Even pathetic. "A dance for a lot of kids," sneers sister. "You'll trample one another to death. Thank heavens *I* don't have to go."

Fuffy's brother, Barlow, is going to take her and he has a friend, Haskell Cummings, who is going to take Judy, if he likes her after he's seen her. Otherwise Barlow will have to take them both. Now, does Mrs. Graves mind if Barlow brings Haskell over to see Judy? Because they're having company at the Adams'—

"Huh! Before I'd be looked over like a prize pig or something!" Lois is scornful.

"I don't mind," chirps Judy. "Barlow says he doesn't like girls."

"All right, they can come up here," agrees Mrs. Graves. "But they can't stay—Judy's got to be in bed by 9:30."

That's fine, and Mrs. Graves certainly is "super," but Judy is pretty scared. She'd like to have Lois sort of stick around, but Lois has other things to do.

There is a ring at the bell, and although Judy runs for the bedroom to hide, it doesn't happen to be the boys. The Curtises are calling—Ellen and J.B., her father. "Ellen is a sweet, rather diffident girl of twenty-nine, who wears glasses and is very much in her father's shade. J.B. is every inch the successful lawyer; a self-made, self-assured, domineering man of about fifty. He is usually in high spirits, but his good spirits are about as hard to bear as his bad spirits."

The greetings are effusive and J.B.'s bubbling spirits are explained by the fact that he feels that the firm is about to close a deal with Cummings, Reade and Barton. All it needs to put it over is Cummings' okay. If J.B. gets that, he hints broadly, anything could happen. A moment later he and Grace have gone to the kitchen to fix up a round of hot toddies, seeing there is no ice.

Left alone, Harry Graves and Ellen Curtis are soon exchanging intimacies. Ellen has found out just what Grace wants for Christmas—an aquamarine set—clips and earrings! And when can they meet for lunch so Harry can look it over?

Harry is worried about Ellen, and about her father's rather overbearing domination. He would like to get her out of the office for a Bermuda vacation. Even if it isn't any of his business—he'd—

"Please, Harry," Ellen is saying, seriously, looking intently into his eyes; "I know perfectly well what you mean—only I've let it go on so long now that Dad is completely dependent on me."

"And the longer you let it go on, the worse it will get."

Harry has put his arm pityingly around Ellen's shoulders, just as Judy comes from the bedroom and is practically struck dumb by what she sees.

"Yes, I know," Ellen continues; "I'll work it out some way—Harry, I don't know what I'd do without you, you're a comfort."

She kisses him on the cheek, impulsively, as Judy's eyes pop. A second later J.B. has arrived with a tray of toddies and everybody rallies 'round—everybody except Judy, who continues to stare at her father and Ellen with a shocked expression.

The doorbell rings. Lois answers, swinging open the door and facing a boy of 16 with skates under his arm. He eyes the adults consciously—

Lois—Good evening, Merrill—
Merrill—Hy'ah, Lois. . . .

Lois (*elegantly*)—How nice of you to be so prompt. . . . Mother, this is Mr. Feurbach. Miss Curtis, Mr. Curtis and my father—Mr. Feurbach.

Merrill (*mumbling*)—Hello. . . .

J.B. (*he can't control himself and chuckles in a horrible way as he surveys them both*)—Ha, ha! Mr. Feurbach, eh? Ha, ha! Well, so you're going skating in the park—

Lois (*coldly*)—We're going to Radio City.

J.B. (*arching his brows*)—Is that so? (*Chuckles again.*) Radio City, eh! Well, the park is a lot less public, Feurbach! (*He bursts into a fresh guffaw.* Lois *and* Merrill *glare at him.*)

Merrill—We'd better get going, Lois!

Lois—I've got my skates here—

Merrill (*left to face the adults alone, he smiles sheepishly*)— I—I guess maybe we'll have an old-fashioned Christmas—it's starting to snow, outside.

J.B.—Just like the one we had in '88, eh, Feurbach? (*He laughs again.*)

Merrill (*after an uncomfortable pause*)—How are you, Mrs. Graves?

Grace—I'm fine, thank you.

Merrill—That's splendid! And how are you, Mr. Graves?

Harry—Fine, thanks.

Merrill—That's splendid.

J.B.—If you want to know my physical condition, I'm splendid. (Lois *comes back with her skates.*)

Grace—Good night, Lois—have a nice time, darling.

Lois—Good night, Mother.

Harry—You'll have Lois back by ten-thirty, Merrill, won't you?

Merrill—Oh, yes, sir! Well— Well—good night. (Lois *smiles to the others.* Merrill *nods foolishly and they exit.* J.B. *shakes his head in amusement.*)

J.B.—Reminds me of Ellen when she was a kid— We always had at least one of those drugstore cowboys hanging around the house!

Ellen (*good-naturedly*)—Yes, and you used to make them just as uncomfortable as you did this one.

J.B. furiously denies the impeachment, but gets little sympathy. When Grace takes Ellen out of the room he is quick to suggest to Harry that there seems to be something wrong with Ellen lately. He can't understand it.

"There's probably a very good reason!" suddenly answers

Judy. J.B. can't understand Judy, either, and Judy's father has long since given up trying. . . .

The Graveses and Curtises are ready to leave. Mrs. Graves calls Judy and finds her daughter acting and talking a little strangely, apparently for no reason.

"Give your little friends some ginger ale or cream soda if you like and remember—I want you in bed by 9:30."

"Very well, Mother," Judy answers, tragically. "Good night—and remember—no matter what happens, I love you very much."

That suggests another mystery, but there is nothing apparently that can be done about it.

When Fuffy Adams comes bounding in shortly after the folks have left she finds Judy squatted on the floor, her legs pulled up under her, her outstretched fingers pressed against her temples, her eyes closed. She is breathing heavily, which means, as Fuffy deduces, that Judy is doing her Yogi exercises. Judy is. And finds a second later that her mind is much clearer. Now she is ready to explain—

"Fuffy, there's a crisis going on in this house," reports Judy, gravely.

"No kidding! Between who?" Fuffy is happily excited.

JUDY—Before I say anything more, I want you to take a sacred vow that this will die with us.

FUFFY (*casually*)—Naturally.

JUDY—Remember that picture with Myrna Loy and Clark Gable—"Wife vs. Secretary"?

FUFFY (*breathes*)—God, yes!

JUDY—Well, I think that same kind of thing is developing between my father and Ellen Curtis.

FUFFY (*whistling her amazement as she slides down the sofa*)—But she's got *glasses!*

JUDY (*impatiently*)—So did Myrna Loy—when she started out! But after she took them off and got those beauty treatments, she looked *gorgeous!*

FUFFY (*nodding*)—Yes, she did. . . . But Ellen's so *old!* Why, she must be—she must be *twenty-nine!*

JUDY—Well, after all, Dad's even older than that!

FUFFY (*suspiciously*)—Judy, are you sure you're not just kickin' the gong around?

JUDY—It's the truth—honestly.

FUFFY—Rat whole?

JUDY—Sure.

Fuffy—Well, *say* it then.

Judy (*holding her hand up*)—May I swallow a live rat whole if I'm lying.

Fuffy (*nodding, convinced*)—Well, you better do something, because Myrna Loy certainly made a dope out of that wife!

Judy (*nodding*)—Gee, I'd hate to see Mom in Joan Crawford's position.

Fuffy—I'll speak to your father if you want me to. He may not resent it, coming from me.

Judy—Fuffy! You took a sacred vow!

Fuffy (*firmly*)—Well, you'd better do *something*—and do it quick—before this all tumbles down like a house of cards!

A ring at the bell throws Judy into another panic. This must be Barlow and Haskell Cummings—and she is certainly in no humor to meet men. Fuffy, however, is able to remain calm and expectant. "All you got to do is to act blasé." That's Fuffy's advice.

Judy decides it would be better if they were to appear preoccupied. What if they should be playing double Canfield? That's an idea. By the time Hilda comes to answer the bell the game is well organized.

"Don't move, ladies," advises Hilda; "you'll tire out those delicate little bodies."

When Hilda opens the door she reveals two kids about 15. Barlow Adams "resembles Fuffy closely, and Haskell Cummings is a slender boy with thin hair that falls over his forehead and an interesting hooked nose."

For a moment the game goes on, though the boys try a couple of times to break it up. Once Barlow sneezes, explaining that it is only a cold in the head. He is advised by his sister not to come too close.

Suddenly Fuffy remembers to introduce Mr. Cummings to Judy, which at least gets that over with. There is an exchange of "Hellos."

Now the card game is over and the conversation turns to Mary Caswell's party. It would be a lot nicer, thinks Fuffy, if Mary were to have games instead of so much dancing. Judy quickly agrees. She has known how to play poker for years. Anyway, Judy hopes they are going to have some fun—like they had at Fuffy's party. They threw water out the window at Fuffy's party.

"Judy, you're crazy. You'll do anything," protests Fuffy, proudly.

"I'll do anything when I happen to feel like it," admits Judy.

FUFFY—And you're the best basket-ball player at school.
JUDY (*modestly*)—Oh, for heaven's sake.
HASKELL—Where do you go in the summer?
JUDY (*trapped*)—Who, me?
HASKELL—Yeah.
JUDY (*getting up and moving around behind* HASKELL)—South Dorset, Vermont. We've been going there for years. Where do you go?
HASKELL—Madison, Connecticut. (FUFFY *nods to* JUDY.)
JUDY—I've been there. I visited my Aunt Julia there one summer. (BARLOW *sneezes.*) God bless you, Barlow.
BARLOW—Thank you.
HASKELL (*poker-faced*)—Do you know Jane Garside? (FUFFY *signals.*)
JUDY—That drip!
HASKELL (*lighting up*)—Drip is right. . . . I can't stomach that Jane Garside. . . . Where did you swim? At the Yacht Club or the Country Club? (FUFFY *takes a swing at an imaginary golf ball.*)
JUDY—At the Country Club.
HASKELL—That's where I swim. (*Turns brightly to* FUFFY.)
FUFFY—Isn't that wonderful?
JUDY (*laughing in relief*)—Well, isn't that the funniest thing. (*She giggles again in excitement.*)
FUFFY—Hey, look out—you'll get the hiccoughs.
JUDY (*gasping*)—Oh, don't! Every time you say that, I do get them, and— (*She draws in her breath.*) I have got them!
FUFFY—Hold your arms over your head and I'll get the vinegar! (*She runs into the foyer.* JUDY *sits there, her arms over her head.*)
JUDY (*after each hiccough*)—Excuse me. . . . Excuse me. . . . Excuse me. (HASKELL *picks up a magazine and hits her sharply over the head.*) Ouch! (FUFFY *runs back into the room with the vinegar bottle.*)
FUFFY—How are they?
JUDY—They're gone. Haskell cured them.
FUFFY—That's the first time I've ever known Judy to have the hiccoughs and get over them like that.
HASKELL (*casually*)—When they get the hiccoughs, the best

thing to do is scare them.

JUDY—You're very scientific, aren't you?
HASKELL—Sort of.
BARLOW (*moving to the door*)—Well, we'd better get going.
JUDY—Wouldn't you like some ginger ale before you go?
BARLOW—We can't—we're late now for our weekly poker game.
JUDY—Well, thanks encore.
HASKELL (*straightening his tie*)—I can almost always cure hiccoughs.

Fuffy follows the boys into the hall to get the dope. A moment later she is back, smiling broadly. Everything's fixed. Haskell will take Judy. "He says you're a darned good sport and not a bit affected," Fuffy reports.

Judy thinks Haskell is nice, too, but she is still sad when she thinks of the impending tragedy facing her father and Ellen Curtis. She knows she will be lying awake all night. Even Fuffy's suggestion that "those kind of women" can always be bought off, fails to cheer Judy.

"Just dangle a grand in front of her kisser and you'll see," advises Fuffy.

"I'll just have to think of some cheaper way," sighs Judy.

After Fuffy has been summoned home Judy takes her ease sprawled out on the sofa, a candy box within reach and a movie magazine in hand. She would put the time to profitable use if Hilda had any imagination at all about why she loves Ivory Flakes. With just a little help Judy could make a bid for a grand prize of $2,000, which she would be glad to split with Hilda. But Hilda, never having heard of anyone winning such a prize, is not at all interested.

Judy has resumed her sofa sprawl when the bell rings. This time she decides to answer in person. When she opens the door Willis Reynolds, "a pleasant-looking man of about thirty-four or -five with a gentle, rather shy air, smiles down at her. He is very pale and wan, and carries a small valise."

Willis is plainly puzzled. He thinks Judy is Lois. Judy is scared. She thinks probably Willis had better come back when her father is there, and Willis good-humoredly agrees, but would leave word for Mrs. Graves that her brother Willis called—

"Uncle Willis!" Now the mystery is cleared and Judy is all excitement and hospitality. Of course she knows her Uncle Willis. Knows that he has been away for a long, long time. He is awfully pale, too— Suddenly Judy is struck with a blinding flash! Of course Uncle Willis is pale, and probably hungry, too. But let him not worry. He'll be back to normal soon. Maybe he'd like a glass of milk and some cake? Judy is willing to have some with him, just to keep him company.

Hilda can quite understand the milk and cake order, but she is still a bit doubtful about Uncle Willis, until Judy explains that he has been away on a trip for a great many years and is hungry.

"You must be terribly bitter, Uncle Willis," bursts out Judy, when Hilda has gone back to the kitchen. "I *hope* you're not bitter!"

"Well, I don't think I am now," answers the surprised Willis.

"That's good. Tyrone Power was *awfully* bitter," sighs Judy.

"Tyrone Power?"

"Yes, in 'Criminal Code.' I guess you didn't see it."

"No. . . ."

"He wanted to go straight and the whole world was against him. Every time he got a job they kept firing him."

"Oh, they did, eh?" Willis is completely at sea.

Hilda has come back with one large slice of cake and one glass of milk. Judy thinks perhaps she had not understood— "You know you're not supposed to eat right after dinner," she reminds Judy.

As a compromise Willis suggests that Judy split the cake with him and drink the milk. "I love all kinds of food," confesses Judy, in hearty agreement with the suggestion. And then, on second thought—

"I hope you've decided to go straight, Uncle Willis."

"Go straight?"

"I don't know what you've done and I don't care! I just want to help you as much as I can!" Judy is very earnest.

"But see here—!"

"Forget the past! There's only one thing you should live for —the *future!*"

"I see. . . . There's an awful lot of truth in what you say, Judy. . . ."

"Do you think so, Uncle Willis?"

"I certainly do."

"Gosh, nobody in this family takes me seriously, but if *you* do, I'd like to help you."

"I'd be very proud and happy to have you help me, Judy," says Willis, extending his hand seriously.

"Gee!" Judy is almost overcome with a new sense of impor-

JUNIOR MISS

tance as she takes Willis' hand.

Now Willis is ready to go, but Judy won't hear of that. He certainly must stay there with them. He can have Judy's and Lois' room—and Judy's bed, which is the best—and Judy can sleep with Hilda—and Lois on the couch—

"It's so much better to be in the bosom of your family than amongst a lot of strangers who ask all kinds of embarrassing questions!" says Judy.

Finally Willis agrees to compromise. He will wait until the folks come back, and he agrees to stretch out and take a nap. He has taken his bag and started for the bedroom. "Thanks, Judy," he turns to say, as Judy lifts her face to his and opens her arms in a very dramatic pose. "Good night, my dear," he adds, kissing her upon the brow. "We shall meet again!"

"Gee!" Judy has dashed for the telephone as soon as Willis closes the door. "Joe, get me Fuffy Adams, quick!" . . .

"Hello, Fuffy! Are you alone? Oh, that's good. . . . Lissen, Fuffy, the most exciting thing has just happened! You won't believe it! (*The curtain begins to descend.*) *Boy!* Am *I* going to have an autobiography!" The curtain is down.

Harry and Grace are getting home from the bridge party when the scene is renewed, Harry muttering in disgust with the whole evening as he flings his coat on a chair—

". . . Sit down at a table with no light even to see the cards, Fred Baker blowing cigar smoke in my face, stale sandwiches, cold coffee, and I'm hooked for seventeen dollars."

"Well, I owe you eight-fifty of it, dear."

"Oh, fine. And you saved twelve dollars on that end table you bought yesterday, so we're really twenty dollars ahead on the week."

There is one small satisfaction—J.B. appeared to have a good time and that may mean something in the long run. J.B. has been hinting at a junior partnership for Harry, and that would clear up a lot of things.

They have started for their room when Grace notices the remains of the cake and milk party. That Judy! Then she discovers a cigarette butt. "My God, she's starting to smoke!" she wails, picking up the cigarette and starting for the girls' room.

There is a flash of light, followed by a terrified shriek, and Grace bounds out, wild-eyed. "A man—in—Judy's bed!" She is breathless. Harry comes rushing in. Quickly he grabs a lamp as a weapon and starts for the bedroom, when Willis appears in the door. His shoes are off and he is looking very sleepy. A second later he has been recognized and is in Grace's arms. Harry is pounding him on the back and everybody is talking at once.

"God, you two haven't changed in ten years!" exclaims Willis, at the first lull. "When I came up here tonight, I didn't know what to expect—"

At which moment Judy and Hilda come rushing from Hilda's room, Judy in pajamas and Hilda trying quickly to cover her nightgown with a robe—

"Mrs. Graves! . . . Did anything happen? What was it?"

"It's all right, Hilda. . . . Mrs. Graves got a sudden shock, that's all . . ." explains Harry.

"Oh, you found Uncle Willis," chimes in Judy, plainly disappointed. "I was going to surprise you."

"We *were* surprised, thanks. . . ."

"Are you all right, Uncle Willis? Is there anything I can get you?"

"No, thanks, Judy, I'm fine."

Now there is more excitement at the door, and a sound of scuffling in the hall. As the door slowly opens Lois backs in slowly, followed by a boy—not Merrill Feurbach. This is Sterling Brown and he is determined to come in for ten minutes to say good night. In their excitement they don't see the gathered family, and when they do they are pretty confused. Lois introduces Sterling with the explanation that she had had an argument with Merrill Feurbach and Sterling had brought her home.

"Well, good night, everybody," calls Sterling, nervously edging toward the door, through which he bolts.

"Nasty little character—I don't want to see him around here again," announces Father.

Willis is for taking his bag and finding himself a hotel, but Grace and Harry will not hear of that. He is to stay right there. The girls can sleep in with their mother. Harry and Willis will take the girls' room—and talk their heads off.

Willis admits being greatly impressed with the children— especially Judy. She certainly has a lively imagination. "She thinks I've done a ten years' stretch," he reports. Willis is amused but Harry and Grace are horrified. "I'll have a talk with Miss Judy at once," promises Harry.

"Not on your life! At least I'm a romantic character," protests Willis.

Grace has gone into the kitchen to make sandwiches when

Judy reappears, carrying her father's pajamas. She is very grim, and eager to have a talk—
"Father, sometimes something happens to a child that turns her into a woman in a couple of hours."
"Some other time, Judy, please. . . ."

JUDY—Father, I hope to be married some day. . . .
HARRY (*fervently*)—I hope so too.
JUDY—And when that day comes, you wouldn't want to stand outside in the snow looking through the window of the church while the ceremony is going on, would you?
HARRY—What's the matter, won't I get a ticket?
JUDY—If they have any pride left that's where they always stand.
HARRY—Look, Judy, when you get married, I promise to be inside the church—in there pitching—and at the moment you say "I do"—I promise to jump right through the window.
GRACE (*coming from the kitchen*)—It's all ready, dear. (*Sees* JUDY.) Haven't you gone to bed yet?
JUDY—I was just going, Mother. . . . (*She starts slowly for the bedroom, lost in thought.*)
GRACE—Willis doesn't look very well, does he, Harry?
HARRY—Sure, he looks fine.
GRACE—He's aged terribly . . . and he seems so worn.
HARRY—All he needs is a regular normal existence and he'll be himself in no time.
JUDY (*turning thoughtfully*)—Father, there's only one thing any man needs—a good woman's love! (*She goes into her bedroom as* HARRY *and* GRACE *stand looking after her.*) The curtain falls.

ACT II

It is early Christmas morning. In the Graves apartment "a small, ornamental table tree, rather bedraggled, is between the windows," with a number of brightly wrapped gift packages around its base. There are holly wreaths on the frosted windows, and the room "somehow manages to convey the Yuletide spirit."

Hilda is the first to appear. She sorts through the packages, picking out her own, sniffing several and concluding, a little patronizingly, that here are "Gloves . . . Handkerchiefs . . . Bedroom slippers . . . and that same tired toilet water I wouldn't use on a dog."

Next Judy appears, all dressed up in her Sunday best. Judy

circles the tree admiringly, casually lifting off a candy cane and starting work on it, as Fuffy's knock announces her arrival. The girls meet at the door, each with a package for the other, and each with the simultaneous greeting—

"Merry Christmas—and here!"

Eagerly they undo their gifts. They are both imitation leather pocketbooks—Judy's red, Fuffy's green—and each with lip stick and lucite cigarette case, which, they allow, will probably have to be hidden until they decide to get the habit.

Fuffy would like a report on the Ellen C. matter. Judy has been working on that, but there are no new developments except that Mr. Graves has been wonderful to Mrs. Graves—which looks suspicious. Fuffy has additional advice to give, but there is a phone call from her "menace"—

"Your mother says she thought she told you not to go out," reports Judy, dutifully, "and if you don't go downstairs right away you won't get your presents."

"Sometimes I wonder," wonders Fuffy, acidly, "are parents worth all we go through for them! . . . Well, Merry Christmas encore, and thanks loads for the bag!" She's gone.

With a furtive look around, Judy goes to the phone and calls Ellen Curtis. She wants to make sure 'that Ellen is coming over to wish them a Merry Christmas. It is important that Judy should see Ellen; a matter of life and death, in fact— "Well, practically life and death! Anyway, it is very vital!"

Judy's Christmas greeting for Dad is hearty, though it isn't easy to explain the candy cane before breakfast. The greeting for Mother is even heartier, but again the candy before breakfast matter comes up. Judy is pretty irritated about that—

"All right, Judy, forget it," Dad compromises, cheerily. "Today you can let that tapeworm of yours run riot."

Judy has gone to call Lois, and Harry has a chance to give Grace the aquamarine earrings and clips that belong naturally in the picture, seeing that they had agreed as usual not to give each other anything.

This time, to Harry, there is an excuse. It looks as though the junior partnership were going through, and if that happens they can prepare to ignore money.

"I take back everything I ever said about J.B.—he's adorable!" Grace is quite happy.

For a moment the spirit of a peaceful Christmas settles over the home of the Graves. After all, the children *are* a good cut above the average and *sweet*, and here is Hilda cheerfully announcing breakfast.

A second later the door of Lois' and Judy's room bursts open. Judy backs out on the defensive and Lois follows threateningly. Judy, it seems, has been practically dousing herself with Lois' cologne, and Lois doesn't intend to stand for it. It is such a waste of cologne. Who wants to smell Judy, anyway? Father has to be firm in restoring order.

Now, by a viva-voce vote, principally by Judy, it is decided to put off breakfast until the packages are opened. The girls have bounded to the tree and begun sorting and tearing open their gifts. There is another bottle of cologne for Lois, which explains everything. Judy was only trying to be rid of the supply on hand so Lois would need more. Now they're friends again.

There are silk stockings for Judy, and a cashmere sweater for Lois, and a lot of other things. Judy has bought her father a Cape Cod barometer. "In bad weather the liquid goes up the spout and in a hurricane it overflows," proudly explains Judy. For her mother she has bought a "peculiar contraption with a frog's head and a long rubber tube."

"It's a combination ash tray and cigarette holder for smoking in bed. . . . The cigarette is in the frog's mouth, and you puff on this end and the ashes automatically drop into the tray. . . . And if you fall asleep nothing can happen."

Judy also gets her first pair of high-heel shoes, and is out of her slippers and into the shoes in no time. They feel absolutely wonderful, even if Judy does have some little difficulty walking in them. "You better walk with crutches until you get used to them," suggests Lois, cattily, and would have been bopped over the head if Judy hadn't tripped on her heels when she tried to rush her.

Now Judy has torn into what proves to be the grandest present of all—a red coat with a squirrel fur collar. The coat is a fair knock-out for Judy and she won't even admit that it may be a size small, which obviously it is. She refuses to take it off, or even to consider changing it—

GRACE—Maybe we can find something in the Junior Miss department—

LOIS (*giving her mother a look, crosses to* JUDY *and pulls the coat from her*)—For heaven's sake, turn around and get into this! (JUDY *looks at her hopefully and struggles into the coat again.*)

GRACE—Lois, if you rip it, we won't be able to take it back.

LOIS (*pulling the coat into place and tying the bow at the front*)—Anybody would think that nobody had ever heard of alterations in this family. Besides, it's perfectly silly to think that Judy could wear a Junior Miss coat. You don't want her to look like her own grandmother, do you?

JUDY (*eagerly*)—Besides, I'll go on a diet. I was only waiting for New Year's to make a resolution!

GRACE (*dubiously*)—Well . . .

JUDY—Please—now that I'm getting the clothes I always wanted, you won't have to worry about my figure, I promise.

LOIS—I think it's perfectly charming. But, really, Judy, you shouldn't wear a bow. It makes you look like a sack of meal—(*Ominously.*)—or worse.

JUDY (*bitterly*)—What do you mean—worse?

LOIS (*meaningly*)—You know what I told you.

JUDY (*lips trembling*)—I do not!

LOIS—Oh, yes, you do! You look it. (*Laughs.*)

HARRY—What are you two talking about?

GRACE—Look what?

JUDY—Look pregnant! (HARRY *chokes back a guffaw.*)

GRACE—I never heard such dreadful talk! You ought to be ashamed of yourselves.

JUDY—Lois is always saying it.

GRACE (*to* LOIS)—If I ever hear you say that again, Lois, no more dates for a month!

From J.B. there is a beautifully dressed doll for Judy, which she thinks is pretty "screwy." The idea! "I'll put it under the tree just for fun until I can think of some child to give it to," announces Judy, giggling excitedly. . . .

Breakfast is spoiling, and Hilda finally gets the family started for the dining room. Judy, however, decides to begin her dieting, seeing she isn't hungry anyway, and Lois has a date to go to church with Albert Kunody.

Judy is alone, admiring her new coat in the mirror, when Uncle Willis arrives. He has brought Judy and Lois beauty aid kits, and that's important, but the thing that is most important to Judy is Willis' willingness to give up church so they will have a chance to talk over a very important matter *alone*—a matter of life and death.

They probably would have gone right to this business, if Fuffy Adams' peculiar knock had not interrupted them. Willis decides to retire to the breakfast room for the moment.

Fuffy is also wearing high-heeled shoes and is all but struck breathless at the sight of Judy's new coat. A moment later she has forgotten everything but the Uncle Willis-Ellen Curtis case. Fuffy is thrilled to know that Judy has contacted E.C. and that she is coming right over. She is also thrilled at the prospect of getting a peek at Uncle Willis. "I've never seen a real criminal," Fuffy confides.

A moment later Harry, Grace and Willis come from breakfast and Fuffy gets her wish. She stares at Willis in such open-mouthed awe that Grace is embarrassed and is at some pains to start the girls off on a walk. They are barging through the door just as the bell rings and another of the men in Lois' life, Albert Kunody, who is 18 and wears horn-rimmed glasses and a studious air, is revealed. Judy and Fuffy have a giggle as they brush past Albert.

Lois has gone to get her things and Albert tries to cover the wait naturally by taking a brand new cigarette case from its chamois bag and offering the other men a cigarette. Even though they do not care to smoke at the moment, he still has a chance to take a new lighter from another chamois bag and light up for himself.

With Lois and Albert gone Harry and Willis have their first chance for a talk. Willis would like to explain that he has never ceased being grateful for all Grace and Harry did for him when he was in trouble—

"Oh, what the hell," breaks in Harry. "We were both a couple of young punks—and whatever you did—it was just bad judgment—"

"They don't try to disbar you for bad judgment."

"But you *weren't* disbarred."

"—Even if it took every nickel you had!"

"I don't want to hear any more about it—and if you ever bring it up again I'm going to get sore! There's only one thing that should be on your mind right now—and that's getting back on your feet!"

"Sold. . . . I just want to say one thing, Harry—the reason I stayed away so long was because I was trying to get enough together to pay you back. But I just couldn't. . . ."

"I know that, Bill. . . ."

Harry and Grace have no more than left for church than Judy

and Fuffy reappear. They had come back through the servants' entrance and are prepared to go on with their conspiracy, somewhat to Willis' bewilderment. A moment later Ellen Curtis is announced.

Judy is all excitement. She hopes they are not going to have any trouble with Uncle Willis' old gang, seeing that they are about to involve an innocent party—

"Now, look, Uncle Willis—I wouldn't talk about my past right away, if I were you," cautions Judy. "I'd wait until you get to know each other better."

"What are you talking about? Know *who* better?"

"You'll see in a minute. . . . Now, would you mind waiting in the bedroom 'til I call you— Please, Uncle Willis."

"Judy, I know you're trying to help me, but I've got to know what this is all about."

"*Please*, Uncle Willis!"

So Uncle Willis is pushed into the bedroom and Ellen Curtis is shown in. It takes some little explaining on Judy's part to convince Ellen that whatever it is that seems to be wrong with her (Judy), it is really all right. Will Ellen please take off her glasses? Will she please take a seat on the couch? Will she stay just as she is?

Willis is brought into the room and introduced. For a moment he and Ellen stare at each other, having some trouble keeping their faces straight.

"Well, there's nothing more *I* can do," announces Judy; "besides I've got a very important date, so I'll just leave you two alone."

With this she dashes into the kitchen to join Fuffy. Willis and Ellen continue their puzzled expressions a second and then burst into laughter. New introductions are in order and a few explanations. Ellen thinks perhaps she had better go, but Willis is anxious that she should stay—

"Miss Curtis," Willis is saying, "I've been away for so long, it's difficult for me to make conversation. But please don't desert me. I'm dying to talk and just keep talking."

"Yes, I know that feeling too," Ellen admits.

WILLIS—It's not just a feeling—it's almost a mania—I've got so many years to make up for—

ELLEN (*smiling sympathetically*)—I promise not to desert you.

WILLIS (*gratefully*)—Thanks. . . . (*Anxiously.*) Has Judy

told you anything about me?

ELLEN—No, not a thing.

WILLIS (*sighs in relief*)—That's good. She's built a whole movie around me and I can't extricate myself.

ELLEN (*laughing*)—I think she's got me worked into the plot, too, but I don't know where.

WILLIS—I'm afraid it's got something to do with a—with a good woman's love.

ELLEN (*blinking*)—That sounds like Judy. . . . (*She looks at her glasses in her hand.*) Oh, now, I understand. (*She puts them on with a quizzical look.*) Can you bear them?

WILLIS (*puzzled*)—I beg your pardon?

ELLEN—Never mind. . . . You know, *you* may not find yourself doing all the talking—I've got a few lost years to make up for myself.

WILLIS (*staring*)—You? I don't understand—

ELLEN (*rising, nervously*)—I don't know what made me say that—

WILLIS (*rising hastily*)—Don't go.

ELLEN—I really must.

WILLIS—Can I drop you somewhere?

ELLEN—Yes, of course.

WILLIS—You know, Miss Curtis, I always used to think that movies were a bad influence on children—but I've changed my mind.

ELLEN—Yes, they can be very educational. I think I'll start going to the movies again.

WILLIS—We *all* should! By the way, have you seen Tyrone Power in "Criminal Code"? I'd like to see that.

With the closing of the door the conspirators' heads pop around the arch. Everything is working to their satisfaction. They rush to the window to see whether Willis and Ellen take a taxi or walk. They walk. That's a good sign, too.

Coming back into the room Fuffy discovers J.B.'s doll under the tree. How perfectly saccharine! "Needless to say I'm just leaving it there for his benefit," Judy is quick to explain. "Naturally!" agrees Fuffy, with deep understanding.

"Before I leave I want to congratulate you," says Fuffy, solemnly offering her hand to Judy. "Not only have you saved a marriage that was heading to the rocks—but you have thrown two people together that may end in a very happy result. Judy, you're a regular Court of Human Relations."

"You're right," admits Judy, proudly. "Thank you, Fuffy."

Fuffy is gone. Judy closes the door and slips off her high-heeled shoes with a sigh of relief. Her eyes catch sight of the doll J.B. has sent her. She glances around stealthily, picks up the doll and is sitting cross-legged on the floor, holding the doll tightly in her arms and humming a lullaby, "Go to sleep. . . . Go to sleep . . ." as the curtain falls.

It is around noon on New Year's Day. Christmas decorations are missing from the Graves' apartment. So, for the moment, are the Graves. Ellen Curtis and Willis Reynolds, who have called with special greetings and a kiss for Judy, discover from Hilda that Mr. and Mrs. Graves just made the bedroom a few hours before, and have not been heard from since. Ellen and Willis are disappointed, but able to take it. They are in each other's arms and very happy when Judy appears.

Willis and Ellen have come to tell her that Ellen knows all; that they are very happy; that Willis is, from that day forth, going straight as a die, and that she (Judy) is an inspired child. Otherwise they will hold their great surprise for Harry and Grace.

One by one the family appears. Lois is holding a wet compress to her aching head, and complaining of a wild night. "I know," says Judy; "the midnight show at Loew's 83d St. and a wild brawl at Childs'." That isn't much to one who had had a glass of champagne with Fuffy and her father. . . .

Harry and Grace are looking and feeling pretty seedy; Harry wearing a robe over his pants and underwear, Grace in her negligee. Nerves are on edge and practically anything irritates them. Grace would like to know if J.B. had said anything more about the junior partnership, but as far as Harry remembers, J.B. spent his time trying to make an impression on old man Cummings, senior member of Cummings, Reade and Barton, whose account, if J.B. could get it, would practically remake Harry's whole world.

Judy has an idea that perhaps they would like to hear her New Year's resolutions, and Grace is sure they would. Without further urging Judy starts to read:

"Resolutions of things to do from now on, by Judy Graves. . . . One—do not eat more than enough to keep healthy—"

"No more than the average family of five," suggests Lois.

"Two—arrange to have ten minutes alone with yourself every day for introspection. . . . Three—try to be tolerant with the rest of the family. . . . Four—keep a cool head and an open mind in all political discussions. . . ."

"Five—honor thy father and mother . . ." This from Dad, which, added to a vigorous ring at the door, breaks up the reading.

The caller is another of Lois' men, this one "a powerful brute of a lad with a booming voice. His name is Tommy Arbuckle and he takes Lois' introduction of her family in high—"

"Don't tell me who *this* little lady is," booms Tommy, turning to Grace. "I could spot your mother anywhere, Lois. She's a dead ringer for you! Looks more like your sister."

"I'm glad you think so, Mr. Arbuckle." Grace is smiling, weakly.

"And this is my baby sister."

"Hy'ah, kid!"

"Nuts!" says Judy, and goes quickly into the kitchen.

Excitements continue. A Western Union messenger boy appears to sing a rhymed greeting to Judy. It is from Haskell Cummings, and was sent, it may be, because she has made an impression on him, but more likely, thinks Judy, because she had sent him one for Christmas.

Fuffy Adams bounds in to wish everybody a loud, "slap-happy" New Year and to report, quietly, to Judy, that her father, plastered the night before, has appeared with "a head out to here" and a cut lip.

Presently J. B. Curtis telephones. He, too, is on his way to call on the Graves, and Judy urges him to come, even if her mother and father are lying down. With Uncle Willis and Ellen the way they are, Judy realizes that Uncle Willis will have to have a job, and J.B. should know about it. She sends Fuffy away so she can talk with J.B. alone.

J.B. is full of New Year's cheer, having had a couple of quick pickups, has brought a box of candy for Grace and insists that Judy call her father—

"These young punks don't know how to drink any more! Why, I'll bet I had two for every *one* of your old man's last night, and look at *me*—fresh as a daisy! . . . Go ahead, wake him up. I've got some news that'll make him feel like a new man."

Judy hesitates. "Mr. Curtis," she says, dipping into her mother's candy, "I want to thank you for the lovely doll you sent me."

"Don't thank me—thank Santa Claus. You still believe in Santa Claus, don't you?"

Judy— Implicitly.
J.B.—Go ahead, wake up your father.

Judy—Mr. Curtis, can I ask you something?

J.B.—Sure, go ahead.

Judy (*sitting near him, earnestly*)—Mr. Curtis, you have a very large business, haven't you?

J.B. (*smugly*)—Just about all we can handle. . . . And your dad's going to be a very important part of it!

Judy (*pursuing her own thoughts*)—Mr. Curtis, if you knew a man that was unjustly convicted of a series of crimes he had never committed, how would you feel toward him?

J.B. (*grinning*)—Like a brother.

Judy (*nodding*)—That's what I thought— And you would want to help that man regain his place in society, wouldn't you, Mr. Curtis? Give him a job, I mean. . . .

J.B.—Any time! Any time! I'd like nothing better than filling my office with ex-convicts.

Judy (*jumping up, happily*)—Gee, that's swell! Account of Ellen, I mean!

J.B. (*sharply*)—*Ellen?* What about Ellen?

Judy—Well, if she's going to get married, he's going to need a job somewhere!

J.B. (*jumping up*)—Ellen—*married!* What the devil are you gibbering about?

Judy (*scared*)—Nothing. . . . I wasn't gibbering about anything. . . .

J.B. (*grabbing her and shaking her furiously*)—You tell me what you started to say!

Judy (*whimpering*)—I was just going to say that I think Ellen and my Uncle Willis are very much in love, that's all. . . .

J.B. (*subsiding a little*)—Your Uncle Willis? Never heard of him!

Judy (*sobbing*)—I know. Nobody's allowed to mention him. He's been away for ten years. . . .

J.B. (*roaring*)—*Away? Where?*

Judy (*backing away*)—You know—he was the one I was telling you about—the one you're going to give a job to . . . Ellen's fiancé—

J.B. (*bellowing*)—Stop saying that, Goddamit! Ellen's not in love with anybody! (*He looks around wildly, springs to the Graves' bedroom door and throws it open.*) Come out here, Harry. I want to talk to you! (*He turns wrathfully on* Judy *who is quivering in fear.*) Ex-convict! I'll be damned!

Harry (*running out anxiously, struggling into his robe, followed by* Grace)—What's the matter, J.B.? What's wrong?

J.B.—Wrong! What the hell's the idea of letting my daughter run around with that jailbird brother of yours?

HARRY (*glaring at* JUDY)—He's not my brother and—

GRACE (*breaking in*)—He's *my* brother, and he's *not* a jailbird!

J.B. is not to be put off with any easy explanations. He knows what Judy told him and he is ready to accept it as the truth.

"Willis Reynolds is the oldest friend I have," Harry is shouting in Willis' defense. "He was my roommate in college and he was my partner when I first started to practice."

"Reynolds"—J.B. recalls the name now, and something of a scandal. Disbarment, that's what it was. A disbarred lawyer—and engaged to his daughter—

A ring at the bell brings a plea from Grace that everybody please be quiet. She opens the door and there stand "Ellen, looking radiant and hugging Willis' arm, and Willis beaming in embarrassment."

Ellen flies to Grace's arms, hardly noticing her apoplectic father until he demands an explanation. Then she turns happily back to Willis, takes his arm and faces her father—

"This is going to be quite a surprise, Dad—Willis—this is my father—Dad, this is Willis Reynolds, my husband."

"Good God!" explodes J.B.

"But—but, Willis—this is fantastic," interrupts Grace. "You never even told us you *knew* Ellen."

ELLEN—I'm afraid it's my fault, Grace. (*She looks at her father.*) I—I wanted it that way. . . . (*She goes to her father.*) Forgive me, Dad. I know it must seem crazy to you, but we're both so terribly happy. . . . (*She sweeps* JUDY *into her arms.*) And just think, Judy darling, if it hadn't been for you, we might never have met. (*The others turn and look at* JUDY *who looks at them with wide-eyed fear.*)

HARRY (*fixing her with a baleful eye*)—That's my Judy.

J.B.—Ellen, have you completely lost your mind?

ELLEN—No, Dad—I just told you—I'm terribly happy. I was sure you would be, too.

J.B.—Not when I find you married to a disbarred jailbird!

WILLIS—Just a moment, Mr. Curtis. I've never been in jail and I've never been disbarred!

J.B.—If I remember the case, you should have been!

ELLEN—Father!

WILLIS—If it wasn't tactless I'd bring up the Angelus Baking Company case—you looked a little frayed around the edges before *that* blew over!

J.B.—How dare you question my integrity? Harry, did you hear that?

HARRY—Yes, and I've heard it on even better authority than Willis.

J.B.—What!

GRACE (*soothingly*)—We all make mistakes, J.B.

J.B.—My only mistake was getting mixed up with you and this whole damn family!

HARRY—That's my family you're talking about!

J.B.—I know it!

HARRY—Lower your voice. My head's splitting as it is!

J.B.—What do I care about your head? I'll yell all I goddam please!

HARRY—Not in *my* house, you won't!

GRACE—Harry, please—

J.B.—Graves, you're *finished!* You're *through!* Get out of my office and stay out!

HARRY—It's a pleasure!

GRACE—Oh, Harry!

ELLEN—Dad!

The door bursts open and in comes Lois, smiling regally and followed by Tom Arbuckle and a couple of other boys. Lois wants them all to meet the family, but her father greets her with a shouted request that she please get out and take her friends with her. Lois is crushed. The boys turn tail and run.

"It'll give me a great deal of pleasure never to see any of you again as long as I live." J.B. has recovered his hat and coat and stalked through the door.

GRACE (*in a small voice*)—Don't believe him, Ellen. He's so excited he doesn't know what he's saying.

ELLEN—I don't care about that . . . (*Turns to* HARRY.) Oh, Harry, I feel so awful for you . . .

HARRY—It had to come. I've been sitting on that keg of dynamite for seven years.

WILLIS—I never should have come back. I've got the damnedest faculty for messing up your lives. . . .

JUDY (*starting to tip-toe out of the room.* HARRY *catches sight of her. She stops and smiles weakly at him*)—Can I get

JUNIOR MISS

you a glass of water, Daddy, dear? (*Turns to* GRACE.) Mother, should I ask Hilda to make some hot chocolate?

FUFFY (*knocking on door and bouncing in cheerfully*)—A slap-happy New Year, everybody! Hi-yah, Judy, did everything work out okay?

HARRY—Judy, go to your room, and stay there 'til I send for you—which may be never! (JUDY *rushes out to her bedroom.* HARRY *turns to* FUFFY.) Fuffy! Get out of here!

FUFFY—What?

HARRY—You heard me, get out!

FUFFY (*retreating*)—Who do you think you are, my father? (*Exits.*)

HARRY—A *slap* happy New Year, everybody!

The curtain falls.

ACT III

It is the following evening. Harry Graves has just got home with a load of his office paraphernalia—"including a desk set, a large, inverted mounted fish, a humidor and a pipe rack, pictures and two bundles of legal volumes tied together with a cord."

The sight is distressing to Grace, but Harry is able to take it. He reports that he and J.B. are still mad, but J.B. is a little the madder of the two.

Judy, coming from a bubble bath and smelling of soap, is a little excited by the prospect of their being poor. Her friends the Bateses are poor, and have a lot of fun cooking and taking turns washing the dishes. From now on, what with her new coat and her being able to wear Lois' cast-off things, Judy can't see that she is going to be any problem at all. Besides, lots of men have to start all over again. Look at Walter Pidgeon. "He was fired from his job," recalls Judy, "but instead of being discouraged, Daddy, he met Don Ameche and they got into a very successful racket and had a very happy ending."

"Will you keep that kid away from the movies?" shouts Harry at Grace. He turns angrily on Judy: "If you don't shut up and keep out of my way *you're* not going to have such a happy ending."

Grace would send Judy to her room to continue dressing for Mary Caswell's party, but Judy must linger on, giving her mother more and more advice until she gets herself slapped for her impudence. At this "Judy blinks and forces back the tears as she looks at her mother with an expression of infinite hurt."

A second later Lois has dashed from her room, her eyes red with weeping, her feelings hurt beyond repair. She is determined that she will not go back to school and have the whole senior body laugh at her because her father had thrown three football stars out of the house "like some kind of a—of a heartless truck driver."

"Oh, bilge!" sneers Judy.

"You insufferable little dope!"

"Aw, go peddle your papers!"

"I ought to sock you!"

"Come on! Come on! I'd like to see you try it!" Judy has squared off threateningly, moving her arms like a wrestler.

With threats of a spanking for them both, Grace has just got the girls quieted when their father comes back prepared to take up matters with his debutante daughter. He is in no mood to consider an apology to the aggrieved football squad. Nor to discuss planned economies for the future with Grace. What he would enjoy most right now is a good deal of being let alone.

But Grace is full of plans. They can let Hilda go. They can cut down the kids' allowances. They can take a cheaper apartment, and Lois can go to Hunter College instead of to Smith—

All very nice, but Harry can't see it. They haven't been able to put anything aside; there will be nothing coming in; therefore they will have to start again from the beginning. Probably the best he will be able to do is another $25 a week junior clerkship in some other law office. Rather than that—why can't he open his own office? He's been making money for other people long enough—

"Grace, darling," Harry explains, gently; "it takes an awful lot of time and cash to build up your own practice. . . . No, I'm afraid I'm just about finished with the law."

GRACE (*jumping up*)—What else could you do? That's your profession!

HARRY—I've been thinking of getting into some other field. . . .

GRACE (*unhappily*)—When you were just beginning to do so well— (JUDY *has come in unnoticed, carrying a tray. She stands in the foyer-archway, listening unhappily.*)

HARRY (*putting an arm around* GRACE *tenderly*)—Darling, you'll have to help me. . . . (*She looks at him anxiously.*) It may take a little while to get started and I thought for the next few months you and the kids might— (*He pauses.*) Well, I was thinking you and the children might visit the folks in Kansas City . . .

GRACE—Oh, darling. . . .

HARRY (*cheerfully*)—It's going to be tough on me too, but with a break I may be able to send for you sooner.

GRACE—Don't look so tragic, darling. We've been through this once before and we can go through it again. Besides, I can't believe anyone as brilliant as you will have any trouble getting just the right thing. (*Cheerfully.*) But you've got to promise me one thing, darling; if you're going to eat in restaurants, you're not going to eat veal cutlets—you know what they do to you. And I'm not going to lie awake nights in Kansas City, wondering if I still have a husband.

HARRY (*tenderly*)—Do you know something, Grace—I'm very fond of you. (*Suddenly he notices* JUDY, *looks warningly at his wife.* JUDY *comes forward slowly, her eyes filled with tears.*)

JUDY—Here— Here's your— (*She goes toward* GRACE, *who takes the tray from her as it starts to tilt over.*)

HARRY (*comfortingly*)—Don't, Judy— Please, baby—

JUDY (*wailing*)—Oh, Daddy! . . .

HARRY—Come on! Didn't you just tell me how much fun it was going to be?

JUDY—Oh, don't, please—I didn't *know*—

GRACE—There's nothing to cry about, Judy. Don't you want to travel, and visit your grandparents?

JUDY—No.

HARRY—You're going to get your eyes all red and swollen for the party.

JUDY (*tragically*)—Who *cares* about the party? It's all my fault—I did it—and I don't blame you for *hating* me!

GRACE Judy, what a thing to say—

HARRY—You had nothing at all to do with . . . (*Cheerfully.*) Now, what are you going to wear at the party?

JUDY (*sobbing louder*)—I don't know—and I don't care! Do you realize what I've done? I've broken up the whole family! (GRACE *and* HARRY *look at each other helplessly.*)

GRACE (*tearfully*)—Judy, I want you to stop saying those silly—those stupid—those idiotic— Oh, Harry— (*Suddenly she breaks and starts to weep. She turns, hurries into the bedroom,* HARRY *looking after her unhappily.*)

HARRY—Don't, Judy, Judy, please, baby . . . Grace—

Her father and mother have gone into the bedroom. Judy, biting her lips to fight back a sob, squats grimly into a Yogi position on the floor and goes into her rhythmic breathing exercises. For a second or two she gets along nicely, then in the middle of a breath, she sobs violently and bursts into tears.

Coming from her bedroom, sniffing, Lois finds Judy sobbing. From her she hears the story of their being sent away to Kansas City. With that announcement their troubles merge and they are sisters in distress—

"Gee, Lois, you're wonderful," sobs Judy. "I don't know how you put up with me as long as you did."

"Don't be a goon! After all, we're sisters, aren't we?"

They are in each other's arms when Fuffy's knock is heard. "Fuffy! At a time like this!" Lois is disgusted.

Fuffy is wearing a wrapper, her hair is up in curlers and she is convinced that she smells beautiful. Also she would like an opinion on nail polishes. She has put a different shade on each nail of one hand, ranging from mother-of-pearl to deep purple.

"Revolting! Does your mother know you're using it?" demands Lois.

"I'm not gonna tell her. I'm just going to walk out with gloves on. . . . (*Holding up her pinkie.*) This is the one *I* like. . . . It's almost black."

"I think it's perfectly disgusting for a child of fourteen to try to act like a *femme fatale!*"

With that Lois sweeps into her own room, leaving Fuffy to stare after her scornfully. "Boy, what a poison puss!" says Fuffy. "Don't you dare call my only sister Lois a poison puss!" answers Judy, threateningly, and that takes Fuffy completely by surprise—

"Okay, okay—I take it back!" She is backing away from the pugnacious Judy. "Say, what's the matter with you? Are you goin' screwy? Boy, you've changed since the last time I saw you!"

JUDY (*nodding profoundly*)—Yes, Fuffy— You know, in the last fifteen minutes I've aged *fifteen years*.

FUFFY (*impressed*)—What happened?

JUDY—I can't tell you anything except that we have suddenly become poverty-stricken.

FUFFY (*awed*)—No kiddin'?

JUDY (*nodding*)—Yes, and what's more—I'm not going to the party.

FUFFY—You're *not?*

JUDY (*enjoying herself tremendously*)—What's the use? It'd

be a farce to pretend that I'm enjoying myself at a time like this.

FUFFY—But what happened?

JUDY—Never mind—you saw the "Grapes of Wrath," didn't you? Well, we're practically Okies.

FUFFY—Oh, Judy! You mean you're migrating away?

JUDY—Yeah—Pop lost his job and we're going to live in Kansas City.

FUFFY—How ghastly! . . . But what about *me?* You're the only true friend I ever had. We've been through so much together!

JUDY (*sadly*)—Yes, we've been bosom friends ever since that first day in the elevator when we first decided to be bosom friends.

FUFFY—And what about the basketball team? We'll never find another roving center like *you!*

JUDY (*nods and sighs*)—It can't be helped. The school is not suffering any more than I am.

FUFFY—Oh, Judy, you just *can't* go. You're the only thing that makes my family bearable.

JUDY—But what can I do?

FUFFY—There must be something. . . . (*Suddenly struck with an idea.*) Maybe you could get a job and take some of the strain off your father.

JUDY—A job! What kind of a job?

FUFFY—Oh, any kind of a job just to begin with. Even if it's only thirty-five or forty dollars a week.

JUDY (*eagerly*)—Oh, that's wonderful, Fuffy. Then I could redeem myself! Wouldn't that be super?

FUFFY—We'll cut school tomorrow and go 'round answering all the classified ads.

JUDY (*offering her hand*)—What a pal!

Willis and Ellen are at the door. They have been to see J.B. and are pretty glum as a result. Ellen had hoped for a new understanding after the first shock, but J.B. had merely "gathered momentum over night," and there was no hope of a reconciliation. Now Willis and Grace are looking for a place to live.

Grace has an idea. Hilda is going; the children can have Hilda's room; Willis and Ellen can have the children's room and everything will be fixed until Willis finds something to do. Nor can Grace see why Willis and Harry, who had been successful in an earlier partnership, should not work together again. Harry is ready to try, but Willis is fearful he would be a handicap—and the idea is dropped.

Now there is new excitement. J.B. is in the lobby and wants to come up. Grace hopes he has realized what a fool he has been and wants to make amends, but Harry is sure J.B. is looking for his daughter. Anyway, Ellen doesn't want to see her father; doesn't want him to know where she is. "It would just mean another awful row," Ellen feels. "I can't go through it again. I don't want to hear myself repeating some of the things I said."

Harry was right. J.B. is looking for Ellen. If she isn't there where is she? "You know where she is, Grace! You better tell me, and damn quick, too!"

"Stop bellowing—you're not in the office now. This is my house!" Harry reminds him.

"Where are they?"

"I don't know where they are. Besides, your daughter doesn't want anything to do with you—and I'm damned if I blame her!"

"Sure! It's all my fault—she did nothing—nothing at all!"

"I'm not going to argue the merits of your case. Would you mind looking for her some place else?"

"If she's not here, she's *coming* here! And I'm not going to leave until I've had a talk with her!"

"Just a minute! You can't wait here. This isn't a Greyhound Bus Terminal!"

"Well, I'm waiting nevertheless! Try to evict me."

"Now, lissen, you—!"

"Oh, come on, Harry—" pleads Grace, taking her husband's arm. "Let him sit here if he wants to make a fool of himself!"

"We're going out to dinner in a few minutes and you can have the house to yourself. Just go on sitting there like an old poop!" Harry follows Grace into the bedroom.

Judy, coming into the room and facing J.B. quite fearfully, is ready to admit that everything has been her fault. Probably she is, as J.B. says, a menace and should be put away some place.

She listens miserably as J.B. mutters to himself, seeking some justification for his attitude toward Ellen and she is relieved when the phone rings. Hilda announces that Mr. Haskell Cummings is in the lobby.

Haskell Cummings! The name is startling to J.B. "Tell him to wait!" he shouts, ready to take the phone away from her. Pushing Judy into her room, J.B. returns a little stealthily to the phone. He is soon connected with his office and trying to make one Fowler understand—

"This is very important, so get this straight," J.B. is saying in a muffled voice. "Graves is trying to steal Haskell Cummings from under our nose. Now I want you to contact Barton right away. Where? White Sulphur Springs? What's he doing down there? He could take a bath up here, couldn't he? All right—I'll have to handle this myself."

He hangs up just as Harry, a dangerous gleam in his eye, comes back into the room.

"Haven't you gone yet?" demands Harry.

J.B. (*very hurt*)—Harry, it's hard for me to believe that you'd do a thing like this. . . .

HARRY (*puzzled*)—Do what?

J.B.—Surely you can get along without stooping to shyster methods!

HARRY (*echoing him*)—Shyster methods? (*He stares at* JUDY.)

J.B.—What else do you call it—sticking a gun in my stomach!

HARRY—What the hell are you talking about?

J.B.—Please, Harry, don't be the innocent with me—I know the game you're trying to play—I know when I'm licked! Here's my proposition—a junior partnership and you bring Cummings, Reade and Barton into the firm! (*The phone rings again. J.B. goes to the phone and grabs it. Listens a moment.*) Tell him to wait! (*He hangs up and turns to* HARRY, *desperately.*) Now look, Harry, I've gone through a great deal in these last two days— I don't claim I've been a hundred per cent right, but God knows I've had provocation. . . . It seems to me you ought to meet me halfway—after all that little monster of yours married off my daughter. How about it, Harry—a junior partnership, and you bring Cummings, Reade and Barton in with us?

HARRY (*bewildered*) J.B., I honestly don't know what you're talking about.

J.B. (*wearily*)—All right, you don't understand—*I* understand. Is it a deal?

HARRY—Deal?

J.B. It's a deal! (*Grabs* HARRY'S *hand, shakes it, then crosses to the phone happily.*) Okay, you can send Mr. Cummings up now!

Now, as junior partner, J.B. should be willing to tell him where his daughter is. Harry does, and the next minute a changed father has rapped on the door and been admitted to a conference with Ellen and her husband.

At the phone Harry confirms the presence of Mr. Cummings in the lobby—Mr. Haskell Cummings, *Jr.* A light dawns. "Oh, my God," explodes Harry, just as Judy arrives to be gathered happily into her excited father's arms. What has he ever done to deserve such a daughter! And they're not going to Kansas City.

"Grace, I want you to meet one of the outstanding personalities of our time—and very likely to be the first woman president of the United States. (*The doorbell rings.*) There he is."

He has given Judy a gentle pat as she starts for her bedroom. Judy stops to give him a hug, and her mother another.

Right royally does Judy's father receive Judy's young man. Takes his hat and coat; offers him the most comfortable chair; offers him a cigarette; compliments him upon the fit of his dinner coat and is pleased to learn that his tailor is Rogers Peet.

"Mr. Graves, may I ask you a question?" ventures Haskell, a little overwhelmed by the attention he is receiving.

"Why, you certainly may, Cummings, you certainly may."

"Mr. Graves, is it considered de rigeur at a formal party to smoke a pipe?"

"Why, it's the derigeurest thing you can do."

J.B., Willis and Ellen come from the children's room, chatting amiably. "When I make a mistake, Willis, it's a beaut!" J.B. is saying.

"Not at all; I've made a few myself," answers Willis, friendly-like.

ELLEN—Don't let him off the hook that easy.
J.B.—Where's Mr. Cummings, Harry?
HARRY—Brace yourself, J.B.
J.B.—Huh?
HARRY—May I present Mr. Haskell Cummings—Junior!
HASKELL—How do you do?
J.B.—What?
HARRY—He's taking Judy to a party.
J.B.—Well, I'll be damned. (*The bedroom door opens and* JUDY *poses there a moment, dramatically. She wears a white net dress, that billows out below the waist. Her dark brown hair lies in soft curls around her neck. On her feet she wears blue satin sandals and over her arm she carries* LOIS' *fur jacket. In her hand she holds a large chiffon handkerchief in which she has wrapped lipstick and powder. Her nails are tinted and she is*

JUNIOR MISS

very carefully made up. JUDY *looks slimmer and older, as pretty as* LOIS—*a Junior Miss.*)

JUDY—Good evening!

HARRY (*staring at her open-mouthed*)—Well! Well. . . .

HASKELL (*turning cheerfully*)—Hi'ya, there, Ju—! (*He stops and stares as he takes her in.*)

JUDY—Haskell! Aren't you nice to be so prompt!

HARRY (*taking her cape*)—Allow me. (*He slips it on her shoulders admiringly.*)

JUDY (*handing* HASKELL *the handkerchief*)—Here, Haskell. Keep these in your pocket for me. I'm simply terrible. I lose everything. (*She turns and kisses her father.*) Well, good night, Daddy. (*She walks across to her mother, her skirts swaying and her soft hair moving gently across the collar of her cape. She bends down and kisses her mother lightly.*) Good night, Mother dear. Don't wait up.

GRACE (*nodding open-mouthed*)—Have a nice time, darling.

JUDY (*shrugging her shoulders, her eyes drooping wearily*)—Well, you know parties. . . . (*She nods brightly to* LOIS.) 'Night, Lois dear . . .

LOIS—Good night, Judy.

JUDY—Good night, all! (HASKELL *mutters a good night as he opens the door.* JUDY *pauses in the doorway.*) I *do* love to dance though—don't you?

HASKELL—Good night! (*To* J.B.) Good night, sir. . . .

JUDY—Good night, Mr. Curtis. (*She kisses him.*)

J.B. (*resignedly*)—Okay, Harry. (*To* HASKELL.) Young man, you're going out with a hell of a girl!

Haskell puts the pipe in his mouth. Judy and he turn to go as

THE CURTAIN FALLS

CANDLE IN THE WIND
A Drama in Three Acts

By Maxwell Anderson

BEING a dramatist of achievement in the theatre carries an obvious handicap. Each successive play is expected to top all its predecessors in both its importance to the theatre and to the times it is written to reflect. Disappointment in a master dramatist's work is spoken with a kind of personal resentment, even by those who are his greatest admirers and strongest wellwishers.

Maxwell Anderson has gone through this experience many times. The quality of his work is no more uneven fundamentally than that of any writer whose sincerity and integrity are beyond question. But often his choice of theme or subject, or his failure to bring theme and subject into effective expression in the theatre, has developed in his plays weaknesses that have been charged against his unevenness as a playwright.

"Candle in the Wind," an October, 1941, contribution to the New York theatre, which was just then desperately in need of an inspiring drama to give the early season a lift, suffered such a reception. The Playwrights' Company and the Theatre Guild joined forces for its production. Helen Hayes played the rôle of its star. The play furnished a thoughtful and interesting evening in the theatre, but there was still that note of disappointment that, as said, inevitably follows the production of a drama by one from whom only great works are expected.

"Since Mr. Anderson is a man of force and principle, and since Miss Hayes is a woman of exalted spirit," Brooks Atkinson wrote in the *New York Times*, "their statement of timeless truths is courageous and sobering. But in spite of the unity of conviction on both sides of the footlights, 'Candle in the Wind' . . . left at least one playgoer last evening unstirred by things in which he deeply believes." Pretty much the same note of qualified approval ran through the reviews of Mr. Atkinson's colleagues.

The playgoing public, however, was more generously responsive. "Candle in the Wind" continued for three months in New York, and was then sent on tour with excellent box office results.

At the opening of Mr. Anderson's drama we are in a corner of the gardens behind the palace at Versailles in the early fall of 1940. There is a flight of steps that runs back to a path leading to and away from the Palace terrace. It is very early in the morning. Fargeau, a workman, is sitting on the terrace balustrade reading a newspaper and Henri, with a park broom in his hand, is looking over his shoulder. What they read, being an account of the fall of occupied France, is emotionally distressing to them. And to Deseze, a park attendant, who shortly comes upon them.

"I tell you they should be shot down, the traitors who write such things, and those who print them," Fargeau is saying, explosively.

"The journalists are merely the historians of the present, my dear Fargeau. They write what exists. They can hardly choose." Deseze is more conservative.

"Why, you fool, do you believe these lies? This is all the doings of the secret agents! This is how they win! Up in Belgium their secret agents ran through the villages crying, 'All is lost! Fly! The Germans have broken through! They are butchering the peasants!' And the peasants believed them, and clogged the roads—and the nation was destroyed! And now you believe them!"

"We saw them take Paris and march on South. It's not difficult to believe the rest."

"I know they took Paris. They can take a city! They have done that before. But France is not taken in a day nor a week! Nor in a hundred years."

Presently a German Captain and a Lieutenant are heard talking in German down the path. They are, it soon appears, in search of the Trianon. Getting their directions they go on, still gossiping volubly.

Now, two New Hampshire schoolteachers, Charlotte and Mercy, have come down the path. They, too, are seeking information. From their Baedeckers and maps they are, as they tell Deseze, "attempting to reconstruct the past, with the most inadequate evidence."

"... There was once a lake here at Versailles," Charlotte announces, while Deseze listens politely. "Lilies grew at the margin, mingled with sedge, and large swans floated about on its surface. Could you tell us where it was?"

"When was that lake here, Madam?"

"At the time of Louis XVIth."

"I fear I cannot help you. Ancient as I appear, and old as is my uniform, my recollection stops this side of Louis XVIth."

Nor can Deseze sympathize with their further desire to reconstruct the picture of the gardens as they appear to Marie Antoinette—

"The whole earth is at war, mesdames," says Deseze, with a touch of impatience. "All nations are in danger, and mine is already overrun. The Germans take Paris and pour down to the Pyrenees, and you hunt for the ghost of Marie Antoinette, in the gardens of Versailles."

A somewhat excited feminine call for "Madeline" is heard in the near distance. A second later a young woman runs down the steps as though in amused flight from the caller beyond.

The newcomer is Madeline Guest, probably in her late twenties, modishly garbed and attractively petite. Madeline is hoping to hear Deseze say that he has seen an officer in the park this morning, but there is no such good news as yet.

Presently Maisie Tompkins, Madeline's companion, appears. She is tall and broad and, not being the long-distance type, is puffing a little from her effort to keep up with Madeline. Neither is Maisie entirely in sympathy with Madeline's determination to keep this particular tryst. Certainly it isn't a very safe place to meet a French officer, for all it may be an "enchanted spot."

"Raoul told me the legend," Madeline explains, happily. "Lost things are found here. And if a woman waits here and wishes hard enough, the man she loves will turn, wherever he is, and come this way."

"I'm not superstitious," says Maisie, curtly, and adds: "Do you mind if I say some things straight from the shoulder, Madeline?"

MADELINE—About Raoul?
MAISIE—Yes.
MADELINE—Yes, I mind a little, but you'll say them anyway, and I can't go away at the moment.
MAISIE—Well, I should have some privileges, darling. After all, I've known you since high school. We ran through our fifteens and twenties together, and you always got the boy I wanted. Then we went on the stage together, and you always got the parts I wanted too. Now you're a star and I'm selling frocks, and I still can't find any malice in my heart for you, just the same old foolish fatty degeneration. (*Opens her bag, taking out bag of chocolates.*)

MADELINE—Maisie, you're an angel.

MAISIE—By Rubens, I know. (*Pops a chocolate into her mouth.*) And so I shall speak my mind. In the first place, I don't think he'll meet you here this morning.

MADELINE—Why?

MAISIE—That message was sent yesterday from Brest, wasn't it? Is it likely that he would get here this morning without a road open or a railroad operating? And all those German patrols about?

MADELINE—Yes, it is likely.

MAISIE—Well, suppose your charm works, and he does get to this enchanted region—and he isn't caught, and everything's all right—then we come to another question. He went through hell to meet you here—how much does it mean to you? And how much would you do for him?

MADELINE—I'd do anything for him. . . . I thought you liked Raoul, Maisie.

MAISIE—I do. I like him a lot. But I feel a bit protective about him—and you. You're an American and he's a Frenchman. He's a serious minded journalist and you're an actress. He's attacked Hitler in his column for years. The Germans probably hate him as much as anybody in France. Well now, what's going to happen to him? He can't stay in this country—

MADELINE—He could come to America with me.

MAISIE—Well—when you get to America—and start living in the same house—are you sure it's all going to be rosy? How much will you have in common—what will you talk about—you don't read editorials.

MADELINE—I know what you mean—that worried me too—but we've talked about these things, Raoul and I.

MAISIE—Well, if you've got it all worked out, I'm wrong.

MADELINE—Shall I tell you what he said to me, Maisie? He said that in the theatre you've played so much at love, are you sure you're in love with me? Are you sure you're not acting?

MAISIE—And what did you say?

MADELINE—I said I was sure.

MAISIE—Is that all?

MADELINE—You know it is true when you're an actress it's easy to put meaning into words you don't mean. I used to do that, even offstage. But not any more. I don't think I could ever play at love again.

MAISIE—Because of him?

MADELINE—Yes. And more than that. You can't play at

serious things any more. The whole world's changed. Maybe it's because the Germans have set out to kill all love and kindness, and instead of killing it, they've made love and kindness more precious than ever.

Maisie feels that she must be getting back to her job, though even that is getting a little difficult. "It's hard to fit a Berlin hausfrau into a Paris model. There's something fundamentally wrong with the combination, and I mean fundamentally. (*Rises.*) I don't like to leave you here. I have a sinking feeling that you'll have to find your way back to Paris alone." At that moment Raoul St. Cloud appears at the head of the path, a little like an apparition. Tall and handsome, hatless and wearing a French officer's uniform, Raoul stands for a moment before he calls softly to Madeline and she answers.

"The gods are with you, and I'll be on my way," says Maisie. "And never listen to me again on any subject, darling. I'm always wrong." She turns and disappears in the park as Raoul comes down to the foot of the stairs.

"I'd have come toward you, but I can't move. You're not wounded?"

"No." She is in his arms now for a long embrace. "Did you pray for me?"

"Yes."

RAOUL—I knew you must have. I've been through miracles. I've prayed to you so long, from so many unimaginary places—that saved me—I think there must be a God.

MADELINE—There must be.

RAOUL (*holding her in his arms*)—How I've wanted you—how I've wanted you.

MADELINE—Oh, my darling—I was so afraid your ship was lost.

RAOUL—It was.

MADELINE—They said it would be impossible for a man to come through free and alive.

RAOUL—Yes, it was impossible, that's how I knew you prayed.

MADELINE—Let me look at you—

RAOUL—I'd have died in the sea if it hadn't been for you. How did you do it, darling?

MADELINE—You had time to think of me?

RAOUL—Every time it got desperate I found myself thinking of you, I could feel you there, saving my life—you were like a

CANDLE IN THE WIND

goddess, with your hand stretched over me. (*They kiss, then break; he looks around nervously.*) I can't stay here too long, there may be mopping up operations.

MADELINE—I didn't know there was fighting still!

RAOUL—Here and there, where men are stubborn.

Henri passes through. Yes, the two Germans are still in the Trianon. He will keep watch of them, and let Mademoiselle know. Raoul goes on with his story. When Dunkirk was taken Raoul's captain had refused to surrender. Their destroyer had fought a lonely battle against four submarines. When finally they were sunk Raoul was thrown into the sea somewhere about the middle of the channel—

"A man can swim just so long in a frigid sea, with salt water chopping over him, and no notion of East or West. I got rid of my clothes in the water, and my coat with the one letter I ever had from you, and in undressing I lost my precious piece of plank, so I had nothing to cling to, but I clung to you—just to you, my darling, and without you I'd be frozen, and drowned and dead."

"It's unfair that men go through such things, and women can't help them!"

"But you haven't listened! You couldn't have helped me more with a lifeline! Darling, you know I'm sane enough, I like to see things as they are, but coming straight out of it this way, with no sleep and no breakfast—it seems like something more than mortal!"

There is a little restaurant outside the grounds. Madeline would take Raoul there, but first he must have a change of clothes, a workman's suit preferably. Madeline will go for these. There is also a matter of getting a wire off to Raoul's friends. He must go to them as soon as possible.

"A few of us are going south to try to find the French fleet. We still have a fleet, you know, even though we have no country."

"But the war's ended," protests Madeline, her eyes wide with anxiety.

"Not for me, dear, not for any of us who isn't helpless." Raoul is confident that soon she will understand; that if it were in her power to make the decision for him, she would tell him to go. If America were in desperate straights she would not think much of those men who ran away—

"My darling!" Raoul is holding Madeline closely in his arms.

"We fell in love so quickly—we were so sure of each other—that I hardly paused to think of what world you came out of—or you to question mine. Now we face these things sharply, in an hour of battle. I am a Frenchman—and fight for France. For years I fought with my pen against them, but not well enough. Not well enough, darling, and so now we must all fight as we can —desperately—with whatever arms there are—"

Oh, I wonder—I wonder—how many chances we're given. If we part again. What if this time it's so long and so cruel, and the iron cuts so deep that we change? It's such a fragile thing —the meeting of lovers. There must be a place, and a time for them to meet—and they must somehow stay alive and somehow reach that tiny focus in eternity which is all they have. And they must want to find each other—the flame must survive the wind. How do we dare part, Raoul, knowing how all the chances are against us?"

"Most lovers of the world are parting just that way these days."

"But those lovers have no gulf between them. Don't you see, Raoul, you're willing to die for something I don't understand. And that comes between us."

"You'd die for it too, if it came to a choice."

"I, Raoul? What would I die for?"

"Rather than live ignobly."

"I don't know."

"But I know. Because I saw you from a long way off—when I was there in the sea. And I know."

"You always do this to me, make me believe in miracles."

Before Madeline can leave Henri is back to warn them. The Germans are leaving the Trianon. Guards have been put at the park exits. Madeline must go and leave Raoul to do the best he can. But he must not fight with the Germans. Better a labor camp than that he should die—

". . . If you're alive there's still at least a chance! A chance to get free! A chance to live!" Madeline has run to Raoul, pleadingly. "Even for France it's wrong to die! It's giving up, saying it's no use any more! Please, darling—"

Now the German Captain and the Lieutenant are heard approaching. Quickly Raoul sits upon the bench, his face turned away, Madeline between him and the approaching officers. They start up the steps and are about to pass on when the Captain sees Raoul. He comes back and demands Raoul's papers which, as Raoul explains, must be somewhere in the sea between France and England—

"Will you stand up, please?" The Captain is very polite, but firm. "We are obliged to arrest all stragglers. We had hoped to find none, but unfortunately for both of us, you are here. We have placed a patrol at each exit, and you will therefore not attempt to use your arms, for you are a sensible person. Your automatic, please."

RAOUL (*starting to remove his gun from holster*)—This is a tame end for a soldier.
MADELINE—No, no, Raoul. Please. (*He unhooks his belt and hands gun to* CAPTAIN.)
RAOUL—For the moment.
CAPTAIN—You see—every man's luck runs out sometime.
RAOUL—Even Hitler's?
CAPTAIN—We shall see.
LIEUTENANT—Das weil uns auf Heilten.
CAPTAIN—Das macht den nicht. Come on, this way.
MADELINE—He's not serving against you, his ship was sunk, he's here only to see me.
CAPTAIN—I can well believe you, my dear.
MADELINE—But you can't take him now. There's to be an armistice now. The war's ended. He's no danger to you, one in so many millions.
CAPTAIN—I'm sorry, we have our orders.
MADELINE—Then we must have a few minutes—to say what must be said—
CAPTAIN—If there's nothing against him, he will be released tomorrow, my dear.
MADELINE—You say that, but it's not true!
CAPTAIN—Will you show me your passport? An American?
MADELINE—Yes.
CAPTAIN—This gentleman is in my custody, mademoiselle. I prefer that there is no interference, no argument, no outcry in the streets. Will you go quietly to your hotel, or shall I detail a soldier to escort you?
MADELINE—I will go quietly.
CAPTAIN—Good. Come on, vorwaerts!
MADELINE—Darling, till I see you—
RAOUL—Yes, Madeline—

Raoul follows the Captain and the Lieutenant into the park. The New Hampshire ladies have returned. They see the soldiers. They would, if they could, help Madeline.

"If there is anything we can do—"

"Thank you—no—there's nothing."

Madeline has followed Raoul and his captors into the park. The curtain falls.

On the outskirts of Paris the Germans have taken a disused pumping station and turned it into a concentration camp. In the "front office" the commandant, Colonel Erfurt, sits at an elaborate desk near a huge metal door before which a guard is stationed. Lieutenant Schoen, his assistant, is seated across the room at a table near a kind of entrance cage fashioned of timbers and heavy wire.

Colonel Erfurt is a handsome and commanding figure; a hard face, a brusque military manner. Lieutenant Schoen is the younger man, a gentler type, but equally brusque.

Proceeding with the business of the day, Colonel Erfurt would continue the interviewing of visitors. At the Lieutenant's suggestion he agrees first to see Corporal Behrens, a new guard assigned to the camp. The Corporal is ushered in through two doors of the wired entrance cage. He is a huge brute of a man, and knows the answers expected of him by rote. The specialty which he has developed is that of punishments. He has had two years of this. Colonel Erfurt is satisfied. Let Lieutenant Schoen continue the examination—

"Why are men punished in the Third Reich?" asks Schoen.

"Because they are guilty."

"And how do you know they are guilty?"

"Because they are condemned by the state, and the state makes no errors."

"If you discovered that the state had made an error, would you report it to the proper authorities?"

"It is impossible, sir, that the state has made an error. In any conflict between the state and the individual, the state is right, and the individual is wrong."

"But suppose God whispers in a man's heart, and tells him truth so that he is right, and the state is mistaken."

"It is impossible, sir. There is no God except the state, and the state carries out our Fuehrer's will."

Colonel Erfurt is satisfied. Let Behrens be sent to assist with the punishments in the third tier.

The outside guard has announced two visitors. They are M. and Mme. Fleury, a country couple, dust-covered, bedraggled and miserable. They have come, with a proper card, hoping to see their son. On order they "Heil, Hitler!" They are permitted to face Colonel Erfurt. He examines them curtly. They are from Tours. They are poor people. They own a small farm.

"Listen to me carefully," Erfurt warns them. "It is my custom to use kindness, but it is not my custom to repeat my words. This camp is here for a special purpose. It does not contain all grades and varieties of prisoners. We have here only political or philosophical offenders who have given us reason to believe them dangerous. It will not be possible for you to see your son."

"But he is the gentlest of men," Mme. Fleury protests.

"Of course. I know."

"M. Director, we have walked here this hundred miles, for there was no transport, even if we could pay, and we could not."

"I'm sorry, Madam—"

On second thought Colonel Erfurt thinks there may be a way. Interviews are permitted only in the public interest. If the Fleurys would be willing to ask their son a simple question—if they would ask him how they can communicate with him without the knowledge of the authorities—

"My son told us that we must never—even to save his life—we must never assist you."

"Your son is ill—he is confined to his cot. He will be up and about in a few days, but he is ill. If you wish to see him—"

"Yes, yes—we will ask the one question."

The Fleurys are turned over to a guard and ushered through the metal door.

And now comes the word that Madeline Guest, the American actress, is waiting. Miss Guest has been there several times and they have looked into her background.

On Erfurt's orders Madeline is admitted to the wire cage. She presents her card. She, too, is commanded to "Heil, Hitler!" She would ignore that issue, even to the extent of flatly refusing the order. Lieutenant Schoen is disturbed. Colonel Erfurt brusquely takes over. Madeline is admitted.

The Colonel is suavely solicitous. He begs Madeline to be seated. He is pained that evil fortune finds one in whom she is interested confined in his prison. It is possible something can be done. If so he will be glad to help.

It is Raoul St. Cloud whom Madeline wishes to see. For sentimental reasons? Madeline does not answer. Is she married? She is not. Would she be willing to make sacrifices—important sacrifices—to see M. St. Cloud? She would. Still, there must be further investigation—

"I'm not entirely a free agent, Miss Guest," explains Colonel Erfurt. "There are rules. I have to look into the case a little further before I can answer that question. And a little earlier or later in the day doesn't matter. Or does it?"

"Yes, it does matter."

"I should have thought the lover would reflect! The sooner I see him, the sooner it's over—the later I see him the fewer hours of absence left in the day. But no lover reflects."

"As you know, Colonel Erfurt, if you wish to make conversation I must listen."

"Ah, I see—you think I am wasting time! No, no—there is a purpose. It is true that I take an artistic pleasure in the beauty and vehemence of a passion, but as I study it I always think of the value it may have, not for me, but for the state. You see?"

"I understand you."

Colonel Erfurt would have Lieutenant Schoen bring him the St. Cloud papers. When they arrive they are studied carefully—

"Oh, yes, I thought I remembered," the Colonel remembers. "M. St. Cloud is by way of being an amateur anthropologist?"

"I believe so, yes."

ERFURT—He has found relief from journalistic routine by examining the facial index and tracing the ancestry of mankind?

MADELINE—Yes.

ERFURT—It would be easier if he had stuck to journalism.

MADELINE—Why do you say so?

ERFURT—I have here a review of "Mein Kampf," written by M. St. Cloud in 1931 for *Le Journal des Debats*. Unfortunately, he analyzes our Fuehrer's theories somewhat to their disadvantage. He also takes occasion to comment on our Fuehrer's anatomical construction.

MADELINE—That was printed in 1931?

ERFURT—Yes.

MADELINE—And it is still held important?

ERFURT—Unfortunately, again, there were recriminations in the press, and to make matters worse, our leader was subjected to personal attack—which he remembers.

MADELINE—Does this—have a bearing—on my request for an interview?

ERFURT—Miss Guest, this dossier carries a stamp, which might be interpreted "No Privileges." Now a visit from you would be considered a privilege, I'm certain.

MADELINE—I may not see him?

ERFURT—I'm sorry, you may not see him.
MADELINE—There was—a promise.
ERFURT—From whom?
MADELINE—He refused his name. But he was a German official.
ERFURT—You should have insisted on the name. Would you accept such a commitment from a stranger?
MADELINE—But he knew you. He has influence with you.
ERFURT—How do you know?
MADELINE—It was he who arranged this appointment.
ERFURT—At a price?
MADELINE Yes.
ERFURT—There is a Latin adage—caveat emptor.
MADELINE—But if he was not a responsible official—how does it happen he could arrange a meeting with you?
ERFURT—Ah, yes—I understand. There perhaps we should be willing to acknowledge a defect. State control is the only efficient control, but it requires a large corps of officials—a bureaucracy, if you like. And under a bureaucracy, there comes a time when the government mills grind slowly, and a modest amount of bribery becomes necessary to the functioning of the state.
MADELINE—Then your government is for sale?
ERFURT—No, no—not at all. But the government, being wise, accepts this unavoidable bribery as a new form of taxation. Of whatever you paid the officer for the interview, he will keep only a part. The government will take its share. And thereby we convert a weakness into a source of strength. You are an American citizen, and therefore not taxable, yet we have collected a tax from you.

There is a rattling at the inner door. The guards are bringing M. and Mme. Fleury from their interview with their son. They appear hopelessly crushed. Schoen unlocks the entrance cage to let them through. As she reaches the gate Mme. Fleury, moaning pitifully, starts to collapse. The guard pulls her up sharply and the Fleurys are hurried through the outer door. Madeline has risen to face Colonel Erfurt, who is apologizing for this interruption—

MADELINE—Colonel Erfurt, I cannot accept what you have said as final. It isn't easy to speak of love in this new world you have made. This wilderness of pain and lost children. I can't defend my love. I only know that since he was taken, I have had no hope of his return, no rest from the torment save in seeking him. Since I have known he was here—the walls of this cruel and ugly prison have gone with me wherever I am. Since I have thought there would come a moment when I might see him—I have lived only in the hope—of that one point in time.

ERFURT—I believe you, Miss Guest, and I would help you if it were possible.

MADELINE—Others go through that door.

ERFURT—No one will ever go through it to see Raoul St. Cloud. (*Rises.*) That is and will remain quite impossible. There is a terrible word written on these papers. The word Sterben. It means "to die." It is not often used. I do not often see it. But when I do, I know for certain that all decisions in that particular case are out of my hands.

MADELINE—I cannot believe you, and I will not. These decisions are out of your hands only if you wish it so. You must let me see him—

ERFURT—It's impossible—

MADELINE—Nothing's impossible! Perhaps I make a difficulty for you, perhaps it is easier to put me aside and go on with your work! But I shan't be put aside! You will not stop me! I shall haunt this prison. I shall not leave France till I have seen Raoul St. Cloud!

ERFURT—Shall I tell you what will happen if you stay in France?

MADELINE—I know what must happen!

ERFURT—You will say to yourself, there must be a way out. There must be a weakness. There must be somewhere a corrupt guard. These hastily constructed camps cannot be impervious. You will go to work to find this one weakness you need, this little crevice which may widen to a crack in our system. You will use all the ardor and the ingenuity of a woman in love, and you will fail! Your love, your talent, your time and your money will be wasted. Now that you have heard this, now that you know this—will you be sensible? Will you give up this living dead man, and your dead love, and go sensibly back to America?

MADELINE—No!

ERFURT—No? You are spoiled and soft, you Americans. You have never been up against sharp iron. It is your destiny to be beaten! Schoen, lassen sie raus.

MADELINE—I will never be beaten. Never. I will stay—and I will win!

The curtain falls.

ACT II

Madeline Guest's sitting room at the Hotel Palza Athenee in Paris is pleasantly furnished. There are French windows looking out on the boulevard, a large and comfortable sofa and the usual desk and chairs common to hotel sitting rooms. One chair has been wedged under the door knob of the door leading to the hall. It is September, 1941.

At the moment Cissie, Madeline's maid, is sitting on the sofa mending a stocking. When there is a knock at the door she listens but does not move. A second knock and a flow of Maisie Tompkins' Americanese convinces Cissie that to remove the chair is safe.

Madeline, Maisie learns, is, as usual, out seeing German officials, but should be home shortly. As for the chair under the door knob, that is Cissie's idea and Cissie knows what she is about. She learned about German soldiers in Vienna, that being her native city, when Austria fell; in Prague when Czecho-Slovakia fell and in Paris when France fell—always in hotels.

"Look, Mademoiselle," Cissie explains. "A German soldier works by what is on his little card. He has orders on a little card. What to do with the proprietor, what to do with the guests. What to do when the door is open, and what to do when the door is locked. But what to do, when a chair is under the door, he does not have. Sometimes he goes away to find out."

"But he comes back."

"Then you have time. You can get the hell out."

At the window Maisie reports the boulevard to be filled with goose-stepping soldiers as far as a person can see in either direction. But it is bad to look out of the windows. Sometimes, says Cissie, the temptation to drop things on them is hard to resist; sometimes someone else drops something, and the Germans, seeing you at the window, shoot you.

The food shortage is becoming more and more acute. Maisie, a meat eater by habit, is beginning to feel a variety of urges. If she could have a whole horse to herself she thinks she might be happy. She has even considered cannibalism. More than a little frightened by the look in Maisie's eye, Cissie quickly finds two water crackers that she has been hoarding and proffers Maisie one of them. Maisie eats it, crumbs and all, and is momentarily appeased.

The matter of getting Madeline away from Paris is of vital interest to both Cissie and Maisie. Cissie has come to work for

Madeline on the promise that she would be taken to America. And as for Maisie—

"Well, I've been sitting around this modern version of hell long enough now waiting for her to give up and go back with me. But she's a monomaniac now. It's really an obsession with her. She won't give up, and she won't go."

There is a knock at the door. Both women listen quietly. The door knob is slowly turned. Then the caller goes away. It is a proof of Cissie's belief. When Maisie insists on opening the door to investigate there is a German soldier named Mueller standing there. He is looking for Madeline, he says, and he will be back.

Shortly Madeline appears. She is glad to see Maisie and would have her stay. She would also have something to eat, if there were anything, which there isn't—nothing but the other water cracker and a little birch bark tea.

Maisie isn't surprised that Madeline looks tired, but Madeline insists that she isn't. "Just shabby, and down at heel and completely out of cold cream," announces Madeline, throwing herself on the couch.

"You've been going it like a soldier for a whole year, Madeline," Maisie reminds her. "And whether you'll admit it or not, you're tired and hungry, and just about done in. I can remember four distinct plots to get Raoul out of that camp. Four times you've built up a fantastic and elaborate machine—complete with corrupt guards, escape, transportation, fake passport, underground passage out of occupied France, and God knows what all, and then it always crashed because somebody squealed and he couldn't get out of camp after all. Now it's about to happen again—I can see there's that same feverish hope in your eyes that's been there so often before. And it won't work, and then you'll be in despair again."

"This time—we have a chance."

"It's come down to that now. This time you have a chance. You used to be sure, remember?"

"Darling, the chance was never so good before. Never once. There are three guards on the inside, helping."

"You believe they're helping?"

"Yes, I've got to, Maisie."

"You believed it before."

"Oh, Maisie—I can't let a chance go by, Maisie. I can't, darling. They torture people there—and they die under it. Suppose we came a day late. And then suppose we came just in time, when they were about—to kill him. I want to come in time, Maisie."

Madeline has only a little money left now. Before that is gone she promises to turn over to Maisie enough to get the three of them back to America. Maisie shall have it tomorrow. And that means that after what she is spending tonight she will be at the end of her resources.

The soldier Mueller is back. He waits patiently while Maisie gets out. He must talk with Madeline alone. He had not met her at the Tabarin, as promised, because he had been followed. He has just been able to shake off the spies. It is not because he, personally, is mistrusted; just a custom; everybody is watched a little to make sure. Mueller brings Madeline a note from Raoul. And now they are discussing a planned daylight escape. Madeline must know about that before she will advance any more money—

MUELLER—It must be tomorrow at three, because we take advantage of something which will happen at the camp tomorrow at that hour—

MADELINE—What will happen?

MUELLER—Sometimes the state wishes prisoners to be free, but cannot dismiss them publicly. Tomorrow it is arranged that certain prisoners depart under fire.

MADELINE—And how do you know this?

MUELLER—I am one of the guards assigned to assist.

MADELINE—Tell me how it will be done. Do you mean that in the confusion—M. St. Cloud will somehow slip out of the enclosure with the others?

MUELLER—Something like that. The fence is being repaired at one point. Guards and prisoners go back and forth through the opening. Now, at exactly three o'clock, an automobile will be drawn up across the road, and certain prisoners are instructed to jump into the car which will drive away. The guards will fire over the car. M. St. Cloud will be among the prisoners chosen for work at the bridge, and he will slip into the car also. The driver is a friend of mine. He will take M. St. Cloud to the room you specified in the Bordeaux Apartments.

MADELINE—And the men for whom the escape was planned?

MUELLER—I will tell them at the last moment that another is to join them.

MADELINE—And the guards who are helping you. You are

sure of them? They are ready and willing to go through with this?

MUELLER—Don't worry, they will carry out their part.

MADELINE—I think that's everything. Have you made my appointment with Colonel Erfurt for three o'clock?

MUELLER—Yes, there is an appointment made for you with Colonel Erfurt at three o'clock. We count on you to keep him at his desk with a discussion of the prison rules.

MADELINE—Yes, I know—I hate that office. I shall hate to go there again. But if it'll help. Did you bring the book?

MUELLER—Yes, and I have marked the page. It would be better if you could get there a little before three, just to keep him in his office.

MADELINE (*rising*)—I shall keep him there if I can. As long as I can. (*Takes book from him.*) I'll study this tonight. (*Puts book on desk, opens drawer and takes out two envelopes.*) Now I have put half the money in this envelope, as I promised. The other half I will give to the driver of the car when he brings M. St. Cloud to the apartment.

MUELLER—I will have to have that now.

MADELINE—That was not our bargain.

MUELLER—The others refuse to take part unless I can put the money in their hands tonight. You see, after the break, we must all three leave France instantly. We have no wish to die here.

MADELINE—Very well.

Mueller has gone, Maisie has come back. There is rejoicing in Madeline's sitting room. Now the packing must go forward. Now they must get Cissie a visa, even if it is expensive. The women will go by plane, Raoul by underground to the coast, where a fisherman will pick him up and take him to England. Maisie isn't quite satisfied with that part of the arrangements. Is it safe?

"Safe?" echoes Madeline. "No, not safe—he couldn't be safe of course. But cared for and watched over. When a prisoner escapes in France, the whole nation hides him, helps him, sends him on his way. And everyone that helps Raoul will be in danger of death—but they'll help him. Oh, Maisie, there are such gallant, such wonderful people in the world. They make one believe in so many things, that England will win, that France will be free, and that he will be free tomorrow—only, Maisie—"

"Yes, darling."

"It's been a year, and I begin to find so much gray in my hair. When I look in the mirror, there are deep lines in my face that he never saw there. Will he turn away from me, Maisie?"

"Nonsense. There'll be plenty of gray in his hair, and lines in his face."

"One thing I know now, I went into this love easily, lightly even, but I shall never see beyond it while I live."

In the prison camp Colonel Erfurt is seated at his desk, facing Raoul St. Cloud. Two additional guards are at the inner door. Colonel Erfurt has sent for Raoul to suggest an arrangement that might be made. Raoul must have noticed that he has been treated better than the other prisoners during the year of his imprisonment. It is because the Fuehrer has thought of a use for him—

"You are influential among French journalists," says Colonel Erfurt. "If you become a friend, if you begin to see virtues in the policy of co-operation with Germany—you will be set free."

"My convictions are unchanged, sir."

"And can you imagine conditions under which they would change?"

"No, I cannot."

"You have seen men here walk into a room strong, confident and defiant. You have seen them reduced inch by inch to the status of the amoeba—reduced to crawling, whimpering, shapeless, mindless blobs of butcher meat."

"Yes, I have seen this, to your shame."

"Could you hold out against us?"

"If the allegiance of the amoeba is of any value to you, that you may have, no doubt, at any time. But while I am able to stand and face you, and my mind is clear, I am my own man, and I fight to keep France free!"

For the moment Raoul is willing to reason with Colonel Erfurt, and to consider the offer of freedom and its conditions. But in the end his conviction stands. He is aware of the weaknesses of all governments, and he knows that of the National Socialists. Within the Fuehrer's government the danger is distrust—

"No man trusts another, no branch of the government trusts another, the leader himself trusts no man," declares Raoul. "You yourself, torturing your prisoners in the leader's name, never know when the purge will strike you, never know when some underling will start up from beneath to denounce you and put you to torture in the Fuehrer's name."

"That is your answer?"

"Among you all there is not one who dares trust even his own brother—for you know that men are devils, all men, and must be devils under your regime."

The guards are called. Raoul is sent back. He is to receive two lashes, "just to taste and try," and then put back to work. Let the guards act quickly!

Colonel Erfurt is in a fiendish mood. He turns now upon Lieutenant Schoen, accusing him, first of laxity in discipline, and then with having been sent there to spy on his superior. The Lieutenant is quick to deny the accusations, but in the end admits what Colonel Erfurt knows—that he (Schoen) has each week made a supplementary report to Berlin. Colonel Erfurt also knows that his lieutenant had been directed to do this and to tell no one.

At five minutes to three Madeline Guest is announced. Colonel Erfurt will see her, though the interview must be short. Madeline has come with two requests: First, as she will not be able to remain much longer in France she would like to beg again an interview with Raoul. That situation, she is informed, remains unchanged.

Second, Madeline, who has read a book of rules, has discovered that it is quite within the powers of a commandant of a prison camp to grant interviews with inmates at his own discretion. Colonel Erfurt admits as much, but insists that for the granting of such an interview he would be held most strictly accountable. He does not intend to take any chances with Raoul St. Cloud.

There is an interruption. Corporal Mueller has come with a request that a pass be stamped. Colonel Erfurt stamps the pass, smiling vaguely at Madeline as he does so.

Yes, he assures her, M. St. Cloud is still there. And well. Thanks partly to her. Because they knew that Madeline was in touch with friends in her own country they did not want reports of a prisoner's mistreatment drifting back. Now, however, since America's attitude has become definitely hostile, there was less reason for leniency.

The clock strikes three. A second later a siren and bell are heard, followed by a series of shots. Lieutenant Schoen goes to the gate and admits two guards. Their pistols are drawn. One guard takes a position at the Colonel's desk; the other goes into the prison. Then the sirens die out. Colonel Erfurt would calm Madeline—

"Don't be disturbed," he is saying; "this is not an alert. Once in a while we allow some prisoners to escape. We blow the siren and do a great deal of shooting and running about, and some certain prisoners drive away in a car, but because we wanted them to go, it is all prearranged. It's a political matter."

Soon Lieutenant Schoen is able to report that everything is again in order. Now Madeline would go. There is no reason why she should prolong the interview. But Colonel Erfurt is not ready to have her leave—

". . . You have kept a long and bitter vigil here in France, I know," he is saying. "Even I am not insensible to that. There is a character in Shakespeare who says—'Some good I mean to do, despite of mine own nature.' Well, I shall take a leaf from Shakespeare. Let them bring in St. Cloud!"

But Madeline, visibly disturbed, does not want to see St. Cloud today; she does not feel well; she has waited so long; she will come tomorrow. Colonel Erfurt is insistent. Lieutenant Schoen is told to order St. Cloud brought in, and does. And now the guard has arrived with Raoul—

"Oh, God!" Madeline has bowed her head in her hands and is crying quietly.

"You weren't expecting this, I know," blandly observes Colonel Erfurt. "You thought him elsewhere. Now I could have arranged that too, only it would have meant the end of my career very definitely. An ordinary escape might have been forgiven, but M. Raoul St. Cloud I must keep safe, or step down into the ranks. Therefore, I keep him safe. Perhaps I should warn you to look well at each other, for this may be your last meeting."

MADELINE—Raoul.
RAOUL—Yes, Madeline.
MADELINE—You know how hard I have tried.
RAOUL—Yes, I know.
MADELINE—We have been betrayed, I think.
RAOUL—Yes, many times. And again today. You must leave France, Madeline, and take up your life again, you've wasted too much time on the impossible.
MADELINE—Are you in pain, Raoul? You moved as if you were in pain.
RAOUL—No, no. We're well treated here. Don't worry about that.
MADELINE—Did you receive my messages?
RAOUL—No, they allow no messages. But sometimes a whisper comes through the prison walls. I've known where you were.

Sometimes even known what you did. When it was ugliest here, the days and nights were filled with words from you to me.

MADELINE—Could I kiss you?

RAOUL—No, not here. It's enough to see you—that's what I've prayed for.

ERFURT (*after a pause*)—If you have no more to say, perhaps we'd better go on to other matters. Is that all?

RAOUL—Never believe we've lost, even though we should lose, we have won. They know what they are, and no words can cover it.

MADELINE—We've not lost yet, never believe I'd say we've lost.

ERFURT—Take him back to his cell. You are dismissed. And don't say that you'll strike me, or that you'll die, for I speak from long experience. And you'll do neither. You'll go home again, and for the last time.

MADELINE—Yes.

ERFURT—You are dismissed. Schoen—

Madeline has gone slowly through the gate, which Lieutenant Schoen closes. "And yet something perishes with them when they are exterminated," Erfurt continues. "A kind of decadent beauty one hates to lose."

Erfurt is studying a ring on his finger. Schoen salutes and returns to his desk as the curtain falls.

It is early evening of the same day. In Madeline Guest's hotel sitting room Maisie Tompkins and Cissie, the maid, are busy tying tags on suit cases. Cissie also is babbling a little excitedly. If she should get her visa she will not need the passage with the fisherman across the channel; is it really true that anyone can buy fruit and cheese and butter on the streets in New York? Surely not all they want; not from wagons!

Cissie is also worried. Would they dare arrest an American lady in Paris? It is four o'clock and Mlle. Guest is not back! And true it is she has tried and tried to get M. St. Cloud out of the camp! Isn't that—

"High treason? It certainly is," interjects Maisie. "It's high treason in this country to steal a cake of soap—it's high treason to think Hitler walks like a woman—but he does. So we're all guilty."

Then Madeline comes. She looks, as Maisie says, as though

she were about to collapse, but insists she isn't tired. She has seen Raoul. He is still in camp. Let Cissie unpack her bags.

"I've been trying to think, but I can't think yet," she says, noting Maisie's despairing expression. "He'd been beaten. I could see it."

"I hate to say this, Madeline, but it's a hard fact, and we must face it. They'll never let go of Raoul." Maisie's tone is firm, yet pleading.

"They've got to, Maisie."

"Don't have the bags unpacked. We must go now. You can't help Raoul without money, you can't even live. Now listen. There's another cable from California today, they're still offering you a fortune."

"I feel that if I let go, just once, for a day—it might be deadly to him."

"But the sooner you're home, the sooner you can return, the sooner you can help."

There is a knock at the door. It is Lieutenant Schoen. He wants to see Miss Guest—alone. Madeline is not interested. If he has any honest business with her he can talk before Miss Tompkins. She is an old and trusted friend.

Lieutenant Schoen decides to talk. He is, as she knows, from Direktor Erfurt's office. He has seen Madeline there many times. He has also seen M. St. Cloud. He feels he knows them well; that they are not ordinary people. He does not blame her for being suspicious, but he feels that he can advise her wisely concerning the possibility of M. St. Cloud's escape from the camp.

Madeline is not impressed. She has heard similar stories from others. These others have all betrayed her to Colonel Erfurt. She has no more money. Schoen is not discouraged. Madeline still has that large diamond on her finger. He is in desperate need of money. He is willing to take any chance to get money. He has a plan—

"Erfurt goes to Berlin tomorrow. I shall be in charge of the camp for some days. I should place M. St. Cloud in solitary confinement and place with him the tools with which to free himself. There is a defect in our solitary system, and it has several times occurred to me that I would know how to escape from it."

Schoen is also certain he could dispose of the diamond for a goodly sum, enough to cover all necessary expenses.

Still Madeline is not impressed. "It always comes to this in the end," she sighs. "A certain amount of money—a plausible plan of escape. And then something always goes wrong."

SCHOEN—How could I prove to you that I am not like the others?

MADELINE—Could it be proved?

SCHOEN—I have glimpsed something in you—and in M. St. Cloud—that I admire. I do honestly wish M. St. Cloud might have his liberty.

MADELINE (*rising, crosses down to* MAISIE *and takes her hand*)—Maisie—Maisie—

MAISIE—What position does this officer occupy at the camp?

MADELINE—I've seen him always in Colonel Erfurt's office.

MAISIE—Are you the director's secretary?

SCHOEN—His assistant.

MAISIE—The game grows fairly obvious, Madeline. They've run out of messengers. They think you may have saved a few dollars—no doubt they've noticed the diamond on your finger, but they can't find a new face in their Gestapo to collect from you. The Direktor looks around him, and here's his old standby, Lieutenant Schoen, as reliable as they come. "We'll send Schoen," he says. "Ah—but she knows Schoen, she's seen him a dozen times!" "Never mind, tell a big enough lie, and it's always believed." That's out of the horse's mouth. But you don't know how to dramatize your story, Lieutenant. I've heard several of Erfurt's little prattlers, and you're easily in last place.

MADELINE (*going behind* MAISIE *and putting her hands on* MAISIE'S *shoulders*)—I have tried to believe you, Lieutenant Schoen. The others I have believed—enough to employ them. But I have heard the story too often, it no longer convinces me.

SCHOEN—I'm sorry. I have never been a good salesman. I'm truly sorry. But I cannot give up so easily. Perhaps you will think better of me later this evening. When you are alone. It must be this evening, or not at all. Let me leave a telephone number. (*Goes to desk, writes number on pad.*) I can be reached at this number at any time before six.

MAISIE—Would an honest man dare to leave his telephone number about? Certainly not!

MADELINE—I will not deal further with Colonel Erfurt or his agents.

SCHOEN—You believe me his agent?

MADELINE—I do.

SCHOEN (*after long pause*)—You are right, Miss Guest. I was

sent by Erfurt; believe none of us.
MADELINE—Thank you.
SCHOEN—But I speak the truth when I say that I wish you well.
MADELINE—Thank you.
SCHOEN—Good night.
MADELINE—Good night.

There does not appear to be anything more to do. Madeline has taken Schoen's telephone number from the desk, torn the card in two and thrown it in the waste basket. Maisie thinks perhaps they had better see about Cissie's visa now. If they don't mind, Madeline will stay in the hotel; she is in no mood to face people.

Maisie and Cissie have gone. Madeline is sitting disconsolately on the sofa as they go out. She gets to her feet quickly and begins pacing the room. Now she has thrown herself on her face on the sofa. She finds her hand-bag and from it takes out a small mirror and stares at her reflection.

"Yes, Madeline," she mutters, sobbingly; "you must learn to live without Raoul. If there's to be no Raoul, you must learn to live without him. Wipe out these lines, and weep less these sleepless nights, for you must go forward without him. That is your lesson, Madeline. Learn it by heart, and never forget. (*Sobbing.*) I can't, I can't— Oh—God help me, I can't!"

She has gone back to the desk and is searching for the torn card with the telephone number on it as the lights fade and the curtain falls.

Madeline is still in her room. It is later the same evening. The heavy velvet drapes have been drawn across the windows and the desk lamp is lighted. There is a knock at the door. A second later Madeline has admitted Lieutenant Schoen.

Madeline had asked him to come. Why? He had warned her that she should trust no one. Madeline is convinced that she can trust him. When the lieutenant had told her that he had come to betray her she knew it to be the first honest word she had heard from him. Whether he intended it or not he had become her friend with that confession. Why did he speak the truth to her?

"I have been sorry for you for many months," admits Lieutenant Schoen. "And for M. St. Cloud. One must look on at many things—but there comes a time when one wishes to put the victim out of his misery. It's not a crime, even in the Reich, to feel sympathy with the suffering."

"But to help, is that a crime?"

"Even in your own country, it is a crime to aid a criminal."

Has the lieutenant ever thought of what it would be like to live in a country where there is freedom of thought? Madeline would know. In his country such freedom is regarded as a diseased condition, Schoen answers. But Madeline knows that he has thought of these things.

"No wild thing was ever put in a cage without wishing for freedom," says Madeline. "And of all wild things in the world, the most uncontrollable—the least tameable—is the human mind. No King or Priest or Dictator has ever tamed it. It cannot rest in captivity. And the mind of Germany is caged."

"Caged by our enemies."

"Do you believe that?" The lieutenant is looking nervously about the room. "No, you are free here. In this room there is no compulsion on you to lie."

"This is not a useful conversation."

"I have seen many men in the world you live in who hate that world. There is a certain veiled regard in the eyes of those who must forever dissemble their unrest, who dare not speak out. And of all those who carry that look about with them, you have seemed to me the most unhappy. This afternoon, in Erfurt's office, that look was on your face. I didn't know what it meant then, but I do know now."

Again Lieutenant Schoen would go, but Madeline holds him back. She gives him the ring, despite his protest.

"You know what I must do with it," repeats Schoen, a note of appeal creeping into his voice. "Yet, how can I, if I remember you here, hoping that it's used for him! Take it back. You don't know what you ask of me! Suppose it's true that I'm caught in a net, that I hate it? That I—it's evil to be in prison, but if you escape, you're an outlaw everywhere. So—one sticks to the prison, and turns to the torture machine, and by and by we shall conquer the earth, no doubt, and give it a rest from torture."

Some of the things that he has told her are true, Schoen admits. It is true that Erfurt is going to Berlin. It is true that escape from the solitary cells might be managed. But how can she tell when he is lying and when he is not? How could she ever be sure that he had ceased to be her enemy?

"I'm sure of it now," insists Madeline. "I was sure of it when

I called you—and if it isn't true you should not have come here, for you knew why I called you."

SCHOEN (*putting the ring in his vest pocket*)—It is my duty to keep the ring. I must go.
MADELINE—I shall wait for your message.
SCHOEN—I think there will be no message. Good night.
MADELINE—Wait, let me look at you. (*Looks into his face.*) You see, there are tears in your eyes.
SCHOEN—Yes, but I have seen tears in Erfurt's eyes, when a man lay dying. And he let the man die. You must not depend on our tears.
MADELINE—I shall depend on yours.
SCHOEN (*back to audience*)—If I call you tonight, then we shall try to work something out together. But if I don't call, then put it all out of your mind, for there's nothing to be done.
MADELINE—But you will call.
SCHOEN—Good night. (*Opens door and goes out.*)
MADELINE—Good night.

Madeline stands at the door a moment, then sinks on to the chair as the curtain falls.

ACT III

Two days later, in the early evening, we find Henri and Deseze in the corner of the garden of Versailles where we first met them. It is Henri who is reading the paper this time, checking on the list of names of those executed recently as hostages. Their old friend and fellow worker, Fargeau, is named in tonight's list.

"He did what we have all wanted to do," sighs Deseze. "Yes, I remember now what he said to me: 'I am too old for many things, but not too old to die.'"

Lieutenant Schoen has walked in from the garden. He is looking for one named Henri. He would have Henri follow him—but as a favor. There is no charge against Henri.

They have gone when Madeline appears. For a moment Deseze does not recognize her. It has been nearly a year since they met. Will she be meeting the officer? No, he will not be coming this evening. He is a prisoner. Nor has it been possible for Madeline to help him—

"I have tried for a year," she tells Deseze, sadly. "I think now I'd have done better to dig a tunnel under Paris with my own hands, till it came up under his cell."

"Yes. One thinks of fantastic things like that."

"And when you've given up hope one clings to fantastic hopes, impossible hopes. I think I came here tonight because of an old superstition about this place. You know it?"

"Yes."

"Nobody believes it of course—and yet I came here."

"I shall pray that as you sit here in the twilight, your hopes will return to you, and that they will come true."

"Thank you."

Now Charlotte and Mercy, the New Hampshire schoolteachers, have come, as they did before. They, too, have changed, but they hold a little more firmly to their dream of restoring the garden as it was in Marie Antoinette's time. It is easier now, because they have found the lake they were looking for.

"Many days we walked here in these gardens," explains Mercy. "A little sad and a little hungry. And then, suddenly, we saw the lake. I think I saw it first."

"Yes, you saw it first," admits Charlotte.

"The lake was there, with the swans, and the sedge, and the water-lilies, and the path to the Orangerie. Oh, all as it was."

"And now we no longer need help with the restoration, because we walk here in that old world daily."

"And every day as we stand at the entrance we see the lake and the old buildings, and the servants carrying fruits and sweetmeats into the *Trianon*. And so we have escaped those new soldiers. We're quite beyond them now. That is our secret."

"Yes, that is our secret. Because they can't touch us there in the gardens of the past. And so we have eluded them, haven't we?"

Madeline isn't sure. "I don't know," she says, sadly. "Perhaps we've all tried to elude them, each in his own way. I'm afraid we haven't succeeded, any of us."

Charlotte and Mercy are worried as they go back to their dream garden. Perhaps they should not have told their secret. "Something goes out of it. Some of the shining goes from it," says Mercy.

Lieutenant Schoen has come down the path. He has come because M. St. Cloud has told him where he will find Madeline. He is not betraying her. He has not tried to reach her before because he has had no chance, but he has done what he could to help her. M. St. Cloud is free. Everything so far has gone miraculously well—

"He came this far in the night in his prison suit," Schoen is saying. "But we have found a workman who will lend him clothes, and he makes the exchange now. We planned to meet here, for he hoped you might be here."

"But he's in grave danger, they must have discovered the escape, they must have followed him."

"I have made an official inspection of the empty cells this morning, he was gone, and I carefully sent the pursuit in the wrong direction. It has all gone well. You have only to wait here until he comes."

"Oh, forgive me, forgive me, for any evil I have thought of you. It was unfair to ask this of you. I knew that, and I can never thank you and repay you. Why are you trembling?"

"Is it so easy to break with all you've ever known? To thrust your neck under the ax? I have seen too many executions, but I have come to the end of this quarrel with myself. This quarrel over whether it is better to be what you are and die for it, or to be what they would have you, and live. Perhaps I have found a sort of courage."

"Where will you go?"

"You must not worry about me, I have my own private war to fight. But, however it goes, not everything is lost. For I am now a soldier against what I hate, and it's good to fight alone. Good-by, and thank you."

Lieutenant Schoen has kissed Madeline's hand and bounded away into the park. A moment later Deseze reappears. He has come to warn Madeline that shortly a workman will pass that way. Yes, he may have time to stop for a moment. Deseze and Henri will guard the paths and warn her should anyone come. The gardens are practically deserted in the early evening.

Raoul comes, making his way furtively through the shadows. Now he lifts his cap, Madeline recognizes him and they are in each other's arms—

RAOUL (*holding her close*)—Dare I believe it?

MADELINE—Dare I believe it? So many times I've thought I saw you, so many times I've heard a voice behind me, and turned, thinking it was yours.

RAOUL—If I could only hold you forever. It's been a year.

MADELINE—Only a year? It's been so many years. (*They kiss.*) Oh, my darling—perhaps you shouldn't have come here.

RAOUL—No place is safe any more. And I had to see you. This is a miracle—a miracle like the others. Madeline, if you hadn't been eternally true, if your love hadn't been stronger than all of them, I'd have been lost long ago. I don't want to leave you again.

MADELINE—Oh, but you must, if we're ever to meet again. You must—and you know it—

RAOUL—Yes, I must—I know, but not yet. I can't go yet. Do many people pass this way?

MADELINE—The park's deserted in the evenings, we can take a few minutes.

RAOUL—But I have a habit of keeping in the shadows. Come. The Lieutenant tells me I must climb these steps, and turn right when I've passed the gate. Beyond that I know nothing. You must tell me, sweet, where do I go?

MADELINE—There's only one way out of France, and that's England. I have your passage. You can reach Cherbourg by tomorrow evening. Yes, with a little luck, I'm sure you can.

RAOUL—Luck never fails me, while you remember me.

MADELINE—Then it won't fail you now. You'll reach Cherbourg in time, and find the little boat, and the Captain will take you across safely, and, oh, I think there must be a God, as you said long ago, for I carried this about with me even after I'd given up!

RAOUL—There must be. Because you are here—and somehow you've got me out of that hell. Your arms are real. (*Takes her in his arms.*) I'm risen from the dead.

MADELINE—And I've been dead, and I'm alive again. (*They kiss.*)

Now Raoul must go and without her. Those who travel underground have taught Madeline the rules: "Travel fast, travel light and travel alone." On an envelope she gives him are three penciled words. Raoul is to go first to where they direct him. There he will receive other instructions.

"Keep safe, my darling," he warns, kissing her. "You must not be seen with me. Perhaps you should wait here a moment and then leave by the other gate."

"Yes, darling, till England!"

"Till England."

Deseze comes soon to report that he has seen Raoul through the gate and away. And Henri has turned up in his makeshift clothes. With a fervent "Thank you!" Madeline finds relief in tears. "I thought I had no tears left, but for happiness I have," she says, struggling to smile. And now she, too, must go.

"I want to be in London before he comes," Madeline explains. "And somehow I will, somehow I will. Once when he came safely out of the sea, he said that my hand had been over him there on the water. Now I know what he meant—for his hand is over me now. Good-by, Henri."

In the distance a whistle is blown. From the top of the steps Deseze and Henri can see soldiers entering the park. Mademoiselle must hurry. Deseze will let her out another gate.

Madeline refuses to go. Let them leave her there. The longer the soldiers spend with her the farther Raoul will be on his way.

Again the whistle is blown, close at hand this time. Now Corporal Shultz appears. It will be necessary for them all to remain there until they are questioned. There has been an escape from the prison camp and the pursuit comes this way. Presently Corporal Shultz is followed by a guard that deploys itself strategically.

Now Captain Hoffman has come to take charge. Soldiers are bringing together all the people in the park. They will be questioned by Colonel Erfurt.

A moment later the Colonel arrives. There is an exchange of reports concerning the pursuit in German. The reports finished, the guard is withdrawn, taking Deseze and Henri along. Now Colonel Erfurt is ready for Madeline, for whom they had looked first at her hotel.

When he returned from Berlin, says Colonel Erfurt, he discovered that there had been an escape from the camp. Obviously Lieutenant Schoen had been connected with it. Schoen has disappeared and they are searching for him. Has Madeline seen him? No.

"Where is Raoul St. Cloud?"

"I don't know."

ERFURT—You do know, of course you do. You told me once you would do this; now, by a combination of chances, you have succeeded. Now, tell me—where is he?

MADELINE—Suppose I did tell you—how would you know I hadn't lied to you?

ERFURT—Of course, it will be necessary to hold you until your lover has been recaptured.

MADELINE—You wouldn't dare!

ERFURT—If you had been a French woman, you would have been arrested and your money confiscated, a year ago. We let you alone because of your nationality, and your name. But now we no longer care greatly what you think of us. You will help me recapture St. Cloud, or face trial for aiding in his escape.

MADELINE—You could let me go—I am only to meet him—some time—a long way from here—if I can find him. There's so little chance of any happiness. You could let me go.

ERFURT—Only if I have him in your place. Ask anything you like for St. Cloud, except his freedom, and you shall have it. I'll make his captivity light. I'll save his life if I can. You shall see him as often as you like—but his freedom, he must not have.

MADELINE—But he is free.

ERFURT—Very doubtfully. We'll catch up with him, wherever he is.

MADELINE—If you're so certain of that, why do you ask my help? I think you've lost him, Colonel Erfurt, and you think so too. As for your promises to treat him well, no child would believe you.

ERFURT (*closing in on her*)—No? As yet you have not quite understood. I must have him, or I must give an accounting to Berlin. I don't think I could find the words to say to my superior, St. Cloud is free. They might be my last words, my last in office, my last as what I am.

MADELINE—But you will say them.

ERFURT—No. I cannot say them. I shall have to employ whatever means I can to make you speak.

MADELINE—And do you believe you could ever make me speak?

ERFURT—Oh, yes, there is no human will—not even a fanatic's, not even a lover's—that can hold out against us.

MADELINE—But I can hold out to the end. A soldier should have no reluctance about dying. You've made soldiers of us all. Women and children and all.

ERFURT—There is no need to discuss your civilization or mine. We are hard because we must be, and your case is like any other, and must be dealt with.

MADELINE—Very well. He's free. Raoul is free. Do as you like with me. Take your revenge, but you must still go to Berlin and tell them Raoul is free!

ERFURT—Hauptmann! (CAPTAIN HAUPTMANN *and three guards enter.*) Take a last look about you at your free world. I have not yet spoken the word that will shut you up, but when I do speak it I will not take it back!

MADELINE—I came into this fight tardily and by chance, and

unwillingly. I never thought to die young, or for a cause. But now that I've seen you close, now that I've known you, I'd give my life gladly to gain one half inch against you. I'd give my life gladly to save one soldier to fight against you. But I took Raoul from you, and I shall not give him back.

ERFURT (*after a pause*)—Give me your passport. You will go with the guard. We take our enemies one at a time, and your country is last on the list. But your time will come.

MADELINE (*as she turns to mount the steps*)—We expect you. In the history of the world there have been many wars between men and beasts. And the beasts have always lost, and men have won.

THE CURTAIN FALLS

LETTERS TO LUCERNE
A Drama in Three Acts
By Fritz Rotter and Allen Vincent

THE acceptance of a war play in war time is inevitably unpredictable. Audience reactions are easily influenced by varied and often biased reasoning. Particularly in a theatre capital in which there live, as the sight-seeing bus lecturers used to shout, "More Germans than there are in Berlin, more Italians than there are in Rome, more Jews than there are in Jerusalem," etc. Successful war plays are usually written some years after the war, or wars, they seek either to chronicle or explain.

During the early part of the season of which this volume is a record there were three dramas inspired by the Second World War produced in New York. "The Wookey," by Frederick Hazlitt Brennan, telling of the bombed and the brave of London in the great blitzkrieg of 1940, was no more than a quasi-success. Norman Krasna's "The Man with the Blond Hair," telling of an escaping Nazi aviator who was reconstructed in the East Side flat of a New York Jewish family, was a quick failure, and even Maxwell Anderson's "Candle in the Wind" was frankly accepted with more enthusiasm for the popular Helen Hayes' playing of its heroine than because it inspired respect for its author's creation.

A fourth war play was this "Letters to Lucerne," of which, both as drama and as a human document, this editor was one of the few enthused champions. "Letters to Lucerne" came from Hollywood, by way of Rosalie Stewart, a dramatists' agent of standing on the coast.

The idea for the play had been submitted to her by Fritz Rotter, a young Viennese song writer who did not yet trust his halting English when it came to putting his ideas into a play script. Stirred by the possibilities of the story, Miss Stewart suggested that Allen Vincent should work on the play, which he did.

Dwight Deere Wiman, in California looking for actors for a revue he had in mind, heard of the play through Miss Stewart and immediately bought it. When he had it cast he was a little set up by the fact that he had included the daughters of no less than five who were celebrities in one artistic field or another.

"LETTERS TO LUCERNE"

Erna (reading letter): "... Hans' good friend, Wilhelm Brandt, was there... He saw Hans deliberately crash-dive his ship— before they ever reached Warsaw... It was partly for Olga.. but it was mostly because it was the only way he could protest and deny this terror that has crept over our country..."

(Gretchen Mosheim, Katherine Alexander, Nancy Wiman, Beatrice Neergaard, Sonya Stokowski, Phyllis Avery, Mary Barthelmess, Faith Brooks)

Photo by Lucas-Pritchard.

There were Sonya Stokowski, daughter of Leopold Stokowski, the conductor; Mary Barthelmess, daughter of Richard Barthelmess and Mary Hay, of stage and screen fame; Faith Brooks, daughter of Clive Brooks, English actor and director; Phyllis Avery, daughter of Stephen Morehouse Avery, author, and Nancy Wiman, daughter of the producer himself. The heroine was played by Greta Mosheim, an actress of standing in Germany before she ran out on Mr. Hitler's Nazi Government.

Because of its cast, which also included Katharine Alexander, a Broadway favorite of other years, the opening night of the play was socially quite on the plush side. The morning after the reviews were pretty depressing, though not without reservations.

As the curtain rises on "Letters to Lucerne" we are facing the main hall of a girls' school in Switzerland, near Lucerne. It is noon of a day in late summer. Brilliant sunshine floods into the room through double doors at back, with windows at either side. "The atmosphere is gay and comfortable." Leading from the main hall at one side are doors to the dining hall, and at the other side a door to the study hall. A curving stairway leads to dormitories and sitting rooms on the floor above.

Olga Kirinski, "about seventeen and very attractive," has the room to herself at the moment. Obviously she is waiting for someone, dividing anxious moments between looking out the door and peering into a mirror to be sure that her hair is still in place.

Presently Gustave the gardener appears, carrying a small bouquet. He is not the one Olga is waiting for. She greets him a little impatiently with the promise that as soon as the folks arrive at the foot of the hill she will warn him. They will not be there for a quarter hour yet. Gustave, too, is anxious. He must not miss the ceremony of greeting Madame.

Olga has had another quick look out the door and patted another stray lock into place when Erna Schmidt, "a young Nordic goddess, with an air of quiet authority, a calm, balanced poise unusual in one of her age," appears on the stairs.

It isn't Erna for whom Olga is waiting, either, but there is evidently a strong bond of friendship and sympathetic understanding between the two. Hans, Erna's brother, it soon appears, is the expected one. Olga is simply mad about Hans, and a little disappointed that Erna will not conspire with her to have him miss his train so he would have to stay over another day. Erna isn't interested—

"I've conspired with you quite enough," says Erna. "I've chaperoned a walking trip through Gstaad Valley—and a very dull walking trip it was too. I did it for myself—I made a match."

"Oh, you did make a match. Think if I had never met him. Think if we had not gone on our walking trip!"

"You would have met him eventually. I planned that from the very first."

Olga is also worried for fear Erna's family is not going to approve of her. But Erna thinks that silly. Surely Olga should know from the letters Erna has read her that the Schmidt family is not like that—

"You cannot tell much from letters," insists Olga. "I did not really know about Hans from them. They did not make him half as wonderful as he is. . . . Erna—I do not think this letter-reading is such a good idea."

"But they are one of the most important parts of our lives. They are why we all know each other so well! You are not fooling me. You're thinking about the letters you will have from now on, aren't you?"

"I *couldn't* read Hans' letters to the others! Think what fun Bingo and Sally would have. They are always teasing me because I haven't any beau."

"But think of the fun you can have now—refusing to read them what Hans writes."

Gretchen Linder, "a cool, collected, efficient, but pleasant woman in her mid-thirties," has appeared to welcome Erna and Olga and to ask about their holiday. It must have been nice for Olga to meet Erna's family. And now the truth comes out. Erna and Olga had not gone to Erna's home, as they were expected to do. They had gone on a walking trip with Erna's brother instead, through the Gstaad Valley. They hadn't intended to tell about it at all, but now that Hans is coming there to get his fare home (he always loses money, so Erna has to keep it for him) they feel it would be better to tell all.

Miss Linder is not too severe. They should have asked Mrs. Hunter first, and doubtless she would have disapproved. But so long as they did nothing wrong—well, Mrs. Hunter is broad-minded, too. Miss Linder is even willing to help them now with their watching for Hans, and to warn them as soon as she sees him. Olga is grateful, and excited, and her eyes are dancing—

A tuneful whistling heralds Hans' approach. A moment later he has passed the window, put down his knapsack and is standing in the door. "He is a fine looking young man with an ingratiating smile, a very masculine kind of gaiety about him."

Hans admits that he is late, and for two very good reasons. First, he doesn't like long farewells; second, he had a little trouble with his English landlady, who had wanted to charge him for the time he had been away, just because he had carelessly left a few things in his room.

"You only do these things because you think they make you picturesque and romantic, when underneath you are entirely sensible," chides Erna. "All this pretending to be unreliable!"

"You do not do Hans justice, Erna," interjects Olga. "He is not . . . humdrum and practical, like other people."

"There—you see? It *is* romantic." Hans is quite pleased.

"When Olga cools down she will probably find it very boring, having to run around picking up things after you—minding your money—"

"I will never cool down, Erna! Not about Hans!"

Erna has gone for the fare money and Hans has turned eagerly to Olga. He is dependable, he is assuring her fervently; and he can be depended on to love her the rest of his life—

OLGA—It does not matter whether you love me or not—because I shall always love you—that is what is so wonderful—the feeling that I have you to love. . . . It is not fair! I do not deserve it.

HANS (*kissing her hand*)—Olga! Don't say that! You make me feel foolish. I am the one who is grateful. I'm what Erna calls a moonstruck moron only for Erna's benefit. She *likes* me to be helpless and unreliable so she can order me around and do things for me. But . . . I know how she feels because I want to do things for *you* now. I want to take care of you and make a wonderful life for you—

OLGA—Because I am helpless?

HANS (*pulling* OLGA *to him*)—I know you are not— But I like to think that you would be—without me.

OLGA—I would, Hans. I will be nothing without you.

HANS—And how did you get along before we met?

OLGA (*taking his face in her hands*)—I was not even alive before we met. I did not know it, but I was not even alive! (*Kissing him. There is a pause.*) It is too long to wait—three and a half months—Christmas will *never* come this year.

HANS (*laughing*)—But it *will*, Olga.

OLGA—You are coming to *Warsaw?* You promise?

HANS (*rising*)—Nothing could keep me away. We'll go to Warsaw—you and Erna and I—then you will stop with us for two or three days in Berlin on the way back to school. We will have a lot of time together at Christmas.

OLGA (*stepping back one step*)—Hans—I want to ask you something foolish. . . . You know when you came in and stood there in the doorway?

HANS—Yes. . . .

OLGA—Do it again—stand there again, just like you were. Erna will come back and she'll want to say good-by . . . and I want to remember you like that—standing in the light.

HANS—I love you, Olga—

She has gone to the dining hall door and stands there, looking back at Hans. For a moment she stands, quietly, and then backs slowly through the door, still staring at him as she goes.

Erna has come with the money. Let him be careful not to lose it on the way to the train. Hans is not listening. There is something he wants to tell Erna. Something is happening. He doesn't know what. But he has had a telegram. Erna must promise him to take care of Olga; always to be her friend; no matter what happens. That she must promise.

"All right—I promise!" agrees Erna, a little impatiently. "But it's so silly—we're friends now and always will be. Olga loves you and some day she and I will be sisters."

"I'm not sure, Erna. . . . I'm not sure."

"What do you mean? Hans!!"

"Whatever happens—*whatever* happens—you're sticking to Olga. Maybe it will come out finally—maybe it will be all right —but I don't see how it can."

"You're just being melodramatic—like when you were a boy—"

"All right—I'm being melodramatic. But remember what I said— You've already promised—that's good enough for me."

"I don't like your going like this—Hans—you've always told me everything—please don't—"

The whistle of the train in the distance can be heard. The next minute Hans has grabbed up his knapsack and started running down the hill. For a long moment Erna stands looking after him, still puzzled by what he has said. . . .

Miss Linder is back. Olga had passed her in the dining hall. She hopes Olga is not going to be unhappy. And what is it that is worrying Erna?

". . . He said something just now, Miss Linder— He said I 'was to take care of Olga.' He said something was happening—

what can it be—he was so serious."

Now there is a commotion outside the door. Gustave, the gardener, is back, waving his bouquet. Margarethe, the cook, takes her position with him in a welcoming line. Olga and Erna have dashed off to meet the arrivals. For a moment there is a wild babble of girlish voices. Then Mrs. Hunter appears. "She is smartly dressed for travel, is about forty, good-looking and gentle." Margarethe curtsies; Gustave advances smiling to proffer his bouquet. It is all in the tradition of the school and pleasing to Mrs. Hunter, as it had been pleasing for years to her predecessor. Remembering the homecomings is one of the things that has always made Mrs. Hunter glad to get back. . . .

Bingo Hill is the first of the girls to come bursting in. She is an American, "smart, full of energy and vitality," and given to drawling one word in a sentence in exaggerated fashion. At the moment Bingo is excited about the glimpse she caught of Erna's brother running for the train. "My dear, he's godlike," she assures Mrs. Hunter. "I could *kill* myself. He's the most beguiling-looking human being I ever laid eyes on!"

Felice Renoir has also arrived, and with a hug for Erna. Felice is petite and French and bubbling with an account of the recipes she has brought Margarethe from Italy. Also baby garlic for her sauces.

Sally Jackson, also American, and definitely from the South, is too concerned about the state of her hair, after a washing in Italy and a long train ride, to pay much attention to the others. Which reminds Mrs. Hunter that the girls have but twenty minutes to get ready for lunch, if they want to change.

Being more interested in their accumulated mail than in a change they decide to wait for François, the postman. Then Marion Curwood arrives. Marion is English and "very tweedy, even though it's summer weather."

Marion has just received a package from the carriage which is to figure in the ceremonies. It is a hand-illumined scroll the travelers have brought for Erna announcing to the world that she is first in her class—"Prima in Schola—Prima in cordibus nostris—Prima in Omnibus"—Madame Hunter had paid for the frame. Erna is a little embarrassed, but plainly moved.

And now François, the aging postman, wearing a uniform a little too large for him, has arrived with the mail and the one English sentence he has been studying hard to learn: "It is with pleasure that one carries the post to the young ladies of the school of Madame." He bows formally to Madame, and to the young ladies, and goes on his way.

There is a concentrated but orderly rush for the mail, with accompanying comment. Bingo is so bored because her one letter is from the Guaranty Trust. She will certainly be glad when she stops being a ward. Sally is losing no time in ripping open one of her letters, which brings a charge from Olga that she is peeking. "You know you ought to wait until tonight," says Olga.

"Oh, this isn't night time mail," insists Sally. "It's not a love one or a family one or anything interesting like that—it's just an old bill. Of course, if you all want me to read my bills aloud to you, I'd be mighty glad to oblige. They're real fancy reading!"

Margarethe has come to sound another warning about lunch and there is a general movement toward the stairs. Out of a babble of inconsequential comments Bingo's voice can be heard declaring a growing resentment of Erna—

"Honestly, Erna, I'm sick and tired of the wonder of you. Best scholar, best tennis, best Latin, and now you've got the best brother!"

"You are the best flatterer."

A moment later Mrs. Hunter and Miss Linder find themselves alone for the first time. They are both happy to be back. A change is good for one but to be back is better.

"We're nothing but a pair of escapists," Mrs. Hunter is saying.

MISS LINDER—The way things go in the world now, everyone with any sense wants to get away from it.

MRS. HUNTER—It's because we're safe here. Until I came back here to stay I always had to fight that feeling that nothing good could really last. . . . Running away from school to marry. . . . Gerald, so proud and happy when he went off to the Argonne. . . . Dead in two weeks. . . . Then that senseless postwar thing. . . . Now, it's starting again! Gretchen, is this another Munich—or is it the real beginning? If it is real, think what it's going to mean to these girls.

MISS LINDER—I don't think there is any question of its being real, Caroline.

MRS. HUNTER—Somehow we've got to keep them away from all that—keep them safe.

MISS LINDER—We'll do it, Caroline. We can try anyway.

MRS. HUNTER—Yes, we can try.

The curtain falls.

In the girls' dormitory at Mrs. Hunter's school that night

Felice, Sally, Marion, Erna, Olga and Bingo are getting settled for the letter reading ceremony that has long been the group's custom. Their six beds are arranged along the back wall, with night tables and lighted lamps between them. Over Erna's bed is the testimonial given her by the girls that afternoon. The girls are in their night clothes or negligees, generally relaxed and comfortable. For a few days they are to have the school to themselves. Then Miss Hartzwig will be back with the junior students.

"Dinner was simply elegant tonight, without all those brats throwing rolls at each other," announces Bingo.

It is nearly 10 o'clock and time for the letters. By general consent it is agreed only those that arrived in the last mail will be read. There isn't time for the accumulations, though Marion thinks it might be nice if everyone would make a précis of the back letters, so they all could keep everything straight—like the notes they put at the top of serials—"The story so far—"

Felice is the first to read. Her letter is from her father. The girls had hoped it would be from Jean Jacques—but it isn't. Felice is reading—

" 'My darling—I am writing you only so that there will be a letter waiting when you return from your journey. There is very little news. Everything is politics, politics, politics and I am afraid I am not very interested in these things. We are most happy and grateful because your brother finishes his military service in three weeks and will be at home again. Your mother is well and busy. We send our love—' "

Felice is sorry she cannot translate better, but that is the best she can do. Sally, who is next, has one from that awful Walker Lee boy that should pin their ears back. Walker Lee is the boy Sally had sent the ring back to. "He had a nerve, anyway, sending me an ol' ring in the mail! Even if it *was* insured and customs paid. Imagine! . . . Just listen: 'My dream girl that was!!!' Isn't that simply sickening! 'I guess these things have to happen to a man.' Man! He's nineteen and a half. 'You have broken my heart, but you will always be enshrined in it. I am glad that you sent the ring back, because Dad didn't know that I had charged it to him and I can return it without getting into any trouble. I will write you soon. My love always—' Isn't that romantic! Isn't that touching and gallant! He'll write me soon!! What a break for a girl!"

Felice is sympathetic. She thinks Walker was quite practical about his father. Bingo hasn't any sympathy to offer. After all, Sally brought it on herself. She knew Walker was a goon. Now, how about Marion?

There is a general shifting of positions to get nearer Marion, who is clearing her throat and taking a swallow of water before she begins the one from "His Nibs." That's Bingo's classification. His name is really Eric. Reads Marion—

" 'My Darling—It's been stifling here, and I ought to have gone to Scotland a week ago, but I've been having a most interesting time of it with an American. Fellow named Johnstone, who was with the MacMullan expedition. We've combed the British Museum from top to bottom but cannot find any justification for Throgood's conclusions . . .' "

"What on earth is he talking about?" Sally wants to know.

"I don't know. Isn't it sweet of him to assume that I do? I suppose it's archeology."

"Anthropology," prompts Erna, and Marion makes a face at her for being superior.

" 'I can't think why you wanted to go off to Italy of all places. I worried a good bit because they said on the wireless that mobs were smashing windows in the Embassy in Rome. Hope you weren't hurt. Do write and let me know how everything was. It is too bad that Italy has to go to pot this way—' There's nothing else but love and all that. . . .' "

Sally likes the love parts, but Bingo doesn't care much for the way the Marquess writes them. And now it is discovered that Erna has forgotten Merriweather and must find her at once. Merriweather is important to Erna because she is a rag doll she has been sleeping with ever since she was seven. Silly, Sally calls it. Marion thinks it sweet, but it interrupts her postscript—to which she returns—

" 'Chamberlain has managed to get an eight weeks' recess for the House of Commons, so the situation can't possibly be really serious, and thank heaven for that, as I hate to think of you there in the middle of things.' "

"Middle of things!" interrupts Bingo. "We couldn't be farther away if we were in Tibet."

" 'If there has to be a war I expect it will be between Russia and Germany over the Northern situation—' What on earth *is* the Northern situation? . . ."

Erna is back with Merriweather, taking Sally's chiding in good spirit. "I know it's silly—but it's a habit. I've had her in my bed so long that I can't go to sleep without her, I honestly can't."

"It's probably a substitution fetish or something," decides

Sally. "You imagine that Merriweather's somebody else—some handsome man—"

"Oh, shut up, Sally—the way you talk!" This from Bingo.

"I'll bet I'm right."

"Nonsense—it's disgusting." It's Marion who settles that.

Erna's turn is next, but Bingo has waited as long as she can to read her guardians' report and proceeds with that. This one is from one of the bank's lawyers relating that a crooked trustee had been caught up with and convicted; that what was returned to the estate was traded in and a thousand shares of American Can bought to replace it, and that another trustee had been appointed to replace the guilty one.

Now something that Bingo has said about Erna's handsome brother, brings Olga quickly into the conversation and before she knows it she is defending and explaining her interest in Hans, both to the surprise and the amusement of the others. Of course they are all wrong, Olga protests; a girl doesn't fall in love in just one afternoon; they're just jumping to conclusions.

Erna is reminded of the time Hans thought of himself as a Greek God. "He made up the most wonderful stories about himself—except that they were all just very mixed up versions of myths and the Bible and Shakespeare and everything like that. Only, whatever the story was, he was always the hero. His favorite one of all was Icarus. What he did to *that* story!"

"Icarus Schmidt," it appears, having been presented with a wonderful pair of wings by his father, was troubled because of a war then raging between his country and certain enemies whom Icarus secretly liked very much. When the Lord Chamberlain suggested that Icarus gather together many spears and fly with them high in the air over the country of the enemy and drop them on the enemy Icarus would have liked to protest but did not dare.

So Icarus told the Lord Chamberlain to have many spears made and when they were ready he lashed on his wings, took the spears and flew high over the country of the enemy. He could hear the cheers of his people growing fainter and fainter as he flew. A lookout on a hill saw Icarus coming and sent a warning to his people, who promptly gathered in the great public square—

" 'When he looked down and saw these people that he loved, he knew that he could not kill them, nor could he betray his own people,' " relates Erna. " 'So he took the spears and put their points against his body, and flew swifter than he had ever flown before, straight down against the rocks of the hill. The spears were driven through him.' "

"Oh, no!" protests Olga, with a shudder. Erna goes on—

" 'When the people saw that he was dead, and when they realized what he had done, they carried word to the country of Icarus and made peace with his people and built a great shrine to his memory. . . .' "

It is a very beautiful story, Marion thinks, but to Felice, it's very sad. Sally has an idea that she would like to fly, seeing Robert Montgomery is in Monte Carlo.

Erna would postpone reading her letter if she could, but the girls won't let her off. It is from her mother, says Erna, who is very sorry not to have had her daughter home for the holidays, but hopes she had a good time with—

"It's really not interesting, really it isn't," protests Erna. "Just about relatives and things—'Your Uncle Ernst has gone away for an extended trip'—that's the one who's the priest—it's all full of things like that—"

BINGO—We want to hear the part about Hans—that's what we want to hear, isn't it, Olga?

ERNA—It just says she hopes I had a nice visit with him. (*She is obviously covering up more than the reference to the girls' walking trip.*) "At last things here look full of hope—the country will certainly have a fine future under our great leader, and I expect all of your father's investments will improve under the new order of things—" It doesn't sound like her writing, somehow—

MARION (*half rising*)—Oh, everyone in your country talks like that now— All those military maneuvers and things— She's probably just caught the spirit of the times.

ERNA—But she's so impractical and—oh, well— "When Hans gets back it will be wonderful to have first-hand news of you. . . ." That's all.

BINGO—As soon as you're asleep I'm going to snitch that thing and find out what she *really* said. There's more in this than meets the eye—you've been up to something about Hans, and you can't tell me different.

MARION—Oh, Bingo, not now. Hurry up, Olga—you're the last.

OLGA (*getting letter*)—This is from my father.

MARION—Oh, good.

OLGA—"You ought to be at home now—Warsaw is so beautiful these summer evenings and I miss you when I take my walk.

When you return for Christmas we have a great surprise for you, but I am so excited that I must spoil it by telling you now. The house has been entirely done over—it was your mother's idea, and at first I did not approve at all, but now that it is done, I am the most enthusiastic of the whole family. Your cousin Antonia comes down next week from Danzig to live with us, as things are so unsettled there. That will please you, I know, as you've always been such friends. This is the first year in so long that everyone in the family seems to be doing well, and to be content and prosperous. I take a lot of satisfaction in this. By all means bring as many friends as you like to stay for the holidays."

SALLY—I haven't a thing to wear.

OLGA—"We will open up the house in the country and have a real old-fashioned Christmas. All my love. . . ."

BINGO—He's a darling. Well, that's all of them. Good night.

Bingo has snapped off her light. Marion follows. Felice puts out her light, then kneels for her prayers. Sally follows Felice, but Sally's prayers are short and snappy and she is back in bed with a jump. Erna, seeing that all the lights are out except Olga's, passes Olga the letter, which Olga reads with glowing eyes and then with puzzled frowns at those parts that trouble her. She has given the letter back to Erna now, and taken up her diary. "I'm so happy, Erna—so happy," she whispers.

ERNA—It's lovely, isn't it?

OLGA—I have so much to catch up—so much to say. . . . "Icarus Schmidt." (*She smiles.*) I wish I had a picture of him.

ERNA—I'll get you one—I have some in my trunk downstairs.

OLGA—*Now, Erna, now!*

ERNA—Of course not. I'd wake up the whole house. Tomorrow.

OLGA—You promise!

ERNA (*lies down*)—Yes.

OLGA—I want to write down everything—how happy I am—how wonderful it is. (*Thumbing diary.*) What's the date, Erna?

ERNA (*sleepily*)—What?

OLGA—The date!

ERNA—The thirty-first of August.

OLGA (*as she hunts for the right page*)—August 31, 1939.
The curtain falls.

ACT II

It is ten days later, mid-morning of a sunny day. Mrs. Hunter is standing at the table in the main hall sorting unopened letters into separate piles and putting rubber bands around them. These are letters that have come for those girls who are not returning to the school. They have to be returned—to England, France, Germany, the United States, Canada, South America—and there is a question whether they will get through.

Gretchen Linder is back from the village. The girls are still in the study hall. Mrs. Hunter had tried to manage a history class, but had had to give up. The girls all want to stay on, Mrs. Hunter reports, and if Madame Rameau had managed to keep the school open all through the First World War Mrs. Hunter doesn't see why it can't be done again—

"Of course Olga can't go now, and I don't think Erna wants to—she mustn't," Miss Linder reminds her. "Bingo has no family—I do not know about her—but the others—"

"I told them I would speak to them when the study hour was over. I wanted a chance to talk to you first."

Gustave has come to suggest that, things being as they are, he would like to take out all the flowers and put in things to eat, as he had done in the other war. He would like to build a hothouse, too, next to the tool shed. He is told he can do whatever he thinks best.

"Twenty girls aren't coming back. Do you realize how much money that means?" Mrs. Hunter is saying, after Gustave has left. "My chemistry teacher gone—the coachman called up—three-fourths of my pupils not coming back—and yet, you know, I have a stubborn, perverse determination to keep going."

MISS LINDER—If the school stayed open during the last war there is no reason it can't stay open now. Somehow I don't feel very much of a threat to Switzerland.

MRS. HUNTER—You know why that is, don't you? They've all got to have a bank—a clearing house—win or lose. Switzerland serves that purpose. No ordinary rules apply any more. We may be bombed tomorrow—but somehow I don't think that very probable as long as Germany has to maintain any kind of exchange with other countries.

MISS LINDER—Doesn't the fact that this is an American School give you some sort of immunity?

MRS. HUNTER—There is no such thing as immunity these

days. However, we have got a chance—(*Crosses to center doors.*)—a slim chance. You know what this place means to me—(*Crosses to* Miss Linder.)—to both of us. It's an island—a refuge. I want to keep it that way.

Miss Linder—You're such an idealist, Caroline!

Mrs. Hunter—Idealist! I've always had a sort of secret contempt for people who died for lost causes! I thought they simply weren't strong enough to fact facts. . . . Now *I* want to fight for a lost cause. Only it's not going to *be* lost!

Miss Linder—But if the girls do stay—think of the complications, think of the trouble there's bound to be.

Mrs. Hunter (*turning to face* Miss Linder)—I'm going to keep that away from here!

Miss Linder—You can't stop them from knowing what's going on in the world, you can't keep them shut up as if they were in jail. You can't stop their letters from home!

Mrs. Hunter—I wish I dared to.

Olga has come from the study-hall to ask if she may go to her room. She cannot make herself study. "Her face is white and stricken," and Mrs. Hunter is worried. Try as she will she has not been able to comfort Olga. There is no news coming through, except the German side. The radio Mrs. Hunter has had taken out. She had come upon Felice and Marion and Erna listening to a news broadcast the night before—

"I couldn't hear what it said—it was turned so low—just that it was news. But I saw one look, one look that Felice gave Erna. After all if I can't control six schoolgirls, it rather looks like I'm in the wrong business, doesn't it?"

Miss Hartzwig will not be coming back, naturally—with her father an officer and her brother in the Gestapo. And Margarethe has a note from Hilda—she'll be at her old job of munitions making. So far as the work is concerned, Margarethe is sure she and Gustave can manage. They can close the dining hall and have their meals there, in the main hall. . . .

Miss Linder will stay on. Already she has been to the village to see about changing her nationality. But there again is a problem—

"Gretchen, if you do change your nationality, I mean, well, suppose Germany wins?" Mrs. Hunter is worried.

"Germany is not going to win. But even if she does—I don't understand my country, Caroline."

"I was only thinking—Margarethe was talking to someone in

the village yesterday. She came back and told me a horrible story. The Germans are supposed to be 'organizing' their nationals here getting ready in case they decide to invade. If that happens—and if you've tried to change your citizenship—"

"I'm *going* to change my citizenship."

"But Margarethe said they have already taken some of their own countrymen—people who wouldn't support the third Reich. They get them across the border and then they shoot them."

"Then I shall be careful about going too near the border."

"But they have men working for them everywhere, Gretchen—men you wouldn't suspect—"

"Please, Caroline."

"François will be here pretty soon. We'll wait and see if there are any new developments with this morning's mail. Please tell the girls I want to speak to them after François's gone."

The girls are called from the study hall. Marion and Felice are putting their books on the table when Erna comes in. "She seems as if she were a young girl at her first party, not quite sure of herself." She looks a little anxiously up the stairs, then turns and goes out the door.

"What are we going to do about her and Olga?" Marion is worried.

"But what is there to do?" Felice is firm.

MARION—It is going to be—well, so awful. I catch myself feeling *oddly* about Erna.

FELICE—Why not?

MARION—Why not! Oh, Felice—

FELICE—There's a war going on—one must expect these things.

MARION (*rising*)—She hasn't anything to do with that—she doesn't even understand what the war is about. But she seems to *believe* in those letters she reads!

FELICE (*coldly*)—Erna is our enemy.

MARION—Felice! That's not true!

FELICE—Of course it's true. The French are supposed to be Latin—the romance languages. The English are cold—Nordic—Anglo-Saxon, whatever you like. And yet they are the dreamers and we are the realists.

MARION—Oh, Felice. . . .

FELICE—You think that just because it seems nicer to have everyone love one another, then that is the way it shall be—that's the way it must be.

MARION—Please don't talk like that, Felice. You don't really mean it—you *know* you don't.

FELICE—I mean a great deal more than I have said! You will see. . . .

With a pleasant "Bon jour, Mademoiselle, voici la poste," François puts the mail on the table. The girls gather round, but without the excitement of other days. Erna, coming back from the yard, quietly takes her own letter and one for Olga, who has come down the stairs. She hands Olga's letter to her and there is an exchange of rather pathetic smiles.

It is easy to guess the contents of the letters from the expressions on the girls' faces. "Felice and Marion's faces are hard and their eyes glow with almost a fanatic hatred, and Marion looks at Felice and suddenly realizes what she meant when she said that Erna was their natural enemy."

The coming of Mrs. Hunter helps to break the tension and soon the girls are settled comfortably to hear her decision.

"I am going to keep the school open," Mrs. Hunter begins. "Naturally I'd like to find out how many of you want to stay here, and how your people feel."

MARION—Of course we want to stay.

MRS. HUNTER—It isn't exactly a question of what we want to do, it's what we can do. What about you, Marion?

MARION—My people simply can't make up their minds, Madame. I put it straight to my father—I asked him if I'd be any good at home. He wrote back and said he'd rather have me stay here until they knew just how things were going to be. Then the very next day I had a letter from Mother saying she thought I ought to come home—

MRS. HUNTER—What do you *want* to do?

MARION—Stay here—of course!

MRS. HUNTER—Felice?

FELICE—Mama and Papa both think it is better for me here. They say that if there is any quick necessity it will be very simple for me to get home. It is not very brave of me, Madame, but—I think it is safer here.

MRS. HUNTER—Sally?

SALLY—I want to stay here, of course—we all want to stay here. Mother says she sent me an air mail last week, maybe it will come this afternoon or tomorrow.

MRS. HUNTER—Erna?

ERNA (*with an effort*)—This is like home to all of us, Madame. Of course I want to stay here, if I may.

BINGO—Madame, I think you ought to tell us what you honestly would like. I want to stay and I don't really see how that old Guaranty Trust can make me come home if I don't want to, but you've got to be considered. Everybody seems to be walking out on you—won't it be pretty difficult.

MRS. HUNTER—If we all work together, it shouldn't be difficult at all. Madame Rameau kept the school open all through the last war, but I know what it means, I was here then. I want to be perfectly frank with you. Later on it may be hard to get provisions—things may not be as comfortable as they have been. I honestly don't think that Switzerland is in any danger. You're all going through the part of your schooling that is most important. To me it is a sort of challenge—a challenge in more ways than one. Now that you all want to stay we have got a chance to demonstrate real practical democracy right here. I'm going to ask you to either cable or send express letters to your people. In a few days' time, we ought to have answers from all of them.

MARION—We're all grateful to you, Madame. We all love and respect you— Oh, blast it! I can't make a speech, but you know what I mean.

SALLY—Madame, I'm going to stay here no matter what anybody says! I'm not going home when things are happening in Europe! If worse comes to worse I'll go to Paris and be an ambulance driver.

MRS. HUNTER (*smiling*)—I think you're just a little young for that, Sally.

MARION—That's the trouble.

MRS. HUNTER—Well, it's decided then—we *do* stay open.

BINGO—Come hell or high water!

At Mrs. Hunter's suggestion the girls have piled out to the stables to help Gustave. They will hitch up the old nags and go careening through the village collecting old windows with which to build the hot house, if Bingo has her way.

Erna and Olga have made their excuses and stayed behind. They want to talk with Madame Hunter. Olga, especially, is grateful because the school is going on. The others do have some place to go. She has none. But she is worried about making it unpleasant for the others—

". . . It's just that I'm glad there will be classes and things to do— Going through ordinary motions seems to help somehow. But what I really wanted to say was this—the other girls are sympathetic—they feel sorry for me because of what is happening—I don't want them to feel any less friendly toward Erna because of that."

"I don't think they'll do that, Olga."

"I just thought—"

"You mustn't worry, Olga. We're all friends—they know that you and I aren't going to let things make any difference."

Margarethe has called Mrs. Hunter away to the phone. Between Erna and Olga there is a renewal of their understanding sympathy. Erna can understand how Olga feels about being self-conscious and unhappy when she is with the others. Even now Olga does not want to wait until Mrs. Hunter comes back—

"I know— You have to be by yourself," says Erna, putting her arms around Olga and hugging her fondly. "Go on, Olga. I'll make some excuse."

"Whatever happens, Erna, we will be friends, always. And not just because of Hans—just because I love him—"

"That's the first time you have mentioned his name. I've been terribly worried about how you must feel because of him."

"But I love him, Erna. You know that. He cannot help it— what Germany's doing, I mean. I would understand even if he was called up, even if he had to go and fight against my own country—I *know* I would understand."

Olga has turned and started up the stairs. Suddenly Erna is conscious of the letter in her own hand. Her arm drops. Olga has turned. "Talking to you helps so much, Erna," she says, smiling a trustful, almost happy smile. Erna somehow manages to smile back. She is staring again at the letter in her hand, "an expression of complete, hopeless despair on her face," when Mrs. Hunter returns. Immediately their talk turns to Olga, and what it may be possible to do to help her. And to Erna's problem, too.

"Madame! When Olga said, a little while ago, that she didn't want the other girls to feel unfriendly toward me—she was only hinting at the truth. She doesn't begin to realize how they really feel about me— Felice and Marion, anyway."

"What do you mean, Erna?"

ERNA—The letters, Madame. Every time I hear François ring the bell now I feel guilty—and frightened.

MRS. HUNTER—Erna!

ERNA—Olga had a letter just now—she was afraid to open it. I know how she feels—it is awful. Only I have been a fool about *my* letters. They are making trouble, Madame.

MRS. HUNTER—What have they said? Do you mean there has been an actual row about them?

ERNA—No, Madame—but I hear from no one but my mother now— She talks of nothing but the war and how wonderful things are going to be for Germany—and of course that makes a difference.

MRS. HUNTER (*putting arm around* ERNA)—Erna—I knew about Felice. I knew that she was feeling—well—patriotic. I think you'll have to stop reading the letters—that all of you will have to stop.

ERNA—It would help.

MRS. HUNTER—I'll speak to the others.

ERNA—No—Madame. They would say that I had been coming to you and complaining.

MRS. HUNTER—Then you suggest it to them, Erna. If it came directly from you it would make everything easier.

ERNA—Maybe it would be better if they don't even know about my letters—if they did not see them coming.

MRS. HUNTER—How could you keep them from knowing?

ERNA—Margarethe could get them from François—he could leave them at her cottage and she could give them to me later.

MRS. HUNTER (*pause*)—If it will make you feel any better about it we can certainly do that.

ERNA—Thank you, Madame. You see, I don't know what to feel about my country. If it is true what they said on the radio—if Germany is really doing those horrible things—I would have to hate my own people. I have to try to believe my mother . . . but I did not mean to make the girls angry.

MRS. HUNTER—Erna—young people can be cruel. They don't mean it. But you can't fight it because you know it isn't deliberate. You just have to stand it. I can help you do that, Erna—because I know in a few days it will be gone.

ERNA—I don't think so, Madame, I think I should even move out of the dormitory, to one of the junior class bedrooms.

MRS. HUNTER—No, Erna! You can't do that. You mustn't divide the school into factions—Olga would certainly be on your side—so would Sally and Bingo. There mustn't be any question of taking sides.

ERNA—I did not think of that—it was foolish of me.

MRS. HUNTER—Erna—I want to see if it isn't possible to live

through whatever comes without its touching you girls. I know it can be done—I know it. And you've got to help me more than any of the others. It's going to take a lot of courage—but I can depend on you.

ERNA (*looking at her letter her attitude changes*)—No. It is a temptation to show you this—to cry on your shoulder about it—but that would only make things worse—*more* complicated.

MRS. HUNTER—But that's what I'm here for, Erna—to take care of complications. What is it? Please tell me—

ERNA—No, Madame. I think I can do this by myself. You said I was to help you.

She is smiling at Mrs. Hunter as she starts up the stairs. The curtain falls.

Later, in the dormitory, Felice, Marion and Sally are excitedly searching around Erna's bed. The other girls are still in the dressing room. The search is for Erna's letter. Sally is sure Erna did not have it on her when she undressed. It was not in her locker downstairs. Marion had looked there.

The girls have fixed up a substitute letter which they hope to slip into the envelope of Erna's letter. It is a kind of comic valentine substitute, Marion explains, to make Erna see how stupid her letters have really been. Sally is sure it's going to be a lot of fun.

Felice has slipped her hand beneath Erna's mattress and come upon the letter just as Bingo's voice heralds the return of the others. The searching three have hopped quickly into their beds and assumed casual, even nonchalant, attitudes as quickly as possible. Felice shoves the discovered letter under her pillow.

"I don't think you belles are making it any easier," Bingo mutters, as she crosses to her bed ahead of Olga and Erna. Erna is the last to appear. She is carrying the doll, Merriweather, with her.

There is an uncomfortable, watchful waiting, as the preparations incident to the letter reading are concluded. Sally works ostentatiously at her night makeup. She is determined to keep her hand in. There might be a fire. But she gives up finally, under a barrage of protests from Bingo and Marion.

When they are all ready, and the letters are called for, Erna makes her suggestion—that they do not go on with the letter reading. "It's time for us to begin growing up, don't you think?

This letter business seems rather childish to me."

The cries of protest are immediate and very strong. Sally thinks Erna needn't get so superior about it. Felice is convinced the letters are more interesting now than they ever have been, since they now reveal both sides of a question. Marion is sure all the rest want to go ahead.

Only Bingo can understand how Erna feels. Olga is inclined to be neutral, but she finds that reading the letters somehow makes the unhappiness easier to bear.

"There!" cries Felice, triumphantly. "You see? It is five against one—or four against two, if Bingo chooses to be on your side. Anyway—the vote is carried. I will start. . . ."

"Wait a minute!" Erna has risen. "There's one thing, it may be no good, but I'd like to try it. We've got to stay here together for some time. We don't *have* to—but apparently we're going to. Don't you think it would make it easier for us to get along together, if we're going on with the letters, if we cut out the parts that might start arguments—the parts where people say things about other countries?"

"But that's what is interesting, Erna—that's what makes it exciting," insists Felice.

"You might try it once—I think it's a hell of a good idea, myself," says Bingo. And when Marion suggests that evidently what is going on in the world is of no interest to her, Bingo adds: "It means a great deal to me—but friendship means more. . . . I think it would be a good idea—to cut out the bitter parts. Won't you try it anyway?"

"There is not much left when the bitter parts are gone—but we will start," protests Felice. She has risen and is sitting at the foot of her bed as she begins—" 'My dearest—"

"That's Jean Jacques, isn't it?" chirps Sally.

"Yes. But— Do not get your hopes up, Sally. This is not one of his *beautiful* letters—"

" 'My dearest—because of the censorship I do not know how much of this letter will get through to you— Here one thinks that this war which is not a war will not last for long. Even though they say that the west wall is impregnable, our Maginot is even stronger and it will soon be stalemate. The enemy have sent a few planes over but there have been no bombs dropped!' Now we come to a few choice phrases that Bingo is too sensitive to hear—'The enthusiasm for Gamelin is formidable, and everyone is in high spirits about our eventual success. I cannot warn you strongly enough about—' "

"About what, Felice?"

"I did not intend to read that—I had forgotten what it says here."

"Oh, go on—it sounds exciting!"

"No. It is not important."

"Is it against Germany?"

"Sally!" Bingo is disgusted.

"It is quite interesting, but it is bitter," says Felice, looking at Erna— "About methods of spreading propaganda and acquiring information— No, I shall not read it."

" 'Your brother has been called back to the service and your mother and father are extremely proud. I am so glad that you have decided to stay there until we have once and for all settled the question of that . . .' Ah, more bitterness! Then he goes into a rather sweet love passage, which, for once, I shall keep to myself. That is all."

Felice has gone back to bed. "You're just being mean," pouts Sally.

"No. I want to keep it to myself. Go on with yours, Sally."

Sally's letter is long and earnest, is from her mother, and is not too clear about anything except that she thinks Sally should stay where she is, however her cables may read. Mrs. Jackson is compelled to submit the cables to Sally's father, and it is Father's idea that Sally should come home.

" 'Let me know if there is anything you need, and don't write your father what I said, as he thinks I agree with him about your coming home. Lots of love—' "

"She's a dream girl—that's what she is," ventures Bingo.

"It's only on paper that she's such an idiot. She really makes sense when you talk to her."

"I'd hate to think she's any different—I love her the way she is on paper."

Marion is next. "Mine are all dull ones—depressing beyond words," she sighs. "They say things like—

" 'This time there are no flags flying—no bands playing. Everything is quiet and calm—in a frightening, sinister way. It is like a horrible inevitable acceptance of doom.' Things like that—definitely not entertaining reading. Let's hear Erna's— hers are so triumphant—they give us all a lift!"

Erna has no letter to read. The letter they saw her get she destroyed. Then what about the letter Felice found? Of course they have it. And they mean to make Erna read it. But Erna does not intend to read any letters, ever again.

Bingo thinks they are stupid trying to make trouble, but Felice, Marion and Sally are not to be put off. Erna pleads with them not to quarrel with Bingo. She knows that it is she they want to fight—and she will not fight—

"You and your damned nobility," sneers Marion, bursting with anger. "You're so above all of it, aren't you? So bloody superior and smug—just because you think your country's going to win. I suppose you think you can *afford* to be big-hearted and gracious about it all!"

"I don't know what to say—I don't know what to do—" Erna has turned to face Olga.

"That tone of the martyr! That is what I cannot face any longer," shouts Felice, holding out Erna's letter. "See if you can be big-hearted and gracious about this—" She has opened the letter and begins to read—

" 'My dearest child—Things are going so well for our armies. In just a few short days so much has been done. The excitement here is beyond all belief—' Of course I cannot get all the delicate shadings in—my German is rather rusty, thank God!"

Erna has jumped up from her bed. "Give me my letter!" she cries. "You do not know what's in it. Please do not read it! I can't stand it!"

"You cannot stand it," shouts Marion, grabbing Erna and holding her. "What of us? Do you think we like it? Do you think we want to pretend that nothing's happened? Isn't it better to face it, in the open?"

Olga, too, would help, but Felice holds her off and goes on triumphantly with her reading—

" 'The censorship makes it hard to know what to say but you must know by now that WARSAW is as good as captured."

"Don't read it—for the love of God don't read it!"

" 'Today we have had word that Hans was there in the first bombing flight over the city, and for his bravery he has been given the Iron Cross—first class . . .' "

Felice has been spacing each word, savagely and viciously. Now she pauses. "Icarus—the great hero," she sneers. "He's a *murderer!*"

Again Erna has tried to break from Marion and reach Felice to tear the letter away from her, but Marion is the stronger. Suddenly Bingo's voice pierces the air and brings them all up with a start—

"Stop it! God damn it, stop it! Give Erna that letter!"

Marion has released Erna and Erna has taken her letter. She

turns pathetically to Olga, realizing what must be going through her mind. Suddenly they have all turned toward Olga, who has taken her own letter from the night table and is opening it. Now she starts to read it in a cold, mechanical voice—

" 'My cousin: I have to tell you that your mother and father are dead. They were killed when your house was completely destroyed by an explosion of a bomb dropped from a German plane. I have tried to think of a way to break this news to you —but there is no other way but to tell the truth. The horrible speed of everything that has happened. There was no place to go, no way to escape—the speed was unreal and paralyzing. I am going to try and reach Bucharest. Perhaps some day I will see you— Perhaps I can try to make up to you for the wonderful kindness you and your mother and father have always shown me. My love—Antonia."

There is an appalling silence. Erna is the first to move. She goes to Olga, who turns her head away. Slowly Erna goes back to her own bed and takes up her bathrobe. The doll Merriweather falls to the floor. Without noticing, Erna slowly takes her traveling clock from the table, walks to the door and goes out.

For a moment the others stare after her. Olga starts as though to follow Erna. She sees the doll on the floor and picks it up. She would take Merriweather with her. Suddenly she stops and is staring at the wall—

"No . . . !" she cries, as the doll falls to the floor. "No . . . !" She has gone back to the foot of Erna's bed as the curtain falls.

ACT III

Three days later, in the Main Hall, Mrs. Hunter, Miss Linder, Felice, Marion, Sally and Bingo are finishing lunch. There is an empty chair next to that of Mrs. Hunter. The day is cloudy. Gustave is serving and Margarethe has just walked through the room and upstairs.

Mrs. Hunter has evidently been lecturing her charges on their failure to restore the friendliness that has previously existed between them. This is the seventh meal that Erna has missed, and Mrs. Hunter is determined that it shall be the last. She has tried to do what she could. She has thought that if she could bring Erna and Olga together the rest of them would make it up, but so far this has not been possible.

Felice would defend the others by insisting that it is all Bingo's fault, because she told Mrs. Hunter, but Mrs. Hunter refuses to accept that excuse. After all neither she nor Miss Linder is blind. They have known that Bingo was taking Erna's side and was still friendly with her—

BINGO—I'm friendly with her, all right, Madame. I love Erna. But I don't blame the others for being sore at me—the other night she was the under-dog and I was just standing up for her—showing off, I guess.

MRS. HUNTER—I thought I could keep the war away from here—I thought we could ignore it—and go on with things the way they were.

FELICE—But Erna is our enemy, Madame.

MRS. HUNTER—Erna! Just because she happens to be born in Germany? You're trying to fight a war—a war you know nothing about. You're trying to reduce it to terms of this school. You can't do that— You simply wanted some excitement—you made it for yourselves.

MARION—That isn't fair, Madame. It isn't just us—it's—

MRS. HUNTER—Wait a minute, Marion. You're going to say something about patriotism and love for one's country. I'm not talking about that. (*Rises.*) I'm talking about—Awareness. I'm talking about knowing what's happening to other people. Erna is your friend—she's the same girl she was two weeks ago.

MARION—It isn't *Erna*, Madame. It's what she stands for.

MRS. HUNTER—Somehow I've got to show you that what's happening is happening to human beings—you can't make one person suffer—somehow you've got to see it through her eyes—

FELICE—Her country is making the whole rest of the world suffer.

MRS. HUNTER—I'm not asking you to be tolerant of an enemy country—I'm asking you to be considerate of a human being! . . . I'm sorry . . . I didn't mean to preach at you. I shouldn't have done it, except that I'm bitterly disappointed in myself. . . . I want you to do something for me. We're going back to classes holding to our regular schedule. And I want Bingo to go and get Erna. Where is she, in the kitchen?

MISS LINDER—I think so, Madame.

MRS. HUNTER—I want her to come in here. I know that if you can only keep up the appearance of friendship that real friendship will come back. It isn't going to be easy. Go on, Bingo.

BINGO (*rising and crossing to door*)—What if she won't come, Madame?
MRS. HUNTER—She will.

There is an awkward silence during which the girls toy guiltily with their food. It is broken finally by Miss Linder's announcement that Olga is improving and will probably be able to sit in the summer house for a little while this afternoon.

Now Bingo and Erna have come from the kitchen, Bingo "smiling with grim determination," Erna "bracing herself for an ordeal." Mrs. Hunter would have Erna take the empty chair beside her and join them with the dessert. Erna has finished her lunch in the kitchen with Margarethe but she does sit down and pretend to eat.

There are awkward attempts at starting conversation and sustaining it after it is started. Mostly it is about the little progress that is being made with the summer house. Also a little about the English class and the themes that have to be finished.

Margarethe has appeared from upstairs to report that Olga has not touched her lunch. The effect is to create another prolonged silence that finally drives Sally to jump up from the table, with a mumbled "Excuse me," and disappear. Felice begs to be permitted to return to her English composition.

Marion makes a brave try at being friendly. She would have Erna come with her and measure the hothouse—after she (Marion) runs up to her room to get her jumper.

Erna makes a brave fight to keep back the tears, but now she has turned and buried her face in her arms on the back of the chair. Her body is shaken by her long-drawn-out sobs. Mrs. Hunter motions Miss Linder to leave, but asks Bingo to stay.

MRS. HUNTER (*rising and crossing to* ERNA)—Erna—Erna! We're your friends—please let us help you.
ERNA—I cannot stay here—they hate me.
MRS. HUNTER—Of course you can stay here—they don't know what they're doing, Erna—they're only hysterical and upset—
ERNA (*stops sobbing; her voice controlled*)—It is frightening —because I feel that it isn't *me*. They are making me into the kind of German they talk about—the kind they hate—just by the way they are treating me.
BINGO—Erna, they're all mixed up and excited—they can't help it.

ERNA—Why is it my fault, what my country is doing. It could happen to Marion or Felice or Bingo or anyone.

MRS. HUNTER—It isn't a question of whose fault it is, Erna. It's everybody's fault if it comes to that. We've got to get this immediate problem settled somehow—we've got to bring peace back to this place.

ERNA—You can do that very easily, Madame—if I go away.

MRS. HUNTER—That isn't solving the problem, Erna—that's evading it.

BINGO—You *can't* go away, Erna—you don't *want* to—you *know* you don't.

ERNA—Of course I don't—but it would be better. Maybe I could make things right with the others—but it is Olga. I can never make it right with her—it is what my brother has done. . . . (*She is crying again.*)

MRS. HUNTER—Let me ask her if she doesn't want to see you, Erna—I know she'll say "yes."

ERNA—Never. If only she— (*Suddenly breaking out.*) Let me *go*, Madame, please let me go away!

MRS. HUNTER—Where, Erna?

ERNA (*after a pause*)—I—I don't know.

BINGO—Wait a while, Erna—wait until Olga's feeling all right—it'll be better then. You see if it isn't.

ERNA—I love this school—I think all of us have been happier here than any place else—why did *I* have to spoil it?—Just because I am a German—just because my brother—

MRS. HUNTER (*in a firm tone*)—Erna—we are starting classes again. I'd like you to be there. You needn't have a theme today—just try sitting with the class. . . . Go for a little walk—you'll feel better.

ERNA—Yes. Of course I want to be in the class . . . I will go to the hothouse—Marion said she was going there— Maybe I can make friends with her—

Erna is starting out. She manages a little smile at the door and disappears past the window. Bingo remembers suddenly that she has a theme to write. Miss Linder appears at the head of the stairs. She has seen a policeman coming up the drive and has come to warn Mrs. Hunter. She is also frightened for herself. It may be the authorities are investigating Germans. Already they have sent some away—

"I'm frightened, Caroline," Miss Linder admits. "If he asks to see me—"

"I'll talk to him, Gretchen. I'll let you know the moment he has gone."

The policeman, it turns out, is Herr Koppler, a brother of Hilda, the kitchen maid who had left Madame Hunter's employ a few days before. He has come to make inquiries concerning a girl named Erna Schmidt. He is not at liberty to say why he wants to know where Erna is, but that is his mission.

Mrs. Hunter does not know where Erna Schmidt is. Nor will she let Herr Koppler question her pupils until she knows why he wants the information. Herr Koppler is reluctant to give up his search, but does finally withdraw.

Bingo has come hurriedly from the study room, but is immediately sent back. "You can watch for Erna through the window in there," Mrs. Hunter tells her, excitedly. "The moment she's near the house, go and ask her to come to the sitting room."

"He's working for Germany, isn't he?"

"There isn't any doubt about that. They hunt out their own nationals—and force them to work with them."

Marion and Olga have come from upstairs, Marion with her arm around Olga. They are on their way to the summer house, where they are hoping they may sit a little while in the sun. But now Sally has come in and is indicating by a fairly frantic dumb show that she wants to talk with Marion. Marion promises to come back as soon as she makes Olga comfortable.

The girls have gone and Margarethe, having cleared the table, is on her way to the kitchen when Bingo comes in from the study hall. It is for Bingo that Margarethe has been looking. She has a new letter for Erna. It is at her cottage.

They will both have to be terribly careful about the letters from now on, Bingo warns Margarethe. Perhaps it would be better if Margarethe were to bring the new letter to Bingo.

Sally and Felice have appeared at the top of the stairs. Sally is acting very mysteriously. She has something awfully important to tell Felice and Marion, but she won't say what it is until Marion comes back. That may be childish, as Felice says, but they'll change their tunes when they hear all.

Marion, like Felice, refuses to be struck dumb with the importance of Sally's discovery, even if it is about Erna—

". . . I thought we were going to drop all that," protests Marion, wearily. "Didn't you hear what Madame said? It's only fair to give Erna a chance—if she's willing to forget it and try to be friendly. I don't see why we shouldn't do the same."

"Anyway, you are being stupid, Sally," Felice adds. "I want to stay here. If staying here means being nice to Erna, then I shall try to be nice to her."

"All right—I'm being *absurd*," declares Sally, her temper rising. "You two can't see what's under your very noses. What do you think she and Margarethe are so thick about? Isn't Margarethe German? Isn't Miss Linder German? Aren't you *fighting* Germans?"

MARION (*sarcastically*)—Now Miss Linder and Margarethe are spies.

SALLY—I don't say they are. But I *do* say you're backing down just because you're scared of Madame. Don't you know what they're doing to Olga's country? Don't you know what they'll do to *yours*? (SALLY *is very near to hysterics. The other two girls are only uncomfortably amused by her outburst.*) You have to spoil the best part. I find out something—something really important and horrible—and all you do is make fun of me.

MARION (*coldly*)—What have you found out?

SALLY—Well, I went down to Margarethe's cottage, like I said I would, but it was locked. She never did *that* before. But I know I saw her giving something to Erna yesterday—

MARION—Is *that* all?

SALLY—No, that isn't all! Then I came back here and there was a man here—a policeman—talking to Madame— I heard him asking her about Erna—then I went upstairs and I listened for just a second on the landing and he said something about questioning the other pupils—then I went into the sitting room and watched him go down the drive, but I had to run because Madame came up the stairs just then—but I saw something else—

FELICE—He was asking about Erna—a policeman?

SALLY—Yes.

MARION—What did you hear him say? What exact words?

SALLY—He wanted to know how long she had been here—and then when I was up on the landing he wanted to know if he could question us—if we could give him any information about her.

MARION—You said you saw something else?

SALLY—I certainly did. I saw the policeman get into his car —and he drove off—but he only went a little way down the road. He stopped behind those trees down there and got out and walked back to the gate. He's standing there right now, watching this place—looking for Erna.

FELICE—Where is Erna?

MARION—Felice!

SALLY—I don't know—but I *do* know it's up to us to find out, and if the police want her, you won't think I'm such a fool. You're scared to do it—but if she's helping Germany, I'll tell 'em about her—you just see if I don't!

FELICE—I think that I will walk down—perhaps the man will ask me questions—I can find out what is the matter—

MARION—No, Felice! Don't!

FELICE—I do not need to give anything away. I can find out what he wants. I will be able to tell from the sort of questions he asks.

SALLY—Maybe it would be better if I did it.

MARION—Neither one of you is going to do it. It may be dangerous. Madame ought to know that he is here.

SALLY—We've got to do *something*. We've got to find out—the police couldn't be looking for Erna except for one reason. One of us has *got* to go and talk to him. . . .

They hear someone coming and are quickly on the watch. Margarethe does not see them as she comes into the room. When they speak to her she tries to hide the letter she is carrying back of her.

Is she looking for Erna? Sally would know. Erna has gone to the summer house to sit with Olga. That is joyful news to Margarethe—that Erna and Olga are friends again is fine. She has forgotten all about the letter. And now Sally has sidled around in back of Margarethe and snatched the letter from her hand. She holds on to it, despite Margarethe's frantic protests—

"It is wrong!" shouts Margarethe. "You are stealing what does not belong to you! I will speak to Madame!"

"You better be careful what you say to *her*—sneaking letters in behind her back!" answers Sally.

"The Ku Klux rides again!" calls Bingo with withering scorn.

Sally stands her ground. The Swiss police are after Erna, and they will probably be very interested in what is in Erna's letter. There's a man down at the gate right now looking for her. They'll see—

Mrs. Hunter is coming down the stairs. "What is the matter?" she demands.

"Please, Madame—Miss Sally has taken a letter that was for

Miss Erna," explains Margarethe.

"She's been sneaking letters in to Erna and I caught her at it, that's all. Helping the Germans . . ."

"That's not true, Sally. There has been no sneaking about it. I knew that Margarethe was getting Erna's letters for her. Give it to me, Sally."

Under protest Sally complies. The situation, she insists, is more serious than Mrs. Hunter thinks. It is, Mrs. Hunter agrees, a situation with which she is unable to go on. She has decided that she will have to send them all home.

Now there is consternation as well as protest. "We can't help it if we are loyal to our countries, Madame," ventures Marion.

"I'd be very much ashamed of you if you *weren't* loyal," says Mrs. Hunter. "But loyalty doesn't mean persecuting someone without any reason."

Marion, Sally and Felice are continuing their argument, their emotions rapidly mounting. Erna has appeared in the doorway. For a moment she listens and then, a little savagely, as she loses control of herself, she shouts—

ERNA—You think you are the only ones who are suffering. Don't you know that I love my people just as much as you love yours?

MARION—Our countries didn't start this war! We're not smashing down farms and killing people and blasting cities off the face of the earth!

MRS. HUNTER—Marion!

ERNA—Madame, it is my letters that have made all the trouble here. It is letters like that, that have done it. I have kept them away from you and that is why you cannot know how impossible it is for me to stay here. I want to read it to you now. I have to show you why you must let me go away. It does not matter what anyone thinks of me any more. I only want to stop all this trouble. I only want to go away. Please, Madame, may I read it?

MRS. HUNTER (*handing her the letter*)—Yes.

ERNA (*staring at the envelope*)—This has been mailed Express from Zurich. But my mother cannot be in Switzerland. (*She opens the letter and starts to read.*)

"My darling—I am praying that this will reach you. Old Heinrich, who used to be our gardener when you were little, is going to try to reach Switzerland. He will try to cross Lake Constance and get to Zurich; it is very dangerous but he has promised that he will get there and that if he is caught he will destroy this before it can be found—" (ERNA's *voice is puzzled —baffled.*)

"I am not a brave woman—if I were I would shield you from the truth—but my only comfort will be that you know the truth —that you can share it with me." (*Her manner changes—her voice is beginning to mount, in realization.*)

"I have not been able to say anything—because of the censors. Even now your father would be horrified if he knew I was writing this to you. But you see, he does not know the truth as he will soon have to know it. . . . Your brother is dead—your brother is dead—" (OLGA *turns to* MISS LINDER *for support.*) "They sent his Iron Cross from the Chancellery, and your father was so proud— He was killed in the first days of fighting near Warsaw—and they said he was a hero. He was, my darling, but not for the reason that they gave." (*There is pride in* ERNA's *voice now.*) "Hans' good friend, Wilhelm Brandt, was there— he saw it happen—he saw Hans deliberately crash dive his ship —before they ever reached Warsaw. It was Wilhelm who reported his death—he was flying next to Hans in the rear of the formation—and he told the officers that it was a lucky antiaircraft shot—but he told *me* the truth. Hans waved to him— then he fell. . . . No matter what happens now—as long as you and I live we can take pride in what he has done. It was partly for Olga—partly for his love—because he loved her deeply—" (OLGA *breaks from* LINDER *and looks at* ERNA.) "—but it was mostly because it was the only thing he could do—the only way he could protest and deny this terror that has swept over our country. . . . Now they are beginning to close in on us. There are signs that they suspect Hans' death—that there may be accusations of treachery—then your father and I will have to face them— They may even try to reach you— But you must not be afraid of them because they cannot hurt you. You have your pride in Hans—your faith in decent people. I am so deeply grateful for the knowledge that you are in a place where you can be safe—where you do not have to suffer for your beliefs— where you have enough to eat—where you are surrounded by kind people who love you—"

Erna stands for a moment, utterly crushed. As she starts for the door Olga runs to her and touches her. Erna turns and they are quickly in each other's arms. Felice has started toward Erna and Olga; Sally, Marion and Bingo are stirring uncertainly as

THE CURTAIN FALLS

JASON

A Comedy in Three Acts

By Samson Raphaelson

NOT the least controversial of the new plays of this laggard season was one called "Jason," written by the Samson Raphaelson whose previous successes had included his study of a temperamental playwright in "Accent on Youth" and that of a lightly egotistical advertising genius in "Skylark." "Jason" continued the dissection of what might be called the creative writing craft by putting a dramatic critic on the fire. The New York reviewers were not taken completely by surprise, having been duly forewarned, but they were a trifle shaken to discover that, far from lampooning the practitioners of their suspect profession, the author had treated them with far more respect than condescension. Mr. Raphaelson, it appeared, was studiedly determined to be fair. Only in those external matters of their living conditions and work routines did the drama critics find themselves extravagantly represented, which was amusing rather than irritating to most of them.

"If drama critics live with the magnificence of Jason, this department is being cheated, and hereby puts in for a stiff raise," protested Brooks Atkinson of the *New York Times*.

"I trust Mr. Raphaelson won't mind if I point out that I have not dictated a review at midnight in the luxurious fashion of his Jason for exactly forty-one years," wrote John Mason Brown in the *World-Telegram*. "Neither, I suspect, have any of my confreres. Nor do dramatic critics drink sherry when they foregather. Or live as snugly as the over fastidious Jason does in a country house in the city without a typewriter in sight."

In general the New York reviewers found the Raphaelson play about one of their kind an acceptable portrait and occasionally even flattering. "My chief disappointment in Mr. Raphaelson's portrait is that Jason Otis seems such a prig," wrote John Anderson in the *Journal-American*. "He is clever, learned and fastidious. Clearly he has a bite much worse than his bark, but he lacks the lustrous urbanity of Mr. Nathan, the infectious enthusiasm of Dr. Woollcott, the shaggy humanity of the late Mr. Broun and warmer qualities which I, as an admittedly prejudiced friend, find among my colleagues along the aisle."

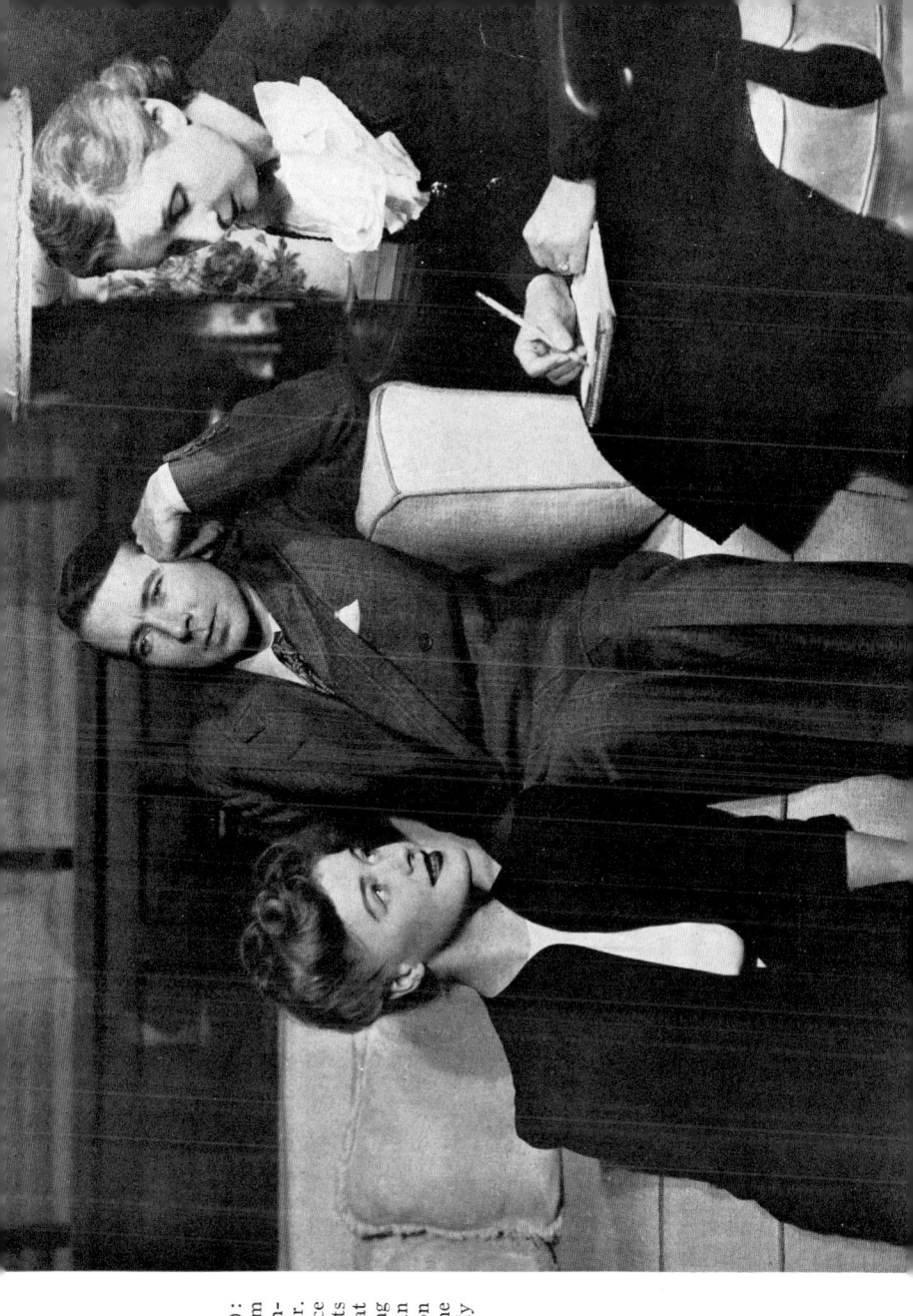

"JASON"

Jason (dictating): "Finally I am forced to the conclusion that Mr. Glencale's elegance is phony. One gets the impression that his plays are being told by a gentleman in full dress, but on closer inspection one discovers it is only the outle..."

(Helen Walker, Alexander Knox, Ellen Hall)

Photo by Talbot.

JASON

"Jason" was produced in mid-January and, to the surprise of many experts, developed a fairly healthy attraction for those average playgoers who are more interested in the theatre and its drama than they are in drama critics and their egos. It continued for 125 performances, the chief rôle being played during that time by three different actors—Alexander Knox, George Macready and Lee J. Cobb—who, naturally, projected three reviewers of separate and distinct virtues. Later Charles Bickford, returned from Hollywood, took over the rôle and played it over a newly formed suburban circuit.

The living room in the New York home of Jason Otis is "a man's room. Warm, friendly, furnished in excellent taste." As we face the room there is a stairway that winds down from the floor above at the left, and at the back "French doors open on a small front yard containing a tree and a patch of grass, bounded by a brick wall with a gate opening to the street." It is about 4.30 of an October afternoon.

As we enter the room Miss Crane, Jason's secretary, "a nondescript person of about thirty," comes from the hall. She is carrying several pages of typed manuscript. She is scribbling an address on an envelope she finds in a desk drawer when Violet, "a middle-aged colored maid," brings in a package and is closely followed by a young man wearing a Western Union messenger's cap. He appears a little old for a messenger and much too alert. Violet would put him out if she could, but she can't. Miss Crane finds the messenger a little impertinent as he follows her about the room asking question after question about her work and the man she works for. She can't do much about that, either.

Does Jason dictate his letters? No. Does he dictate his criticisms? Yes. With that much information Miss Crane leaves him. The messenger is not discouraged. He continues the inquiry. Violet is more responsive.

Does Mr. Otis have enough to do to keep him busy all day? If so, what? "He sees a show, writes it up the same night—and then what does he do with the rest of his time?"

Mr. Otis reads books, Violet tells him. All those books in the book cases. He writes books, too. He writes more books than all the other drama critics put together. Is he a bachelor? He was until a month ago. Now he's married.

"Do you suppose his wife likes this perfect room?" demands the messenger.

"Huh?" Violet is beginning to wonder about this strange young man.

"I'm not really asking you," explains the messenger. "I'm talking to myself. I bet she married him for it. . . . *You* wouldn't care for a room like this. Neither would I. Now, you and I . . . If we thought up a room together . . . For instance, you wouldn't want a roof, would you?"

"I certainly *would* want a roof," protests Violet.

"All right—then *I* wouldn't want a roof. And you'd want at least one wall out. . . . Hmm . . . (*He reads a few lines of the manuscript.*)"

"Why would I want a wall out?"

"So you could breathe. So you could see the world. Suppose a bird flew by, and you had to talk to it . . ."

"Why would I have to do that?"

"You're black, aren't you? That's reason enough."

"I never talked to a bird in my life."

"Sure. And the *birds* don't think they talk to *me*, either."

"Well, *do* they?"

"Why, it all depends on the bird. Some birds are pretty stupid. I'm no promiscuous bird-lover, but every once in a while you run into a bird that's so damn smart . . ."

"Young man, are you right in your mind? I think you'd better come to . . ."

At that moment Jason Otis comes down the stairs, humming cheerfully to himself. "Jason is in his late thirties, worldly, intellectual." As Violet instinctively withdraws, and the messenger follows Jason's movements with obvious fascination, the writer goes straight to his desk for the typewritten sheets Miss Crane has left there. They are to go to the *Evening World*. He is looking them over when the fascinated messenger calmly interrupts him—

"You thought that play was terrible, didn't you?"

"How do you know?" parries Jason.

MESSENGER—I read your opening paragraph.

JASON (*staring at the* MESSENGER, *amused*)—Oh, did you? I hope you liked it!

MESSENGER—It wasn't bad, but what fascinates me is . . . (*He takes the sheets out of* JASON'S *hand so casually that* JASON *is paralyzed for the moment.*) Take something like this: "If you write a play wherein your hero has tuberculosis, can't pay the interest on the mortgage, and at the same time gets appendicitis and pleurisy, don't call in an audience: call in a doctor . . ." Did you write that because it sounds good?

JASON (*taking the papers from him*)—That's none of your business, my boy.

MESSENGER—What do you mean it's none of my business? I'm one of your readers. Whom do you write for—me, or the owner of the *New York Evening World?*

JASON (*after a pause*)—What did you want to know?

MESSENGER—Well—that's a clever little paragraph. I'd like to know how a critic works out something like that. Does it come easily?

JASON (*after studying the* MESSENGER *for a moment and deciding, with some humor, to accept the situation*)—Very.

MESSENGER—No walking up and down the room all night, maybe, trying to figure out your opinion?

JASON—I usually dictate it with my feet on the sofa, a whiskey and soda by my side, and two cuties on my knee.

MESSENGER—You're kidding me, aren't you?

JASON—If you're asking whether I know what I think you, I always know what I think. Every critic should.

MESSENGER—Suppose you didn't know—would you say so?

JASON (*half to himself*)—I never faced that problem.

MESSENGER (*sitting down—solemnly*)—That's very interesting—*very* interesting.

JASON (*sitting down, too, and leaning toward the* MESSENGER—*sweetly*)—Incidentally, I'm taking your number, and I'm going to ask Western Union to fire you.

MESSENGER (*taking off his hat*)—Oh, that. That's not mine. I gave the boy a dollar—he's having an ice-cream soda around the corner. But let's get back to you. Do you get any excitement when you knock off a paragraph like this—any joy? Do you want to run out on the streets and holler: "Hey, mister—listen to what I just found out—we can get drunk together on it!"

Now the truth begins to dawn upon Jason. This is the young man who has been asking for an appointment; the young man who has written a play which he has tried to induce Jason to read. His name is Mike Ambler.

As for Mike, he is not at all startled by being discovered. He is indeed the young playwright in question. He is quite disappointed to find that the drama critic's routine is so ordinary. He thought they always went through hell in composing their criticisms. He can't understand. He goes through hell with everything he writes, and he writes only about imaginary people.

"... I don't know what I really think of about them," admits Mike; "whether they're bright or dull, good or bad, strong or weak. All I know is they're wonderful."

"What's that—your play?" demands Jason, as Mike draws a green manuscript from his coat.

"It's my first play, and it's so beautiful that sometimes I think I'll never write another as good—but that's just a passing mood. Better read it tonight. We're in rehearsal—we open next Monday."

Jason isn't interested. He had told Mike over the telephone that he never read plays before they were produced. Mike is still puzzled. "I should think, now that you've talked to me, you'd realize that I was a genius."

"Well, you must be patient," reasons Jason. "Next Monday, when your play opens, I'll probably find it out—to my amazement."

Mike isn't sure. Jason might not like the play. After all he (Mike) is the first great American playwright and it isn't always easy for anyone to digest a masterpiece. Mike would, with Jason's permission, explain his play, but Jason's impatience increases. He is expecting friends. Good! Mike would love to meet Jason's friends. Especially his fellow critics—

"Are they anything like you?" Mikes wants to know.

"From your viewpoint—yes," answers Jason.

MIKE—That's fascinating. Listen, I can do something for you *all*. I can disturb you. I can remind you of the days when you weren't critics. I can make you hear the birds sing again. Why, I can tell all of you about my play.

JASON (*wistfully*)—Mr. Ambler, if I asked you to get to hell out of here—do you think that would help?

MIKE—Jason, I'm going to give you a quick picture of the play, and then you'll realize . . . Listen, Jason—it's humanity the way God would see it. Why, He's crazy about people. He and I both, get me? Take Mama, for instance. Mama is semi-symbolic—one moment representing motherhood, the next moment lust and corporation dividends. . . . Jason, this play is mysterious, like a baby, like the Einstein Theory. It's as real as what's going to happen yesterday, or what has happened tomorrow. It's full of lies like every truth, and full of truth like every lie. It's me—it's you—it's what you don't know you are, because you're being it. It's every bum in the park . . . The title is "Hooray for the Madam." Do you like it?

JASON—Do you know what you're talking about?
MIKE—Occasionally. I figure I do about twenty-five per cent of the time. What's your average?
JASON—Ninety-nine.
MIKE (*impressed*)—Really?
JASON—But it's easier for me, I'm sure, because I don't find myself as difficult to understand as you must find yourself.
MIKE—I don't understand myself at all. I'm too dazzling. Do oxygen and nitrogen understand themselves? Does a locomotive, a flower, a woman's shoulder coming out of the bathtub? (*By now* MIKE *has dropped the manuscript on the table again, and* JASON *picks it up*.)
JASON (*with finality, as he gives* MIKE *the manuscript*)— Listen, Woman's Shoulder—take your manuscript. Locomotive, go away! (*Picking up the* MESSENGER'S *hat and throwing it to* MIKE.) Good-by, Flower!
MIKE (*after a pause*)—Let me thank you. This has been a deeply moving experience. You've presented me with the problem of yourself, but my shoulders are broad enough to carry it. (*Brightening.*) I'm beginning to get ideas already. Do you know what you need, Jason?
JASON—Yes—solitude.
MIKE—No! Just the opposite! You need people. Look at this beautiful house—it has too many walls. Break down one of those walls! Walk out on the street—pass the time of day with a stranger waiting for a bus or sitting on a park bench. Ask him to drop in. Offer him a sandwich and a glass of beer. Then walk up to another—a plumber out of work—and still another— maybe a young couple who can't afford to go to Coney Island. . . . You don't think it's practical, huh?
JASON (*a little wearily*)—You guessed it.
MIKE (*studying him*)—There's something about you . . . I don't know what it is . . . but I think you're a good guy. You make me sad, but optimistic. So long, Jason.

With obvious relief Jason calls to Violet to get another messenger. Then he would talk with Mrs. Otis, who is upstairs and has, at the moment, advanced from her toenails to her fingernails, by Violet's report.
Lisa Otis "is a beautiful girl of about twenty-three, wearing a house-robe smart to the point of absurdity and very becoming to her." She stops at the bend in the stairs that her husband may not miss the picture, and is "brimming with affection for

him" when she completes the descent.

Jason had some idea of talking with Lisa about Violet, who is getting a little on his nerves. When they were married Lisa had told Jason that she was without kith or kin. That was true, Lisa reassures him. Her father was the last of his branch of the Breckinridges of Virginia and her mother—

"Oh, Jason, you would have worshiped her! She was so sweet and fragile, and she looked so lovely in the morning out in the garden."

"Sometimes you make your mother sound as if she lived in the *Woman's Home Companion,* instead of the sunny South," ventures Jason.

It was the wrong thing to say. Lisa is on the verge of tears, even after Jason has taken her in his arms and comforted her with a kiss. And now Jason has forgotten what it was he wanted to report about Violet, as well as everything else that was in his mind. He has helped Lisa unwrap the most beautiful pair of shoes he has ever seen and cheerfully adjusted himself to the news that there is one hell of a dress to go with them.

"Darling, when are you going to tell me about money, and things like that?" Lisa is asking, sweetly.

"You mean you'd like to know whether we can afford the shoes and the dress which you have already bought."

"Yes, dear."

"My idea of an attractive woman is a woman I can't afford."

Lisa remembers that one. Jason did not just make it up. It was in one of his little books he wrote ten years ago. So was the one he delivered to his managing editor the other night at dinner: " 'A liberal is a nice fellow who doesn't know he's a Communist, or a nice fellow who doesn't know he's a Fascist . . .' " repeats Lisa.

"But he's always a nice fellow," adds Jason.

"That's it."

"Darling—(*He drops onto the sofa beside her and puts his arm around her.*) if I'd ever dreamt that after one month of marriage you would be doing this to me, I'd have avoided you like a rattlesnake."

"You've been awfully cross for the last week," pouts Lisa, snug in his embrace. "What's the matter? Honeymoon over? Reaction?"

"For a kid of twenty-three, you're awfully slick and smart. You dress your mind the way you dress your body."

Jason holds his wife closely for a moment, wishing fervently the while that she will shut up. Which she does presently, at the appearance of Miss Crane. Lisa does not leave, however, even when Jason takes up the task of dictating an addition to his Sunday article—

"Ready?" he calls to Miss Crane, whose pencil is poised above her notebook. "Ready," she answers, and the dictation begins—

" 'Finally, I am forced to the conclusion that Mr. Glendale's elegance is phony. One gets the impression that his plays are being told by a gentleman in full dress, but on closer inspection, one discovers it is only the butler. In other words, Mr. Glendale wears his subtlety on his sleeve.' "

"That's awfully clever, dear." Lisa is interested.

" 'The rumor that . . .' I hate the word clever, darling . . . (*To* Miss Crane.) Where was I?"

" '. . . wears his subtlety on his sleeve.' "

" 'The rumor that it takes Mr. Glendale only a week to write a play, and that he does it in bed, fails to alienate me. I believe many a good play can be, and has been, written swiftly and in bed. And many splendid novels . . . And many brilliant opinions, Mr. Ambler—penetrating, sincere and true . . .' "

"Mr. Who?"

"I was thinking of something else. Cut that out, and keep the rest. That's all, Miss Crane."

The added copy is to be sent by a new messenger. Lisa is enormously impressed with her husband's brilliance—if he will permit her to substitute "brilliant" for "clever"—

"Because I really mean brilliant," protests Lisa. "These things come out of you so *easily*. When I'm writing a letter, I bite my nails, and I tear up one sheet after another. . . . (Jason *stops fondling her knee*.) Am I saying something wrong again?"

"It's not you. It's me. Darling," Jason says, slowly, "I've been a critic too long. It's getting me. And I don't know what to do about it."

"I do!" proudly announces Lisa, picking up a large box from a nearby chair. "I think a great big gasp is what you need." And she draws from the box a gorgeous evening gown. "Well?" she demands.

"I'm gasping," admits Jason. But he does wish that she would cultivate a greater resourcefulness. She might think up something "more diverting than extravagance."

Lisa agrees, and she has done just that. She has thought up an enormous party to which shall be invited all the people Jason doesn't know, but who know him. Katharine Cornell, for instance. Helen Hayes and Jock Whitney. Lisa has prepared a list—a wonderful list—including the Mayor. And Herbert Marshall. Gertrude Lawrence. Jascha Heifetz. A couple of Whitneys, Orson Welles, a couple of Vanderbilts, Sinclair Lewis—

"I know him—does that matter?" interrupts Jason. Lisa squelches him with a withering "Wise guy!"

Jason is soon tired of even thinking of the new game. He knows that he has, as she says, everything in the world to make him happy, *but*—

"Everything *but*. I've been living for artistic pleasure, just as a roué lives for sensual pleasure. I've absorbed wine and women like works of art, and works of art like wine and women. There's nothing creative in my life. I've lived like a critic. I haven't lived. It's not unusual. Millions of people haven't lived. But it's bad when you begin to suspect it . . . The roué can find salvation with Dr. Buchman or the Salvation Army. (*He goes to* LISA, *strokes her hair*.) Not I. I'm too clever. I'm stuck."

"You are in a bad way, aren't you? I wish I knew more about men."

"I wish you did too. I wish *I* did."

Lisa thinks she may have been to blame. Perhaps she has been following his written formula too closely. She is free to confess that she landed him by being "capricious and shallow and extravagant." Now she is going to change. What Jason needs is somebody deeper, and Lisa will become deeper. No more smart magazines. Lisa will start on "Hamlet" that very night. . . .

Violet has come to announce Mr. Bronson. She has sent for a new messenger, but the old one is still in the kitchen. He has been telling Violet about his play. Very interesting . . .

George Bronson is one of Jason's colleagues, "a solid fellow of about fifty, unpretentious, neatly dressed, competent." Perhaps a little on the gloomy side. George doesn't think much of himself as a hack reviewer. "I do my stint every day for the half million readers of the *Globe*," says he. "I don't publish any books or give lectures or go on the radio. I'm an ordinary citizen —and that makes me a much better risk as a husband than Jason."

"Oh, stop bragging about your mediocrity, will you?"

Lisa doesn't understand, but Jason explains: "It's very simple. George pleases five hundred thousand and one people—namely, the readers of the *Globe* and his wife. He's a failure. I please one person—namely, myself. I'm a success."

Violet has brought in the sherry and reported the playwright messenger getting along famously in the kitchen. He is right in the middle of the second act at the moment. That is about all Jason can stand, but before he can move into action Lisa takes over and agrees to get rid of the brash young man.

Bronson has brought a play script with him. As it soon turns out this is another copy of the same play the eager author is now trying to read in the kitchen. Nevertheless, it has impressed Bronson tremendously. Either it is "a remarkably good or a terribly bad piece of work." And how did Bronson come by it? Why, the young man telephoned that he was a photographer on *Life* and would like to take a few intimate shots of George. Being invited to come he brought his play instead of a camera.

"I'll tell you all about this script," Jason finally explodes. "It's flashy, it's insolent, it's full of bright, unexpected phrases—and it's phony from cover to cover. . . . It took me a few minutes to get his number, but when I did, I tossed him out. He's a shallow anarchist posturing as a profound individualist."

"I thought he was refreshing, in a way," admits Bronson.

Now Bill Squibb, another of Jason's critical colleagues, has arrived. "Squibb is in his late thirties; keen, sensitive, well-dressed." In his hand he, too, carries a green manuscript, and very shortly this is discovered to be a third copy of the messenger's play.

"I bet he's been at every drama reviewer in New York," growls Jason. "The fellow is impudent and vulgar, dazzling those who are so afraid to admire themselves that they get a kick out of anybody who climbs into their lap and hollers, 'I'm Napoleon!'"

Before they can agree on what they really think of the intruding dramatist and his work Lisa is back in a state of some excitement. She has come to get some yellow paper. In the kitchen, she reports, Mr. Ambler has just had an idea for improving his third act—

"Can you imagine, he got his idea just through something I said," Lisa is explaining, with shining eyes. "It had nothing whatever to do with his play—but it gave *him* an idea about something else, which made his mind leap way back to his play, which had nothing whatever to do with the *other* thing, either."

JASON—Well, what's he going to do write it here in the house?
LISA—Oh, yes. He has to get it down while it's hot. (*She starts for the hall.*)
JASON—Wait a minute . . .

Lisa—I can't, darling. He might lose his inspiration. You see, he started on Violet's kitchen pad—but he's superstitious about yellow paper, and all she had was a pencil. . . . Oh, yes! May I borrow your fountain pen? (*As she goes back to the desk, opens the center drawer and brings forth a fountain pen.*) He's *much* more comfortable with a fountain pen.

Jason—Now, see here, Lisa—do you realize that I've been trying to get rid of this fellow?

Lisa—Yes, I know—he explained it to me—it's only because you don't like to read manuscripts. But, darling, this is different. I never saw a creative artist creating before. And you always say the creative artist is the most important of all; and I thought they wrote quietly at home, but he doesn't—and I really think this is a chance for me to learn all about it from the bottom. . . . (*The silence overwhelms her. She looks from one of the men to the other, then back to* Jason.) Or am I wrong?

Jason—Well—ahem—as usual, not exactly!

Lisa (*eagerly*)—That's what I thought! Thank you, darling. . . . (*She starts for the hall, but at the same moment* Mike *enters.*)

Mike (*on fire with creativeness, ignoring the men*)—Oh, there you are. . . . (*Grabbing the paper and the fountain pen.*) That's it—that's what I want! (*Going quickly to the desk and getting set to write.*)

Squibb—Oh, hello.

Mike (*to himself*)—God, I hope I don't lose this! (*As the three men, paralyzed, watch him.*) It'll put cornets and the perfume of honeysuckle into that third act . . . (*Half shutting his eyes to hold the mood.*) I can see it like a painting, like a sweetly tragic dream—honeysuckle and cornets against a background of Papa's red flannel drawers hanging on the clothesline! (*He plunges into his work, writing away with the fountain pen, oblivious to everything else.* Jason *looks with dismay at* Bronson *and* Squibb, *who look back at him helplessly but with a slight touch of humor.* Lisa *stands near* Mike, *but not too near, watching him in fascination. Pretty soon she goes closer and reads over his shoulder as he works. There is a silence of several moments, during which* Jason *doesn't know what to do.*)

Jason (*finally, to* Lisa)—Well—I hope we're not intruding!

Lisa—Oh, not at all. And you can go right on talking—Mr. Ambler doesn't mind. Why, when he gets an inspiration, just so long as he has yellow paper . . . Why, he can work in bars, in the park, down by the river—oh, anywhere! Go right ahead!

(*She goes back to watching* MIKE.)
JASON (*after a slight pause*)—That's—that's just dandy.

Jason has turned to his friends. Let them continue their conversation. What were they talking about? Oh, yes—so it was. Mike, the playwright. Well, let them choose another subject. Jason will be damned if he is going to be driven from that room.
They try the Critics' Circle election as a topic, but that doesn't go too well. "Frankly, I'm fed up with the Critics' Circle," admits Jason. "We get to know each other, to understand each other—we rub the edges off each other, and pretty soon we'll talk alike, think alike, write alike."
Presently they are aware that they are beginning to feel pretty uncomfortable. Even a little flabbergasted. Mike writes on and Lisa continues a fascinated observer over his shoulder. Still Jason refuses to admit defeat. Perhaps if they tried singing—
The next minute they are grouped in approved barber-shop style and have swung lustily into "I've Been Workin' on the Railroad." By the time they have reached the first chorus Lisa has turned to stare at them. Mike "has gradually come up from his work, a look of pleasure dawning on his face." Now Mike has decided to join the singers. He throws one arm chummily around Jason's shoulders and catches up with the melody just as they swing into "Can't you hear the darkies callin'? . . . Dinah—blow—your horn!"
One by one the others, as they become aware of Mike, stop singing. In fact, Mike is the only one left to do justice to the final and proudly sustained "Ho-o-o-orn!" But he is not in the least discouraged. "That was great!" he declares, slapping Jason jovially on the back. But even this thrill must not be permitted to interfere with his work. Mike goes quickly back to the desk. Lisa follows to continue looking over his shoulder.
"Boys, I give up!" sighs Jason, turning to face his friends. "Who knows—maybe he *is* a genius; maybe this is a historic moment. . . . Let's give him five minutes, and then, if the son of a bitch is still here, I'll kick him out—and the hell with posterity!"
For a moment after Jason, Bronson and Squibb have marched out through the garden, Mike and Lisa are unaware of having been left alone. Mike writes on feverishly. Lisa picks up each page as he finishes and reads it avidly. Suddenly she stops reading. She has found something that displeases her. "Oh, I don't like this!" she says. "This is terrible! Listen, you . . ."

But Mike can't be bothered. He continues to write. Lisa refuses to be put off. The people he is writing about—the white trash of the South—are dirty and stupid—

"Are you calling my play dirty and stupid?" demands an outraged Mike, jumping up and grabbing the yellow sheets from her hands.

"I call it vile. The way that girl talks is all wrong. . . . She's vile!"

MIKE—Are you crazy? You never read anything more beautiful in your life than this: (*He reads.*) "Listen, Mister, you heard me when I said five dollars. Don't get funny, Mister, or I'll raise the price to what I'm worth, and that's a million."

LISA—That's dirty—just dirty!

MIKE (*going on*)—"I was the girl in the bus you didn't have the nerve to talk to. I was Hedy Lamarr in the moonlight. . . . I gave you consolation for your obscurity . . . I gave you that thing you crave most of all, the swaggering, wicked sense of being a man."

LISA—I don't want you in my house!

MIKE (*picking up to get rhythm*)—". . . the swaggering, wicked sense of being a man. I did something glorious for you, Mister—and two and a half dollars will not pay for it. Three dollars . . . That's my best and final price!" (*During the last part of this speech* LISA *stands with her hands over her ears. He goes over to her and pulls one of her hands down.*) What's the matter with you, anyway?

LISA (*pulling away from him—breathing hard*)—I don't like you or your play. I loathe mean, cheap, common people. They're not beautiful—they're filthy. They're diseased, and miserable, and nasty, and low . . .

MIKE (*interrupting sharply*)—How do you know?

LISA—I—it's none of your business.

MIKE—How do you know?

LISA—I—I'm from a fine old Southern family . . . My father was Colonel Breckinridge—and I've heard about the poor people. . . . Why, every Southerner knows . . . Those *lint-heads!*

MIKE—Lint-heads? That's a mill-town word. It's a fighting word. Honey, you swung that one from the floor. That word came right off your shoe tops.

LISA (*frightened*)—What do you mean?

MIKE—I mean, you poor kid, you're no lady.

LISA (*with a childish desperation*)—My father was Colonel

Breckinridge of Virginia, and if he was here right now . . .

MIKE (*as he grabs her wrist*)—You made that up. No lady ever hated the poor the way you do.

LISA (*struggling*)—Let me go—you—you trash!

MIKE—Listen, I spent five years down South. I know the back country and the mill-towns. Why are you ashamed? You should be proud!

LISA—Proud of being a *lint-head?*

MIKE—Sure. The sidewalks of Tenth Avenue made me, and the dust of the mill-towns made you. . . .

LISA (*out of control*)—Take that back! I'll kill you if you say that—if you ever say that again! What do you think I've been fighting all my life? Those ignorant girls in their torn dresses—I saw what happened to them . . . My cousins, and the kids next door, and the kids on the street . . . My mother stupid enough to work herself to the bone, and the house still dirty . . . My father out of a job half the time and drunk the rest of the time, and me with never a pair of shoes to my name—not one pair . . .

MIKE (*suddenly*)—How old were you when you ran away?

LISA—Fifteen. . . .

MIKE—You poor, tortured, confused kid! (*She is limp as he puts his arm around her and draws her to him tenderly.*) God, how dumb you are!

LISA (*breaking away, almost snarling*)—Don't you call me dumb! I'm as smart as anything, and don't you forget it. I've got guts. I made a lady of myself . . . My diction is better than yours . . . I talk as well as Herbert Marshall, see? And I've got the most cultured husband in America!

MIKE (*putting his arm around her again*)—I only said you were dumb, darling. I didn't say you weren't wonderful. I love dumb people—and you're beautiful inside. . . . (*He draws her closer to him.*)

LISA—You don't know anything about what I am inside. I'm everything inside.

MIKE—And you're beautiful outside, too.

LISA—What are you trying to do?

MIKE (*gently*)—This is great. I like this. I was beginning to get discouraged. I haven't been in love for at least two weeks.

LISA (*breaking away, coldly*)—You *are* trash, all right. Do you think you're going to blackmail me?

MIKE (*puzzled*)—Blackmail . . . ?

LISA (*picking up his pages of writing*)—Better not try it!

(*Handing them to him, grimly.*) Go on—get out.

MIKE (*staring at her*)—You make me want to cry.

JASON (*coming in*)—Oh—finished, are you?

LISA (*taking* JASON'S *arm possessively*)—Mr. Ambler was just going, darling.

JASON—Good! And if you ever get the impulse, don't drop in again.

MIKE (*going to the desk and picking up the remaining sheets and the fountain pen*)—Jason, I'll always love your house, because I wrote a beautiful scene in it, and because I've already done more living here than you have. I'll never forget the sight of either one of you. The sight of something dying is always vivid. . . . I'm not giving up. I'm going to talk to God about you both. There's one spark of hope. You sang "I've Been Workin' on the Railroad"—and she sang "Dixie." . . . Goodby.

JASON—I hope God doesn't mind—but I'll have that fountain pen!

Mike calmly returns the pen, salutes them both and is gone. Lisa is greatly relieved, but Jason apparently is troubled. He can't quite understand Lisa's violent change of attitude. As a matter of fact Mike is beginning to grow on Jason. He thinks now he wants to read his plays—

"He is everything that I'm not," admits Jason, in an effort to explain his feelings to the puzzled and outraged Lisa. "He believes; I am skeptical. He is full of himself; I am full of good taste. . . . I'm sick and tired of my bright, neat, pungent, sophisticated and puny little mind."

"Shut up," shouts Lisa, picking up an ashtray and smashing it on the floor. But Jason goes on—

"I'm sick and tired of the intricate bookkeeping system with which I could add up everything—for myself, and for the not so many thousands of literary snobs who read me. I have a secret suspicion that I never really had a thought in my life—that thinking begins with feeling, and that feeling has something to do with all the people in the world. . . ."

Lisa has been ranging the room savagely. Now she picks up Jason's beloved antique and holds it poised, ready to smash it, too—

"If you break that vase I'll hate you," says Jason, firmly, without raising his voice. "I mean it. That vase is very old—and very beautiful."

"You hate me already."

"I love that vase. . . . Now will you please leave me alone with this manuscript—which, for all I know, may bring something *new* and beautiful into my life—if not into yours. . . ."

Lisa has slowly put down the vase. They look at each other for a silent moment. Lisa has turned and gone up the stairs. Jason takes up the Ambler manuscript and begins to read as the curtain falls.

ACT II

The following Monday morning, in the Otis living room, we find Jason and Mike sipping highballs. Mike is lolling contentedly on the sofa and Jason is sprawled upon a nearby chair.

Their adventures of the day have been revealing and amusing to them both. Jason actually has had fun. Mike is pleased at that discovery. It means that Jason is breaking through his shell. Jason is free to admit that he is also Mike's friend. Now he would like to play craps, if Mike is ready.

Mike is ready, and pleased, but crap shooting is a serious business with him. "I used to make my room and board with dice and poker," admits Mike.

Jason has gone to find money and dice. Mike, turning his gaze upward, begins a little prayer: "Oh, Lord, You did a wonderful job when you made me, and I want to thank You," he recites. "You have granted me the divine gift of loving myself. I love myself deeply, Lord. I'm sure that pleases You. . . . I observe my deeds with gentle indulgence. Therefore, I find all men infinitely delightful and engaging—for have You not made them in my image? (*Unobserved by* MIKE, JASON *comes down the stairs. He stops on the last step, listening with a gradually widening smile.*) Their sins are my sins, and thus I can forgive them with Your heavenly smile. Oh, Lord, follow my example and have mercy on those who do not understand me—but don't let it be the critics of New York! And don't let it be tonight! A little luck—just a little—would help, Lord. . . . And one of these days I promise to do the same for You!"

Jason has come down the stairs. "You don't change your style even for God, do you?" he says.

"Why should I kid Him, of all deities? He knows me. He knows I'm a poseur, full of uncertainty and guile, but noble, yet foolish, but great. . . ."

The crap game starts haltingly. Mike has trouble concentrating. Suddenly he is greatly worried about how he is to get through the night. How can he stand the adventure of having his play acted? Suddenly his confidence is leaving him. He is afraid of many things, including the critics. Only Jason is sure now—

"Now, look here," says Jason, comfortingly; "you're a nincompoop if you don't realize that you're a profound and beautiful artist; and if you don't grasp the fact that your work is saturated with the grandeur of simple human beings, then your mind is trivial and petty—and we both ought to be ashamed of yourself!"

"Okay— Let's have those dice," shouts Mike, and the game is resumed.

Jason doesn't know much about craps, but he learns readily and loses gracefully. Still Mike finds it hard to concentrate. He is relieved when Lisa comes to report that all is in readiness for the party—with plenty of sandwiches (roast beef, ham and turkey) and plenty of drinks (three cases of beer and four gallons of red wine). Neither Jason nor Mike has much idea of how many guests they have invited to the party. They can only count seven, really. Lisa thinks seven should be enough to give Jason the "cross section" he is looking for.

"Darling, you're not really excited about this party, are you?" asks Jason, sensing Lisa's lack of enthusiasm.

"Don't be silly. I've got Swiss cheese in my fingernails—and butter all over your face," she adds, running her hands playfully over Jason's cheek.

"Do you know—Lisa didn't like the people in your play when she first read it," comments Jason, wiping his cheek. Lisa continues on upstairs.

"Didn't she?" Mike is watching Jason closely.

"The only snobbery I can endure is that of the well-born Southerner. It has the fragrance of all decaying things. But I think she's getting over it."

"I don't like the way you talk about that girl, Jason. She's a great woman."

"I like the way *you* talk about her," admits Jason with simple sweetness.

They have returned to their crap game when George Bronson arrives. Bronson is puzzled, first, as to what kind of party it is that Jason is giving and, second, why should Mike Ambler be there? Seeing that they are to review the Ambler play that night Bronson, for one, would prefer to be free from the charm of the author's personality until after he has seen "Hooray for the Madam."

"You fill me with melancholy, George," declares Mike. "We got up this party for you and Squibb. (*Turning to* JASON.) Didn't we?"

"No, we didn't," corrects Jason. "But it's a thought. . . . George, I dropped in on Mike this morning, and we took a stroll along the docks. Mike and I got to chatting with some people."

"You mean—strangers?"

"Oh, naturally."

"What's natural about it?"

"You see?" Jason has turned to Mike. "We talk different languages already!"

"George, haven't you ever walked up to a stranger and passed the time of day?" Mike is serious.

"Not that I can remember."

"Whom *do* you talk to?"

"Other critics, women's organizations, relatives, his managing editor, the desk clerk at the Harvard Club, and his wife—in the order named."

"Well, that makes everything clear!"

"Not to me."

"George, you've spent your whole life in the fifth row on the aisle," says Jason. "Mike has spent his life among *people*. His play defies the footlights, the customary mood of audiences. And until you get the feel of people, you'll never understand 'Hooray for the Madam.'"

Bronson is going, still uncertain about Jason and whatever it is that has come over him. Jason thinks he will walk along with his friend. Mike would go, too, but Jason doesn't want Mike. What further experimenting he does talking with strangers he prefers to try alone.

Left to himself, Mike is suddenly conscious that there is quite a bit of money left from the unfinished crap game. He throws the dice, apparently makes his point and picks up the dice just as Lisa comes down the stairs.

"Hello, Wonderful!" Mike calls. Lisa is in no mood for banter. She is looking for Jason who, Mike tells her, is out soliciting customers for his party. Lisa would go on, but Mike stops her—

"One question: Were you ever actually in Virginia?"

LISA (*with great deliberateness*)—I was born there and lived there until Father died—didn't you know?

MIKE—The aristocracy fascinates me. Give me a picture of

a typical day in a Southern mansion.

Lisa (*after a moment's hesitation*)—Gladly. I was awakened in the morning by a chorus of a hundred darkies singing plantation songs, then twenty mammies, in yellow bandannas, lifted me gently out of my bed and carried me to a solid gold bathing pool. (*With a deadly change of tone.*) And, after tomorrow morning, you lousy heel, when you'll have your good reviews and all you want out of Jason, I never expect to set eyes on you again!

Mike (*after pause*)—Take your shoes off.

Lisa—What?

Mike—Take those high-heeled pretty shoes off, and your silken stockings, and come out and get your naked feet into the grass again.

Lisa—Can't you see me doing it? Listen, you—I'm never going barefoot again—never in all my life—except on a deep, soft rug.

Mike—Take your shoes off.

Lisa—The rug in my bathroom is the most gorgeous that money could buy. And when I step out, I wear the most beautiful bedroom slippers anyone ever saw. I have five pairs of bedroom slippers, see? And I have twenty pairs of shoes!

Mike—Even if you had a million shoes, you still couldn't run away from yourself.

Lisa—You cheap, ready-made, unpressed organ-grinder—I warn you: after tomorrow, *you're out*.

Mike—If I were a gentleman, I'd slink away—but being an artist, wild horses couldn't keep me from Jason. Do you know what kind of kid he was?

Lisa (*turning away from him*)—No.

Mike—You should. It's important. He never had a fight with another kid, and yet they were all afraid of him—can you imagine that? He had words. The other kids were not perfect, and he had the knack of seeing perfection and nailing it. Words! They were better than a left jab, a right hook, the one-two to the chin. He wore them in his belt like cartridges. That's how critics are born! His mother devoted her life to him. It's a lousy idea, but she did. So after she died, when he felt he ought to go around with girls, do you know how he went at it? He read Freud, Jung and Adler—found out that he had a mother fixation, kissed a couple of those girls at the right intellectual moment, and the net result was that he danced a little, wooed a little, and revered his mother's memory without pain. . . . Isn't that sweet?

LISA (*harshly*)—Is that why you're hanging around?

MIKE—Sure. I can't get the guy out of my mind. Him on the green lawns of Boston Back Bay, and me on the streets of New York. Him with books piled high in his crib, and me stealing them from the public library. Him terrifying the other kids with unforgettable epithets, and me—well, I hope to God when I licked them, that wasn't what they remembered. There's no love sweeter than the love you have for kids you lick; a licked kid is reasonable and attentive; you should fill his listening heart with bright hope—and I did, always.

It may be his interest in Jason that holds Mike's interest, but, seeing that he had tried to kiss her, Lisa thinks that may have something to do with it, too. Mike is contemptuous of the suggestion— "Hell, no!" says he. "I embrace a woman the way I write a beautiful sentence. I mean it—that's why it doesn't last. . . ."

They have moved close together now. Lisa, "sensing another kind of closeness," moves away. Mike is following her, with his eyes, with his questioning. How did she get away from the South? he would know.

Lisa, "remembering deeply," recalls some of those experiences. She had hitch-hiked; she had said she was seventeen; she had stolen a dress, and money, and bought shoes; she used to steal magazines like *Vogue* and *Harper's Bazaar*.

How had she learned to talk so pretty? By listening to a radio; by listening to Herbert Marshall. In New York she had worked as a salesgirl, and as a model and finally in a bookshop, where she met Jason.

"Were you a virgin?" demands Mike.

"Jeez, do you think I'm a goddam fool? Of course I was a virgin!"

There is a pause. "Take your shoes off!" orders Mike, approaching her.

"Don't be funny."

MIKE—You're beautiful—and you don't love him.

LISA—Don't make me laugh.

MIKE—You *want* to love him. You want to love him so badly that it's tearing you to pieces. But you can't, because you don't love yourself. You're hating yourself with every breath you draw. . . .

Lisa—Listen, you—you *handyman*—I could have had a Wall Street millionaire. I could have had a lawyer with a yacht. But I went after *him*—because he's a gentleman!

Mike—What's a gentleman? I'm better than all the gentlemen in the world.

Lisa—You! Why, if you were the greatest writer that ever lived—he'd still be top man. He's the one who *criticizes* you! He's criticized Rockefeller, Mrs. Astor, and the President of the United States. I've been smart enough to land him, and if you think I'd waste my time spitting on you . . .

Mike—Take your shoes off.

Lisa—Guttersnipe!

Mike—Lint-head . . . (Lisa, *breathing hard, suddenly slaps him across the face.* Mike *watches her, fascinated. They stand looking at each other breathlessly for a moment, and then suddenly* Mike *slaps her.*)

Lisa (*in a strange voice*)—Don't! You mustn't . . . Please don't!

Mike—You liked it!

Lisa (*backing away from him, wide-eyed*)—I hated it! It's what I ran away from. . . . My father . . .

Mike—You *loved* your father! (*He goes over to her.*) I'm not a sadist, but this is very interesting. I think I'll have to slap you again.

Lisa (*fascinated and terrified*)—Don't! Please don't! Oh, Mike, don't slap me. . . .

Lisa is facing Mike, trembling and cowering. They hear someone coming and move apart. It is Jason. He is back from another adventure and full of it. He had dragged Bronson along the street, threatening to speak to every shabby person they passed. Bronson was terribly fussed.

Suddenly Jason notices Lisa. What's wrong? Nothing, Lisa insists. He had been talking out of turn to Lisa, Mike explains. She'll be all right if Jason will leave her alone for awhile.

"She's a racehorse two-stepping around the paddock; she's a dream coming back like thunder in the middle of the day," says Mike.

Jason goes on with his adventure. He had spoken to several people. After awhile he had lost Bronson. Mike is worried. He thinks he had better be looking for George at the Harvard

Club. Maybe he can pick up Squibb, too. . . .

Lisa and Jason are alone. Lisa is desperate. Mike had made love to her, she confesses, a little hysterically. She doesn't want him in the house. Jason is interested, but not excited. ". . . There is such a thing as an atmosphere of gallantry," he says. "But men don't create that by themselves—"

Lisa is attractive. Jason expects his friends will always be paying her compliments, flirting with her—

"Aren't you jealous?" demands an outraged Lisa.

"Darling, please—don't. I've seen too many plays."

He has gone to her now, and is caressing her. "You've read everything I ever wrote about women," he is saying. "By your own confession, you used it to trap me. Well, use it some more. Be amiable, be friendly, and make it clear to Mike and all the others that you're not interested. I promise you'll have no more trouble."

"I don't like him!"

"I'm sorry—but I've taken him into my life, for better or for worse." Jason's decision is abrupt.

"What is this, for heaven's sake, a triangle?"

"Well, you're doing your best to make it one."

"I? *You've* taken *Mike* for better or worse—and I . . . My God, I'm the Lady in Red!"

"You're getting redder every minute."

For a second Lisa is quiet. Then she resumes her argument. Jason, she insists, is making himself the laughing stock of New York with this ridiculous party; with his prancing around talking about poetry; sneaking up on strangers and snooping into their personal business. Lisa has had her experiences and she knows. Poor people are no good. "I tell you they're ignorant because they want to be ignorant! They're dirty because they want to be dirty. And I hate Mike Ambler!"

"Oh, this isn't your fault, I suppose," counters Jason. "If you were older, or—or wiser . . . Oh, I don't know . . . You think you love me, don't you?"

"Don't say that!" shrills Lisa, remembering what Mike had said.

"You love my furniture, my reputation, the style of the girls I used to go with, my bright remarks. I love your face, your voice, your high spirits. I love what may eventually be in your heart. . . . It's not a bad beginning—if we let this party stream into us and fill us with something bigger than all that. A poet has dropped into our lives. The things he stands for—humanity, color, song, reality—are coming into this house today. If we can learn to take them in our arms, we'll end up in each other's arms."

"And if we can't?"

"Then we're through."

Mike has come through the garden gate, followed by an old man. "The old man is dressed neatly but shabbily, and is a little the worse for wear. His eyes are watery, his face is weak—but there is a flicker of spirit in him somewhere."

Mike introduces his companion as Mr. Humphrey Crocker, a gentleman with plenty of time for the party, seeing this is "his day off, his year off, his century off—"

"Look him over, folks. Mr. Crocker is a capitalist. There, but by the grace of God, stands J. P. Morgan, John D. Rockefeller, Henry Ford. His mind is rotten with money—the money he hasn't got—the money the other fellow has. Look at his smile—it's sweet, the smile of an angel."

Mr. Crocker's reaction to Mike's explanatory eulogy is one of placid acceptance. He evidently enjoys hearing himself described as a prince of the earth who enjoys a great contentment because of the things for which he is *not* responsible. And yet a prince of the earth who is ashamed and bitter with disappointment.

Then Mike leaves them to continue his search for Squibb. "I'm in great form today—and I don't want him to miss me," announces Mike, as he disappears again across the yard.

There isn't much that Jason and Lisa can do for Mr. Crocker. He doesn't drink and he's just et. Presently Lisa has left them, plainly disgusted, and Jason carries on as a sort of interested interrogator. Mr. Crocker, it transpires, is a curiously self-contained person who has sailed the seven seas and never been stirred by a single adventure. Maybe there ought to be stories he could tell, but there ain't. He just minded his own business and was content.

Presently Bill Squibb arrives, also curious about Jason's party. He, too, meets Mr. Crocker and takes part in the quiz, but without changing the results.

"What boat were you on, Mr. Crocker?" asks Jason.

"Sailing vessel—three-master—schooner type."

"Sailing vessel!"

"Carried freight between nineteen-ten and nineteen-twenty."

"What was your job?"

"Started as a second-class seaman, ended up as a—second-class seaman."

"I see. Steady, eh?" Squibb is interested.

"Always. Never got anywhere."

Mr. Crocker's sailing carried him all through the First World War period, but, he repeats, without adventure. He'd never run across a U-boat. He'd been in lots of colorful ports—Bombay! Calcutta! Rio de Janeiro! Nothing ever happened. Been through a coupla hurricanes. Excited? Nah! "Seasick!"

Before he took to sailing, Mr. Crocker had been a stagehand at the Metropolitan. Sure, he knew Caruso. Interesting? "Nah! Jist a kinda fat Eyetalian. He tended to his business and we tended t' ours."

"What line of work you in?" Crocker finally asks Jason.

"I'm a drama critic. And so is this gentleman."

"Well, what do you know. A drama critic."

"I measure, and I weigh."

"Sounds bad."

"That's why I'm trying to fill my house with people—people whom I meet, not professionally, not socially, but by the simple process of seeing them and saying Hello. That's why you're in my house, Mr. Crocker. I hope to get something from you— I'm willing to give in return."

"Mister, you depress me. I thought I was going to have some fun. Excuse me—but I'll be saying good-by."

At the French doors Crocker turns and surveys Jason and Squibb quizzically. "Peculiar people!" he mutters as he goes through the yard.

Squibb can take no more. He is willing to promise on his word of honor that he will not say a word about what has happened— but he is leaving. "If I encounter a noble soul in patched pants with a universal message, I'll send him to you. So long, Jason."

The next three guests to arrive are Nick Wiggins, "a nondescript young fellow"; Kennedy, "a husky Irish-American of about fifty"; and Mrs. Kennedy, "a fine, solid woman." Jason, the host, would have them all sit down. But they prefer to stand.

Kennedy, it soon appears, is in a belligerent mood. Being assured by Wiggins that Jason is, indeed, the man, Kennedy would like to know if Jason did, at such and such a time, on such and such a Second Avenue bus, engage Mr. Wiggins and his fiancée (the Kennedy daughter) in conversation? He did.

Then, is it true that, after enticing them into a discussion of the cost of living, did he or did he not invite the young people to something by way of a party? He did.

"Why?" Mr. Kennedy wants to know.

"I—I see what you mean," stutters Jason, after an awkward pause.

"He said there'd be ham, and roast beef, and cheese, and pickles," Mr. Wiggins chimes in; "and the other fellow said there was a room with a piano in it if we wanted to dance—and this one said we'd have all the beer we could drink."

"Well? I haven't heard anything out of you except 'Yes' and 'Certainly' and 'I wouldn't be surprised.' "

"I don't quite know what to say. I assure you I have no ulterior motive. I merely wanted the pleasure of these people's company. Others are coming, too. If you and Mrs. Kennedy would join us, I'd be more than pleased."

"Who are you, anyway?"

"I—I'm a drama critic."

"Woman, what's that?"

"It's like Louella Parsons—only they write about plays instead of pictures."

"What does one of them fellows want with the likes of us?"

"Don't ask me."

"Hasn't he got friends of his own?"

"I wouldn't know."

"Aren't there people living next door, if he wishes to pass the time of day? He must have relatives somewhere! There's something funny here. I don't like it. (*Turning to the others.*) Let's go!"

Before they can leave Lisa has come gaily down the stairs and greeted the Kennedys with genuine cordiality. She is Mrs. Otis and she is glad to welcome any of her husband's friends. His wife? The Kennedys are surprised and pleased. That puts an entirely different complexion on the matter. Now Mr. Kennedy is ready to relax. Why hadn't Jason said he was a married man? Sure, Kennedy could do with a drop of whiskey. And Mrs. Kennedy wouldn't mind a sandwich and a bottle of beer. Nick, too—but no mustard on his, please!

Soon the spirits of the party have risen noticeably. Lisa is all for having fun. Perhaps they would like to go into the other room and dance. Nick has brought his mouth organ along and is soon playing "Tavern in the Town" with enthusiasm.

Now Lisa has danced around the couch and pulled Jason to his feet. The Kennedys are clapping their hands to the music. A moment later Kennedy has taken Jason's place. "Man—I don't doubt you're a good drama critic—but you're a terrible dancer. Out of the way!" says Kennedy, as he waltzes away with Lisa and Nick changes the tune to the livelier "Turkey in the Straw."

Violet has come to announce that the sandwiches are ready in the dining room, which is inviting news to the guests. Lisa, a bit overwrought emotionally, is trying to catch her breath. She evidently is in a strange mood. Jason, flushed with a new interest, is looking at her deeply—

"Darling—you *are* wonderful," he is saying. "I'm crazy about you."

"I—I want to be alone for a little while," she answers.

"I'm trying to tell you something, dear."

"Listen, damn you—you asked for this, and you're going to get it." Lisa is almost sobbing. Suddenly her voice is hard and cold. "I'm no Breckinridge of Virginia. My father was an unemployed millhand. I was never in Virginia in my life. My name is Breckinridge, but it's Lizzie Breckinridge from Cooperstown, South Carolina. I'm no gentlewoman—and I never was—and I never want to be any more."

"Now I'm beginning to realize why I married you . . . I must have known instinctively that you were not a lady!"

"Go away, will you?"

"Darling—don't you understand—I'm in love with you!"

"Don't tell me that now—I don't want to hear that now! I have to get used to—to what I am! I'm common . . . (*Sobbing.*) You got me into this, and—and—*leave me alone, will you!*"

"All right, dear," says Jason, gently, as he quietly leaves her. From the other room comes the sounds of the continuing party. Nick has returned to "Tavern in the Town."

For a moment Lisa stands quite still, breathing heavily. Then she sits down and kicks off her shoes. She is starting to take off her stockings as Mike comes through the gate into the yard. She does not see him at first and he stands watching her intently. Now Lisa stands up. For a moment she and Mike stand looking at each other. The next moment they are in each other's arms. Lisa has relaxed completely as Mike kisses her fervently.

Jason has come into the hall looking for a chair. He sees Lisa in Mike's arms, still kissing. He turns and quietly carries the chair back into the other room. Presently he can be heard talking to someone. Now he backs into the room, as though deliberately giving Mike and Lisa a chance to separate and pull themselves together. When Jason turns Lisa has quickly put her shoes on and is standing leaning on the door frame looking into the yard.

Mike reports no success at the Harvard Club. He could not find Squibb. Jason would have them both go into the other room and join the party. Quickly Lisa turns to face him—

LISA—Jason . . . I have something to tell you about Mike and me . . .

MIKE—You can't do that. Not now. It's a long subject—it has to do with your whole family tree. Right now Jason's big adventure is waiting in the other room. Here—have a cigarette. (MIKE *picks up a cigarette and offers it to her. There is a rise in the chatter of the unseen guests. After a moment's hesitation, she takes the cigarette.*) Jason, it's after five. In four hours "Hooray for Madam" will be on the stage, launched, like a ship in the sea—and I'll be helpless . . . Jason—do you think Squibb is coming to the party?

JASON (*concentrating with an effort*)—Why—he was here for a little while . . .

MIKE (*anxiously*)—You mean he came and went?

JASON—Yes.

MIKE—What do you mean yes? Did he get disgusted? Did he disapprove? Was he skeptical? Or did he just have another engagement? Jason, wouldn't it be ghastly if he and Bronson—

JASON—It doesn't matter how they feel about your party. Or about your manuscript. When they see it on the stage, they'll really see it.

MIKE—You mean—when they see it, they'll like it?

JASON—That's what I mean.

LISA—Jason!

MIKE—Take it easy. Here—have a light. (*He strikes a match, waits until, after a moment's hesitation, she decides to take the light. She realizes he is trying to steady her and accepts the breathing spell. To* JASON.) I wonder if *you'll* still like it by tonight.

JASON—Nothing will change my mind about your play . . .

MIKE—I'm glad to hear that . . .

JASON—Well, let's go . . .

LISA (*putting her cigarette down*)—*Listen* to me!

VIOLET (*entering*)—There's four more people just came—

JASON—Show them into the dining room, Violet.

VIOLET—Yes, sir. (*She goes.*)

MIKE (*to* LISA)—Come on—hold your horses. The three of us have a job to do. This is Jason's big moment, don't forget.

JASON—That's very true, dear.

LISA (*to* JASON)—I don't care. I've got to say this . . . He knows all about me, see? He knew it the first day he came. And today—

JASON—I'm not surprised at all . . . I've been thinking about you, too—alone in here with the discovery of yourself . . . (*Noise of party grows louder.*) and . . . Look, dear—the guests are pouring into the house—they're Mike's contribution to my ludicrous and obstinate quest for a new life . . .

MIKE (*taking her arm*)—Come on—let's give them everything we've got.

LISA (*breaking away*)—I'm not going. I can't. I've got to have this out right now!

JASON (*with sudden violence*)—Shut up, damn it. I know you kissed him! (LISA *and* MIKE *stand paralyzed.*) I've been standing here trying to forget it, to forgive it, to imagine it never happened—for if it means anything at all, it means I've lost you both. And I'm not blind—I can see it means something. Well, I don't want to face it now—I haven't the wit, nor the courage. . . . I'll face it later—after I've gone through with this party as I must, and after I've seen your play and written about it. And then I'll fight. I'll put up a struggle. I won't give you up lightly—either of you! . . . In the meantime—(*He steps into the hall, the party noises surging up again.*)—shall we join the people?

"There's a moment's hesitation. Then Lisa, followed by Mike, goes through into the hall. Jason goes after them. The party grows louder. We can hear Nick's harmonica again, playing 'Turkey in the Straw.'" The curtain falls.

ACT III

At eleven o'clock the evening of the party the Otis living room is in half darkness, only the lamp on the desk being lighted. When Violet comes down the stairs and starts to clean up the glasses, bottles, etc., she finds Mrs. Kennedy playing solitaire, and Kennedy, his coat off, asleep on the sofa.

Violet reports Lisa as still upstairs and still suffering a headache. It may have come from the overstrain of dancing with

Kennedy, suggests Mrs. Kennedy, but Kennedy, waking slowly, doesn't think so. "I never overstrained a woman in me life—dancing, or any other way," asserts Kennedy with conviction.

However, as to the party Kennedy is a little vague. "Did we have a good time?" he would know from Mrs. Kennedy.

"Yes—I think we did," says she. "A little on the unusual side, but good."

Kennedy has a faint recollection of having broken Jason's favorite vase, and the memory of that makes him uncomfortable. "Oh, God. I hate breaking things—it doesn't do the Irish any good," he says.

Mike Ambler drifts in. He has changed his shirt, but otherwise he is as he was in the afternoon. He has just come from the theatre and is pretty sick about it. "My God, I'll never write another play as long as I live. I'm a wreck!" he says.

"What's the matter—didn't the people like it?" Kennedy asks.

"How do I know?"

"Wasn't you there?"

"Sure I was there. Up in the balcony. They laughed at the most unexpected places. All of them. They all laughed. You'd think they gave each other a signal. And when it was funny, they didn't laugh. I ran away between the acts—I didn't dare listen to what they might say. Why did I ever write a play?"

"Maybe a bit of nourishment is what you need. Violet!"

But Mike will have nothing to do with food. He'll try a drink instead. And he would like to know about the party. It was, Mrs. Kennedy assures him, a very nice party. Nobody got drunk except Kennedy. "After Mr. Otis went the ladies made each other's acquaintance, while the gentlemen had a friendly game of pinochle," says she.

His experience at the theatre is still worrying Mike. He knows that after the second act three of the critics—Bronson and two others—didn't like his play. An usher had heard them talking to each other.

Now Jason is on the phone. Mike is burning with curiosity to know what he thought of the play, but he won't let Violet ask. Jason has called to say that he is walking home.

"I couldn't have stood it if he said it was lousy," wails Mike, trying to explain to Kennedy the reactions of a playwright at a first night. "It all looked different there on the stage, with people sitting in the dark, not saying anything. I hate silent people! . . . Oh, Kennedy, Kennedy . . . these eleven men speak to millions of people in New York—and they're syndicated all over the country. If they say one word like 'second-rate,' it'll hang around my neck for years. Half the critics all over the country will say 'second-rate.' All the club women—can you imagine five hundred thousand women standing in a row, pointing at you, and saying 'Phooey!'"

"Every time I read bad remarks about the President or the Mayor," puts in Mrs. Kennedy, "I think, my goodness, how grand it is to be so important that they can call you names and you don't even bother to punch them in the nose."

"Yeah—that's the way you feel about it. But the President and the Mayor and I—we suffer. The city, that's the Mayor's baby. The country, that's the President's baby. And 'Hooray for the Madam' is my city and my country and my mother and my child. I'd kill, I'd steal, I'd lie—I'd even use clichés—there's nothing so low that I wouldn't do it to protect my play —or it's author."

Now Bill Squibb has arrived, and Mike is upon him with a rush. Did he like the play? Was it clear? Does Bronson— The rush is stopped by Squibb's smiling admission that yes, he liked it; he thought it was glorious in fact; he would like to congratulate the author, and he is positively not kidding.

Mike is "inarticulate with happiness." He would introduce Squibb to the Kennedys—two really great people; he would know more about Squibb's reaction to the play; and Bronson's. His hysteria is mounting when Squibb stops him. Does Mike know where his (Squibb's) copy of "Hooray for the Madam" is? He wants to quote from it—"some of the dialogue between the two elephants at the zoo."

That sets Mike off again. He's glad Squibb wants to quote from it, he's glad Squibb liked that scene—and will Squibb please be careful in the traffic on his way home?

Squibb has gone and Mike is proposing that they all have a drink. They're great people, the Kennedys; if they weren't great Jason Otis wouldn't have them in his house. "You're America," announces Mike; "you're the original hunk of wood out of which it's all cut. . . . Here's to all the people in this house—beautiful people."

Kennedy and Mike raise their glasses. Mrs. Kennedy, having no glass, takes a swig from the bottle.

Now Mike, grown suddenly thoughtful, thinks he will have a look at the lady upstairs. . . . When he comes back he is very happy. When Mrs. Kennedy would know how he found Lisa he is ready to shout. "She's the dawn in Carolina—the dew on the fence railing. She's the distant rumble of the train over the hill. . . ."

Jason has come through the hall door. He is haggard and nervous, but he brightens at the sight of the Kennedys and is again the perfect host. He is pleased that they liked the party. When Kennedy shamefacedly admits the breaking of the vase Jason's poise does not desert him. "I'll never forgive myself," Kennedy is saying. "I can't forget it. Was it expensive?"

"Yes. It was expensive." Jason has put his hand on Kennedy's shoulder. "And every time I look at the table it stood on, I'll remember you both—and when I do, I'll see something more beautiful in its place. I want you to remember it that way, too."

"He makes it out that you did him a favor by breaking it," says Mrs. Kennedy, in awed tones.

"You're right—everybody in this house is beautiful." Kennedy agrees with Mike.

The Kennedys have gone. Mike and Jason are alone. "You were heroic about that vase," says Mike. "I could have killed them," admits Jason.

MIKE (*his anxiety overcoming him*)—Jason—
JASON—Why are you here?
MIKE—Jason—I can't stand the suspense any longer. Aren't you going to tell me what you think? Do you still like it?
JASON (*slowly*)—Yes—I still like it. Did you see Lisa?
MIKE—Do you still think it's great?
JASON—Did you see Lisa?
MIKE (*after an almost imperceptible hesitation*)—No.
JASON—I'm glad. I didn't want you to see her—and *I* don't want to see *you*, either—until I'd finished my notice. I asked you to telephone me at midnight.
MIKE (*humbly*)—I'm sorry, Jason. You haven't told me—do you still think it's *great?*
JASON (*slowly*)—Well, the word great shouldn't be used lightly. I thought the manuscript was great. But tonight I saw it on the stage—in its final form. I had to think it over. That's why I walked home.
MIKE—And . . . ?
JASON—It's never taken me so long to form an opinion. You see, somehow you and your play have become one and the same thing to me. I found myself standing on the corner of Forty-

ninth Street and Sixth Avenue—and doubting you, you as a person. I was visualizing what had happened between you and Lisa today when you were alone—and my imagination took an unhealthy leap.

Mike—Let me tell you about this afternoon—and about this evening too. I might as well tell you.

Jason—No! You see, in that moment of doubt, I had the extraordinary experience of seeing your play in a different light. What had seemed eloquent became glib. Sincerity became superficial . . .

Mike—But, Jason—if you'll only let me tell you—

Jason—Not now. I'm all right now. I was all right by the time I reached Fifth Avenue. I think your play is great.

Mike (*thrilled*)—You mean it?

Jason—Yes.

Mike—You won't change your mind—you really think so?

Jason—Go away. Telephone me at midnight, will you please?

Mike (*offering* Jason *his hand*)—In the name of drama and literature we're friends.

Jason (*taking* Mike's *hand*)—That's how I want it to be.

Mike—And in the name of humanity.

Jason—Don't say any more. (Mike *drops* Jason's *hand*.)

Mike—All right, Jason.

Miss Crane has come to take Jason's dictation. She has called a messenger for a quarter to one instead of twelve-thirty, she explains. Now she has settled herself at the desk, with pencil poised. Jason begins—

Jason (*dictating slowly, fighting to retain his detachment*)— In "Hooray for the Madam" the American theatre welcomes an enchanting new personality. Mike Ambler, in this, his first play, brings innocence and beauty to Broadway. (*He pauses, looks up the stairs.*) Let us forget all the formulas for the well-made drama. Ambler is both more and less than a playwright—he is a poet who reports, with the wondering eyes of a child, the heartbreak and the laughter of the common man. The common man is beautiful . . . (*He happens to glance into the wastebasket, and pauses. He reaches into the wastebasket, bringing forth a large, easily recognizable chunk of the vase which had decorated the living room. After a moment, he drops the chunk back into the wastebasket.*) . . . is beautiful. To imply that one therefore must rush out and embrace the first taxidriver or plumber who comes along is perhaps going too far—but that is because not only the plumber has his limitations, but also the party of the first part. It would take Walt Whitman, Abraham Lincoln, or Mike Ambler to achieve it—and even then, the plumber might not respond neatly by shaking hands and crying "Brother!" . . . And yet when Mike Ambler cries "Brother!" he does it with supernal music.

He pauses to inquire about Lisa, when Violet appears on the stairs. Lisa is better and would have him call her when he is through working. He tries to go on with his dictation and changes his mind. He will call Lisa now.

When Lisa appears on the stairway, she is dressed for the street. Why? She will tell him when he has finished his review. He insists on an answer now—and gets it. Lisa has decided that after what has happened, she can't stay there. She must go to Mike. She must find out what his kiss meant. Is she in love with Mike?

"I don't know! How do I know? I've only seen him twice in my life—and I kissed him." Lisa is quite evidently in pain. "I never kissed anybody—not one person—before I met you." . . .

"How did you happen to be kissing him?" Jason demands, with difficulty.

LISA—Oh—(*She lights a cigarette.*)—he was nagging at me, telling me to take off my shoes and stockings. He wanted me to go out in the garden and stand on that little hunk of grass.

JASON—What for?

LISA—Because I was always barefoot when I was a kid. I slapped him. And then he slapped me—and then somehow, it made me feel like a kid again—when my father would slap me. I got all scared and excited—and he seemed to know . . .

JASON—Know what?

LISA—*Something*. . . . It was as if we were both in Carolina—both being kids. (*She sits.*) I—I wanted my mother all of a sudden—although she never cared a damn about me . . . Then you came along—and you said if I didn't roll in his mud, you were through with me. I didn't want to lose you.

JASON—Didn't you?

LISA—No, I didn't. And all the time I was still feeling that slap—and the things he said . . . And I was hating you, for throwing me at him. And the Kennedys—they did something to me, too. When I got through dancing, I was really back in Carolina—I was suddenly remembering a lot of forgotten things that happened—glorious things—*feeling* them. . . . I had to be alone.

JASON—And then he came in. (*Pause.*) Well! (*With growing relief.*) That's not so bad! Why, it looks to me as if—by heaven, this man Ambler *is* amazing! He's actually done something for you. He made you meet yourself!

LISA (*with a strange, disturbed manner*)—Is that what he did?

JASON—Of course! (*He sits beside her.*) Why, it's obvious! He's done the same thing for me! If not for him, I wouldn't be loving you so much right now. . . .

LISA (*suffering*)—Wouldn't you?

JASON (*moving closer to her*)—I love you more than ever. (LISA *moves away almost imperceptibly.*) Why, darling, this is wonderful! I never felt about a woman the way I feel about you—the way I began feeling this afternoon. . . . It's been a horrible day for both of us, dear—but it's been a good day, too.

Violet comes in. She is carrying a folded sheet of note paper, and is disconcerted at finding Mrs. Otis downstairs. At his demand Violet obediently hands the note to Jason. Now let her tell Mr. Ambler to come in. Jason reads the note to Lisa—

"My darling, my love—it lifted my heart to see you again, so pale and bright. Please be sure not to talk to him until he has finished his review. I'll be on the corner, listening for your step like the roar of a distant train over the hills. Mike. P.S. Bring along some money. We'll need at least twenty-five dollars."

Why hadn't Lisa told him that she had seen Mike? Because Mike had asked her not to. What had they talked about? . . .

Mike has joined them. "He is a little frightened, but maintains a surface air of friendliness." Jason turns on him—

"Now, Jason—you asked me not to tell you. I was trying to —to explain. . . ."

JASON (*hating him*)—You weren't trying to explain anything. You were going to lie. You told me you hadn't seen her.

MIKE—I didn't want to upset you. But I'm glad we're all together now. Everything is becoming beautiful again. The truth is always beautiful. (*Drunk with his own logic, he relaxes, sits.*) Let's all remember this night as the night we faced the truth. It'll keep our friendship perfect—the way you wanted it, Jason.

JASON (*after pause, to* LISA)—You can see my lawyer tomorrow—or any other lawyer. (LISA *rises, picks up her coat.*) Go to Reno—or stay in New York—there'll be no trouble about alimony. And good luck to you both.

MIKE—Now, Jason, you're getting romantic. I wasn't thinking about marriage. Were you, Lisa? Of course, it's possible I'll love her tomorrow as much as I do tonight. Maybe she'll be crazy about me—she probably will. It might even last a week or two—there was one time in my life when it lasted three and a half months.

JASON (*quietly*)—I think I know what to do about you.

MIKE (*rises, comes to* JASON)—Now wait a minute—if you don't like this idea— Say! How about my moving in here? You've got a guest room. Then she won't have to go. With me in the house, everything will come to a head in a few days, instead of dragging on the way it would with conventional people. Why waste some of the best years of your life—and Lisa's? (*Suddenly aware of the murderous expression on* JASON'S *face.*) You're sore! What is this? When you said this afternoon that you didn't want to lose us both, you touched my heart.

JASON—You're a swine.

MIKE—I don't get this! She's a young girl. Do you think you're the only man she'll ever love? And if it's somebody else, why not me—your friend?

JASON (*raging*)—I'm going to kill you!

MIKE (*retreating solemnly*)—My God, Jason—I'm frightened.

JASON (*following him*)—You'll be *unconscious* in a minute.

MIKE—Wait! (*Pushing a chair between them.*) This is a matter of life and death—I have to tell you something!

JASON (*circling the chair*)—Not me! I'll twist your tongue out!

MIKE—Jason—you mustn't touch me—I've got another play in me! I'm very strong, but suppose accidently you hurt me?

JASON—It won't be accidentally!

MIKE—I knew a fellow once and another fellow threw a bottle at him and he injured his brain. (*With terrible anxiety.*) Jason, this is a great play—it's bigger than "Hooray for the Madam" —let me just tell you the opening scene!

JASON (*throws chair out of way, grabs* MIKE *and claps his hand over* MIKE'S *mouth*)—I'll shut you up, all right!

MIKE (*pulling* JASON'S *hand down*)—You've got to admit I'm a genius—I may write the great American drama—those were your own words—

JASON

Jason (*full of loathing*)—You're a fraud and a mediocrity. You're an eloquent half-wit. You're the idiotic victim of your malevolent self. (Mike *stands staring at him.*) You're a nightmare licking its chops under the impression that it's a daydream. (Mike *slowly backs away.*) Your work is lazy fantasy masquerading as imagination.

Jason has stopped suddenly. Without turning his head he calls to Miss Crane. Let her read him the opening paragraph of his review. She does. Now let her tear that up and start over—

Jason (*dictating—his eyes blazingly on* Mike)—"Hooray for the Madam" is a play cunningly designed to dupe literary fellows, which critics are often said to be. It seems original, but it is merely novel. All the symbols of innocent pleasure, of childlike joy, and the deeper symbols of humanity, are juggled and flashed in a manner to delude the unwary sophisticate.

Mike (*numbly*)—Jason, there are three critics at least who don't like the show. If you do this, it may destroy me!

Jason (*never taking his eyes off* Mike)—Mr. Ambler's writing seems heartfelt, but it is merely sentimental with trimmings. It is the product of an articulate half-wit, of a writer who is the cheerful, idiotic victim of his malevolently prankish self.

Mike—You're murdering me in cold blood.

Jason—Where Steinbeck in his "Tortilla Flat" gives us the eternal godhead through the vagaries of wine-guzzling, shiftless trash, Mr. Ambler offers a troupe of incredible eccentrics.

Mike—I have a new play in my heart, but I'm losing it . . . I'll never be able to write again.

Jason (*inexorably going on*)—The play is overburdened with feeble fantasy masquerading as virile imagination. And even here it is full of clumsy plagiarisms from Tchekov and Gorky. If this man's work is original, then Eugene O'Neill, Franz Werfel, Sinclair Lewis, Thomas Mann and Evelyn Waugh are hacks. You can find equal originality in the nearest lunatic asylum.

Mike (*with a cry of great pain*)—You've said enough! (*Pause. He moves slowly to the French doors, stops.*) I'm going. (*It is, in a way, an invitation to* Lisa. *But she is immovable, as if she hadn't seen or heard* Mike.) I'm going. . . . (*Still no response from* Lisa, *whose eyes never leave* Jason. *Now the coat falls from her hand.*) They say it's good for a poet to have his heart broken. They say it's good for him to be ridiculed and scorned by the world. They say it all turns into bigger and better poetry. In that case, I ought to thank you both. I wish I could. (*He goes.* LISA *turns away from* JASON, *thinking.* JASON, *looking at her, starts dictating again.*)

JASON—The egotistical challenge of this sort of writing is dangerous also to the unformed, imaginative mind. It can split a maturing person in two and toss him, or her, back into the limbo of adolescence. It turns black into white and white into black—not with the disarming malice of an Oscar Wilde, but with evangelical fervor.

LISA (*unable to control herself any longer, goes to him with great excitement*)—Jason, you've made me see him so clearly! You've taken him apart! You've shown me what he really is!

JASON (*turning to* MISS CRANE, *continuing as if she hadn't spoken*)—Almost any night, standing on a soapbox, you will find Mr. Ambler's counterpart, some hyper-thyroid uttering words and ideas wondrous to behold, full of meaningless excitement, bearing a startling resemblance to the things which gifted people say and think. The so-called plot defies description, but I will sandpaper my finger and try to hold down one typical episode. . . . (*He pauses to think.*)

LISA (*rushing to him, tears in her eyes*)—Oh, Jason, I'm just beginning to understand you, to appreciate you. You love me! You really love me! You love me in a way that I never knew anything about until tonight. You're fighting for me with—Oh, your words are like—why, you're out in the ring right now swinging with both fists! This is thrilling—don't stop!

JASON (*shouting—in pain*)—I've got a deadline to meet!—will you leave me alone, for God's sake?

LISA (*with utter meekness*)—Yes, darling. (*He stands, waiting impatiently. She reaches to him with her hands, timidly, hesitates, then goes over to her hat and coat, picks them up and, with her tearful eyes still on him, goes up the stairs, looking at him happily until she disappears.* JASON *stands still a moment.*)

JASON (*to* MISS CRANE)—Where was I?

MISS CRANE—"I will sandpaper my finger and try to hold down one typical episode."

JASON (*after pause*)—Throw it away, Miss Crane. We can't use it.

MISS CRANE—All of it?

JASON—All of it.

MISS CRANE—Oh, it sounds *awfully* good.

JASON (*deeply thinking*)—It doesn't happen to be my opinion.

Miss Crane—I still have the first one you dictated.

Jason—I'm afraid that's not my opinion either. (*Pause.*) I'm just beginning to find out what I think of a man. Both the hate and the love are true.

Miss Crane—Excuse me—but it's a quarter after twelve.

Jason (*after another pause*)—Yes. All right. Ready?

Miss Crane—Ready.

Jason (*dictating slowly, in control, many emotions underneath*)—In seeking a proper evaluation for a living work of art, the reviewer faces himself as well as it. A balanced opinion is not a mild, bloodless compromise. It is a struggle, sometimes involving sweat and tears. The critic, like the artist, must go through fire. It is thus, humble and burnt, that I present my conclusions about "Hooray for the Madam," by Mike Ambler, which is both a work of art and a trap for the fastidious. One moment it is an ineffectual nightmare; the next moment it is a rhapsody straight from heaven, more real than automobiles or governments. Call Ambler a fool, a mountebank—and you won't be wrong. But, however reluctantly, you must also call him an angel. . . . As he talks,

THE CURTAIN FALLS

ANGEL STREET
A Melodrama in Three Acts

By Patrick Hamilton

IT had been a pretty dull season in the New York theatres, up to early December. Nothing resembling a "smash" hit, as the Broadway classicists describe it, had occurred through the busier production months of October and November. Nothing very promising in the way of drama was in sight.

When Shepard Traube announced the production of a melodrama he had brought back from the Pacific Coast and renamed "Angel Street" he did not raise expectations so much as the fraction of a degree. The play had been known previously as "Gaslight." Under that title it had had some little success in London, but it had been tried in several summer theatres in America without causing anything resembling a stampede, and its reception in Hollywood had been quite conservative.

Traube, being the author of an informative brochure entitled "So You Want to Go into the Theatre?" had cannily protected himself by selling shares in the venture to something like fifteen angels, who contributed approximately $15,000. Hope ran high with the angels opening night, when the curtain rose on "Angel Street," but audience expectations were, if anything, a little below normal. The Messrs. Shubert, lessees of the John Golden Theatre, had ordered just enough tickets printed to cover the first three performances—a Friday night opening and two performances Saturday—evidently expecting a quick failure.

And then occurred one of those fantastic theatre surprises that serve to keep speculative investors producing bank rolls and keep experienced, but incorrigibly optimistic, playgoers approaching each new play with the hope in their hearts that something like "Angel Street"—or "Men in White" or "The Children's Hour"—will happen.

The reviewers' notices were on the rave side. This correspondent ran gaily from the theatre to his typewriter, there to deliver himself a little wildly of the statement that he had, indeed, just seen the theatre really come alive for the first time that season.

Curiously, all this excitement was caused by nothing more important than a modest but skillfully wrought bit of theatre.

ANGEL STREET

"Angel Street" is one of those good old Victorian thrillers, common to the stage thirty or forty years ago, which depends entirely upon the interest it builds in its characters and the suspense it holds as to their adventure of the evening. True, this is an especially well-written thriller. The author, Patrick Hamilton, has a gift for words and scenes equaled by few of his contemporaries. But after it is all added up, it is no more than a good melodrama exceptionally well staged.

"Angel Street" was an immediate, though never exactly a sensational, success. It ran through the season easily, and to good profits. Naturally, there were those who did not always respond to the drama with the same enthusiasm that moved the first audience. A majority, however, were thrilled and made happy by this particular theatre experience.

The first scene of "Angel Street" is properly terrifying. We are in a gloomy living room on the first floor of a four-story house in London the latter part of the last century. "The room is furnished in all the heavily draped and dingy profusion of the period, and yet, amidst this abundance of paraphernalia, an air is breathed of poverty, wretchedness and age."

It is late afternoon, "the zero hour, as it were, before the feeble dawn of gaslight and tea." Stretched out on the sofa in front of the fire Jack Manningham is sleeping heavily. "He is tall, good-looking, about forty-five, heavily mustached and bearded and perhaps a little too well dressed."

Sitting near Mr. Manningham at a center table, Bella Manningham is sewing. "She is about thirty-four, has been almost a beauty, but now has a haggard, wan, frightened air, with rings under her eyes, which tell of sleepless nights and worse." Big Ben has just struck 5. From a distance the jingle of a muffin man's bell can be faintly heard. It is the bell that first attracts Mrs. Manningham's attention. She listens to it "furtively and indecisively, almost as if she were frightened even of this," then decides upon action and goes to the bell cord. Elizabeth, cook and housekeeper, "a stout, amiable, subservient woman of about fifty," answers and is given whispered instructions.

Mr. Manningham, however, is not sleeping as heavily as supposed. His position has not changed the fraction of an inch, but his eyes are open now and he is demanding in rather particular detail a report as to what is going on. What is Mrs. Manningham doing, and why? And why does she seem so apprehensive about doing it? The fire's in ashes. Will she please call and have it replenished? No, no, no, no—she is not to put the coal on. Haven't they had that out many times before? What does she suppose servants are for? And why should they be considered—

"Consider them?" Mr. Manningham is quite firm. "There's your extraordinary confusion of mind again. You speak as though they work for no consideration. I happen to consider Elizabeth to the tune of sixteen pounds per annum. And the girl ten. Twenty-six pounds a year all told. And if that is not consideration of the most acute and lively kind, I should like to know what is."

"Yes, Jack, I expect you are right."

"I have no doubt of it, my dear. It's sheer weak-mindedness to think otherwise."

Mr. Manningham is up and moving about, now. When Nancy, the second maid, arrives to put on the coal he becomes quite chatty. Nancy, being a "self-conscious, pretty, cheeky girl of nineteen," is not displeased with this attention nor with its effect upon Mrs. Manningham. Nancy likes to be called impudent and an evident heart-breaker. Of course she isn't, but— "Won't you tell us the name of your chemist?" Mr. Manningham persists. "Perhaps you could pass it on to Mrs. Manningham—and help banish her pallor. She would be most grateful, I have no doubt."

"I'd be most happy to, I'm sure, Sir."

"Or are women too jealous of their discoveries to pass them on to a rival?"

"I don't know, Sir. . . . Will that be all you're wanting, Sir?"

"Yes. That's all I want, Nancy— (*She stops.*) Except my tea."

"It'll be coming directly, Sir."

Mr. Manningham is quite surprised when Mrs. Manningham reproaches him for humiliating her before the servants. He certainly must have seen how he was hurting her, she insists; that Nancy was really laughing at her; has long been laughing at her in secret. No, Mr. Manningham has not noticed any such thing. And if Nancy does laugh at her, isn't it her own fault?

"You mean that I'm a laughable person?" demands Mrs. Manningham.

"I don't mean anything," insists Mr. Manningham. "It's you who read meanings into everything, Bella, dear. I wish you weren't such a perfect little silly. Come here and stop it. I've just thought of something nice."

The something nice that Mr. Manningham has thought of is a visit to the theatre. He has heard that Mr. MacNaughton, a celebrated actor, is playing a season of comedy and tragedy and he thought Bella would like to see him.

Mrs. Manningham is completely thrilled at the prospect. What perfect heaven that would mean! To go with Jack to the theatre! Mrs. Manningham can hardly realize such joy. And would she prefer seeing Mr. MacNaughton in comedy or tragedy? Would she prefer to laugh or to cry?

"Oh—I want to laugh," laughs Mrs. Manningham. "But then, I should like to cry, too. In fact, I should like to do both. Oh, Jack, what made you decide to take me?"

She has gone to the little stool beside his chair and leans against him as she talks.

"Well, my dear, you've been very good lately, and I thought it would be well to take you out of yourself."

Mrs. Manningham—Oh, Jack dear. You have been so much kinder lately. Is it possible you're beginning to see my point of view?

Mr. Manningham—I don't know that I ever differed from it, did I, Bella?

Mrs. Manningham—Oh, Jack dear. It's true. It's true. (*Looks at him.*) All I need is to be taken out of myself—some little change—to have some attention from you. Oh, Jack, I'd be better—I could really try to be better—you know in what way—if only I could get *out* of myself a little more.

Mr. Manningham—How do you mean, my dear, exactly, *better?*

Mrs. Manningham (*looking away*)—You know. . . . You know in what way, dear. About all that's happened lately. We said we wouldn't speak about it.

Mr. Manningham (*drawing away and looking away*)—Oh, no—don't let's speak about that.

Mrs. Manningham—No, dear, I don't want to—but what I say is so important. I *have* been better—even in the last week. Haven't you noticed it? And why is it? Because you have stayed in, and been kind to me. The other night when you stayed in and played cards with me, it was like old days, and I went to bed feeling a normal, happy, healthy, human being. And then, the day after, when you read your book to me, Jack, and we sat by the fire. I felt all my love for you coming back, then, Jack. And I slept that night like a child. All those ghastly dreads and terrible, terrible fears seemed to have vanished. And all just because you had given me your time, and taken me from brooding on myself in this house all day and night.

Mr. Manningham (*raising her head*)—I wonder if it is that—or whether it's merely that your medicine is beginning to benefit you?

Mrs. Manningham—No, Jack, dear, it's not my medicine. I've taken my medicine religiously—haven't I taken it religiously? Much as I detest it! It's more than medicine that I want. It's the medicine of a sweet, sane mind, of interest in something. Don't you see what I mean?

Mr. Manningham—Well—we are talking about gloomy subjects, aren't we?

Mrs. Manningham—Yes. I don't want to be gloomy, dear—that's the last thing I want to be. I only want you to understand. Say you understand.

Mr. Manningham—Well, dear. Don't I seem to? Haven't I just said I'm taking you to the theatre?

Mrs. Manningham—Yes, dear . . . Yes, you have. Oh, and you've made me so happy—so happy, dear.

There is still the question of comedy or tragedy to be settled. Mrs. Manningham is too happy to care greatly. To go to the play with her husband—that is enough.

But when Nancy comes with the tea Mrs. Manningham puts the question to her. What would she choose—comedy or tragedy? It's comedy for Nancy, every time. Mrs. Manningham makes a note of that. When Nancy turns to leave the room she sticks her tongue out at the girl. "The little beast! Let her put that in her pipe and smoke it!"

"But what has she done?" demands Mr. Manningham.

"Ah—you don't know her. She tries to torment and score off me all day long. You don't see these things. A man wouldn't. She thinks me a poor thing. And now she can suffer the news that you're taking me to the theatre."

"I think you imagine things, my dear."

They are at tea now, and Mrs. Manningham's happiness convinces Mr. Manningham that he should have thought of taking her to the theatre oftener. He, too, is fond of the theatre. As a young man he had wanted to be an actor; thought seriously of trying to be. If he were an actor, Mrs. Manningham suggests, she should have a free seat and come every night to see him—and to protect him from all the designing hussies who would be after him. The idea is not displeasing to Mr. Manningham.

Mrs. Manningham is still chattering gaily when Mr. Manningham suddenly stiffens. He is looking fixedly at the back wall. Now he rises and going to the fireplace, turns his back on Mrs. Manningham. When he calls to her his voice is calm, yet menacing.

"Bella!"

"What is it? What's the matter? What is it now?" Mrs. Manningham's voice has dropped almost to a whisper; her face is ashen.

MR. MANNINGHAM (*walking over to fireplace and speaking with his back to her*)—I have no desire to upset you, Bella, but I have just observed something very much amiss. Will you please rectify it at once, while I am not looking, and we will assume that it has not happened.

MRS. MANNINGHAM—Amiss? What's amiss? For God's sake don't turn your back on me. What has happened?

MR. MANNINGHAM—You know perfectly well what has happened, Bella, and if you will rectify it at once I will say no more about it.

MRS. MANNINGHAM—I don't know. I don't know. You have left your tea. Tell me what it is. Tell me.

MR. MANNINGHAM—Are you trying to make a fool of me, Bella? What I refer to is on the wall behind you. If you will put it back, I will say no more about it.

MRS. MANNINGHAM—The wall behind me? What? (*Turns.*) Oh . . . yes . . . The picture . . . Who has taken it down? Why has it been taken down?

MR. MANNINGHAM—Yes. Why has it been taken down? Why, indeed. You alone can answer that, Bella. Why was it taken down before? Will you please take it from wherever you have hidden it, and put it back on the wall again?

MRS. MANNINGHAM But I haven't hidden it, Jack. (*Rising.*) I didn't do it. Oh, for God's sake look at me. I didn't do it. I don't know where it is. Someone else must have done it.

MR. MANNINGHAM—Someone else? (*Turning to her.*) Are you suggesting perhaps that I should play such a fantastic and wicked trick?

MRS. MANNINGHAM—No, dear, no! But someone else. (*Going to him.*) Before God, I didn't do it! Someone else, dear, someone else.

MR. MANNINGHAM (*shaking her off*)—Will you please leave go of me? (*Walking over to bell.*) We will see about "someone else."

Mrs. Manningham (*crossing to front of couch*)—Oh, Jack—don't ring the bell. Don't ring it. Don't call the servants to witness my shame. It's not my shame for I haven't done it—but *don't* call the servants! Tell them not to come. (*He has rung the bell. She goes to him.*) Let's talk this over between ourselves! Don't call that girl in. Please!

Mr. Manningham has shaken himself free of his wife and rung the bell. Elizabeth answers. Let Elizabeth have a look at the room, at the walls, particularly, and see if she notices anything wrong. It is not hard for Elizabeth to note the missing picture. With that she had nothing to do. Nor ever has had. Will she fetch the Bible from the desk and kiss it as a token of her truthfulness? Elizabeth hesitates a moment but finally does as she is bid. So much for Elizabeth. Now let Nancy be sent.

"Jack—spare me that girl," pleads Mrs. Manningham, wildly. "Don't call her in. I'll say anything. I'll say that I did it. I did it, Jack, I did it. Don't have that girl in. Don't!"

"Will you have the goodness to contain yourself?" calmly demands Mr. Manningham.

Nancy is quick to notice the missing picture and to add her denial of any knowledge concerning it. Kiss the Bible? Why not? Nancy is smiling as she leaves the room.

As Mr. Manningham moves to replace the Bible on the desk, Mrs. Manningham intercepts him, snatching the book from his hands.

"Give me that Bible!" she screams. "Give it to me! Let me kiss it, too! There! There! There! Do you see that I kiss it?"

Mr. Manningham (*putting out his hand for the Bible*)—For God's sake be careful what you do. Do you desire to commit sacrilege above all else?

Mrs. Manningham—It is no sacrilege, Jack. Someone else has committed sacrilege. Now see—I swear before God Almighty that I never touched that picture. (*Kisses it.*) There!

Mr. Manningham (*grabbing the Bible*)—Then, by God, you are mad, and you don't know what you do. You unhappy wretch—you're stark gibbering mad—like your wretched mother before you.

Mrs. Manningham—Jack—you promised you would never say that again.

Mr. Manningham—The time has come to face facts, Bella.

If this progresses you will not be much longer under *my* protection.

Mrs. Manningham—Jack—I'm going to make a last appeal to you. I'm going to make a last appeal. I'm desperate, Jack. Can't you see that I'm desperate? If you can't, you must have a heart of stone.

Mr. Manningham (*turning to her*)—Go on. What do you wish to say?

Mrs. Manningham—Jack, I may be going mad, like my poor mother—but if I am mad, you have got to treat me gently. Jack—before God—I never lie to you knowingly. If I have taken down that picture from its place I have not known it. *I have not known it.* If I took it down on those other occasions I did not know it, either. Jack, if I steal your things—your rings —your keys—your pencils and your handkerchiefs, and you find them later at the bottom of my box, as indeed you do, then I do not know that I have done it. . . . Jack, if I commit these fantastic, meaningless mischiefs—so meaningless—why should I take a picture down from its place? If I do all these things, then I am certainly going off my head, and must be treated kindly and gently so that I may get well. You must *bear* with me, Jack, *bear* with me—not storm and rage. God knows I'm trying, Jack, I'm trying! Oh, for God's sake believe me that I'm trying and be kind to me! (*Lays her head on his chest.*)

Mr. Manningham—Bella, my dear—have you any idea where that picture is now?

Mrs. Manningham—Why, yes, I suppose it's behind the cupboard.

Mr. Manningham—Will you please go and see?

Mrs. Manningham (*vaguely*)—Yes . . . yes . . . Yes, it's here.

Mr. Manningham—Then you did know where it was, Bella. You did know where it was.

Mrs. Manningham—No! No! I only *supposed* it was! I only supposed it was because it was found there before! It was found there twice before! Don't you see? I didn't know . . . I didn't!

Mr. Manningham remains studiedly calm through Mrs. Manningham's threatened hysteria. Sooner or later, he warns, they will have to face facts, but for the moment he will say no more. He is going out and he thinks Bella should go to her room and lie down. This suggestion causes Mrs. Manningham further distress. She begs not to be sent to her room. Why must he always go and leave her alone after one of these terrible scenes?

Mr. Manningham is of no mind to argue the point. He is going out and while he is out he will pay the grocer's bill—if she will tell him where she put the bill. On the top of the secretary? No, it isn't there. Mr. Manningham searches carefully. The bill is not to be found. Mrs. Manningham is again frantic with fear. Soon she is pawing excitedly through all the drawers of the secretary, screaming that she knows she put the bill there that morning. Now Mr. Manningham has followed her to the desk and with his hands on her shoulders, is shaking her violently—

"Will you control yourself?" he shouts. "Will you control yourself? . . . Listen to me, Madam, if you utter another sound I'll knock you down and take you to your room and lock you in darkness for a week. I have been too lenient with you, and I mean to alter my tactics."

"Oh, God help me! God help me!" She has sunk to her knees.

"May God help you indeed." He has lifted her to her feet. "Now listen to me. I am going to leave you until ten o'clock. In that time you will recover that paper, and admit to me that you have lyingly and purposely concealed it . . . if not, you will take the consequences. You are going to see a doctor, Madam, more than one doctor. And they shall decide what this means. Now do you understand me?" He has taken his coat and hat and is moving toward the door.

"Oh, God—be patient with me. If I am mad, be patient with me."

"I have been patient with you and controlled myself long enough. It is now for you to control yourself, or take the consequences. Think upon that, Bella. (*Opens doors.*)"

"Jack . . . Jack . . . don't go . . . Jack . . . You're still going to take me to the theatre, aren't you?"

"What a question to ask me at such a time. No, Madam, emphatically, I am not. You play fair by me, and I'll play fair by you. But if we are going to be enemies, you and I, you will not prosper, believe me."

The door slams behind Mr. Manningham. Whimperingly Mrs. Manningham picks her way to the secretary and renews her search for the bill. She finds her medicine and takes that, with a shudder of disgust. She has thrown herself down on the couch and is sobbing bitterly when there is a knock at the door. Elizabeth has come to say that a gentleman has called and is quite determined to see Mrs. Manningham. Elizabeth, too, is anxious that her mistress see the man—

"Madam, Madam. I don't know what's going on between you and the Master, but you've got to hold up, Madam. You've got to hold up."

"I am going out of my mind, Elizabeth. That's what's going on."

"Don't talk like that, Madam. You've got to be brave. You mustn't go on lying here in the dark, or your mind *will* go. You must see this gentleman. It's *you* he wants—not the Master. He's waiting to see you. Come, Madam, it'll take you out of yourself."

The caller is Detective Rough of Scotland Yard. "He is middle-aged, graying, short, wiry, active, brusque, friendly, overbearing. He has a low warming chuckle." His attitude toward Mrs. Manningham is gentle, almost paternal, and plainly aimed at inspiring her trust.

He knows that she doesn't know him from Adam; he doesn't wonder that she thought he had come to see her husband, but she is wrong. Detective Rough has come to see her, and has chosen this particular time because Mr. Manningham is not there.

"You're the lady who is going off her head, aren't you?" blurts Detective Rough, while busily divesting himself of coat, hat and scarf. The thought makes him chuckle, but it terrifies Mrs. Manningham.

"What made you say that?" she all but screams. "Who are you? What have you come to talk about?"

ROUGH—Ah, you're running away with things, Mrs. Manningham, and asking me a good deal I can't answer at once. Instead of that, I am going to ask you a question or two. . . . Now, please, will you come here, and give me your hands? (*Pause. She obeys.*) Now, Mrs. Manningham, I want you to take a good look at me, and see if you are not looking at someone to whom you can give your trust. I am a perfect stranger to you, and you can read little in my face besides that. But I can read a great deal in yours.

MRS. MANNINGHAM—What? What can you read in mine?

ROUGH—Why, Madam, I can read the tokens of one who has traveled a very long way upon the path of sorrow and doubt—and will have, I fear, to travel a little further yet before she comes to the end. But I fancy she is coming to the end, for all that. Come now, are you going to trust me, and listen to me?

Mrs. Manningham (*after a pause*)—Who are you? God knows I need help.

Rough (*still holding her hands*)—I very much doubt whether God knows anything of the sort, Mrs. Manningham. If he did I believe he would have come to your aid before this. But I am here, and so you must give me your faith.

Mrs. Manningham (*withdrawing her hands and withdrawing a step*)—Who are you? Are you a doctor?

Rough—Nothing so learned, Ma'am. Just a plain police detective.

Mrs. Manningham (*shrinking away*)—Police detective?

Rough—Yes. Or was some years ago. At any rate, still detective enough to see that you've been interrupted in your tea. Couldn't you start again, and let me have a cup? (*He stands back of chair and holds it for her.*)

Mrs. Manningham—Why, yes—yes. I will give you a cup. It only wants water.

Rough (*crossing around above table and to back of chair*)—You never heard of the celebrated Sergeant Rough, Madam? Sergeant Rough, who solved the Claudesley Diamond case—Sergeant Rough, who hunted down the Camberwell dogs—Sergeant Rough, who brought Sandham himself to justice. (*He has his hand on back of chair as he looks at her.*) Or were all such sensations before your time?

Mrs. Manningham (*looking up at* Rough)—Sandham? Why, yes—I have heard of Sandham—the murderer—the throttler.

Rough—Yes—Madam—Sandham the Throttler. And you are now looking at the man who gave Sandham to the man who throttled him. And that was the common hangman. In fact, Mrs. Manningham—you have in front of you one who was quite a personage in his day—believe it or not.

With a cup of fresh tea to toy with, Detective Rough starts a kindly cross-examination from which he learns that the Manninghams have been married five years; that they had traveled some, lived in Yorkshire and then, about six months ago, bought the house in Angel Street. Mrs. Manningham had a bit of money, and Mr. Manningham thought this a very good investment.

Does Mr. Manningham always leave her alone in the evenings? Yes, he goes to his club on business. And does he give her the

"ANGEL STREET"

Mrs Manningham: But my husband! My husband is up there!
Rough: Precisely that, Mrs. Manningham. Your husband. You see, I am afraid you are married to a tolerably dangerous gentleman. Now drink this quickly, as we have a great deal to do. Detective Rough has recovered both their drinks from the mantel and stands holding Mrs. Manningham's glass out to her as the curtain falls.

(*Judith Evelyn, Leo G. Carroll*)

run of the house while he is out? Yes, all except the top floor.

Detective Rough would have Mrs. Manningham know that he has been keeping track of things in her house through information that he gets through the maid, Nancy. Nancy, it appears, has been walking out with a young man who is an operator in Detective Rough's employ and there isn't much that Nancy knows or has surmised about her employers that Detective Rough doesn't know also. Nor would Detective Rough think of permitting Mrs. Manningham the satisfaction of discharging Nancy. To the contrary, before they are through Mrs. M. will probably be greatly indebted to Nancy. For the present, however, Detective Rough's plan must remain a secret.

But, to get back to the top floor. Does no one ever go up there? No one—not even a servant to dust. That, to Detective Rough, is a little funny. And how about this idea of Mrs. Manningham's—that her reason was playing her tricks? When did she first get that notion into her head—

"I always had that dread," admits Mrs. Manningham. "My mother died insane, when she was quite young. When she was my age. But only in the last six months, in this house—things began to happen—

ROUGH—Which are driving you mad with fear?

MRS. MANNINGHAM (*gasping*)—Yes. Which are driving me mad with fear.

ROUGH—Is it the house itself you fear, Mrs. Manningham?

MRS. MANNINGHAM—Yes. I suppose it is. I hate the house. I always did.

ROUGH—And has the top floor got anything to do with it?

MRS. MANNINGHAM—Yes, yes, it has. That's how all this dreadful horror began.

ROUGH—Ah—now you interest me beyond measure. Do tell me about the top floor.

MRS. MANNINGHAM—I don't know what to say. It all sounds so incredible. . . . It's when I'm alone at night. I get the idea that—somebody's walking about up there. . . . (*Looking up.*) Up there. . . . At night, when my husband's out. . . . I hear noises, from my bedroom, but I'm afraid to go up. . . .

ROUGH—Have you told your husband about this?

MRS. MANNINGHAM—No. I'm afraid to. He gets angry. He says I imagine things which don't exist. . . .

ROUGH—It never struck you, did it, that it might be your own husband walking about up there?

Mrs. Manningham—Yes—that *is* what I thought—but I thought I must be mad. (*As she turns to* Rough.) Tell me how you know.

Rough—Why not tell first how *you* knew, Mrs. Manningham.

Mrs. Manningham (*rising and going toward fireplace*)—It's true, then! It's true. I knew it. I knew it! When he leaves this house he comes back. He comes back and walks up there above—up and down—up and down. (*Turning to fireplace.*) He comes back like a ghost. How does he get up there?

Rough (*rising, crossing to* Mrs. Manningham)—That's what we're going to find out, Mrs. Manningham. But there are such commonplace resources as roofs and fire escapes, you know. Now please don't look so frightened. Your husband is no ghost, believe me, and you are very far from mad. (*Pauses.*) Tell me now, what made you first think it was him?

Mrs. Manningham—It was the light—the gaslight. . . . It went down and it went up. . . . (*Starts to cry.*) Oh, thank God I can tell this to someone at last. I don't know who you are, but I must tell you. (*Crosses to* Rough.)

Rough (*taking her hands*)—Now try to keep calm. You can tell me just as well sitting down, can't you? Won't you sit down? (*He moves back.*)

Mrs. Manningham—Yes . . . yes. (*She sits down on end of sofa.*)

Rough (*looking around*)—The light, did you say? Did you see a light from a window?

Mrs. Manningham—No. In this house. I can tell everything by the light of gas. You see the mantel there. Now it is burning full. But if an extra light went on in the kitchen or someone lit it in the bedroom then this one would sink down. It's the same all over the house.

Rough—Yes—yes—that's just a question of insufficient pressure, and it's the same in mine. But go on, please.

Mrs. Manningham (*after pause*)—Every night, after he goes out, I find myself waiting for something. Then all at once I look around the room and see that the light is slowly going down. Then I hear tapping sounds—persistent tapping sounds. At first I tried not to notice it, but after a time it began to get on my nerves. I would go all over the house to see if anyone had put on an extra light, but they never had. It's always at the same time—about ten minutes after he goes out. That's what gave me the idea that somehow *he* had come back and that it was *he* who was walking about up there. I go up to the bedroom but I daren't stay there because I hear noises overhead. I want to scream and run out of the house. I sit here for hours, terrified, waiting for him to come back, and I always know when he's coming, always. Suddenly the light goes up again and ten minutes afterwards I hear his key in the lock (*A look at doors.*) and he's back again.

Other things have been happening lately to cause Mrs. Manningham to wonder about the stability of her mind. For one, her memory has been playing her tricks. Often Mr. Manningham will give her things to keep and she will lose or mislay them. His rings and studs have disappeared and been found in the bottom of her workbox. The key to a certain door has disappeared, after the door had been locked, only to turn up again also among her things. Just this morning there was the matter of the picture that had been taken from the wall. Then—

"We have a little dog," Mrs. Manningham continues. "A few weeks ago it was found with its paw hurt. . . . He believes . . . Oh, God, how can I tell you what he believes—that I had hurt the dog. He does not let the dog near me now. He keeps it in the kitchen and I am not allowed to see it! I begin to doubt, don't you see? I begin to believe I imagine everything. Perhaps I do. Are you here? Is this a dream, too? Who are you? (*Rises and steps away.*) I'm afraid they are going to lock me up."

Now Detective Rough is all sympathy. It has occurred to him that Mrs. Manningham could do with a little medicine. Not the horrible, bitter stuff that she has been taking—a little medicine the detective knows about, and that he always carries with him—

"You see," he explains, "it has been employed by humanity for several ages, for the purpose of the instantaneous removal of dark fears and doubts. That seems to fit you, doesn't it?"

"The removal of doubt. How could a medicine effect that?"

"Ah—that we don't know. The fact remains that it does. Here we are. (*Produces what is obviously a bottle of whiskey.*) You see, it comes from Scotland. Now, Madam, have you such a thing handy as two glasses or a couple of cups?"

"Why—are you having some, too?"

"Oh, yes. I am having some above all things. . . ."

They have had their medicine, which tastes like "something between ambrosia and methylated spirits," as Rough sees it, and they have settled again to their exchange of confidences. Now it is the detective's turn, for he must tell Mrs. Manningham the revealing story of the cabman's friend. She was an old lady who had died many years ago. She was a kindly person of great wealth and decided eccentricities, and her principal mania was the protection of cabmen. She had provided them with shelters, clothing and pensions, and saved them much of the world's pain—

"It was not my privilege to know her," Detective Rough is saying, "but it was my duty, on just one occasion, to see her. (*Turns to her.*) That was when her throat was cut open, and she lay dead on the floor of her own house."

MRS. MANNINGHAM—Oh, how horrible! Do you mean she was murdered?

ROUGH—Yes. (*Crosses to end of sofa.*) She was murdered. I was only a comparatively young officer at the time. It made an extremely horrible, in fact I may say lasting, impression on me. You see the murderer was never discovered but the motive was obvious enough. Her husband had left her the Barlow rubies. (*Crosses to other end of sofa.*) And it was well known that she kept them, without any proper precautions, in her bedroom on an upper floor. (*Turns to her.*) She lived alone except for a deaf servant in the basement. Well, for that she paid the penalty of her life.

MRS. MANNINGHAM—But I don't see—

ROUGH—There were some sensational features about the case. The man seemed to have got in at about ten at night, and stayed till dawn. Apart, presumably, from the famous rubies, there were only a few trinkets taken, but the whole house had been turned upside down, and in the upper room every single thing was flung about, or torn open. Even the cushions of the chairs were ripped up with his bloody knife, and the police decided that it must have been a revengeful maniac as well as a robber. I had other theories, but I was a nobody then, and not in charge of the case.

MRS. MANNINGHAM—What were your theories?

ROUGH (*crossing up right*)—Well, it seemed to me, from all that I gathered here and there, that the old lady might have been an eccentric, but that she was by no means a fool. It seemed to me—(*Crossing to back of sofa.*)—that she might have been one too clever for this man. We presume he killed her to silence her, but what then? What if she had *not* been so careless? (*Slowly crossing to her.*) What if she had got those jewels cunningly hidden away in some inconceivable place, in the walls, floored down, bricked in, maybe? What if the only person who could tell him where they were was lying dead on the floor! Would not that account, Mrs. Manningham, for all that strange confusion in which the place was found? (*Crosses back of sofa.*) Can't you picture him, Mrs. Manningham, searching through the night, ransacking the place, hour after hour, growing more and more desperate, until at last the dawn comes and he has to slink out into the pale street, the blood and wreckage of the night behind. (*Turns to her.*) And the deaf servant down in the basement sleeping like a log through it all.

Mrs. Manningham—Oh, how horrible! How horrible indeed. And was the man never found?

Rough—No, Mrs. Manningham, the man was never found. Nor have the Barlow rubies ever come to light.

Mrs. Manningham—Then perhaps he found them after all, and may be alive today.

Rough—I think he is almost certainly alive today, but I don't believe he found what he wanted. That is, if my theory is right.

Mrs. Manningham—Then the jewels may still be where the old lady hid them?

Rough—Indeed, Mrs. Manningham, if my theory is right the jewels *must* still be where she hid them. The official conclusion was quite otherwise. The police, naturally and quite excusably, presumed that the murderer had got them, and there was no reopening of matters in those days. Soon enough the public forgot about it. They always do. I almost forgot about it myself. But it would be funny, wouldn't it, Mrs. Manningham, if after all these years I should turn out to be right.

Mrs. Manningham is still confused. What has all this to do with her? What, indeed? echoes Detective Rough. That is what he, too, would like to know and what he hopes to find out. It is just possible that the man who had murdered old Mrs. Barlow had, after fifteen years, decided to have another search of the Barlow house. The criminal, it is said, often returns to the scene of his crime. And in this case there is something more than morbid compulsion. There are still the Barlow jewels to be accounted for. There is real treasure to be unearthed if a man could take his time for a thorough search of the house without arousing suspicion. And how would he most likely go about—

Mrs. Manningham has suddenly leaped to her feet. The lights are going down! Mr. Manningham has come back! He is in the house and Detective Rough must get out, quietly, quickly—

"Quiet, Mrs. Manningham, quiet!" cautions the detective,

going to her, taking her arms in his hands. "You have got to keep your head. Don't you see my meaning, yet? Don't you understand that this was the house?"

"House? What house?"

"The old woman's house, Mrs. Manningham. . . . This house, here, these rooms, these walls. Fifteen years ago Alice Barlow lay dead on the floor in this room. Fifteen years ago the man who murdered her ransacked this house—below and above—but could not find what he sought. What if he is still searching, Mrs. Manningham? *(Indicating upstairs.)* What if he is up there—still searching? Now do you see why you must keep your head?"

"But my husband, my husband is up there!"

"Precisely that, Mrs. Manningham. Your husband. You see, I am afraid you are married to a tolerably dangerous gentleman. Now drink this quickly, as we have a great deal to do."

Detective Rough has recovered both their drinks from the mantel and stands holding Mrs. Manningham's glass out to her as the curtain falls.

ACT II

There has been no lapse of time. Mrs. Manningham accepts the drink Detective Rough offers her, her eyes staring bewilderedly at him. When she finds her voice she demands to know how the detective knows that this is indeed the Barlow house. Rough knows because he was one of those assigned to the case. How can he possibly believe that Mr. Manningham may have had anything to do with the murder? Because it was a part of his work to interview a variety of the murdered lady's acquaintances and relatives, nephews and nieces. Among these he most vividly remembers a young man named Power—Sydney Power—of whom it isn't likely that Mrs. Manningham has ever heard. No, she has not—

"Well, he was a kind of distant cousin," the detective is saying, pouring himself another drink as he continues; "apparently much attached to the old lady, and even assisting her in her good works. The only thing was that I remembered his face. Well, I saw that face again just a few weeks ago. It took me a whole day to recollect where I had seen it before, but at last I remembered."

Mrs. Manningham—Well—what of it? What if you did remember him?

Rough—It was not so much my remembering Mr. Sydney

Power, Mrs. Manningham. What startled me was the lady on his arm and the locality in which I saw him.

Mrs. Manningham—Oh—who was the lady on his arm?

Rough—*You* were the lady on his arm, Mrs. Manningham, and you were walking down this street.

Mrs. Manningham—What are you saying? Do you mean you think my husband—my husband is this Mr. Power?

Rough—Well, not exactly, for if my theories are correct—

Mrs. Manningham—What are you saying? (*Sits.*) You stand there talking riddles. You are so cold. You are as heartless and cold as he is.

Rough (*coming down to left of table*)—No, Mrs. Manningham, I am not cold, and I am not talking riddles. (*Sets his drink down on the table.*) I am just trying to preserve a cold and calculating tone, because you are up against the most awful moment in your life, and your whole future depends on what you are going to do in the next hour. Nothing less. You have got to *strike* for your freedom, and strike *now*, for the moment may not come again.

Mrs. Manningham—Strike—

Rough (*leaning across the table*)—You are not going out of your mind, Mrs. Manningham, you are slowly, methodically, systematically being driven out of your mind. And why? Because you are married to a criminal maniac who is afraid you are beginning to know too much—a criminal maniac who steals back to his own house at night, still searching for something he could not find fifteen years ago. Those are the facts, wild and incredible as they may seem. His name is no more Manningham than mine is. He is Sydney Power and he murdered Alice Barlow in this house. Afterward he changed his name, and he has waited all these years, until he found it safe to acquire this house in a legal way. He then acquired the empty house next door. Every night, for the last few weeks, he has entered that house from the back, climbed up onto its roof and come into this house by the skylight. I know that because I have seen him do it. You have watched the gaslight, and without knowing it been aware of the same thing. He is up there now. Why he should employ this mad, secretive, circuitous way of getting what he wants, God himself only knows. For the same reason, perhaps, that he employs this mad, secretive, circuitous way of getting rid of you: that is, by slowly driving you mad and into a lunatic asylum.

Mrs. Manningham—Why?

Rough—The fact that you had some money, enough to buy this house, is part of it, I expect. For now that he's got that out of you, he doesn't need you any longer. Thank God you are not married to him, and that I have come here to save you from the workings of his wicked mind.

Mrs. Manningham—Not married? . . . Not married? . . . He married me.

Rough—I have no doubt he did, Mrs. Manningham. Unfortunately, or rather fortunately, he contracted the same sort of union with another lady many years before he met you. Moreover, the lady is still alive, and the English law has a highly exacting taste in monogamy. You see, I have been finding things out about Mr. Sydney Power.

Mrs. Manningham—Are you speaking the truth? My God —are you speaking the truth? Where is this wife now?

Rough—I'm afraid she is the length of the world away—on the Continent of Australia to be precise, where I know for a fact he spent two years. Did you know that?

Mrs. Manningham—No. I—did—not—know—that.

Of course, if Detective Rough could find that other Mrs. Manningham, his work would be easier, but as he can't, his most earnest hope is that the present Mrs. Manningham will help him get the evidence he needs. Of course, if she were really married to Mr. Manningham the detective could understand her shock at the thought of betraying him. But perhaps if she knew how slight is her real obligation to the man she married; if she knew, as Detective Rough knows, how the persuasive Mr. Manningham comes really to life at night, and how exciting are many of his less serious excursions into the resorts of the town; if she knew his taste in unemployed actresses, for instance, she would feel differently—

"Mrs. Manningham, it is hard to take everything from you," admits Detective Rough, "but you are no more tied to this man, you are under no more obligation to him than those wretched women in those places. You must learn to be thankful for that."

"What do you want me to do? What do you want?"

"I want his papers, Mrs. Manningham—his identity. There is some clue somewhere in this house, and we have got to get at it."

So far as Mrs. Manningham knows, the only place that Mr. Manningham keeps any papers is in his bureau—his desk, there in that room, and that is always locked. Locked it may be, but it doesn't look too formidable to Detective Rough, who long has boasted to himself that if he had developed a turn for burgling he might easily have been a genius.

A cursory examination of the desk convinces Rough that it will not be hard to master. He has his coat off, and is starting to work on the locks when the lights begin slowly to go up. Mr. Manningham evidently has left the top floor and is coming back. Mrs. Manningham is the first to notice the lights. Her hysteria mounts with her fear, and she pleads with Detective Rough please to get out of the house quickly.

The detective is not unduly excited. He would have a talk with Elizabeth before he leaves, if Mrs. Manningham will call the maid. Mr. Manningham may be on his way, but it will take him at least five minutes to get around to the front of the house. Much can be accomplished in five minutes.

Elizabeth, too, is effected by the tenseness of the moment. Would she be willing to help her mistress, blindly, without asking questions? Elizabeth would. Could she, then, hide Detective Rough in her kitchen for a short space of time—in the oven if necessary—that Mr. Manningham may not see him leaving the house? Elizabeth could, and would, but unfortunately Nancy is entertaining a young man in the kitchen at the moment. Elizabeth had agreed not to summon the detective if Nancy were there, but Nancy, who was going out, had suddenly changed her plans. No, Nancy did not know that Detective Rough was in the house. He might hide in their bedroom—Elizabeth's and Nancy's—but what if Nancy should go up there before she went out—

There is Mr. Manningham's dressing room adjoining the living room. There is a big wardrobe in the dressing room at the back. Detective Rough decides to investigate. He is back in a moment to declare the accommodations perfect. And just in time too. Mr. Manningham is at the front door—

"Now, we really have got to hurry," announces the detective. "Get off to bed, Mrs. Manningham, quick! And you, Elizabeth, go to your room. You can't get downstairs in time. Hurry, please. . . ."

"To bed? Am I to go to bed?" wails Mrs. Manningham.

"Yes, quick. He's coming." For the first time Detective Rough loses his professional calm.

"Don't you understand? Go there and stay there. You have a bad headache—a bad headache." He has turned down the gas bracket above the fireplace. "Will you go, in heaven's name?"

Mrs. Manningham hurries up the stairs and Elizabeth disappears in the hall. Rough is still taking his time as he turns down another gas jet and tiptoes toward the dressing room. The front door is heard to slam. Rough is just disappearing into the dressing room when suddenly he feels his head and realizes he has left his hat behind. Quickly he turns about, recovers the hat and disappears through the dressing room door.

A second later Mr. Manningham appears in the doorway. He looks guardedly about the room, closes the hall doors after him, glances inquiringly up the stairs and, being satisfied, turns up the gas jets. Now he has taken off his hat and coat, thrown them on the sofa and rung the bell for Elizabeth.

Elizabeth reports that so far as she knows Mrs. Manningham has gone to bed with a bad headache. She will clear away the tea things, and would Mr. Manningham care for supper? Mr. Manningham would not. He is having supper out, and has come home only to change his linen. Elizabeth suggests quickly that, if he likes, she will fetch him a fresh collar from his dressing room, but Mr. Manningham prefers to make his own selection.

Mr. Manningham disappears in the dressing room. Elizabeth stands motionless, taut with suspense, until he returns, leisurely buttoning his collar, which he adjusts in front of the living room mirror.

It is about Mrs. Manningham and her condition that Mr. Manningham wants to talk to Elizabeth. She probably has noticed a definite change in her mistress recently. For his own part he is at his wit's end—

"I have tried everything," says Mr. Manningham. "Kindness, patience, cunning—even harshness, to bring her to her senses. But nothing will stop these wild, wild hallucinations, nothing will stop these wicked pranks and tricks."

Mr. Manningham has decided that he wants a different tie, and again disappears in the dressing room for a tense moment. He is still talking as he returns.

"I suppose you know about Mrs. Manningham's mother, Elizabeth. . . . She died in the madhouse, Elizabeth, without any brain at all in the end. . . . You know, don't you, that I shall have to bring a doctor to Mrs. Manningham before long, Elizabeth? I have fought against it to the last, but it can't be kept a secret much longer."

"No, Sir. . . . No, Sir. . . ."

"I mean to say, you know what goes on. You can testify to what goes on, can't you?"

"Indeed, Sir. Yes."

"Indeed, you may *have* to testify in the end. Do you realize that? (*Pause. Then sharply.*) Eh?"

"Yes, Sir. I would only wish to help you both, Sir."

"Yes, I believe you there, Elizabeth. You're a very good soul. I sometimes wonder how you put up with things in this household—this dark household. I wonder why you do not go. You're very loyal."

"Always loyal to you, Sir. Always loyal to you."

"There, now, how touching. I thank you, Elizabeth. You will be repaid later for what you have said, and repaid in more ways than one. You understand that, don't you?"

"Thank you, Sir. I only want to serve, Sir."

Having completed his dressing Mr. Manningham is ready to depart. He is going out, he repeats, and he is even going to try to be a little gay. Surely Elizabeth cannot think that that is wrong. Elizabeth agrees that Mr. Manningham should get all the pleasure he can, while he can.

With the slamming of the front door, Rough pops out of the dressing room and a moment later Mrs. Manningham appears on the stairs. Now they must get back to work on the desk drawers. Even though there is no way of their being warned of Mr. Manningham's return, this is a chance they will have to take. . . .

It doesn't at first appear that they have found anything in the desk. Detective Rough has found a brooch, and a watch and finally a grocery bill—all of which Mr. Manningham had accused his wife of having lost, or hidden— And a letter! A letter addressed to Mrs. Manningham—from her cousin—which is exciting to Mrs. Manningham.

"Is your husband's correspondence with your relations very much to the point at the moment?" inquires the detective, with a slight impatience.

"You don't understand," explains the excited Mrs. Manningham. "When I was married I was cast off by all my relations. I have not seen any of them since I was married. They did not approve my choice. I have longed to see them again more than anything in the world. When we came to London—to this house, I wrote to them, I wrote to them twice. There never was any answer. Now I can see why there never was any answer."

It is a pleasant affectionate letter, as Mrs. Manningham reads it. Her cousins were overjoyed at hearing from her again and were looking forward to their renewing old ties. If she would come to them in Devonshire they would give her their Devonshire cream to fatten her cheeks and their fresh air to bring the sparkle back to her eyes— The thought is too much for her, and she breaks down. "Dear God, they wanted me back!" she sobs.

"They wanted me back all the time—"

She is crying softly on the sympathetic shoulder of Detective Rough, and being reassured by his promise that she will yet see her cousins and be happy again. Then back to the desk goes Rough. Finally he gets out his tools and forces the most stubborn of the locks. There is nothing else for him to do.

Again they are disappointed. There seems to be nothing but papers in the drawer and these of no great significance. They have, sighs the detective, apparently lost their gamble. And how can they account for the forcing of the desk? Mrs. Manningham grows a little panicky at the thought.

Detective Rough is putting the things back in the first drawer —the watch and the brooch—and trying to remember just where they were placed, when something about the brooch attracts his eye. It was only second-hand, Mrs. Manningham tells him. She discovered that when she found an affectionate inscription to someone else inside it.

That inscription adds to the detective's interest. He has a feeling he has seen this brooch before. That feeling is strengthened when Mrs. Manningham shows him how to pull a tiny pin which she had discovered by accident. That permits the brooch to open out like a star. There were several beads inside it originally, she explains, but they were all loose and Mrs. Manningham had taken them out and put them in an old vase. Can she find them? She can. The vase is still on the mantel. Did there happen to have been nine of them originally, Rough would like to know. Yes, there were. But some may have been lost. Detective Rough's excitement is mounting as he fits the beads back into the brooch and is examining them with his jeweler's glass.

"Did you happen to read this inscription at any time, ma'am?" he is asking. " 'Beloved A.B. from C.B. Eighteen fifty-one.' Does nothing strike you about that?"

"No. What of it? What should strike me?"

ROUGH—Really, I should have thought that as simple as A.B.C. Have you got the others? There should be four more.

MRS. MANNINGHAM—Yes. Here they are.

ROUGH (*taking them*)—Thank you. That's the lot. (*He is putting them in brooch on the table.*) Now tell me this—have you ever been embraced by an elderly detective in his shirt sleeves?

MRS. MANNINGHAM—What do you mean?

ROUGH—For that is your immediate fate at the moment.

(*Puts down brooch and comes to her.*) My dear Mrs. Manningham— (*Kisses her.*) My dear, dear Mrs. Manningham! Don't you understand?

Mrs. Manningham—No, what are you so excited about?

Rough (*picking up brooch*)—There, there you are, Mrs. Manningham. The Barlow rubies—complete. Twelve thousand pounds' worth before your very eyes! Take a good look at them before they go to the Queen.

Mrs. Manningham—But it couldn't be—it couldn't. They were in the vase all the time.

Rough—Don't you see? Don't you see the whole thing? *This* is where the old lady hid her treasure—in a common trinket she wore all day long. I knew I had seen this somewhere before. And where was that? In portraits of the old lady—when I was on the case. She wore it on her breast. I remember it clearly though it was fifteen years ago. Fifteen years! Dear God in heaven, am I not a wonderful man!

Mrs. Manningham—And I had it all the time. I had it all the time.

Rough—And all because he could not resist a little common theft along with the big game. . . . Well, it is I who am after the big game now.

Detective Rough is hurrying into his things now. He has a lot to do and it must be done quickly. Leave her? Of course he will have to leave her. But— First they will have to put the brooch right back where they found it. Then he must summon Sir George Raglan, "the power above the powers that be." The broken desk they will have to risk for the present. As for Mrs. Manningham—

"You will serve the ends of justice best by simply going to bed," the detective is saying. . . . "Go there and stay there. Your headache is worse. Remember—be ill. Be anything. But stay there, you understand. I'll let myself out."

He has started for the door when Mrs. Manningham is again attacked by a great fear. Pitifully she pleads with him not to leave her. She has a feeling that something will happen. But Detective Rough is not too sympathetic—

"Have the goodness to stop making a fool of yourself, Mrs. Manningham," he says. "Here's your courage." He hands her his flask. "Take some of it, but don't get tipsy and don't leave it about. Good-by."

Mrs. Manningham starts up the stairs. Rough is at the door.

He turns again. "Mrs. Manningham," he calls. She stops. "Good-by," he repeats, motioning her on up the stairs.

When she is out of sight he goes through the doors and closes them after him. The curtain falls.

ACT III

It is eleven o'clock that night. The Manningham living room is practically blacked out until Mr. Manningham appears from the hall and turns up the lights. Ringing for a maid, he discovers that everyone has gone to bed. A second later, however, Nancy puts her head around the hall door. She has just come in, but is perfectly willing to substitute for Mrs. Manningham or Elizabeth. She fetches Mr. Manningham's milk and biscuits and then goes to call Mrs. Manningham. Her husband would like to see his wife immediately.

Mrs. Manningham, Nancy reports, has a headache and is trying to sleep. Mr. Manningham is not surprised. It is hard to remember when his wife was not suffering from a headache. For the moment he turns his attention to Nancy.

Does Nancy realize that she enjoys considerable liberty in that house? Liberty that includes two nights off a week; liberty that permits her to stay out as late as her master, and probably in the company of young men? Nancy is not loathe to admit the charges. As for the gentlemen friends—Nancy feels sure that she can take care of herself. Perhaps at times she is not too particular about that.

"You know, Nancy, pretty as your bonnet is, it is not anything near so pretty as your hair beneath it," says Mr. Manningham. "Won't you take it off and let me see it?"

"Very good, sir. It comes off easy enough. There (*It's off.*)—Is there anything more you want, sir?"

MR. MANNINGHAM—Yes. Possibly. Come here, will you, Nancy?

NANCY (*dropping hat on chair*)—Yes, Sir. . . . Is there anything you want, Sir? (*He puts his hands on her shoulders.*) What do you want? . . . eh . . . What do you want? (MANNINGHAM *kisses* NANCY *in a violent and prolonged manner. There is a pause in which she looks at him, and then she kisses him as violently.*) There! Can she do that for you? Can she do that?

MR. MANNINGHAM—Who can you be talking about, Nancy?

NANCY—You know who I mean all right.

MR. MANNINGHAM—You know, Nancy, you are a very remarkable girl in many respects. I believe you are jealous of your mistress.

NANCY—She? She's a poor thing. There's no need to be jealous of her. You want to kiss me again, don't you? Don't you want to kiss me? (MR. MANNINGHAM *kisses* NANCY.) There! That's better than a sick headache—ain't it—a sick headache and a pale face all the day.

MR. MANNINGHAM—Why, yes, Nancy, I believe it is. I think, however, don't you, that it would be better if you and I met one evening in different surroundings?

NANCY—Yes. Where? I'll meet you when you like. You're mine now—ain't you—cos you want me. You want me—don't you?

MR. MANNINGHAM—And what of you, Nancy. Do you want me?

NANCY—Oh, yes! I always wanted you, ever since I first clapped eyes on you. I wanted you more than all of them.

MR. MANNINGHAM—Oh—there are plenty of others?

NANCY—Oh, yes—there's plenty of others.

MR. MANNINGHAM—So I rather imagined. And only nineteen.

NANCY—Where can we meet? Where do you want us to meet?

MR. MANNINGHAM (*slowly crossing to fireplace*)—Really, Nancy, you have taken me a little by surprise. I'll let you know tomorrow.

NANCY—How'll you let me know, when she's about?

MR. MANNINGHAM—Oh, I'll find a way, Nancy. I don't believe Mrs. Manningham will be here tomorrow.

NANCY—Oh? Not that I care about her. I'd like to kiss you under her very nose. That's what I'd like to do.

MR. MANNINGHAM—All right, Nancy. Now you had better go. I have some work to do.

It isn't easy for Nancy to be turned away. She would, if she could, convince her master that his work at the moment is quite unimportant. But she gives way, reluctantly, to wait until he finds a chance to communicate with her the next day. She closes the hall doors as she goes out.

Now Mr. Manningham has found certain papers on the secretary and takes them to the desk. He gets out his keys and is about to unlock the drawer when he discovers that it has been opened. Further investigation reveals that the second drawer has been opened. Quickly he goes back to the bell cord and summons Nancy. This time she is to summon Mrs. Manningham and bid her come downstairs, whatever her ailments—a mission Nancy undertakes with undisguised pleasure.

A moment later Nancy is back with the announcement that Mrs. Manningham not only refuses to come downstairs, but that she has closed and locked her door. Just shamming, she is, in Nancy's opinion, and she would like to see Mr. Manningham batter the door in.

Mr. Manningham has a better plan. He will write a note to Mrs. Manningham which Nancy can slip under the door. But, first, let her go into the basement and bring up the little dog. On second thought Mr. Manningham decides that will not be necessary. They will just let Mrs. Manningham assume that they have the dog.

While Nancy is gone Manningham busies himself changing the scene by placing an armchair in front of the fireplace, as though for a ceremony. He is standing calmly waiting when Nancy returns to report that the note had done the trick—her mistress is on her way down. Nancy is still curious. She would like to have a more intimate part in the experiment.

"Good night, old dear. Give her what-for, won't you?" she advises, cheerily, as she throws her arms about Manningham's neck and kisses him. "Ta-ta!"

Mrs. Manningham hesitates as she comes down the stairs. Her eyes are wide with fear and wonder. Mr. Manningham has taken his position in front of the fireplace, facing a chair he has placed for his wife. He meets her excitement with an exaggerated calm. He would have her come and take the seat he has indicated. The dog? What has he done with the little dog? Not a thing. That was only a ruse to get her to pay some attention to his commands. Why will she not sit in the chair in front of him? Is she afraid of him? No, she is not afraid.

Slowly Mrs. Manningham comes toward the chair. Mr. Manningham's eyes are fixed steadily upon her. Now there is a smirk at the corners of his cruel mouth. As she walks across the room she reminds him greatly of a somnambulist. Has she ever seen a somnambulist? No?

"Not that funny, glazed, dazed look of the wandering mind—the body that acts without the soul to guide it? I have often thought you had that look, but it's never been so strong as tonight."

"My mind is not wandering!" insists Mrs. Manningham.

In that case Mr. Manningham would like to know how it happens that, although she had reported that she had gone to bed, she appears fully dressed? Mrs. Manningham does not know. That, Mr. Manningham insists, is a curious oversight.

"You know, you give me the appearance of having had a rather exciting time since I last saw you," Mr. Manningham is saying, as he leans menacingly over her. "Almost as though you have been up to something. Have you been up to anything?"

"No. I don't know what you mean."

"Did you find that bill I told you to find?"

"No."

"Do you remember what I said would happen to you if you did not find that bill when I returned tonight?"

"No."

"No?" Mr. Manningham has gone to the table and poured himself a glass of milk. "Am I married to a dumb woman, Bella, in addition to all else? The array of your physical and mental deficiencies is growing almost overwhelming. I advise you to answer me."

Mrs. Manningham—What do you want me to say?

Mr. Manningham—I asked you if you remembered something. (*Going back to fireplace with glass of milk.*) Go on, Bella—what was it I asked you if you remembered?

Mrs. Manningham—I don't understand your words. You talk round and round. My head is going round and round.

Mr. Manningham—It is not necessary for you to tell me, Bella. I am just wondering if it might interrupt its gyratory motion for a fraction of a second, and concentrate upon the present conversation. (*Sips milk.*) And please, what was it I a moment ago asked you if you remembered?

Mrs. Manningham (*labored*)—You asked me if I remembered what you said would happen to me if I did not find the bill.

Mr. Manningham—Admirable, my dear Bella! Admirable! We shall make a great logician of you yet—a Socrates—a John Stuart Mill! You shall go down in history as the shining mind of your day. That is, if your present history does not altogether submerge you—take you away from your fellow creatures. And there is danger of that, you know, in more ways than one. (*Puts milk on mantel.*) Well—what did I say I would do if you did not find that bill?

MRS. MANNINGHAM (*choking*)—You said you would lock me up.

MR. MANNINGHAM—Yes. And do you believe me to be a man of my word? (*Pause in which she does not answer.*) You see, Bella, in a life of considerable and varied experience I have hammered out a few principles of action. In fact, I actually fancy I know how to deal with my fellow-men. I learned it quite early actually—at school in fact. There, you know, there were two ways of getting at what you wanted. One was along an intellectual plane, the other along the physical. If one failed, one used the other. I took that lesson into life with me. Hitherto, with you, I have worked with what forbearance and patience I leave you to judge, along the intellectual plane. (*Crosses down and over to her.*) The time has come now, I believe, to work along the other as well— You will understand that I am a man of some power. . . . (*She suddenly looks at him.*) Why do you look at me, Bella? I said I am a man of some power and determination, and as fully capable in one direction as in the other. . . . I will leave your imagination to work on what I mean. . . . However, we are really digressing. . . .

Craftily Mr. Manningham returns to the cross-examination. Where had she looked for the bill? In his desk? No? Why should she try to lie to him? He knows. He knows that her poor, dark, confused, rambling mind has led her into playing some pretty tricks. Her mind is tired? Indeed, it is tired. So tired that it can no longer work. She dreams. She dreams "maliciously and incessantly—"

"You sleep-walking imbecile, what have you been dreaming tonight—where has your mind wandered—that you have split open my desk? What strange diseased dream have you had tonight—eh?"

MRS. MANNINGHAM—Dream? Are you saying I have dreamed. . . . Dreamed all that happened? . . .

MR. MANNINGHAM—All that happened when, Bella? Tonight? Of course you dreamed all that happened—or rather all that didn't happen.

MRS. MANNINGHAM—Dream. . . . Tonight . . . are you saying I have dreamed? . . . Oh, God—have I dreamed . . . Have I dreamed again . . .

Mr. Manningham—Have I not told you—?

Mrs. Manningham (*storming*)—I haven't dreamed. I haven't. Don't tell me I have dreamed. In the name of God don't tell me that!

Mr. Manningham (*forcing her down into a small chair*)—Sit down and be quiet. Sit down! (*More quietly and curiously.*) What was this dream of yours, Bella? You interest me.

Mrs. Manningham—I dreamt of a man—(*Hysterical.*)—I dreamt of a man—

Mr. Manningham (*now very curious*)—You dreamed of a man, Bella? What man did you dream of, pray?

Mrs. Manningham—A man. A man that came to see me. Let me rest! Let me rest!

Mr. Manningham—Pull yourself together, Bella. What man are you talking about?

Mrs. Manningham—I dreamed a man came in here.

Mr. Manningham (*grasping her neck*) I know you dreamed it, you gibbering wretch! I want to know more about this man of whom you dreamed. Do you hear! Do you hear me?

Mrs. Manningham—I dreamed . . . I dreamed . . .

Suddenly her gaze is fixed on the door of the dressing room. Detective Rough is standing there. He advances toward them as Manningham releases Bella's throat and she falls back into the chair.

"Was I any part of this curious dream of yours, Mrs. Manningham?" Rough is asking, quietly. ". . . Perhaps my presence here will help you to recall it."

"May I ask who the devil you are, and how you got in?" shouts Manningham.

"Well, who I am seems a little doubtful. Apparently I am a mere figment of Mrs. Manningham's imagination. As for how I got in, I came in, or rather I came back—or better still, I effected an entrance a few minutes before you, and I have been hidden away ever since."

"And would you be kind enough to tell me what you are doing here?"

"Waiting for some friends, Mr. Manningham, waiting for some friends. Don't you think you had better go up to bed, Mrs. Manningham? You look very tired."

Rough can see no reason for his going into a long explanation as to who he is or what he is there for, seeing he is only a figment. But he does agree with Mr. Manningham that Mrs. Manningham should go to her room. Mrs. Manningham, still staring at both of them wonderingly, goes slowly up the stairs. Again Manningham would have an explanation from Rough, and again an explanation is denied him. Suddenly Rough is impressed with the idea that the gaslights are being lowered. Can't Manningham see that the lights are going down? They surely are—

"—Eerie, isn't it?" Rough is saying, as the lights become noticeably lower. "Now we are almost in the dark. . . . Why do you think that has happened? You don't suppose a light has been put on somewhere else. . . . You don't suppose that strangers have entered the house? You don't suppose there are other spirits—fellow spirits of mine—spirits surrounding this house now—spirits of justice, even, which have caught up with you at last, Mr. Manningham?"

MR. MANNINGHAM—Are you off your head, Sir?

ROUGH—No, Sir. Just an old man seeing ghosts. It must be the atmosphere of this house. (*He looks about.*) I can see them everywhere. It's the oddest thing. Do you know one ghost I can see, Mr. Manningham? You could hardly believe it.

MR. MANNINGHAM—What ghost do you see, pray?

ROUGH—Why, it's the ghost of an old woman, Sir . . . an old woman who once lived in this house, who once lived in this very room. Yes—in this very room. What things I imagine!

MR. MANNINGHAM—What are you saying?

ROUGH—Remarkably clear, Sir, I see it. . . . An old woman getting ready to go to bed—here in this very room—an old woman getting ready to go to bed at the end of the day. Why! There she is. She sits just there. (*Pointing to chair.*) And now it seems I see another ghost as well. (*He is looking at* MANNINGHAM.) I see the ghost of a young man, Mr. Manningham—a handsome, tall, well-groomed young man. But this young man has murder in his eyes. Why, God bless my soul, he might be you, Mr. Manningham—he might be you! (*Pause.*) The old woman sees him. Don't you see it at all? She screams—screams for help—screams before her throat is cut—cut open with a knife. She lies dead on the floor—the floor of this room . . . of this house. There! (*Pointing to floor in front of table.*) Now I don't see that ghost any more.

MR. MANNINGHAM—What's the game, eh? What's your game?

ROUGH (*confronting* MANNINGHAM)—But I still see the ghost of the man. I see him, all through the night, as he ransacks the house, hour after hour, room after room, ripping everything up, turning everything out, madly seeking the thing he cannot find. Then years pass and where is he? . . . Why, Sir, is he not back in the same house, the house he ransacked, the house he searched —and does he not now stand before the ghost of the woman he killed in the room in which he killed her? A methodical man, a patient man, but perhaps he has waited too long. For justice has waited too, and here she is, in my person, to exact her due. And justice found, my friend, in one hour what you sought for fifteen years, and still could not find. See here. Look what she found. (*Going to desk*.) A letter which never reached your wife. Then a brooch which you gave your wife but which she did not appreciate. How wicked of her! But then she didn't know its value. How was she to know that it held the Barlow rubies! (*Opening it out*.) See. Twelve thousand pounds' worth before your eyes! There you are, Sir. You killed one woman for those and tried to drive another out of her mind. And all the time they lay in your own desk, and all they have brought you is a rope around your neck, Mr. Sydney Power!

Mr. Manningham—You seem, Sir, to have some very remarkable information. Do you imagine you are going to leave this room with such information in your possession? (*Going up to door as though to lock it*.)

Rough—Do you imagine, Sir, that you are going to leave this room without suitable escort?

Mr. Manningham—May I ask what you mean by that?

Rough—Only that I have men in the house already. Didn't you realize they had signaled their arrival from above, your own way in, Mr. Manningham, when the lights went down?

A second later Manningham has made a rush for the door. As he throws it open, he faces two officers. He would turn and try another way out, but the men have grabbed him. It is a lively struggle during which Rough feels impelled to take some part. He delivers a kick in Manningham's shins, another in his groin, that are quite discouraging to the prisoner, and he pulls down the bell cord for the men to tie Manningham with. Then he takes a paper from his pocket and begins to read—

"Sydney Charles Power, I have a warrant for your arrest for the murder of Alice Barlow. I should warn you that anything you may say now may be taken down in writing and used as evidence at a later date. Will you accompany us to the station in a peaceful manner? You will oblige us all, and serve your own interests best, Power, by coming with us quietly. (MAN-NINGHAM *renews struggle.*) Very well—take him away. . . ."

As the men are about to follow instructions Mrs. Manningham appears on the stairs. She would, if the Inspector will permit it, like to speak to her husband—alone. Rough, at first inclined to refuse the request, decides to grant it. Manningham is tied securely to the chair. The detective and his men withdraw, Rough promising not to listen.

When they are alone, Mrs. Manningham goes slowly to the door and locks it. Now she is back, looking at her husband fixedly, and listening as he begs her to help him. In his room she will find a razor. Let her cut his bonds. Then he can make a jump for it from his dressing room window.

Dutifully, still mumbling to herself, Mrs. Manningham goes for the razor and returns with it. As she takes it from its case, a scrap of paper falls out. It is the missing grocery bill! Found at last! And she didn't lose it! Bella is hysterically happy at the discovery. It takes her mind so completely off the razor she can remember nothing of it. His pleading that she cut the cords comes vaguely to her. Now she is moving toward him looking wonderingly at the razor and he cringes before her—

"You are not suggesting that this is a razor I hold in my hand?" she intones. "Have you gone mad, my husband?"

MR. MANNINGHAM—Bella, what are you up to?

MRS. MANNINGHAM (*with deadly rage that is close to insanity*)—Or is it I who am mad? (*She throws the razor from her.*) Yes. That's it. It's I. Of course it was a razor. Dear God— I have lost it, haven't I? I am always losing things. And I can never find them. I don't know where I put them.

MR. MANNINGHAM (*desperately*)—Bella!

MRS. MANNINGHAM—I must look for it, mustn't I? Yes—if I don't find it you will lock me in my room—you will lock me in the madhouse for my mischief. (*Her voice is compressed with bitterness and hatred.*) Where could it be now? (*Turns and looks around.*) Could it be behind the picture? Yes, it must be there! (*She goes to the picture swiftly and takes it down.*) No, it's not there—how strange! I must put the picture back. I have taken it down, and I must put it back. There. (*She puts it back askew.*) There! (*She is raging like a hunted animal.*) Where shall I look? The desk. Perhaps I put it in the desk. (*Goes to the desk.*) No—it is not there—how strange! But here is a letter. Here is a watch. And a bill— See, I've found them at last. (*Going to him.*) You see! But they don't help you, do they? And I am trying to help you, aren't I?—to help you to escape. . . . But how can a mad woman help her husband to escape? What a pity. . . . (*Getting louder and louder.*) If I were not mad I could have helped you—if I were not mad, whatever you had done, I could have pitied and protected you! But because I am mad I have hated you, and because I am mad I am rejoicing in my heart—without a shred of pity—without a shred of regret—watching you go with glory in my heart!

MR. MANNINGHAM (*desperately*)—Bella!

MRS. MANNINGHAM—Inspector! Inspector! (*Up to door, pounds on door, then flings it open.*) Come and take this man away! Come and take this man away! (ROUGH *and the others come in swiftly.* MRS. MANNINGHAM *is completely hysterical and goes down to lower end of desk.*) Come and take this man away! (ROUGH *gestures to the men. They remove* MANNINGHAM. MRS. MANNINGHAM *stands apart, trembling with homicidal rage. She is making tiny animal sounds.* ROUGH *takes her by the shoulders sternly. She struggles to get away. He slaps her across the face. She is momentarily stunned. He puts her down into a chair.* ELIZABETH *enters, quickly takes in the situation. Gets a glass of water from table and standing back of* MRS. MANNINGHAM, *holds her head and gives her a drink.*)

ROUGH (*watching them for a second and . . . his eyes on* MRS. MANNINGHAM *whose wild fury has dissolved into weeping*)—I came from nowhere and gave you the most horrible evening of your life. Didn't I?

MRS. MANNINGHAM—The most horrible? Oh, no—the most wonderful!

THE CURTAIN FALLS

UNCLE HARRY
A Drama in Three Acts
By Thomas Job

THERE were several satisfying factors developed in the production of "Uncle Harry" late in the season. It had been a particularly disappointing season, for one thing, as report has frequently been made, and there was practically no hope at all of seeing even a halfway worthy drama uncovered late in May. Also the venture presented Eva Le Gallienne and Joseph Schildkraut in acting partnership again. That fact was hailed with satisfaction by both their individual followings, which are of healthy proportions, and the joint public that came to admire them when they first played "Liliom" for the Theatre Guild the season of 1920-21.

As a third satisfying factor, Thomas Job, the author, had been accepted as a native dramatist of more than average promise with his first play, a dramatization of Anthony Trollope's "Barchester Towers," in which Ina Claire was starred by the Theatre Guild the season of 1937-38. It was therefore a rewarding experience to have him prove that such promise had not been misplaced.

"Uncle Harry" is, as the saying goes, "pure theatre." Meaning that it is an artificially contrived drama depending on nothing as serious as a theme, social or political, and with no more than a single hope that it would furnish an evening's intelligent entertainment offered as an excuse for its production.

Mr. Job boldly reveals his murderer's identity in the first scene of the play. Thereafter he proceeds, with definite skill, both to guide and follow that murderer through the commission of a perfect crime. The attention of the audience is held taut, not with the suspense that is the major sustaining force of nine out of ten mystery murder plays, but by building the evidence by which the wrong person is convicted of the crime with such circumstantial perfection that the story interest is never dulled.

In the parlor of the Blue Bell Tavern, in a small town in Canada, a matter of thirty years ago, Miss Phipps, "a very much the barmaid" type, shows Mr. Jenkins, "a small commercial traveler," into the back room where she thinks he will be more comfortable. The back room is just off the end of the bar, being set in a sort of inglenook, with a small table surrounded by benches on three sides.

Mr. Jenkins is properly appreciative of Miss Phipps' consideration. He sips his tankard of ale, allows that a man has to be up and coming to get anywhere in these hard times and prepares to make out his report to the manufacturers of Pelham's Perfection Soap. He barely has spread out his papers and begun to write when he is joined by a man who has been sitting at the bar, apparently absorbed in his newspaper.

In his casual give and take with Miss Phipps, Mr. Jenkins had referred to the hanging that day of a murderer named Tomkins. It was the murderer's faulty reasoning that had tricked him, declared Mr. Jenkins. He had buried his poor wife's legs in the chicken yard, but had tried to burn her head in the fireplace, and that is why he was eventually hanged.

It was about this hanging that the man who has come from the bar would like to talk to Mr. Jenkins. It is the man's opinion that Tomkins, the murderer, was well pleased at the way things turned out. "The end crowns the work, Mr. Jenkins," ventures the newcomer. "Murderers, like artists, must be hung to be appreciated."

"I don't agree with you there," protests Jenkins. "Murderers have to lie low. They owe it to themselves."

"Yes, that's the paradox of murder. It's very sad. Because murder is a beautiful art if you look at it properly. Yes, that's the pathetic part of it."

Take, as the man insists on doing, the Quincey case. Does Jenkins remember? That was one of the few perfect murders. True, it was settled "just like that," as Mr. Jenkins illustrates with a snap of his fingers, but the authorities were wrong. Quite wrong.

"I'll have to convince you, I see," the stranger continues, with practically no encouragement from Mr. Jenkins. It'll be a pleasure, since your analysis of the Tomkins' case struck me as shrewd. But Tomkins was too ingenious, and ingenuity always betrays itself. Tomkins tried to create circumstances, not take advantage of them. An artist, Mr. Jenkins, must create from what he knows. He invents nothing, he arranges."

"Does he?"

"Have you ever read 'Murder as One of the Fine Arts' by Thomas de Quincey? Ah, you should—you'd find it instructive. De Quincey emphasizes the fact that your true murderer works with a few bold decisive strokes. Some say that the Quincey family here was descended from him, but the relationship was never established."

Mr. Jenkins, having his way, would concentrate on his home work, but the man must tell his story. He calls for Miss Phipps and proceeds—

MAN—The Quinceys lived in a pleasant little house on Union Street, here in town. You know, respectable—
JENKINS—Stuffy, like?
MAN—Precisely, precisely, Mr. Jenkins. You'll find its parallel all over—Europe, the States . . .
JENKINS—My wife's cousin lives in Boston, and we go there . . .
MAN—Exactly. Exactly. Well, Harry Quincey lived here with his two unmarried sisters, Hester and Lettie. The family was not important, but quite beyond reproach. One of these mixed marriages, father English, mother French.
JENKINS—Me, I'm pure English.
MAN—Extraordinary. The parents died, and these three were left a legacy. Not much, but enough to keep them in comfort if they lived together. Note that, Mr. Jenkins, if they lived together. You can see at once the situation that a clause like that would create.
JENKINS—Private incomes, huh? I'm against private incomes. I'm a salaried man myself.
MAN—So I should judge from your air of skeptical self-importance.
MISS PHIPPS (*coming from bar*)—What do you want?—
MAN—This gentleman could do with another beer. (*She stares at him but does not move.*) What's the matter, Miss Phipps? Don't you want to fill the order? (*She goes.*) Everyone called Quincey Uncle Harry—
JENKINS—Uncle Harry?
MAN—A term of affection and contempt which the boys of the local grammar school fastened on him. He used to teach drawing there gratuitously since he wasn't a qualified teacher. The name Uncle Harry clung, but he never really liked it.
JENKINS—Why not?
MAN—We all like to be considered sharp fellows, sir, and the term "Uncle" somehow irritates by its suggestion of ineffectuality.

Mr. Jenkins again grows restless. If this is to be a long tale— It is, admits the man, and calls Miss Phipps to change the gentleman's order to brandy. When the drink is brought the barmaid is caught obviously staring at the man—

"A bit afraid of you, isn't she?" ventures Mr. Jenkins.

"Naturally," quietly answers the man. "You see, I'm the murderer. I'm Uncle Harry."

With a start Mr. Jenkins jumps to his feet. "What?" he cries.

"Now take it easy, Mr. Jenkins. I just want you to listen."

"Why are you running around loose?"

"Because of the cunning ways of God. I'm trying to circumvent them. Through you and through thoughtful men like you. I tell lots of people."

"What are you trying to get out of it?"

"I want the world to know me for what I am. Then I won't be Uncle Harry any more. Then perhaps Lettie will let me be."

"Don't be impatient. I'll explain it all. Ironic, isn't it? Tomkins hangs on the gallows and Uncle Harry walks the streets as free as air—yet he's far from satisfied. Now follow me closely, Mr. Jenkins, and you'll see how success, like a curse, has a curious way of coming home to roost."

The curtain falls.

Briefly the lights are dimmed. When they are raised we are in the living room of the Quinceys, "very neat and comfortable and indicating a conservative though not particularly old-fashioned taste." A stairway to the upstairs room rises from the back. It is a wet afternoon in October and a fire is burning in the fireplace. Hester and Lettie Quincey are sitting facing each other, talking to a visitor, Lucy.

"Hester is 48, a large, domineering woman. Lettie is 44, smaller and less obviously aggressive, though she has a touch of waspishness that can be effective enough when she chooses to use it. Both women share an indefinable air of self-righteousness. Lucy is obviously a visitor, a perfectly nice, healthy young woman of about thirty. Her outstanding characteristic is her extreme normality. She has obviously dressed up for the occasion and is determined not to show how triumphant she feels."

Lucy is proudly showing Hester and Lettie her engagement ring. It has three rubies—small, but still three—and the setting makes them look larger. Lucy is, she admits, a lucky girl. She's only 30. Her fiancé, Lucy admits, is 38.

"Any children?" Lettie would know.

"Not yet," laughs Lucy.

HESTER—Lucy, you're a caution.

Lettie—Imagine what a surprise this will be to Harry.
Lucy—A nice one, I hope.
Hester—Bound to be.
Lettie—Thinking he left you high and dry has bothered him no end.
Hester—Harry's so sensitive.
Lucy—Glad to take a load off his conscience.
Lettie—I said to Harry at the time, "If that girl doesn't sue you for breach of promise, Harry, well, she's a saint, that's all."
Lucy (*looking at her pointedly*)—If I'd sued anyone, it wouldn't have been Harry.
Hester (*covering up*)—And I can't tell you how sweet I think you were to call and tell us about Mr.—or Mr.—
Lucy—Waddy. George Waddy.
Hester—Oh, yes . . . Waddy.
Lettie—Aren't you glad now, Lucy, that you decided to wait?
Lucy—Did I decide? I don't remember?
Hester—Home's the best place for Harry.
Lucy—That's what you said at the time, Hester.
Hester—Did I? Doesn't that show you now?
Lucy—It does, Hester dear, it shows me.
Lettie (*after a brief, uncomfortable pause*)—Oughtn't we start tea?
Hester—Without Harry?
Lucy—I don't think you ought to go to the trouble. Besides I've about a million things to do and—
Lettie—I bet you're buying the trousseau.
Lucy—Oh—a little here and there. It's all going to be quite simple.

There is a knock at the door. That would be Harry. Lettie would let him in, but it is Hester's turn. Lucy is quite fussed wondering what Harry will say. They have, Lettie calls, a great surprise for him.

Harry "is a quiet, unobtrusive man who gives the impression of being little. His features are delicate and fine but marred by a pudginess, the result of being spoiled for about forty years. His hands are small and beautiful, and he has a warm, hesitant way of talking."

For a second Harry and Lucy stare at each other, then their greetings are casual. It will be four years in March since they have seen each other. Harry has missed Lucy, he says, but Lucy refuses to believe that. And now for the surprise. The girls insist Lucy should tell it—

Lucy—Well—I hardly know how to start. It—it's like this.
Uncle Harry—Yes?
Lettie—She's engaged. That's the long and short of it.
Hester—To Mr. George Waddy, engineer.
Lucy—And doing nicely, too.
Lettie—Show Harry your ring, dear.
Lucy (*showing*)—It isn't much.
Uncle Harry—Very lovely.
Hester—Three rubies, did you notice?
Uncle Harry—I noticed, all right. Did you come to tell me this, Lucy?
Lucy—I just wanted you to know.
Lettie—She knew how interested we'd be.
Uncle Harry—*Is* tea ready?
Hester—In two shakes of a lamb's tail. I was baking a cake—so we'll celebrate.
Lettie—And I'm making a pie. This is going to be high tea.
Uncle Harry—It's the least we can do for the lady . . . Excuse me. (*He goes upstairs.*)
Hester—He turned pale. Did you see, Lettie?
Lettie—I'm sure I didn't. And besides why should he?
Hester—White as a sheet. You never keep your eyes open for these little—
Lucy (*uneasily*)—Really, Hester, I don't feel I should stay to tea. The train leaves at 5:30 and I've got such a lot—
Hester—Nonsense, Lucy. This is a celebration. You wouldn't let us down.
Lettie—Harry'd be heartbroken, too.
Lucy—Heaven forbid.

Nona, a healthy retainer and chatty, does not help matters by greeting Lucy with a welcome based on the assumption that she has come to "kiss and be friends" with Harry. Lucy only hopes to be friends, she admits, embarrassedly. Lettie also would explain her feeling. She has never disliked Lucy; she just thought Lucy wasn't the right girl for Harry.

"Is there a right girl for him?" Lucy asks, with a trace of hurt.

"Probably. She'll show up sometime. And if she doesn't, where's the tragedy?"

"Harry will never get married. But you might have given him a chance."

"Who's stopping him? . . . Lucy, you didn't come here to compare the two, did you?"

Before Lucy can answer there is an interruption from Hester. She would have Lettie come to the kitchen to watch her cake. Then Harry appears. He has changed into a youngish tweed suit a bit too tight for him, and is wearing a tie that is quite lively.

One after the other they each have something to say about Harry's resurrection of the old suit. "Men either shrink or spread after forty," Lucy suggests, rather enjoying the situation. . . .

As soon as they are alone Lucy extends the hand of friendship to Harry. So far as she is concerned all is forgiven. As for that, there is nothing for which she has to forgive him, insists Harry. She knows he had wanted to marry her—

"Not enough to give up Hester and Lettie, though," Lucy reminds him.

"And all these years I've thought—"

"So have I— And thank God that's over."

"Time's a great healer, eh?"

"So is another man."

"So you did come to gloat after all."

Lettie, coming in to set the table, must take another fling at Harry's tight suit. She was just about to give it to the Salvation Army. But perhaps, now that he is taking an interest in his clothes, he will get him a new suit. She had seen one in the tailor's window that she decided was just the thing for him. But Harry is content with the old one.

LETTIE—That's Harry for you. He collects old things like a magpie. You should see your letters, Lucy.

UNCLE HARRY—Lettie—

LETTIE—Just my fun. He keeps them all tied up, Lucy.

LUCY—In a pink ribbon?

LETTIE—In a shoelace.

UNCLE HARRY—Easier to untie.

LETTIE—Remind me to dust them, Harry, when I clean your top right-hand drawer on Saturday. Shan't be long now. (*Exits to kitchen.*)

UNCLE HARRY—Some day I'll throw something at her. Something hard.

LUCY—She wouldn't notice it. (*A pause.*)

UNCLE HARRY (*fingering his lapel*)—Remember?

Lucy—Unhuh.
Harry—Beacon Hill.
Lucy—I know.
Harry—The evening we climbed up there. (Lucy *turns away*.) Did you ever tell George Waddy about that evening?
Lucy (*defiantly*)—Yes, I did.
Harry—You do believe in cards on the table, don't you? What did he say?
Lucy—He said forget it.
Uncle Harry—Modern sort of man, isn't he?
Lucy—Yes.
Uncle Harry (*fingers her ring*)—It's not as easy to forget as George seems to think. At least it isn't to me. Look. (*Points to a canvas.*) Like it?
Lucy—Harry . . . Harry, that's lovely.
Harry—I did it from memory. I didn't dare go back.
Lucy—Why didn't you?
Uncle Harry—It wouldn't have looked the same.
Lucy—No—no, it wouldn't. Not any more.
Uncle Harry—There's the tree, our tree, you notice.
Lucy—Where you cut our names.
Uncle Harry—I've put them in. Hearts and all.
Lucy—Like a couple of kids.
Uncle Harry—Grand, wasn't it?
Lucy—It was . . . I like the view of the town in the sunset light. Remember how we picked out your house and I said it was following us around?
Uncle Harry—It was following us around. You had flowers in your hair.
Lucy—And we talked of the life we were going to have and it was all so perfect—and so easy.
Uncle Harry—Well—well—you're not crying, Lucy?
Lucy (*a bit shaky*)—Yes. It was so long ago.

Hester has brought a steaming cake from the kitchen and gone back to help Lettie with her pie. Hester, Lucy remembers, always was jealous of Lettie's cooking. "Jealous! Of her? Rubbish!" There is scorn in Hester's voice.

Now Lucy and Harry have returned again to their own adjustments. Harry is hoping Lucy will be happy with this George. Lucy is thinking of George, not as she thought of Harry, but as giving her a home and family. "No lady's complete without babies, you know," laughs Lucy.

"Is George also eager for babies?"

"He says he can hardly wait to start. The devil."

"Hot-blooded."

"Why shouldn't he be? What's wrong, Harry? Jealous?"

"What do you think?"

"You mustn't be a dog in the manger."

"Having a hell of a good time, aren't you?"

"Do you blame me? Harry, *what* are you trying to do?"

Harry has grabbed Lucy and is kissing her with fervor. "Not so easy to forget, is it, Lucy?" he says.

"Not so easy," Lucy admits.

From the kitchen comes the sound of Hester's and Lettie's voices. They are still jabbing at each other about their respective housewifely virtues.

"Lucy—Lucy, if it weren't for those two, would you—would you come back to me?"

"Would there be any 'you' to come back to? It would be the same all over again."

"Not this time."

"No? You've been spoiled so much, that I don't believe you could live as a man ought to.—You're too used to being smothered."

"Lucy—"

"Don't torture yourself, Harry. Hester and Lettie are eternal."

"Would you marry me? George or no George?"

"That, Uncle Harry, is a leading question."

"That's all I wanted to know."

Hester and Lettie have brought the tea. At table the talk turns again to Lucy's engagement and how it came about. That was simple enough, Lucy relates. George, being an engineer, was there building a bridge. He had taken Lucy home a few times in his automobile and one night she had frankly told him that if that was the way he felt about it he had better ask her father—and that was all there was to it.

Nona has come in with a dog in a basket. It is the same Weary Willie that Lucy remembers. Very old now and with impaired hearing. Lettie can't understand why Nona should bring the animal in—spoiling their tea that way.

"It isn't her fault you're not dead already," Nona whispers in Weary Willie's ear. "But Mr. Harry stuck up for you."

The tea proceeds with another quarrel about the food. Lettie's "pièce de résistance" a canned gooseberry pie, is much too acid for Harry, insists Hester, who promptly takes his piece away from

by Alfredo Valente.

"UNCLE HARRY"

Lettie: After all my good work you should pick a piece to suit me. . . .
Uncle Harry: Here we are. The loveliest swan song ever written. Shakespeare's. Dirge from Cymbeline."

(*Joseph Schildkraut, Eva La Gallienne*)

him. Gooseberry pie is much better for him than Hester's hot cake, insists Lettie. It is a wonder Harry doesn't go mad with Hester constantly bothering him—

"Bothering—you call it bothering and me devoting my whole life to him?"

"It would be better for everyone if you didn't. . . . I sometimes think one of us would be all that Harry needs to look after him."

"You, I suppose."

Now Harry has interfered. After all he is able to decide for himself what is best for him. He will eat a half piece of Lettie's pie, and give the other half to Hester.

" 'Pièce de résistance!' " sneers Hester, glancing contemptuously at her plate. . . .

George Waddy has called. Everybody is surprised, especially Lucy. What can George be up to now? she wonders.

George is revealed as "a good-looking practical man of about forty, dressed in tweeds, a bit self-conscious and very much the fiancé." He is very happy at finding his darling. Just happened to be in the neighborhood on business, and, having the automobile, he thought—

Of course, he did. Lucy is very proud of George. She introduces him to the nice Quincey family, about which he has already heard so much he feels quite well acquainted. Especially Harry. George feels greatly indebted to Harry—

"I—I'm glad to meet the better man," says Harry, as they shake hands.

"Not the better—just the luckier," answers George. "If I'm half as good as she deserves I'd be an angel."

The sisters invite George to tea, but he has just had lunch and can only take a cup—and a piece of cake. Then he would like to see Mr. Quincey's paintings—

"You must call him Uncle Harry—everybody does," corrects Lucy, and George willingly complies. Harry hasn't been painting much the last three years, according to Harry, but Hester insists he is at it all the time. Both sisters have their favorite studies. Hester's is that tiger behind bars. Lettie likes the "Beacon Hill" number, which is also Lucy's favorite. Perhaps Uncle Harry will do them a picture for a wedding present, Lucy suggests. They would be proud to hang it over the mantel and boast of knowing the artist personally. . . .

Lucy and George have to hurry on. And when will Uncle Harry be seeing Lucy again? At the wedding, Lucy thinks.

"Good-by, Uncle Harry," George is saying. "It's been a treat to have met you. I used to be mighty jealous of you, I don't mind saying."

"And you're not jealous any more?"

"Not a scrap. Not any more."

"That's good."

Now Lettie has come running downstairs with a surprise package for Lucy. It is something that might make George furious—in a nice way—so Lucy better not open it until she gets home.

Lucy and George have gone. Harry is inclined to show a bit of temper when he thinks of George, but Lettie is quite pleased with everything.

"Lucy's idea of a husband," she says, "is a man who spends half his time getting increases in salary and the other half in kissing her and so forth."

Not a bad program, Harry agrees. He realizes, however, as Lettie says, that Lucy would never have spoiled him as his sisters do. And Harry is one, as his mother had said, who has to be spoiled.

There is a call from Hester in the kitchen. She wants Lettie to come and help her. Lettie prefers to sit and talk with Harry. She sometimes thinks Hester doesn't realize what a sympathetic understanding she and Harry really enjoy. Hester doesn't know what it means to be together, as they are now.

"We're pretty well off, really," Lettie is saying. "Hester or no Hester. Sort of settled. Father knew a thing or two when he left us just enough to stick together. He was a great one for family."

"Yes. His family." There is a pause. "Hadn't you better go and give Hester a hand before she blows the kitchen roof off?" Harry suggests.

LETTIE—I must, I suppose. Yes, it's all very comfortable, and to think that that Lucy—well, she's got a nice little surprise waiting for her when she gets home.

UNCLE HARRY—Surprise!

LETTIE—I gave her back her old letters.

UNCLE HARRY—My letters!

LETTIE—Bootlace and all. You won't want them any more. Will you? (*Waits for an answer.*) Will you, Harry?

UNCLE HARRY (*very quiet*)—No, no. Why should I?

LETTIE—It will show her we're done with her. For good. (*Pause again. She becomes anxious.*) Won't it?

UNCLE HARRY—Unquestionably.
LETTIE (*very hurt*)—You're cross with me.
UNCLE HARRY (*violently*)—Cross with you! (*Quiet again.*) All you do is make me look like a fool.
LETTIE—Oh, don't be cross with me. I couldn't bear it. It was nasty of me, I know, now I look back on it. Horrid. But I knew you'd understand. I just had to. It's all right, Harry, isn't it?
UNCLE HARRY—Yes, it's all right.
LETTIE—Kiss and be friends then. (*Kisses him on cheek.*) We've got to put up with each other's little ways, haven't we? It's the only way to get along. Smile at me, sir, or I'll go and drown myself in the teapot. There.
UNCLE HARRY—Go and help Hester.
LETTIE (*going to fireplace*)—Besides I always hated them.
UNCLE HARRY—What?
LETTIE—Those damn letters.

Lettie has no sooner disappeared through the kitchen door than Harry has begun pacing the room angrily. Stopping at the mantel he picks up a cup and deliberately breaks it.

Hester, Lettie and Nona, coming from the kitchen, are still discussing their triumph over Lucy. Much good it has done her to come there to crow over Harry. Still, Letty thinks, Hester should not have acted as she had at the table. And Hester is convinced that Lettie had asked for all she got. Again Harry must step in to halt the battle and Hester flounces back to the kitchen.

Now Lettie has found the broken cup. Who did that? Harry thinks perhaps George Waddy had left it too near the edge of the mantelpiece, and— "Thank heaven it's only the second best set," interrupts Lettie.

There are bits of cake left from the tea. Harry takes them into the kitchen for Weary Willie. Weary is a sick dog—too sick ever to get well again, probably.

"He'd be better off out of his misery," suggests Lettie.

"Nonsense, Lettie, he—" And then Harry has a better idea. "Perhaps you're right, Lettie. Perhaps you're right at that."

LETTIE—Harry, you really agree with me?
UNCLE HARRY—He knows he isn't necessary any more.
LETTIE—It would be for the best all 'round.
UNCLE HARRY—But Hester—

LETTIE—She'd boil, that's all. Simply boil.

UNCLE HARRY—Yes, indeed. We'll have to keep it dark from Hester.

LETTIE—That'll be fun.

UNCLE HARRY—Hardly fun, Lettie. It's an unpleasant business. I hate to do it.

LETTIE—It's better than letting him suffer. When will we do it?

UNCLE HARRY—The sooner the better . . . Tonight, perhaps.

LETTIE (*leans over the back of the sofa*)—How does one go about it?

UNCLE HARRY—Poison, Lettie. Poison will be quickest and Hester will never know.

LETTIE (*pause*)—Chloroform?

UNCLE HARRY—No—he'll struggle too much. Hydrocyanic acid will do the trick.

LETTIE—What's that?

UNCLE HARRY—Something very quick—same as Prussic acid.

LETTIE—Will it hurt?

UNCLE HARRY—It'll be over too soon.

LETTIE—Ugh! (*Silence.*)

UNCLE HARRY (*after pause*)—Lettie! You might get some if you're down town tonight.

LETTIE—I was going to the Post Office.

UNCLE HARRY—Drop in at the druggust's and get some.

LETTIE—Can you buy it just like that?

UNCLE HARRY—You have to sign for it. You sign your name. . . . Ben's will be the best place. Ben won't make any difficulty.

LETTIE—I'll go right away—then I won't have to help wash up.

UNCLE HARRY—Sneak out, eh?

LETTIE—It'll serve her right for the way she behaved at tea. (*Goes to the hall tree.*) How much of this stuff shall I get? (*At door.*)

UNCLE HARRY—Tell Ben what you want it for. Say you want a good dose.

LETTIE—Oh, I hate to, somehow. (*Appears with mackintosh and umbrella.*)

HARRY—The poor devil.

HESTER (*from kitchen*)—Lettie!

UNCLE HARRY (*after pause*)—She's calling you. Think how she'll feel when she finds you gone!

LETTIE—That's just what she needs.
UNCLE HARRY—Don't forget—Ben's.
LETTIE—I'll remember.

Again Hester has burst in from the kitchen determined that Lettie shall come and do her share of work. She is pretty mad when she finds Lettie gone. And who broke the cup? Harry! Nonsense! Harry never broke anything in his life. It probably was Lettie—that's why she ran away.

"She's going to say that George broke it," murmurs Harry.

"She is, is she? Oh, won't I give it to her for this?"

Harry would regret that. But if she must, won't she please wait until he gets back from the Blue Bell? He must go to the Blue Bell. It is Wednesday and the boys will be expecting him to play the piano. He couldn't let them down.

"Harry, when are you going to stop being a little martyr?"

"Soon, very soon now."

"No one gives a thank-you for all you do."

"That's right, Hester. You've got to be a devil to make people really esteem you. Wait till I get back, before hauling poor Lettie over the coals."

"All right. I want you to be here when I face her with it, anyway. And don't you defend her."

"I won't lift a finger to defend her . . . Not a little finger!"

Harry is looking at Hester "speculatively and almost gleefully." Then he begins to chuckle.

"What are you looking at me like that for?"

"Just taking a good look at you, Hester. You're such a big live woman."

"Don't be a fool, Harry. And what in heaven's name is there to laugh at?"

Uncle Harry is chuckling—

" 'When the rain rains and the goose winks,
   Little knows the gosling what the goose thinks.' "

The curtain falls.

The boys in the back room at the Blue Bell are singing "A Capital Ship." They are D'Arcy, Blake and Albert with Uncle Harry at the piano. Their tendency, according to D'Arcy, is to "Americanize" the harmony, and there should be no "Americanizing"—no harmonizing in correct quartet singing.

They get around to "I Want to See My Sister Flo," and also to another round of drinks. Uncle Harry has been calling for double Scotches, which is going a bit strong for Harry, thinks D'Arcy. But Harry wants to be happy. "Blessed are the meek for they shall inherit the earth," quotes D'Arcy, and Harry smiles a little vacantly. He would like to go on with the discussion, but already it has led Albert to blurt out—

"If you weren't so meek—your sisters—"

"Yes. What have you to say about my sisters?"

"Oh, nothing, nothing. When did they have their last little tiff?" The others would stop Albert, but he must finish. Everybody knows the sisters quarrel—"just like cats and dogs."

UNCLE HARRY—It is not true!

D'ARCY—Of course it's not true. The thing to do with Albert is to pay no attention to him. He's a gossip.

ALBERT—Who's a gossip?

D'ARCY—Let's face the facts—you are.

ALBERT—It isn't a question of gossip—you can see for yourself, whenever he comes in after they've been fighting you've only got to look at him. Like someone who's been kicked in the seat of his trousers and is doing his damnedest to act as if he hadn't been kicked in the seat of his trousers. Oh, you can't miss it. I bet there's been more trouble tonight.

UNCLE HARRY—Just a slight argument.

ALBERT—There you are. I know. (*Pats* HARRY *on the shoulder*.) I'm sorry, old man. It's too bad. We're all sorry for you. Aren't we, gents?

D'ARCY—Now you bring the subject up—we are. You're a lesson, Uncle Harry, a great moral lesson. We all ought to be like you. We aren't and we don't want to be, but we ought to want to be like you, make no mistake about that.

BLAKE—That's putting the matter in a nutshell.

UNCLE HARRY—This is kind of you, gentlemen. But I assure you the reports are grossly exaggerated. If there is some slight bickering, who's to blame for it? I'm to blame.

ALBERT—You're to blame! He says he's to blame. Anyone would as soon blame Jesus.

D'ARCY—Albert!

ALBERT—All right. I wasn't being blasphemous, what's more. He does remind me of Jesus in the small.

UNCLE HARRY (*apparently a little drunk*)—Hester and Lettie are too fond of me.

BLAKE—It's because they're not married.

UNCLE HARRY—That's right. Lettie wants to do all the work

and Hester says no—and there you are! Still Lettie shouldn't have said it.

D'ARCY—Said what, Uncle Harry?

UNCLE HARRY—Oh, it was just nothing, just nothing.

ALBERT—But what was it? Harry, we're all friends here.

D'ARCY—Of course we are.

BLAKE—Sure.

UNCLE HARRY—That's right. Does a man good to get these things off his chest. Lettie said this afternoon that one of them was enough to look after me. That hurt Hester.

BLAKE—H-m. Too bad!

UNCLE HARRY—Just in the heat of the moment, of course. But still—

D'ARCY—We should never let our tempers get the best of us.

UNCLE HARRY—That's right.

ALBERT—That's damn right. Shake hands on it, Uncle Harry.

Ben, the druggist, has arrived. "Ben is a young, sociable fellow. Obviously accustomed to being the life and soul of the party." He would have Miss Phipps hurry his beer. He wants to catch up with the others. When he gets his drink his eyes fall on Harry, and a mysterious smile twinkles in his eye. "Old Caesar Borgia" he calls Harry. Harry's sister, "Lucrezia Borgia," had just been in Ben's place.

"Sounds like a couple of foreigners to me," ventures Albert.

"So they were, Albert, my boy—historical foreigners. They'd poison you at the drop of a hat."

"I'm afraid I don't quite follow you, Ben," says Uncle Harry.

BEN—See, he's trying to cover up his tracks. Sending your sister to get poison.

UNCLE HARRY (*quickly*)—Was it Lettie?

BEN—Certainly it was and she signed your name.

UNCLE HARRY—Signed my name for what?

BEN—For the poison. Didn't you know you have to sign for it?

UNCLE HARRY—Do you?

BEN She seemed to know more about this than you do.

UNCLE HARRY—What did she get?

BEN—Hydrocyanic acid.

UNCLE HARRY—Beg your pardon.

BEN—Prussic acid.

UNCLE HARRY—I suppose she wanted it to clean clothes.

BEN—That's a good one. Clean clothes, eh? One whiff of that stuff and that's the last clothes you'll ever clean. So you be careful.

UNCLE HARRY—Is it as deadly as all that?

BEN—It's quick—that's the best you can say for it. Weary Willie won't suffer long—but it'll pinch him a bit at first.

UNCLE HARRY—My dog?

BEN—She said that something ran out of his poor ears all the time.

UNCLE HARRY—That's all wrong.

BEN—What?

UNCLE HARRY—Nothing—it's all right.

BEN—You're sure, aren't you?

UNCLE HARRY—It's all right—it's quite all right.

BLAKE—That's the sad part about dogs; they die.

ALBERT—This acid stuff, Ben. What does it do to you?

BEN—Plenty. Hydrocyanic acid if taken internally unites with the haemogloben in the blood to the exclusion of oxygen.

D'ARCY—That's bad.

BEN—And that causes a unique type of chemical suffocation.

ALBERT—Is that worse than just plain suffocation?

BEN—Anything chemical is worse than anything plain. I saw a case once of prussic acid poisoning. It wasn't nice.

BLAKE—A human case!

BEN—Human! It had been human.

ALBERT—Geeze!

Suddenly Harry decides to go home. Let Ben play for them. What time is it? Only 9. Harry usually stays until 10:15. But he isn't feeling very well tonight. Might be the whiskey.

Harry's gone. Ben has confirmed Lettie's purchase of the acid. It's just possible, he thinks, that Lettie is planning to kill the dog behind poor old Harry's back—

"You should have seen Sister Lettie buying the stuff," says Ben. "Sly as if she had murder up her sleeve. Wouldn't talk to my Pop either. Nothing would do for her but she had to see me."

"Why did Harry leave so early?" Albert wants to know.

"It was the whiskey, he said."

"Whiskey has its faults but it doesn't make a man go home early," allows Ben, as the curtain falls.

It is 9:30 the same evening. The wind has risen and a rain

is beating against the window in the Quinceys' living room. The gas has been lit and the fire is burning brightly in the fireplace. Lettie is sitting reading at one side of the fireplace. At the other side a man's slippers have been placed in front of a chair and a smoking jacket is laid over the back of it.

Presently there is a knock at the door. Harry is back from the Blue Bell. He has been drinking water, he says, with three friends—Haig and Haig and Johnny Walker—which, he explains, is supposed to be a joke.

Hester is sitting in her room, in the cold and dark, Lettie reports. If she wants to make a martyr of herself, let her.

Did Lettie get that stuff? She did. And did she have a time getting it! Ben wouldn't give it to her at first, not until she told him it was for Harry. There was enough of it, Ben had said, to settle the hash of a whole kennel.

Lettie had better put the stuff out of the way, Harry thinks. Some place where Hester won't see it. Or Nona. Let her put it in the jar with the matches. Harry is the only one who uses the jar. But, first, perhaps she had better write something on the wrapper. It says "Poison" on the bottle plain enough, but no one ever notices print. It would be better if Lettie were to write "Danger!" or "Don't touch!" on it, Harry thinks. Lettie does— and puts the package in the matches jar.

Now Harry is ready to read to Lettie, but he thinks they should calm Hester down first. Lettie is for letting Hester stew in her own juice. "She's really cross because Lucy preferred my pie," says Lettie.

"There's the matter of the cup too."

"What cup?"

"The broken one. She thinks you've done it."

"How dare she? Why, I've never in my life—"

"I told her that," says Harry.

Nona is home, after dismissing her depressed fiancé at the back door. He wouldn't come into the kitchen. Miss Lettie kept coming in too often, he said. "Tell him he should be more charitable," laughs Harry. "Lettie likes a little excitement, too."

"Did you see me break a cup, Nona?" demands the still angry Lettie.

"What cup?"

"The cup that George Waddy used. Did I break it or didn't I?"

"Why should you?"

"There!" announces Lettie, and flounces up the stairs.

There's been another scene. Nona can see that. But Harry would warn her not to criticize people. Will she please reach him a match from the jar? She does. But Harry lets it go out. She reaches for another, and finds a package—a package Miss Lettie has been writing something on—"Danger!" "Don't touch!" Should she open it? She should not. Harry will look after it. He'll ask Miss Lettie what it is.

"And the sooner I know the better I'll feel," admits Nona. "I don't mind 'Danger'—it's the 'Don't touch' part that gets me."

From upstairs comes the sound of angry voices. Lettie and Hester are evidently having a lively exchange of words. Uncle Harry decides he had better investigate. He dashes up the stairs.

"Poor Uncle Harry! You do have a dreadful time!" mutters Nona. She has unwrapped the package and read the label: "Hy-dro-cyanic acid!" Lettie suddenly appears on the stairs and shouts to her to put that package down. "Put it down, you little fool! If you even smelt it you'd be a sick woman."

It isn't plain to Nona what anyone would want prussic acid in a decent house for and Lettie, to satisfy the maid's curiosity, finally has to tell her that they are planning to put Weary Willie out of his misery. Mr. Harry had ordered it. Mr. Harry? "Yes," Lettie repeats, "Mr. Harry ordered it!" Nona is still muttering doubtfully as she goes into the kitchen.

Now Harry has brought a very quiet, but evidently still angry Hester down from upstairs and would start the way to a family reconciliation. They have both acted as though they were about five years old—

"We all know you do it out of high spirits, but other people don't believe that," Harry is saying. "You're a fine, dignified couple of women but as soon as you start in on each other, bang goes the dignity and you behave—"

"I won't be talked to that way."

"It's just for your own good. You don't want to be the laughingstock of the town, do you?"

"Who is?"

"I'm afraid you both are rapidly becoming so. You know how they talk. That business this afternoon was most unfortunate."

They all know that Lucy has a tongue, Harry points out, which is all the more reason why they should be careful when she is around. They are both agreed to that.

"You are, Harry, quite right," Lettie admits. "I sometimes think though that Hester and I will only be at peace in our graves."

"Lettie Quincey, what a dreadful thing to say!" Hester is quite shocked.

"Oh, shut up!" snaps Lettie.

"There—nothing like letting the sun go down upon your wrath. Now we'll have a cup of cocoa to seal the treaty." Harry is again the successful conciliator and calls to Nona to make the cocoa. "The trouble is that you need such a little thing to start you off," Harry goes on. "If it were a really big cause you'd stick together like glue, but give you a tiny reason and it's all up."

Nona will have to make the cocoa over the fire in the fireplace, seeing the kitchen stove is out. During her preparations Lettie and Hester try for an understanding without success. It isn't that Hester cares about the broken cup—or wants to keep the set full—it's the principle of the thing. If Lettie had come to her and admitted she had broken the cup in place of sneaking out—

Who sneaked out? That was just for fun, Harry tries to explain. Anyway, why should she consult Hester about everything she does? Lettie wants to know. "Simply because you bullied us when we were children you think you can do it now. And you call it 'showing consideration.'"

"Oh, I understand. You wish I weren't here at all. Then you'd be free to gallivant as you please and let the house go to rack and ruin. Don't think I've forgotten what you said this afternoon."

"The cocoa's ready," announces Nona, going into the kitchen for the cups.

"What *did* you say this afternoon, Lettie?" Harry wants to know.

"You said I wasn't wanted," continues Hester. "You said that one of us was enough to look after Harry."

"And I meant it too. So the cup was just an excuse for your bad temper?"

"Excuse!"

"That's true—you don't need an excuse. I wish you'd stayed upstairs. I wish you weren't here. It was so peaceful till you came down."

"Yes, I'm just a nuisance, I know."

"Why don't you break that china dog and call it quits?" Harry suggests.

"Yes, why don't you? Heaven knows it's the only thing I can call my own."

"I will, too," shrills Hester. The next moment she has seized the china dog from the mantelpiece and is threatening to throw it into the fireplace. Lettie jumps to grab her hand. There is a struggle ending when Hester slaps Lettie soundly in the face. With a cry of "You—you devil!" Lettie sinks to the sofa, sobbing. "You asked for it!" Hester answers defiantly.

Again Harry must step in and stop the fight. He forces Hester to put the china dog back on the mantel. Then Hester storms upstairs.

"Well, I will say this: the house doesn't lack for entertainment—of a sort," says Nona as, taking a hint from Harry, she withdraws to the kitchen.

"I hate her!" mutters Lettie, sobbing afresh.

"She's always been jealous of you," agrees Harry. Even when they were children, catching tadpoles in a pond in Clark's meadow, Hester had broken Lettie's jampot when Harry had said she (Lettie) was the best fisherman in the world. "We're still children," insists Harry.

"She is. That's evident," agrees Lettie.

"You can't be cross with a child."

"She isn't a child—she's a vicious, bad-tempered old woman—"

It is Harry's idea that Lettie should make the first advances toward a further reconciliation. Hester has gone to bed, and is probably crying her eyes out. If Lettie will take Hester's nightcap of cocoa to her— Lettie positively refuses. Very well, then, Harry will do it. That, Lettie insists, would be worse. Finally Lettie agrees. She'll take Hester her cocoa, but she'll not kowtow to her.

First, however, Hester's cocoa should be sweetened. Hester likes it sweet. If Lettie will bring the sugar bowl from the kitchen—Harry would like more sugar, too. Lettie has gone for the sugar. Quickly Harry pours the poison into Hester's cup. Now he adds the sugar and bids Letty hurry before Hester goes to sleep.

"You should do this with forgiveness in your heart," Harry says, sweetly.

"I'm a Christian, I hope, but I'm a Christian within decent limits," answers Lettie, taking the cocoa upstairs.

Harry goes nervously to the window. "A vicious gust of wind

UNCLE HARRY

and rain blows into the room. He closes the window, pulls down the blind and carefully wipes his face with the handkerchief." He turns as he hears Lettie's step on the stair. She still has the cup of cocoa. Hester had refused to take it. "She says anything that I gave her would be like poison to her," reports Lettie, and Harry doubles up with laughter. Lettie can see nothing funny in what she has said.

Lettie thinks now they should let Hester enjoy her sulks while they drink their cocoa. Harry has decided that he doesn't want any at the moment, though he had ordered it. And he shouts at Lettie when she is about to drink from Hester's cup—

"Now you're angry, too. And with me," pouts Lettie.

"Sulks are catching," admits Harry.

LETTIE—Don't you want to read that poetry?
UNCLE HARRY—Not interested.
LETTIE—Please, I'd love to hear it. (*Pause.*) Would you if I went up and talked to Hester?
UNCLE HARRY—If you don't go all the squabbling will start again in the morning. And I'm sick of your squabbles.
LETTIE—But you saw her strike me. How can you expect— Where are you going?
UNCLE HARRY—Up to Hester.
LETTIE—I'd rather go myself.
UNCLE HARRY—You'd fail again.
LETTIE—I wouldn't. You'll see.
UNCLE HARRY—And the peace offering will be getting cold. Well— (*Makes for the stairs.*)
LETTIE—I insist on going. You sit down and pour out for both of us and I'll be back in a jiffy—and you'll see that everything will be all right.
UNCLE HARRY—Since you insist.
LETTIE—She'll drink it this time if I have to pour it down her throat.
UNCLE HARRY—Lettie!
LETTIE—Yes.
UNCLE HARRY—Lettie—if it was just you and me and there was no Hester—
LETTIE—We'd be much happier.
UNCLE HARRY—And I wanted to get married—what would you say?
LETTIE—What would become of me?
UNCLE HARRY—Yes, that's what I thought you'd say.

LETTIE—Well, what else should I say?

Lettie has again disappeared up the stairs. Harry goes to the kitchen door and calls Nona. He would have her come in and drink her cocoa with him. Nona is quite pleased. Delighted, too, to hear of what Lettie has done—

"I wish I could do a thing like that," admits Nona, stirring her cocoa. "That's the kindest thing that I ever heard of."

"It's just what Miss Lettie would do," insists Harry.

"H'm. It's more like what you'd do, Mr. Harry, if I may say so. Maybe you used your blarney on her."

"No blarney at all. She seemed very anxious to do it. Simply insisted."

"If things go on like this we'll have a nice house of it here— Good night, Mr. Harry."

Nona is starting away when Harry stops her. Does she remember where he had hidden the package she had found in the match jar? He had not hidden it, Nona remembers. He was going to, but he left it on the table.

"Then where is it?" demands Harry.

"Miss Lettie found me with it and did I get a bawling out. She—"

Lettie is coming down the stairs. "It's all settled," she calls, cheerily. "You'd better go to bed, Nona. Ironing tomorrow!"

"I know." Nona has started upstairs. "It's wonderful what a fuss we can make by just living."

"Did she drink it?" Harry demands of Lettie, as Nona disappears.

"She will as soon as she's finished the serial she's reading in 'Leslie's.'"

"It'll get cold."

"She likes it cold. (*Pours cocoa.*) Shall we have ours now?"

"You've earned it, Lettie," says Uncle Harry, passing his cup.

It is all cozy and peaceful now, Lettie agrees. Shall they go on with their reading? Harry is agreeable. Seeing Hester is not there, it might be nice to find something appropriate for her.

"She was mighty condescending," Lettie is saying, as she sips her cocoa. "I'll never give in to her again."

"You won't have to," says Harry.

LETTIE—Kindness is just lost on her.

UNCLE HARRY—This will be a great moment for Hester. Imagine her reaching out for it victoriously. She's beaten you, hands down. It's at such a time that a person should be careful.

LETTIE—What things you say! (*Pause.*) After all my good work you should pick a piece to suit me.

UNCLE HARRY—It will suit you, too. Eventually.

LETTIE—I don't see how anything could suit us both.

UNCLE HARRY—Here we are. The loveliest swan song ever written. Shakespeare's. Dirge from Cymbeline. (*Reads.*):

> "Fear no more the heat o' the sun
> Nor the furious winter's rages;
> Thou thy worldly task hast done,
> Home art gone and ta'en the wages:
> Golden lads and girls all must,
> Like chimney sweepers, come to dust.
>
> "Fear no more the lightning flash,
> Nor the all dreaded thunder-stone;
> Fear not slander, censure rash;
> Thou hast finished—" (*There is a choked scream from above.*)

LETTIE (*after a silence*)—That's Hester.

UNCLE HARRY—There's no need to hurry.

LETTIE—She's ill. She may need— (*Sound of* HESTER'S *dropping to the floor.*)

UNCLE HARRY—Hester needs nothing any more.

LETTIE—What do you mean? (UNCLE HARRY *indicates bottle.*) You've used it.

UNCLE HARRY—The cocoa you gave her.

LETTIE—You—

UNCLE HARRY—Murdered her . . . Why should she go on living?

LETTIE—You'll be hanged for this.

UNCLE HARRY—Somehow I don't believe that I will be hanged.

LETTIE—*You,* Harry, *you* of all people.

UNCLE HARRY—Yes. I rather depend upon that attitude.

LETTIE—Where are you going?

UNCLE HARRY (*at stairs*)—Just to see.

LETTIE (*almost in a collapse*)—I can't believe it—I can't believe it!

UNCLE HARRY—Better that two of us should die than three rot together.

LETTIE—I can't believe it and go on living.

UNCLE HARRY—I'm glad you see it that way.

NONA (*entering*)—I've been in . . . I heard the noise she made and I ran into her room—I saw her.

LETTIE—She's dead?

NONA—Yes. I won't ever forget her face. It was no illness that took her off and you can't tell me that it was. (*She sees the bottle in* LETTIE's *hand.*) So that's why you got that stuff—that's why you said that Mr. Harry . . . You tried to put it off on him. (*Becomes hysterical.*) Oh, God! God! I didn't think you had it in you. No, I didn't think you had it in you.

UNCLE HARRY (*from the stairs, quietly*)—You see, Lettie, the way it is?

Lettie is looking up at him as the curtain falls.

In the parlor of the Blue Bell Tavern the following December a couple of Uncle Harry's friends are awaiting the verdict of the jury that has tried Lettie Quincey for the murder of her sister, Hester. It is 5:30 in the afternoon and so far nothing has come from the jury room. But, as Ben remarks to Albert, the jury has only been out half an hour. And there is no doubt about the verdict. It's certain to be "Guilty."

"Bad business, hanging a woman," says Albert. "If she hadn't tried to put the blame on poor Uncle Harry, I'd have been sorry for her. You certainly helped settle her hash for her there, Ben. How did it feel to be on the witness stand?"

"How did I do?"

"Fine. You spoke up smart as a whip."

"I wanted to do all I could to help the poor chap."

"Where you were best was the way you laid it on about how guilty she looked when she came in to buy the stuff."

"I thought I was better where I told how Harry was upset when he found out she bought the poison."

"You were good there, too."

"But he helped himself more than anybody without knowing he was helping himself. The prosecution didn't need to treat him as a hostile witness."

"Every time he tried to help her he put his foot in it worse. It was a fair treat to see the way the prosecution balled him up."

"We'll have to be very kind to him."

It is Miss Phipps, the barmaid, who sounds the first note of doubt. Miss Phipps never has believed entirely in Uncle Harry. "He's too good to be possible," is the way she puts it. Miss Phipps has seen a lot of men in her time, and she still insists there is something queer about Harry.

"If you don't believe in him you got to believe in the facts," insists Ben, sticking up a handful of fingers to be used as markers. "Look at them fair and square: First—those two had always hated each other. Second—as the plain evidence of that girl and Nona shows, they had a real set-to on the day of the murder with slapping included. Third—Lettie said Hester would be better out of the way. Fourth—she buys the poison. Fifth—she gives the poison. It's open and shut. The only point in doubt is: Did she buy the poison to give the dog and change her mind and give it to her sister, or did she mean to give it to her sister right from the first? In any case it comes to the same thing."

Now Uncle Harry himself appears, looking very solemn and a little abused. Awkwardly Ben and Albert try to show their sympathy for him, and he as awkwardly accepts it. Harry can't drink with them. He is expecting to meet a lady there, but there is no reason for them to hurry away. She hasn't come yet. He thinks perhaps if Ben would play something lively it would help him get his mind off his trouble.

Ben is at the piano, playing softly, when Blake rushes in with the news. "She's done for!" he reports from the doorway, without noticing Harry.

"Guilty?" asks Albert.

"Guilty—yes, guilty as hell!"

"I—I must go to her," mutters Harry, rising quickly from the bench. "Excuse me."

There is nothing he can do, the boys convince him. The law will not let anyone see her before the next morning, after her jailors have given her something to make her sleep. Harry sinks back on the bench. He could do with a cup of tea, now.

Soon after his friends have left Harry, Lucy appears. He greets her with a nervous eagerness he tries to restrain. He had not wanted to send for her before—not until it was settled. But now it is settled.

It must be dreadful for him, Lucy feels. "I think you're splendid," she is saying. "That moment in the witness box when you said that if there were any justice you should be in the dock and not Lettie—well, it was the most touching thing I've ever seen."

Miss Phipps has arrived with the tea, taken a good look at Lucy and departed. Lucy will pour. She is glad that Harry does not blame her for testifying against Lettie. It was the only thing she could do. She is glad, too, though it may sound brutal to say it, that Harry will have his own life to lead now. He is free, and still young.

"It's queer what a strange business life is," Harry is saying, with increased eagerness. "You go on for years and nothing happens and all of a sudden—bang, your old life's gone and there's a new one coming up. Nothing's eternal, thank God. I remember once getting up at dawn and catching a train and before breakfast I was a hundred miles away. I thought of my old self lying in bed doing nothing when I could always be doing that. It's like that now."

"Is it?" Lucy is a little puzzled. She starts to leave. "That's all I had to say.—Except whatever happens you can depend on me."

UNCLE HARRY (*quietly but triumphant*)—Before you go, Lucy, what are we going to do about George?
LUCY (*amazed*)—George!
UNCLE HARRY—It'll be a blow to George and it's a pity.
LUCY—What difference can it possibly make to George?
UNCLE HARRY—He seemed pretty fond of you, that's all.
LUCY—Of course he is fond of me.
UNCLE HARRY—Then we'll have to make him understand?
LUCY—Understand what?
UNCLE HARRY—That you're mine.
LUCY (*muttering*)—Good God.
UNCLE HARRY—What's wrong, Lucy?
LUCY (*walking away with her back to him*)—But—
UNCLE HARRY—I know it's too early to talk about it. But I couldn't bear the thought of George going around with you any longer. Kissing you whenever he wanted and—
LUCY—You poor man!
UNCLE HARRY—I'm not a poor man. Not any more.
LUCY—You're not yourself and I'm not surprised. A tragedy like yours is enough to upset anyone.
UNCLE HARRY—It isn't a tragedy to me. I'm free, Lucy. You said so yourself.
LUCY—I didn't mean it that way.
UNCLE HARRY—Sit down. (LUCY *sits*.) Now. Remember the afternoon when you came to tea with us— I asked you then would you marry me if it weren't for Hester and Lettie. Do you know what you said?
LUCY—Something. I don't know. I've forgotten whatever it was.
UNCLE HARRY—You said, "That, Uncle Harry, is a leading

question—" Very well. It's time to answer it now. And there's only one answer to a leading question and that's yes. I depended on that.

LUCY—You were terribly mistaken, Harry.

UNCLE HARRY—But how could I have been?

LUCY—I suppose I might have encouraged you. I was a fool, but you were so pathetic and then there was some—some nostalgia mixed up in it too. Yes, that's what it was but I swear I never had the slightest intention of—

UNCLE HARRY—But you're not going to marry George as things are?

LUCY—I certainly am.

UNCLE HARRY—No.

LUCY—It's quite final, Harry.

UNCLE HARRY (*after a pause*)—After what I've done for you!

LUCY—What have you done?

UNCLE HARRY—Lucy . . .

LUCY Please don't make me say nasty things to you. It'll make me feel worse than I feel already.

No, Lucy insists, it is not that George stands between them. It would be the same, George or no George. There would still be the question of the disgrace! "Haven't you heard that it isn't the person who gets hanged who suffers most? It's his family," says Lucy. "They have to live with the murder." And when Harry would protest she goes on—

"How could I marry you? How could any girl marry you? How could you have the nerve to ask her? And if a woman was mad enough to do it and didn't care if she were stared at all her life, what about the children? It wouldn't be fair to them."

"That's a cruel way to look at it."

"Not cruel—just the ordinary way and I'm afraid I'm a very ordinary person. Good-by, Uncle Harry."

"Can't I see you again?"

"No."

"Lucy, stay with me, Lucy." He has gone to her and taken her hand. She is staring at him. "Don't look at me like that!" She steps away from him and quickly leaves the room.

"Lucy!" He calls wildly. She has gone on. For a moment Harry stares after her. "So, it was all useless!" he mutters, sinking down on the piano stool.

Harry is picking out the notes of a song as Miss Phipps looks in at the door and beckons to Blake, Albert and Ben in the bar.

They are all staring at him silently through the door as the curtain falls.

Three weeks later, about four in the afternoon, the Governor of the Prison is sitting in his room interviewing a man across the desk from him. It is a large formal room with a large, log-burning fireplace and an armchair standing in front of it.

The Governor is "a decent, unimaginative man, obviously of the military type." The man to whom he is talking is a Mr. Burton, "a neat, eager little man, smoking a cigar."

Mr. Burton has come to report that his assistant, Perce Downsberry, who is to officiate at the hanging, has fortified himself with a pint of whiskey. That's against the rules, but Mr. Burton is of the opinion that an exception will have to be made in this instance.

"Funny about Perce," Burton reports. "As long as it's a man no cucumber could be cooler than he. But when it comes to a woman, well, he gets rattled."

The Governor is inclined to overlook Perce's infraction of the rules this once, which eases Mr. Burton's conscience and leads him to predict that everything will go off with a "minimum of embarrassment," seeing that the Quincey woman is the quiet rather than the noisy type.

Suddenly Uncle Harry appears. His appointment was for 7, but as he wanted to talk with the Governor before he saw his sister, he has come early. Harry has brought a manuscript he wants the Governor to read. This, it transpires, is Uncle Harry's confession. The Governor reads it with a mounting amazement—

". . . 'Here I gave her the little bottle. It was my hope that she would hold it until the servant found her with it. This she did. Thus I entangled my sister in a net of evidence from which escape was as impossible as for a fly in the web of a spider. No hand could unspin the painstaking lies I had drawn about her. Only the reputation of a lifetime . . .'"

UNCLE HARRY—You realize, Mr. Governor, the implication in those last remarks.
GOVERNOR—Astonishing! Why are you confessing all this? (*Stands.*)
UNCLE HARRY—There's no longer any reason why I should live.
GOVERNOR—You're not doing this to save your sister?
UNCLE HARRY—There's no point in Lettie dying any more.

How long will it be before you can release her? I suppose there'll be a few formalities.

GOVERNOR—This is magnificent of you, Mr. Quincey. (*Picks up confession.*)

UNCLE HARRY—Not at all!

GOVERNOR—And now you'd better be going.

UNCLE HARRY—Why don't you arrest me? I've confessed.

GOVERNOR—It doesn't hold water, old man.

UNCLE HARRY (*rising*)—I killed my sister Hester and involved Lettie. That's clear enough.

GOVERNOR—Too clear. You can't expect the government to hang you on your mere assertion, sir. This way, Mr. Quincey. (*Crosses to door.*) We respect your attempt, we honestly do.

UNCLE HARRY—I rather expected that this might happen. Red tape seldom has much vision. Why do you think I wrote all this out?

GOVERNOR—You had your reasons, probably.

UNCLE HARRY—Excellent ones, I assure you. The proof is right here. (*Taps manuscript.*) Now look. You've read all the conversation Lettie and I had on the night Hester died. It didn't come out in the trial. But Lettie will remember it. She's bound to remember it. Suppose her account agrees with what I've written here?

GOVERNOR—I wouldn't care to trouble her now.

UNCLE HARRY—You must, sir, you must! It's your duty.

GOVERNOR—The whole thing is impossible.

UNCLE HARRY—The world is full of impossibilities.

GOVERNOR—It's devilish irregular. However... (*He crosses to desk, picks up phone.*) Bring up the prisoner from the condemned cell. Yes, bring her here.

The Governor is not sure he is doing the prisoner a kindness in confronting her with Harry. She has refused to see him the last three weeks. Harry is not surprised. Lettie never was one to forgive a wrong.

When Lettie comes, accompanied by a matron, Harry speaks to her. She ignores him and walks quickly to the armchair in front of the fire. It will be a novelty to sit in an armchair again—perhaps she could have one in her—her room, this being her last night—

"There's going to be no last night for you, Lettie," breaks in Harry.

"Mr. Governor, you shouldn't have made me look at that

man," protests Lettie, quietly. "He has been dreadful to me. . . . Send him away, please. He's wicked. Beyond belief."

She is not to be troubled long, the Governor agrees. First he would like to ask her a few questions: She had maintained during the trial that her brother was responsible for the crime. She had, admits Lettie, but no one would believe her. They will believe her now, Harry insists, because he has told them that he did it, and she will be cleared—

"You know what red tape is, Lettie," Harry says, with some eagerness. "I was afraid they might not believe me, so I've written the whole business down. All you've got to do is to tell the Governor word for word what we said after Hester screamed. If what you say agrees with this, then you're free."

"At least, it will create a reasonable doubt," admits the Governor.

Lettie is puzzled. She would get things straight. Harry has admitted that he killed Hester. That being so, Lettie would like to talk with Harry alone, before they go any further. This, the Governor is agreed, would be quite irregular, and could not be permitted. In that case Lettie will say nothing more. What she has to say to her brother must be said to him alone.

The Governor stands firm until the Matron points out that no harm could come from such an interview and it might prove important. The Governor weakens—

"Very well, Miss Quincey, we'll give you five minutes. . . . You will be under surveillance, you understand. You remain here."

With the Governor and the Matron gone, Lettie would know coldly what it is that Harry is up to now. He is, he says, trying to save her life. Yes, he admits, it is a bit dull at home, especially since Nona had left right after the verdict. Lettie is not surprised. This sort of thing does drive people away.

"That's what Lucy pointed out," admits Harry.

"Lucy! Does she come to see you?"

"She married George last week."

"A fair weather friend," chortles Lettie. "I always said so. . . . So it was Lucy, was it, who was the cause of all this? So that's why you're here! Can't live without her! Selfish Harry. Selfish as ever. . . . Do you suppose I don't see through you? It's just like the little trick you had of giving your toys away when you'd broken them and you'd act so big and generous about it too, and everyone was supposed to look, oh, so grateful, and then they'd all say how fine you were. Now you've broken your life and you want to give that away. But it won't do, Harry. Not this time."

The thought of dying doesn't worry Lettie any more. Nor is she moved by Harry's argument that it will be great fun to go on living, now that she can be the Lord of the Manor.

"What would be the good of that?" demands Lettie. "What would I want to be bossing an empty house for? It would be silly. I've always been a good woman and now I've finally found peace. I'm all right. I'm not afraid and that's much better for me than trying to go back to a life that's over and done with. But you— No, be quiet a minute because this is my last word. What are you going to do, Uncle Harry? You've a nasty time ahead of you. You're a great one for company, and where your company's coming from now I'm sure I don't know. You'll walk up and down the streets and people will smile at you and cross to the other side of the road and then you'll go home and the memory of Hester and me will be there to meet you at the door. And everything you do in that house will remind you of something I did, or Hester said, and you'll sit in your chair in an empty room—alone—and my little china dog will stare down at you and you'll be alone. And so it will go on and on. I wouldn't be in your shoes for anything in the world."

"Lettie, you can't do that. You'll tell the truth! You've spoilt everything for me. Don't spoil this. Please don't spoil this."

The Governor and the Matron have returned. No, Lettie has nothing to say. Who did the murder? It has been agreed that she did. Let the verdict stand.

"He's always been headstrong, sir," Lettie is saying to the Governor, indicating Harry. "Full of the wildest ideas. First he wanted to go to Paris to paint pictures as if he couldn't paint all he wanted to at home. He's done some lovely ones too, I must say. Then he wanted to marry a perfectly ordinary girl and it was hard to make him see sense about that. And now he wants to die. That shows you, doesn't it?"

"That will be all, Miss Quincey."

LETTIE—I hate to leave this fire. I always was like a cat about fires. You won't forget about that armchair, will you?

GOVERNOR—You shall have it. You are a brave woman to refuse to take advantage of your brother's sacrifice.

UNCLE HARRY—You're not going?

LETTIE—You wouldn't care to say good-by, Uncle Harry? (*Goes to the door.*)

UNCLE HARRY—You've got to delay it. Just for a little while, Mr. Governor. Then she'll break down and tell the truth. She wouldn't be so cruel as to keep on lying. You see, if she dies tomorrow I'll be alone with what I've done.

LETTIE (*with a smile*)—You see, Harry, the way it is. (*She exits with* MATRON.)

UNCLE HARRY (*rushing to* GOVERNOR)—She said it! That's what I said to her last night. That proves it! Look in this and you'll see. (*Shows confession to* GOVERNOR.) I'll find it for you. I know precisely where it is. (*He looks hurriedly through the confession.*) I'm sure I put it down. Maybe I didn't think those words important. But I did say them. I swear I did. (*He goes to door.*) Come back, Lettie. Can't I have a say in my own life? Only this once, that's all I ask. Oh, God damn you, Lettie. Don't you see what you've done to me! (*He breaks down weeping.*)

GOVERNOR (*filling water glass from decanter on desk, gives it to* UNCLE HARRY)—Drink this.

UNCLE HARRY—Thank you.

GOVERNOR—You'll be all right.

UNCLE HARRY—Yes, I'll be all right.

GOVERNOR (*handing him confession*)—Take this with you.

UNCLE HARRY—I don't need to. I'll tell everyone myself. I'll make you all see some day. I'll be free of her yet.

GOVERNOR—Better be on your way now, Mr. Quincey.

UNCLE HARRY—On my way— (*Takes hat. Laughs ironically.*) They say murder will out! Murder will out! But not my murder! Not Harry Quincey's murder! My God! That's a good one. (*He starts out the door.*)

THE CURTAIN FALLS

HOPE FOR A HARVEST
A Comedy in Three Acts

By Sophie Treadwell

THE second Theatre Guild play of the season was Sophie Treadwell's "Hope for a Harvest," with Fredric March and Florence Eldridge playing the leads. This family acting combination, second only to the Lunts in country-wide popularity, had tried the Treadwell play on the road. Starting in the Spring they had played it in such centers as Boston, Pittsburgh, Baltimore and Washington and had been received with a good deal of enthusiasm.

As so frequently happens, the New York reception of the play was slightly chilled by the reactions of the professional play reviewers. These exacting worthies were quick to admit the seriousness of Miss Treadwell's theme, and to credit her complete sincerity in its statement, but they were depressed because the play was not more exciting dramatically.

Richard Watts, Jr., of the *Herald Tribune* summed up this reaction intelligently when he wrote: "Because 'Hope for a Harvest' has something of importance to say, and says it with unmistakable sincerity, one has from the start a sympathetic concern with it and a far deeper respect for its heart and mind than for far more expert dramas of a lesser integrity. It really is striving to speak to the soul of America with gravity and idealistic fervor. The unfortunate thing is that in expressing the author's heartfelt interest in the future of the nation in a time of desperate crisis the play goes in for some unpersuasive and undramatic theatrical matters which destroy the greater part of its effectiveness."

Individual reactions to the effectiveness of a drama being as varied in character as the individuals expressing them differ in mind, temperament and general biological conditioning, the Marches shook themselves free of the critics' chill and continued. They had a good deal of audience warmth to sustain them for five weeks. Then they returned to Hollywood and their cinema chores.

"Hope for a Harvest," in pattern, belongs to that simple type of folk drama that flourished twenty or thirty years ago, when experts were fewer and audiences were larger. It has its scenes of drama, frequently flaring into touches of melodrama, alternating with scenes of comedy relief provided by character types common to the native drama. It even revels in an old-fashioned happy ending that ties up loose ends, loose characters and loose emotions.

Standing directly on a country highway in the San Joaquin Valley, in California, and on land that once was known as the Thatcher ranch, is the house of Mrs. Matilda Martin—"a typical, ugly, five-room, one-floor house of thirty years ago." We enter the Martin house by way of the kitchen—"a mixture of shining new improvements against a background of old-fashioned shabbiness." An old wood stove is flanked by a new gas stove with oven and cupboard; there is a bright new radio on a small table and a shiny new refrigerator in the corner. A tall Hoover cabinet sits in an alcove, and a large oval table is covered with a worn oilcloth. Through the window can be seen the top of a Tydol gas pump and a coca-cola sign.

It is 11 o'clock on a Sunday morning in the early summer. Matilda Martin is sitting at the table sorting eggs, taking them from a bucket, weighing them and assigning them to a variety of bowls in front of her. Mrs. Martin "is a bright, still vigorous old lady of over seventy; she has blue eyes, fine, regular features, and her white hair is drawn into a small, neat knot at the top of her head. . . . There is an unmistakable air of refinement, of race, of gentleness about her, as though her sharp, almost grim way of talking were a shell—a defensive shell—against the hardness of her life."

The radio is going. Mrs. Martin is hearing the last of the romance of Elizabeth and Jack Manders, when in bursts her niece, Tonie Martin, "a small, dark-eyed girl of sixteen, her pretty face over made-up, her hair short and tousled, worn down in her eyes." Tonie wears colored slacks, a white shirt, cheap cut-out red sandals, and yet "in spite of this cheap, vulgar exterior there is in her beautiful black eyes a look, not only of passion, but of loneliness, bewilderment and appeal." Under her arm Tonie carries a Sunday paper. She is no sooner in the room than she shuts off the radio, spreads out the paper and is soon at her puzzles.

By her half-hearted replies to Mrs. Martin's queries Tonie reports that she has been selling gas to Al, the duster; that she does a lot of flying with Al and doesn't consider it as dangerous as "doing sixty on this lousy old highway," and that she has her own ideas as to what her part of the work around the house should be. She serves the customers at the gas pump and doesn't think it's fair that she should also be expected to get her father's Sunday dinner. As for that, she's got everything ready for dinner—in cans. Soup, spaghetti, chow-mein, corn. Besides—

"I got to help Al dust the De Lucchi orchard tomorrow morning," says Tonie. "Got to get out at four."

"You better get to bed before three then," grimly advises Mrs. Martin. "Where were you last night?"

"Oh, driving around."

"Driving around where?"

"Oh, I don't know—up at Pete's place and—"

"Out every night till morning chasing around with Billie. Up every morning before it's light flying around with that old Al. I'd give up one or the other if I were you."

"Which?"

"Maybe I'd give up both of 'em—if I were you!"

"Well, you ain't me, Granma."

Granma turns on the radio again, but not for long. Tonie turns it off. Let Granma look at the funnies while she (Tonie) concentrates on the puzzles. ·If Tonie wins a million dollars—or even ten thousand—she'll be buying herself an airplane. And she might win if she could think of a "cinnamon" for love. Which reminds Tonie that personally she doesn't think much of love. She isn't ever going to get married. Neither does she intend to be an old maid—

"They say if you're an old maid you go daffy or get dopey or something," says Tonie.

"Good Godfrey! So that's the latest, eh?" Mrs. Martin is plainly irritated. "Well, when I was a girl, it was the married women who were daffy and got dopey. The old maids were up on their feet from dawn till night doing all the work for the rest of them, taking care of the kids and—"

"That was just it, Granma. Married women had a lot of kids then. Now they don't have any. That makes a difference."

It is getting pretty late for Tonie's father. He ought to be getting up, even if he did get in late the night before. Tonie has an explanation for that, too—

"I think Pa's got a girl," says Tonie.

"What are you talking about?" demands a shocked Granma.

"He's got a girl and he's sleeping with her. He started to sleep with her last Saturday night."

"Antoinette Martin, how you talk!" Mrs. Martin is shocked but her curiosity is also high. "Who said so?"

"I said so. Last Sunday didn't you notice how good-humored he was—and at the same time kind of hangdog?"

"That's nothing."

"But he went in—and put flowers on Ma's grave!" Tonie's lip is trembling.

"Well?"

"Because he was guilty! He felt guilty!" cries Tonie.

A moment later Elliott Martin has appeared. He is "a man about forty-five, a Westerner, a rancher—a characteristic fine American type—but gone to seed."

Neither his daughter nor his mother is very cordial in response to Elliott's good mornings. Mrs. Martin is ready to get his breakfast—eggs, of course—and Tonie grudgingly answers his queries about the puzzles. This is the last batch. If she wins, she is, as she has told him, going to buy herself an airplane. Even if she only wins the third prize she can get a Cub. . . .

The talk has turned to Victor de Lucchi. A boy at the gas pump wants to know where Victor lives. He doesn't live where he did any more, Tonie calls to the boy. Victor's gone away to school to be a priest. He's coming back, the boy insists. That's bad news for Elliott—

"Good God!" he exclaims, lowering his paper with a swish. "Is that going to start again? I thought we were rid of that fellow. I thought he was gone for good. I'm not going to have it, I tell you! You're going to get outa here and be somebody! What do you think I'm giving Al all his gas and oil for? To make an aviator out of you! Then let you marry this Dago—this—"

"Dago? He's one of the finest boys in the country. He's—"

"He's a foreigner!"

"He's not. He was born here, he went to school here—he—"

"His folks are foreigners!—Just common immigrants—"

"And what were ours?"

"Ours!" Elliott is completely astonished.

"We're Americans!" announces Mrs. Martin, stopping halfway to the stove. "You got good blood on your father's side—Scotch and English."

"Got good blood on my mother's side too—Irish and Indian!" snaps Tonie.

Her father has put down his paper and faced Tonie, angrily. "No more of that, young lady. I'm not going to let you get bogged down here like I was. No! You're going to get out—

get away—be something—be somebody—be—"

"Oh, shut up!" answers Tonie, jumping up and starting for the door.

"Did I ever talk to you like that, Ma? (*Suddenly, to* TONIE.) And look at you—wearing those pants on Sunday! Didn't I ask you not to wear pants on Sunday? Didn't I? Didn't I?"

"Oh, Pa!" Tonie has started for the door when it suddenly opens and Carlotta Thatcher walks in. Carlotta "is an interesting-looking woman—dressed in worn but beautifully cut and becoming Summer traveling clothes. She looks weary to the point of exhaustion, but there is a nervous intensity about her that gives her personality—excitement."

Carlotta is looking for the Martin place—and doesn't recognize it. Doesn't recognize her cousin Elliott or her Aunt Mat at first. And they have some difficulty recognizing her—

"Lot! God! I can't believe it!" exclaims Elliott as he moves around the table toward her. "All these years—and you walk in just like— Where did you drop from?"

"Paris."

"For cripe's sake! How did you get here?"

"I started on foot—then trains—then the boat—then—America! From New York I drove."

The queries come thick and fast, but Mrs. Martin manages to hold Elliott off until she gets the all but exhausted Carlotta into a chair and comfortable. Carlotta does look tired—and sick—but—

"This place will make me well," she says, with a smile; "this earth, this sun and all of you."

Carlotta won't let Elliott bring her things in. She plans to go on to the ranch. That would be the old ranch Granma Thatcher left Carlotta, Elliott explains to Tonie, who seems a little startled by the news.

"This is my girl, Antoinette," Elliott explains to Carlotta. "Her mother died last winter—and—" His excitement having subsided, a buried resentment begins to trouble Elliott. "Pretty well lost touch with us altogether, haven't you, Lot?"

"I know, but ever since the war started—I—"

"This war or the last? Ever since you went away."

"No, Elliott, ever since she married," Mrs. Martin puts in.

"Well, she married right away, didn't she?"

"You haven't written us a real good letter since—not 'til he died."

Carlotta will not join Elliott at breakfast, but she would like to be invited to dinner. She has been thinking a good deal about those fried chicken-hot biscuit dinners she used to get at the ranch. It's Tonie who gets the Sunday dinners now, they explain to her, and there isn't much cooking goes with them.

Little by little Carlotta is made acquainted with the new conditions under which the family has been living the last several years. Tonie, for example, is going to be an aviator; there isn't anything she doesn't know about an engine already. A mechanical genius her father would call her. Of course Tonie's mother hadn't been much—one of the "squatter" McCanns, according to Aunt Mat, and that's nothing to joke about.

"You say you drove out, Lot?" Elliott is saying.

"Yes," answers Carlotta, eagerly. "And you know, Elliott, I drove the same road that Grandma Thatcher drove her ox team over ninety years ago—as near as I could figure it. I stayed at Emigrant Gap last night and I came down out of the mountains with the sun this morning. You remember, Elliott, how Grandma Thatcher used to tell us how the great valley looked that day they drove down into it? Miles and miles of just the land and the sky and the great oak trees. The Promised Land. Not a human being or a house anywhere."

The trip had taken her ten days in a second-hand Ford. No, Carlotta is not rich! Hadn't her artist husband left her well off when he died?

"Oh, I had some money in the Paris bank—but that's all gone, of course," sighs Carlotta. "Everything's gone—everything— I sold my engagement ring to buy this old car—"

The news is evidently a surprise to Elliott and Aunt Mat, and a silence falls momentarily upon them. Elliott drinks his coffee slowly and Mrs. Martin fusses with the eggs at the stove—

"How long are you going to stay?" asks Elliott, after a pause.

"The rest of my life," promptly answers Carlotta.

ELLIOTT—You going to live here?

LOTTA—Yes. I've come home.

ELLIOTT (*exchanging glances with his mother*)—Well—what are you going to live on if—

LOTTA—The ranch. How does the old place look?

MRS. MARTIN—Oh, it's just gone to ruin, Lottie!

ELLIOTT—It's not the only one. All the old ranches are nothing but dumps now.

LOTTA—Yes—I saw the Pearson place as I came down the road from the hills, and the Merrills'—and the Gordons'!—

all the fine old ranches I used to know! The trees cut down, the barns falling in—the— What's happened?

ELLIOTT—Oh, nobody lives in 'em any more but Dagoes and Japs. They've driven us out, Lot!

LOTTA—How?

ELLIOTT—Oh, undercut us—underlived us—overbred us—an inferior race will always breed out a superior one—

LOTTA—I thought—when I left Europe I was getting away from all that!

ELLIOTT—You walked right into it again! Wait till you see your mail box—there's a whole row of 'em there—where just our one Thatcher box used to be—Cadematori, Yamaguchi—Sanguinetti—Matsumoto—Cardozo—Ito—all living on what was just our one ranch—and all despising each other—and—

LOTTA—But I thought in America!

ELLIOTT—Oh, they all have automobiles and lipsticks and washing machines—but underneath they are just what they were! —New soil but old roots—

LOTTA—How do they all make a go of it if—

MRS. MARTIN—By hard work!

ELLIOTT (*defensively*)—And big families!

MRS. MARTIN—That all work!

ELLIOTT—And a low standard of living—a low standard of living! (*To* LOTTA.) They're just a lot of peasants!

LOTTA—Peasant?

ELLIOTT—You know what a peasant is, don't you? You lived in Europe long enough!

LOTTA—I didn't think the word existed in America!

ELLIOTT—A lot of words don't exist, but the thing itself does.

A carload of "Okies" has driven up to the gas pump. They are the "peasants" of the new order. "They used to come in broken down old wagons—now they come in broken down old cars," says Mrs. Martin.

"Well, that's a difference," protests Elliott. "It took guts to start out that long haul in a wagon—and it took endurance not to fall by the way— Now it doesn't take a damn thing—just hoist yourself into an old wreck of a car—turn it west on the finest highways in the world and just keep sitting till an ocean stops you. The old car'll get you there—it's dumb and lazy proof."

Tonie has disappeared and there is no one there to sell gas to the "Okies." Presently a spokesman for the bunch arrives.

He is Nelson Powell, "a thin, dilapidated man, yellow hair burnt by the sun and fair skin, tanned a deep brown."

Powell and his folks are looking for work. He'd like to pick Elliott's peaches, if they are going to be picked. They aren't. Elliott plans to leave 'em hang on the trees and rot. There's no price for 'em.

"Let 'em hang, eh?" meditates Powell. "Well, I reckon that's all you can do— No price. Cherries was good and apricots— We cleaned up on cots. Now, we was counting on peaches. Well, I reckon all we can do is wait for grapes, but, Jesus, grapes is a hell of a long ways off. Well, I reckon we'll just have to go back on relief—till grapes. (*Pause.*) We wasn't figuring on going back till Winter."

The Powells have gone on to the village, fortified with a "coke and three straws." They'll find a free camp in the village. "Pure old American stock, Lotta," says Elliott, with a shrug. "Deteriorated."

"But where do they come from?"

"Oklahoma—Texas—Missouri—Kansas—Illinois. From all over. They've turned the place into a regular slum! Their lousy camps all over—and their rotten little shacks."

"Poor people!" mutters Carlotta, watching the departure from the window.

Carlotta finds it hard to understand why Elliott is letting his peach crop rot on the trees. She remembers when peaches were his life's work, and he was experimenting enthusiastically with a new brand of his own. Elliott insists that it hasn't paid him to harvest his crop since he was married. He has a service station now. That keeps him going. And he hasn't any land. Just a patch his mother gave him—an old river bed that he had filled in—

"I put up a sign 'Dump Here' and all the Dagoes and Japs in the neighborhood dumped in all their junk," laughs Elliott. "First thing I knew I owned a nice little piece of land right on the highway—put my gas tanks up, bought that shack out there from a fellow down the road, got a Dago to move it up here for me on a truck and there I was—independent. That's all the land I own—that little piece of fill-in—Grandma cut me out of the ranch—you know—gave you my share."

LOTTA—I guess she figured you had your share of it, Elliott— through your marriage. Grandma always considered that McCann place still our land, you know.

"HOPE FOR A HARVEST"

Elliott: What do you say Joe. We drink to you and me?
Joe (as he pours): O.K. Me and you.

(Alan Reed, Florence Eldridge, Fredric March)

Photo by Vandamm Studio.

ELLIOTT (*darkly*)—I was tricked out of that piece.

LOTTA—Tricked out of it? How?

ELLIOTT—By a damned Dago. I guess you don't remember that de Lucchi? That first Dago that bought into the old ranch?

LOTTA—Oh, yes—how Grandma hated to have to sell to him! Don't you remember, Elliott, how she shut herself up in her room and cried? We tiptoed to the door to listen.

ELLIOTT—We had never heard her cry before. It scared us to death.

LOTTA—Afterwards, you went out to the barn—and hid up in the hay.

ELLIOTT—I took a solemn vow out there then, I'd drive him off some day! (*Grimly.*) Well—I haven't. He's driven me off. That Dago that started there with ten acres! And borrowed every cent from the bank to do that, well, he owns everything around here now— He always had his eye on the McCann place and just after my wife died, just that week—he went over and persuaded my father-in-law to sell it to him. He knew the old man never wanted me to have it. The old man never wanted that piece of land to come back to us, any of us, so he sold it to this de Lucchi and went into town and went on a big spree and died. I didn't even get any of the money, nor Tonie either, because he made a will that all of it should be spent on his funeral.

LOTTA (*smiling*)—Was it a good funeral?

ELLIOTT—I'll say it was. It was a hell of a good funeral.

Tonie is still missing and Mrs. Martin must work in and out of the house, selling gas to the motorists that stream up and down the highway. On Sunday they just drive one way till they get tired and then turn around and come back, according to Aunt Mat.

The talk turns to other cousins and Carlotta learns still more of the family activities. Cousin Bertha, for example, is still gallivanting around. She and her folks have three automobiles, but they're still broke, like everybody else. Bertha's son, Billie, has turned out to be a good deal of a "flibbitty jibbitt," good for nothing but to chase girls. "Know what he is making a collection of?" demands Mrs. Martin. "Brazeers! Whenever he goes out with a new girl, he dares her to give him her brazeer and they're such little fools, they do it."

His parents have spoiled Billie, Mrs. Martin is convinced. They've tried to make a big shot of him. Now they're bent on sending him to college. "You know what your grandmother used to say—'No use to give a ten-thousand-dollar education to a ten-cent boy.'"

As for Elliott, both Carlotta and Mrs. Martin are agreed that he is a changed man. He's gone to seed, in Aunt Mat's estimation. And he began to go to seed the day that Carlotta went away—

"You and Elliott were awful close, Lottie— I guess you never knew how much you meant to him," says Aunt Mat. "I guess he never knew it either till you were gone. Elliott's one of those people can't get along alone."

LOTTA—I guess everybody's that way—really—Auntie— I know I am.

MRS. MARTIN—Some are—some aren't—like horses—some horses are only good single—and some only good in a team. Elliott's like that. After you went he moped around with his head hanging over the corral fence—for days. Then he got to moseying over to Verna's place—and the first thing we knew he'd married her.

LOTTA—Were they happy?

MRS. MARTIN (*sharply*)—What's happy? I don't know. (*Irritably.*) You could never get anything out of Elliott. But that was no marriage for a fine boy like Elliott.

LOTTA—You must be awfully glad to have him back again, Aunt Mat.

MRS. MARTIN (*tartly*)—Can't say as I am. There's the both of 'em now—they just take up the whole place. They're always sittin' in my chair—and playing the radio!—What they want to hear—not what I want to.

LOTTA—It must keep you from being lonesome?

MRS. MARTIN—There're worse things than being lonesome. (*Pause.*) Anyway you don't get lonesome any more—with a radio. A radio is the finest company there is—and you can turn it off if you get sick of it—that's more than you can do with humans. I have my chickens too—chickens are a lot of company—and they don't talk back. I used to see Elliott every day anyway. All those years he was working with his peaches—he was over here every day working. Now he's out at that gas station all day—gassing! "Gas Station"—that's a good name for it—gas and gas. That's all most of 'em do around here—sit around—talk hard times—wait for a boom. Something for nothing! Something for nothing! Elliott is just like all the rest of 'em now. That service station's just been his finish!

LOTTA—Oh, Aunt Mat!

MRS. MARTIN (*defending him now*)—He does the best he can I guess. He pays all the living—and he bought me all this stuff. (*Indicating refrigerator, etc.*) Bought it all on tick, of course. That's the way everybody does. They count up the stuff they owe for like it was money in the bank. Tonie says I'm old-fashioned and Bertha says so too, because I won't even take out enough to get me a permanent and I've been wanting to get me a permanent ever since they had 'em. I've always hated my hair stringing down, ever since I was a girl.

LOTTA (*gently*)—Why not, if you want it?

MRS. MARTIN—Because it's spending my money and I won't spend it!

LOTTA—But why not, if—

MRS. MARTIN—Because it's independence! Money is independence! And I'm going to be independent till I die! I've got my chickens and money in the bank—and—

There's excitement at the gas pump now. A truck load of Japs has driven up. Tonie is back to fill their tank for them, but there is a white boy holding the hose for her. The white boy is Victor de Lucchi. That starts Elliott from his chair with a vengeance. He has told the de Lucchis to keep off his place and that's the way it's going to be, whatever Aunt Mat or anybody else may think of it. As for Victor—

"He's a De Lucchi and a Dago and I'm not going to have him hanging around my place. I'm not going to have him hanging around my girl. I'm not—"

The door opens and in walks Victor. "He is a boy about 18 —a handsome boy—but there is something of a pallor in his dark skin, something of strain in the corners of his mouth and his black eyes shine with nervous excitement."

Victor would like to know what Elliott wants. For him to stay off the place? That's all right with Victor. He had no intention of coming there anyway. He had caught a ride on the truck and the truck had run out of gas. As for his father's having cheated Elliott, Victor doesn't believe his father ever cheated anybody. He worked hard for everything he's got.

"Damned Dago—" Elliott mutters.

"You say that again and I'll—"

Immediately Tonie is between them, pleading with Victor not to fight. He can't fight, if he's going to be a priest! But Victor isn't going to be a priest—

Now Cousin Bertha's boy, Billie—William Jennings Barnes—"a good-looking, typical small town boy of about twenty—a country boy who has become a town boy—dressed in his best suit for Sunday—" has come through the door. For a moment Billie and Victor stare at each other. Billie is surprised that Victor is back, and more surprised that he is back to stay—

"We'll take that up later," growls Elliott, not liking the way Victor is looking at Tonie. . . .

Billie is pleased to meet Carlotta. "Your mother and she are first cousins—like her and Elliott," explains Mrs. Martin. But he is more interested in knowing when Tonie is going to get off—

"These kids are just about as big chums as we were, Lot—always together," says Elliott.

Billie's mother is on the phone, and Billie is anxious that she should not know where he is. She thinks he's calling on the social Irma Belding in town. Hearing of Carlotta's arrival, Bertha would have her up for luncheon right away—

"We used to have dinner around here in the middle of the day," laughs Elliott; "then it was lunch, now it's luncheon."

Elliott and Carlotta have gone on to Bertha's, Elliott all dressed up in his new suit for the first time in months. Aunt Mat has gone to look after her chickens.

Billie and Tonie, left alone, are not exactly at their ease. Billie, hearing that Carlotta plans on going to the old Thatcher ranch house, is worried. Won't she get on to something if she should go upstairs? She won't, Tonie explains, because she had gone over and straightened things up. "Boy! That was a narrow squawk!" says Billie.

He can't quite understand what makes Tonie act so funny, however. Or why she pushes him away when he would put his arm around her. If that's the way she is going to act he is going into town. Which will be all right with Tonie. Let him go and let him stay. She is perfectly willing to be left alone—

"All right! Suits me—you'll be left alone all right," snaps Billie. "You're not the only oo in my goo—you're not the only—"

"Going to take Irma Belding up to Pete's?"

"You've said it!"

"Well, you'll see me there if you do."

"Say—you going to start going out with that Dago again? (TONIE *does not answer.*) Pass the garlic, dear! (*He waves his hand in front of his nose.*) Phew!"

"Good-by!" shouts Tonie, running to the door and looking after him. Now she has turned back into the room and has begun to glide around, making a whirring noise with her mouth, like an airplane. Around the table she glides, making sharp banks at the corners. She is just passing the door when Carlotta opens it and smiles at what she sees. Tonie laughs, too, but a second later she is feeling dizzy and has to reach out for support. It must be the smell of gas all day that gets her down, Tonie thinks. A moment later she has gone back to the gas tank and Carlotta is left holding the glass of water she had brought for her.

For a moment Carlotta stares after Tonie. Then she turns and looks around the room, which "seems to close in on her"—she begins to cry. She is trying to control her sobs when Elliott comes back—

"I'm so sorry, Elliott—so ashamed," apologizes Carlotta. "I don't like to make a mess of myself like this. I'm just a little tired, I guess."

"But what's wrong?"

LOTTA—It's just that—I don't know—there is just nothing I—recognize—here any more.

ELLIOTT—You mean—me?

LOTTA (*swiftly*)—I mean everything! All these little shacks—and the hot dog stands—and the cheap dance halls—all so shabby—and dirty—and dreary. Don't you remember how it used to be?—Now it's just a slum!

ELLIOTT—Everything changes, Lotta—we can't—

LOTTA—A country slum! I didn't suppose there was such a thing!

ELLIOTT—You must have seen it!—all along the way! Miles after miles of it—why—

LOTTA—Yes! But I thought when I got home! Now you tell me that, too, is gone—just a dump—that's what you said—an old dump—

ELLIOTT—Old places are like old people, Lotta—they come to the end of their lives and—

LOTTA—They should die! They're weary and exhausted and they want to die! Their life is finished— They haven't anything to go on for—they— (*She breaks into a paroxysm of weeping.*)

ELLIOTT (*moving toward her comfortingly*)—You need rest.

LOTTA—That's what I came here to find, Elliott. I thought

I could rest here—maybe sleep. I haven't been able to sleep for—oh, I don't know—it seems to me years.

ELLIOTT—You mean the bombing—the—

LOTTA—Everything—the war and—oh, before that—when Ted died—and afterwards—you don't know what it's like, Elliott, to lie awake nights—wide awake—and—yet tired—it just exhausts you—eats up all your strength—your strength to deal with life. You begin to break down inside—and then all the fears come, and—

ELLIOTT—Fears, Lotta? What fears?

LOTTA—Oh, the fear of being alone—of getting old—getting old alone. Of being poor—destitute, maybe—and—oh, I know how terribly neurotic all this must sound to you, Elliott. You're such a normal, matter-of-fact person—

ELLIOTT—Are you sure this all isn't just the war, Lot?

LOTTA—No! The war just made it worse! I'd been through it all before. I knew what it meant. I just couldn't stand it any more! It was like living through some frightful insanity again. Even before I was bombed out I knew I had to get back to this place—there'll be peace there, I thought. Peace. There I won't be alone—can rest—there I can work again—there I can hope again—hope for a harvest—and have a home.

ELLIOTT—Well, you're here, Lot.

LOTTA (*eagerly*)—You'll help me, Elliott? advise me—and—

ELLIOTT (*brusquely*)—I ought to be pretty good at that! Failures are always good at—

LOTTA—Don't say that!

ELLIOTT (*suddenly*)—It's good to have you back, Lot!

LOTTA—I guess that's what I've been waiting to hear!—

ELLIOTT (*patting her shoulder*)—God . . . Well, I guess we better get going—huh? Bertha'll be wondering what's happened to us— (*In doorway.*) Oh, for the love of Mike! There's still those Okies! Got a flat and can't fix it!

LOTTA (*going to the door and calling*)—Say you!

POWELL'S VOICE—Yeah?

LOTTA—I've got work for you!

POWELL'S VOICE—Where at?

LOTTA—My ranch!

ELLIOTT—Oh, Lot! For Pete's sake! You're walking right into it! (LOTTA *laughs—throws the door open and walks out. He follows her.*) Walking right into it!

The curtain falls.

ACT II

A week later, in the living room of the old Thatcher ranch house, Carlotta is standing on a stepladder in front of the fireplace restoring a picture of Grandma Thatcher to its rightful place on the wall. "It is a beautiful picture and when it is hung seems to add a presence to the room."

The living room is worn and shabby, furnished in the fashion of fifty years ago, but "there are several good pieces of old walnut and mahogany, among them a beautiful old desk and a table."

Presently Tonie appears. She has come across the slough from the Martin place and is eager to talk with Carlotta. "You're not a sap and yet you're not a wise guy," ventures Tonie, in explanation of her urge for a confidential chat. "You seem to be on to everything all right, and yet you don't seem to be hardboiled . . . you're good, but you're not mean. People around here— it they're good they're mean. . . . If I tell you something, Cousin Lot, will you keep it?"

Carlotta's word being given, the confession proceeds. Tonie and Victor de Lucchi are going to be married. That's why Victor came home from the priest school; that's why he gave up being a priest. Nor does Tonie care what her father says—he gives it to Tonie for going with a Dago and he's going with one himself.

To prepare herself for standing up before a priest some day, Tonie has been going to church. To Victor's church. She doesn't like church as well as she does flying—she feels pretty near like being an angel when she's flying—but she'd like to understand better what they talk about in church. What exactly do they mean by "confession"? Tonie would know. The priest was giving the people in church hell about confession. Tonie would like to know how it's done.

Carlotta tries to explain that when one person tells another what he's done that's wrong, that's a confession, and the confessor is freed of his sense of guilt. "You don't have to be religious to believe this," explains Carlotta. "Doctors believe it —lots of people. They know that almost everybody at one time or another has a feeling inside of having done something wrong and this feeling makes them unhappy—makes them sick sometimes. And they don't seem to get rid of it except by telling it."

"Does it have to be the church? Couldn't you just tell it to somebody—somebody good?"

"I don't know, dear. We're getting in pretty deep now. Doctors think it's enough to tell it, but the church says—"

The appearance of Elliott breaks up the conference. He has come looking for Tonie. His ma wants Tonie to take her to the village to get a permanent. Everybody's getting spruced up since Carlotta came back.

Elliott has come to see if Lotta has any more furniture moving jobs for him. They've moved about everything in the room three or four times, but Carlotta is making a home there, and, as she explains, she must have harmony—

"There's a sort of enchantment about it to me," admits Carlotta; "a sort of enchantment in this whole place—of the old and the familiar and—"

"And the lost."

"But it isn't lost. It's all here. Look at that desk. Grandma's beautiful old desk—that she sent all the way home to Concord for—look at this old table—where we used to do our homework nights."

"Oh, yeah! Gosh! You used to keep my nose to the grindstone all right—(*Mocking*.)—'Now we'll do our arithmetic—now we'll do our spelling—'"

The man Powell is in to report that he is finished with the fence job Carlotta gave him and is wondering what he should do next. One look at the fence is completely discouraging to Carlotta, but she thinks perhaps Mr. Powell can lay a few bricks in the path if he can follow the pattern previously set down. A child of six could do it, but Elliott assures her that Powell won't be able to—

"And if you think he's no good, have you tried to get anything out of his wife?" asks Elliott. "I tell you their women are so damned lazy they won't even do their own day-dreaming—want a machine to do that for them—they'll sit around all day with a sink full of dirty dishes listening to 'Valiant Lady' and 'Life Can Be Beautiful.'"

Powell, Lotta admits, is a good deal of a problem but she hasn't the heart to fire him—with a wife and three kids. "They're so utterly helpless; I just can't turn them loose," insists Carlotta. "What's he got to face the world with?"

"He's not your responsibility," insists Elliott.

"Well, who is responsible for what happens to the people of a country—their rulers?"

"This fellow's his own ruler, ain't he?"

There being no immediate answer to that, Elliott would have Carlotta sit down and enjoy some of the harmony she has been creating. He would also like to justify his own life to her if he could. He had to quit experimenting with his peaches because he married and had to make a living. And he did all right for a while, even without the college education Grandma Thatcher wanted to give him the year she sent Lotta to Europe—

"Maybe she shouldn't have," Carlotta is saying. "Maybe I should have stayed home—where I belonged and—here—it's as though I'd found myself again. Do you know that feeling—of being on the right road after—"

"I know how it feels to be on the wrong road. I've felt that most of my life."

"You have, Elliott?"

"Yep."

"Since when?"

"Oh—I don't know—always, I guess."

"Europe was what did it to me. I always felt an outsider there—really. Of course as long as Ted lived—any place seemed to be home. But this—is home!"

Elliott doesn't appreciate Carlotta's reverence for the old place. There are only two things an American can do with his ancestral home—restore it or destroy it, says he. In that case Carlotta proposes to restore hers. She may even have some effect on restoring the whole neighborhood—

"Why, when people drive by and see this beautiful old pioneer house back here . . . they'll think how fine we are in this neighborhood!—how strong—how proud—how—"

ELLIOTT (*grimly*)—They won't think anything of the kind.

LOTTA—What will they think?

ELLIOTT (*turning to her*)—It's only a mile more to the next hot dog stand—two miles to the next gas station—and only three to Pete's. You're such a dreamer, Lot! You always were—even as a kid—full of hop! Everything's gone! Lotta! Gone—can't you—

LOTTA (*tears in her eyes*)—No! It hasn't! It's just—gone down—been neglected! It just needs what everything needs—care—love—and a lot of hard work.

ELLIOTT—And a lot of hard money! All this costs money! And you say—

LOTTA—I know I haven't any money! But I've got land! Rich land! Don't you remember, Elliott, how the geography said that this valley and the Nile Valley had the richest growing earth in the world!

ELLIOTT—But what good is it—if you can't sell the stuff it grows? Listen, Lot. I grew the finest peaches in the world. That's no joke! I grew the finest peaches in this county. This county grows the finest peaches in California—and California grows the finest peaches in the world! And for eight years—it hasn't paid me to take them off the trees.

LOTTA—Oh, Elliott! That's heart-breaking!

ELLIOTT—I'll say it's heart-breaking! Take the heart out of anybody to work and plan—struggle and contend—year after year—year after year—and for nothing!

LOTTA—Is it every year the same?

ELLIOTT—No! It's every year different! One year, no prices—one year, no crop—another year swell crop but Europe's quit buying—another year swell price but the canneries have a strike—next year the teamsters take a hand—they wouldn't let us haul our own fruit in our own trucks—I drove up to the cannery gate—they pulled me off, tipped my whole load over—all my peaches lying there in the dirt—I tell you, a man gets fed up.

LOTTA—Oh, Elliott—don't say that! That's what happened in Europe! People were fed up! Tired—disillusioned—they wanted order and a chance to do their work—and something to work for—they were fed up and so they gave up— I was in Rome when it first happened—then Germany—and now France. I've just come from France! It's the people like you, when you give up! Elliott, you mustn't give up!

Elliott remains entirely unconvinced. What does Lotta know about farming? What had she ever learned before she went to Paris? She rode horseback, helped a little in the house, monkeyed around trying to paint and went to school. And she thinks she can come back now and do better as a farmer than those who had stayed there and worked their whole life at it!

Carlotta refuses to give up. At least she can make her living there—if Grandma Thatcher did. Grandma had nine children to look out for. Carlotta has none. She'll have to have money to start with, Elliott warns. She'll have to put a mortgage on the old place—probably two or three mortgages. She'll have to have an electric pump. She'll have to have a well. She'll have to have a tractor. She can't go back to horses and mules. And how is she going to keep paying for these things, plus interest and taxes and insurance?

"I was counting on the big grain field," ventures Lotta.

"There isn't any money in grain any more! Doesn't pay to put it in! No price! Too much of everything! The government pays us not to plant."

"Not to plant!"

"Yes, didn't you know that—not to plant! There's just too much of everything—that's why we're all starving to death! Anyway—if you could get a price—you can't raise a crop on that field now!—it's worn out!"

"Worn out?—the earth?"

"Yes. Land wears out, just like a house does, or a person—or—"

"Like a person!"

"You want to be a farmer!—and you don't even know that! You think just because you love the land—the earth! Well, just wait until you've fought weeds—and bugs—and rot—and drought—and rain—and frost for a few years—maybe you won't love it so much. All you people that talk about coming back to the land! You all give me a pain in the neck. Farming needs highly specialized training nowadays! Why, just to grow a decent peach is a life's work, and you have to know how to handle men and handle machines—and how to buy and sell— A farmer's a trader! And a gambler! There's no other work on earth that's as big a gamble as farming! And when a man's all that!—has got the knowledge and the training and the character to be all that—what good does it do him? He just can't make a living, that's all! He just can't—"

Bertha Barnes is standing in the doorway. "Bertha is a strong-looking woman in her forties; elaborate permanent, over-made-up, red nails, wearing cheap, loud, unbecoming clothes; a country woman trying to look like a town woman; she has a hearty, insensitive voice."

Bertha has come over to show them her brand new car, a black sedan with nickel trim. "How do you all have all these cars and everything when you say you are starving to death?" Carlotta wants to know. "We are starving to death," Bertha insists. "Why, just to keep up the payments keeps us broke."

Bertha would add her protest to Elliott's about Carlotta's crazy notion of trying to restore the Thatcher place. It's a terrible old house; not a place in it fit to lay your head. Grandma's beautiful old room? Nobody's been in that for years.

That is where Bertha's wrong, Carlotta tells her. Somebody has just walked out of Grandma's room—and left the bed nicely made up. Who? Carlotta thought Elliott would know.

"There were two coca-cola bottles—and an empty whiskey flask on the shelf," Carlotta reports. Evidently somebody had broken in. So far as Elliott knows the house has always been locked.

"They were just a harmless couple—glad of a place to sleep," Carlotta decides. "One of them was a woman. There was a cigarette stub with lipstick on it—under the bed."

Elliott decides not to wait for Bertha to take him home in the new car. He'll try it some other time. But he suspects Tonie will enjoy it—with Billie. Which reminds Bertha, after Elliott has gone, that she wants to talk to Carlotta about Tonie. She isn't going to have her Billie running around with Tonie. She just isn't good enough for him.

"Why, she is only a child," Carlotta protests.

"Child nothing!—anyway, that doesn't make any difference. I'm not going to have her out in my new car with Billie, parking with him up some dark road—you know what that means."

"Nonsense—didn't we used to go out with our beaux in a buggy?"

"A buggy ain't a car—anyway, times have changed—girls have changed. Why, these kids around here, they'll pile in a car with some fellow they hardly know, tear up to a roadhouse, get a drink, a couple of drinks, tear on to another till they're so full of the devil—so excited and exhausted that—"

"Why do their parents let them?"

"Let them! It's easy for you to talk, you've never had a child. Oh, I look out for Billie. Why, Billie goes with the nicest people in town!—the Belding girl is crazy about him, and I guess you know who the Beldings are! He's the President of the First National and she's President of the Friday Morning Club. And Irma's the Junior League! That's the kind of people we want Billie to go around with. Just because we're farmers doesn't mean we can't go with nice people. We want to get Billie off the farm."

Bertha is continuing her argument against Carlotta's attempting to make even so much as a living out of the farm when Joe de Lucchi walks in on them. "Joe is a man over sixty; a strong Italian farmer with bright eyes, a red face and a lusty good humor, all of which is partly his nature and partly good red wine." He has brought a huge coolie-basket filled with fruit and melons that he has just picked for Carlotta. Carlotta remembers Joe. She was just a little girl peeking in the door the day Joe had come to buy his land from Grandma Thatcher, and she remembers that after the deal was closed that Grandma cried and cried. That was the first piece of Thatcher land to go. Now Joe has come to buy the last piece, if Carlotta will sell. Carlotta insists she has no intention of selling.

"What are you goin' to do? Mortgage?" demands Joe.

Carlotta doesn't answer, but her gesture indicates her helplessness.

"That's no good, Missa Thatch," Joe goes on. "What's you want to do that for? You worry, and you work and you worry and what ees the end? You loosa your place. The bank get the place and you get nothin'. Better sella Missa Thatch. Better have something in the bank than something owe the bank."

LOTTA—You began with a bank.

JOE—I began, but I'm a no finish! I was a young man, I was a strong man and I work lika dog, all the days and half the nights, me and my old lady both, and all our kids. You ain't so young no more, and you ain't got nobody. How you end up, huh? You end up an old lady without no shirt on you. . . . I tella you what you do, Missa Thatch. You don't sella all your land. You sella justa one piece. That's the way your grandmother did . . . when times is hard and she feel, maybe she a little old—a little weak. She don't make no mortgage. She sella a piece here—a piece there. You sella justa one piece—to me.

LOTTA—What piece?

JOE—That piece between my place and the old McCann place I gotta now.

LOTTA—Where the slough goes?

JOE—That the place.

LOTTA—But they say that land isn't good for anything any more. They say it's—worn out—

JOE—Sure! I know. She's neglect! But she's a good land too. The land is like human, Missa Thatch. Sometimes she's just no good—born no good. Sometimes she born good—but she neglect. This land neglect but she don't have to stay like that. This land work hard for somebody. Now somebody work hard for this land. You just leave her to me.

LOTTA—You can bring it back?

JOE (*roaring*)—Sure, I can bring her back! Why you think I want to buy, huh? I nobody's fool. Why—we got twenty—twenty-five feet top soil here! (*Laughs.*) The land issa no spoil. Itsa people who are spoil. Nobody don't want to work it no more. Nobody's gotta no patience. All thisa farmer around here—all they wanta do is—one crop. And they don't want to work to do that! Pay somebody to put it in. Pay somebody to take it off! This they call farming! Your cousin Jim Barnes—he put in wheat. Wheat no price—psshh! he's broke. Your cousin Elliott Martin—he got peaches. Peacha no price—broke. My peacha no price—I gotta plums. Plums no price—I gotta bean. Beana no price—I gotta tomato. Tomato no price—I gotta potato. Potato no price—what the Hell!—that's all the more we gotta eat! We live—me and my old lady and my kids—we live. Live good! Farming no just a business—a one crop selling business—farming is a way you live—it's a life!

LOTTA (*eagerly*)—That's just what I want to find here, Mr. De Lucchi! A life!

JOE—Sure. You sella me this piece and you keepa the rest, huh? Then you have money to get what you need. (*Coaxing.*) You can dig a well—you can buy a pump! The water come out—whsshh!—like that!—and spread on the ground—wida like that! And the sun come down—everything grow. Your whole place look like a garden— Plenty fruit, plenty veg—some chick! In the morning you get up—you take a fresh egg—a fresh egg!—you go out—you pick a little parsley—you chop. You put a little oil in the pan—or a little sweet butter—oh! You must have a cow!

LOTTA—Who'll milk her?

JOE (*roaring*)—You will! You'll milk her! A nice, gentle, easy cow! My old lady she use to milk twelve cow!

LOTTA (*doubtfully*)—I don't think I'm strong enough for that.

Joe's picture of Carlotta as a farmer expands with his eloquence until she, too, becomes enthused and the deal is made. Carlotta agrees to sell him the piece of slough land that he wants, and Joe rushes to the door to call Victor to bring in a jug of wine from the back of the car so they can drink on the deal. Now the only thing to settle is the price. Joe would drive a bargain there. The land, of course, isn't worth as much as it was when he bought from Grandma Thatcher. It isn't worth as much as he paid for the McCann place, which was $50 an acre.

Carlotta thinks it is—and more. She wants $100 an acre. Joe argues and pleads and tries to wheedle her, but Carlotta sticks to her price.

Joe's attention is momentarily diverted by the arrival of Victor with the wine. It is then that he learns for the first time that Carlotta and Victor have already met—which means that Vic has been over to the Martins'—and that's against orders. Victor is not going to be allowed to marry—he's going to be a priest—

"I told you the day I come home I'm not going to be no—"

Victor can get no further. His father is standing over him menacingly, wild with anger—

"But you didn't say why! We don't know why! Now we know why!" Joe is throwing himself around as though he were in pain. "Jesu Maria! You aren't going to marry no Tonie Martins! No and no!" He has turned apologetically to Carlotta. "Excuse me, Miss Thatch. This nothing against you, but I don't want my boys marry no American girls. We got one already! That's enough! My boy, Gino, he marry American girl—troub'—troub'—troub'—all the time troub'! She don't like what he eat—she don't like what he drink—she don't like what he say. The shirt on his back she no like—fine silk shirt, she no like. Dago shirt. 'I'ma no Dago,' she say. My boy getta mad and give her a slap in the face shesa talk like that. Then she go away—she go 'way all right—but two three days she come back. In the day shesa no like no Dago—but at night she's like all right—all right."

Presently Joe's anger is spent. He is still mad at Victor, but not too mad to let him write a check for $500 for Miss Thatch. That would be a down payment—the rest to be paid with the deed. A moment later Joe has gone with Carlotta to show her the line to be surveyed to determine his new holdings.

As soon as Carlotta and Joe disappear Tonie comes in from the kitchen. She had seen Victor drive into the Thatcher place with his father and had been waiting for a chance to talk with him. Victor and Tonie are happy together. So long as they are going to get married sometime, Victor doesn't see any reason for waiting. Why can't they run away to Reno and get married right away? Nobody would stop them there, even if they were not of age.

They can't do that, Tonie explains, suddenly becoming very serious. There is something she must tell him—something he will understand because it is a confession and because he's good. Tonie has been living with Billie Barnes and she is in trouble.

For a second Victor is too shocked fully to understand. Tears come to his eyes as he puts his head in his hands on the desk. Tonie, too, has some trouble understanding. She did not think he would take it that way. She thought he would forgive her like a priest would. "We can get married, Vic—just the same Nobody will know."

"I'll know," answers Victor, pitifully.

TONIE—But if you forgive me and I'm free of it—why—
VICTOR—Doesn't Billie know?
TONIE (*shaking her head*)—No.
VICTOR—You've got to tell him!
TONIE—I won't either tell him!
VICTOR—You got to!
TONIE—I won't! I'm not going to let him have any claim on me! I don't like him!
VICTOR—You don't like him!
TONIE—No.
VICTOR (*seizing her by the arms*)—Then why did you—
TONIE—Why?—I don't know! It just happened! We was up to Pete's drinkin' and dancin' one night and when we was going home in the car— What's the use pretending! Irma Belding and those girls—they go out with a fellow in a car and pet—and pet—pretend it's nothing—pretend they're just too nice. Billie was telling me about 'em—how they act! It made me sick! I thought if I ever want a fellow—I'll—
VICTOR (*turning to her*)—Was that the only time?
TONIE (*hesitating*)—No—no—then we started coming over here.
VICTOR—Here?
TONIE (*crying out*)—I never loved him, Vic! I never loved anybody but you, but he was always after me. And you were gone—gone forever. (*Looking at him.*) There was never anything like this between you'n me, Vic. Before you went away we just looked at each other! That's all—hardly touched a hand— (*With sudden passion.*) But I tell you there's more for me in just the touch of your little finger than in his whole body!
VICTOR—But you got to marry him!
TONIE—I won't either marry him.
VICTOR—What are you going to do?
TONIE—I'm going to marry you!
VICTOR—Now?
TONIE—Why not? *It* can grow up with ours, Vic!
VICTOR—No!
TONIE—Why not?
VICTOR—You're not straight!

TONIE—I am, too, straight. I'm just as straight as anybody—I didn't have to tell you—did I? I could have gone off with you tonight—couldn't I? You'd never know—never!—if I hadn't told you.

VICTOR—I wish you hadn't told me. Why did you?

TONIE—Because I didn't want to make a sap out of you!—that's why! I just couldn't bear—to make a sap out of you, Vic! (*Takes his arm.*) Oh, marry me, Vic, please—I've—

VICTOR—I'm going back to the Fathers.

TONIE—No—Victor—no, you mustn't do that!

VICTOR—I've got to, now.

TONIE—But you aren't right for that life! You told me they said you weren't right for that life! Because you never could get rid of me in your mind—

VICTOR—I'll get rid of you, now.

TONIE (*clinging to him*)—No—you won't, Victor! No, you won't! (*At the door.*) Victor—please!—please don't leave me like this! What's to become of me! What—

VICTOR (*pulling away from her*)—You got to marry—him!

TONIE—No!—I won't! I won't marry him! I'll get rid of it first! I won't have it! I'll—

Before Tonie can get through the door Carlotta and Joe de Lucchi are back. Joe is suspicious, but he accepts Tonie's statement that Victor has gone. Now the check is signed and accepted. They'll postpone the drink until the deed is transferred, but Joe will leave the wine for Carlotta to put in her cellar.

After Joe has left Carlotta turns to the unhappy Tonie. She would like to have Tonie come and live with her, but Tonie isn't interested. In fact Tonie is frankly belligerent and resentful. Carlotta makes her sick! All that business Carlotta's been telling her— It makes her sick! Tonie is out the door and away before Carlotta can stop her.

Powell, the Okie, has come for his pay. The Powells are leaving. Work's too hard, the wages too low. Powell and his missus can do better. Sometimes they make as much as eight dollars a day—sometimes. Besides Mrs. Powell don't like it here. Too lonesome. She likes the camps better.

Elliott is back. He doesn't like the thought of Carlotta staying in the old ranch house alone. But it seems pretty safe to Carlotta, after Europe. Now Elliott has discovered the basket of fruit that De Lucchi has brought Carlotta. Fine fruit it is. Elliott can remember when he was raising as fine peaches as those— His reawakening enthusiasm is crushed when he hears that Carlotta has decided to go back to farming again; to "work like a mule—and live like a hog" if necessary.

"Work isn't the answer to life—work and more work—what we want is more leisure," spouts Elliott.

LOTTA—What's leisure good for if it just means sitting around —empty and dreary—gassing—and—

ELLIOTT—That's a dig at me, I suppose, and my service station—well, what if I do sit around, dishing out gas— I'm not being pushed around by a lot of Dagoes—I'm not—

LOTTA—Oh, Elliott! This Dago business. It's so cheap and insulting—and ignorant.

ELLIOTT—I know I'm ignorant! I've never been to college! I've never been to Europe! I'm just a nobody—a—

LOTTA—That's childish!

ELLIOTT—All right—I'm childish, too!

LOTTA—This prejudice of yours—is childish—

ELLIOTT—You try sitting there on a bunch of old tin cans all day—while all the land around you—the land that was your people's—

LOTTA—That's just rationalizing your own— (*Stops abruptly.*)

ELLIOTT—Failure! Say it! I know I'm a failure! Why don't you—

LOTTA (*going to him*)—You're not a failure, Elliott. You just have to take hold again. Why, you can start tomorrow!

ELLIOTT (*grimly*)—No—I can't!

LOTTA—You can begin experimenting again! You can begin working in your orchard again!

ELLIOTT—No—not again.

LOTTA—Why not?

ELLIOTT (*swiftly*)—Everything I had I gave that orchard, Lot. I can't do it again! I staked my life on it! I—

LOTTA—Everybody stakes his life. On somebody or something.

ELLIOTT—But when your stake breaks up under you—

LOTTA—Then you've got to find another one—that's all— That's what I came back here for—to find a new stake! Elliott! Let's find our new stake together. This place! Let's bring this place back together. It's your home as much as mine. Oh, I know the land is a little worn out—but we can subsoil and—

ELLIOTT—Subsoil! Say! Where did you get that?

LOTTA—And dig a well and buy a pump and—

ELLIOTT—Sure—if we had the money.
LOTTA—I've got the money!
ELLIOTT—How?
LOTTA—I've sold some land, Elliott.
ELLIOTT—Land? What land? Who to?
LOTTA—To Mr. De Lucchi.
ELLIOTT (*waving angrily at basket of fruit*)—Joe? Did he bring— That piece that joins the McCann place to his?
LOTTA—Yes.
ELLIOTT (*suddenly*)—What about the slough? You didn't let him have the slough, did you?
LOTTA—Why, yes.
ELLIOTT—Good God! You know what this means to me, don't you?
LOTTA—No!
ELLIOTT—He's going to drown me out—that's what it means!

Elliott's excitement grows with the thought of what is going to happen. Of course De Lucchi will fill in the slough and the water will back up on Elliott's place. Just as it backed up on the McCann place when Elliott filled in his slough. But that was different. No Dago is going to play the same trick on Elliott, by God! Carlotta will have to call the deal off.

Carlotta has no thought of going back on her word to De Lucchi. "What if he does drown out your service station," she says. "Maybe it will be a good thing. Maybe you'll get back to work then! Your own work! Oh, I know things haven't been easy for you. They've been full of disappointments. I know things have broken down around you—but that doesn't mean you have to break down inside, too! Quit! sit around—dish out gas all day—to a lot of—"

"And what if I dish out gas?" shouts Elliott, furiously. "I'm making my living, ain't I? Not asking anything of anybody, am I? Not you! Nor this Dago! Nor anybody else. And I'm going to stay here dishing out gas—and not you—nor this Dago—nor anybody else is going to stop me! I'll see you all in hell first!"

"Oh—Elliott! Please don't!" Carlotta has followed him to the door.

"That's all right!" he calls back. "You've shown where you stand all right! You've shown where you stand!"

Elliott has slammed the door. Carlotta stands looking after him, her hand on the fruit basket, as the curtain falls.

ACT III

One morning, a month or so later, the sun is streaming in the living room of the Thatcher ranch house. There are fresh curtains at the windows and the furniture has been rearranged. Presently a large middle-aged woman, elaborately overdressed, appears on the porch and rings the tinkle bell before helping herself to a chair.

She has come in answer to Carlotta's ad in the village paper. She thinks she might like to be Carlotta's housekeeper if there isn't too much work and if all the conveniences have been modernized, she admits when Carlotta greets her. She is a widow, but her money is disappearing rapidly and she cannot get on relief so long as she has any money left. She has decided to work out until her writing begins to pay.

No, she never has done any writing before, but she is taking a course. The man in the East with whom she is studying by correspondence, and to whom she has paid $100 down, has assured her that after one learns to write one can often sell a single piece for as much as a thousand dollars.

It is Carlotta's cow that discourages her. "No, I guess the place wouldn't suit me," she concludes with a sigh. "There's too much work. You got a cow—and you ain't got an automatic hot water heater—and then, too—I kinda like a man around—you know how it is—they're kinda handy."

Tonie Martin is at the door. She is dressed in her best and appears a little excited. Her appearance is a surprise to Carlotta, who had about given up seeing her again. Tonie has come to apologize for the things she said. Also, if Carlotta hasn't anybody to help her, Tonie would like to apply for that job. She didn't win the puzzles prize. Didn't win a thing.

Carlotta will be glad to have Tonie live with her, but she is afraid Elliott may have something to say about it. Elliott has also been keeping away from Carlotta; didn't even answer a letter she had written him proposing a new plan that might work to their mutual advantage.

That letter would be the one Elliott tore up without reading the day the notice of Carlotta's deed transfer to Joe de Lucchi appeared in the paper, Tonie thinks. Elliott has been an unhappy man ever since—"Just keeps by himself most of the time," Tonie says.

Tonie would like to draw an advance on her wages, if Carlotta doesn't mind. She would like $20 for something that she has to do in town. After that is attended to she will be glad to come to work. No, Tonie hasn't been seeing anything of Victor recently. So far as she knows he has gone back to the priest's school. Nor has she been seeing anything of Billie. She is, she thinks, going to enjoy working for Carlotta—while she is waiting to be an aviator—but she would appreciate it if Carlotta didn't tell any of the town folk about their arrangement. It might affect her social standing.

"But what is finer for a girl than to know how to make a home?" Carlotta would like to know. "Even an aviator has to have a home. Everybody has to have a home. . . . I can teach you about all kinds of homes. Irma Belding and those girls won't know anything about making a home when they get married, but you— (*Gently.*) The only thing I can't teach you, darling, is about your children when you have them."

"I'm not going to have any."

"You're not?"

Tonie shakes her head. "You never did," she says.

"I know, but—"

"Did you ever want one?"

"Oh, yes."

"Then why didn't you?"

"I guess—because—I was a coward."

"Coward?"

"You see when I first married—it was in the war—and that made me afraid. And afterwards, we were poor—and that made me afraid."

"But afterwards—why didn't you have one then?"

"Then—I couldn't." For a second Carlotta hesitates. "That sometimes happens," she goes on. "If a woman doesn't have her child—when she can—sometimes—afterwards—she can't have one—at all."

"She can't?"

"There seems to be some sort of law in life that if we don't take things when they come—"

Joe de Lucchi is at the door. He is ready to begin work on the slough, but he doesn't want to go on the Martin place without Elliott's O.K. Tonie will fetch Elliott. As she rushes past De Lucchi he is struck by her appearance. Tonie doesn't look too good to Joe. Whassa mat? It is because she has lost Victor, Carlotta explains. Tonie is unhappy. Joe has insisted that Victor be a priest, and that—

"Isa my old lady, Missa Thatch," Joe explains, confidentially. "She want—so—what the hell—I want too. But longa time—I no like so much—I thinka betta stay on the place—worka hard—getta married—plenty kids. (*Loudly.*) No Tonie Martins!"

"Why, she's a wonderful little girl. You just don't understand her. She'll make a wonderful little wife for the right boy. She's got grit. She's happy and loving—and—"

"Loving, all right—sure—but no work! . . . She's a spoiled. All theesa girl is the same—everybody is a tell she's a wonderful! Every dat goes a moofies—what she see?—just girla girla girla—girl is wonderful—iss come home—turns radio—what she hear—girla girla girla—Martha—Betty—Jane—all wonderful—so she think—I'm a girl—I'm wonderful! I no gotta work—I no gotta cook—I no gotta have kids—I no gotta do nothing—I'm a girl—it's enough—I'm wonderful!"

There is a racket outside. That would be Joe's new three-thousand-dollar Diesel tractor, the virtues of which he is explaining when Elliott appears. The men greet each other with explosive grunts. Mr. De Lucchi, Carlotta explains, wants to start work filling in his part of the slough. He has agreed to put pipes under Elliott's fill-in to carry the water through to the drain canal along the road, and Carlotta has taken enough off the price of the land to pay him for it.

Elliott will have nothing to do with the plan. He's not accepting charity from anyone, including Carlotta.

That's all right with Joe de Lucchi. He'll take his tractor and go home, though he was planning that the money he saved on the land would help pay for the Diesel. A moment later he has bounced out.

"Why didn't you let him do the work, Elliott? . . . Why do you keep this up?"

"I don't know— Damn it!—I can't help it," admits a slightly chastened Elliott. "I been telling myself for the last month—everything you told me here—but just the first minute I see him—damn Dagoes—I just don't like 'em—it's in the blood—I guess."

"Nonsense! It's in your head!"

"I know—prejudice—ignorance and all the rest—you needn't tell it to me again."

"I wish I hadn't said all those things, Elliott."

"That's all right—did me good—I guess."

Elliott confirms the report that he is pulling up his trees.

They've deteriorated from one year's neglect to the extent of being no good any more. He'll take the trees out and put in some quick turn-over crops. Prices are going up with the war— The situation has set Elliott thinking—and that's hard work, too, when you're not used to it— "Thinkin' and diggin'—diggin' and thinkin'—"

"There's something awful wrong, Lot—about what people like us have let happen to our land," admits Elliott. "Two hundred million acres of it just plain used up since we took it over from the Indians. You see, the Indians respected the land—they knew there are gods in it. We ain't got any gods any more. Just a lot of machines— (*Hears the tractor.*) Like that— Hear that thing out there? God, look at it tearin' into the earth—pulling for sixty horses—sixty horses that ain't there any more—to eat, and to fertilize. Just one smart machine. It's smart, all right. But maybe what we're lettin' it do to us is stupid. We been too damn busy making things to think what they're doing to us. They've made us damn lazy for one thing! There isn't a kid around here who'll put a shovel in the ground for you. He'll sit on the seat of that damned thing—but he won't put a shovel in the ground—a shovel brings him down! Think of that!—a democracy—and work brings you down— Everybody wants to be something they ain't—bigger—not better! Bigger! As Ma says—'something for nothing—something for nothing.'"

Elliott has stopped, more than a little surprised at himself. "God—I thought I had given up gassing," he laughs.

Now the talk has turned to Tonie. Carlotta would like to have Tonie come here to live, if Elliott is willing. Something's gone wrong with Tonie, Carlotta thinks—

"She's lost her way, somehow—you know how it is when you're that age—you can lose your way so easily. Life suddenly isn't anything the way you thought it was—and—"

"What do you mean?"

"Oh, she's in love with Victor and—"

"That's all over. He's gone back to—"

"And it's made her ill. She's sick with love of him! She's a passionate—primitive girl, Elliott, and a child—she needs someone who—"

Elliott guesses the rest. That's why Tonie had fainted dead away when she heard she hadn't won a puzzles prize! Elliott might have guessed—

"When I used to see her playing around in the dirt at the feet of her lazy, drunken, half-breed grandfather—I knew then!—

I knew enough from working with my fruit stock to know—then—"

"Nonsense! You used to cross all kinds of stock. How could you tell how she was going to turn out?—How could you?"

"Where is she? Where did she go?" With that Elliott has stormed out of the house, unheeding Carlotta's pleading call.

A moment later Tonie comes in through the kitchen. She wants Carlotta to take back her money and to release her from her promise to take the housekeeper's job. She's been thinking things over and she has made other plans. She's going to try and get in touch with Billie—

Aunt Mat has arrived. She thought she would find Tonie there. Her father's looking for her—and he's on the warpath for fair. Now Cousin Bertha has appeared—full of news that she is almost too excited to deliver. Her Billie's married!! And to Irma Belding! Can they beat that! They had driven up to Reno, where they didn't have to file a notice, and did it.

And is Bertha pleased! Now they won't have to send Billie to college. Mr. Belding will surely give him a job in the bank. Being in a bank is just as good as going to college.

"Tonie, did you know what was up?" Bertha suddenly asks. Tonie has been standing with her back to them while Bertha has been telling the news. No, Tonie had not known.

"I thought maybe Billie told you. You haven't been ringing him up for weeks. Well, I gotta get along—going in to call on Mrs. Belding . . ."

Bertha and Aunt Mat have gone. Tonie has collapsed in a chair, sobbing. Carlotta would comfort her, but Tonie doesn't want that. Nor will she tell what is wrong.

The sound of the De Lucchi tractor coming up the road is heard. A moment later Victor de Lucchi has appeared in the doorway. "He looks strong and is elated with work and the new tractor." No, he had not gone back to school. Not yet. He's going to help finish the work on the slough first. He has come to warn Carlotta to close her windows against the dust. They'll be working the tractor for the next two days and nights —under flood lights at night. That's what you call farming these days.

Vic has started for the door when Tonie comes in from the kitchen and calls to him. She has news for Victor. Billie Barnes and Irma Belding were married yesterday. They drove to Reno and—

Tonie can get no farther. Her helpless gesture toward Victor ends in a dead faint. Victor tries to catch her as she sinks to the floor. He is holding her when Carlotta starts for the phone. She will call a doctor. "She wouldn't want no doctor," Victor advises, picking Tonie up in his arms. She wouldn't want nobody to know—except him. It's Billie— She told him, Vic says, because she didn't want to make a sap out of him

Tonie is opening her eyes now. "I'm here," Vic is saying; "and we're going to get married right away."

"You can't, Victor," protests the confused Carlotta.

"But there isn't anybody now—but me."

"You're going back to school—you're going to be a priest."

"No. I'm going to stay here and work and marry Tonie."

"But you aren't of age—your parents won't let you."

"They will when I tell 'em—they'll make me."

"But it isn't yours, Victor."

"I don't care. I'm going to marry her anyway."

They can be in Reno in four hours, Vic says, and Carlotta is eager they should take her car. But there still is Elliott to deal with. He stalks into the problem now with the statement that Tonie is not going to marry Victor, no matter what has happened, but is less belligerent about it when he hears that it is Billie's child that Victor is demanding his right to father.

"Victor wants to marry Tonie," Carlotta explains, "because he loves her and he has been taught what love means."

Then Joe de Lucchi strides into the scene. Joe, too, would like to know whassa matter? He sends Victor to tell Carlotta to close her windows and now what does he find—

"I'm going to marry Tonie, Papa—"

"No! No! And no! Yousa go back to school! Yousa be a—"

"No! No! And no! They said I ain't right for that life, Papa. And you said so too. You told Mama better I marry and have kids and—"

"But no Tonies!" Joe is shouting now.

"She's going to have one already, Papa."

"Whassa you say?"

"She's going to have a kid."

Joe wheels on his son and slaps him soundly in the face. "So the Fathers say you no right for that life! I say it so too and no right for it! You betcha my life you no right for it! What you do now, eh? What you going to do?"

"I told you, Papa, I'm going to get married."

"What they going to live on? Where are you going to live?

You no come backa my place!"

"They can come here. Tonie will have this place some day. This place will be theirs."

"Wait a minute— The whole place?"

"Yes, the whole place. I haven't anyone to leave it to."

"—And the old lady's place, too?"

"Some day. All that's left of the old Thatcher ranch."

"By Jeez—all my life I look at this place—since that first day I come—I look at this place, and now! Good! O.K.! It's a go!—We gotta drink on this."

Carlotta has gone to the kitchen to get the wine Joe had left at their last sales talk and Joe has followed to help her bring in both wine and glasses, when the children decide not to wait for the drinking. With Elliott's decision that they had better get going they are on their way.

"That's a good boy you got there, Joe! A great boy!" declares the suddenly expanding Elliott, with the second toast.

"You betcha my life he's a good boy," agrees the now affable Joe. "Kid already, eh? Alla my boys isa good boys. Isa good girl you got there, too. A great girl. Works hard—plenty kids —and thisa place."

"To our children!" proposes Carlotta.

It would be nice, Carlotta thinks with her second glass, if Joe would give the children the McCann place. That's a nice little house. All right. Joe give.

Now Elliott and Joe decide to drink to each other. Then Joe must go back to work. He has an idea how he can make the McCann place nice—now he has the new tractor.

"Joe's all right," decides Elliott, finishing another drink. And straightway decides that he will give the children his service station. They couldn't make a living out of the McCann place— and, anyway, Elliott has decided to go back to farming. He'll go in on the Thatcher ranch with Carlotta—

"That is—if the offer's still good," adds Elliott, to which Carlotta makes a happy gesture of assent. "You don't know anything about farming—and I'm the best damned farmer in the county—there isn't a Jap or a damned Italian in the whole place that can—of course I can't promise anything big—but we can make us a living— If we stick together we can make us a living."

LOTTA—We can make us a life!—

ELLIOTT—Yeah. You know, Lot—we'll be a good team—

that's what Ma always says about me—that I'm only good in a team—she don't know the half of it—like that big, strong sorrel we used to have—Chief—just lay back in the traces—wouldn't pull for a damn—till you hitched him up with Daisy—then he'd pull like all hell! (*Moves up to wine—pours another glassful.*) You never should a gone away! You never should have gone!

LOTTA—Haven't you had about enough of that?

ELLIOTT (*pours—then crosses to her and gives her a glass*)— No! We've drunk to everybody else around here—now we're going to drink to you and me— How does that sound to you, eh? You and me—how does that sound?

LOTTA—Sounds good.

ELLIOTT—You know what I'm going to do?—I'm coming in here with you.

LOTTA (*soothing*)—I know, Elliott—we're going to run the ranch together and—

ELLIOTT—No! In here! Here. Right in here! Yep! — I've made up my mind!—made up my mind the first week you got here—probably wouldn't have told you for a year or so yet—if it wasn't for the kids going off like this—and maybe—this Dago red—anyway— It's the thing to do—the sound practical thing to do— Everything for it—nothing against it—not a thing —why shouldn't we marry?

LOTTA—Elliott, please.

ELLIOTT—Why not? We're both alone. I haven't anybody now—neither have you. Alone we haven't anything to look forward to—not a damn thing.

LOTTA—I know—but—

ELLIOTT—Me?

LOTTA—No!—but to make a new life now—to—

ELLIOTT—It wouldn't be a new life, Lot. Just a new graft on an old root.

LOTTA—All those delicate adjustments one has to go through to make a go of it. We're beginning to get old, Elliott.

ELLIOTT—That's just why we got to stick together. We'll keep each other young—don't you know that? People like you and me who knew each other young—they keep seeing each other that way— you look just the girl to me, Lot, you used to be—only a little better-looking—(*She looks away archly. He laughs.*)— it's people like us who need love the most, Lot—and who know how to live together—not kids! Kids expect too much —and give too little. People like us—we learned not to expect too much of people—and we have time to be kind to each other—

Why, just to be there—to talk to each other and eat with each other—sit in a chair alongside of each other— Just to keep each other from being so damned lonesome all the time. Why!

LOTTA—Are you so very lonesome, Elliott?

ELLIOTT—Lonesome? I've been lonesome my whole life—ever since you went away—anyway— You never should have gone, Lot—never should have gone.

LOTTA—Well—now I've come home.

ELLIOTT—Yep. Now you've come home. (*Takes her hand.*) I guess you got what you come for too—a home and a harvest—isn't that what you said?

THE CURTAIN FALLS

THE PLAYS AND THEIR AUTHORS

"In Time to Come," a drama in prologue and seven scenes by Howard Koch and John Huston. Copyright, 1940, by Mr. Koch as "Woodrow Wilson." Copyright and published, 1942, by The Dramatists' Play Service.

Howard Koch, one of the leading scenario writers in Hollywood, wrote the first draft of "In Time to Come" and called it "Woodrow Wilson." John Huston was called in later. When certain suggested changes were made in the script the result of their collaboration was given the new title. Mr. Koch is a New Yorker by birth, has an A.B. from Bard College and an LL.B. from Columbia. He gave up a career as a lawyer to write for the stage and the screen. His first play was one called "Great Scott," and his first production to attract attention was that of "Give Us This Day," produced in 1933. He also wrote a Lincoln Play, "The Lonely Man," which had a Chicago production with John Huston playing the Lincoln rôle. It was Koch who wrote the famous Martian incident which, with Orson Welles reading it over the radio, scared the daylights out of certain simple New Jersey farmers who heard it. He and Huston did the scenarios for both "Sergeant York" and "In This Our Life." Mr. Koch has just finished the American version of "Girl from Leningrad," now called "Russian Girl," which is to be the first Soviet film to be made in America. He has been writing a drama called "If This Be Treason," and looks forward to a routine that will permit him to write one play and one picture each year.

John Huston is Actor Walter Huston's son. His writing life, which he took up after a variety of adventures, including one as a professional prizefighter and another as a lieutenant in the Mexican cavalry, has been largely devoted to the screen drama. He also has been a contributor to the *American Mercury* magazine. He has collaborated on many successful pictures, including "Juarez," "Dr. Ehrlich's Magic Bullet" and "High Sierra." Recent achievements have included the writing and directing of "The Maltese Falcon," "In This Our Life" (with Mr. Koch) and "Across the Pacific."

"The Moon Is Down," a drama in three acts by John Steinbeck, from his novel of the same title. Copyright, 1940, 1941, by the author. Copyright and published (as a novel), 1942, by The Viking Press, Inc., New York.

John Steinbeck's last appearance in this series of playbooks was in the issue of 1937-38, the season he wrote "Of Mice and Men." That play also had been written first as a novel, with an idea to its later dramatization, which was made by George S. Kaufman. Mr. Steinbeck followed the same pattern with "The Moon Is Down," though this time he made his own dramatization. The playwright was born 41 years ago in California, educated in the public schools and later took special courses at Stanford University. He tried free-lance writing in New York as a young man, resented the attitude of certain editors, returned to California to write his first novels, "Cup of Gold," "Pictures of Heaven," "To a God Unknown," "Tortilla Flat," "Of Mice and Men."

"Blithe Spirit," a comedy in three acts by Noel Coward. Copyright, 1941, by the author. Copyright and published, 1941, by Doubleday, Doran & Co., Garden City, New York.

Noel Coward has been more active in war work than he has been in the theatre the last two or three seasons. He did manage to write "Blithe Spirit" with the deliberate and expressed hope that it would take the minds of as many of his countrymen as saw it off their war miseries for a few hours. The farce has been a great success in both England and America, though it has not got farther than New York and Chicago up to now. Mr. Coward has lived forty-three years and done a lot of writing. His recent successes have included an autobiography, "Present Indicative," and a volume of short stories, "To Step Aside." He was born in the parish of Teddington, near London; went on the stage when he was 12; enlisted in the last war. He was represented in these volumes with "Design for Living" in 1932-33. His popular plays have included "Private Lives," "Hay Fever," "Bitter Sweet" and "Cavalcade."

"Junior Miss," a comedy in three acts by Jerome Chodorov and Joseph Fields, based on the book by Sally Benson. Copyright, 1942, by the authors. Copyright and published, 1942, by Random House, Inc., New York.

The Messrs. Chodorov and Fields broke into the lists of top-flight playwrights last season with their first dramatization of Ruth McKenney's *New Yorker* magazine stories entitled "My Sister Eileen." Turning again to their favorite magazine source for a second inspiration, they decided to whittle a comedy out of the sub deb sketches that Sally Benson had also contributed to the *New Yorker,* and had later put into a book. "Junior Miss" was the happy result. George Kaufman having staged their "Eileen" play, it was perfectly natural that Moss Hart should want to stage "Junior Miss," Mr. Hart being Mr. Kaufman's favorite collaborator, and vice versa. Both Mr. Fields, who is the son of the late Lew Fields of Weber and Fields, and Mr. Chodorov were born in New York and went to school in their home town. Fields thought he'd be a lawyer, but took to writing instead. Chodorov went into newspaper work as soon as possible after he left school. They have been successful as scenarists in Hollywood, where their present writing partnership was formed.

"Candle in the Wind," a drama in three acts by Maxwell Anderson. Copyright, 1941, by the author. Copyright and published, 1941, by Anderson House, Washington, D. C. Distributed through Dodd, Mead & Co., New York.

Maxwell Anderson has been a frequent contributor to "The Best Plays" series, this being his twelfth appearance. His first plays were written in the early 1920's, the first being "The White Desert," which failed, his second the "What Price Glory?" on which he collaborated with Laurence Stallings, and which was a great success. His verse dramas, "Elizabeth the Queen," "Mary of Scotland" and "Valley Forge," established his position as one of the topflight American dramatists. He won a Pulitzer prize with "Both Your Houses" and two New York Drama Critics' Circle awards with "Winterset" and "High Tor." He was born in Atlantic, Pa., in 1888, the son of a minister, and has done considerable writing for newspapers and magazines, also a little schoolteaching, in addition to his playwriting.

"Jason," a comedy in three acts by Samson Raphaelson. Copyright, 1942, by the author. Copyright and published, 1942, by Random House, Inc., New York.

This is Samson Raphaelson's third contribution to this theatre record. In 1934-35 he wrote "Accent on Youth," included in the volume of that year, and in 1939-40 he was the author of the very successful comedy called "Skylark," which was the springboard from which Gertrude Lawrence sprang to "Lady in the Dark." He has been a writing man since he left the University of Illinois, has sold short stories and magazine articles, advertising copy and dramas. His "Jazz Singer," which George Jessel played for two seasons, was his first success. "Young Love" and "The Wooden Slipper" were also his. He was born in New York, but lived, worked and went to school in Chicago.

"Letters to Lucerne," a drama in three acts by Fritz Rotter and
   Allen Vincent. Copyright, 1941, by the authors. Copyright and published, 1942, by Samuel French, New York.

This moving drama of the second World War resulted from the joining of two definite Hollywood talents—those of Fritz Rotter, formerly of Vienna, Austria, and Allen Vincent, always of these United States, he having been born in Spokane, Washington, and graduated from Dartmouth College. Mr. Rotter, having made a career as a song writer (some 1,200 songs written by him include "I Kiss Your Hand, Madame" and "Two Hearts in Three-quarter Time") he decided the writing of the lyrics for these, and often the composing of the scores as well, was really a trivial business. So he turned to writing and supplying ideas for the screen, and to writing for the theatre. In 1936 he came to America, went to Hollywood, struggled with the language and the bosses and finally became a superior sort of "idea man." He couldn't write out his scenarios very well, but he could tell the stories so well he sold most of them before a word had been put on paper.

Mr. Vincent, meantime, having left college, decided to become an actor. He played parts with Doris Keane in "Romance," and in Noel Coward's "The Vortex," "The Grand Street Follies," the first "Little Show" and "The Vinegar Tree." He went to Hollywood as a juvenile and remained to take up writing. That is how he met Rosalie Stewart, the play agent who has mothered the genius of many writers, including George Kelly. Miss Stewart introduced Mr. Vincent to Mr. Rotter. Mr. V, she said, wrote the best dialogue in screenland and Mr. R sparked the best ideas. Let them work together. They did and "Letters to Lucerne" was the result of their first joint effort.

THE PLAYS AND THEIR AUTHORS 389

"Angel Street," a drama in three acts by Patrick Hamilton. Copyright, 1939, by the author. Copyright and published as "Gaslight," 1939, by Constable & Co. Ltd., London. Copyright and published as "Angel Street," 1942, by Samuel French, New York.

The author of this Victorian thriller, which he called "Gaslight," was born in London in 1904 and educated at Westminster. He took to the stage, playing in companies touring the provinces, as soon as he could get away from school and later, because he wanted to be a writer, became a stenographer in London. He was 21 when his first novel, "Monday Morning," was published. "Craven House" and "Two Pence Coloured" followed. His first play to be produced in London and New York was one called "Rope" and later "Rope's End." He went back to novel writing and did a "Midnight Bell" trilogy. "Gaslight" came along in 1938, was something of a success in London but was unsuccessfully hawked about America for two years before Shepherd Traube took it, made a few alterations as to scene sequence, and produced it as "Angel Street." It proved an overnight success in New York. Mr. Hamilton's newest work is again a novel, another Victorian thriller called "Hangover House," published the spring of 1941 by Random House. He is a keen student of Victorian literature and the spectacular crimes of the period. His sister is Diana Hamilton of the London stage. She is the wife of the Sutton Vane who wrote "Outward Bound."

"Uncle Harry," a drama in three acts by Thomas Job. Copyright, 1941, by the author. Copyright and published, 1942, by Samuel French, New York.

This is Thomas Job's second play to be given a Broadway hearing. His first was the "Barchester Towers" in which Ina Claire was starred by Guthrie McClintic in 1937. He was born in the small village of Conwil in South Wales, his father being Welsh and his mother English. He was graduated from the University of Wales and took his M.A. in 1924. He majored in literature and the history of languages. He came to America in 1925 and for ten years taught English in a Midwestern college, eventually establishing a department of drama. Began writing dramas to provide his students with stage material for their class work. He has written three plays since "Barchester Towers"—"Rue with a Difference," "Dawn in Lyonnese" and "Uncle Harry." He is now teaching playwriting and dramatic literature at Carnegie Tech. in Pittsburgh, and hopes eventually to make playwriting his chief concern.

"Hope for a Harvest," a drama in three acts by Sophie Treadwell. Copyright, 1940, by the author. Copyright and published, 1942, by Samuel French, New York.

In the 1928-29 volume of "The Best Plays" Sophie Treadwell was represented by a drama called "Machinal," one of the outstanding productions of that season. Of recent years she has devoted most of her time to story and scenario writing, working in her native California. During her junior and senior years at the University of California she did a good deal of acting with the dramatic clubs and societies. After her graduation she played in stock and did some singing in vaudeville. She was for a time a protege of the late Mme. Helena Modjeska and helped compile the Modjeska memoirs. Two of her early dramas were "Gringo" and "Oh, Nightingale."

PLAYS PRODUCED IN NEW YORK

June 15, 1941 — June 15, 1942

(Plays marked with asterisk were still playing June 15, 1942)

IT HAPPENS ON ICE

(386 performances)

A skating show in two acts. Second edition resumed by Sonja Henie and Arthur M. Wirtz at the Center Theatre, New York, July 15, 1941.

Principals engaged—

Hedi Stenuf	Georg Von Birgelen
Jo Ann Dean	Gene Berg
Betty Atkinson	Charles Hain
Mary Jane Yeo	Skippy Baxter
Edwina Blades	Le Verne
Freddie Trenkler	Fritz Dietl
Tommy Lee	Charlie Slagle
Dorothy Allan	A. Douglas Nelles
Rona and Cliff Thael	The Four Bruises
June Forrest	Jack Kilty

Staged by Leon Leonidoff; dances directed by Catherine Littlefield; settings and costumes by Norman Bel Geddes.

"It Happens on Ice" ran for 180 performances at the Center Theatre from October 10, 1940, to March 8, 1941. The second edition opened April 4, 1941, and ran until June 14, 1941. The two engagements totaled 276 performances. The second edition resumed after a month's vacation on July 15, 1941, making a total of 662 performances (not consecutive).

(Closed April 26, 1942)

PAL JOEY

(104 performances)

A musical comedy in two acts by John O'Hara; music by Richard Rodgers; lyrics by Lorenz Hart. Returned by George Abbott to the Shubert Theatre, New York, September 1, 1941. (Moved to St. James Theatre, Oct. 21, 1941.)

Cast of characters—
Joey Evans..Gene Kelly
Max..Averell Harris
The Kid..Janet Lavis

```
Gladys..............................................Vivienne Allen
Agnes...............................................Diane Sinclair
Linda English........................................Anne Blair
Valerie............................................Charlene Harkins
Albert Doane..........................................Phil King
Vera Simpson......................................Vivienne Segal
Escort................................................Edison Rice
Terry.................................................Jane Fraser
Victor...............................................Van Johnson
Ernest...............................................John Clarke
Stagehand............................................David Jones
The Tenor.......................................Norman Van Emburgh
Melba Snyder..........................................Jean Casto
Waiter.............................................Dummy Spevlin
Ludlow Lowell........................................David Burns
Commissioner O'Brien.................................James Lane
Assistant Hotel Manager.............................Cliff Dunstan
Specialty Dancer: Shirley Paige.
```

Act I.—Scenes 1, 3 and 5—Night Club in Chicago's South Side. 2—Pet Shop. 4—Vera's and Joey's Rooms. 6—Tailor Shop. 7—Joey Looks into the Future. Act II.—Scenes 1 and 3—Chez Joey. 2 and 4—Joey's Apartment. 5—Pet Shop.

Staged by George Abbott; dances directed by Robert Alton; settings and lighting by Jo Mielziner; costumes by John Koenig.

"Pal Joey" ran for 270 performances from December 25, 1940, to August 16, 1941, at the Barrymore Theatre, New York, returning after a two weeks' vacation to the Shubert Theatre, New York. The two runs made a total of 374 performances (not consecutive).

(Closed November 29, 1941)

LADY IN THE DARK

(305 performances)

A musical play by Moss Hart; music by Kurt Weill; lyrics by Ira Gershwin. Returned by Sam H. Harris to the Alvin Theatre, New York, September 2, 1941.

Cast of characters—

```
Dr. Brooks........................................Donald Randolph
Miss Bowers.........................................Jeanne Shelby
Liza Elliott......................................Gertrude Lawrence
Miss Foster.........................................Evelyn Wyckoff
Miss Stevens.............................................Ann Lee
Maggie Grant.......................................Margaret Dale
Alison Du Bois.....................................Natalie Schafer
Russell Paxton.....................................Eric Brotherson
Charley Johnson......................................Walter Coy
Randy Curtis.......................................Willard Parker
Joe.................................................Ward Tallmon
Tom................................................George Bockman
Kendall Nesbitt.....................................Paul McGrath
Helen..............................................Virginia Peine
Ruthie..............................................Gedda Petry
Carol................................................Beth Nichols
Marcia...........................................Margaret Westberg
Ben Butler...........................................Dan Harden
Barbara...........................................Patricia Deering
```

The Albertina Rasch Group Dancers: Rita Charise, Audrey Costello, Patricia Deering, June MacLaren, Beth Nichols, Wana Wenerholm, Margaret Westberg, Jerome Andrews, George Bockman, Andre Charise, Fred Hearn, John Sweet, William Howell, Edward Browne.
The Singers: Catherine Conrad, Jean Cumming, Carol Deis, Stella Hughes, Gedda Petry, June Rutherford, Florence Wyman, Robert Arnold, Robert Lyon, Evan K. Taylor, Carl Nicholas, Len Frank, Frank Sherman, William Marel, Larry Siegle.
The Children: Anne Bracken, Sally Ferguson, Jacqueline Macmillan, Lois Volkman, Joan Volkman, Bonnie Baken. Kenneth Casey, Robert Mills, George Ward, William Welch, Roger Smith.
Act I.—Scenes 1 and 3—Dr. Brooks' Office. 2 and 4—Liza Elliott's Office. Act II.—Scenes 1 and 3—Liza Elliott's Office. 2—Dr. Brooks' Office.
Staged by Moss Hart; production and lighting by Hassard Short; choreography by Albertina Rasch; music directed by Maurice Abravanel; settings by Harry Horner; costumes by Irene Sharaff and Hattie Carnegie.

First New York opening of "Lady in the Dark" was at the Alvin Theatre on January 23, 1941. After 162 performances it closed June 15, 1941, re-opening September 2, 1941. This made an interrupted run of 467 performances.

After the eleven-week rest Gertrude Lawrence resumed the run of "Lady in the Dark" at the Alvin with four new leading men—Eric Brotherson, succeeding Danny Kaye; Paul McGrath, succeeding Bert Lytell; Walter Coy replacing Macdonald Carey and Willard Parker taking over Victor Mature's rôle. There were also minor changes in the ensemble.

(Closed May 30, 1942)

VILLAGE GREEN

(30 performances)

A comedy in three acts by Carl Allensworth. Produced by Dorothy and Julian Olney and Felix Jacoves at the Henry Miller Theatre, New York, September 3, 1941.

Cast of characters—
Judge Homer W. Peabody...........................Frank Craven
Zeke Bentham......................................Joseph Allen
Margaret Peabody................................Laura Pierpont
Harriet Peabody...................................Perry Wilson
Jeremiah Bentham..................................John Craven
Henry Ames...Matt Briggs
Hubert Carter.......................................Henry Jones
The Reverend Horace Shurtleff...................Calvin Thomas
Walter Godkin......................................John Ravold
Harmony Godkin....................................Maida Reade
George Martin..................................Joseph R. Garry
A Boy Scout.....................................Julian Olney, Jr.
The Reverend Arthur McKnight.....................Frank Wilcox
Dawson..Norman Lloyd
Acts I, II and III.—In Judge Peabody's Home, North Oxford, New Hampshire.
Staged by Felix Jacoves; setting by Raymond Sovey.

Homer Peabody had been running for Congress on the Democratic ticket in the Republican stronghold of Connecticut for 16 years, and laughing amusedly at defeat. Now comes a progressive young artist to paint a symbolical nude in a postoffice mural. The artist is in love with Judge Peabody's daughter and the nude just naturally takes on Harriet Peabody's features. Town scandal threatens and the Judge takes a stand for freedom of expression in art which rallies the progressives of both parties to his aid and gets him elected.

(Closed September 27, 1941)

THE WOOKEY

(134 performances)

A drama in three acts by Frederick Hazlitt Brennan. Produced by Edgar Selwyn at the Plymouth Theatre, New York, September 10, 1941.

Cast of characters—

Ernie Wookey	George Sturgeon
Aunt Gen	Carol Goodner
Mrs. Wookey	Nora Howard
Primrose Wookey	Heather Angel
Constable Simpson	Henry Mowbray
Walt Gibbs	Neil Fitzgerald
Mr. Wookey	Edmund Gwenn
Rory McSwiggin	Horace McNally
Cousin Hector	Victor Beecroft
Mr. Archibald	Byron Russell
A. R. P. Warden	Roland Bottomly
Dr. Lewishohn	Everett Ripley
First Boy	Allen Shaw
Second Boy	Gilbert Russell
Third Boy	John Moore
First Girl	Grace Collins
Second Girl	Cora Smith
The Vack Lady	Olive Reeves-Smith
The Curate	Sean Dillon
First-Aid Man	Harry Sothern
Messenger	Allen Shaw
Subaltern	Gilbert Russell
Colonel Glenn	Charles Francis
Navvies	{ John Tervor / Milton Blumenthal }

Act I.—Parlor of the Wookey Home in the East End Dock Area of London, the day before England's Entrance into World War II. Act II.—Scene 1—Back Yard of Wookey Home, June, 1940. 2—Parlor. Act III.—Scene 1—Back Yard, September, 1940. 2—Mr. Wookey's Basement.

Staged by Robert B. Sinclair; settings by Jo Mielziner.

Mr. Wookey was a tugboat captain who served in the B.E.F. in the First World War but disagreed with the government on the Second. He wrote 10 Downing Street, telling Churchill exactly what to do, and then quit the whole bally mess. When he heard a relative was in trouble at Dunkirk he took the tugboat over to help. He made seventeen crossings after that. When his own home was bombed he realized that Britain's war was every free man's war, got himself a machine gun and went out to meet Jerry face to face.

(Closed January 3, 1942)

BROTHER CAIN

(19 performances)

A drama in three acts by Michael Kallesser and Richard Norcross. Produced by American Civic Theatre at the Golden Theatre, New York, September 12, 1941.

Cast of characters—
```
Mom ................................................ Kasia Orzazewska
Pete ............................................... William T. Terry
Hugo ...................................................... Jack Lambert
Joe ..................................................... Royal Raymond
Annie ..................................................... Anita Lindsey
Paul .................................................... Frederic deWilde
Marion ..................................................... Grace Linn
Mr. Tyler .............................................. Richard Karlan
Process Server ........................................... George Edwards
```
Acts I and III.—The Kowalski Home-Kitchen and Living Room. Act II.—Gangway in a Coal Mine.
Staged by Charles Davenport; settings by Louis Kennel.

Paul was a coal miner's son whose brothers chipped in to help him realize his thirst for learning by sending him to college. When he came back with a degree from the law school he found his old Polish mother still loyal but his stupid brothers resentful and bitter. He tried to help them by going back into the mines. No good. He brought suit against the company under a New Deal compensation act, got his brothers fired and his mother dispossessed. He was pretty sure of a settlement out of court, however, and planned to marry a mine executive's daughter.

(Closed September 27, 1941)

THE MORE THE MERRIER

(16 performances)

A comedy in three acts by Frank Gabrielson and Irvin Pincus. Produced by Otto Preminger and Norman Pincus at the Cort Theatre, New York, September 15, 1941.

Cast of characters—

Miss Craig	Dorrit Kelton
Harvey Royal	Louis Hector
Senator Broderick	J. C. Nugent
Jackson	Herbert Duffy
Crivers	Robert Gray
Daniel Finch	Frank Albertson
Bugs Saunders	Grace McDonald
Joseph Dolma	Keenan Wynn
Mr. Cartwright	John McKee
Mrs. Cartwright	Mrs. Priestly Morrison
Bus Driver	Scott Moore
Mrs. Keek	Lucia Seger
Lucille Keek	Brenda Struck
Fat Man	Ralph Chambers
Young Man with a Radio	Saint Subber
Mr. Jupiter	Max Beck
Sinister Man	Daniele Porise
Miss Hogben	Doro Merande
Al Goblin	Teddy Hart
Harry Scravvis	Millard Mitchell
George Smith	Jack Riano
Forrest Lockhart	Will Geer
Capt. James	John Barnes
First State Trooper	Lee Frederick
Second State Trooper	James Albert
Mr. Dewey	Guy Sampsel
Mrs. Dewey	Jane Standish
Doc Strube	G. Albert Smith

Acts I, II and III.—Main Hall of Harvey Royal's Castle in the Colorado Rockies.
Staged by Otto Preminger; setting by Stewart Chaney.

Harvey Royal, egocentric owner of a chain of newspapers, is trying to be elected Governor of Colorado. He leaves his castle in the mountains in charge of Daniel Finch, a publicity man, while he goes to the convention. A storm comes up, a bus is stalled and the passengers swarm in, mistaking the castle for a hotel. Two crooks have blackjacked a passenger with funds and are trying to get the body out of the house when Harvey Royal returns. He tosses the cadaver off a balcony and thinks he is responsible for the victim's death. Some fun. Turns out there was a reward on the murdered man's head anyway.

(Closed September 27, 1941)

CUCKOOS ON THE HEARTH

(129 performances)

A comedy in three acts by Parker W. Fennelly. Produced by Brock Pemberton at the Morosco Theatre, New York, September 16, 1941. Moved to Mansfield Theatre, November 2 and to the Ambassador, November 21, 1942.

Cast of characters—

Amos Rodick	Walter O. Hill
Lulu Pung	Janet Fox

THE BEST PLAYS OF 1941-42

```
Charlotte Carlton..............................Margaret Callahan
Donald Carlton..................................Carleton Young
Sheriff Preble.....................................Percy Kilbride
Zadoc Grimes...................................Howard Freeman
"Doc" Ferris.....................................George Mathews
The Professor....................................Frederic Tozere
The Rev. Dr. Clarence Underhill................Howard St. John
Peck..................................................James Coots
Dr. Gordon..........................................Henry Levin
A State Trooper...................................Arthur Hughes
```
    Prologue.—Outside Harmony Hearth, the Home of the Carltons in Maine. Acts I, II and III.—Living Room of Harmony Hearth.
    Staged by Antoinette Perry; setting by John Root.

Donald Carlton is summoned to Washington. He is obliged to leave Charlotte, his young and pretty wife, alone on their lonely Maine farm, with a dim witted cousin, Lulu Pung, and an eccentric novelist who is practically stone deaf. A blinding storm threatens and the Sheriff stops in to announce that a sex-crazed patient has escaped from the sanitarium up the road. Three strangers are blown in by the storm; they threaten Mrs. Carlton with death and worse unless she gives them the formula for a poison gas Mr. Carlton has gone to tell Washington about. Mrs. C. is being strangled at the end of the second act when Amos Rodick, from the General Store, appears to explain that that is only what the novelist imagined happened. What really did happen is revealed in a second second act, and includes the outwitting of the three spies.

(Closed January 3, 1942)

THE DISTANT CITY

(2 performances)

A play in three acts by Edwin B. Self. Produced by John Tuerk at the Longacre Theatre, New York, September 22, 1941.

Cast of characters—

```
Mom Quigley.....................................Gladys George
Pete Quigley........................................Ben Smith
Edna Scott.......................................Gertrude Flynn
David Hacket.....................................Robert Vivian
Reverend Jonas West...............................Lee Baker
Mrs. Beatrice Prentiss West.....................Merle Maddern
Lester Prentiss..................................Leonard Penn
Mrs. Laura Prentiss..............................Louise Stanley
Sergeant McKiernan.................................Len Doyle
Policeman........................................Gilbert Morgan
Chaplain.........................................Morgan Farley
Warden............................................Burke Clarke
Guard..............................................Larry Hugo
```
    Act I.—Kitchen in Home of Mom and Pete Quigley. Act II.—Garden Porch in Home of Reverend West. Act III.—The Warden's Office. A Big City in the Middle West.
    Staged by Edward Byron; settings by Samuel Leve; costumes by Helene Pons.

Mom Quigley had been something of a trollop in her youth, but her life had yielded her a son, Pete. Pete became a respected collector of garbage and was good to his Mom, hanging her on the wall in an armchair when she got in his way. Pete had for years been in love with Edna Scott. When Edna tells him the minister's son has got her into trouble, he is willing to marry her anyway, but the minister's son, fearing repercussions, strangles Edna and throws the blame on Pete. Pete is convicted and sent to the electric chair, which distresses Mom. Having been an atheist, she prays for help. Then she realizes that in the distant city of Heaven she and Pete will be just as important as anybody and quits praying.

(Closed September 23, 1941)

GHOST FOR SALE

(6 performances)

A comedy in three acts by Ronald Jeans. Produced by Daly's Theatre Stock Company and Alex Cohen at Daly's Theatre, New York, September 29, 1941.

Cast of characters—

Martin Tracey	Evan Thomas
Pope	Jack Lynds
Eleanor Tracey	Mary Heberden
Geoffrey Tracey	Leon Janney
Sir Gilbert Tracey	Austin Fairman
Judy	Ruth Gilbert
Fluff (Lady Tracey)	Elsie Mackie
Pleasance Ambleton	July Blake
Basil Pennycook	Guy Tano
Hermione Proudfoot	Sara Fanelle
Mr. Blow	Martin Balsam
Mr. Whiteside	Ronald Alexander
Mr. Quale	Anthony Kent
Mr. Wilberforce	Steve Colton

Acts I, II and III.—Library of Tracey Manor, Hertfordshire, England.

Staged by Ilia Motyleff; setting by Cleon Throckmorton.

Martin Tracey wants to buy the Tracey ancestral estate from Sir Gilbert and tries to frighten Sir Gilbert into the sale by hiring a ghost to haunt it. The sale is made, but the ghost stays on to haunt Martin, who finally sells to young Geoffrey Tracey, who had been cheated out of it in the first place.

(Closed October 4, 1941)

MR. BIG

(7 performances)

A comedy in three acts by Arthur Sheekman and Margaret Shane. Produced by George S. Kaufman at the Lyceum Theatre, New York, September 30, 1941.

Cast of characters—

Henry Stacey	George Baxter
Paula Loring	Fay Wray
Leo Orton	Judson Laire
Myra Davenport	Nina Doll
Joan Starling	Ann Evers
Mack	James MacDonald
Dr. Willoughby	Richard Barbee
Bill	Ray Mayer
Stanwood	Le Roi Operti
Mrs. Jessup	Eleanor Phelps
Oscar Cullen	Harry Gribbon
Mr. Jessup	Jack Leslie
Harley L. Miller	Hume Cronyn
Charles G. Wakeshaw	Florenz Ames
The Little Man	E. J. Ballantine
Amy Stevens	Betty Furness
Carter	George Petrie
Nesbitt	Robert Whitehead
Kennedy	David Crowell
Eric Reynolds	Barry Sullivan
Rodney	Oscar Polk
Broadway Sarah	Mitzi Hajos
Johnny Tilley	Sidney Stone
Mrs. Tarpin	Sarah Floyd
Man From Brooklyn	Harry M. Cooke
Molly Higee	Ruth Thane McDevitt
Jack Lamperson	John Parrish
The Man From Boston	Harold Grau
Check Room Boy	James Elliott
Photographers	William Layton / Edward Fisher
Policemen	Benson Springer / Robert Rhodes / Rodney Stewart / Peter Lawrence / Irwin Wilcox / Fred O'Dwyer

Acts I, II and III.—In a Theatre.
Staged by George S. Kaufman; setting by Donald Oenslager.

Henry Stacey, actor producer of a New York stock company, is taking a bow with his actors at the close of a first night opening when he is shot and killed by a poisoned needle dart. Attending the show are a Police Commissioner and a District Attorney who is a candidate for the Gubernatorial nomination. The D.A. takes charge of the investigation, holds the audience in its seats, takes advantage of the occasion to deliver several short political pleas for support, and finally, by 11 o'clock, having been aided by a variety of fortuitous circumstances arranged by the playwrights, uncovers the guilty party.

(Closed October 4, 1941)

* BEST FOOT FORWARD

(302 performances)

A musical comedy in two acts by John Cecil Holm; music and lyrics by Hugh Martin and Ralph Blane. Produced by George Abbott at the Ethel Barrymore Theatre, New York, October 1, 1941.

Cast of characters—

Dutch Miller	Jack Jordan, Jr.
Fred Jones	Lou Wills, Jr.
Freshman	Richard Dick
Junior	Danny Daniels
Hunk Hoyt	Kenneth Bowers
Satchel Moyer	Bobby Harrell
Goofy Clark	Lee Roberts
Chuck Green	Tommy Dix
Dr. Reeber	Fleming Ward
Old Grad	Stuart Langley
Minerva	June Allyson
Ethel	Victoria Schools
Miss Delaware Water Gap	Betty-Anne Nyman
Blind Date	Nancy Walker
Bud Hooper	Gil Stratton, Jr.
Professor Lloyd	Roger Hewlett
Waitress	Norma Lehn
Jack Haggerty	Marty May
Gale Joy	Rosemary Lane
Chester Billings	Vincent York
Helen Schlessinger	Maureen Cannon
Prof. Williams	Robert Griffith

Other principals: Billy Parsons, George Staisey, Stanley Donen, Buddy Allen and Art Williams.

Act I.—Scenes 1 and 8—Gymnasium. 2 and 5—Room at Eagle House. 3—Room in Boys' Dormitory. 4 and 7—Hall Outside Girls' Cot Room. 6—Girls' Cot Room. Act II.—Scenes 1, 4 and 8—Gymnasium. 2—Room in Boys' Dormitory. 3—Exterior of Dormitory. 5 and 7—Hall. 6—Room in Eagle House.

Staged by George Abbott; dances directed by Gene Kelly; settings and lighting by Jo Mielziner; costumes by Miles White.

Bud Hooper thought it would be a good joke to invite Gale Joy, the movie glamour girl, to be his date at the Winsocki prom, never thinking he would get more than a refusal and an autograph out of it. Miss Joy, about to toss the invitation aside, is advised by her press agent to accept Bud's invitation for the good the publicity might do her. Gale arrives in Winsocki, accompanied by her agent, arouses the jealousy of Bud's regular girl and, at the prom, is stripped down to her silhouette by souvenir-hunting classmen. This threatens a scandal when the principal walks in. Everybody clothed and happy at the finale.

AH, WILDERNESS!

(29 performances)

A comedy in three acts by Eugene O'Neill. Revived by The Theatre Guild, Inc., at the Guild Theatre, New York, October 2, 1941.

Cast of characters—

```
Nat Miller...........................................Harry Carey
Essie................................................Ann Shoemaker
Arthur...............................................Victor Chapin
Richard..............................................William Prince
Mildred..............................................Virginia Kaye
Tommy................................................Tommy Lewis
Sid Davis............................................Tom Tully
Lily Miller..........................................Enid Markey
David McComber.......................................Hale Norcross
Muriel McComber......................................Dorothy Littlejohn
Wint Selby...........................................Walter Craig
Belle................................................Dennie Moore
Nora.................................................Philippa Bevans
Bartender............................................Zachary Scott
Salesman.............................................Edmund Dorsay
```
Act I.—Scene 1—Sitting Room of Miller Home in Large Small-Town in Connecticut. 2—Dining Room. Act II.—Scene 1—Back Room of Bar in Small Hotel. 2—Sitting Room. Act III.—Scenes 1 and 3—Sitting Room. 2—Strip of Beach on Harbor.
Staged by Eva Le Gallienne; production under supervision of Theresa Helburn, Lawrence Langner and Eva Le Gallienne; settings by Watson Barratt.

The original production of Eugene O'Neill's "Ah, Wilderness!" was staged at the Guild Theatre, New York, in October, 1933. It had 289 performances before starting a country-wide tour that lasted the better part of two years. George M. Cohan was the star of a cast that included Gene Lockhart, Eda Heinemann, Marjorie Marquis and Elisha Cook, Jr.

(Closed October 25, 1941)

ALL MEN ARE ALIKE

(32 performances)

A farce in two acts by Vernon Sylvaine. Produced by Lee Ephraim at the Hudson Theatre, New York, October 6, 1941.

Cast of characters—

```
Sydney Butch.........................................Eustace Wyatt
Mrs. Featherstone....................................Ethel Morrison
Major Gaunt..........................................A. P. Kaye
Collins..............................................Stapleton Kent
Alfred J. Bandle.....................................Reginald Denny
MacFarlane...........................................Ian Martin
Wilmer Popday........................................Bobby Clark
Frankie Marriott.....................................Lillian Bond
Miss Trellow.........................................Mary Newnham-Davis
```

```
Albert Butch..........................................Milton Karol
Olga................................................Jeraldine Dvorak
Constable........................................William Valentine
Cyrano DeVeau.........................................Rolfe Sedan
Thelma Bandle....................................Cora Witherspoon
Elizabeth Popday......................................Velma Royton
    Acts I and II.—Lounge Hall of Alfred Bandle's Country Residence
in Surrey, England.
    Staged by Harry Wagstaff Gribble; setting by Frederick Fox.
```

Alfred Bandle takes his pretty secretary, Frankie Marriott, and retires to the country to work. He is shortly followed by his curious, but hopeful, partner, Wilmer Popday, and later by his own wife as well as Wilmer's. Complications certainly ensue.

(Closed November 1, 1941)

ANNE OF ENGLAND

(7 performances)

A drama in three acts by Mary Cass Canfield and Ethel Borden based on a play, "Viceroy Sarah," by Norman Ginsbury. Produced by Gilbert Miller at the St. James Theatre, New York, October 7, 1941.

Cast of characters—

```
Mr. Throstlewaite...............................Oswald Marshall
Lady Mary Churchill............................Elizabeth Inglise
Anne, Lady Sunderland..........................Frances Tannehill
Sarah, Duchess of Marlborough ("Mrs. Freeman")....Flora Robson
John Churchill, 1st Duke of Marlborough..........Frederic Worlock
Footman to the Marlboroughs......................Geoffrey Borden
Lord Godolphin, Lord Treasurer....................Reginald Mason
Abigail Hill (Afterwards Mrs. Masham)..............Jessica Tandy
Mr. Harley........................................Leo G. Carroll
Mrs. Danvers......................................Margery Maude
Duchess of Somerset ................................Cherry Hardy
Captain Vanbrugh..........................Anthony Kemble Cooper
Anne, Queen of England ("Mrs. Morley")...........Barbara Everest
George, Prince of Denmark..................Hans Von Twardowski
Mr. St. John......................................Edward Langley
Colonel Parke........................................Colin Hunter
    Footmen to the Queen...................... { Raymond Johnson
                                                { Thaddeus Suski
    Pages to the Queen........................ { Kenneth Leroy
                                                { Jack Leach
    Act I.—Scene 1—Marlborough House.  2—Kensington Palace.  Act
II.—Kensington Palace.  Act III.—Scenes 1 and 3—Kensington Palace.
2—Marlborough House.
    Staged by Gilbert Miller; settings by Mstislav Dobujinsky.
```

Sarah, Duchess of Marlborough, long the friend and confidant of Queen Anne of England (1665-1714), seeks to promote her own importance at court by inducing Anne to appoint Abigail, Sarah's young cousin, a lady of the bedchamber. Abigail, being sly and ambitious, comes to resent Cousin Sarah's patronizing domination and craftily worms her way into the good graces of the Queen. As a result of the intrigue a good deal of trouble develops between Queen Anne and the Marlboroughs. The Duke (Winston Churchill's ancestor) resigns his commission in the army, peace at any price is sought with the France of Louis XIV, and there are depressing days ahead for England.

(Closed October 11, 1941)

VIVA O'BRIEN

(20 performances)

A musical comedy in two acts by William K. and Eleanor Wells; lyrics by Raymond Leveen; music by Marie Grever. Produced by John J. Hickey, Chester Hale and Clark Johnson at the Majestic Theatre, New York, October 9, 1941.

Cast of characters—

Jeeves	Cyril Smith
Emilio Morales	Milton Watson
Betty Dayton	Ruth Clayton
Manuel Estrada	Roberto Bernardi
Lupita Estrada	Victoria Cordova
Tom	Harold Diamond
Dick	Hugh Diamond
Harry	Tom Diamond
J. Foster Adams	Edgar Mason
Professor Sherwood	John Cherry
Mrs. Sherwood	Ann Dere
Senora Estrada	Adelina Roatina
Pedro Gonzales	Gil Galvan
Don Jose O'Brien	Russ Brown
Carol Sherwood	Marie Nash
Gateman	Hugh Diamond
Maria	Mara Lopez
Dolores	Tanya Knight
Ramon	Rudy Williams
Juan	Joe Frederic
Native Carrier	Pete Desjardins
Zambrano	James Phillips
Boatman	Joe Frederic
Vicente	Gil Galvan
Rani	Tony (Oswald) Labriola
Ship's First Officer	Cyril Smith
Secretary of Mexican Consulate	Terry La Franconi
The Divers	Pete Desjardins / Ray Twardy / Betty O'Rourke

Act I.—Scene 1—Swimming Pool, J. Foster Adams Estate, Miami Beach, Fla. 2—Airport, Pan-American Airways, Miami. 3—Interior of Airliner. 4—South of the Border. 5.—La Casa de Estrada, Merida, Mexico. 6—Edge of the Forest, Yucatan. 7—The Sacred Pool. Act II.—Scene 1—Street in Merida, Mex. 2—Edge of the Forest, Yucatan. 3—Floating Gardens of Xochimilco, Mexico. 4—Plaza del Toros, Mexico City. 5—Deck of a Cruise Ship. 6—Walking the Plank.

7—Swimming Pool on Adams Estate.
  Staged by Robert Milton; settings by Clark Robinson; comedy scenes directed by William K. Wells; dances by Chester Hale; costumes by John N. Booth, Jr.

A party organized at cocktail hour in Miami starts South in search of a fabled wishing stone. The progress through Mexico and Yucatan to a Malayan jungle is frequently interrupted by hordes of dancing girls, fancy divers and hopeful comedians.

(Closed October 25, 1941)

AS YOU LIKE IT

(8 performances)

A comedy by William Shakespeare with incidental music by Henry Holt. Revived by Ben A. Boyar and Eugene S. Bryden at the Mansfield Theatre, New York, October 20, 1941.

Cast of characters—

Orlando	Alfred Drake
Adam	Ross Matthew
Oliver	Arthur L. Sachs
Dennis	Kenneth Tobey
Charles	Peter Cusanelli
Celia	Carol Stone
Rosalind	Helen Craig
Touchstone	Leonard Elliott
Le Beau	John Lorenz
Duke Frederick	David Leonard
Corin	Harry Sheppard
Silvius	John Call
Jacques	Philip Bourneuf
Amiens	Murvyn Vye
Duke	David Leonard
Audrey	Valentine Vernon
Sir Oliver Martext	James O'Neill
Phoebe	Paula Trueman
William	Kenneth Tobey

Lords, Pages, Foresters, Attendants: Randolph Echols, Wallace House, Florence Winston, John Lund, Allyn Rice, Ruth Krakovska, Doloris Hudson.

Scene: In the Usurper's Court and in the Forest of Arden.

Staged by Eugene S. Bryden; settings and costumes by Lemuel Ayers.

The last previous revival of "As You Like It" on Broadway was that of the Surrey Players in October, 1937. It was done in 1932 by the Shakespeare Repertory Company, in 1930 by the Chicago Civic Repertory and in 1923 by the American National Theatre with Marjorie Rambeau the Rosalind, Ian Keith the Orlando, Jerome Lawlor the Oliver and Walter Abel the Jacques.

(Closed October 25, 1941)

GOOD NEIGHBOR

(1 performance)

A play in three acts by Jack Levin. Produced by Sam Byrd at the Windsor Theatre, New York, October 21, 1941.

Cast of characters—

```
Yankel Barron....................................Gustav Shackt
Hannah..........................................Anna Appel
Heinrich........................................Howard Fischer
Whitey..........................................Albert Vees
Mrs. Jacobs.....................................Edith Shayne
Mrs. Kurtmann...................................Grace Mills
Officer Glydesdale..............................Donald Arbury
Luther..........................................Arthur Anderson
Bessie..........................................Edna Mae Harris
Miss Jolly......................................Helen Carter
Barney..........................................Lewis Charles
Miss Jaffrey....................................Susanne Turner
Western Union Boy...............................Leslie Barrett
Doctor..........................................Henry Sherwood
Hildie..........................................Marcella Powers
Dave............................................Sam Byrd
Leader of the Cavaliers.........................Winfield Smith
Second Cavalier.................................John A. Stearns
```

Act I.—Hannah's Second-Hand Shop in an American City. Acts II and III.—Hannah's Kitchen.
Staged by Sinclair Lewis; settings by Frederick Fox.

Hannah Barron has her problems. Her husband is a hypochondriac. Her son Dave goes to sea and sends her a thousand dollars which she is supposed to save, but which she doles out to suffering neighbors, and her son Barney marries a no-good wife. Dave comes ashore and wants his money to get married. Mama could get it by turning over a half-wit German boy she has hidden in her house to save him from hooded Cavaliers who want to lynch him. But Mama holds to the principles of the Golden Rule and Good Neighborliness. The Cavaliers shoot her, but Dave gets her life insurance and she is content.

(Closed October 21, 1941)

CANDLE IN THE WIND

(95 performances)

A drama in three acts by Maxwell Anderson. Produced by The Theatre Guild, Inc., and The Playwright's Company at the Shubert Theatre, New York, October 22, 1941.

Cast of characters—

```
Fargeau.........................................Philip White
Henri...........................................Benedict MacQuarrie
Deseze..........................................Robert Harrison
```

406 THE BEST PLAYS OF 1941-42

Charlotte	Leona Roberts
Mercy	Nell Harrison
Madeline Guest	Helen Hayes
Maisie Tompkins	Evelyn Varden
Raoul St. Cloud	Louis Borell
German Captain	Harro Meller
German Lieutenant	Knud Kreuger
Col. Erfurt	John Wengraf
Lieut. Schoen	Tonio Selwart
Corporal Behrens	Mario Gang
Madame Fleury	Michelette Burani
M. Fleury	Stanley Jessup
First Guard	Brian Connaught
Second Guard	Ferdi Hoffman
Cissie	Lotte Lenya
Corporal Mueller	Joseph Wiseman
Third Guard	George Andre
Fourth Guard	Guy Moneypenny
Corporal Schultz	William Malten
Captain	Bruce Fernald

Act I.—Scene 1—Garden at Versailles, June, 1940. 2—Pumping Station on Outskirts of Paris, Now Office of Concentration Camp. Act II.—Scenes 1 and 3—Madeline's Apartment in the Plaza Athenae. 1941. 2—Office of Concentration Camp. Act III.—Garden at Versailles.

Staged by Alfred Lunt; production supervised by Lawrence Langner and Maxwell Anderson; settings and lighting by Jo Mielziner.

See page 180.

(Closed January 10, 1942)

THE LAND IS BRIGHT

(79 performances)

A drama in three acts by George S. Kaufman and Edna Ferber. Produced by Max Gordon at the Music Box, New York, October 28, 1941.

Cast of characters—

Blake	Herbert Duffy
Matt Carlock	Jack Hartley
Jesse Andrews	Roderick Maybee
Ollie Pritchard	Grover Burgess
Lacey Kincaid	Ralph Theadore
Tana Kincaid	Martha Sleeper
Deborah Hawks	Ruth Findlay
Ellen Kincaid	Phyllis Povah
Letty Hollister	Flora Campbell
Count Waldemar Czarniko	Arnold Moss
Grant Kincaid	Leon Ames
Flora Delafield	Muriel Hutchison
Dan Frawley	G. Albert Smith
Miss Perk	Edith Russell
Dorset	Walter Beck
Anne Shadd	Louise Larabee
Clare Caron	K. T. Stevens
Linda Kincaid	Diana Barrymore
Wayne Kincaid	Hugh Marlowe
Chauffeur	Norman Stuart
Maid	Elaine Shepard
Jerry Hudson	Robert Shayne
Theodore Kincaid	William Roerick

THE BEST PLAYS OF 1941-42

```
Joe Tonetti..........................................James La Curto
Greta................................................Lili Valenty
Bennet...............................................Russell Conway
Timothy Kincaid......................................Dickie Van Patten
Ellen Hudson.........................................Constance Brigham
Lacey Kincaid........................................John Draper
Bart Hilliard........................................Charles McClelland
Count Waldemar Czarniko II...........................Arnold Moss
```
Acts I, II and III.—Fifth Avenue Home of the Kincaids, New York City.

Staged by George S. Kaufman; setting by Jo Mielziner; costumes by Irene Sharaff.

Lacey Kincaid amassed a fortune of $200,000,000 by various questionable industrial triumphs in the West and founded the Kincaid dynasty. Coming East he built a Fifth Avenue mansion for Ellen, the boarding house keeper's daughter he married, and sought to force his way into New York's social life by buying a decaying French Count for their daughter Tana. The generation of Kincaids that followed Lacey ran with the hounds and hunted with the rats of society, but the third generation, sobered by events leading up to and including the Second World War, were on their way to a social and moral reform at the last curtain.

(Closed January 3, 1942)

* LET'S FACE IT

(263 performances)

A musical comedy in two acts by Herbert and Dorothy Fields, based on "The Cradle Snatchers"; music and lyrics by Cole Porter. Produced by Vinton Freedley at the Imperial Theatre, New York, October 29, 1941.

Cast of characters—
```
Madge Hall...........................................Marguerite Benton
Helen Marcy..........................................Helene Bliss
Dorothy Crowthers....................................Helen Devlin
Anna.................................................Kalita Humphreys
Winnie Potter........................................Mary Jane Walsh
Mrs. Fink............................................Lois Bolton
Mrs. Wigglesworth....................................Margie Evans
Another Maid.........................................Sally Bond
Maggie Watson........................................Eve Arden
Julian Watson........................................Joseph Macaulay
Nancy Collister......................................Vivian Vance
George Collister.....................................James Todd
Cornelia Abigail Pigeon..............................Edith Meiser
Judge Henry Clay Pigeon..............................Fred Irving Lewis
Molly Wincor.........................................Marion Harvey
Margaret Howard......................................Beverly Whitney
Ann Todd.............................................Jane Ball
Phillip..............................................Henry Austin
Jules................................................Tony Caridi
Eddie Hilliard.......................................Jack Williams
Frankie Burns........................................Benny Baker
Muriel McGillicuddy..................................Sunnie O'Dea
```

THE BEST PLAYS OF 1941-42

```
Jean Blanchard..................................Nanette Fabray
Lieutenant Wiggins............................Houston Richards
Jerry Walker......................................Danny Kaye
Gloria Gunther....................................Betty Moran
Sigana Earle...................................Miriam Franklin
Master of Ceremonies...........................William Lilling
Private Walsh.......................................Fred Nay
Dance Team..........................Mary Parker, Billy Daniel
Mrs. Wiggins..................................Kalita Humphreys
```
   Royal Guards: Tommy Gleason, Ollie West, Roy Russell, Ricki Tanzi, Henry Austin, Toni Caridi.
   Vocalists: Marguerite Benton, Helene Bliss, Janice Joyce, Beverly Whitney, Lisa Rutherford, Frances Williams.
   Guests: Billie Dee, Mary Ann Parker, Sally Bond, Jane Ball, Peggy Carroll, Sondra Barrett, Jean Scott, Jean Trybom, Marilynn Randels, Marion Harvey, Miriam Franklin, Peggy Littlejohn, Pat Likely, Zynaid Spencer, Renee Russell, Pamela Clifford, Edith Turgell.
   Selectees: Garry Davis, George Florence, Fred Deming, Dale Priest, Mickey Moore, Jack Riley, Joel Friend, Fred Nay, Frank Ghegan, Randolph Hughes.
   Act I.—Scene 1—The Alicia Allen Milk Farm on Long Island. 2—Service Club at Camp Roosevelt. 3—Parade Grounds. 4—Mrs. Watson's Summer Home, Southampton, L. I. Act II.—Scene 1—Mrs. Watson's Home. 2—Boathouse of Hollyhock Inn. 3—Hollyhock Inn Gardens. 4—Exterior of Inn. 5—Service Club.
   Staged by Edgar MacGregor; dances and ensembles by Charles Walters; music directed by Max Meth; settings by Harry Horner; costumes by John Harkrider.

Maggie Watson, Nancy Collister and Cornelia Pigeon, suspicious of their husbands' hunting trips, invite Jerry Walker, Frankie Burns and Eddie Hilliard from a nearby army camp to come over and help entertain them. Complications ensue when the husbands return and the boys' girl friends show up unexpectedly. The story stems from the farce, "The Cradle Snatchers," a 1925 hit written by Russell Medcraft and Norma Mitchell.

HIGH KICKERS

(171 performances)

A musical comedy in two acts by George Jessel, Bert Kalmar and Harry Ruby from a suggestion by Sid Silvers. Produced by Alfred Bloomingdale at the Broadhurst Theatre, New York, October 31, 1941.

Cast of characters—

—IN THE PROLOGUE—
```
The Candy Spieler........................................Billy Vine
High Kickers Chorus.....................................Themselves
Two American Showgirls.................Joyce Mathews, Rose Teed
Schultz....................................................Joe Marks
Geo. M. Krause, Sr. (Kelly)...........................George Jessel
Sophia....................................................Mary Marlow
The Doctor...............................................Rollin Bauer
George M. Krause, Jr. ..................................Dick Monahan
The Stylish Four........................Shaw, Bay, Young, Griffin
Mamie....................................................Betty Bruce
```

THE BEST PLAYS OF 1941-42

—IN THE PLAY—

Sophie Tucker	Herself
Geo. M. Krause, Jr.	George Jessel
S. Kaufman Hart	Jack Mann
Kitty McKay	Lois January
Jimmy Wilberforce	Lee Sullivan
Frank Whipple	Franklyn Fox
Mayor John Wilberforce	Chick York
Hortense Wilberforce	Rose King
Chief of Police	Jack Howard
Betty	Betty Bruce
Stuart Morgan Dancers	Themselves
Betty Jane	Betty Jane Smith
The Pianist	Ted Shapiro
A Stage Hand	Chaz Chase

Stuart Morgan Dancers

Showgirls: Sunny Ainsworth, Barbara Brewster, Gloria Brewster, Lucille Casey, Bonita Edwards, Eleanor Hall, Joyce Mathews, Betty Stewart, Rose Teed.
Dancing Girls: Jean Anthony, Helen Barrie, Stephenie Cekan, Marilyn Hale, Frances Hammond, Ann Helm, Ellen Howard, Marjorie Jackson, Dorothy Jeffers, Mary-Robin Marlow, Ray McGregor, Bobbie Prieser, Helen Spruill, Marion Warnes.
Boys: Bob Bay, Bob Shaw, Harry Mack, Victor Griffin, Harold Young, Donald Weissmuller.
Act I.—Scene 1—Inside Piners Burlesque Theatre—Year 1910. 2—The High Kickers in Paris. 3—A Dressing Room in the Cellar. 4—Dancing Time Away. 5—Stage Door of a Theatre in Chamberville, U. S. A.—Year 1941. 6—Backstage. 7—The Opening Night. 8—In Panama. 9—Sophie Tucker's Dressing Room. 10—The Strip. Act II.—Scene 1—Courtroom in Chamberville. 2—On the Street Outside the Court. 3—Hotel Lobby. 4—Boudoir of Mrs. Wilberforce. 5—Specialty—Chaz Chase. 6—Outside of Mayor's Estate. 7—In the Garden.
Staged by Edward Sobel; music directed by Val Ernie; dances by Carl Randall; settings by Nat Karson.

George M. Krause, Jr., inherits his father's "High Kickers" burlesque troupe. Sophie Tucker goes along as a sort of guardian and friend. The troupe is arrested in Chamberville, O., but Sophie is able to expose the Mayor's wife as an old trouper and gets them off.

(Closed March 28, 1942)

THE MAN WITH BLOND HAIR

(7 performances)

A play in three acts by Norman Krasna. Produced by Frank Ross at the Belasco Theatre, New York, November 4, 1941.

Cast of characters—

Harry	Coby Ruskin
Matt	Robert Williams
John	Alfred Ryder
Frank Connors	James Gregory
Ruth Hoffman	Eleanor Lynn
Sidney	Curt Conway
Carl	Rex Williams
Sturner	Bernard Lenrow

Mrs. Hoffman..................................Dora Weissman
Messenger Boy................................George Wallach
McCarthy.....................................Francis DeSales
Harvey...Owen Martin

Act I.—Scenes 1 and 2—Roof of East Side Tenement on Summer Evening. 3—The Hoffman Living Room. Acts II and III.—The Hoffman Living Room.

Staged by Norman Krasna; settings by Howard Bay.

Carl and Sturner, German aviators, escape from a prison camp in Canada, get to New York and are picked up by the police. While being held for the Federal government a group of East Side boys, one a rookie policeman, get them out of the police station with the intention of beating them up. Sturner escapes. Carl is given a chance to throw himself off a tenement roof. Ruth Hoffman, hoping to keep her boy friends out of trouble, hides Carl in her Jewish mother's apartment. After two days with the kindly Hoffmans, Carl discovers the truth about American Democracy. Given a chance to shoot it out with police captors he begs for help.

(Closed November 8, 1941)

* BLITHE SPIRIT

(257 performances)

A farce in three acts by Noel Coward. Produced by John C. Wilson at the Morosco Theatre, New York, November 5, 1941. Moved to Booth Theatre, May 18, 1942.

Cast of characters—
Edith..Jacqueline Clark
Ruth..Peggy Wood
Charles..Clifton Webb
Dr. Bradman.......................................Philip Tonge
Mrs. Bradman.....................................Phyllis Joyce
Mrs. Arcati.....................................Mildred Natwick
Elvira..Leonora Corbett

Acts I, II and III.—Living Room of the Charles Condomines House in Kent.

Staged by John C. Wilson; setting by Stewart Chaney.

See page 109.

THE WALRUS AND THE CARPENTER

(9 performances)

A comedy in three acts by A. N. Langley. Produced by Alfred de Liagre, Jr., at the Cort Theatre, New York, November 8. 1941.

Cast of characters—

Corder	Ivan Triesault
Grant Magill	Gordon Oliver
Nurse Pyngar	Mary Boylan
Bickey	Frances Heflin
Essie Stuyvesant	Pauline Lord
Gerda	Karen Morley
Wilfred Marks	Alan Hewitt
Roland Wayne	Harold Landon
Yipper Pickford	Frank Albertson
Doctor Drew	Nicholas Joy
Policeman	Charles Knox

Acts I, II and III.—Living Room of Essie Stuyvesant's House on East 88th Street, New York City.

Staged by Alfred de Liagre; setting by Raymond Sovey.

Essie Stuyvesant is a flibbertigibbet with a family on her hands. Her oldest daughter is about to give birth to her first child. Her youngest daughter is in the throes of a particularly violent calf-love affair. Her sister is gradually discovering that her husband is a cad if not a scoundrel. The rent collector is about to toss Essie and her brood into the street, and the family doctor, an old flame, is hoping Essie will light long enough to consider his proposal of marriage. Everything is settled by curtain time.

(Closed November 15, 1941)

SPRING AGAIN

(241 performances)

A comedy in three acts by Isabel Leighton and Bertram Bloch. Produced by Guthrie McClintic at the Henry Miller Theatre, New York, November 10, 1941. Moved to the Playhouse, January 12, 1942.

Cast of characters—

Halstead Carter	C. Aubrey Smith
Nell Carter	Grace George
Elizabeth	Betty Breckenridge
Edith Weybright	Ann Andrews
Girard Weybright	Richard Stevenson
Millicent Cornish	Jayne Cotter
Tom Cornish	John Craven
Bell Boy	Joe Patterson
Robert Reynolds	Ben Lackland
Dr. Lionel Carter	Robert Keith
Joe Crumb	Michael Strong
L. J. O'Connor	Lawrence Fletcher
A Western Union Boy	George Spelvin, Jr.
William Auchinschloss	Joseph Buloff
Arnold Greaves	William Talman

Acts I, II and III.—Living Room of the Carter's Apartment, in New York City.

Staged by Guthrie McClintic; setting by Donald Oenslager.

Nell Carter has lived with her husband, Halstead, for a good many not too happy years. Nell's chief irritation is Halstead's hero worship of his father, the late General Carter, who did something heroic at Shiloh and has been done into statues and brochures periodically ever since. During one spell of rebellion Nell writes the true history of all the stuffy Carters and sells it as a radio serial. She has to recall it in the end, however, to avoid a family scandal and also to guarantee peace in her own home.

(Closed June 6, 1942)

MACBETH

(131 performances)

A tragedy by William Shakespeare, arranged in two acts and 19 scenes; incidental music by Lehman Engel. Produced by Maurice Evans in association with John Haggott at the National Theatre, New York, November 11, 1941.

Cast of characters—

First Witch..Grace Coppin
Second Witch...Abby Lewis
Third Witch..William Hansen
Duncan, King of Scotland...........................Harry Irvine
Malcolm..Ralph Clanton
Donalbain...William Nichols
Menteith...Ernest Graves
Angus...Philip Huston
Lennox...Erford Gage
Caithness..Walter Williams
Fleance..Alex Courtnay
Sergeant..John Ireland
Ross...Harry Brandon
Macbeth..Maurice Evans
Banquo...Staats Cotsworth
Lady Macbeth.....................................Judith Anderson
A Messenger...John Straub
Seyton..Irving Morrow
A Porter...William Hansen
Macduff..Herbert Rudley
An Old Man..John Parish
A Page..Jackie Ayers
First Murderer......................................John Ireland
Second Murderer.....................................John Straub
Lady Macduff...Viola Keats
Boy...Richard Tyler
A Doctor...Harry Irvine
A Waiting-Gentlewoman..............................Grace Coppin
A Young Soldier....................................Alex Courtnay
Siward, Earl of Northumberland...................Gregory Morton
    Lords, Gentlemen, Gentlewomen, Officers, Soldiers, Attendants and
        Messengers: Evelyn Helmore, Abby Lewis, Ada McFarland,
        Jackie Ayers, John Parish, William Nichols, Melvin Parks, Alfred Paschall.
    Act I.—Scene 1—Desert Place. 2 and 4—Camp Near Forres. 3—A Heath. 5—Room in Macbeth's Castle. 6 and 7—The Castle. Act II.—Scenes 1 and 3—Palace. 2—Park. 4—A Heath. 5—Fife.

Macduff's Castle. 6—Before King's Palace, England. 7—Macbeth's Castle. 8—Country near Dunsinane. 9—Room in Castle. 10—Camp Near Birnam Wood. 11 and 12—The Castle.
 Staged by Margaret Webster; settings by Samuel Leve; costumes by Lemuel Ayers.

Recent revivals of the tragedy of "Macbeth" in New York have been those of Philip Merivale and Gladys Cooper in 1935, Lynn Harding and Florence Reed in 1932. Jack Carter and Edna Thomas played a Negro version in 1936 under WPA auspices, and John Cromwell and Margaret Wycherly gave a single performance in 1937, sponsored by the Barter Theatre.

(Closed February 28, 1942)

THEATRE

(69 performances)

A comedy in three acts by Guy Bolton and Somerset Maugham. Produced by John Golden at the Hudson Theatre, New York, November 12, 1941.

Cast of characters—

Julia Lambert	Cornelia Otis Skinner
Mr. Purkiss	Leon Shaw
Evie	Viola Roache
Michael Gosselyn	Arthur Margetson
Roger Gosselyn	Frederick Bradlee
Tom Fennell	John Moore
Jevons	J. Colvil Dunn
Dolly De Vries	Helen Flint
Lord Charles Temperley	Francis Compton
Avice Crichton	Jane Gordon
A Stage Manager	George Spelvin
Sergeant	Stanley Harrison

Acts I and II.—Living Room of Julia and Michael in Hampstead. Act III.—Scenes 1 and 2—Julia's Dessing Room at Siddons Theatre. 3 The Stage.
 Staged by John Golden; settings by Donald Oenslager.

Julia Lambert, the most popular actress in London, has divorced her actor husband, Michael, but continues to live publicly as his wife. She is worried both about her advancing years and her possible loss of sex appeal. She is anxious that her growing son, Roger, should continue to appear as young as possible, and she deliberately welcomes an affair with her husband's secretary, Tom Fennell, to reassure herself of her continuing attraction for men. Finally, deciding against further experiment, Julia tricks her husband into a remarriage.

(Closed January 10, 1942)

LITTLE DARK HORSE

(9 performances)

A comedy in three acts by Theresa Helburn, adapted from a French comedy by Andre Birabeau. Produced by Donald Blackwell and Raymond Curtis at the Golden Theatre, New York, November 16, 1941.

Cast of characters—

```
Agatha.....................................Wauna Paul
Dr. Roubert................................Rolfe Sedan
Louise Monfavet............................Leona Powers
Madame Onzain..............................Cecilia Loftus
Catherine..................................Anita Magee
Jean-Pierre (Jipe).........................Raymond Roe
Patrick (Patoche)..........................Edmund Abel
Madame Vellenaud...........................Katheryn Givney
Madame Monfavet............................Ann Mason
Emil Onzain................................Walter Slezak
Noel.......................................R. V. Whitaker
François Monfavet..........................Grant Mills
```
Acts I, II and III.—Living Room of the Monfavet House in Provincial France, Some Years Before the Present War.

Staged by Melville Burke; setting by John Koenig; costumes by Frank Spencer.

François Monfavet, living in a provincial French village, is taken suddenly ill. In going through his desk the family discovers that he has been paying tuition for a boy at a military school. They assume the boy is illegitimate, and that, under the circumstances, he should be taken into the family. They send for the boy and discover him to be black. François, the father, had spent three years in the Congo and little Noel is one of the results. A threatened community scandal is averted when Noel is turned over to Emil Onzain, a bachelor uncle.

(Closed November 22, 1941)

RING AROUND ELIZABETH

(10 performances)

A comedy in three acts by Charl Armstrong. Produced by Allen Boretz and William Schorr in association with Alfred Bloomingdale at the Playhouse, New York, November 17, 1941.

Cast of characters—

```
Laurette Carpenter Styles..................Katherine Emmett
Hubert Cherry..............................Herbert Yost
Mercedes...................................Marilyn Erskine
Vida.......................................Ruth Chorpenning
Jennifer...................................Katharine Bard
Elizabeth Cherry...........................Jane Cowl
Irene Oliver...............................Diantha Pattison
Harriet Gilpin.............................Lea Penman
```

THE BEST PLAYS OF 1941-42

```
Ralph Sherry........................................McKay Morris
Andy Blayne........................................Barry Sullivan
Policeman..........................................Gilbert O. Herman
Dr. Hollister......................................Edwin Cooper
```
    Acts I, II and III.—Living Room of Elizabeth Cherry's House, in Small Mid-Western City.
    Staged by William Schorr; setting by Raymond Sovey.

Elizabeth Cherry finds herself revolving closer and closer to a nervous breakdown in her squirrel cage of a home. Suddenly she decides to forget everything and become a stranger to her own family. Amnesia, the doctor calls it. As a stranger Elizabeth is able to straighten out a few family problems before she permits herself to recover.

(Closed November 25, 1941)

*JUNIOR MISS

(246 performances)

A comedy in three acts by Jerome Chodorov and Joseph Fields. Produced by Max Gordon at the Lyceum Theatre, New York, November 18, 1941.

Cast of characters—
```
Harry Graves.......................................Philip Ober
Joe................................................Kenneth Forbes
Grace Graves.......................................Barbara Robbins
Hilda..............................................Paula Laurence
Lois Graves........................................Joan Newton
Judy Graves........................................Patricia Peardon
Fuffy Adams........................................Lenore Lonergan
J. B. Curtis.......................................Matt Briggs
Ellen Curtis.......................................Francesca Bruning
Willis Reynolds....................................Alexander Kirkland
Barlow Adams.......................................John Cushman
Western Union Boy..................................James Elliott
Merril Feurbach....................................Peter Scott
Sterling Brown.....................................Robert Willey
Albert Kunody......................................Jack Manning
Tommy Arbuckle.....................................Walter Collins
Charles............................................Jack Geer
Henry..............................................John Hudson
Haskell Cummings...................................Billy Redfield
```
    Acts I, II and III.—The Graves' Apartment.
    Staged by Moss Hart; setting by Frederick Fox.

See page 145.

WALK INTO MY PARLOR

(29 performances)

A drama in three acts by Alexander Greendale. Produced by Luther Greene at the Forrest Theatre, New York, November 19, 1941.

Cast of characters—

Theresa	Rosina Galli
Ilio	Silvio Minciotti
Salvatore	Duane McKinney
Carmella	Rita Piazza
Gino	Nicholas Conte
Grace	Helen Waren
Nick	Lou Polan
Luigi	Joseph De Santis
Rose	Hildegarde Halliday
Aurora	Rachel Millay
Dadish	Joseph Julian

Acts I, II and III.—Living Room of the Sarellis in an Italian Section of Chicago.

Staged by Luther Greene; setting by Paul Morrison.

The Sarellis family is living precariously in the Italian section of Chicago. Ilio, the father, and his good son, Salvatore, can make no more than $11 a week selling fruit. Gino, a bad boy, goes in for crime, and induces his mother, Theresa, an honest soul but weak, to take up the passing of counterfeit money. Carmella, married to Luigi, loves Gino, and things get depressingly mixed before Gino decides to leave home and mother and reform.

(Closed December 13, 1941)

THE SEVENTH TRUMPET

(11 performances)

A drama in three acts by Charles Rann Kennedy; music by Horace Middleton. Produced by Theatre Associates at the Mansfield Theatre, New York, November 21, 1941.

Cast of characters—

Sam Brodribb	A. G. Andrews
Percival	Peter Cushing
Deborah Broome	Leslie Bingham
Lady Madeleine	Carmen Mathews
Father Bede	Ian Maclaren
Brother Ambrose	Thaddeus Suski
Bomber 666	Alan Handley

Acts I, II and III.—Lawn of a Primitive Chapel of Saint Lazarus, Near Glastonbury, England.

Staged by Charles Rann Kennedy; supervised by Jean Rosenthal; lighting and setting by Jo Mielziner.

Percival, a London bobby who plucked a time bomb off Ludgate Hill at the expense of a shattered body, arrives at Glastonbury, England, the morning after Nazi bomber 666 has blown the Monastery of St. Lazarus to bits. Thereafter Percival, Lady Madeleine, Deborah Broome, Father Bede, Brother Ambrose (from Greece) and Sam Brodribb, all Christian socialists variously advanced, expound the call to faith and an international brotherhood to meet the Nazi menace.

(Closed November 29, 1941)

HOPE FOR A HARVEST

(38 performances)

A drama in three acts by Sophie Treadwell. Produced by The Theatre Guild at the Guild Theatre, New York, November 26, 1941.

Cast of characters—

Mrs. Matilda Martin	Helen Carew
Antoinette Martin	Judy Parrish
Elliott Martin	Fredric March
Carlotta Thatcher	Florence Eldridge
Nelson Powell	John Morny
Victor de Lucchi	Arthur Franz
Billy Barnes	Shelley Hull
Bertha Barnes	Edith King
Joe de Lucchi	Alan Reed
A Woman	Doro Merande

Act I.—Kitchen of Mrs. Martin's House. Acts II and III.—Living Room of the Old Thatcher Ranch-House.

Staged by Lester Vail; supervised by Lawrence Langner and Theresa Helburn; settings by Watson Barratt.

See page 349.

(Closed December 27, 1941)

* SONS O' FUN

(231 performances)

A vaudeville revue in a prologue and two acts by Ole Olsen, Chic Johnson and Hal Block; songs by Jack Yellen and Sam E. Fain. Produced by the Messrs. Shubert at the Winter Garden, New York, December 1, 1941.

Principals engaged—

Ole Olsen	Chic Johnson
Carmen Miranda	Ella Logan
Frank Libuse	Joe Besser
Rosario Perez	Antonio Ruiz
Lionel Kaye	James Little
Ben Beri	Kitty Murray
Valentinoff	Ivan Kirov
Vilma Josey	Stanley Ross
Margaret Brander	Milton Charleston
Richard Craig	Martha Rawlins
Catherine Johnson	Eddie Davis
Moran & Wiser	Parker & Porthole
Watson & O'Rourke	Carter & Bowie
Statler Twins	Mullen Twins
Crystal Twins	Blackburn Twins

The Pitchmen: Al Ganz and Al Meyers.
The Biltmorettes: Edna Isenburg, Joan Baker and Beverly Sweet.

Staged and lighted by Edward Duryea Dowling; supervised by Harry Kaufman; dances directed by Robert Alton; settings by Raoul Pene Dubois.

After three years of the Olsen and Johnson "Hellzapoppin," this "Sons o' Fun" might just as well have been called "More of the Same."

TWELFTH NIGHT

(15 performances)

A comedy in a prologue and two acts by William Shakespeare; music by Joseph Wood. Revived by The Chekhov Theatre Players at the Little Theatre, New York, December 2, 1941.

Cast of characters—

```
Viola..............................................Beatrice Straight
Sea Captain.............................................Frank Rader
Sebastian............................................Ronald Bennett
2nd Sea Captain.....................................Charles Barnett
Orsino...................................................John Flynn
Curio................................................Nelson Harrell
Valentine..........................................Lester Bacharach
Sir Toby Belch..........................................Ford Rainey
Maria..............................................Mary Haynsworth
Sir Andrew Aguecheek..................................Hurd Hatfield
Feste................................................Alan Harkness
Malvolio...............................................Sam Schatz
Olivia.............................................Mary Lou Taylor
Fabian.................................................Youl Bryner
```
Servants: Daphne Moore, Eleanor Barrie, Alfred Boylen, Margaret Boylen, and Penelope Sack.

Prologue—Seacoast of Ilyria. Act I.—Scene 1—Apartment in Duke's Palace. 2—Street Before Olivia's House. 3 and 6—Room in Duke's Palace. 4—Room in Olivia's House. 5—Cellar in Olivia's House. 7—Olivia's Garden. Act II.—Scene 1—Street Before Olivia's House. 2—A Prison. 3—Room in Olivia's House.

Staged by Michael Chekhov and George Shdanoff; settings and costumes by Michael Chekhov.

A stylized staging of the Shakespearean comedy which is well known to the college campuses of the West and Middle West.

(Closed December 13, 1941)

SUNNY RIVER

(36 performances)

A musical comedy in two acts by Oscar Hammerstein, 2nd; music by Sigmund Romberg. Produced by Max Gordon at the St. James Theatre, New York, December 4, 1941.

Cast of characters—

```
Children..........Carol Renee, Joan Shepherd, Edwin Bruce Moldow
Old Henry.............................................Richard Huey
Gabriel Gervais....................................Ainsworth Arnold
```

THE BEST PLAYS OF 1941-42

```
Mother Gervais..................................Ivy Scott
Jean Gervais...................................Bob Lawrence
Jim............................................Donald Clark
Harry..........................................George Holmes
Emil...........................................Gordon Dilworth
Emma...........................................Vicki Charles
Lolita.........................................Ethel Levey
Aristide.......................................Oscar Polk
George Marshall................................Dudley Clements
Judge Pope Martineau...........................Frederic Persson
Marie Sauvinet.................................Muriel Angelus
Daniel Marshall................................Tom Ewell
Cecilie Marshall...............................Helen Claire
Madeleine Caresse..............................Joan Roberts
Martha.........................................Peggy Alexander
Specialty Dancer...............................Jack Riano
Specialty Dancer...............................Miriam LaVelle
Achille Caresse................................William O'Neal
The Drunk......................................Howard Freeman
```

Act I.—Scene 1—Levee Street, New Orleans. 1806. 2—Patio of the Cafe des Oleandres. 3—Upstairs Sitting Room of M. and Mme. Jean Gervais. 1911. 4—Jean's Dressing Room. 5—Reception Hall. Act II.—Scene 1 and 3—Patio of Cafe des Oleandres. 2—Levee Street.

Staged by Oscar Hammerstein, 2nd.; dances by Carl Randall; settings by Stewart Chaney; costumes by Irene Sharaff.

Marie, with a voice, was making her way with the other girls at Lolita's place called the Cafe des Oleandres when Jean Gervais, a highborn young man, fell in love with her. This so greatly upset Cecilie Marshall, who hoped to marry Jean, that she told Marie she (Cecilie) and Jean had been lovers for ages. Marie thereupon took a loan of $5,000, ran away to Paris, became a great opera singer and came back to sing Jean into subjection a second time. They were about to continue the old love when Cecilie was found fainting on their doorstep and they gave up.

(Closed January 3, 1942)

*ANGEL STREET

(224 performances)

A drama in three acts by Patrick Hamilton. Produced by Shepard Traube at the Golden Theatre, New York, December 5, 1941.

Cast of characters—
```
Mrs. Manningham................................Judith Evelyn
Mr. Manningham.................................Vincent Price
Nancy..........................................Elizabeth Eustis
Elizabeth......................................Florence Edney
Rough..........................................Leo G. Carroll
```
Acts I, II and III.—House on Angel Street, Pimlico District of London. 1880.

Staged by Shepard Traube; setting and costumes by Lemuel Ayers; lighting by Feder.

See page 282.

GOLDEN WINGS

(6 performances)

A drama in three acts by William Jay and Guy Bolton. Produced by Robert Milton at the Cort Theatre, New York, December 8, 1941.

Cast of characters—

Pam	Margot Stevenson
Bessie	Valerie Cossart
John, Acting Flight Lieutenant	Lowell Gilmore
Jane, a Member of the W.A.A.F.	Cathleen Cordell
Joe, an Aircraftsman	Edmond Stevens
Geoffrey ⎫	Hughie Green*
Babe ⎬ Pilot Officers	Peter Boyne
Winks ⎪	William Rykey
Norman ⎭	Gerald Savory
Rex, Flight Lieutenant	Lloyd Gough
Tom, Pilot Officer	Gordon Oliver
Judith, a Flyer in the Ferry Service	Signe Hasso
Kay, a Farmerette in the Land Service	Fay Wray
Wing-Commander Forbes	Evan Thomas
Hunt, a Pilot Officer	William Packer
Dillon ⎫ Newspaper Men	J. W. Austin
Jepson ⎭	Len Mence

Acts I, II and III.—Lounge of Chilgrove Service Club. December, 1940.

Staged by Robert Milton; setting by Watson Barratt.

* On leave of absence from the Royal Canadian Air Force.

Rex and Tom are fliers in the RAF. Rex, an aristocrat on the loose, takes a fancy to Tom's girl, Judith. Judith doesn't mind, but Rex's fiancée, Kay, feels pretty bad about it. Rex and Tom work up to a fight in which Tom strikes Rex, his superior officer. The fight is patched up, but Rex advises Tom to keep out of range of his guns the next time they are in the air. In the next fight Tom is killed. Rex swears he had forgotten all about the quarrel once he was tailing Heinkels, but a court-martial and a scandal threaten.

(Closed December 12, 1941)

BROOKLYN, U.S.A.

(57 performances)

A drama in three acts by John Bright and Asa Bordages. Produced by Bern Bernard and Lionard Stander at the Forrest Theatre, New York, December 21, 1941.

Cast of characters—

The Dasher	Tom Pedi
Smiley Manone	Eddie Nugent

THE BEST PLAYS OF 1941-42

```
Nick Santo.........................................Victor Christian
Josephine..........................................Irene Winston
Si Ornitz..........................................Ben Ross
Lena Rose .........................................Adelaide Klein
Louis Cohen........................................Martin Wolfson
A Customer.........................................Lou Leif
Willie Berg........................................Sidney Lumet
Mike Zubriskie.....................................Robert H. Harris
Jean...............................................Julie Stevens
McGill.............................................Byron McGrath
Philadelphia.......................................Henry Lascoe
Tony Mazzini.......................................David Pressman
Albert.............................................Roger De Koven
A Guard............................................Eli Siegel
```
  Act I.—Scene 1—Section of Brooklyn Waterfront. 2—Brooklyn Candy Store. 3—Brooklyn Barber Shop. Act II.—The Candy Store. Act III.—Scene 1—Pre-execution Cells in Sing Sing. 2—Candy Store.
  Staged by Lem Ward; settings by Howard Bay.

  Nick Santo is a comparatively innocent and honest representative of organized labor whom the bosses want put out of the way. They engage Smiley Manone's mob to do the job. Nick is murdered in a barber's chair. Smiley and the mob are eventually rounded up by an honest and persistent District Attorney. (Plot and details have been credited to a Brooklyn murder syndicate known to the press as "Murder, Inc.," which District Attorney William O'Dwyer recently ran into Sing Sing.)

(Closed February 7, 1942)

PIE IN THE SKY

(6 performances)

  A comedy by Bernadine Angus. Produced by Edgar MacGregor and Lyn Logan at the Playhouse, New York, December 22, 1941.

Cast of characters—
```
Monte Trenton, Jr. ................................Oscar Shaw
Vera Trenton.......................................Luella Gear
Nellie.............................................Marjorie Peterson
Dan Harmon.........................................Ben Laughlin
Art Winton.........................................Lucian Self
Roger Montgomery Trenton, III......................Herbert Evers
Sylvia Kent........................................Leona Powers
Corinne Bassett....................................Enid Markey
Suzy Bransby.......................................Barbara Arnold
Lily de Lacy.......................................Lyn Logan
Pepino Rodrigo.....................................Kirk Alyn
Mr. Sterling.......................................Ted Emery
Homer Bassett......................................Herbert Corthell
William Taylor.....................................Bram Nossen
Emile LeBeau.......................................Rafael Corio
```
  Acts I, II and III.—Living Room of the Trenton Residence, Fifth Avenue, New York City.
  Staged by Edgar MacGregor; setting by Donald Oenslager.

The Monte Trentons are practically bankrupt. If they can marry their personable son, Roger, to Lily de Lacy, a man hunter with a lot of widow money, they can be saved. Could have happened if Roger hadn't preferred brunettes.

(Closed December 27, 1941)

LETTERS TO LUCERNE

(23 performances)

A drama in three acts by Fritz Rotter and Allen Vincent. Produced by Dwight Deere Wiman at the Cort Theatre, New York, December 23, 1941.

Cast of characters—

Olga Kirinski	Sonya Stokowski
Gustave	Alfred A. Hesse
Erna Schmidt	Grete Mosheim
Gretchen Linder	Beatrice De Neergaard
Hans Schmidt	Carl Gose
Margarethe	Lilia Skala
Mrs. Hunter	Katherine Alexander
Bingo Hill	Nancy Wiman
Felice Renoir	Mary Barthelmess
Sally Jackson	Phyllis Avery
Marion Curwood	Faith Brook
Francois	Kenneth Bates
Koppler	Harold Dyrenforth

Act I.—Scene 1—The Main Hall. 2—A Dormitory. Act II.—Scene 1—The Main Hall. 2—The Dormitory. Act III.—The Main Hall. Staged by John Baird; settings by Raymond Sovey.

See page 212.

(Closed January 10, 1942)

BANJO EYES

(126 performances)

A musical comedy in two acts by Joe Quillan and Izzy Elinson, from a play by John Cecil Holm and George Abbott; lyrics by John La Touche and Harold Adamson; music by Vernon Duke. Produced by Albert Lewis at the Hollywood Theatre, New York, December 25, 1941.

Cast of characters—

Miss Clark	Jacqueline Susann
Mr. Carver	E. J. Blunkall
Erwin Trowbridge	Eddie Cantor
Sally Trowbridge	June Clyde
Harry, the Bartender	Richard Rober
Charlie	Bill Johnson
Ginger	Virginia Mayo

```
The De Marcos........................Sally and Tony De Marco
Patsy................................................Lionel Stander
Frankie................................................Ray Mayer
Mabel.............................................Audrey Christie
Tommy.............................................Tommy Wonder
The General..........................................John Ervin
The Captain........................................James Farrell
The Filly.....................................Ronnie Cunningham
"Banjo Eyes"..................................Mayo and Morton
The Quartette.....................George Richmond, Phil Shafer,
                                Doug Hawkins, Geo. Lovesee
```

Act I.—Scene 1—The Display Salon of Carver Greeting Card Co. 2—Bar in Midtown Hotel. 3 and 5—Mabel's Room. 4—The Dream Pastures. Act II.—Scene 1—Bar. 2 and 4—Erwin's Home, Jackson Heights. 3—Dream Pastures. 5—Camp Dixon. 6—Clubhouse, Belmont Park. 7—Grandstand, Belmont Park.

Staged and lighted by Hassard; book directed by Albert Lewis; dances by Charles Walters; settings by Harry Horner; costumes by Irene Sharaff.

Erwin Trowbridge is the greeting card salesman who figured out a system of beating the races in "Three Men on a Horse." In "Banjo Eyes," an adaptation of that comedy, he gets his information in dreams that take him to the stables of the racers. The horses give him the tips on condition that he will not gamble. Erwin is practically shanghaied by a gang of touts and has a lot of trouble before it is time to call it an evening.

(Closed April 12, 1942)

CLASH BY NIGHT

(49 performances)

A drama in two acts and seven scenes by Clifford Odets. Produced by Billy Rose at the Belasco Theatre, New York, December 27, 1941.

Cast of characters—
```
Jerry Wilenski...........................................Lee J. Cobb
Joe W. Doyle...........................................Robert Ryan
Mae Wilenski....................................Tallulah Bankhead
Peggy Coffey.....................................Katherine Locke
Earl Pfeiffer..................................Joseph Schildkraut
Jerry's Father...................................John F. Hamilton
Vincent Kress.......................................Seth Arnold
Mr. Potter.......................................Ralph Chambers
Tom...................................................Art Smith
A Waiter...........................................William Nunn
A Man...............................................Harold Grau
Abe Horowitz..................................Joseph Shattuck
An Usher.....................................Stephan Eugene Cole
```

Acts I and II. Wilenski Home, Staten Island, New York. Summer of 1941.

Staged by Lee Strasberg; settings by Boris Aronson.

Mae Wilenski is fed up with life and her husband, the cloddish but honest Jerry Wilenski. When Earl Pfeiffer, a fairly dashing young motion picture projectionist, comes to board with the Wilenskis Mae, after a short struggle, decides to submit to his advances. Jerry, sluggishly awakening to the situation, stalks Earl to his projection booth and strangles the life out of him.

(Closed February 7, 1942)

IN TIME TO COME

(40 performances)

A drama in prologue and seven scenes by Howard Koch and John Huston. Produced by Otto Preminger at the Mansfield Theatre, New York, December 28, 1941.

Cast of characters—

Woodrow Wilson	Richard Gaines
Edith Bolling Wilson	Nedda Harrigan
Captain Stanley	Randolph Preston
Tumulty	William Harrigan
Colonel House	Russell Collins
Judge Brandeis	Bernard Randall
Dillan	James Gregory
Terry	Harold J. Kennedy
Smith	Philip Coolidge
Price	Edgar Mason
Gordon	Robert Gray
Dr. Cary Grayson	Alexander Clark
Henry White	John M. Kline
Professor Seymour	Maurice Burke
Signor Orlando	Vincenzo Rocco
Signor Martino	Joseph Quaranto
Monsieur Pichon	Arnold Korff
Sonino	Rene Roberti
Clemenceau	Guy Sorel
Lloyd George	Harold Young
Senator Lodge	House Jameson

Prologue—Congress in Joint Session, April 6, 1917. Scenes 1, 6 and 7—President Wilson's Study in the White House, Washington, D. C. 2—An Enclosed Deck Reserved to American Delegation on S.S. *George Washington* Approaching Brest Harbor. 3 and 5—Living Room in House Occupied by the President Near Parc Monceau. 4—Conference Room at Quai Dorsay. The action ends on March 4, 1921.

Staged by Otto Preminger; settings by Harry Horner; costumes by John Koenig.

See page 34.

(Closed January 31, 1942)

THE FIRST CROCUS

(5 performances)

A comedy in three acts by Arnold Sundgaard. Produced by T. Edward Hambleton at the Longacre Theatre, New York, January 2, 1942.

Cast of characters—

Henrik Jorislund	Edwin Philips
Inga Jorislund	Martha Hedman
Avis Jorislund	Barbara Engelhart
Milford Jorislund	Eugene Schiel
Lars Hilleboe	Lewis Martin
Ansgar Jorislund	Herbert Nelson
Herman Nelson	Hugo Haas
Violet Melby	Jocelyn Brando
John Hanson	Jack Parsons
Trygve Knutsen	Clarence Nordstrom
Miss Engebretsen	Joan Croydon
Mrs. Jens Oppedal	Elizabeth Moore
Alfred Oppedal	Harry Maull
Sigvald Pickett Nordahl	Robert Pastene
Paul Johnson	Charles Furcolowe
Richard Johnson	Milton Karol
Borghild Jensen	Connie Maull
Muriel Fevold	Josephine McKim

Acts I and III.—The Jorislund Living Room in Albion, Minnesota. Act II.—Scene 1—The Albion Schoolhouse. 2—The Jorislund Living Room.

Staged by Halsted Welles; settings by Johannes Larsen.

Inga Jorislund is determined that her children shall become persons of social consequence in the new world to which the Jorislunds are devoted. She is temporarily defeated in her ambitions when her youngest son, Milford, cheats himself into a school prize given to the student who finds the first crocus in the Spring and is exposed, and when her daughter, Avis, becoming disgusted with being too rigidly ruled at home, determines to leave home and live her own life elsewhere. Inga also borrows money from the school fund, which her husband has to sell his overcoat to pay back before a scandal results. Only mother's ambition survives the defeats.

(Closed January 6, 1942)

PAPA IS ALL

(63 performances)

A comedy in three acts by Patterson Greene. Produced by Theatre Guild, Inc., at the Guild Theatre, New York, January 6, 1942.

Cast of characters—

Mama	Jessie Royce Landis
Jake	Emmett Rogers
State Trooper Brendle	Royal Beal
Emma	Celeste Holm
Mrs. Yoder	Dorothy Sands
Papa	Carl Benton Reid

Acts I, II and III.—Kitchen of the Aukamp Farmhouse, North of Lancaster, Pa.

Staged by Frank Carrington and Agnes Morgan; supervised by Lawrence Langner and Theresa Helburn; setting and costumes by Emeline Roche.

Papa is a Hitler in the home. He won't let Mama go to the movies. He won't let Emma have a beau. He won't let Jake study engineering. When he discovers that Emma has sneaked out with a boy he goes gunning for the boy. Jake gets the family Ford stalled on a railroad track, whacks Papa over the head with a wrench and leaves his body in an empty freight car. When the Ford is demolished he reports that Papa is "all" (meaning dead in Pennsylvania German). There is much happiness until Papa turns up again. Finally the law closes in on Papa and he is definitely "all" for at least a few years.

(Closed February 28, 1942)

JOHNNY ON A SPOT

(4 performances)

A comedy in three acts by Charles MacArthur, from a story by Parke Levy and Alan Lipscott. Produced by John Shubert at the Plymouth Theatre, New York, January 8, 1942.

Cast of characters—

Cameraman	Jack Brainard
McClure	Arthur Marlowe
Danny	William Foran
Ben Kusick	Paul Huber
Creeper	Sanford Bickert
Julie Glynn	Edith Atwater
Heeler	Tom Morrison
Doc Blossom	Will Geer
Nicky Allen	Keenan Wynn
Salesman	Jack McCauley
Barbara Webster	Florence Sundstrom
Lucius	Olvester Polk
Colonel Wigmore	Michaell Harris
Mayor Lovett	Charles Olcott
Pepi Pisano	Tito Vuolo
Pearl Lamonte	Dennie Moore
Judge Webster	Joseph Sweeney
Chronicle Reporter	Richard Karlan
Chronicle Cameraman	Burton Mallory
Chief of Police	G. Swayne Gordon
Sergeant of State Troopers	John O'Malley
Flanagan	Harry Meehan
Warden	Ben Roberts
Dapper	Garnay Wilson
Captain of State Troopers	Phil Sheridan

Acts I, II and III.—The Governor's Office in a Southern State.
Staged by Charles MacArthur; setting and costumes by Frederick Fox.

Nicky Allen is campaign manager for the Governor of a Southern State who is trying to get himself elected to the U. S. Senate. On the eve of the election the Governor, an alcoholic, passes out in the resort of his favorite trollop. Later Nicky learns that the Governor is dead and the rest of his day is given over to getting the body out of the bordello and into the state house, that his patron may die decently and be buried with dignity.

(Closed January 10, 1942)

THE LADY COMES ACROSS

(3 performances)

A musical comedy in two acts by Fred Thompson and Dawn Powell; music and lyrics by Vernon Duke and John LaTouche. Produced by George Hale in association with Charles R. Rogers and Nelson Seabra at the 44th Street Theatre, New York, January 9, 1942.

Cast of characters—

```
Jill Charters..................................Evelyn Wyckoff
Tony Patterson................................Ronald Graham
Otis Kibber...................................Joe E. Lewis
Elmer James...................................Morton L. Stevens
Mary..........................................Betty Douglas
Alberto Zorel.................................Stiano Braggiotti
4 Shoppers....................................The Martins
Mrs. Riverdale................................Ruth Weston
Campbell......................................Gower (Champion)
Kay...........................................Jeanne (Tyler)
Babs Appleway.................................Wynn Murray
Ernie Bustard.................................Mischa Auer
Baroness Helstrom.............................Helen Windsor
Ballerina Comique.............................Eugenia Delarova
Ballerina.....................................Lubov Rostova
The Phantom Lover.............................Marc Platt
```
  Models: Betty Douglas, Evelyn Carmel, Patricia Donnelly, Judith Ford, Dorothy Partington, Arline Harvey, Joan Smith, Drucilla Strain.
  Autograph Seekers, Reporters, Guests, Etc.
  Act I.—Scene 1—A Railroad Station. 2—Jill's Room in a Hotel. 3—Blue Room at Chez Zoral. 4—Red Room. Act II.—Scene 1—At Mrs. Riverdale's Estate. 2—On Way to Bathing Pavilion. 3—Bathing Pavilion. 4—After the Party. 5—Bedroom. 6—Garden. 7—Railroad Station.
  Staged by Romney Brent; choreography by George Balanchine; settings and costumes by Stewart Chaney; production under supervision of Morrie Ryskind.

Jill Charters dreams she is a spy and when she awakens, by golly, she is a spy. Her adventures involve several distressed comedians and a few comediennes, including Ruth Weston, who has to hide the papers in her girdle.

(Closed January 10, 1942)

THE RIVALS

(54 performances)

A comedy in two acts by Richard Brinsley Sheridan with songs and lyrics by Arthur Guiterman and Macklin Marrow. Produced by The Theatre Guild at the Shubert Theatre, New York, January 14, 1942.

Cast of characters—

Lydia Languish	Haila Stoddard
Lucy	Helen Ford
Julia	Frances Reid
Mrs. Malaprop	Mary Boland
Sir Anthony Absolute	Walter Hampden
Captain Absolute	Donald Burr
Faulkland	Robert Wallsten
Acres	Bobby Clark
Boy	Walt Draper
Sir Lucius O'Trigger	Philip Bourneuf
David	Horace Sinclair
Footman	George Boots
Footman	William Whitehead

Act I.—Scenes 1 and 4—Mrs. Malaprop's Lodgings. 2—Captain Absolute's Lodgings. 3—The North Parade. 5—Acres' Lodgings.
Act II.—Scenes 1 and 3—Mrs. Malaprop's Lodgings. 2—The North Parade. 4—King Mead Fields. Bath.

Staged by Eva Le Gallienne; production under supervision of Theresa Helburn and Lawrence Langner; settings and costumes by Watson Barratt.

A major revival of "The Rivals" was made by the Players' Club in 1922, with Francis Wilson as Acres, Mary Shaw as Malaprop and Tyrone Power as Sir Anthony. In 1923 the Equity Players staged a revival, again with Miss Shaw and Mr. Wilson, Maclyn Arbuckle playing the Sir Anthony. Minnie Maddern Fiske organized a "Rivals" company in 1924-25 with herself as Malaprop, James T. Powers as Acres and Tom Wise as Sir Anthony. Again in 1930 she played Malaprop to the Acres of Powers and the Sir Anthony of John Craig.

(Closed February 28, 1942)

ALL IN FAVOR

(7 performances)

A comedy in three acts by Louis Hoffman and Don Hartman. Produced by Elliott Nugent, Robert Montgomery and Jesse Duncan at the Henry Miller Theatre, New York, January 20, 1942.

Cast of characters—

Tony	Ralph Brooke
Wack Wack (Harry McDougal)	Raymond Roe
Weasel	Arnold Stang
Flip	Bob Readick
Marco (Lover)	Leslie Barrett
Mr. Piper	Frank Conlan
Peewee (Edgar McDougal)	Tommy Lewis
Helen	Gloria Mann
Jean	Claire Frances
Cynthia	Frances Heflin
Bixby	J. C. Nugent
Gorman	James R. Waters
Officer Callahan	Harry Antrim
The Professor ⎫	Milton Herman
Sasha ⎪	Hank Wolf
Myron ⎬ (Radio Voices)	Freddie Geffen
Raymond ⎪	George Spelvin, Jr.
Young Lady ⎭	Joy Geffen

Acts I, II and III.—Club Revel, Washington Heights, New York.
Staged by Elliott Nugent; setting by Samuel Leve.

Harry (Wack Wack) McDougal and a gang of his Washington Heights pals in New York organize a Club Revel. Running into debt for their basement rooms they decide to take in a few girls to help the treasury. Cynthia, one of the girls, loses her purse, can't get back to Brooklyn and stays the night in the club rooms with Wack Wack. From the perfectly innocent adventure scandal threatens which, added to continued financial difficulties, is about to break up the club when Wack Wack's younger brother, Peewee, wins the jackpot at a radio quiz show.

(Closed January 24, 1942)

JASON

(125 performances)

A drama in three acts by Samson Raphaelson. Produced by George Abbott at the Hudson Theatre, New York, January 21, 1942.

Cast of characters—

Miss Crane	Ellen Hall
Violet	Eulabelle Moore
Messenger	Nicholas Conte
Jason Otis	Alexander Knox
Lisa Otis	Helen Walker
George Bronson	Raymond Greenleaf
Bill Squibb	William Niles
Humphrey Crocker	E. G. Marshall
Nick Wiggins	Abraham Knox
Mr. Kennedy	Tom Tully
Mrs. Kennedy	Edna West

Acts I, II and III.—Living-Room of the New York Home of Jason Otis.
Staged by Samson Raphaelson; setting by John Root.

430   THE BEST PLAYS OF 1941-42

Jason Otis is a dramatic critic. Mike Ambler (Messenger) is a slightly wacky playwright who loves humanity. Mike has a play accepted and seeks out Jason to explain its meaning. Jason would throw Mike out of his house if he could, but Mike is tenacious. He not only stays on, but he makes love to Jason's wife. The night Mike's play is produced Jason catches Mrs. Jason in the playwright's arms. In spite of which he writes an honest (and favorable) criticism of Mike's play.

(Closed May 9, 1942)

BOSTON COMIC OPERA COMPANY—JOOSS BALLET DANCE THEATRE

(63 performances)

Presenting a repertory of Gilbert and Sullivan operettas and Kurt Jooss dance drama. Produced by the Messrs. Shubert at the St. James Theatre, New•York, beginning January 21, 1942.

H.M.S. PINAFORE

(18 performances)

Cast of characters—

The Rt. Hon. Sir Joseph Porter, K.C.B. ....Florenz Ames
Captain Corcoran................................Bertram Peacock
Ralph Rackstraw....................................Morton Bowe
Dick Deadeye.......................................Robert Pitkin
Bill Bobstay...John Henricks
Bob Becket..Edward Platt
Tommy Tucker........................Master Arthur Henderson
Josephine..Kathleen Roche
Cousin Hebe..Margaret Roy
Little Buttercup.....................................Helen Lanvin
First Lord's Sisters, His Cousins, His Aunts, Sailors, Marines, Etc.
  Scene: The Quarterdeck of H.M.S. *Pinafore,* Off Portsmouth, England.
  Staged by R. H. Burnside; music directed by Louis Kroll.

THE GREEN TABLE

A dance drama in eight scenes by Kurt Jooss; music by Frederic Cohen.

Cast of characters—

Death..Rolf Alexander
The Standard-Bearer.................................Jack Gansert
The Old Soldier.....................................Jack Skinner
The Woman..Bunty Slack
The Old Mother....................................Eva Leckstroem
The Young Soldier.................................Henry Shwarz
The Young Girl..................... ....Noelle de Mosa
The Profiteer..Hans Zullig
  Directed by Kurt Jooss; costumes by H. Heckroth.

THE MIKADO

(February 3, 1942)

(19 performances)

Cast of characters—

The Mikado of Japan	Robert Pitkin
Nanki-Poo	Morton Bowe
Ko-Ko	Florenz Ames
Poo-Bah	Bertram Peacock
Pish-Tush	Frederic Persson
Yum-Yum	Kathleen Roche
Pitti-Sing	Mary Roche
Peep-Bo	Margaret Roy
Katisha	Helen Lanvin

Chorus of School Girls, Nobles, Guards and Coolies.

Act I.—Courtyard of Ko-Ko's Palace in Titipu. Act II.—Ko-Ko's Gardens in Titipu.

THE BIG CITY

Cast of characters—

The Young Girl	Noelle de Mosa
The Young Workman	Hans Zullig
The Libertine	Jack Gansert

Scene 1—The Street. 2—The Workers' Quarters. 3—The Dance Halls.

Costumes by H. Heckroth. Ballet by Kurt Jooss. Music by Alexander Tansman.

A BALL IN OLD VIENNA

Cast of characters—

The Debutante	Ulla Soederbaum
Her Admirer	Hans Zullig
Her Aunts	Elsa Kahl, Bunty Slack
The Eligible Young Man	Lucas Hovinga
His Sweetheart	Noelle de Mosa
The Dancing Master	Henry Shwarz
His Partner	Eva Leckstroem
Dancing Couples	Lydia Kocers, Jack Skinner, Joy Bolton-Carter, Alfredo Corvino, Marguerite De Anguera, Jack Gansert

Scene—Vienna in the 1840's.

Staged by Leon Greanin; costumes by Aino Sllmola. Choreography by Kurt Jooss. Music by Joseph Lanner; arranged by Frederic Cohen.

THE PIRATES OF PENZANCE

(February 17, 1942)

(11 performances)

Cast of characters—

The Pirate King	Bertram Peacock
Samuel	Frederic Persson
Frederic	Morton Bowe

```
Major-General Stanley..................................Florenz Ames
Sergeant of Police.....................................Robert Pitkin
Mabel................................................Kathleen Roche
Edith...................................................Mary Roche
Kate..................................................Margaret Roy
Isabel................................................Marie Valdez
Ruth..................................................Helen Lanvin
General Stanley's Wards; Pirates and Police.
    Act I.—A Rocky Seashore on the Coast of Cornwall. Act II.—A
Ruined Chapel by Moonlight.
```

THE PRODIGAL SON

Cast of characters—

```
The Father............................................Jack Skinner
The Mother..............................................Elsa Kahl
The Son.............................................Rolf Alexander
The Mysterious Companion.............................Jack Gansert
The Young Queen...................................Noelle de Mosa
The Seductress........................................Bunty Slack
Two Harlots...................Joy Bolton-Carter, Lydia Kocers
    Young Men and Women, Mob: Alfredo Corvino, Lucas Hovinga,
    Lydia Kocers, Eva Lekstroem, Alida Mennen, Peter Michael,
    Lavina Nielson, Marguerite de Anguera, Henry Shwarz, Ulla
    Soederbaum, Richard G. Wyatt, Hans Zullig, Jack Dunphy.
    Staged by Kurt Jooss; costumes by Dimitri Bouchene. Legend in
dance by Kurt Jooss. Music by Frederic Cohen.
```

IOLANTHE

(February 23, 1942)

(5 performances)

Cast of characters—

```
The Lord Chancellor..................................Florenz Ames
Earl of Mountararat..................................Robert Pitkin
Lord Tolloller........................................Morton Bowe
Private Willis...................................Frederic Persson
Strephon.............................................Phillip Tully
Queen of the Fairies................................Helen Lanvin
Iolanthe............................................Margaret Roy
Celia..................................................Mary Roche
Fleta................................................Marie Valdez
Phyllis.............................................Kathleen Roche
    Fairies—Peers.
    Act I.—An Arcadian Landscape. Act II.—Palace Yard, West-
minster. Date—Between 1700 and 1882.
```

TRIAL BY JURY

(February 28—March 1, 1942)

(7 performances)

Cast of characters—

```
Judge................................................Florenz Ames
Plaintiff..............................................Mary Roche
Counsel for Plaintiff..............................Bertram Peacock
Defendant...........................................Phillip Tully
```

Foreman of Jury..............................Frederic Persson
Usher..Robert Pitkin
  Chorus of Bridesmaids, Jury and Spectators.
  Scene—A Court of Justice.
  Followed by H.M.S. *Pinafore*.

THE GONDOLIERS

(March 3, 1942)

(3 performances)

Cast of characters—

  The Duke of Plaza-Toro..........................Florenz Ames
  Luiz...Phillip Tully
  Don Alhambra Bolero............................Robert Pitkin
  Marco Palmieri..................................Morton Bowe
  Giuseppe Palmieri............................Bertram Peacock
  Antonio...Edward Platt
  Francesco....................................Lawrence Shindel
  Giorgio......................................Frederic Persson
  The Duchess of Plaza-Toro........................Helen Lanvin
  Casilda...Margaret Roy
  Gianetta.......................................Kathleen Roche
  Tessa..Mary Roche
  Fiametta.......................................Marie Valdez
  Vittoria..Phyllis Blake
  Giulia..Mary Lundon
  Inez..Florence Keezel
    Act I.—The Piazzetta, Venice. Act II.—The Pavilion in the Palace of Bataria.

(Closed March 14, 1942)

*PORGY AND BESS

(165 performances)

A folk opera in three acts by DuBose Heyward; music by George Gershwin; lyrics by DuBose Heyward and Ira Gershwin, founded on play by DuBose and Dorothy Heyward. Revived by Cheryl Crawford at the Majestic Theatre, New York, January 22, 1942.

Cast of characters—

  Maria..Georgette Harvey
  Lily..Helen Dowdy
  Annie.......................................Catherine Ayers
  Clara...Harriett Jackson
  Jake..Edward Matthews
  Sportin' Life....................................Avon Long
  Mingo..Jimmy Waters
  Robbins..Henry Davis
  Serena...Ruby Elzy
  Jim..Jack Carr
  Peter..Robert Ecton
  Porgy..Todd Duncan
  Crown...Warren Coleman
  Bess..Anne Brown

1st Policeman..................................William Richardson
2nd Policeman....................................Paul Du Pont
Detective..Gibbs Penrose
Undertaker..John Garth
Frazier.................................J. Rosamund Johnson
Nelson..William Bowers
Strawberry Woman................................Helen Dowdy
Crab Man..William Woolfolk
Coroner..Al West
    Residents of Catfish Row, Fishermen, Children, Stevedores, Etc.
  The Eva Jessye Choir.
    Act I.—Scene 1—Catfish Row. 2—Serena's Room. Act II.—Scenes 1 and 3—Catfish Row. 2—A Palmetto Jungle. 4—Serena's Room. Act III.—Catfish Row.
    Staged by Robert Ross; settings by Herbert Andrews; costumes by Paul du Pont.

A dramatization of Du Bose Heyward's "Porgy," made by the author and his wife, Dorothy, was produced by the Theatre Guild in New York October 10, 1927, with Frank Wilson in the name part. On the same date in 1935 an operatic version was produced, also by the Guild, at the Alvin Theatre, New York, with Todd Duncan as Porgy and Anne Brown as Bess. The drama had 231 performances, the opera 120. Including an engagement in London Wilson played the rôle of Porgy 850 times.

CAFE CROWN

(141 performances)

A comedy in three acts by H. S. Kraft. Produced by Carly Wharton and Martin Gabel at the Cort Theatre, New York, January 23, 1942.

Cast of characters—

Customer..Mervin Williams
Rubin...Jed Cogut
Sam..Jay Adler
Kaplan..Alfred White
Mendel Polan......................................Daniel Ocko
Jacobson...Frank Gould
Mrs. Perlman......................................Paula Miller
Hymie...Sam Jaffe
Looie..Lou Polan
Walter...Whitner Bissell
Beggar...Solen Burry
Toplitz...Eduard Franz
Lester Freed....................................Sam Wanamaker
Norma Cole...Mary Mason
Ida Polan...Mitzi Hajos
David Cole...................................Morris Carnovsky
George Burton....................................George Petrie
Lipsky..Robert Leonard
Anna Cole......................................Margaret Waller
Florist...Michael Gorrin
Messenger Boy......................................Tom Jordan
    Acts I, II and III.—Cafe Crown, Theatrical Restaurant on Second Avenue, New York City.
    Staged by Elia Kazan; setting by Boris Aronson.

David Cole, for years the leader of the Yiddish Theatre in New York, returns to his old haunts in Second Avenue after a considerable absence, following quarrels with his wife and daughter. He has a play for which he is seeking backing. Hymie, the busboy at the Cafe Crown, who has previously put his savings into all the Cole ventures, agrees to help with the new play until he discovers it is a modernized version of Shakespeare's "King Lear." No more Shakespeare for Hymie. Backing is found, Hymie relents, the play goes into rehearsal and the Cole family is reunited.

(Closed May 23, 1942)

* GUEST IN THE HOUSE

(129 performances)

A drama in three acts by Hagar Wilde and Dale Eunson. Produced by Stephan and Paul Ames at the Plymouth Theatre, New York, February 24, 1942.

Cast of characters—

```
Ann Proctor........................................Louise Campbell
Lee Proctor..........................................Joan Spencer
Hilda................................................Hildred Price
The Rev. Dr. Shaw...................................Walter Beck
Aunt Martha Proctor..........................Katherine Emmet
Miriam Blake.........................................Pert Kelton
Dan Proctor........................................William Prince
Douglas Proctor......................................Leon Ames
John...............................................Oscar Sterling
Evelyn Heath.....................................Mary Anderson
Frank Dow........................................Richard Barbee
Mrs. Dow...........................................Helen Stewart
Miss Rhodes.......................................Frieda Altman
Cam Tracy.....................................J. Robert Breton
```
Acts I, II and III.—Living Room of Proctor Home Near Trumbull, Connecticut.
Staged by Reginald Denham; setting by Raymond Sovey.

Evelyn Heath is taken in by her relatives, the Douglas Proctors. Presumably she is suffering from a heart ailment. Deliberately she plays on the sympathies of Mr. Proctor, causing him to take to drink and neglect his work. This brings about an inharmonious home condition that starts Mrs. Proctor toward a nervous breakdown and sets little 10-year-old Joan copying Evelyn's neurotic invalidism. When the Proctors finally decide to be rid of Evelyn, she tears open her blouse and calls the authorities to witness that she has been attacked by Mr. Proctor. In the end Evelyn is a victim of one of her own traps.

LILY OF THE VALLEY

(8 performances)

A drama in three acts by Ben Hecht. Produced by Gilbert Miller at the Windsor Theatre, New York, January 26, 1942.

Cast of characters—

Smaley	Edmund Dorsey
Butch	David Kerman
Beitler	Charles Mendick
Andy Miller	Joseph Pevney
Joe	Will Lee
Man	Paul R. Lipson
Lieutenant Balboa	Clay Clement
Bum	John Philliber
Emma Jolonick	Minnie Dupree
Mag	Alison Skipworth
Blakie Gagin	Richard Taber
Frances	Katharine Bard
Shorty	Myron McCormick
Willie	David Hoffman
Annie	Grania O'Malley
Mr. Whittleson	Eugene Keith
Rev. Swen Houseman	Siegfried Rumann
Mike	John Shellie

Acts I, II and III.—Office of Lieutenant Balboa in the County Morgue, New York City.

Staged by Ben Hecht; setting and lighting by Harry Horner.

Lieutenant Balboa, in charge of the County Morgue in New York, is discussing with Andy Miller, official photographer, the recent collection of unclaimed dead. As they talk the deceased file solemnly into the Lieutenant's office. A fire in a nearby Bowery Mission sends the Rev. Swen Houseman in search of shelter. He is the only one to whom the shades are visible. When he sets up his paraphernalia for a regular nightly gospel meeting the shades are his audience and give their life's testimony. A miser among the dead reveals the hiding place of his savings; the Rev. Houseman recovers the money; a morgue attendant murders Houseman for the money and is headed for the chair.

(Closed January 31, 1942)

SOLITAIRE

(23 performances)

A comedy in two acts by John Van Druten from a novel by Edwin Corle. Produced by Dwight Deere Wiman at the Plymouth Theatre, New York, January 27, 1942.

Cast of characters—

Celia	Anna Franklin
Virginia Stewart	Pat Hitchcock
Claire Ensley	Joan McSweeney
Mrs. Stewart	Sally Bates

THE BEST PLAYS OF 1941-42

```
Mr. Stewart..........................................Ben Smith
Ben................................................Victor Kilian
Gosh.............................................Harry Gresham
Tex..................................................Tony Albert
Heavy............................................Howard Smith
Dean............................................Frederic Tozere
First Officer.......................................Blair Davies
Second Officer.................................Charles George
Third Officer....................................Robert Gilbert
Ryland..........................................John D. Seymour
```
    Act I.—Scenes 1 and 5—The Stewarts' House and Garden in Pasadena, California. 2, 3 and 4—The Arroyo. Act II.—Scenes 1 and 3—The Arroyo. 2 and 4—The Stewarts' House.
    Staged by Dudley Digges; settings by Jo Mielziner.

Virginia Stewart, aged 12, meets Ben, a philosophic drifter, on a streetcar the day Ben is taking a pet rat back to his shack at the bottom of the arroyo below the Stewarts' bungalow. Fascinated by the adventure, Virginia goes to call on Ben and the rat. A warm, understanding friendship springs up between them and is happily continued until the rougher element in the arroyo, led by Dean, a communistic tramp, brings the law down on the drifters and gets Ben arrested with the others. Virginia's father pays Ben's fine and sends him on his way.

(Closed February 14, 1942)

HEDDA GABLER

(12 performances)

A drama in three acts by Henrik Ibsen; translated by Ethel Borden and Mary Cass Canfield. Revived by Luther Greene at the Longacre Theatre, New York, January 29, 1942.

Cast of characters—
```
Miss Juliana Tesman......................Margaret Wycherly
Berta...........................................Octavia Kenmore
George Tesman...................................Ralph Forbes
Hedda Tesman.................................Katina Paxinou
Mrs. Elvsted......................................Karen Morley
Judge Brack...................................Cecil Humphreys
Eilert Lovborg...................................Henry Daniell
```
    Acts I, II and III.—The Tesmans' Drawing-Room.
    Staged by Luther Greene; setting by Paul Morrison.

Other recent revivals of "Hedda Gabler" have been modernized adaptations of the Ibsen text. One of recent importance was that of Alla Nazimova in 1936, with Harry Ellerbe playing Tesman, Edward Trevor the Lovborg, McKay Morris the Judge Brack and Viola Frayne the Mrs. Elvsted. This ran for 32 performances at the Longacre Theatre in New York and met with considerable success on tour. Other recent Heddas include Eva Le Gallienne, who played Hedda through the middle 1930s, Blanche Yurka in 1929, Emily Stevens in 1926.

(Closed February 7, 1942)

THE FLOWERS OF VIRTUE

(4 performances)

A comedy in three acts by Marc Connelly. Produced by Cheryl Crawford at the Royale Theatre, New York, February 5, 1942.

Cast of characters—

Ezequiel	Leon Belasco
Tomasina	Maria Morales
Sheldon Williams	Jess Barker
Rafael Garcia	Charles Bell
Carlotta Garcia	Isobel Elsom
Paco Perez	Peter Beauvais
General Orijas	Vladimir Sokoloff
Maude Bemis	Kathryn Givney
Tona	Carmelita Fortson
Serafina	Maria Ferreira
Nancy Bemis	Virginia Lederer
Grover Bemis	Frank Craven
Trinidad Perez	S. Thomas Gomez
Colonel Gomez	Samson Gordon
First Orijista	William Roerick
Second Orijista	Jose Willie
Third Orijista	Kumar Goshal
Fourth Orijista	Tony Mannino

Acts I, II and III.—Carlotta's Garden in Las Flores de la Virtud, Mexico.

Staged by Marc Connelly; setting by Donald Oenslager.

Grover Bemis has been working for months as a dollar-a-year man in Washington, trying to stimulate interest in the defense of the United States. He suffers a nervous breakdown and his family takes him to the little town of Las Flores de la Virtud in Southern Mexico to get back his health. There he runs into General Orijas, just out of jail, who is starting a Hitlerian putsch with which he hopes to eliminate the honest leader of the people, Trinidad Perez, and reduce the inhabitants to slavery. Grover Bemis takes a hand. Through his knowledge of electrical machinery he is able to start the power plant General Orijas has crippled. The natives accept this as a miracle and the General is given the heave-ho.

(Closed February 7, 1942)

OF V WE SING

(76 performances)

A topical revue in two acts and twenty-five scenes, lyrics by Alfred Hayes, Lewis Allen, Roslyn Harvey, Mike Stratton, Bea Goldsmith, Joe Barian and Arthur Zipser; music by Alex North, George Kleinsinger, Ned Lehack, Beau Bergersen, Lou Cooper and Toby Sacher; sketches by Al Geto, Sam D. Locke and Mel

THE BEST PLAYS OF 1941-42

Tolkin. Produced by American Youth Theatre in association with Alexander Cohen at Concert Theatre, New York, February 11, 1942.

Principals engaged—

Adele Jerome	Phil Leeds
Lee Barrie	Perry Bruskin
Betty Garrett	John Wynn
Susanne Remos	Buddy Yarus
Eleanore Bagely	Daniel Nagrin
Letty Stever	Curt Conway
Mary Titus	John Flemming
Connie Baxter	Robert Sharron
Ann Garlan	Byron Milligan

Staged by Perry Bruskin, music directed by Lou Cooper, dance directed by Susanne Remos.

A semi-professional revue produced first as "V for Victory" in September, 1941, at the Malin Studio Theatre.

(Closed April 25, 1942)

HEART OF A CITY

(28 performances)

A drama in three acts by Lesley Storm. Produced by Gilbert Miller at the Henry Miller Theatre, New York, February 12, 1942.

Cast of characters—

Judy	Gertrude Musgrove
Frenchie	Jean McNally
Betty	Terry Fay
Bubbles	Virginia Bolen
Diana	Leone Wilson
Ann	Cora Smith
Pamela	Augusta Roeland
Toni	Margot Grahame
George	Skelton Knaggs
Valerie	Frances Tannehill
Patsy	Caroline Bergh
Rosalind	Beverly Roberts
Joan	Virginia Peine
Leo Saddle (L.S.)	Dennis Hoey
Tommy	Romney Brent
Mrs. Good	Bertha Belmore
Anna	Miriam Goldina
Gloomy	Victor Beecroft
First Pilot Officer	Peter Boyne
Second Pilot Officer	Bertram Tanswell
Third Pilot Officer	Fred Stewart
Czech Officer	Richard Stevens
Fourth Pilot Officer	Edward Langley
June	Harda Normann
Fifth Pilot Officer	John Ireys
Bob	Rodney Stewart
Polish Officer	Jonathan Harris
Wing Commander	Robert Whitehead
Group Captain	Austin Fairman
Sergeant	Louis Meslin

Paul Lundy..Richard Ainley
 Act I.—The Star Dressing Room of Windmill Theatre, London.
Act II.—Scene 1—Officers' Mess at Bomber Station and The Field.
2 and 3—The Dressing Room. Act III.—The Dressing Room.
 Staged by Gilbert Miller; settings by Harry Horner.

Judy of the Windmill Theatre, "the little theatre in Shaftesbury Avenue that carried on through the great London blitz," is in love with Tommy, a song writer. Tommy, for his part, loves Rosalind, the leading lady, who finds out quite suddenly that she loves Paul, a handsome R.A.F. flyer she meets at a camp concert. Rosalind and Paul are married, Judy and Tommy are killed in a bombing. Life and the show at the little Windmill Theatre go on.

(Closed March 7, 1942)

THEY SHOULD HAVE STOOD IN BED

(11 performances)

A comedy in three acts by Leo Rifkin, Frank Tarloff and David Shaw. Produced by Sam H. Grisman in association with Alexander H. Cohen at the Mansfield Theatre, New York, February 13, 1942.

Cast of characters—

Al Hartman...Grant Richards
Barney Snedeker....................................Jack Gilford
Sam Simpkins.......................................Sanford Meisner
Mr. Cooper...LeRoi Operti
Harry Driscoll.....................................Russell Morrison
Vivian Lowe..Florence Sundstrom
Henry Angel..Edwin Philips
George Jensen......................................John Call
Julius P. Chatfield................................Richard Irving
A Policeman..Robert Williams
Killer Kane..Tony Canzoneri
Mike Gilroy..William Foran
Peggy Chatfield....................................Katherine Meskill
Announcer..Randolph Preston
Referee..Arnold Spector
First Man..George Matthews
Second Man...Martin Ritt
Third Man..Norman Budd
Hornblower...Topper Jordan
 Acts I and II.—An Office in New York City. Act III.—Scene 1—The Garden. 2—The Office.
 Staged by Luther Adler; settings by Samuel Leve.

Al Hartman and a group of associate promoters are seeking to induce Killer Kane, a title-holding pugilist, to lend his name to a restaurant for which they will furnish a chef named Henry Angel. A further scheme to raise money is to match Henry, the chef, with Kane, the pugilist, for a fight in which Kane will "take a dive" and his backers will clean up. With Kane and Henry both determined to lose the fight matters become complicated, not to say confused.

(Closed February 21, 1942)

PLAN M

(6 performances)

A play in three acts by James Edward Grant. Produced by Richard Aldrich and Richard Myers at the Belasco Theatre, New York, February 20, 1942.

Cast of characters—
```
Private Stuart.........................................Guy Spaull
Private Russell...................................Thaddeus Suski
Orderly Horton.........................................A. P. Kaye
Mrs. Bodleigh.......................................Joanna Duncan
Marjorie Barr..........................................Anne Burr
Colonel Clegg.......................................Stapleton Kent
Wing Commander Rambeau..............................Ellieo Irving
Mrs. Barr..........................................Margery Maude
Rear Admiral Spring................................Charles Gerrard
Brigadier Husted...................................Neil FitzGerald
General Sir Hugh Winston..............................Len Doyle
Dr. Hawes.........................................Lumsden Hare
Colonel Corliss...................................Douglas Gilmore
Private Thurston..................................Lathrop Mitchell
Private McCoy.....................................Edward LeComte
Sir Ethan Foy........................................Stuart Casey
Admiral Farnsworth..............................Reynolds Denniston
```
Acts I, II and III.—General Hugh Winston's Headquarters, War Office, London, England.
Staged by Marion Gering; setting by Lemuel Ayers.

Gen. Sir Hugh Winston, British chief of staff, has been taking electric cabinet treatments under the direction of Dr. Hawes. On an appointed day Dr. Hawes locks Sir Hugh in the cabinet, places a cyanide of potassium gag in his mouth, and turns the British War Office over to Colonel Corliss and other German agents. Colonel Corliss's chief assistant turns out to be an exact physical duplicate of Sir Hugh. The substitute Sir Hugh takes command, substitutes a false "Plan M" for that being held to meet a German invasion and brings the invasion to the verge of a complete success.

(Closed February 23, 1942)

UNDER THIS ROOF

(17 performances)

A drama in three acts by Herbert Ehrmann. Produced by Russell Lewis and Rita Hassan at the Windsor Theatre, New York, February 22, 1942.

Cast of characters—

Granny Warren	Louise Galloway
Abner Warren	George L. Spaulding
Cornelia Warren	Barbara O'Neil
Ezra Warren	Russell Hardie
Horace Drury	Howard St. John
Nora	Hilda Bruce
Gibeon Warren	Peter Hobbs
David Warren	John Draper
Mr. Gassaway	Harlan Briggs
Senator Flower	Watson White
Eileen O'Shaughnessy	Alexandra Brackett
Shawn O'Shaughnessy	Walter Burke
Sidney Snow	James O'Neill

Acts I, II and III.—Living Room of Farm House Built by Zebulon Warren During the 1770's Outside of Boston and Near Wachussett.

Staged by Russell Lewis; setting by Perry Watkins; costumes by Ernest Shrapps.

Abner Warren had two sons, Ezra and Gibeon. In 1846 Gibeon, inspired by the radicals who were supporting the abolitionists, decided to cast his lot with the fight for freedom. Cornelia Warren, who had planned on marrying Gibeon, decided radicals were nothing to wait for and married his brother Ezra instead. In 1864 the son, David, born to Cornelia and Ezra, decides also to fight for liberty, joins the forces of the North in Missouri Territory, and is later killed in the Battle of the Wilderness. After the war Ezra gets mixed up in a crooked transcontinental railway deal, and finally crashes in the panic of 1873. Cornelia decides she will stand by Ezra.

(Closed March 7, 1942)

A KISS FOR CINDERELLA

(48 performances)

A comedy in three acts by Sir James M. Barrie. Produced by Cheryl Crawford and Richard Krakeur in association with John Wildberg and Horace Schmidlapp, at the Music Box Theatre, New York, March 10, 1942.

Cast of characters—

Mr. Bodie	Cecil Humphreys
Policeman	Ralph Forbes
Miss Thing	Luise Rainer
Mr. Jennings	Victor Morley
Mrs. Maloney	Emily Loraine
Marion	Doris Patston
Coster	Le Roi Operti
Gladys	Abby Bonime
Delphine	Elizabeth Leland
Ching Ching	Marilyn Chu
Gretchin	Patsy O'Shea
Godmother	Edith King

THE BEST PLAYS OF 1941-42

—AT THE BALL—
Courtiers: Elinor Breckenridge, Helen Kramer, Jean Reeves, Lukas Hovinga, John Taras, Robert Wilson
Pages...................................Victor Chapin, Fred Hunter
Lord Mayor.....................................Victor Morley
Lord Times...................................Roland Bottomley
Censor..Glen Langan
King..Cecil Humphreys
Queen..Ivy Troutman
Prince...Ralph Forbes
Beauties: Jacqueline Gately, Blanche Faye, Olga Daley, Doris Hughes, Beatrice Cole.
Venus...Eunice Lee
Bishop..Le Roi Operti

Ellen..Jacqueline Gateley
Dr. Bodie..Edith King
Danny...Glen Langan
Nurse..Sarah Burton
Act I.—Mr. Bodie's Studio in London. Act II.—Scene 1, 3 and 5—Street. 2—Celeste et Cie. 4—The Ball. Act III.—Dr. Bodie's Home in the Country.
Staged by Lee Strasberg; settings by Harry Horner; choreography by Catherine Littlefield; costumes by Paul du Pont.

Miss Thing, a little London drudge, decides during the first World War that she can best help Britain by adopting an assortment of war orphans. She collects boards to build pens for them so they may be safely left when she goes out to work. The police become suspicious and the policeman on her street decides to make an investigation. After his visit Miss Thing is romantically interested in her memory of him. The night she tells the children she is going to Cinderella's ball she falls asleep in her doorway, is all but frozen to death, and in her delirium dreams that she is Cinderella and that her Policeman is her Prince. In the hospital later she learns the truth, but is made happy with a pair of glass slippers. Maude Adams first played "A Kiss for Cinderella" at the Empire Theatre, New York, December 25, 1916.

(Closed April 18, 1942)

*PRIORITIES OF 1942

(209 performances)

A variety show assembled by Clifford C. Fischer; ensemble music and lyrics by Marjery Fielding and Charles Barnes. Presented by Clifford C. Fischer by arrangement with the Messrs. Shubert at the 46th St. Theatre, New York, March 12, 1942.

Principals engaged—

Lou Holtz
Willie Howard
Phil Baker and
 Paul Draper
Joan Merrill

Hazel Scott
Helen Reynolds Skaters
The Nonchalants
Gene Sheldon and
 Loretta Fischer

444 THE BEST PLAYS OF 1941-42

   The Barrys   Diane Denise
   Johnny Masters and   Lari and Conchita
    Rowena Rollins   Beverley Lane
  Choreography by Marjery Fielding; music directed by Lou Forman.

JOHNNY 2 x 4

(65 performances)

A melodrama in three acts by Rowland Brown. Produced by Rowland Brown at the Longacre Theatre, New York, March 16, 1942.

Cast of characters—

Creepy	Lester Lonergan, Jr.
Pete	Lew Eckels
Bottles	Yehudi Wyner
Mike Maloney	Ralph Chambers
Johnny 2 x 4	Jack Arthur

 The Yacht Club Boys: Charles Adler, George Kelly, Rod McLennan, Don Richards.

Laundry Man	Frank Verigun
Coaly Lewis	Barry Sullivan
Beetle-Puss	Bert Reed
Mary Collins	Evelyn Wyckoff
Dutch	Jack Lambert
Martin	Arthur L. Sachs
Mabel	Isabel Jewell
Knuckles Kelton	Harry Bellaver
Butch	Marie Austin
Rudy Denton	Douglas Dean
Burns	Sam Raskyn
Ohio Customer	Eddie Hodge
Midal	Bert Frohman
Apples	Leonard Sues
Billy the Booster	James La Curto
Harry, a Waiter	Al Durant
Cigarette Girl	Monica Lewis
Maxine	Karen Van Ryn
Dot	Wilma Drake
Jerry Sullivan	Russel Conway
Kean	Thom Conroy
Bottles, Grown Up	Lance Elliott

 The B Girls: Marianne O'Brien, Muriel Cole, Irene Charlott, Josi Johnson, Natalie Draper, Carolyn Cromwell.
 Acts I, II and III.—Johnny 2 x 4 Club in Greenwich Village. 1926-1933.
 Staged by Anthony Brown; setting by Howard Bay.

In the flush prohibition period "Johnny 2 x 4" opened a speakeasy for the sale of liquor to thirsty violators of the law in Greenwich Village, New York. He was given his name because of his skill playing a 2 x 4 portable piano. Shortly Johnny ran into trouble, principally with the beer racketeers. Then his gangster friends fell into the habit of getting themselves shot up and trying to hide out in his night club. Finally the worst of his gangster enemies was bumped off by a sympathetic horn player. Johnny started in 1926 and went out in 1936, with repeal.

(Closed May 9, 1942)

THE BEST PLAYS OF 1941-42

NATHAN THE WISE

(28 performances)

A drama in two acts and eight scenes adapted by Ferdinand Bruckner from a play by Gotthold Ephraim Lessing. Produced by Erwin Piscator in association with the Messrs. Shubert at the Belasco Theatre, New York, April 3, 1942.

Cast of characters—
Nathan..Herbert Berghof
Daja..Bettina Cerf
Rahel...Olive Deering
A Knight Templar..............................Alfred Ryder
A Lay Brother.................................Ross Matthew
The Patriarch.................................Gregory Morton
The Sultan Saladin............................Bram Nossen
Monks...........................Liebert Wallerstein, Jack Bittner

Act I.—Scenes 1, 3 and 4—Courtyard of Nathan's House. Act II.—Scene 1—Cloister. 2—Palace of Sultan. 3—Courtyard of Nathan's House. 4—Judgment Room in Palace of Sultan.

Staged by James Light; settings by Cleon Throckmorton; costumes by Rose Bogdanoff.

Rahel, daughter of Nathan the Jew, is saved from a burning building by a Knight Templar from Germany, held as a prisoner by the Sultan Saladin in the Third Crusade. The young people fall desperately in love. When the Templar learns by Nathan's confession that Rahel is really a Christian reared as a Jew he is horrified to the point of seeking the advice of the Church. Death, according to the Christian law, should be Nathan's punishment. Saladin sits in judgment on both Christian and Jew, hears Rahel plead for Nathan's life, which shames the Templar into a broader tolerance and permits the joining of the lovers.

"Nathan the Wise" was produced at the Studio Theatre, New York, by the New School for Social Research, March 11, 1942, and ran for 11 performances before being transferred to the Belasco. The Ferdinand Bruckner version is in a free English verse, and represents a fairly drastic cutting of the Lessing classic.

(Closed April 25, 1942)

THE MOON IS DOWN

(71 performances)

A drama in two parts and eight scenes by John Steinbeck. Produced by Oscar Serlin at the Martin Beck Theatre, New York, April 7, 1942.

Cast of characters—

Dr. Winter	Whitford Kane
Joseph	Joseph Sweeney
Sergeant	Edwin Gordon
Captain Bentick	John D. Seymour
Mayor Orden	Ralph Morgan
Madame Orden	Leona Powers
Corporal	Charles Gordon
Colonel Lanser	Otto Kruger
George Corell	E. J. Ballantine
Annie	Jane Seymour
Soldier	Kermit Kegley
Major Hunter	Russell Collins
Lieutenant Prackle	Carl Gose
Captain Loft	Alan Hewitt
Lieutenant Tonder	William Eythe
Soldier	Victor Thorley
Molly Morden	Maria Palmer
Alex Morden	Philip Foster
Will Anders	George Keane
Tom Anders	Lyle Bettger

Part I.—The Drawing-Room of the Mayor's House in a small Mining Town. Part II.—Scenes 1, 3 and 4—The Drawing-Room. 2—Living-Room of Molly Morden's House.

Staged by Chester Erskin; settings by Howard Bay.

See page 72.

(Closed June 6, 1942)

AUTUMN HILL

(8 performances)

A drama in three acts by Norma Mitchell and John Harris. Produced by Max Liebman at the Booth Theatre, New York, April 13, 1942.

Cast of characters—

Gussie Rogers	Beth Merrill
Mary Barton	Dorrit Kelton
Bob Ferguson	William Roerick
Judge Hendricks	Clyde Franklin
Tony Seldon	Jack Effrat
Julie Smith	Elizabeth Sutherland
Al	Robert Williams
Frank	James Gregory

Acts I, II and III.—Living Room of Remodeled Colonial Dwelling in a New England Village.

Staged by Ronald Hammond; setting by Lemuel Ayers; lighting by Feder.

Gussie Rogers has lived as companion to Matilda Hatfield for twenty years, expecting to be left something when Matilda passes. After Matilda's death it is discovered she has left no will. A nephew, Tony Seldon, moves in to collect his inheritance as next of kin. The lonely Gussie grows fond of Tony, but he, being a crook, sets up a counterfeiting plant in the basement of the Hatfield house while waiting for a court decision. With discovery imminent Tony kills a man and Gussie kills Tony to keep him from being sent to the electric chair.

(Closed April 18, 1942)

YESTERDAY'S MAGIC

(55 performances)

A drama in three acts by Emlyn Williams. Produced by The Theatre Guild at the Guild Theatre, New York, April 14, 1942.

Cast of characters—
Mrs. Banner.................................Brenda Forbes
Barty.......................................Patrick O'Moore
Fan..Cathleen Cordell
Bevan......................................James Monks
Maddoc Thomas.............................Paul Muni
Cattrin....................................Jessica Tandy
Robert.....................................Alfred Drake
Mrs. Lothian...............................Margaret Douglass
   Acts I, II and III. Room at the top of a House in Long Acre, London, W.C.2.
   Staged by Reginald Denham; production under supervision of Theresa Helburn and Lawrence Langner; setting by Watson Barratt.

Maddoc Thomas in his day was a great actor on the London stage, but the liquor got him. For eight years he suffered a succession of failures that brought him finally to impersonating Santa Claus in the Selfridge department store. His loyal daughter, Cattrin, sticks by him and, when he is offered a small straight part in a musical comedy, helps him back on his feet. This touch of success impells Cochran, the famous manager, to give Maddoc a chance to revive King Lear as a test of his ability to come back. Before his first performance Maddoc hears that Cattrin, feeling that her father will soon be re-established on the stage, is planning to marry and go to America. The shock sends Maddoc back to the bottle, and finally to his death.

(Closed May 30, 1942)

WHAT BIG EARS

(8 performances)

A comedy in three acts by Jo Eisinger and Judson O'Donnell. Produced by L. Daniel Blank and David Silberman at the Windsor Theatre, New York, April 20, 1942.

Cast of characters—
Jean Martin...............................Ruth Weston
Joey Smithers.............................Edwin Philips

448 THE BEST PLAYS OF 1941-42

Gabby Martin	Taylor Holmes
Lucas	Owen Martin
Betty Leeds	Joy Geffen
Milford	Ralph Bunker
McCall	Owen Lamont
The Professor	Reynolds Evans
Muldoon	George Church
Police Lieutenant	Herbert Duffy
Olympe Grogan	Ethel Morrison
Dr. Treadle	Hans Robert
Brewster	Frederick Howard

Nick Dennis, Sterling Mace, Pitt Herbert, Royal Rompel, Louis Charles, Warren Goddard, Tom Daly.

Act I.—A Furnished Room in Los Angeles. Act II.—A Victorian Cottage in Beverly Hills. Act III.—Room in Hotel Savoy, New York.

Staged by Arthur Pierson; settings by Horace Armistead; costumes by Kenn Barr.

Joey Smithers used to dress up as an old lady and act as a stooge for Gabby Martin the time they were running a patent medicine pitch at the carnivals. Going broke in Hollywood Joey gets a day's work as an extra by again getting into his make-up. The picture people are impressed to the point of offering him a contract to play Whistler's Mother. The explosion occurs when the bankers summon the little old lady (Joey) to New York.

(Closed April 25, 1942)

KEEP 'EM LAUGHING

(77 performances)

A variety show assembled by Clifford C. Fischer; sketches by Arthur Pierson and Eddie Davis. Produced by Clifford C. Fischer by arrangement with the Messrs. Shubert at the 44th Street Theatre, New York, April 24, 1942.

Principals engaged—

William Gaxton
Hildegarde
Zero Mostel
Fred Sanborn
Miriam La Velle
Shirley Paige
Peggy French
Jack Tyler
Victor Moore
Paul and Grace Hartman
Stuart Morgan Dancers
Jack Cole and Dancers
Kitty Mattern
The Bricklayers
Al White Beauties
George E. Mack
Phil Romano and His Orchestra

Staged by Clifford Fischer; settings and draperies by Frank W. Stevens.

(Closed May 28, 1942)

CANDIDA

(27 performances)

A comedy in three acts by George Bernard Shaw. Revived by the American Theatre Wing War Service, Inc., for the benefit of the Army Emergency Fund and the Navy Relief Society for four matinees and one evening performance at the Shubert Theatre, New York, April 27, 1942.

Cast of characters—

Miss Proserpine Garnett	Mildred Natwick
Alexander Mill	Stanley Bell
James Mavor Morell	Raymond Massey
Mr. Burgess	Dudley Digges
Candida	Katharine Cornell
Eugene Marchbanks	Burgess Meredith

Acts I, II and III.—Sitting Room in St. Dominic's Parsonage in the Northeast Suburb of London.

Staged by Guthrie McClintic; setting and costumes by Woodman Thompson.

Katharine Cornell first played "Candida" in 1924, revived it in 1937, and played the Shaw heroine this year as a benefit for both Army and Navy relief associations. This particular cast of volunteers represents what many insist is the greatest company to appear in the comedy in America. Other American Candidas have included Dorothy Donnelly, Peggy Wood, Ellen Von Volkenberg and Hilda Spong.

(Closed May 31, 1942)

THE LIFE OF REILLY

(5 performances)

A comedy in three acts by William Roos. Produced by Day Tuttle and Harald Bromley at the Broadhurst Theatre, New York, April 29, 1942.

Cast of characters—

Johnny Ramsay	George Mathews
Snake Foote	John Call
Mike	Norman Tokar
Rocket Reilly	Peter Hobbs
Hankins	Len Hollister
Frank	Francis Nielsen
Jackie Moultrie	Glenda Farrell
Smitty	John Shellie
Horace Moultrie	Loring Smith
Miss Collins	Theodora Bender
Mildred Walker	Charita Bauer
Harriet	Guerita Donnelly
Miss Hook	Polly Walters
Cooper	Howard Smith

Act I.—Writing Room on Mezzanine, Crescent Hotel, Brooklyn, N. Y. Acts II and III.—Scene 1—The Moultries' Room. 2—Rocket's Room.

Staged by Roy Hargrave; settings by Samuel Leve.

Rocket Reilly is the star southpaw of the Brooklyn Dodgers. He has been suspended for several days, but is to be allowed to pitch a crucial game against the N. Y. Giants. Rocket is under the influence of a fortune teller, who insists that he is going to commit a murder before midnight the day before the game. Just to oblige, Rocket does shoot a gambler and insists on being arrested. The Brooklyn police refuse to keep him from the game and give him the third degree in an effort to force him to deny the crime. Rocket insists on dying to prove his belief in capital punishment. He is finally restrained, and the man he shot comes to life.

(Closed May 2, 1942)

HARLEM CAVALCADE

(49 performances)

A Negro vaudeville show assembled and produced by Ed Sullivan, at the Ritz Theatre, New York, May 1, 1942.

Principals engaged—

Noble Sissle
Flournoy Miller
Hawley and Lee
Moke and Poke
The Gingersnaps
Jesse Crior
Pops and Louie
Monte Hawley
Garland Wilson
Tim Moore
Maude Russell
5 Crackerjacks

Amanda Randolph
Una Mae Carlisle
The Peters Sisters
Jimmie Daniels
The Harlemaniacs
Tom Fletcher
Red and Curley
Johnny Lee
Edward Steele
Joe Byrd
Wini and Bob Johnson
Miller Brothers and Lois

Staged by Ed Sullivan and Noble Sissle; music directed by Bill Vodery; dances by Leonard Harper; costumes by Veronica.

(Closed May 23, 1942)

THE WALKING GENTLEMAN

(6 performances)

A drama in three acts by Grace Perkins and Fulton Oursler. Produced by Albert Lewis and Marion Gering at the Belasco Theatre, New York, May 7, 1942.

Cast of characters—

Mrs. Shriver.....................Margery Maude
Doris............................Arlene Francis
Dr. Blake........................Richard Gaines
Miss Marshall....................Ruth Thea Ford
Savage...........................Clay Clement
Father Benoit....................Arnold Korff
Frazier..........................George Spaulding
Sam Hertz........................Clarence Derwent
Jim Lake.........................Cledge Roberts

THE BEST PLAYS OF 1941-42

Electrician	Roderick Maybee
Elsie Ellis	Margo Railton
Newcome	Ross Chetwynd
Connie	Jane Forbes
Lanyon	David Stewart
Poole	A. J. Herbert
Marmot	Oscar Polk
Basil Forrest	Victor Francen
Wrinkles	Lew Hearn
Myrtle Tracey	Toni Gilman
Officer Blum	Roderick Maybee

Act I.—Scene 1—Dr. Gerald Blake's Office in Large New York Hospital. 2—The Avenue Theatre, New York City. Acts II and III.—An Apartment in New York City.

Staged by Marion Gering; settings by Harry Horner; lighting by Feder.

Doris Forrest, having divorced her husband, Basil Forrest, the actor, is eager to marry Dr. Blake, the famous psychiatrist. She still feels that Basil has a fascination for her and thinks to break the spell by accepting his invitation to return to acting with him when his leading woman is found hanged in her dressing room. Basil is connected by the police with the death of the actress, as well as with the deaths of several other women who have come into his life. His impulse to murder is traced by the psychiatrist to his lost love for Doris, whom he would also have strangled if the police had not stepped in.

(Closed May 12, 1942)

THE STRINGS, MY LORD, ARE FALSE

(15 performances)

A drama in two acts by Paul Vincent Carroll. Produced by Edward Choate in association with Alexander Kirkland and John Sheppard, Jr., at the Royale Theatre, New York, May 19, 1942.

Cast of characters—

Alec	Ralph Cullinan
Geordie	Sherman MacGregor
Sarah	Frances Bavier
Canon Courtenay	Walter Hampden
Councilor Bill Randall	Colin Keith-Johnson
"Ma" Morrisey	Ruth Vivian
Maisie Gillespie	Constance Dowling
Jerry Hoare	Philip Bourneuf
Madge	Joan Hayden Shepard
Sadie O'Neill	Margot Grahame
Ross	John McKee
Louis Liebens	Will Lee
Iris Ryan	Ruth Gordon
Ted Bogle	Art Smith
Monsignor Skinner	Reynolds Evans
Inspector Steele	Gordon Nelson
Councilor McPearkie	Tom Tully
Provost Grahamson	Hale Norcross
Veronica	Alice MacKenzie
Religious Man	Hurd Hatfield

R. P. Messenger	Anna Minot

Act I.—Scenes 1 and 2—Refuge Room in Presbytery of Canon Courtenay of St. Bride's Church, Port Monica, a Steel Town in Firth of Clyde, Scotland. Act II.—Scene 1—Crypt Underneath Church of St. Bride's. 2—The Refuge Room.

Staged by Elia Kazan; settings by Howard Bay.

Canon Courtenay was shepherding his flock at St. Bride's church in Port Monica, a steel town in the Firth of Clyde, and taking in all the strays who applied, when the Luftwaffe bombed Scotland in the spring of 1941. Large was the Canon's heart, broad was his understanding and many were his adventures. Iris Ryan, the most aristocratic of his canteen workers, found herself with child by the wrong man; Veronica might have lost the baby born to her during a blitz if it had not been for the kindly sympathy and help of Sadie O'Neill, a noble harlot with flaming hair and a heart of gold; grafting Councilor McPearkie would never have been exposed and honest Councilor Bill Randall might never have discovered that he loved Iris Ryan enough to forgive her her adventure with sex if it had not been for the good Canon and the shelter he offered his people.

(Closed May 30, 1942)

*UNCLE HARRY

(29 performances)

A drama in seven scenes by Thomas Job. Produced by Clifford Hayman and Lennie Hatten at the Broadhurst Theatre, New York, May 20, 1942.

Cast of characters—

Miss Phipps	Wauna Paul
Mr. Jenkins	Guy Sampsel
A Man	Joseph Schildkraut
Hester	Adelaide Klein
Lettie	Eva Le Gallienne
Lucy	Beverly Roberts
Nona	Leona Roberts
George Waddy	Stephen Chase
D'Arcy	John McGovern
Albert	A. P. Kaye
Blake	Ralph Theodore
Ben	Karl Malden
The Governor	Colville Dunn
Mr. Burton	Bruce Adams
Matron	Isabel Arden

Scenes 1 and 7—The Tavern. A small town in Eastern Quebec, Canada. 2—Tea Time. 3—Musical Interlude. 4—The Nightcap. 5—The Verdict. 6—The Confession.

Staged by Lem Ward; settings by Howard Bay; costumes by Peggy Clark.

See page 316.

ALL THE COMFORTS OF HOME

(8 performances)

A farce in two acts adapted by William Gillette from a play by Carl Laufs; revised by Helen Jerome. Revived by Edith C. Ringling in association with Mollie B. Steinberg at the Longacre Theatre, New York, May 25, 1942.

Cast of characters—
Alfred Hastings...................................Gene Jerrold
Tom McDow......................................Oliver B. Prickett
Theodore Bender, Esq. ....Nicholas Joy
Josephine Bender.................................Dorothy Sands
Evangeline Bender...............................Florence Williams
Mr. Egbert Pettibone............................William David
Rosalie Pettibone...............................Grace McTarnahan
Emily Pettibone.................................Peggy Van Vleet
Christopher Dabney..............................Wallace Acton
Judson Langhorne................................Guy Spaull
Fih Oritanski...................................Celeste Holm
Augustus McSnath................................Percy Helton
Victor Smythe...................................Stuart Lancaster
Thompson..Richard Stevens
Katy..Virginia Runyon
Gretchen..Jordie McLean
Bailiff...John Regan

Acts I and II.—Parlor in Egbert Pettibone's House.
Staged by Arthur Sircom; setting by Harry G. Bennett; costumes by Paul duPont.

Alfred Hastings, serving as caretaker for his Uncle Egbert's house, rents out lodgings to an assortment of comedy characters. He is variously aided by Tom McDow, who gets half the profits and most of the laughs. When Uncle Egbert and his family return, Alfred and Tom are exposed, but not before Alfred and Evangeline, the ingénue, have made a match of it. "All the Comforts of Home" was adapted from a German original fifty-two years ago by William Gillette. In the first New York production at Proctor's 23d St. Theatre in 1890 Maude Adams played Evangeline and Henry Miller was the Alfred.

(Closed May 30, 1942)

COMES THE REVELATION

(2 performances)

A comedy in three acts by Louis Vittes. Produced by John Morris Chanin and Richard Karlan at the Jolson Theatre, New York, May 26, 1942.

454   THE BEST PLAYS OF 1941-42

Cast of characters—

Benjamin Barney	G. Swayne Gordon
Ma Flanders	Mary Perry
Zachary Flanders	Peter Hobbs
Grandpa Crane	Wendell K. Phillips
Sophronia Flanders	Carroll Hartley
Joe Flanders	Wendell Corey
Pa Flanders	Will Geer
Orris Hockett	Grover Burgess
Oliver Sampson	John Thomas
Ellen Crale	Lesley Woods
William Garrett	Richard Karlan
David Garrett	William Thornton
Judy Garrett	Audra Lindley
James Q. Silsbury	Mitchell Harris
Grammus	George Leach
Lily Milland	June Stewart
Mrs. Barney	Sara Floyd
Mrs. Hockett	Mona Moray
Mrs. Garrett	Kathryn Cameron
Sheriff	Maurice Minnick
Sheriff's Deputy	Clay Yurdin

Acts I, II and III.—Kitchen of House on Flanders Farm, Dorking, New York.

Staged by Herman Rotsten; setting by Ralph Alswang.

Joe Flanders buys a book that advances the theory that the American Indians were really the lost tribes of Israel. Having a gift for preaching, Joe trades on the credulity of his neighbors, draws a crowd of excited religious fanatics to his drunken father's home and proceeds to trick and rob them. Ellen Crale, the girl he seduced and later married, convinced of his deceit and aware of his unfaithfulness, assists in his exposure in the end.

(Closed May 27, 1942)

* TOP-NOTCHERS

(37 performances)

A variety show assembled by Clifford C. Fischer. Produced by Clifford C. Fischer and the Messrs. Shubert at the 44th Street Theatre, New York, May 29, 1942.

Principals engaged—

Gracie Fields
Argentinita
Walter O'Keefe
Jack Stanton
Pilar Lopez
Evelyn Brooks
Benigno Medina
Carlos Mintaya
Bricklayers
Al White Girls

A. Robins
Al Trahan
Zero Mostel
The Hartmans
Marguerite Adams
Pablo Miquel
Frederico Rey
Hoffman
Six Willys
Phil Romano's Orchestra

"Keep 'Em Laughing" produced by Mr. Fischer and the Messrs. Shubert at the 44th Street Theatre, April 24, 1942, after its seventy-seventh performance changed into "Top-Notchers" with new principals, new songs and new acts added to much of the old program which was retained. Gracie Fields and Argentinita took the places left by William Gaxton and Victor Moore.

*BY JUPITER

(14 performances)

A musical comedy in two acts by Richard Rodgers and Lorenz Hart based on "The Warrior's Husband" by Julian F. Thompson; music arrangements by Don Walker and Buck Warnick. Produced by Dwight Deere Wiman and Richard Rodgers at the Shubert Theatre, New York, June 3, 1942.

Cast of characters—

Achilles	Bob Douglas
A Herald	Mark Dawson
Agamemnon	Robert Hightower
Buria	Jayne Manners
First Sentry	Martha Burnett
Second Sentry	Rose Inghram
Third Sentry	Kay Kimber
Sergeant	Monica Moore
Caustica	Maidel Turner
Heroica	Margaret Bannerman
Pomposia	Bertha Belmore
First Boy	Don Liberto
Second Boy	Tony Matthews
Third Boy	William Vaux
Hippolyta	Benay Venuta
Sapiens	Ray Bolger
Antiope	Constance Moore
A Huntress	Helen Bennett
An Amazon Dancer	Flower Hujer
Theseus	Ronald Graham
Homer	Berni Gould
Minerva	Vera-Ellen
Slaves	Robert and Lewis Hightower
Amazon Runner	Wana Wenerholm
Hercules	Ralph Dumke
Penelope	Irene Corlett
First Camp Follower	Vera-Ellen
Second Camp Follower	Ruth Brady
Third Camp Follower	Helen Bennett
Fourth Camp Follower	Joyce Ring
Fifth Camp Follower	Rosemary Sankey

Act I.—Scene 1—A Greek Camp, a Week's March from Pontus. 2—Terrace of Hippolyta's Palace in Pontus. Act II.—Scene 1—Before Hippolyta's Tent. 2—The Greek Camp. 3—Inside Theseus' Tent.

Staged by Joshua Logan; dances by Robert Alton; music directed by Johnny Green; settings and lighting by Jo Mielziner; costumes by Irene Sharaff.

DANCE DRAMA

The fourth New York season of the Ballet Russe de Monte Carlo ran from October 8 until November 2, 1941, at the Metropolitan Opera House under the management of S. Hurok, the direction of Leonide Massine and the musical direction of Efrem Kurtz and Franz Allers. A repertory of about thirty productions started with "Poker Game," by Balanchine, with Stravinsky music; "Labyrinth" by Leonide Massine and Salvador Dali with Shubert C Major Symphony music, and "Gaite Parisienne," by Massine, with Offenbach music. "Labyrinth" and "Saratoga" were new to New York. "Saratoga" with music by Jaromir Weinberger, choreography by Massine and setting by Oliver Smith had its world premiere. Other dance dramas were from the regular repertory. "St. Francis," by Massine and Paul Hindemith, was added to the repertory in a later engagement.

Ballet Theatre, produced by the New Opera Company in association with S. Hurok, began a month's engagement November 12 and ended December 14, 1941, at the 44th Street Theatre. "Bluebeard," by Michel Fokine, Meilhac and Halevy, with music by Jacques Offenbach, had its first New York showing, as also had "Stavonika," by Vania Psota based on Dvorak's music and designed by Alvin Colt, and "Beloved" by Bronislava Nijinska with Schubert-Liszt music. Other dance dramas were from the repertory.

A return engagement in April at the Metropolitan opened with Michel Fokine's new ballet, "Russian Soldier," to music of Prokofieff. Another new work was "Pillar of Fire," by Antony Tudor, music of Schoenberg.

The Jooss Ballet, under the management of Leon Greanin and directed by Frederic Cohen, opened at the Maxine Elliott Theatre, September 22, 1941. The repertory included the premieres "Chronica," by Kurt Jooss and Berthold Goldschmitt, "Drums Sound in Hackensack," by Agnes de Mille with music by Frederic Cohen, and "A Spring Tale," by Kurt Jooss, with music by Frederic Cohen.

The Jooss Ballet returned for a brief engagement in the Fall at the Windsor Theatre in a joint program with a repertory of Gilbert and Sullivan operettas presenting "The Green Table," "The Big City," "A Ball in Old Vienna" and "The Prodigal Son."

THE BEST PLAYS OF 1941-42

Ruth St. Denis and a small company of dancers began a series of four performances at the Carnegie Chamber Music Hall opening December 4, 1941, with "Radha," "Incense," "The Cobras," "The Nautch" and "Yogi."

Le Meri and Natya Dancers presented three dance dramas of India at the Guild Theatre in December.

Martha Graham and company presented three dance dramas at the Concert Theatre, with Louis Horst as music director, in December. "Punch and Judy," with music by Robert McBride, spoken text by Gordon Craig, was presented for the first time.

Doris Humphrey and Charles Weidman opened their second repertory season at the Studio Theatre, December 26, 1941, with "Decade" by Miss Humphrey, music by Aaron Copland, spoken text by Alex Kahn, Lionel Nowak the musical director. Other dance dramas included "Flickers," by Weidman, with music by Nowak, "On My Mother's Side," by Weidman and Nowak and "Alcina Suite," with Handel music and "Variations from New Dance," by Doris Humphrey and Wallingford Riegger.

Argentinita with her company of dancers appeared at the Cosmopolitan Opera House February 12, 1942, and again at the Shubert Theatre for a series of three week-ends in March.

Dance Players, Inc., under the management of Eugene Loring, opened April 21, 1942, at the National Theatre, New York, with "Billy the Kid." During the engagement the following dance dramas were presented for the first time: "The Man from Midian," based on a poem by Winthrop B. Palmer, with score by Stefan Wolpe; "Jinx," by Lew Christensen with music by Benjamin Britten, and "City Portrait," by Eugene Loring with music by Henry Brant and decor by Reginald Marsh. Other selections were from the repertory.

OFF BROADWAY

The Savoy Opera Guild under the direction of Lewis Denison, leased the Cherry Lane Theatre in Greenwich Village and gave three performances a week of Gilbert and Sullivan operas continuously through the season of 1941-42, starting with "Mikado," June 19, 1941. During the season Sylvia Cyde, Charles Kingsley, Well Clary, Bernard O'Brien, Seymour Penzner, Ruth Giorloff and others sang "Cox and Box," "Pirates of Penzance," "Ruddigore," "Iolanthe," "Trial by Jury," "Yeoman of the Guard," "Pinafore," and "The Gondoliers." Arthur Lief was the music director.

Other Gilbert and Sullivan operas produced during the season were "Pirates of Penzance" produced by Bluehill Troupe and staged by Richard Skinner at the Heckscher Theatre, April 15; "Patience," "Pinafore" and "Trial by Jury," staged by Allen Hinckley and produced by the Village Light Opera Group at the Heckscher Theatre, beginning December 12, 1941, and "Cox and Box" and "Pinafore," directed by John F. Grahame and Alexander Maissel at the Provincetown Playhouse, N. Y., June 11, 1942.

The Studio Theatre of the New School for Social Research, under the direction of Erwin Piscator, produced four plays during the season, one of which, "Nathan the Wise," was later moved to the Belasco Theatre. "The Days of Our Youth," by Frank Gabrielson, opened the season in November and closed after 12 performances. Leon Janney and Curt Conway headed the cast and James Light staged the production. Ferdinand Bruckner's "The Criminals," translated by Edwin Denby and Rita Matthias, opened December 20 and continued for 15 performances. Sanford Meisner directed. The cast included Lili Darvas, Warner Anderson, Paul Mann and Herbert Berghof. The third production was "Nathan the Wise" (11 performances) and the fourth and last play was "War and Peace" dramatized from the Tolstoi novel by Erwin Piscator and Alfred Neumann in collaboration with Harold L. Anderson and Maurice Kurtz. Hugo Haas, Alfred Urban, Warner Anderson, Paul Mann, R. Ben Ari and Dolly Haas were in the cast. Erwin Piscator directed.

The Blackfriars' Guild opened its season October 30, 1941, with "Up the Rebels," by Sean Vincent. Dennis Gurney directed. In December "Song of Sorrows," by Felix Doherty, was presented for the first time and "The Years Between," by Edward Burbage, another premiere, opened February 5, 1942. "The White Steed," by Paul Vincent Carroll, was played by the Irish Repertory Players and staged by J. Augustus Keogh. The season closed with "Savonarola," by Urban Nagle, with 12 performances. An all male cast of 22 was headed by Brandon Peters. The drama was directed by Dennis Gurney.

In December Madison Square Garden housed the "Ice Follies of 1942," and at the end of the season, in June, the "Skating Vanities of 1942," a musical comedy on roller skates, had a brief engagement.

The American Actors Company produced "Out of My House," by Horton Foote, at the Humphrey-Weidman Studio January 7, 1942. The play was staged by Mary Hunter, Horton Foote and Jane Rose. In the cast were William Hare, Casey Walters and Thomas Hughes.

William Saroyan's one act play, "Across the Board on Tomorrow Morning," preceded by "Theatre of the Soul," a one-act play by Nicolas Evreinov, was produced by Theatre Showcase, March 20, 1942. Staging by William Boyman and Bernarr Cooper.

Martin Blaine presented "It's About Time," a revue in two acts, at the Barbizon-Plaza Concert Hall, March 28, 1942. Sketches were written by Peter Barry, Arnold Horwitt, Arthur Elmer, Sam Locke, David Greggory and Reuben Shipp; lyrics by Mr. Greggory; music by Will Lorin, Al Moss and Genevieve Pitot; settings by William Martin and Walter Ketchum.

Robert Henderson staged and presented a play in three acts called "Me and Harry" at the Studio Theatre, April 2, 1942. The play was written by Charles Mergendahl.

"Mexican Mural," by Ramon Naya, was presented and staged by Robert Lewis at the Chanin Theatre, New York, April 25, 1942. Included in the cast were Libby Holman, Perry Wilson, Montgomery Clift, Norma Chambers, Mira Rosovskaya and Kevin McCarthy.

Three interesting productions were "The Valiant" and "Bound for Mexico," produced by the Victory Players, a group of blind performers, May 28, 1942; the Lighthouse Players' production of "Women Without Men," by Philip Johnson; "Gallant Lady," by C. C. Clements, and "Silent Voice," by Esther Shephard. A performance of "Arsenic and Old Lace" by Joseph Kesselring was played entirely in sign language by the Gallaudet College Dramatic Club May 10, 1942.

As a result of the war many pageants, patriotic revues and

plays were presented. The first of these was "Fun To Be Free," a revue and pageant by Ben Hecht and Charles MacArthur with music by Kurt Weill and staged by Brett Warren, was produced by Fight for Freedom, Inc., October 5, 1941, at Madison Square Garden. In charge of the presentation was Laurence Schwab and prominent stage, screen and radio actors were in the cast. The show was under the supervision of Billy Rose.

"Johnny Doodle," a musical play in two acts by Jane McLeod and Alfred Saxe, with incidental music and direction by Lan Adomian, was produced by the Popular Theatre at the Popular Theatre, March 18, 1942.

The Navy Relief Benefit Show at Madison Square Garden, March 10, 1942, was under the direction of Marvin Schenck and Sidney Pierpont. Lieutenant Commander Walter Winchell, Tyrone Power, Bert Lytell, Ray Bolger, George Jessel and Jack Haley were alternating masters of ceremony. Andre Kostelanetz led his own orchestra and many celebrities assisted.

"Salute to Negro Troops," by Carleton Moss, was presented at the Apollo Theatre, Harlem, for a week's run starting March 27, 1942. It had previously been given at the Cosmopolitan Opera House. This was a pageant of the history of the Negro in America and was staged by Brett Warren.

"Gratefully Yours," a revue by Peter Jackson with sketches contributed by John Van Druten, Herbert Farjeon, Harold Rome, Patricia Collinge, Howard Lindsay and Russel Crouse, was presented at the Imperial Theatre under the direction of Constance Collier and Robert Ross, April 7 and April 12, 1942. Fifty-four British refugee children from 8 to 16 years old, sons and daughters of actors and actresses, gave the performance for the American Theatre Wing War Service and the British and American Ambulance Corps. Miss Collier and Gertrude Lawrence took part in the prologue.

College Plays in New York

The Mask and Wig Club of the University of Pennsylvania produced its fifty-fourth annual musical, "Out of this World," at the Hollywood Theatre, New York, December 13, 1941. The musical was based on a scenario by John C. Parry. Dr. Clay A. Boland wrote the score, S. B. Reichner the lyrics, John C. Parry, Louis de V Day, Sidney Wertimer, Jr., and Fred Griffiths the dialogue. The production was under the supervision of Dr. Boland. Proceeds turned over to the relief fund for Pearl Harbor.

The Triangle Club of Princeton University presented their fifty-third annual production, "Ask Me Another," at the Mansfield Theatre, New York, December 18, 1941. This friendly satire on quiz programs was written by Mark Lawrence, W. C. Matthews, J. A. Nevius, Charles H. Burr, Gordon Bent, F. O. Birney, Clinton E. Wilder and Norman Cook; music and lyrics by Mark Lawrence, Howard Anderson, William Jamison, Roger W. Bissell, J. A. Schumann and Gordon Bent. The production was supervised by Norris Houghton.

The Columbia University Players presented their forty-ninth annual varsity musical in the Grand Ballroom of the Hotel Astor, March 26, 1942. "Saints Alive," in two acts, was written by Edward Falasca, Jean Sosin and Robert Bergman with music by Albert Sherwin, Edgar J. Carver and Morton Lippman. The production was supervised by Paul Winkopp; music directed by Lee Wainer; dances by Frank Gagen.

The Mimes and Mummers of Fordham College presented Goldoni's "A Servant of Two Masters" as their annual varsity production at the Penthouse Theatre, New York, April 23, 1942.

The Yale Dramatic Association presented "The Waterbury Tales" at the Hotel Waldorf-Astoria, December 22, 1941. This musical comedy was based on an idea by William H. Schubart, Jr. The sketches and lyrics were by John W. Leggett, Samuel J. Wagstaff and William Schubart; music by Dudley P. Felton, Franklin B. Young, Albert W. Selden, Richard L. Brecker and John Gerald. Directed by Burton G. Shevelove; dances staged by Dean Goodelle; settings by Peter Wolf; costumes by Joe Fretwell, III.

STATISTICAL SUMMARY

(LAST SEASON PLAYS WHICH ENDED RUNS AFTER JUNE 15, 1941)

Plays	Number Performances	
Hellzapoppin	1,404	(Closed December 17, 1941)
Johnny Belinda	321	(Closed June 21, 1941)
Native Son	114	(Closed June 28, 1941)
Pal Joey	374	(Closed November 29, 1941)
Panama Hattie	501	(Closed January 3, 1942)
Separate Rooms	613	(Closed September 6, 1941)
The Beautiful People	120	(Closed August 2, 1941)
The Corn Is Green	477	(Closed January 17, 1942)
The Doctor's Dilemma	121	(Closed June 21, 1941)
The Man Who Came to Dinner	739	(Closed July 12, 1941)
Watch on the Rhine	378	(Closed February 21, 1942)

"Claudia" closed March 7, 1942, with 453 performances and reopened May 24, the return engagement adding 24 performances by June 15, making a total of 477. "Pal Joey" ran for 270 performances in the first engagement and 104 in the return engagement, making a total of 374 performances.

LONG RUNS ON BROADWAY

To June 15, 1942

(Plays marked with asterisk were still playing June 15, 1942)

Plays	Number Performances
Tobacco Road	3,182
Abie's Irish Rose	2,327
Hellzapoppin	1,404
Lightnin'	1,291
Pins and Needles	1,108
*Life with Father	1,093
The Bat	867
White Cargo	864
You Can't Take It with You	837
Three Men on a Horse	835
The Ladder	789
The First Year	760
The Man Who Came to Dinner	739
Seventh Heaven	704
Peg o' My Heart	692
The Children's Hour	691
Dead End	687
East Is West	680
Irene	670
Boy Meets Girl	669
The Women	657
A Trip to Chinatown	657
Rain	648
The Green Pastures	640
*My Sister Eileen	624
Is Zat So	618
Separate Rooms	613
Student Prince	608
Broadway	603
Adonis	603
Street Scene	601
Kiki	600
*Arsenic and Old Lace	598
Blossom Time	592
Brother Rat	577
Show Boat	572
The Show-Off	571
Sally	570
Rose Marie	557
Strictly Dishonorable	557
Good News	551
Within the Law	541
The Music Master	540
What a Life	538
The Boomerang	522
Blackbirds	518
Sunny	517
Victoria Regina	517
The Vagabond King	511
The New Moon	509
Shuffle Along	504
Personal Appearance	501
Panama Hattie	501
Bird in Hand	500
Sailor, Beware!	500
Room Service	500

DRAMA CRITICS' CIRCLE AWARD

For the second time in its seven years' existence the New York Drama Critics' Circle failed to select a best play of American authorship to represent the theatre season. In an official announcement covering its deliberations the Circle pointed out that "while it was organized to encourage native playwrights and honor native dramatists, it had also the third obligation of maintaining the standards of the theatre and of dramatic criticism, and that it felt it would cause a serious confusion of standards if it merely made a selection from a group of plays, none of which seemed up to the standards of the previous awards." The vote was 11 to 6 in favor of abiding by this decision. Of the six reviewers favoring the selection of a best play, four voted for the Koch-Huston "In Time to Come" and two for John Steinbeck's "The Moon Is Down." Noel Coward's "Blithe Spirit" received practically the unanimous endorsement of the Circle as being the best of the imported plays of the season. It received 12 votes, to two for "Angel Street" and four "no decisions." The only previous "no decision" season was that of 1938-39, when Robert Sherwood's "Abe Lincoln in Illinois" and Lillian Hellman's "The Little Foxes" split the vote. Drama Critics' Circle Awards have been:

1935-36—Winterset, by Maxwell Anderson
1936-37—High Tor, by Maxwell Anderson
1937-38—Of Mice and Men, by John Steinbeck
1938-39—No decision. ("The Little Foxes" and "Abe Lincoln in Illinois" led voting.)
1939-40—The Time of Your Life, by William Saroyan
1940-41—Watch on the Rhine, by Lillian Hellman
1941-42—No award.

PULITZER PRIZE WINNERS

"For the original American play performed in New York which shall best represent the educational value and power of the stage in raising the standard of good morals, good taste and good manners."—The Will of Joseph Pulitzer, dated April 16, 1904.

In 1929 the advisory board, which, according to the terms of the will, "shall have the power in its discretion to suspend or to change any subject or subjects . . . if in the judgment of the board such suspension, changes or substitutions shall be conducive to the public good," decided to eliminate from the above paragraph relating to the prize-winning play the words "in raising the standard of good morals, good taste and good manners."

The committee awards to date have been:

1917-18—Why Marry? by Jesse Lynch Williams
1918-19—None
1919-20—Beyond the Horizon, by Eugene O'Neill
1920-21—Miss Lulu Bett, by Zona Gale
1921-22—Anna Christie, by Eugene O'Neill
1922-23—Icebound, by Owen Davis
1923-24—Hell-bent fer Heaven, by Hatcher Hughes
1924-25—They Knew What They Wanted, by Sidney Howard
1925-26—Craig's Wife, by George Kelly
1926-27—In Abraham's Bosom, by Paul Green
1927-28—Strange Interlude, by Eugene O'Neill
1928-29—Street Scene, by Elmer Rice
1929-30—The Green Pastures, by Marc Connelly
1930-31—Alison's House, by Susan Glaspell
1931-32—Of Thee I Sing, by George S. Kaufman, Morrie Ryskind, Ira and George Gershwin
1932-33—Both Your Houses, by Maxwell Anderson
1933-34—Men in White, by Sidney Kingsley
1934-35—The Old Maid, by Zoe Akins
1935-36—Idiot's Delight, by Robert E. Sherwood
1936-37—You Can't Take It with You, by Moss Hart and George S. Kaufman
1937-38—Our Town, by Thornton Wilder
1938-39—Abe Lincoln in Illinois, by Robert E. Sherwood
1939-40—The Time of Your Life, by William Saroyan
1940-41—There Shall Be No Night, by Robert E. Sherwood
1941-42—No award.

PREVIOUS VOLUMES OF BEST PLAYS

Plays chosen to represent the theatre seasons from 1909 to 1941 are as follows:

1909-1919

"The Easiest Way," by Eugene Walter. Published by G. W. Dillingham, New York; Houghton Mifflin Co., Boston.

"Mrs. Bumpstead-Leigh," by Harry James Smith. Published by Samuel French, New York.

"Disraeli," by Louis N. Parker. Published by Dodd, Mead and Co., New York.

"Romance," by Edward Sheldon. Published by the Macmillan Co., New York.

"Seven Keys to Baldpate," by George M. Cohan. Published by Bobbs-Merrill Co., Indianapolis, as a novel by Earl Derr Biggers; as a play by Samuel French, New York.

"On Trial," by Elmer Reizenstein. Published by Samuel French, New York.

"The Unchastened Woman," by Louis Kaufman Anspacher. Published by Harcourt, Brace and Howe, Inc., New York.

"Good Gracious Annabelle," by Clare Kummer. Published by Samuel French, New York.

"Why Marry?" by Jesse Lynch Williams. Published by Charles Scribner's Sons, New York.

"John Ferguson," by St. John Ervine. Published by the Macmillan Co., New York.

1919-1920

"Abraham Lincoln," by John Drinkwater. Published by Houghton Mifflin Co., Boston.

"Clarence," by Booth Tarkington. Published by Samuel French, New York.

"Beyond the Horizon," by Eugene G. O'Neill. Published by Boni & Liveright, Inc., New York.

"Déclassée," by Zoe Akins. Published by Liveright, Inc., New York.

THE BEST PLAYS OF 1941-42

"The Famous Mrs. Fair," by James Forbes. Published by Samuel French, New York.

"The Jest," by Sem Benelli. (American adaptation by Edward Sheldon.)

"Jane Clegg," by St. John Ervine. Published by Henry Holt & Co., New York.

"Mamma's Affair," by Rachel Barton Butler. Published by Samuel French, New York.

"Wedding Bells," by Salisbury Field. Published by Samuel French, New York.

"Adam and Eva," by George Middleton and Guy Bolton. Published by Samuel French, New York.

1920-1921

"Deburau," adapted from the French of Sacha Guitry by H. Granville Barker. Published by G. P. Putnam's Sons, New York.

"The First Year," by Frank Craven. Published by Samuel French, New York.

"Enter Madame," by Gilda Varesi and Dolly Byrne. Published by G. P. Putnam's Sons, New York.

"The Green Goddess," by William Archer. Published by Alfred A. Knopf, New York.

"Liliom," by Ferenc Molnar. Published by Boni & Liveright, New York.

"Mary Rose," by James M. Barrie. Published by Charles Scribner's Sons, New York.

"Nice People," by Rachel Crothers. Published by Charles Scribner's Sons, New York.

"The Bad Man," by Porter Emerson Browne. Published by G. P. Putnam's Sons, New York.

"The Emperor Jones," by Eugene G. O'Neill. Published by Boni & Liveright, New York.

"The Skin Game," by John Galsworthy. Published by Charles Scribner's Sons, New York.

1921-1922

"Anna Christie," by Eugene G. O'Neill. Published by Boni & Liveright, New York.

"A Bill of Divorcement," by Clemence Dane. Published by the Macmillan Company, New York.

"Dulcy," by George S. Kaufman and Marc Connelly. Published by G. P. Putnam's Sons, New York.

"He Who Gets Slapped," adapted from the Russian of Leonid Andreyev by Gregory Zilboorg. Published by Brentano's, New York.
"Six Cylinder Love," by William Anthony McGuire.
"The Hero," by Gilbert Emery.
"The Dover Road," by Alan Alexander Milne. Published by Samuel French, New York.
"Ambush," by Arthur Richman.
"The Circle," by William Somerset Maugham.
"The Nest," by Paul Geraldy and Grace George.

1922-1923

"Rain," by John Colton and Clemence Randolph. Published by Liveright, Inc., New York.
"Loyalties," by John Galsworthy. Published by Charles Scribner's Sons, New York.
"Icebound," by Owen Davis. Published by Little, Brown & Company, Boston.
"You and I," by Philip Barry. Published by Brentano's, New York.
"The Fool," by Channing Pollock. Published by Brentano's, New York.
"Merton of the Movies," by George Kaufman and Marc Connelly, based on the novel of the same name by Harry Leon Wilson.
"Why Not?" by Jesse Lynch Williams. Published by Walter H. Baker Co., Boston.
"The Old Soak," by Don Marquis. Published by Doubleday, Page & Company, New York.
"R.U.R.," by Karel Capek. Translated by Paul Selver. Published by Doubleday, Page & Company.
"Mary the 3d," by Rachel Crothers. Published by Brentano's, New York.

1923-1924

"The Swan," translated from the Hungarian of Ferenc Molnar by Melville Baker. Published by Boni & Liveright, New York.
"Outward Bound," by Sutton Vane. Published by Boni & Liveright, New York.
"The Show-off," by George Kelly. Published by Little, Brown & Company, Boston.
"The Changelings," by Lee Wilson Dodd. Published by E. P. Dutton & Company, New York.
"Chicken Feed," by Guy Bolton. Published by Samuel French,

New York and London.

"Sun-Up," by Lula Vollmer. Published by Brentano's, New York.

"Beggar on Horseback," by George Kaufman and Marc Connelly. Published by Boni & Liveright, New York.

"Tarnish," by Gilbert Emery. Published by Brentano's, New York.

"The Goose Hangs High," by Lewis Beach. Published by Little, Brown & Company, Boston.

"Hell-bent fer Heaven," by Hatcher Hughes. Published by Harper Bros., New York.

1924-1925

"What Price Glory?" by Laurence Stallings and Maxwell Anderson. Published by Harcourt, Brace & Co., New York.

"They Knew What They Wanted," by Sidney Howard. Published by Doubleday, Page & Company, New York.

"Desire Under the Elms," by Eugene G. O'Neill. Published by Boni & Liveright, New York.

"The Firebrand," by Edwin Justus Mayer. Published by Boni & Liveright, New York.

"Dancing Mothers," by Edgar Selwyn and Edmund Goulding.

"Mrs. Partridge Presents," by Mary Kennedy and Ruth Warren. Published by Samuel French, New York.

"The Fall Guy," by James Gleason and George Abbott. Published by Samuel French, New York.

"The Youngest," by Philip Barry. Published by Samuel French, New York.

"Minick," by Edna Ferber and George S. Kaufman. Published by Doubleday, Page & Company, New York.

"Wild Birds," by Dan Totheroh. Published by Doubleday, Page & Company, New York.

1925-1926

"Craig's Wife," by George Kelly. Published by Little, Brown & Company, Boston.

"The Great God Brown," by Eugene G. O'Neill. Published by Boni & Liveright, New York.

"The Green Hat," by Michael Arlen.

"The Dybbuk," by S. Ansky, Henry G. Alsberg-Winifred Katzin translation. Published by Boni & Liveright, New York.

"The Enemy," by Channing Pollock. Published by Brentano's,

New York.

"The Last of Mrs. Cheyney," by Frederick Lonsdale. Published by Samuel French, New York.

"Bride of the Lamb," by William Hurlbut. Published by Boni & Liveright, New York.

"The Wisdom Tooth," by Marc Connelly. Published by George H. Doran & Company, New York.

"The Butter and Egg Man," by George Kaufman. Published by Boni & Liveright, New York.

"Young Woodley," by John Van Druten. Published by Simon and Schuster, New York.

1926-1927

"Broadway," by Philip Dunning and George Abbott. Published by George H. Doran Company, New York.

"Saturday's Children," by Maxwell Anderson. Published by Longmans, Green & Company, New York.

"Chicago," by Maurine Watkins. Published by Alfred A. Knopf, Inc., New York.

"The Constant Wife," by William Somerset Maugham. Published by George H. Doran Company, New York.

"The Play's the Thing," by Ferenc Molnar and P. G. Wodehouse. Published by Brentano's, New York.

"The Road to Rome," by Robert Emmet Sherwood. Published by Charles Scribner's Sons, New York.

"The Silver Cord," by Sidney Howard. Published by Charles Scribner's Sons, New York.

"The Cradle Song," translated from the Spanish of G. Martinez Sierra by John Garrett Underhill. Published by E. P. Dutton & Company, New York.

"Daisy Mayme," by George Kelly. Published by Little, Brown & Company, Boston.

"In Abraham's Bosom," by Paul Green. Published by Robert M. McBride & Company, New York.

1927-1928

"Strange Interlude," by Eugene G. O'Neill. Published by Boni & Liveright, New York.

"The Royal Family," by Edna Ferber and George Kaufman. Published by Doubleday, Doran & Company, New York.

"Burlesque," by George Manker Watters. Published by Doubleday, Doran & Company, New York.

THE BEST PLAYS OF 1941-42

"Coquette," by George Abbott and Ann Bridgers. Published by Longmans, Green & Company, New York, London, Toronto.

"Behold the Bridegroom," by George Kelly. Published by Little, Brown & Company, Boston.

"Porgy," by DuBose Heyward. Published by Doubleday, Doran & Company, New York.

"Paris Bound," by Philip Barry. Published by Samuel French, New York.

"Escape," by John Galsworthy. Published by Charles Scribner's Sons, New York.

"The Racket," by Bartlett Cormack. Published by Samuel French, New York.

"The Plough and the Stars," by Sean O'Casey. Published by the Macmillan Company, New York.

1928-1929

"Street Scene," by Elmer Rice. Published by Samuel French, New York.

"Journey's End," by R. C. Sherriff. Published by Brentano's, New York.

"Wings Over Europe," by Robert Nichols and Maurice Browne. Published by Covici-Friede, New York.

"Holiday," by Philip Barry. Published by Samuel French, New York.

"The Front Page," by Ben Hecht and Charles MacArthur. Published by Covici-Friede, New York.

"Let Us Be Gay," by Rachel Crothers. Published by Samuel French, New York.

"Machinal," by Sophie Treadwell.

"Little Accident," by Floyd Dell and Thomas Mitchell.

"Gypsy," by Maxwell Anderson.

"The Kingdom of God," by G. Martinez Sierra; English version by Helen and Harley Granville-Barker. Published by E. P. Dutton & Company, New York.

1929-1930

"The Green Pastures," by Marc Connelly (adapted from "Ol' Man Adam and His Chillun," by Roark Bradford). Published by Farrar & Rinehart, Inc., New York.

"The Criminal Code," by Martin Flavin. Published by Horace Liveright, New York.

"Berkeley Square," by John Balderston. Published by the Macmillan Company, New York.

"Strictly Dishonorable," by Preston Sturges. Published by Horace Liveright, New York.
"The First Mrs. Fraser," by St. John Ervine. Published by the Macmillan Company, New York.
"The Last Mile," by John Wexley. Published by Samuel French, New York.
"June Moon," by Ring W. Lardner and George S. Kaufman. Published by Charles Scribner's Sons, New York.
"Michael and Mary," by A. A. Milne. Published by Chatto & Windus, London.
"Death Takes a Holiday," by Walter Ferris (adapted from the Italian of Alberto Casella). Published by Samuel French, New York.
"Rebound," by Donald Ogden Stewart. Published by Samuel French, New York.

1930-1931

"Elizabeth the Queen," by Maxwell Anderson. Published by Longmans, Green & Co., New York.
"Tomorrow and Tomorrow," by Philip Barry. Published by Samuel French, New York.
"Once in a Lifetime," by George S. Kaufman and Moss Hart. Published by Farrar and Rinehart, New York.
"Green Grow the Lilacs," by Lynn Riggs. Published by Samuel French, New York and London.
"As Husbands Go," by Rachel Crothers. Published by Samuel French, New York.
"Alison's House," by Susan Glaspell. Published by Samuel French, New York.
"Five-Star Final," by Louis Weitzenkorn. Published by Samuel French, New York.
"Overture," by William Bolitho. Published by Simon & Schuster, New York.
"The Barretts of Wimpole Street," by Rudolf Besier. Published by Little, Brown & Company, Boston.
"Grand Hotel," adapted from the German of Vicki Baum by W. A. Drake.

1931-1932

"Of Thee I Sing," by George S. Kaufman and Morrie Ryskind; music and lyrics by George and Ira Gershwin. Published by Alfred Knopf, New York.
"Mourning Becomes Electra," by Eugene G. O'Neill. Published by Horace Liveright, Inc., New York.
"Reunion in Vienna," by Robert Emmet Sherwood. Published

by Charles Scribner's Sons, New York.
"The House of Connelly," by Paul Green. Published by Samuel French, New York.
"The Animal Kingdom," by Philip Barry. Published by Samuel French, New York.
"The Left Bank," by Elmer Rice. Published by Samuel French, New York.
"Another Language," by Rose Franken. Published by Samuel French, New York.
"Brief Moment," by S. N. Behrman. Published by Farrar & Rinehart, New York.
"The Devil Passes," by Benn W. Levy. Published by Martin Secker, London.
"Cynara," by H. M. Harwood and R. F. Gore-Browne. Published by Samuel French, New York.

1932-1933

"Both Your Houses," by Maxwell Anderson. Published by Samuel French, New York.
"Dinner at Eight," by George S. Kaufman and Edna Ferber. Published by Doubleday, Doran & Co., Inc., Garden City, New York.
"When Ladies Meet," by Rachel Crothers. Published by Samuel French, New York.
"Design for Living," by Noel Coward. Published by Doubleday, Doran & Co., Inc., Garden City, New York.
"Biography," by S. N. Behrman. Published by Farrar & Rinehart, Inc., New York.
"Alien Corn," by Sidney Howard. Published by Charles Scribner's Sons, New York.
"The Late Christopher Bean," adapted from the French of René Fauchois by Sidney Howard. Published by Samuel French, New York.
"We, the People," by Elmer Rice. Published by Coward-McCann, Inc., New York.
"Pigeons and People," by George M. Cohan.
"One Sunday Afternoon," by James Hagan. Published by Samuel French, New York.

1933-1934

"Mary of Scotland," by Maxwell Anderson. Published by Doubleday, Doran & Co., Inc., Garden City, N. Y.

"Men in White," by Sidney Kingsley. Published by Covici, Friede, Inc., New York.
"Dodsworth," by Sinclair Lewis and Sidney Howard. Published by Harcourt, Brace & Co., New York.
"Ah, Wilderness," by Eugene O'Neill. Published by Random House, New York.
"They Shall Not Die," by John Wexley. Published by Alfred A. Knopf, New York.
"Her Master's Voice," by Clare Kummer. Published by Samuel French, New York.
"No More Ladies," by A. E. Thomas.
"Wednesday's Child," by Leopold Atlas. Published by Samuel French, New York.
"The Shining Hour," by Keith Winter. Published by Doubleday, Doran & Co., Inc., Garden City, New York.
"The Green Bay Tree," by Mordaunt Shairp. Published by Baker International Play Bureau, Boston, Mass.

1934-1935

"The Children's Hour," by Lillian Hellman. Published by Alfred Knopf, New York.
"Valley Forge," by Maxwell Anderson. Published by Anderson House, Washington, D. C. Distributed by Dodd, Mead & Co., New York.
"The Petrified Forest," by Robert Sherwood. Published by Charles Scribner's Sons, New York.
"The Old Maid," by Zoe Akins. Published by D. Appleton-Century Co., New York.
"Accent on Youth," by Samson Raphaelson. Published by Samuel French, New York.
"Merrily We Roll Along," by George S. Kaufman and Moss Hart. Published by Random House, New York.
"Awake and Sing," by Clifford Odets. Published by Random House, New York.
"The Farmer Takes a Wife," by Frank B. Elser and Marc Connelly.
"Lost Horizons," by John Hayden.
"The Distaff Side," by John Van Druten. Published by Alfred Knopf, New York.

1935-1936

"Winterset," by Maxwell Anderson. Published by Anderson House, Washington, D. C.

"Idiot's Delight," by Robert Emmet Sherwood. Published by Charles Scribner's Sons, New York.
"End of Summer," by S. N. Behrman. Published by Random House, New York.
"First Lady," by Katharine Dayton and George S. Kaufman. Published by Random House, New York.
"Victoria Regina," by Laurence Housman. Published by Samuel French, Inc., New York and London.
"Boy Meets Girl," by Bella and Samuel Spewack. Published by Random House, New York.
"Dead End," by Sidney Kingsley. Published by Random House, New York.
"Call It a Day," by Dodie Smith. Published by Samuel French, Inc., New York and London.
"Ethan Frome," by Owen Davis and Donald Davis. Published by Charles Scribner's Sons, New York.
"Pride and Prejudice," by Helen Jerome. Published by Doubleday, Doran & Co., Garden City, New York.

1936-1937

"High Tor," by Maxwell Anderson. Published by Anderson House, Washington, D. C.
"You Can't Take It with You," by Moss Hart and George S. Kaufman. Published by Farrar & Rinehart, Inc., New York.
"Johnny Johnson," by Paul Green. Published by Samuel French, Inc., New York.
"Daughters of Atreus," by Robert Turney. Published by Alfred A. Knopf, New York.
"Stage Door," by Edna Ferber and George S. Kaufman. Published by Doubleday, Doran & Co., Garden City, New York.
"The Women," by Clare Boothe. Published by Random House, Inc., New York.
"St. Helena," by R. C. Sherriff and Jeanne de Casalis. Published by Samuel French, Inc., New York and London.
"Yes, My Darling Daughter," by Mark Reed. Published by Samuel French, Inc., New York.
"Excursion," by Victor Wolfson. Published by Random House, New York.
"Tovarich," by Jacques Deval and Robert E. Sherwood. Published by Random House, New York.

1937-1938

"Of Mice and Men," by John Steinbeck. Published by Covici-Friede, New York.
"Our town," by Thornton Wilder. Published by Coward-McCann, Inc., New York.
"Shadow and Substance," by Paul Vincent Carroll. Published by Random House, Inc., New York.
"On Borrowed Time," by Paul Osborn. Published by Alfred A. Knopf, New York.
"The Star-Wagon," by Maxwell Anderson. Published by Anderson House, Washington, D. C. Distributed by Dodd, Mead & Co., New York.
"Susan and God," by Rachel Crothers. Published by Random House, Inc., New York.
"Prologue to Glory," by E. P. Conkle. Published by Random House, Inc., New York.
"Amphitryon 38," by S. N. Behrman. Published by Random House, Inc., New York.
"Golden Boy," by Clifford Odets. Published by Random House, Inc., New York.
"What a Life," by Clifford Goldsmith. Published by Dramatists Play Service, Inc., New York.

1938-1939

"Abe Lincoln in Illinois," by Robert E. Sherwood. Published by Charles Scribner's Sons, New York and Charles Scribner's Sons, Ltd. London.
"The Little Foxes," by Lillian Hellman. Published by Random House, Inc., New York.
"Rocket to the Moon," by Clifford Odets. Published by Random House, Inc., New York.
"The American Way," by George S. Kaufman and Moss Hart. Published by Random House, Inc., New York.
"No Time for Comedy," by S. N. Behrman. Published by Random House, Inc., New York.
"The Philadelphia Story," by Philip Barry. Published by Coward-McCann, Inc., New York.
"The White Steed," by Paul Vincent Carroll. Published by Random House, Inc., New York.
"Here Come the Clowns," by Philip Barry. Published by Coward-McCann, Inc., New York.

THE BEST PLAYS OF 1941-42

"Family Portrait," by Lenore Coffee and William Joyce Cowen. Published by Random House, Inc., New York.

"Kiss the Boys Good-bye," by Clare Boothe. Published by Random House, Inc., New York.

1939-1940

"There Shall Be No Night," by Robert E. Sherwood. Published by Charles Scribner's Sons, New York.

"Key Largo," by Maxwell Anderson. Published by Anderson House, Washington, D. C.

"The World We Make," by Sidney Kingsley.

"Life with Father," by Howard Lindsay and Russel Crouse. Published by Alfred A. Knopf, New York.

"The Man Who Came to Dinner," by George S. Kaufman and Moss Hart. Published by Random House, Inc., New York.

"The Male Animal," by James Thurber and Elliott Nugent. Published by Random House, Inc., New York, and MacMillan Co., Canada.

"The Time of Your Life," by William Saroyan. Published by Harcourt, Brace and Company, Inc., New York.

"Skylark," by Samson Raphaelson. Published by Random House, Inc., New York.

"Margin for Error," by Clare Boothe. Published by Random House, Inc., New York.

"Morning's at Seven," by Paul Osborn. Published by Samuel French, New York.

1940-1941

"Native Son," by Paul Green and Richard Wright. Published by Harper & Bros., New York.

"Watch on the Rhine," by Lillian Hellman. Published by Random House, Inc., New York.

"The Corn Is Green," by Emlyn Williams. Published by Random House, Inc., New York.

"Lady in the Dark," by Moss Hart. Published by Random House, Inc., New York.

"Arsenic and Old Lace," by Joseph Kesselring. Published by Random House, Inc., New York.

"My Sister Eileen," by Joseph Fields and Jerome Chodorov. Published by Random House, Inc., New York.

"Flight to the West," by Elmer Rice. Published by Coward, McCann, Inc., New York.

"Claudia," by Rose Franken Maloney. Published by Farrar & Rinehart, Inc., New York and Toronto.

"Mr. and Mrs. North," by Owen Davis. Published by Samuel French, New York.

"George Washington Slept Here," by George S. Kaufman and Moss Hart. Published by Random House, Inc., New York.

WHERE AND WHEN THEY WERE BORN

(Compiled from the most authentic records available.)

Abba, Marta	Milan, Italy	1907
Abbott, George	Hamburg, N. Y.	1895
Abel, Walter	St. Paul, Minn.	1898
Adams, Maude	Salt Lake City, Utah	1872
Addy, Wesley	Omaha, Neb.	1912
Adler, Luther	New York City	1903
Adler, Stella	New York City	1904
Aherne, Brian	King's Norton, England	1902
Akins, Zoe	Humansville, Mo.	1886
Allgood, Sara	Dublin, Ireland	1883
Ames, Florenz	Rochester, N. Y.	1884
Anders, Glenn	Los Angeles, Cal.	1890
Anderson, Judith	Australia	1898
Anderson, Mary	Trussville, Ala.	1917
Anderson, Maxwell	Atlantic City, Pa.	1888
Andrews, A. G.	Buffalo, N. Y.	1861
Andrews, Ann	Los Angeles, Cal.	1895
Angel, Heather	Oxford, England	1909
Anglin, Margaret	Ottawa, Canada	1876
Anson, A. E.	London, England	1879
Arden, Eve	San Francisco, Cal.	1912
Arling, Joyce	Memphis, Tenn.	1911
Arliss, George	London, England	1868
Ashcroft, Peggy	Croydon, England	1907
Astaire, Fred	Omaha, Neb.	1899
Atwater, Edith	Chicago, Ill.	1912
Atwell, Roy	Syracuse, N. Y.	1880
Atwill, Lionel	London, England	1885
Bainter, Fay	Los Angeles, Cal.	1892
Baker, Lee	Michigan	1880
Bankhead, Tallulah	Huntsville, Ala.	1902
Banks, Leslie J.	West Derby, England	1890
Barbee, Richard	Lafayette, Ind.	1887
Barrett, Edith	Roxbury, Mass.	1904
Barry, Philip	Rochester, N. Y.	1896
Barrymore, Diana	New York City	1921

Barrymore, Ethel .... Philadelphia, Pa. 1879
Barrymore, John .... Philadelphia, Pa. 1882
Barrymore, Lionel .... London, England 1878
Barton, James .... Gloucester, N. J. 1890
Baxter, Lora .... New York 1907
Behrman, S. N. .... Worcester, Mass. 1893
Bell, James .... Suffolk, Va. 1891
Bennett, Richard .... Cass County, Ind. 1873
Bergner, Elisabeth .... Vienna 1901
Berlin, Irving .... Russia 1888
Best, Edna .... Sussex, England 1900
Binney, Constance .... Philadelphia, Pa. 1900
Boland, Mary .... Detroit, Mich. 1880
Bolger, Ray .... Dorchester, Mass. 1906
Bondi, Beulah .... Chicago, Ill. 1892
Bordoni, Irene .... Paris, France 1895
Bourneuf, Philip .... Boston, Mass. 1912
Bowman, Patricia .... Washington, D. C. 1912
Brady, William A. .... San Francisco, Cal. 1863
Braham, Horace .... London, England 1896
Brent, Romney .... Saltillo, Mex. 1902
Brian, Donald .... St. Johns, N. F. 1877
Brice, Fannie .... Brooklyn, N. Y. 1891
Broderick, Helen .... New York 1891
Bromberg, J. Edward .... Hungary 1903
Brotherson, Eric .... Chicago, Ill. 1911
Brown, Anne Wiggins .... Baltimore, Md. 1916
Bruce, Nigel .... San Diego, Cal. 1895
Bryant, Charles .... England 1879
Buchanan, Jack .... England 1892
Burke, Billie .... Washington, D. C. 1885
Burr, Ann .... Boston, Mass. 1920
Byington, Spring .... Colorado Springs, Colo. ... 1898
Byron, Arthur .... Brooklyn, N. Y. 1872

Cabot, Eliot .... Boston, Mass. 1899
Cagney, James .... New York 1904
Cahill, Lily .... Texas 1891
Calhern, Louis .... New York 1895
Cantor, Eddie .... New York 1894
Carlisle, Kitty .... New Orleans, La. 1912
Carminati, Tullio .... Zara, Dalmatia 1894
Carnovsky, Morris .... St. Louis, Mo. 1898

THE BEST PLAYS OF 1941-42

Carpenter, Edward Childs	Philadelphia, Pa.	1871
Carroll, Earl	Pittsburgh, Pa.	1892
Carroll, Leo G.	Weedon, England	1892
Carroll, Nancy	New York City	1906
Catlett, Walter	San Francisco, Cal.	1889
Chandler, Helen	Charleston, N. C.	1906
Chaplin, Charles Spencer	London	1889
Chase, Ilka	New York	1900
Chatterton, Ruth	New York	1893
Christians, Mady	Vienna, Austria	1907
Churchill, Berton	Toronto, Can.	1876
Claire, Helen	Union Springs, Ala.	1908
Claire, Ina	Washington, D. C.	1892
Clive, Colin	St. Malo, France	1900
Coburn, Charles	Macon, Ga.	1877
Cohan, George M.	Providence, R. I.	1878
Cohan, Georgette	Los Angeles, Cal.	1900
Colbert, Claudette	Paris	1905
Collier, Constance	Windsor, England	1882
Collier, William	New York	1866
Collinge, Patricia	Dublin, Ireland	1894
Collins, Russell	New Orleans, La.	1901
Colt, Ethel Barrymore	Mamaroneck, N. Y.	1911
Colt, John Drew	New York	1914
Conklin, Peggy	Dobbs Ferry, N. Y.	1912
Conroy, Frank	London, England	1885
Conte, Nicholas	Jersey City, N. J.	1916
Cook, Donald	Portland, Ore.	1902
Cook, Joe	Evansville, Ind.	1890
Cooper, Gladys	Lewisham, England	1888
Cooper, Violet Kemble	London, England	1890
Corbett, Leonora	London, England	1908
Cornell, Katharine	Berlin, Germany	1898
Corthell, Herbert	Boston, Mass.	1875
Cossart, Ernest	Cheltenham, England	1876
Coulouris, George	Manchester, England	1906
Courtleigh, Stephen	New York City	1912
Coward, Noel	Teddington, England	1899
Cowl, Jane	Boston, Mass.	1887
Craig, Helen	Mexico City	1914
Craven, Frank	Boston, Mass.	1880
Crews, Laura Hope	San Francisco, Cal.	1880
Cronyn, Hume	Canada	1912

Crosman, Henrietta	Wheeling, W. Va.	1865
Crothers, Rachel	Bloomington, Ill.	1878
Cummings, Constance	Seattle, Wash.	1911
Dale, Margaret	Philadelphia, Pa.	1880
Davis, Donald	New York	1907
Davis, Owen	Portland, Me.	1874
Davis, Owen, Jr.	New York	1910
De Cordoba, Pedro	New York	1881
Digges, Dudley	Dublin, Ireland	1880
Dinehart, Allan	Missoula, Mont.	1889
Dixon, Jean	Waterbury, Conn.	1905
Dowling, Eddie	Woonsocket, R. I.	1895
Dressler, Eric	Brooklyn, N. Y.	1900
Dressler, Marie	Cobourg, Canada	1869
Dudley, Doris	New York City	1918
Duncan, Augustin	San Francisco	1873
Duncan, Todd	Danville, Ky.	1900
Dunn, Emma	England	1875
Dunning, Philip	Meriden, Conn.	1890
Dupree, Minnie	San Francisco, Cal.	1875
Durante, Jimmy	New York City	1893
Edney, Florence	London, England	1879
Eldridge, Florence	Brooklyn, N. Y.	1901
Ellerbe, Harry	Georgia	1905
Emery, Gilbert	Naples, New York	1875
Emery, Katherine	Birmingham, Ala.	1908
Erickson, Leif	California	1917
Errol, Leon	Sydney, Australia	1881
Ervine, St. John Greer	Belfast, Ireland	1883
Evans, Edith	London, England	1888
Evans, Maurice	Dorchester, England	1901
Farley, Morgan	Mamaroneck, N. Y.	1901
Farmer, Frances	Seattle, Wash.	1914
Farnum, William	Boston, Mass.	1876
Fassett, Jay	Elmira, N. Y.	1889
Ferber, Edna	Kalamazoo, Mich.	1887
Ferguson, Elsie	New York	1883
Ferrer, Jose	Puerto Rico	1909
Field, Sylvia	Allston, Mass.	1902
Fields, W. C.	Philadelphia, Pa.	1883

Fischer, Alice .... Indiana 1869
Fitzgerald, Barry .... Dublin, Ireland 1888
Fletcher, Bramwell .... Bradford, Yorkshire, Eng... 1904
Fontanne, Lynn .... London, England 1887
Forbes, Ralph .... London, England 1905
Foster, Phœbe .... New Hampshire 1897
Foy, Eddie, Jr. .... New Rochelle, N. Y. 1906
Fraser, Elizabeth .... Brooklyn, N. Y. 1920
Friganza, Trixie .... Cincinnati, Ohio 1870

Gahagan, Helen .... Boonton, N. J. 1902
Gaxton, William .... San Francisco, Cal. 1893
Geddes, Norman Bel .... Adrian, Mich. 1893
George, Grace .... New York 1879
Gerald, Ara .... New South Wales 1902
Gershwin, Ira .... New York 1896
Gielgud, John .... London, England 1904
Gillmore, Frank .... New York 1884
Gillmore, Margalo .... England 1901
Gish, Dorothy .... Massillon, Ohio 1898
Gish, Lillian .... Springfield, Ohio 1896
Gleason, James .... New York 1885
Golden, John .... New York 1874
Goodner, Carol .... New York City 1904
Gordon, Ruth .... Wollaston, Mass. 1896
Gough, Lloyd .... New York City 1906
Granville, Charlotte .... London 1863
Granville, Sydney .... Bolton, England 1885
Green, Martyn .... London, England 1899
Green, Mitzi .... New York City 1920
Greenstreet, Sydney .... England 1880
Groody, Louise .... Waco, Texas 1897
Gwenn, Edmund .... Glamorgan, Wales 1875

Haines, Robert T. .... Muncie, Ind. 1870
Hall, Bettina .... North Easton, Mass. 1906
Hall, Natalie .... North Easton, Mass. 1904
Hall, Thurston .... Boston, Mass. 1882
Halliday, John .... Brooklyn, N. Y. 1880
Halliday, Robert .... Loch Lomond, Scotland ... 1893
Hampden, Walter .... Brooklyn, N. Y. 1879
Hannen, Nicholas .... London, England 1881
Hardie, Russell .... Griffin Mills, N. Y. 1906

Hardwicke, Sir Cedric .... Lye, Stourbridge, England . 1893
Hargrave, Roy .... New York City 1908
Harrigan, William .... New York 1893
Harris, Sam H. .... New York 1872
Haydon, Julie .... Oak Park, Ill. 1910
Hayes, Helen .... Washington, D. C. 1900
Hector, Louis .... England 1882
Heflin, Van .... Walters, Okla. 1909
Heineman, Eda .... Japan 1891
Heming, Violet .... Leeds, England 1893
Henie, Sonja .... Oslo, Norway 1912
Hepburn, Katharine .... Hartford, Conn. 1907
Hernreid, Paul .... Trieste, Italy 1905
Hobart, Rose .... New York 1906
Hoey, Dennis .... London, England 1893
Holm, Celeste .... New York City 1916
Hopkins, Arthur .... Cleveland, Ohio 1878
Hopkins, Miriam .... Bainbridge, Ga. 1904
Holmes, Taylor .... Newark, N. J. 1872
Howard, Leslie .... London, England 1890
Huber, Paul .... Wilkes-Barre, Pa. 1895
Hull, Henry .... Louisville, Ky. 1893
Humphreys, Cecil .... Cheltenham, England 1880
Hunter, Glenn .... Highland Mills, N. Y. ... 1896
Huston, Walter .... Toronto 1884
Hutchinson, Josephine .... Seattle, Wash. 1898

Inescort, Frieda .... Hitchin, Scotland 1905
Ingram, Rex .... Dublin, Ireland 1892

Jagger, Dean .... Columbus Grove, Ohio ... 1904
Joel, Clara .... Jersey City, N. J. 1890
Johann, Zita .... Hungary 1904
Jolson, Al .... Washington, D. C. 1883
Johnson, Harold J. (Chic) .... Chicago, Ill. 1891
Joslyn, Allyn .... Milford, Pa. 1905
Joy, Nicholas .... Paris, France 1892

Kane, Whitford .... Larne, Ireland 1882
Karloff, Boris .... Dulwich, England 1887
Kaufman, George S. .... Pittsburgh, Pa. 1889
Kaye, A. P. .... Ringwood, England 1885
Kaye, Danny .... New York City 1914

THE BEST PLAYS OF 1941-42

Keith, Ian	Boston, Mass.	1899
Keith, Robert	Scotland	1899
Kelly, Gene	Pittsburgh, Pa.	1912
Kerrigan, J. M.	Dublin, Ireland	1885
Kerr, Geoffrey	London, England	1895
Kilbride, Percy	San Francisco, Cal.	1880
King, Dennis	Coventry, England	1897
Kingsford, Walter	England	1876
Kingsley, Sydney	New York	1906
Kirkland, Alexander	Mexico City	1904
Kirkland, Muriel	Yonkers, N. Y.	1904
Kruger, Alma	Pittsburgh, Pa.	1880
Kruger, Otto	Toledo, Ohio	1895
Landi, Elissa	Venice, Italy	1904
Landis, Jessie Royce	Chicago, Ill.	1904
Lane, Rosemary	Indianola, Ia.	1916
Larimore, Earl	Portland, Oregon	1899
Larrimore, Francine	Russia	1898
Lauder, Harry	Portobello, Scotland	1870
Laughton, Charles	Scarborough, England	1899
Lawford, Betty	London, England	1904
Lawrence, Gertrude	London	1898
Lawson, Wilfred	London, England	1894
Lawton, Frank	London, England	1904
Lawton, Thais	Louisville, Ky.	1881
Lederer, Francis	Karlin, Prague	1906
Lee, Canada	New York City	1907
Le Gallienne, Eva	London, England	1899
Lenihan, Winifred	New York	1898
Leontovich, Eugenie	Moscow, Russia	1894
Lillie, Beatrice	Toronto, Canada	1898
Locke, Katherine	New York	1914
Loeb, Philip	Philadelphia, Pa.	1892
Loftus, Cecilia	Glasgow, Scotland	1876
Logan, Stanley	Earlsfield, England	1885
Lord, Pauline	Hanford, Cal.	1890
Love, Montagu	Portsmouth, Hants	1877
Lukas, Paul	Budapest, Hungary	1895
Lunt, Alfred	Milwaukee, Wis.	1893
Macdonald, Donald	Denison, Texas	1898
March, Fredric	Racine, Wis.	1897

Margetson, Arthur	London, England	1897
Margo	Mexico	1918
Marshall, Everett	Worcester, Mass.	1902
Marshall, Herbert	London, England	1890
Massey, Raymond	Toronto, Canada	1896
Matthews, A. E.	Bridlington, England	1869
Mature, Victor	Louisville, Ky.	1916
May, Marty	New York City	1900
McClintic, Guthrie	Seattle, Wash.	1893
McCormick, Myron	Albany, Ind.	1906
McGrath, Paul	Chicago, Ill.	1900
McGuire, Dorothy	Omaha, Neb.	1918
Menken, Helen	New York	1901
Mercer, Beryl	Seville, Spain	1882
Meredith, Burgess	Cleveland, Ohio	1909
Merivale, Philip	Rehutia, India	1886
Merman, Ethel	Astoria, L. I.	1909
Merrill, Beth	Lincoln, Neb.	1916
Mestayer, Harry	San Francisco, Cal.	1881
Miller, Gilbert	New York	1884
Miller, Marilyn	Findlay, Ohio	1898
Miranda, Carmen	Portugal	1912
Mitchell, Grant	Columbus, Ohio	1874
Mitchell, Thomas	Elizabeth, N. J.	1892
Mitzi (Hajos)	Budapest	1891
Moore, Grace	Del Rio, Tenn.	1901
Moore, Victor	Hammonton, N. J.	1876
Moran, Lois	Pittsburgh, Pa.	1909
Morley, Robert	Semley, Wiltshire, England	1908
Morgan, Claudia	New York	1912
Morgan, Helen	Danville, Ill.	1900
Morgan, Ralph	New York City	1889
Morris, Mary	Boston	1894
Morris, McKay	San Antonio, Texas	1890
Moss, Arnold	Brooklyn, N. Y.	1910
Muni, Paul	Lemberg, Austria	1895
Nagel, Conrad	Keokuk, Iowa	1897
Natwick, Mildred	Baltimore, Md.	1908
Nazimova, Alla	Crimea, Russia	1879
Nolan, Lloyd	San Francisco, Cal.	1903
Nugent, J. C.	Miles, Ohio	1875
Nugent, Elliott	Dover, Ohio	1900

O'Brien-Moore, Erin	Los Angeles, Cal.	1908
O'Connell, Hugh	New York	1891
Odets, Clifford	Philadelphia	1906
Oldham, Derek	Accrington, England	1892
Olivier, Laurence	Dorking, Surrey, England	1907
Olsen, John Siguard (Ole)	Peru, Ind.	1892
O'Malley, Rex	London, England	1906
O'Neill, Eugene Gladstone	New York	1888
Ouspenskaya, Maria	Tula, Russia	1876
Overman, Lynne	Maryville, Mo.	1887
Pemberton, Brock	Leavenworth, Kansas	1885
Pennington, Ann	Philadelphia, Pa.	1898
Philips, Mary	New London, Conn.	1901
Pickford, Mary	Toronto	1893
Pollock, Channing	Washington, D. C.	1880
Powers, Leona	Salida, Colo.	1900
Powers, Tom	Owensburg, Ky.	1890
Price, Vincent	St. Louis, Mo.	1914
Pryor, Roger	New York City	1901
Quartermaine, Leon	Richmond, England	1876
Rains, Claude	London, England	1889
Rambeau, Marjorie	San Francisco, Cal.	1889
Rathbone, Basil	Johannesburg	1892
Raye, Martha	Butte, Mont.	1916
Reed, Florence	Philadelphia, Pa.	1883
Rennie, James	Toronto, Canada	1890
Revelle, Hamilton	Gibraltar	1872
Ridges, Stanley	Southampton, England	1891
Ring, Blanche	Boston, Mass.	1876
Robinson, Edward G.	Bucharest, Roumania	1893
Robson, Flora	South Shields, Durham, Eng.	1902
Robson, May	Australia	1868
Roos, Joanna	Brooklyn, N. Y.	1901
Ross, Thomas W.	Boston, Mass.	1875
Royle, Selena	New York	1905
Ruben, José	Belgium	1886
Sanderson, Julia	Springfield, Mass.	1887
Sands, Dorothy	Cambridge, Mass.	1900
Savo, Jimmy	New York City	1895

Scheff, Fritzi	Vienna, Austria	1879
Schildkraut, Joseph	Bucharest, Roumania	1896
Scott, Cyril	Ireland	1866
Scott, Martha	Jamesport, Mo.	1914
Segal, Vivienne	Philadelphia, Pa.	1897
Selwart, Tonio	Munich, Germany	1906
Selwyn, Edgar	Cincinnati, Ohio	1875
Shannon, Effie	Cambridge, Mass.	1867
Shean, Al	Dornum, Germany	1868
Sherman, Hiram	Boston, Mass.	1908
Sherwood, Robert Emmet	New Rochelle, N. Y.	1896
Sidney, Sylvia	New York	1910
Skinner, Cornelia Otis	Chicago	1902
Skinner, Otis	Cambridgeport, Mass.	1858
Slezak, Walter	Vienna, Austria	1902
Smith, Ben	Waxahachie, Texas	1905
Smith, Kent	Smithfield, Me.	1910
Sondergaard, Gale	Minnesota	1899
Starr, Frances	Oneonta, N. Y.	1886
Stenuf, Hedi	Vienna, Austria	1922
Stickney, Dorothy	Dickinson, N. D.	1903
Stoddard, Haila	Great Falls, Mont.	1914
Stone, Fred	Denver, Colo.	1873
Stone, Dorothy	New York	1905
Strudwick, Sheppard	North Carolina	1905
Sullavan, Margaret	Norfolk, Va.	1910
Tandy, Jessica	London, England	1909
Taylor, Laurette	New York	1884
Tearle, Conway	New York	1878
Tearle, Godfrey	New York	1884
Terris, Norma	Columbus, Kansas	1904
Thomas, Frankie	New York	1922
Thomas, John Charles	Baltimore, Md.	1887
Thorndike, Dame Sybil	Gainsborough, England	1882
Tobin, Genevieve	New York	1901
Tobin, Vivian	New York	1903
Toler, Sidney	Warrensburg, Mo.	1874
Tone, Franchot	Niagara Falls, N. Y.	1907
Tracy, Lee	Atlanta, Ga.	1898
Travers, Henry	Berwick, England	1874

Truex, Ernest	Red Hill, Mo.	1890
Tynan, Brandon	Dublin, Ireland	1879
Ulric, Lenore	New Ulm, Minn.	1897
Vallée, Rudy	Island Pond, Vermont	1902
Varden, Evelyn	Venita, Okla.	1893
Venuta, Benay	San Francisco, Cal.	1912
Waldron, Charles	New York	1877
Walker, June	New York	1904
Walsh, Mary Jane	Davenport, Ia.	1915
Warfield, David	San Francisco, Cal.	1866
Waring, Richard	Buckinghamshire, England	1912
Warwick, Robert	Sacramento, Cal.	1878
Waters, Ethel	Chester, Pa.	1900
Watkins, Linda	Boston, Mass.	1908
Watson, Lucile	Quebec, Canada	1879
Watson, Minor	Marianna, Ark.	1889
Webb, Clifton	Indiana	1891
Weber, Joseph	New York	1867
Webster, Margaret	New York City	1905
Welles, Orson	Kenosha, Wis.	1915
Westley, Helen	Brooklyn, N. Y.	1879
Weston, Ruth	Boston, Mass.	1911
White, George	Toronto, Canada	1890
Whorf, Richard	Winthrop, Mass.	1908
William, Warren	Aitkin, Minn.	1896
Williams, Emlyn	Mostyn, Wales	1905
Wiman, Dwight Deere	Moline, Ill.	1895
Winwood, Estelle	England	1883
Witherspoon, Cora	New Orleans, La.	1891
Wood, Peggy	Brooklyn, N. Y.	1894
Worlock, Frederick	London, England	1885
Wright, Haidee	London, England	1868
Wycherly, Margaret	England	1883
Wynward, Diana	London, England	1906
Wynn, Ed.	Philadelphia, Pa.	1886
Wynn, Keenan	New York City	1917
Young, Roland	London, England	1887
Yurka, Blanche	Bohemia	1893

NECROLOGY

June 15, 1941—June 15, 1942

Barrymore, John, actor, 60. Stage, screen and radio actor for forty years; son of Maurice and Georgia Drew Barrymore; first appeared with his father in "A Man of the World" in Philadelphia; first appearance in New York in "Glad of It," 1903; in London in "The Dictator," 1904; gained stage fame in "Hamlet," "Richard III," "Justice," "Peter Ibbetson," "Redemption" and "The Jest"; starred in half a hundred films; wrote "The Confessions of an Actor." Born Philadelphia, Pa.; died Hollywood, Calif., June 29, 1942.

Bates, Blanche, actress, 69. Leading American actress for thirty years; starred in "Madame Butterfly," "Under Two Flags," "The Darling of the Gods" and "The Girl of the Golden West"; debut in New York in "The Taming of the Shrew"; retired in 1926; returned in 1933, to support Katharine Hepburn in "The Lake"; married George Creel, author and chairman of the Committee on Public Information during first World War. Born Portland, Ore.; died San Francisco, Calif., December 25, 1941.

Benrimo, J. Harry, actor, playwright, director, 67. Wrote "The Yellow Jacket," with George C. Hazelton, Jr.; "The Willow Tree," with Harrison Rhodes; first New York appearance in "The First Born," 1897; supported many stars; was director for the Messrs. Shubert. Born San Francisco, Calif.; died New York, March 26, 1942.

Bowers, Robert Hood, composer, conductor, 64. Conducted for Victor Herbert; best known compositions "Chinese Lullaby" and "East Is West." Born Chambersburg, Pa.; died New York, December 29, 1941.

Cameron, Hugh, actor, 62. Started as callboy in San Francisco with James O'Neill in "The Count of Monte Cristo"; co-starred with Fannie Brice; leading comedian in Music Box revues; recently in pictures. Born Duluth, Minn.; died New York, November 9, 1941.

Calvé, Emma, singer, 83. Metropolitan Opera House debut as Santuzza in "Cavalleria Rusticana"; popular in grand opera from 1893 to 1906; best remembered rôle name part in

THE BEST PLAYS OF 1941-42

"Carmen"; married Alnor Gaspari, tenor. Born Bastide, France; died Millau, France, January 5, 1942.

Carle, Richard (Charles Nicholas Carleton), actor and playwright, 69. Thirty years on stage in America and England; debut in "Niobe," 1911; wrote and appeared in "The Tenderfoot" and "The Spring Chicken"; played many film rôles in recent years. Born Somerville, Mass.; Died Hollywood, Calif., June 28, 1941.

Cooke, Eddie, manager and press agent, 73. Represented Klaw & Erlanger, Kiralfy Bros., Nixon, Zimmerman, William A. Brady, Winchell Smith and John Golden for fifty years. Born New York City; died New York, January 15, 1942.

Duncan, Malcolm, actor, 60. Started with Richard Mansfield in Boston in "Cyrano de Bergerac," 1899; appeared in New York in "Five Star Final," "Dinner at 8," and "Merrily We Roll Along." Born Brooklyn, N. Y.; died Bayshore, L. I., May 2, 1942.

Fields, Lew (Lewis Maurice Schanfields), actor and producer, 74. Famous comedy team of Weber and Fields; started partnership in 1877 at Bowery, Music Hall; partnership continued until 1904; opened Lew Fields Theatre with "It Happened in Nordland"; appeared recently with Weber in radio plays and pictures, notably in "Blossoms on Broadway" and "Lillian Russell." Born New York City; died Beverly Hills, Calif., July 20, 1941.

Franklin, Irene, actress and song writer, 65. Famous on stage, screen and in vaudeville in America, Europe and Australia; prominent as entertainer during first World War; started as child actress with Minnie Palmer; toured United States and England with her husband, Burt Green, with whom she wrote many songs. Born St. Louis, Mo.; died Englewood, N. J., June 16, 1941.

Gest, Morris, producer, 61. Famous as a producer of spectacles; started in Boston 1900; associated with F. Ray Comstock from 1905 to 1928; produced more than 50 plays, including "Aphrodite," "The Wanderer," "Chu Chin Chow," "The Miracle" and "Chauve Souris"; brought Moscow Art Theatre, Russian Ballet and Max Reinhardt to America; managed Midget Village at New York World's Fair, 1939-40; married Rene Belasco. Born Vilna, Russia; died New York, May 16, 1942.

Goodrich, Arthur F., playwright, 63. First play "Yes and No," 1917; best known plays "Caponsacchi," with Rose A. Palmer; "So This Is London"; wrote new version of "Richelieu" for Walter Hampden. Born New Britain, Conn.; died New York, June 26, 1941.

Grattan, Lawrence, actor and playwright, 71. Many years in stock and vaudeville; headed Lawrence Grattan Players in Chicago; wrote 21 vaudeville sketches in which he acted with his wife, Eva Taylor, on Orpheum circuit. Born Concord, N. H.; died New York, December 9, 1941.

Hackett, Charles, singer, 52. Widely known internationally as opera singer and concert artist; debut Metropolitan Opera House in "Barber of Seville," 1919; last appearance in "Mignon," 1939; with Chicago Civic Opera Company ten years; born Worcester, Mass.; died Jamaica, N. Y., January 1, 1942.

Hamilton, Hale, actor, 62. Twenty years on stage, twelve in pictures; played name part in "Get-Rich-Quick Wallingford" for years in America and England; last outstanding part in picture, "Adventures of Marco Polo." Born Topeka, Kan.; died Hollywood, Calif., May 19, 1942.

Harris, Sam H., producer, 69. Partner of George M. Cohan, with whom he produced fifty plays, many of them written by Cohan; on his own since 1919; recent productions included "Of Thee I Sing," "You Can't Take It with You," "Once in a Lifetime," "Dinner at 8," "Stage Door" and "Lady in the Dark"; president Producing Managers' Association. Born New York City; died New York, July 3, 1941.

Intropodi, Josie, actress, 75. Light opera comedienne known for rôles in Gilbert and Sullivan operas and popular musical comedies; last New York engagement in "Oh, Evening Star," 1936. Born New York; died New York, September 19, 1941.

Jackson, Joe (Joseph Francis Jiranek), comedian, 62. Internationally known for trick tramp bicycling act; first appearance in New York at Fifth Avenue Theatre, 1911; last appearance backstage at the Roxy Theatre, New York, where he collapsed and died at the end of his performance. Born Vienna, Austria; died New York, May 14, 1942.

Kramer, Wright, actor, 71. Supported Fanny Davenport and other stars in early years of century; toured extensively in vaudeville; recently in pictures. Born Chicago, Ill.; died Hollywood, Calif., November 14, 1941.

Lee, Auriol, actress and director, 60. Staged "There's Always Juliet," "The Distaff Side," "The Wind and the Rain," and others in New York and London; first appearance in London, 1900; with Forbes-Robertson in "The Light That Failed," 1903; toured United States in "The Man Who Stayed at Home." Born London, England; died near Hutchinson, in automobile accident July 2, 1941.

Leonard, Eddie (Lemuel Gordon Toney), comedian and songwriter, 70. Minstrel and vaudeville headliner for forty-five years; began with Primrose & West; wrote many songs, including "Ida," "Roly Boly Eyes," and "Just Because She Made Them Goo-goo Eyes"; last engagement Billy Rose's "Diamond Horseshoe," 1940. Born Richmond, Va.; died New York, July 29, 1941.

Lombard, Carole (Carol Jane Peters), actress, 32. Gained fame in motion pictures; co-starred with William Powell in "Ladies' Man," George Raft in "Bolero," John Barrymore in "Twentieth Century," etc. Born Fort Wayne, Ind.; died in airplane crash returning to California from patriotic warbond campaign in East, January 16, 1942.

McIntosh, Burr, actor, author, 79. First appearance in New York in 1885; remembered as Taffy in first American production of "Trilby"; as Squire Bartlett in the first "Way Down East" company, and in the title rôle of "The Gentleman from Mississippi"; pioneer in motion pictures. Born Wellsville, Ohio; died Hollywood, Calif., April 28, 1942.

Mordant, Edwin, actor, 74. Began career in Baltimore as member of Ford Stock company; with Charles Frohman in New York; leading man in Henry W. Savage Stock Co. in Philadelphia; leading man first American stock company in Mexico City. Born Baltimore, Md.; died Hollywood, Calif., February 15, 1942.

Morgan, Helen, actress, singer, 41. Began in Chicago's neighborhood theatres; first appearance in New York in "Sally"; appeared in White's "Scandals," "Show Boat," Ziegfeld's "Follies," "Sweet Adeline," etc.; in vaudeville; remembered for songs "My Bill" and "Why Was I Born?" Born Danville, Ill.; died Chicago, Ill., October 8, 1941.

Morton, Sam, actor, 79. Famous as leader of The Four Mortons, including his wife and children, in vaudeville for years; last appeared in "The Sidewalks of New York," 1931; one of the founders of the White Rats in New York. Born Detroit, Mich.; died Detroit, Mich., October 28, 1941.

Paderewski, Ignace Jan, pianist and statesman, 80. Internationally famous for many years; professional debut in Vienna at 18; first appeared in New York in 1891; his twentieth and last American tour in 1939; made film appearance in "Moonlight Sonata" 1937. Born Kurilovka, Poland; died New York, June 29, 1941.

Pidgeon, Edward Everett, drama editor, 75. In charge of drama departments New York Evening World, Evening Post, Globe, Sun and Journal of Commerce; president of Theatrical Press Representatives of America. Born Charlottestown, Nova Scotia; died New York, August 30, 1941.

Pitman, Richard, actor and theatrical agent, 67. Started stage career with E. H. Sothern in "Hamlet"; appeared with Maude Adams in "The Little Minister" and "The Pretty Sister of Jose"; last appearance with Nat Goodwin in "Why Marry?"; represented many well known actors and actresses. Born Boston, Mass.; died Jamaica, N. Y., November 13, 1941.

Pollock, Allan, actor, 64. British actor first seen in New York in support of Mrs. Patrick Campbell; played with Eleanor Robson in "The Dawn of a Tomorrow"; brought "A Bill of Divorcement" to New York in which Katharine Cornell scored her first Broadway success; last New York engagement with Billie Burke in "Jerry." Born London, England; died England, January 18, 1942.

Royle, Edwin Milton, actor, playwright, 79. Played in support of Booth and Barrett, Louis James and other old-time stars; co-starred with Selena Fetter (Mrs. Royle) in "Friends," "Captain Impudence" and other plays which he wrote; biggest success "The Squaw Man," starring William Faversham. Born Lexington, Mo.; died New York, February 6, 1942.

Saxon, Marie, actress, 37. Dancing ingénue in musical comedies; started with her mother, Pauline Saxon, in vaudeville; last Broadway appearance in "Ups-a-Daisy," 1928; appeared in pictures, notably "Broadway Hoofer." Born Lawrence, Mass.; died Harrison, N. Y., November 12, 1941.

Scribner, Samuel A., theatrical manager, 82. Active in theatre and amusement world for nearly 70 years; headed Burlesque Wheel, 40 theatres, 40 road shows, from Boston to Omaha; organized Columbia Amusement Co.; president of Theatre Authority, Inc.; actively associated with Actors' Fund and Percy Williams Home. Born Brookville, Pa.; died Bronxville, N. Y., July 8, 1941.

Skinner, Otis, actor, producer, author, 83. In sixty years played more than 325 parts; gained international fame for Shakespearean rôles; won citations for outstanding diction; first appearance 1877, Philadelphia Museum; first New York appearance Niblo's Gardens in "Enchantment," 1879; member Augustin Daly's company; launched his own company 1894, remembered as star of "Kismet," "The Honor of the Family," "Mister Antonio," etc.; wrote many books, including his autobiography, "Footlights and Spotlights"; appeared in picture "Kismet." Born Cambridge, Mass.; died New York, January 4, 1942.

Stevens, Thomas Wood, author, director, 62. Director of Goodman's Theatre, Chicago; headed drama department of Carnegie Institute of Technology; head of University of Arizona Art Department; wrote masque, "Drawing of the Sword," for Red Cross during first World War; his pageant, "Joan of Arc," was produced at Doremy, France, in 1918; wrote "The Theatre from Athens to Broadway." Born Daysville, Ill.; died Tucson, Ariz., January 29, 1942.

Stewart, William G., singer and director, 74. Comic opera baritone well known in early 1900's; authority on Gilbert and Sullivan repertory, which he staged for Federal Theatre project in California. Born Cleveland, Ohio; died Glendale, Calif., July 16, 1941.

Taylor, Charles A., producer, playwright, 78. Wrote and produced many melodramas, including "Yosemite" and "Rags and Riches," in which his wife, Laurette Taylor, first appeared in New York; prominent as picture director. Born South Hadley, Mass.; died Glendale, Calif., March 20, 1942.

Weber, Joseph M., actor and manager, 74. First appearance at Bowery Music Hall, 1877, with Lew Fields; became famous comedy team, presenting a series of musical travesties at the Weber and Fields Music Hall, New York, from 1895 to 1904, including "Fiddle-de-Dee," "Hoity-Toity," "Pousse Cafe," etc.; later became a producer, scoring a big success with "The Climax," "Alma, Where Do You Live?", etc. Born New York; died Los Angeles, Calif., May 10, 1942.

Zweig, Stefan, playwright, 60. Wrote "Volpone" and "Jeremiah," produced by the New York Theatre Guild; many of his books widely read and freely translated; screen drama of "Marie Antoinette" adapted from his work. Born Vienna, Austria; died Petropolis, Brazil, February 23, 1942.

THE DECADES' TOLL

(Persons of Outstanding Prominence in the Theatre
Who Have Died in Recent Years)

	Born	Died
Aborn, Milton	1864	1933
Ames, Winthrop	1871	1937
Anderson, Mary (Navarro)	1860	1940
Baker, George Pierce	1866	1935
Barrymore, John	1882	1942
Belasco, David	1856	1931
Benson, Sir Frank	1859	1939
Bernhardt, Sarah	1845	1923
Campbell, Mrs. Patrick	1865	1940
Crabtree, Charlotte (Lotta)	1847	1924
De Koven, Reginald	1861	1920
De Reszke, Jean	1850	1925
Drew, John	1853	1927
Drinkwater, John	1883	1937
Du Maurier, Sir Gerald	1873	1934
Duse, Eleanora	1859	1924
Fiske, Minnie Maddern	1865	1932
Frohman, Daniel	1851	1940
Galsworthy, John	1867	1933
Gorky, Maxim	1868	1936
Greet, Sir Philip (Ben)	1858	1936
Herbert, Victor	1859	1924
Patti, Adelina	1843	1919
Pinero, Sir Arthur Wing	1855	1934
Pirandello, Luigi	1867	1936
Rejane, Gabrielle	1857	1920
Rogers, Will	1879	1935
Russell, Annie	1864	1936
Schumann-Heink, Ernestine	1861	1936
Sembrich, Marcella	1859	1935
Shaw, Mary	1860	1929
Skinner, Otis	1858	1942
Sothern, Edwin Hugh	1859	1933
Terry, Ellen	1848	1928
Thomas, Augustus	1857	1934
Yeats, William Butler	1865	1939

INDEX OF AUTHORS

Abbott, George, 8, 422, 469, 470, 471
Adamson, Harold, 422
Akins, Zoe, 465, 466, 474
Allen, Lewis, 438
Allensworth, Carl, 4, 393
Alsberg, Henry G., 469
Anderson, Maxwell, 5, 180, 212, 387, 405, 464, 465, 469, 470, 471, 472, 473, 474, 475, 476, 477
Andreyev, Leonid, 468
Angus, Bernardine, 421
Ansky, S., 469
Anspacher, Louis Kaufman, 466
Archer, William, 467
Arlen, Michael, 469
Armstrong, Charlotte, 7, 414
Atlas, Leopold, 474

Bagnold, Enid, 29
Baker, Melville, 468
Balderston, John, 471
Barian, Joe, 438
Barnes, Charles, 443
Barrie, James M., 12, 442, 467
Barry, Philip, 468, 469, 471, 472, 473, 476
Baum, Vicki, 472
Beach, Lewis, 469
Behrman, S. N., 473, 475, 476
Benelli, Sem, 467
Benson, Sally, 7, 145, 386
Bergenson, Beau, 438
Bernstein, Henri, 23
Besier, Rudolf, 472
Biggers, Earl Derr, 466
Birabeau, Andre, 414
Blane, Ralph, 4, 400
Bloch, Bertram, 6, 411
Block, Hal, 417
Bodeen, De Witt, 30, 33
Bolitho, William, 472
Bolton, Guy, 7, 18, 413, 420, 467, 468
Boothe, Clare, 475, 477

Bordages, Asa, 8, 420
Borden, Ethel, 5, 10, 402, 437
Bradford, Roark, 471
Brennan, Frederick Hazlitt, 4, 212, 394
Bridgers, Ann, 471
Bright, John, 8, 420
Brown, Rowland, 444
Browne, Maurice, 471
Browne, Porter Emerson, 467
Bruckner, Ferdinand, 445
Butler, Rachel Barton, 467
Byrne, Dolly, 467

Canfield, Mary Cass, 5, 10, 402, 437
Capek, Karel, 468
Carroll, Paul Vincent, 14, 451, 476
Casella, Alberto, 472
Chodorov, Jerome, 7, 145, 386, 415, 477
Coffee, Lenore, 477
Cohan, George M., 466, 473
Cohen, Frederic, 430, 431, 432
Colton, John, 468
Conkle, E. P., 476
Connelly, Marc, 11, 438, 465, 467, 468, 469, 471, 474
Cooper, Lou, 438
Corle, Edwin, 436
Cormack, Bartlett, 471
Cowan, William Joyce, 477
Coward, Noel, 6, 31, 109, 386, 388, 410, 464, 473
Craven, Frank, 467
Crothers, Rachel, 467, 468, 471, 472, 473, 476
Crouse, Russell, 477

Dane, Clemence, 467
Davis, Donald, 475
Davis, Eddie, 448
Davis, Owen, 465, 468, 475, 478
Dawless, Smith, 33
Dayton, Katharine, 475
Dell, Floyd, 471

INDEX OF AUTHORS

Deval, Jacques, 475
Dodd, Lee Wilson, 468
Drake, W. A., 472
Drinkwater, John, 466
Duke, Vernon, 422, 427
Dunning, Philip, 470

Ehrmann, Herbert, 441
Eisinger, Jo, 447
Elinson, Izzy, 422
Eliscu, Edward, 31
Elser, Frank B., 474
Emery, Gilbert, 468, 469
Engel, Lehman, 412
Ervine, St. John, 466, 467, 472
Eunson, Dale, 11, 435

Fain, Sam E., 417
Fauchois, Rene, 473
Fennelly, Parker W., 4, 396
Ferber, Edna, 5, 406, 469, 470, 473, 475
Ferris, Walter, 472
Field, Salisbury, 467
Fielding, Marjery, 443
Fields, Herbert and Dorothy, 407
Fields, Joseph, 7, 145, 386, 415, 477
Fischer, Clifford C., 12, 443, 448, 454
Flavin, Martin, 471
Forbes, James, 467
Franken, Rose, 3, 18, 473, 478

Gabrielson, Frank, 395
Gale, Zona, 465
Galsworthy, John, 467, 468, 471
George, Grace, 468
Geraldy, Paul, 468
Gershwin, George, 9, 433, 465, 472
Gershwin, Ira, 392, 433, 465, 472
Geto, Al, 438
Gilbert, W. S., 10, 430
Gillette, William, 453
Ginsbury, Norman, 5, 402
Glaspell, Susan, 465, 472
Gleason, James, 469
Goff, Madison, 30
Goldsmith, Bea, 438
Goldsmith, Clifford, 476
Gore-Brown, R. F., 473
Gorney, Jay, 18, 31
Goulding, Edmund, 469
Granville-Barker, H., 467, 471

Grant, James Edward, 11, 441
Green, Paul, 465, 470, 473, 475, 477
Greendale, Alexander, 7, 415
Greene, Luther, 415
Greene, Patterson, 9, 425
Grever, Marie, 403
Guiterman, Arthur, 428
Guitry, Sacha, 467

Hagan, James, 473
Hamilton, Patrick, 8, 28, 282, 389, 419
Hammerstein, Oscar, 2d, 8, 418
Harris, John, 446
Hart, Lorenz, 14, 391, 455
Hart, Moss, 392, 465, 472, 474, 475, 476, 477, 478
Hartman, Don, 428
Harvey, Roslyn, 438
Harwood, H. M., 473
Hayden, John, 474
Hayes, Alfred, 438
Hecht, Ben, 10, 436, 471
Helburn, Theresa, 401, 414
Hellman, Lillian, 21, 464, 474, 476, 477
Heyward, Dorothy, 433
Heyward, Du Bose, 9, 433, 471
Hoffman, Louis, 428
Holm, John Cecil, 4, 8, 400, 422
Holt, Henry, 404
Hopwood, Avery, 17, 24
Horwin, Jerry, 33
Housman, Laurence, 475
Howard, Sidney, 465, 469, 470, 473, 474
Hughes, Hatcher, 465, 469
Hurlbut, William, 470
Huston, John, 9, 34, 385, 424, 464

Ibsen, Henrik, 10, 437

Jay, William, 420
Jeans, Ronald, 398
Jerome, Helen, 453, 475
Jessel, George, 5, 408
Job, Thomas, 14, 316, 389, 452
Johnson, Chic, 417
Jooss, Kurt, 430, 432

Kallesser, Michael, 395
Kalmar, Bert, 408

INDEX OF AUTHORS

Katzin, Winifred, 469
Kaufman, George S., 5, 386, 406, 465, 467, 468, 469, 470, 472, 473, 474, 475, 476, 477, 478
Kaye, Sylvia Fine, 5
Kelly, George, 465, 468, 469, 470, 471
Kennedy, Charles Rann, 7, 416
Kennedy, Mary, 469
Kesselring, Joseph, 477
Kingsley, Sidney, 465, 474, 475, 477
Kleinsinger, George, 438
Koch, Howard, 9, 34, 385, 424, 464
Kraft, H. S., 10, 434
Krasna, Norman, 6, 212, 409
Kummer, Clare, 466, 474

Langley, A. N., 410
Lanner, Joseph, 431
Lardner, Ring W., 472
La Touche, John, 422, 427
Laufs, Carl, 453
Lavery, Emmett, 33
Leback, Ned, 438
Leighton, Isabel, 6, 411
Lessing, Gotthold Ephraim, 445
Leveen, Raymond, 403
Levin, Jack, 405
Levy, Benn W., 473
Levy, Parke, 426
Lewis, Sinclair, 474
Liebman, Max, 5
Lindsay, Howard, 477
Lipscott, Alan, 426
Locke, Sam D., 438
Lonsdale, Frederick, 470

MacArthur, Charles, 426, 471
Marquis, Don, 468
Marrow, Macklin, 428
Martin, Hugh, 4, 400
Maugham, Somerset, 7, 18, 413, 468, 478
Mayer, Edwin Justus, 469
McGuire, William Anthony, 468
McKenney, Ruth, 387
Medcraft, Russell, 408
Meloney, Rose Franken, 478
Middleton, George, 467
Middleton, Horace, 416
Milne, Alan Alexander, 468, 472
Mitchell, Norma, 446
Mitchell, Thomas, 471
Molnar, Ferenc, 467, 468, 470

Morris, Ray, 33
Myers, Henry, 31

Nichols, Robert, 471
Norcross, Richard, 395
North, Alex, 438
Nugent, Elliott, 477

O'Casey, Sean, 471
Odets, Clifford, 9, 423, 474, 476
O'Donnell, Judson, 447
Olsen, Ole, 417
O'Hara, John, 391
O'Neill, Eugene, 5, 24, 29, 401, 465, 466, 467, 469, 470, 472, 474
Osborn, Paul, 476, 477
Oursler, Fulton, 14, 450

Parker, Louis N., 466
Perkins, Grace, 14, 450
Pierson, Arthur, 448
Pincus, Irvin, 395
Pollock, Channing, 468, 469
Porter, Cole, 5, 19, 407
Powell, Dawn, 427

Quillan, Joe, 422

Randolph, Clemence, 468
Raphaelson, Samson, 8, 9, 244, 387, 429, 474, 477
Reed, Mark, 475
Reizenstein, Elmer, 466
Rice, Elmer, 465, 471, 473, 477
Richman, Arthur, 468
Rifkin, Leo, 440
Riggs, Lynn, 472
Rodgers, Richard, 14, 391, 455
Romberg, Sigmund, 8, 418
Roos, William, 13, 449
Rotter, Fritz, 8, 212, 388, 422
Ruby, Harry, 408
Ryskind, Morrie, 465

Sacher, Toby, 438
Saroyan, William, 29, 464, 477
Self, Edwin B., 397
Selwyn, Edgar, 469
Shairp, Mordaunt, 474
Shakespeare, William, 404, 412, 418
Shane, Margaret, 399
Shaw, George Bernard, 13, 29, 448
Shaw, David, 440

INDEX OF AUTHORS

Sheekman, Arthur, 399
Sheldon, Edward, 466
Sheridan, Richard Brinsley, 428
Sherriff, R. C., 471, 475
Sherwood, Robert, 464, 465, 470, 472, 474, 475, 476, 477
Sierra, G. Martinez, 470, 471
Silvers, Sid, 408
Smith, Dodie, 475
Smith, Harry James, 466
Spewack, Bella and Samuel, 475
Stallings, Laurence, 387, 469
Steinbeck, John, 13, 34, 72, 386, 445, 464, 476
Stewart, Donald Ogden, 472
Storm, Leslie, 11, 439
Stratton, Mike, 438
Sturges, Preston, 472
Sullivan, A. S., 10, 430
Sullivan, Ed, 13, 450
Sundegaard, Arnold, 424
Swann, Francis, 25
Sylvaine, Vernon, 401

Tansman, Alexander, 431
Tarkington, Booth, 466
Tarloff, Frank, 440
Thomas, A. E., 474
Thompson, Fred, 427
Thompson, Julian F., 14, 455
Thurber, James, 477
Tolkin, Mel, 438
Totheroh, Dan, 469
Treadwell, Sophie, 7, 349, 390, 417
Trollope, Anthony, 316
Turney, Catherine, 33
Turney, Robert, 475

Underhill, John Garrett, 470

Van Druten, John, 10, 436, 470, 474
Vane, Sutton, 389, 468
Varesi, Gilda, 467
Vincent, Allen, 8, 212, 388, 422
Vittes, Louis, 453
Vollmer, Lula, 469

Walker, Don, 455
Walter, Eugene, 466
Warnick, Buck, 455
Warren, Ruth, 469
Watkins, Maurine, 470
Watters, George Manker, 470
Weill, Kurt, 392
Weitzenkorn, Louis, 472
Wells, William K. and Eleanor, 403
Wexley, John, 472, 474
Wilde, Hagar, 11, 435
Wilder, Thornton, 465, 476
Williams, Emlen, 13, 447, 477
Williams, Jesse Lynch, 465, 466, 468
Wilson, Harry Leon, 468
Winter, Keith, 474
Wodehouse, P. G., 470
Wolfson, Victor, 475
Wood, Cyrus, 17, 24
Wood, Joseph, 418
Wright, Richard, 477

Yellen, Jack, 417

Zilboorg, Gregory, 468
Zipser, Arthur, 438

INDEX OF PLAYS AND CASTS

Abe Lincoln in Illinois, 464, 465, 476
Abie's Irish Rose, 27, 463
Abraham Lincoln, 466
Accent on Youth, 21, 244, 387, 474
Across the Board on Tomorrow Morning, 29
Adam and Eva, 467
Adonis, 463
Ah, Wilderness, 5, 30, 401, 474
Alien Corn, 473
Alison's House, 465, 472
All in Favor, 428
All Men Are Alike, 401
All the Comforts of Home, 453
Ambush, 468
American Sideshow, 17, 21
American Way, The, 476
Amphitryon, 38, 476
Angel Street, 8, 19, 20, 28, 282, 389, 419, 464
Animal Kingdom, The, 473
Anna Christie, 24, 29, 465, 467
Anne of England, 5, 402
Another Language, 473
Arsenic and Old Lace, 3, 18, 20, 25, 28, 463, 477
As Husbands Go, 472
As You Like It, 404
Autumn Hill, 446
Awake and Sing, 474

Baby's Name Is Oscar, The, 33
Bad Man, The, 467
Ball in Old Vienna, A, 431
Banjo Eyes, 8, 422
Barchester Towers, 316, 389
Barretts of Wimpole Street, The, 472
Bat, The, 463
Beautiful People, The, 462
Beggar on Horseback, 32, 469
Beggar's Opera, 25
Behold the Bridegroom, 471
Berkeley Square, 471
Best Foot Forward, 4, 400
Beyond the Horizon, 465, 466

Big City, The, 431
Bill of Divorcement, A, 467
Biography, 473
Bird in Hand, 463
Bitter Sweet, 25, 31, 386
Blackbirds, 463
Blackouts of 1942, 32
Blithe Spirit, 6, 18, 20, 21, 28, 109, 386, 410, 464
Blossom Time, 21, 24, 30, 463
Boomerang, The, 463
Both Your Houses, 387, 465, 473
Boy Meets Girl, 463, 475
Bride of the Lamb, 470
Brief Moment, 473
Bright Champagne, 33
Broadway, 463, 470
Brooklyn, U. S. A., 8, 420
Brother Cain, 395
Brother Rat, 463
Burlesque, 470
Butter and Egg Man, The, 470
By Jupiter, 14, 455

Cabin in the Sky, 24, 30
Cafe Crown, 10, 434
Call It a Day, 475
Candida, 13, 21, 448
Candle in the Wind, 5, 20, 180, 212, 387, 405
Catch as Catch Can, 33
Cavalcade, 386
Changelings, The, 468
Charley's Aunt, 19, 21
Charlot's Revue, 30
Chicago, 470
Chicken Feed, 468
Children's Hour, The, 21, 282, 463, 474
Circle, The, 468
Clarence, 466
Clash by Night, 9, 423
Claudia, 3, 18, 20, 21, 25, 28, 462, 478
Comes the Revelation, 453

501

INDEX OF PLAYS AND CASTS

Constant Nymph, The, 30
Constant Wife, The, 470
Coquette, 471
Corn Is Green, The, 3, 20, 462, 477
Cradle Snatchers, 5, 407, 408
Cradle Song, 470
Craig's Wife, 465, 469
Criminal Code, The, 471
Cuckoos on the Hearth, 4, 396
Cynara, 473

Daisy Mayme, 470
Dance Drama, 456
Dancing Mothers, 469
Daughters of Atreus, 475
Dawn in Lyonnese, 390
Dead End, 463, 475
Death Takes a Holiday, 472
Deburau, 467
Déclassée, 466
Design for Living, 386, 473
Desire Under the Elms, 469
Devil Passes, The, 473
Devil's Disciple, The, 29
Dinner at Eight, 32, 473
Disraeli, 466
Distaff Side, The, 474
Distant City, The, 397
Doctor's Dilemma, The, 21, 23, 30, 462
Dodsworth, 474
Don't Feed the Actors, 33
Dover Road, The, 468
Drunkard, The, 32
Dulcy, 467
Dybbuk, The, 469

Easiest Way, The, 466
East Is West, 463
Elizabeth the Queen, 387, 472
Emperor Jones, The, 467
End of Summer, 475
Enemy, The, 469
Enter Madame, 467
Escape, 471
Escape to Autumn, 30
Ethan Frome, 475
Excursion, 475

Fall Guy, The, 469
Family Portrait, 477
Famous Mrs. Fair, The, 467
Far Off Hills, The, 33

Farmer Takes a Wife, The, 474
Firebrand, 469
Firefly, The, 25
First Crocus, The, 424
First Lady, 475
First Mrs. Fraser, The, 472
First Year, 463, 467
Five-Star Final, 472
Flight to the West, 33, 477
Flowers of Virtue, The, 11, 438
Fool, The, 468
Front Page, The, 471
Fun for the Money, 31

Gaslight, 8, 28, 283, 389
George Washington Slept Here, 32, 478
Ghost for Sale, 398
Girls in Uniform, 17
Give Us This Day, 385
Golden Boy, 476
Golden Wings, 420
Gondoliers, The, 433
Good Gracious, Annabelle, 466
Good Neighbor, 5, 405
Good News, 463
Good Night, Ladies, 16, 17, 20, 21, 24
Goose Hangs High, The, 469
Grand Hotel, 472
Grand Street Follies, The, 388
Great American Family, The, 33
Great God Brown, The, 469
Great Scott, 385
Green Bay Tree, The, 474
Green Goddess, The, 467
Green Grow the Lilacs, 472
Green Hat, The, 469
Green Pastures, The, 463, 465, 471
Green Table, The, 430
Gringo, 390
Guest in the House, 11, 435
Gypsy, 471

Harlem Cavalcade, 13, 450
Hay Fever, 386
He Who Gets Slapped, 25, 468
Heart of a City, 11, 439
Hedda Gabler, 10, 437
Hell-bent fer Heaven, 465, 469
Hello Out There, 29
Hellzapoppin, 3, 8, 15, 18, 21, 24, 32, 418, 462, 463

INDEX OF PLAYS AND CASTS

Her Master's Voice, 474
Here Come the Clowns, 476
Hero, The, 468
High Kickers, 6, 21, 408
High Tor, 387, 464, 475
Hit the Deck, 25, 31
H.M.S. Pinafore, 430
Holiday, 471
Home from Home, 33
Hope for a Harvest, 7, 349, 390, 417
House of Connelly, The, 473

Icebound, 465, 468
Ice Follies of 1942, 25
Idiot's Delight, 465, 475
In Abraham's Bosom, 465, 470
In Time to Come, 9, 34, 385, 424, 464
Iolanthe, 432
Irene, 463
Is Zat So, 463
It Happens on Ice, 4, 391

Jane Clegg, 469
Jason, 8, 9, 244, 387, 429
Jazz Singer, 388
Jest, The, 467
Jim Dandy, 29
John Ferguson, 466
Johnny 2 x 4, 12, 444
Johnny Belinda, 462
Johnny Johnson, 475
Johnny on a Spot, 426
Journey's End, 471
Jump for Joy, 31
June Moon, 472
Junior Miss, 7, 28, 145, 386, 415

Keep 'Em Laughing, 12, 448
Key Largo, 477
Kiki, 463
Kingdom of God, The, 471
Kiss for Cinderella, A, 12, 442
Kiss the Boys Good-bye, 477
Knickerbocker Holiday, 25

Laburnum Grove, 4
Ladder, The, 463
Ladies in Retirement, 33
Ladies in Waiting, 33
Ladies' Night, 17, 24
Lady Comes Across, The, 427
Lady in the Dark, 4, 388, 392, 477

Land Is Bright, The, 5, 406
Last Mile, The, 472
Last of Mrs. Cheyney, The, 470
Late Christopher Bean, The, 473
Left Bank, The, 473
Let's Face It, 5, 407
Let's Have a Baby, 16, 20
Letters to Lucerne, 8, 212, 388, 422
Let Us Be Gay, 471
Life of Reilly, The, 13, 449
Life with Father, 3, 13, 16, 18, 21, 23, 25, 27, 28, 463, 477
Lightnin', 463
Liliom, 14, 316, 467
Lily of the Valley, 10, 436
Little Accident, 471
Little Dark Horse, 414
Little Foxes, The, 33, 464, 476
Little Show, The, 388
Lonely Man, The, 385
Lost Horizons, 474
Lottie Dundass, 29
Louisiana Purchase, 21
Lovely Miss Linley, 33
Loyalties, 468

Macbeth, 6, 21, 412
Machinal, 390, 471
Male Animal, The, 23, 31, 33, 477
Mamba's Daughters, 24, 30
Mamma's Affair, 467
Man Who Came to Dinner, The, 23, 30, 32, 462, 463, 477
Man with Blond Hair, The, 6, 8, 212, 409
Marco Millions, 25
Margin for Error, 477
Mary of Scotland, 387, 473
Mary Rose, 467
Mary the 3d, 468
Meet the People, 18, 27, 31
Men in White, 282, 465, 474
Merrily We Roll Along, 474
Merry Widow, The, 25
Merton of the Movies, 468
Michael and Mary, 472
Mikado, The, 10, 431
Minick, 32, 469
Miss Lulu Bett, 465
Moon Is Down, The, 13, 34, 72, 386, 445, 464
More the Merrier, The, 395
Morning's at Seven, 477

INDEX OF PLAYS AND CASTS

Mourning Becomes Electra, 472
Mr. and Mrs. North, 19, 20, 25, 33, 478
Mr. Big, 399
Mrs. Bumpstead-Leigh, 466
Mrs. Partridge Presents, 469
Much Ado About Nothing, 33
Murder in a Nunnery, 33
Music in the Air, 25, 31
Music Master, The, 463
Music to My Ears, 31
My Dear Children, 17
My Sister Eileen, 3, 18, 20, 21, 23, 24, 28, 30, 145, 387, 463, 477

Nathan the Wise, 13, 445
Native Son, 20, 462, 477
Nest, The, 468
New Moon, The, 463
Nice People, 467
No More Ladies, 474
No Strings Revue, 31
No Time for Comedy, 23, 476

Of Mice and Men, 386, 464, 476
Of Thee I Sing, 465, 472
Of V We Sing, 11, 438
Oh, Nightingale, 390
Old Maid, The, 465, 474
Old Soak, The, 468
Ol' Man Adam an' His Chillun, 471
On Borrowed Time, 476
On Trial, 466
Once in a Lifetime, 32, 472
One Sunday Afternoon, 33, 473
Our Town, 465, 476
Out of the Frying Pan, 25, 33
Outward Bound, 389, 468
Overture, 472

Pal Joey, 3, 4, 19, 21, 391, 462
Panama Hattie, 3, 19, 21, 462, 463
Papa Is All, 9, 16, 18, 20, 425
Paris Bound, 471
Patricia, 23
Patsy, The, 23
Peg o' My Heart, 463
Personal Appearance, 463
Petrified Forest, The, 474
Philadelphia Story, The, 33, 476
Pie in the Sky, 421
Pigeons and People, 473
Pins and Needles, 463

Pirates of Penzance, 431
Plan M, 11, 441
Play's the Thing, The, 470
Plough and the Stars, The, 471
Porgy, 434, 471
Porgy and Bess, 10, 433
Pride and Prejudice, 475
Priorities of 1942, 12, 443
Private Lives, 386
Prodigal Son, The, 432
Prologue to Glory, 476

Quiet, Please, 23

Racket, The, 471
Rain, 463, 468
Rally Round the Girls, 31
Rebound, 472
Reunion in Vienna, 472
Riddle for Mr. Twiddle, A, 30
Ring Around Elizabeth, 7, 414
Rivals, The, 9, 20, 21, 428
Road to Rome, 470
Rocket to the Moon, 476
Romance, 388, 466
Room Service, 463
Rope, 389
Rope's End, 389
Rose Burke, 23, 30
Rose Marie, 32, 463
Royal Family, The, 32, 470
Rue with a Difference, 389
R.U.R., 468

Sailor, Beware, 463
St. Helena, 475
Sally, 463
Saturday's Children, 470
Separate Rooms, 462, 463
Serena Blandish, 29
Seven Keys to Baldpate, 466
Seventh Heaven, 463
Seventh Trumpet, The, 7, 416
Shadow and Substance, 476
She Lost It in Campeche, 32
Shining Hour, The, 474
Show Boat, 463
Show-Off, The, 23, 463, 468
Show Time, 32
Shuffle Along, 463
Silver Cord, The, 470
Sim Sala Bim, 24
Six Cylinder Love, 468

INDEX OF PLAYS AND CASTS

Skin Game, The, 467
Skylark, 33, 388, 477
Solitaire, 10, 436
Sons o' Fun, 8, 417
Spring Again, 6, 411
Springtime for Henry, 23, 31
Stage Door, 475
Star and Garter, 6
Star-Wagon, The, 476
Strange Interlude, 465, 470
Street Scene, 463, 465, 471
Strictly Dishonorable, 463, 472
Strings, My Lord, Are False, The, 14, 451
Student Prince, The, 21, 463
Sunny, 463
Sunny River, 8, 418
Sun-up, 469
Susan and God, 476
Swan, The, 468

Take My Advice, 16, 20
Tarnish, 469
Theatre, 7, 18, 20, 413
There Shall Be No Night, 477
They Can't Get You Down, 18, 21, 31
They Knew What They Wanted, 465, 469
They Shall Not Die, 474
They Should Have Stood in Bed, 11, 440
Three Men on a Horse, 8, 423, 463
Time of Your Live, The, 464, 477
To Live Again, 32
Tobacco Road, 24, 30, 463
Tomorrow and Tomorrow, 472
Top-Notchers, 454
Tovarich, 475
Trial by Jury, 432
Trip to Chinatown, A, 463
Twelfth Night, 418

Unchastened Woman, The, 466
Uncle Harry, 14, 316, 389, 452
Under This Roof, 441

Vagabond King, The, 25, 31, 463
Valley Forge, 387, 474
Varieties of 1942, 25

Viceroy Sarah, 5, 402
Victoria Regina, 463, 475
Village Green, 4, 16, 20, 393
Vinegar Tree, The, 23, 388
Viva O'Brien, 403
Vortex, The, 388

Walk into My Parlor, 7, 415
Walking Gentleman, The, 14, 450
Walrus and the Carpenter, The, 410
Warrior's Husband, The, 14, 455
Watch on the Rhine, 3, 20, 25, 28, 462, 464, 477
We, the People, 473
Wedding Bells, 467
Wednesday's Child, 474
Western Union, Please, 18, 20
What a Life, 463, 476
What Big Ears, 447
What Price Glory, 387, 469
When Ladies Meet, 473
White Cargo, 463
White Collars, 27
White Desert, The, 387
White Steed, The, 476
Why Marry?, 465, 466
Why Not?, 468
Wild Birds, 469
Wings over Europe, 471
Winterset, 387, 464, 474
Wisdom Tooth, The, 470
Within the Law, 463
Women, The, 463, 475
Wooden Slipper, The, 388
Woodrow Wilson, 34, 385
Wookey, The, 4, 212, 394
World We Make, The, 477

Yellow Jacket, 33
Yes, My Darling Daughter, 475
Yesterday's Magic, 13, 447
You and I, 468
You Can't Take It with You, 32, 463, 465, 475
Young Love, 388
Young Woodley, 469
Youngest, The, 469

Zis Boom Bah, 31

INDEX OF PRODUCERS, DIRECTORS AND DESIGNERS

Abbott, George, 4, 392, 400, 429
Abravanel, Maurice, 393
Adler, Luther, 440
Aldrich, Richard, 441
Alswang, Ralph, 454
Alton, Robert, 392, 417, 455
American Civic Theatre, 395
American Theatre Wing War Service, 13, 448
American Youth Theatre, 11, 439
Ames, Stephen and Paul, 11, 435
Anderson, John Murray, 32
Anderson, Maxwell, 406
Andrews, Herbert, 434
Armistead, Horace, 448
Aronson, Boris, 423, 434
Ayers, Lemuel, 404, 413, 419, 441, 446

Baird, John, 422
Balanchine, George, 427
Barr, Kenn, 448
Barratt, Watson, 401, 417, 420, 428, 447
Bay, Howard, 410, 421, 444, 446, 452
Bennett, Harry G., 453
Bernard, Bern, 420
Blackwell, Donald, 414
Blank, L. Daniel, 447
Bloomingdale, Alfred, 408, 414
Bogdanoff, Rose, 445
Booth, John N., Jr., 404
Boretz, Allen, 414
Boston Comic Opera Company, 430
Bouchene, Dimitri, 432
Boyar, Ben A., 404
Brent, Romney, 427
Bromley, Harald, 449
Brown, Anthony, 444
Brown, Rowland, 444
Bruskin, Perry, 439
Bryden, Eugene S., 404
Burke, Melville, 414
Burnside, R. H., 430
Byrd, Sam, 405

Byron, Edward, 397

Carnegie, Hattie, 393
Carrington, Frank, 425
Carroll, Earl, 32
Chaney, Stewart, 396, 410, 419, 427
Chanin, John Morris, 453
Checkhov, Michael, 418
Choate, Edward, 451
Clark, Peggy, 452
Cohen, Alexander H., 11, 398, 439, 440
Connelly, Marc, 438
Cooper, Lou, 439
Crawford, Cheryl, 9, 12, 433, 438, 442
Curran, Homer, 25
Curtis, Raymond, 414

Daly's Theatre Stock Company, 398
Davenport, Charles, 395
de Casalis, Jeanne, 475
de Liagre, Alfred, Jr., 24, 410, 411
Denham, Reginald, 435, 447
Digges, Dudley, 437
Dobujinsky, Mstislav, 402
Dowling, Edward Duryea, 417
Dubois, Raoul Pene, 417
Duffy, Henry, 23, 30
Duncan, Jesse, 428
duPont, Paul, 434, 443, 453

Elliott, Clyde, 16
Ephraim, Lee, 401
Ernie, Val, 409
Erskin, Chester, 446
Evans, Maurice, 6, 412

Feder, 419, 446, 451
Fielding, Marjery, 444
Fischer, Clifford C., 12, 443, 448, 454
Forman, Lou, 444
Fox, Frederick, 402, 405, 415, 426
Freedley, Vinton, 5, 407
Freeman, Charles K., 17

INDEX OF PRODUCERS, DIRECTORS, DESIGNERS 507

Gabel, Martin, 434
Geddes, Norman Bel, 391
Gering, Marion, 441, 450, 451
Golden, John, 18, 413
Gordon, Max, 8, 406, 415, 418
Greanin, Leon, 431
Green, Johnny, 455
Greene, Luther, 415, 416, 437
Gribble, Harry Wagstaff, 402
Grisman, Sam H., 11, 440

Haggott, John, 412
Hale, Chester, 403, 404
Hale, George, 427
Hambleton, T. Edward, 424
Hammerstein, Oscar, 2d, 419
Hammond, Ronald, 446
Hargrave, Roy, 449
Harkrider, John, 408
Harper, Leonard, 450
Harris, Sam H., 392
Hart, Moss, 145, 387, 393, 415
Hassan, Rita, 441
Hassard, 423
Hatten, Lennie, 452
Hayman, Clifford, 452
Hecht, Ben, 436
Heckroth, H., 430, 431
Helburn, Theresa, 401, 417, 425, 428, 447
Henie, Sonja, 391
Hickey, John J., 403
Horner, Harry, 393, 408, 423, 424, 436, 440, 443, 451
Houseman, John, 24

Jacoves, Felix, 393
Johnson, Clark, 403
Jooss Ballet Dance Theatre, 430
Jooss, Kurt, 430, 431, 432

Karlan, Richard, 453
Karson, Nat, 409
Kaufman, George S., 387, 399, 407
Kaufman, Harry, 417
Kazan, Elia, 434, 452
Kelly, Gene, 400
Kennedy, Charles Rann, 416
Kennel, Louis, 395
Kirkland, Alexander, 451
Koenig, John, 392, 414, 424
Krakeur, Richard, 442
Krasna, Norman, 410

Kroll, Louis, 430

Lang, Howard, 17
Langner, Lawrence, 401, 406, 417, 425, 428, 447
Larsen, Johannes, 425
LeGallienne, Eva, 401, 428
Leonidoff, Leon, 391
Leve, Samuel, 397, 413, 429, 440, 449
Lewis, Albert, 422, 423, 450
Lewis, Russell, 441, 442
Lewis, Sinclair, 5, 405
Liebman, Max, 446
Light, James, 445
Littlefield, Catherine, 391, 443
Logan, Joshua, 455
Logan, Lyn, 421
Lunt, Alfred, 406

MacArthur, Charles, 426
MacGregor, Edgar, 408, 421
McClintic, Guthrie, 13, 389, 411, 449
Meth, Max, 408
Mielziner, Jo, 392, 394, 400, 406, 407, 416, 437, 455
Miller, Gilbert, 11, 402, 436, 439, 440
Milton, Robert, 404, 420
Montgomery, Robert, 428
Morgan, Agnes, 425
Morrison, Paul, 416, 437
Motyleff, Ilia, 398
Myers, Richard, 441

New School for Social Research, 445
Nugent, Elliott, 428, 429

Oenslager, Donald, 399, 411, 413, 421, 438
Olney, Dorothy and Julian, 393
Olsen and Johnson, 8

Pasadena Community Playhouse, 32
Pemberton, Brock, 4, 396
Perry, Antoinette, 397
Pierson, Arthur, 448
Pincus, Norman, 395
Piscator, Edwin, 445
Playwrights' Company, 5, 180, 405
Pons, Helene, 397
Preminger, Otto L., 34, 395, 396, 424

Randall, Carl, 409, 419

INDEX OF PRODUCERS, DIRECTORS, DESIGNERS

Raphaelson, Samson, 429
Rasch, Albertina, 393
Remos, Susanne, 439
Ringling, Edith C., 453
Robinson, Clark, 404
Roche, Emeline, 425
Rodgers, Richard, 455
Rogers, Charles R., 427
Root, John, 397, 429
Rose, Billy, 9, 423
Rosen, Al, 17
Rosenthal, Jean, 416
Ross, Frank, 409
Ross, Robert, 434
Rotsten, Herman, 454
Ryskind, Morrie, 427, 472

Schmidlapp, Horace, 442
School for Social Research, 13
Schorr, William, 414, 415
Seabra, Nelson, 427
Selwyn, Edgar, 394
Selznick, David O., 24, 29
Serlin, Oscar, 13, 27, 72, 445
Sharaff, Irene, 393, 407, 419, 423, 455
Shdanoff, George, 418
Sheppard, John, Jr., 451
Short, Hassard, 393
Shrapps, Ernest, 442
Shubert, John, 426
Shubert, Lee, 12
Shubert, Messrs., 282, 417, 430, 443, 445, 448, 454
Shumlin, Herman, 20
Silberman, David, 447
Sinclair, Robert B., 394
Sircom, Arthur, 453
Sissle, Noble, 13, 450
Sllmola, Aino, 431
Sloan, Lee, 16

Sobel, Edward, 409
Sovey, Raymond, 393, 411, 415, 422, 435
Spencer, Frank, 414
Stander, Lionel, 420
Steinberg, Mollie B., 453
Stevens, Frank W., 448
Strasberg, Lee, 423
Students' Theatre, 13
Sullivan, Ed, 13, 450

Theatre Associates, 416
Theatre Guild, 5, 7, 9, 13, 14, 18, 20, 180, 316, 349, 401, 405, 417, 425, 428, 434, 447
Thompson, Woodman, 449
Throckmorton, Cleon, 398, 445
Todd, Michael, 6
Traube, Shepard, 8, 282, 389, 419
Tuerk, John, 397
Tuttle, Day, 449

Vail, Lester, 417
Veronica, 450
Vodery, Bill, 450

Walters, Charles, 408, 423
Ward, Lem, 421, 452
Watkins, Perry, 442
Webster, Margaret, 413
Welles, Halsted, 425
Wells, William K., 404
Wharton, Carly, 434
White, Miles, 400
Wildberg, John, 442
Wilson, John C., 19, 410
Wiman, Dwight Deere, 8, 10, 18, 212, 422, 436, 455
Wirtz, Arthur M., 291